HOUSE OF SUNS

HOUSE OF SUNS

Alastair Reynolds

The right of Alastair Reynolds to be identified as the author
of this work has been asserted by him in accordance with
the Copyright, Designs and Patents Act 1988.

First published in Great Britain in 2008 by
Gollancz
An imprint of the Orion Publishing Group
Orion House, 5 Upper St Martin's Lane,
London WC2H 9EA
An Hachette UK Company

This edition published in Great Britain in 2009 by Gollancz

10 9 8 7

A CIP catalogue record for this book
is available from the British Library.

ISBN 978 0 575 08237 3

Typeset by Input Data Services Ltd,
Bridgwater, Somerset

Printed and bound in the UK by
CPI Group (UK) Ltd, Croydon, CR0 4YY

The Orion Publishing Group's policy is to use papers that
are natural, renewable and recyclable products and made
from wood grown in sustainable forests. The logging and
manufacturing processes are expected to conform to the
environmental regulations of the country of origin.

www.orionbooks.co.uk

To Tracy and Grace:
big and little sister,
with love

PART ONE

PART ONE

I was born in a house with a million rooms, built on a small, airless world on the edge of an empire of light and commerce that the adults called the Golden Hour, for a reason I did not yet grasp.

I was a girl then, a single individual called Abigail Gentian.

During the thirty years of my childhood, I only saw a fraction of that vast, rambling, ever-changing mansion. Even as I grew older, and gained the authority to wander where it suited me, I doubt that I ever explored more than a hundredth of it. I was intimidated by the long, forbidding corridors of mirror and glass, the corkscrewing staircases rising from dark cellars and vaults where even the adults never went, the rooms and parlours that – although the adults and housekeepers never said as much in my presence – were alleged to be haunted, or in some way not convivial to anything other than transitory occupation. The elevators and dumb waiters alarmed me when they moved without apparent instruction, obeying some inscrutable whim of the house's governing persona. It was a mansion of ghosts and monsters, with ghouls in the shadows and demons scuttling behind the wainscotting.

I had one true friend, although I cannot now remember his name. He arrived occasionally, but only ever for short visits. I would be allowed to watch the approach and docking of his private shuttle, viewing it from the airtight vantage of a glass-windowed belvedere perched above the mansion's highest tower. I was always pleased when Madame Kleinfelter allowed me up to the belvedere, and not just because such an occurrence signalled the arrival of my only true companion. From there I could see the entirety of the house, and much of the world on which it was built. The house curved away in all directions until it met the sharp bend of the planetoid's jagged horizon, a thin margin of rock marking the limit of my home.

It was a strange building, although for a long time I had nothing to compare it with. There was no organised plan to it, no hint of symmetry or harmony – or if there ever had been, that underlying order had been lost beneath countless additions and alterations – work that was still ongoing. Though the planetoid had no atmosphere, and therefore no weather, the house was designed as if it belonged on a world where it rained and snowed. Every distinct part of it, every wing and tower, was surmounted by a steep-sided, blue-tiled roof. There were thousands of roofs, meeting each other at odd, unsettling angles. Chimneys and turrets, belvederes and clock towers punctuated the haphazard, dinosaur-backed roofline. Some parts of the house were only one or two storeys high; others had twenty or more levels, with the tallest parts rising like mountains from the foothills of surrounding structures. Windowed bridges spanned the gaps between towers, a silent, distant figure occasionally stealing behind their illuminated portholes. It was less a house than a city in which you could walk from one side to the other without ever stepping outside.

Later in life I would learn the reason for my home being the way it was, the reason why the building work never ceased, but as a child I simply accepted it unquestioningly. I knew the house was different from the ones I saw in books and story-cubes, but then nothing in those books or cubes resembled any significant aspect of my life. Even before I could read, I knew that we were rich, and it had been impressed on me that there were only a handful of other families whose wealth could be compared to our own.

'You're a very special young lady, Abigail Gentian,' was what my mother told me on one of the many occasions when her ageless face addressed me from one of the house's panes. 'You're going to do great things with your life.'

She had no idea.

It did not take me long to realise that the little boy must also be the child of a rich family. He came on his own ship, not one of the company-owned liners that occasionally conveyed lesser mortals to and from our planetoid. I would watch it arrive from deep space, slowing down on a spike of cobalt flame before stopping above the outer wings of the house, pirouetting into a landing configuration, flinging out skeletal landing legs and lowering with elegant precision onto the designated touchdown pad. Our family's symbol was a black cinquefoil; his was a pair of intermeshing cogs, the emblem painted on the ship's sleek, flanged hull.

As soon as the shuttle was down I would rush from the belvedere, almost tumbling down the tightly wound spiral stairs threading the tower. Whichever clone nanny was looking after me that day would take me to one of the elevators and we would travel up, down and sideways until we reached the docking wing. We usually got there just as the little boy was coming out, taking hesitant steps down the long, carpeted ramp from his ship, with two robots gliding alongside him.

The robots scared me. They were hulking things of dull, weather-worn silver, with heads, torsos and arms, but only a single huge wheel in place of legs. Their faces consisted of a single vertical line, like an arrow slit in a castle wall, at the leading edge of a fierce wedge-shaped skull. They had no eyes, no mouth. Their arms were segmented and ended in three-clawed hands, good for nothing except crunching flesh and bone. In my imagination, the robots were keeping the little boy prisoner when he was not visiting me, doing horrible things to him – so horrible that he could never quite speak of them even when we were alone. It was only when I was older that I grasped that they were his bodyguards, that deep within the dim architecture of their minds was something perilously close to love.

The robots only came to the bottom of the carpet, never rolling off it onto the wooden reception floor. The boy would hesitate, then step off, shiny black shoes clicking on the varnished blocks. His clothes were black except for white cuffs and a wide lacework collar. He wore a little backpack, and his black hair was glued back from his brow with strong-smelling lacquer. His face was pale and slightly pudgy, with round, dark eyes of indeterminate colour.

'Your eyes are funny,' he always told me. 'One blue and one green. Why didn't they fix that when you were born?'

The robots would spin around at the waist and reverse back into the shuttle, where they would wait until it was time for the boy to leave.

'It's hard to walk here,' the boy always said, his footsteps unsteady. 'Everything's too hard.'

'It feels normal to me,' I said.

It was a long time before I realised that the boy came from a place in the Golden Hour where the local gravity had been fixed at half-standard, which meant he found it difficult to move around when visiting the planetoid.

'Father says it's dangerous,' the boy said as we made our way to the playroom, two nannies trailing behind.

'What's dangerous?'

'The thing inside your world. Or has no one told you about that yet?'

'There's nothing inside the world but rock. I know – I looked it up in the story-cube, after you told me there were snakes living in the caves under the house.'

'The story-cube was lying to you. They do that when they think you need to be protected from the truth.'

'They don't lie.'

'Then ask your parents about the black hole. It's under your house right now.'

He must have known that my father was dead, and that I could only ask my mother something when her face appeared on one of the panes.

'What's a black hole?'

The boy thought about this for a moment. 'It's a kind of monster. Like a giant black spider, hanging in an invisible web. Anything that comes too close, it grabs them and stings them and then eats them alive. And there's a very big one under your house.'

Thinking I was being clever, I said, 'So what happened to the snakes? Did it eat them?'

'I lied about the snakes,' the boy said insouciantly. 'But this is real – ask the story-cube about black holes if you don't believe me. Your family had it put under the house to make everything heavier – if it wasn't there, we'd be floating now.'

'How can a spider make things heavier?'

'I said it's *like* a spider, not that it really is one.' He gave me a pitying look. 'It's a sucking, hungry mouth that you can't ever fill. That's why it pulls everything in towards it, making us feel heavier. But it's also why it's dangerous.'

'Because your father said so?'

'It's not just Father. The story-cube will tell you everything, if you ask it the right questions. You can't just come at it headlong – you have to go in sideways, like a cat stalking a mouse. Then you can fool it into telling you things it isn't meant to. A black hole swallowed up a whole planetoid once – bigger than this one. It swallowed up the planetoid and everyone living on it. They all went down the plug, like water after a bath. Glug, glug, glug.'

'That won't happen here.'

'If you say so.'

'I don't believe you anyway. If you weren't telling the truth about the snakes, why should I listen to you now?'

Quite suddenly, the malice vanished from his face. I felt as if my friend had only just arrived – the teasing, spiteful boy who had accompanied me until now had just been an impostor.

'Have you got any new toys, Abigail?'

'I've always got new toys.'

'I mean, anything special.'

'There is something,' I said. 'I was looking forward to showing it to you. It's a kind of doll's house.'

'Doll's houses are for girls.'

I shrugged. 'Then I won't show it to you.' Echoing the words he had spoken to me earlier, I announced, 'I said it's a *kind of* doll's house, not that it really *is* one. It's called Palatial; it's like a castle you control, with its own empire. It's a pity; I think you would have liked it. But there are other games we can play. We can play in the mood maze, or the flying room.'

I could be manipulative as well, and I had already gained some dark insights into the boy's mind – I knew that he would feign indifference for at least part of the afternoon, while his curiosity to see the doll's house was burning a hole right through him. And he was right to be curious, for the doll's house was the toy I was most eager to show off.

With the nannies in tow, I brought the little boy to the playroom. In the dark-shuttered, gloomily lit room I rolled out boxes and trunks and unpacked some of the things we had played with on his last visit. The boy shrugged off his backpack, undid the top flap and pulled out some of his own favourite toys. There were things I remembered from his last visit: a scaly-winged dragon that flew around the room, spitting pink fire before landing on his arm and coiling its tail several times around it; a soldier who would hide himself somewhere in the room when we closed our eyes – it had taken us hours to find him the last time. There were marbles, little glass balls cored with whirls of colour, which rolled on the floor and organised themselves into shapes and figures according to shouted commands, or formed shapes which we then had to guess at before they were complete. There was a puzzle board and a lovely machine ballerina who would dance on anything, even the tip of a finger.

We played with these things, and eventually the nannies brought us lemonade and biscuits on a floating trolley. Somewhere in the house a long-case clock chimed.

'I want to see the doll's house now,' the boy said.

'I thought you didn't want to see it.'

'I do. Really.'

So I showed him Palatial, taking him into the room-within-a-room where it was kept, and although I revealed only a fraction of its capabilities, he was fascinated by it, and I knew even then that he was jealous, and that Palatial would be the first thing he would want to see on his next visit.

It was the first time I had felt him in my power. I decided that I liked the feeling very much.

CHAPTER ONE

I lifted the glass of wine, already drunk on the scenery before a drop had touched my lips.

'To the future security of your civilisation and solar system, Mister Nebuly.'

'To your civilisation,' Purslane said, from the other side of the table.

'Thank you,' said Mister Nebuly.

We were sitting by the beach, enjoying wine on a warm evening. Night on the Centaurs' world was not the same as on most planets. Since the world orbited a star heavy in ultraviolet radiation, Scapers had thrown a protective bubble around the atmosphere – a transparent shield that the Centaurs tolerated, as opposed to the armoured shell that would have been necessary if the House of Moths had moved their solar system. By day the bubble served only to screen out the rays and take the edge off that scalding blue brilliance. By night, it amplified the faintest star or gas cloud until the hues were intense enough to trigger the colour receptors in the human eye. The Milky Way was a luminous, many-boned spine arcing from horizon to horizon. A nearby supernova remnant was a smear of ruby red, dulling to sable at its curdled edges. The pulsar at its heart was a ticking lighthouse. An open cluster of blue stars, no more than a few hundred lights away, spangled like a clutch of electric gems. The dwarf stars within a few lights of this system were warm ambers and golds, promising life and sanctuary and the ten-billion-year stability of a slow fusion cycle. Even the Absence was visible: that thumb-sized smudge of starless, galaxyless darkness in the direction where Andromeda used to lie.

The sky was beautiful, as luscious as a drug-induced vision, but I did not care to be reminded of the Absence. It brought to mind my promise to Doctor Meninx, the promise I had so far failed to keep and which now hung by the slimmest of threads.

My only hope was that the Centaurs would come through.

'And you're absolutely certain the stardam won't give us any cause for concern in the future, shatterling Campion?' asked the four-legged being standing at our table.

'You can rest easy, Mister Nebuly. Your civilisation is safe again.'

'Not that it was ever in *grave* danger,' Purslane said, swirling the wine in her glass. 'Let's be clear about that.'

I smiled. 'A leaking stardam's not something you can ignore, but the fault is repaired. We installed it; we'll fix it if it goes wrong. That's how we do things in Gentian Line.'

'You can understand why we're concerned. When the other survival options were presented to us, it was emphasised that repairing the stardam involved the minimum of risk.'

'And it did,' I said.

One and a half million years ago, a supermassive star within eleven lights of the Centaurs' world had grown unstable. Rebirthers had attempted to siphon matter from the star's core using wormhole taps, but the fierce densities and temperatures had thwarted the throat-stabilising devices that held the wormholes open. Scaper intervention could not protect the Centaurs' biosphere. That left only two other options, apart from evacuation of the system. Mellicta Line, the House of Moths, were experts in the movement of stars. They offered to relocate either the star or the system, promising to accomplish either task for free provided they received exclusive trading rights with the Centaurs for the next two million years. Neither option was without risk. The point of moving a star was to eject it out of the galactic disc before it had a chance to explode, but the very act of movement had occasionally led to premature detonation. And while the Centaurs' system could be moved, their planet would need to be encapsulated against interstellar radiation and debris for the duration of the voyage. This was deemed unacceptable by the Centaurs, who had a horror of claustrophobia.

At this point Gentian Line, the House of Flowers, had made the Centaurs' acquaintance. Seeking prestige within the Commonality, we offered them the option of remaining where they were *and* being protected from the ailing star. A stardam would be erected around the supergiant. When the star blew up, its energies would be contained within the dam, trapped for ever inside a screen of perfect mirrors.

The Centaurs were naturally sceptical. But Gentian Line could point to some experience in this matter. If it had any specialisation within the Commonality, it was in stardams. We had been making them for dozens of circuits – millions of years.

At the time of the Centaur negotiations, no Gentian stardam had ever collapsed.

We could only take so much credit for this, of course. We made the dams, but all we really did was put together the ready-made components left behind by the Priors. They had done all the hard work. They forged ringworlds in their millions, large and small, then threw them like hoops around stars. Then they abandoned them and became extinct.

A billion or so years later, we began to collect them. We scour space for the occluding signatures of orphaned, starless ringworlds. We fix pushers to their dark sides and launch them across the galaxy at miserable, snail-like fractions of light. It must be done with care, lest the structures shatter into a trillion twinkling fragments. Ringworlds are immensely strong, but they are not indestructible. What they are is shiny. In fact, there is nothing shinier in the known universe. That mirrored inner surface reflects everything, including neutrinos that would happily sail through fifty light-years of solid lead.

To dam a star, to enclose it completely, would require the construction of a Dyson shell. Humans can shroud a star with a swarm of bodies, a Dyson cloud, but we cannot forge a sphere. Instead we approximate one by surrounding a star with thousands of ringworlds, all of similar size but with no two having exactly the same diameter. We make a discus and then start tilting, until each ringworld is encircling the star at a unique angle. The light of the star rams through the narrowing gaps as the ringworlds tighten into their final orientation. Shutters close on a fierce, deadly lantern.

Then suddenly there is no star, just a dark sphere. Inside that shell, the energies of the dying star are held in reflected fury, allowed to bounce back and forth between those flawless reflecting surfaces until, photon by photon, they gradually leak out into space at a harmless intensity.

It takes an unthinkably long time. Should the stardam collapse before most of that pent-up energy has been allowed to dissipate, the results would be more disastrous than the explosion the dam was designed to contain.

I had exaggerated when I said that we had saved the local civilisation, but that was not to say there had not been a problem with the stardam. One of its pushers – the engines that keep the ringworlds in check – had begun to fail. An eye-shaped gap had opened in the dam, allowing furious light to burn through.

I had been sent to repair it. A new pusher had followed *Dalliance* from the last reunion, tailing my ship like a loyal puppy. In my hold was the string of linked brass spheres called a single-use opener, a device keyed to that specific stardam which permitted limited adjustment of its nested mechanisms. Before visiting the Centaurs I had deployed the opener – it had shattered into glittery dust after emitting its graviton pulse – and installed the new pusher. Over the course of several days the eye had closed, the dam sealing over again.

Our work here was done. Purslane thought the decent, honourable thing would have been to leave without contacting the Centaurs, without soliciting their gratitude.

She was right, beyond any measure of doubt.

'You were right to pick the stardam,' Purslane said, doubtless aware that she was talking to the distant descendant of one of the creatures the Line had first done business with. 'But you're also right to express disappointment that the fault arose in the first place. You expected better of us.'

Mister Nebuly scuffed a hoof against the ground. 'No great harm came of it.'

'Regardless, you have the Line's apology, and our assurance that nothing like this will ever be permitted to happen again.' Purslane was making no secret of her being a Gentian shatterling as well. Though the Line frowned on the practice of consorting during circuits, our hosts had a well-earned reputation for discretion. 'In the meantime,' she continued, 'if there's anything else Gentian Line can do for your civilisation, I'll be glad to raise the matter at the next reunion. You've been gracious hosts – beyond anything we deserve. The arrangements you've made for our guest, Doctor Meninx—'

'Speak of the devil,' I said, lifting a pair of antique binoculars from the table.

'Is that him now?' asked Mister Nebuly.

'One and the same.'

'He's travelling in a most curious contraption. What are those circular things along the side, turning round?'

'Wheels,' said Purslane.

'It's his bathing machine,' I said.

The bathing machine was a rust-streaked black rhomboid mounted on four sets of independent undercarriage. It had emerged from the hold of my ship, descended the loading ramp and made its ponderous, plodding, smoke-belching way from the landing area, through the low, shuttered buildings of the sleepy seaside town, to the cracked concrete of the ancient revetments above the beach. Negotiating a steep slipway, it had crossed the sands and entered the water, continuing until the machine was submerged up to the depth of its wheels. At the front, a single door folded up onto the roof of the machine and allowed seawater to slosh inside.

The sea was the midnight blue of ink, awash with shimmering micro-organisms. The waves foamed pink and cerise when they dashed against the chrome-white sands. I levelled the binoculars at the seaward end of the bathing machine, hoping for a clear glimpse of Doctor Meninx as he emerged into the sea. Disappointed, all I saw was a barnacled form slipping away from the machine, vanishing beneath the surface before I could make out more than the rudimentary details. The door closed and the bathing machine crept back out of the water.

'Might I ask how you came by such an unusual specimen, shatterling? It's been a very long time since we saw the likes of Doctor Meninx – several hundred thousand years, at the very least.'

'I can't take any credit for him. He was foisted on me.'

'You make it sound like a punishment.'

'It was. The rest of my Line felt it would give me ample opportunity to demonstrate that I could shoulder responsibility, and put up with a difficult guest.'

Purslane said, 'It was Campion's bad luck, Mister Nebuly. Gromwell – another shatterling – showed up at our last reunion with Doctor Meninx as a guest. By then, Gromwell was looking for any excuse to fob him off onto someone else. That was around the time that Campion threaded a strand that happened to include a visit to the Vigilance.'

'You know all about the Vigilance,' I said.

Mister Nebuly looked to the sky, in the approximate direction of the Absence. He wore a tight-fitting pinstripe suit that reached down to the point where his human torso merged seamlessly with the groomed chestnut of his horse body. 'This and that, shatterling. Which is not to say we've ever had direct contact with them.'

Purslane sipped her wine. 'The thing is, it turned out that Doctor Meninx's ultimate goal was to reach the Vigilance. Apart from being a staunch Disavower, he fancies himself a scholar of remote history.'

'Which is how Campion came to be burdened with the doctor's presence,' Mister Nebuly said.

'In addition to monitoring the stardam, I was told to ferry Doctor Meninx to the Vigilance and use my contacts there to secure him privileged scholar status – unrestricted access to the deep archives, that kind of thing. They don't much like Disavowers, and they definitely don't like aquatics, but it was assumed I'd be able to talk them around.'

Mister Nebuly flexed his torso to look out to sea again, a thoughtful expression appearing on his face. 'One can only conclude that you were not entirely successful in that venture, shatterling?'

'No, everything's still on track,' I said. 'Since this was the doctor's last chance for a swim before the Vigilance, he jumped at it. I second Purslane's thanks for making the necessary arrangements, by the way.'

The Centaur waved a dismissive hand at the twinkling barrier on the horizon, beyond which Purslane's hovering ship – much too large for the landing area – rose like a tarnished silver moon. 'It was nothing. There are no large predators in this ocean, but for your guest's peace of mind it was a simple matter to establish the impasse across the bay. I just hope we adjusted the salinity to his tastes.'

The conversation lulled. Mister Nebuly had not come up to our table to pass the time of day. He was here to tell me what value he placed on the items I had offered for sale. Much depended on his offer, though I was doing my utmost not to let him know it.

'It was good of you to open your trove for examination,' Mister Nebuly said.

I nodded encouragingly, while Purslane maintained a tense, diplomatic smile. 'I hope you found something of interest in it.'

'I found much of interest in it. You have travelled far, traded intelligence with other starfarers and amassed a great deal of knowledge, much of it of considerable rarity. It was a privilege to sift through your data.'

'And did you find anything in there that you might like to purchase?'

Mister Nebuly shifted on his iron-shod hooves. 'I did find several things, shatterling, but I must confess that much of what you have to offer is not of direct value to me, despite its rarity. If you had arrived twenty kilo-years ago, things might have been different. But it is only eleven since we were visited by a shatterling of Gentian Line, and only two since a Marcellin was in our airspace.'

'Those Marcellins get everywhere,' Purslane said, through tight lips.

'The items that did interest you ...'

'I have a breakdown here,' the Centaur said, reaching into a pocket of his business suit to remove a handkerchief-sized square of material. He flicked it open and it enlarged to the width of our tabletop. He let it hang in the air, where it hovered against the breeze. It was a series of tabulated columns, in the written variant of Tongue.

The Centaurs had been known to Gentian Line for more than eight circuits. They were the thirteenth form of human to live in this system, having emerged from the post-civilisational ruins of the last culture. They owned this system and the handful of scaped worlds inside it, but had never ventured further than their cometary halo. Their main world was a panthalassic, a superoceanic planet smothered in water, with a thick, blue atmosphere containing photo-disassociated oxygen. Scapers had thinned out that atmosphere and made it less corrosive, dropped floating landmasses onto the world-enveloping sea and scattered a multitude of hardy pelagic organisms into that sterile ocean. The planet's gravity had never been adjusted, which was why the Centaurs had attained their present, sure-footed form. They had a dim recollection of where they had come from, which was more than could be said for all postemergents. According to the statistical forecast of the Universal Actuary, they stood an excellent chance of persisting for at least another one or two million years, provided their ambitions remained modest. In the long run, the best strategy for cultural longevity was either to sit tight in a single system, or become like the Lines, entirely unshackled from planetary life. Expansionism worked for a while, but was ultimately futile. Not that that stopped new emergents from trying, even when they had six million years of sobering history to mull over.

We called it turnover: the endless, grinding procession of empires. The Centaurs had done well not to climb onto that wheel.

'As you can see,' Mister Nebuly said, 'our offers are not un-reasonable.'

'No, your terms are very generous,' I said. 'I was just hoping you'd bid for some of the larger items in the trove.'

'I wish that were possible. Unfortunately there would be little sense in bidding for data we already possess.'

'Are you absolutely certain we can't find some middle ground?'

'We are inclined to generosity, shatterling, but there have to be limits. We feel that these terms are fair. It's a shame that your trove does not contain more of value to us, but that does not preclude you from visiting us again, when you have something new to offer.' The Centaur paused, three of his hooves in full contact with the ground, the rear left touching only by its tip. 'Would you like a moment alone, to discuss our offer?'

'If you wouldn't mind.'

'I shall return shortly. Would you like some more wine?'

'We're fine,' I said, raising a hand.

Mister Nebuly turned and trotted away along the curving road that lay on this side of the revetments. In the distance stood two other Centaurs, dressed in red uniforms and carrying the pennanted staffs of some civic guild.

Mister Nebuly joined his compatriots and watched us patiently.

'We're doomed,' I said, not really caring if my words were intercepted.

Purslane finished off her wine. 'Could be worse. He's prepared to offer you something.'

'Not enough to make a difference.' Parked in orbit around the Centaurs' world was an assortment of second-hand ships, most of which were up for sale. If Nebuly had liked enough of the data in my trove, he could have made me an offer sufficient to buy one of those vehicles. With a faster ship, I could have kept my promise to Doctor Meninx and made it back to the reunion only slightly later than anticipated. 'I suppose I could hold out, see if he changes his mind.'

'He'd have to change it a lot. He could double his offer and it wouldn't buy you a quarter of one of those ships. The best thing we can do now is take Mister Nebuly's money. You can't replace *Dalliance*, but you can still upgrade some of her systems.'

'It won't make her faster.'

'I'd settle for safer, if I were you. If you turn him down, we might as well never have come here. We could have gone straight to the Vigilance and got fish-face off our backs.'

It was as if Doctor Meninx had heard Purslane, for as she spoke the bathing machine bellowed its engine and began to labour back into the sea, clouds of filthy smoke emerging from slats in its rear. I watched as the door swung up and water sluiced in. I half-considered raising the binoculars again, but my curiosity had dissipated. The barnacled form crested the waves momentarily and vanished back into the bathing machine. The door clammed down and the machine began to crawl back onto dry land.

'There's another possibility,' I said quietly.

Purslane looked at me with practised scepticism. 'There always is, where you're concerned.'

'Before we landed I had a look at the nearby systems, just in case Mister Nebuly wasn't as forthcoming as I'd hoped. Less than a hundred lights from here, and more or less on our way home, is a place called Nelumbium. According to the trove—'

'"According to the trove." Where have I heard that before?'

'Hear me out. There's supposed to be an entity, a posthuman, called Ateshga. He's supposed to have ships, a lot more than Nebuly, and he's unlikely to charge as steeply.'

'Why didn't we go there first?'

'The trove entry isn't as up to date as I'd like, so there's an element of uncertainty.'

'An element. I've heard that before as well.'

'Also, it would have taken us even further from the Vigilance – if we'd gone straight to Nelumbium, there'd have been no possibility of dropping off Doctor Meninx.'

'If the trove isn't up to date, what's to say Ateshga's there at all?'

'I ran the Actuary – the prognosis looked good.'

Purslane leaned back in her wickerwork seat, measuring me with those mismatched Gentian eyes. 'So what you're proposing is, you limp to the Vigilance, deliver the doctor, then continue to Ateshga.'

'Actually ... no. What I'm proposing is, I skip the Vigilance completely.'

The hard notch of a frown ate into her brow. 'Leave him here?'

'The choice'll be his. If he wants, I'll take him all the way back to the reunion world.'

'He won't like it.'

'He doesn't *like* anything – haven't you noticed?'

A thin figure was stalking across the sand from the direction of the bathing machine. As the walker neared, climbing the crumbling steps up to the road, it revealed itself to be a paper cut-out of a harlequin, inked in watery diamonds. The two-dimensional figure – which resisted the breeze just as effectively as Mister Nebuly's hanging sheet – was a humanoid avatar of Doctor Meninx. At the same time as the avatar approached, Nebuly left the red-suited centaurs and started trotting back in our direction. He arrived first, the avatar still a good hundred metres away.

'Might I assume that you've reached a decision, honoured shatter-ling?' he asked.

'I'm afraid I'm going to have to turn you down,' I said. 'I'm not saying your terms aren't generous, but I have to be realistic. I think I can get a better deal for my trove somewhere else.'

'If you are thinking of Ateshga, I'd caution against it. He has a very bad reputation.'

I scratched sand from my eyes. 'Ateshga – who's he?'

'Merely a warning, shatterling – it's up to you whether you heed it.' He brushed his hands against the breast of his pinstripe suit. 'Well, I am sorry we could not close a deal, but it won't stop us parting as friends. We are very happy that you visited our world, and I trust your stay here has been rewarding.'

'It has,' Purslane said. 'You've been excellent hosts, Mister Nebuly; I'll be sure to put in a good word for you with the rest of the Line.'

'That is very kind of you.' He turned around to greet the approaching avatar, bowing slightly from the point where his human torso joined his horse body. 'You finished your swim very quickly, Doctor: I trust all was satisfactory?'

'No,' the avatar said in his high-pitched, piping voice. 'The swim was very far from satisfactory, which is why I aborted it at the earliest opportunity. There were things in the water – dark, moving things that my sonar could not easily resolve – and the temperature and salinity were not at all to my tastes.' The paper face bent in my direction. 'I was given to understand that you had communicated my needs to the relevant authorities, Campion.'

I shifted on my seat. I had told the Centaurs what the doctor needed, and I had no doubt that they had done their best to meet his requirements. Nothing was ever good enough for Doctor Meninx, though; no effort ever sufficient.

'I'm sorry,' I said. 'I must have mixed up the figures. All my fault, I'm afraid.'

'I shall lay the blame where I choose to lay it,' the avatar said. 'And I was so looking forward to my swim. But what's done is done; shortly I shall take my leave of this dreary world and continue my odyssey to the Vigilance. Perhaps they will know the fit way to treat a guest.'

'I'm sure Mister Nebuly did his best,' I said.

'Yes, he probably did,' the avatar said, as if our host was not present.

The moment, the one I had been dreading since Mister Nebuly had delivered his verdict on my trove, was now upon me. I could postpone it no longer, though at that instant there was nothing I would rather have done than walk into the sea and swim all the way to that twinkling horizon, where, depending on the effectiveness of its setting, the impasse would have dissuaded, rebuffed, stunned, wounded or simply annihilated me.

'Doctor Meninx,' I said, after drawing a deep, invigorating breath, 'there's something we need to discuss.'

CHAPTER TWO

It would be a mistake to say that Campion was lazy, laziness being a trait that Abigail went out of her way to scrub from our personalities. But Campion was certainly a masterful prevaricator. He did not just put things off until tomorrow; he put them off for tens of kilo-years, until his delays and evasions consumed significant chunks of an entire circuit. His motto might have been *Why do today what you can still do in a quarter of a million years?*

He had got away with it for thirty-one circuits, too. But now this business with Doctor Meninx was going to make up for that glorious streak of good luck. Campion joked about censure and excommunication, as if to immunise himself from those outcomes. But the Line's tolerance of his antics had been wearing perilously thin for several circuits, which is why he had been saddled with Doctor Meninx in the first place. He should have discharged that obligation as urgently as possible, instead of dilly-dallying from star to star with the doctor still aboard.

It was a short hop from the Centaurs' system to Nelumbium – barely ninety years of flight by planetary time – but it was still necessary to enter some form of abeyance. Campion preferred stasis; I – much to his incomprehension – preferred to be frozen and thawed. As soon as the cryophagus released me, I called up the information from *Silver Wings'* sensors, and apart from a whisper of residual energies – which might mean only that a ship had passed through this system in recent centuries – there was no evidence at all of human habitation.

No Ateshga, no ships.

Once I had digested *Silver Wings'* analysis, I whisked over to *Dalliance*, then up-ship to the bridge, where Campion and Doctor Meninx were already waiting for me. Campion was seated, reclining back in one of the couches, while the avatar stood close to him. They were both facing the enormous, illuminated wall of the displayer.

Although I could not make out their words, the acoustics of the bridge were such that I could tell they were lost in quiet, slightly strained conversation, a petulant or defensive note rising every now and then.

I did not need to be told what they were talking about.

Most of the displayer was filled with a plan-view of the Milky Way, based on the trove's knowledge of real conditions. The spirals were traced with wispy filaments of white and yellow, ochre and tan and dulling, fire-brick orange, with the individual stars too countless to separate, discernible only by their groupings into associations, streams and clusters. The only stars one saw as distinct entities were the very brightest: end-phase supergiants burning their way to supernova, or Tauri-phase youngsters, glaring out of that barred spiral in hot blues and venomous reds.

The main disc, excluding the outer band of the Monoceros Ring, was ninety thousand lights across. Settled worlds spread from the core to the outermost extremities of the spiral arms, but the highest density of human habitation was in the thick band of the Comfort Zone, the region where planets required the least adaptation to make them liveable. Provided it stayed within the Zone, a ship could circumnavigate the galaxy in two hundred kilo-years and still have time to stop off at a hundred systems en route. That was a circuit, the two-hundred-kilo-year interval between Gentian reunions.

The last reunion world had been a planet on the coreward extremity of the Norma Spiral Arm. Since then we had travelled clockwise, looping out to cross the Local Spur, passing within a thousand lights of the Old Place, then diving back through the Sagittarius, Scutum-Crux and Perseus Arms, before returning to the other side of the Scutum-Crux Arm. A wavery red line traced our progress. The Centaurs' panthalassic had been in Scutum-Crux, and the distance we had travelled since then was barely a scratch against the scale of the spiral, not even enough to take us out of the arm. Marked in dashed red was the distance we still had to travel to make it to the reunion; it was less than a thousand lights in the direction of the Sagittarius Arm.

In circuit terms, we were nearly home. Yet as far as our punctuality was concerned, it may as well have been ten thousand lights, or ninety thousand.

We were going to be late, very late, and that was very much not the done thing.

'Ah, here comes the lovely Purslane,' said Doctor Meninx, his voice rising to a note of shrill indignation. 'She will lend a sympathetic ear to my complaints even if you choose not to, Campion. Is that not so, Purslane?'

'I don't know, Doctor Meninx. What exactly are you complaining about?'

'Need I explain?' the avatar said, raising a limp origami arm in the direction of the displayer. 'Once again Campion has let me down! Not only did he fail to deliver me to the Vigilance, not only did he attempt to fob me off on those stinking, ill-mannered horse-people with their revolting bodily habits, not only did he stand by as I nearly drowned in their horrid, flotsam-infested bay, but now he has the temerity to tell me that I will not even return to the reunion in time to be entrusted to someone else's better care!'

'I didn't say that,' Campion replied, sounding like a man drained of argument. 'All I said was that we might be just a tiny bit late.'

'And this reunion of yours – they will delay starting it until you have arrived?' The avatar's tone was needling. 'Is that what you are telling me?'

'I can't make any guarantees. If Ateshga's here, and if he agrees to replace my ship, we might not be very late at all.'

I walked across the narrow tongue that connected the main part of the bridge to the circular platform where Campion and Doctor Meninx were waiting.

'So where do you think he is?'

'I don't know, hiding or something,' Campion said.

Doctor Meninx pounced. 'Oh, yes – hiding – that well-known business model, embraced by profit-conscious traders the galaxy over.'

I smiled. 'At least the view's nice.'

Ateshga's world – shown beneath the map of the galaxy – was an outrageous confection of a planet: a striped marshmallow giant with a necklace of sugary rings, combed and braided by the resonant forces of a dozen glazed and candied moons. We were crossing the ecliptic, so the rings were slowly tilting to a steeper angle, revealing more of their loveliness. There was no doubt that it was one of the most glorious worlds I had ever seen, and I had seen quite a few.

But we had not come here to gawp at a picturesque planet, even if it was a spectacular exemplar of the form.

'Did you get anything I missed?' Campion asked.

I kissed Campion, then took one of the unoccupied couches.

'There were some hints of technological activity, but nothing you'd bet your life on. Maybe a ship came through with a noisy drive, or perhaps I'm just seeing some leakage from the private network of another Line. *We* don't appear to have a functioning node in this system.'

'I'll make sure we leave one. It might be the kind of thing that will placate Fescue.'

'I'm afraid it'll take rather more than that.'

'I notice it's all right when he's late.'

I pressed a finger to my brow, feeling a throbbing between my eyes. 'Don't start on about Fescue again.'

'We all had to wait in abeyance until he deigned to arrive. How long was it? Seven, eight kilo-years easily. I didn't see him getting censured.'

'That's because Fescue had been invited by the Rebirthers to witness a Kindling. He couldn't leave until it was finished, as you well know. Your situation is very different.'

'Go on, kick a man when he's down.'

'Perhaps I should entrust myself to Purslane instead,' Doctor Meninx said. 'That way I might at least get back to the reunion before it finishes.'

'You know, that's not such a bad idea. Why don't both of you leave now, and I'll catch up when I'm able?'

'As if I'd ever do that,' I said, shooting an apologetic glance at the avatar. 'Sorry, Doctor Meninx, but I can't abandon Campion here.'

'There'll be repercussions.'

'And you're still my guest,' Campion said.

'More's the pity.'

'Indeed. And wouldn't it be a tragedy if something happened to you between now and the reunion? Something obscure and undocumented, like a sudden breakdown of tank chemistry? Can't be too careful, you know: that apparatus already looks as if it belongs back in some museum of horrors from the Golden Hour. It's just begging for something to go wrong with it.'

The paper figure's face creased in anger. 'Are you *threatening* me, shatterling?'

'No, just indulging in a little wishful thinking.'

Things might have taken a turn for the worse at that point had *Dalliance* not chosen to interrupt with a report. Someone – something – was signalling our two ships. A vehicle had emerged from the atmosphere of the giant, near its lusciously banded equator:

a vehicle that had been completely hidden until that moment, but which was now keen to announce its existence.

'And to think you doubted me,' Campion said.

The other vessel was reassuringly old-fashioned: a solid, reliable example of Eleventh Intercessionary shipbuilding. It was all severe angles and dark, lustrous facets, like a mountain-sized lump of coal chiselled into the shape of an arrowhead. It had continued to signal us since its emergence, sending a single repeating transmission in Tongue. There had been no need to respond; the message had simply instructed us to decelerate from our trans-ecliptic trajectory and await further instructions.

The vessel curved past the ring system without penetrating it and came to a dead stop in the local reference frame defined by *Dalliance* and *Silver Wings of Morning*. The three ships formed an approximate equilateral triangle, with only a thousand kilometres between their centres of mass. Campion's ship was an Art Deco rhomboid; mine a headless chrome swan with wings curved and raised as if in courtship.

'Now what?' I asked.

'We wait and see. Ateshga – whoever he is – probably hasn't had much company lately. I don't think he's going to be particularly bothered about keeping us waiting a bit longer.'

I touched a finger against the side of my head. I had felt a shivery, someone-walking-over-my-grave sensation. '*Silver Wings* has just been scanned with deep-penetration sensors.'

'Attack him now,' shrilled Doctor Meninx. 'Why are you waiting? Attack him immediately!'

'*Dalliance* is requesting permission to realise an imago,' Campion said.

'Nothing ventured,' I said.

A hooded figure resolved into existence before us, rendered with just enough translucence and artificial flicker to affirm that this was a projection, not a physical presence. The voice – slow and deep and sonorous – was modulated to sound as if it had passed through a primitive transmitting apparatus.

'State your business here, *Dalliance* and *Silver Wings of Morning*.' The figure spoke a variant of Tongue, the only thing approaching a universal language for star-travellers.

'I'm looking for someone called Ateshga,' Campion said, using Trans, the private language of the Commonality of Lines, trusting *Dalliance* to translate his outgoing message into Tongue. He could speak Tongue as well as I could, but preferred to let the ship do the hard work.

'I ask again: what is your business here? Why have you arrived in this system?'

'I need a new ship,' Campion answered. 'I was led to believe I might find one here.'

The figure hovering before us wore a hooded gown of dark-red material, patterned with fine chrome wires in the branching forms of ancient circuitry. His hands were clasped, but otherwise hidden under voluminous sleeves. Of his face, nothing was visible under that dark, sagging hood.

'A ship?' he asked, as if it was the last thing in the world Campion might have been looking for. 'Why would you want a ship, traveller?'

'Mine's getting a bit worn out.'

I had the sense of something staring at me from under the hood, something with superhuman acumen.

'Do you see many ships here, traveller?'

'They're not exactly leaping out at me, no.'

'In which case it would appear that you have come to the wrong place, would it not?'

'Except my trove says otherwise,' Campion said. 'Now, if you hadn't popped out of that Jovian I might have put it down to faulty data, but your arrival is a coincidence too far. I *am* speaking to Ateshga, aren't I?'

'What would your trove have to say about this Ateshga?'

'Very little. His prices are said to be fair, and apparently he has a large assortment of used vessels. But if he sells ships, that's really all I need to know.'

The sleeves fell back to reveal thin white wrists and even thinner white fingers, curiously jointed and tipped with obsidian nails. The hands reached up to throw back the hood. Ateshga's face was a ghoulish mask: gauzy white skin papered over a hollow-cheeked skull. His eyes were set deep into shadowed sockets. His teeth were jagged chips of blood-red glass, pushed into his gums at irregular angles.

'I might have some ships.'

Campion looked at me before answering. 'Can we see them?'

'Follow me. I will show you what is on offer.'

'I do not trust this man,' said Doctor Meninx. 'I insist that we leave immediately.'

My thoughts flicked back to the warning Mister Nebuly had given us. It was like touching a raw nerve.

'Campion,' I said, 'maybe we ought to think—'

Ateshga's ship wheeled around and accelerated back towards the gas giant. Exotic particles twinkled into existence in its wake as tortured, addled spacetime relaxed back towards its normal tension. Stars and one edge of the ring system blurred as if seen through moiled water.

'We're going in,' Campion said.

CHAPTER THREE

At the last possible instant, Ateshga's ship threw an impasse around itself as armour against the atmosphere as it plunged into the cloud deck. *Dalliance*'s impassor was less effective and we experienced moderate buffeting as the aerodynamic forces increased. Purslane grimaced and muttered something about how we should have gone in her ship instead. *Silver Wings* was standing watch in orbit, monitoring our descent.

Ateshga took us one hundred kilometres into the clouds, disengaging his parametric engine and using sequenced field rippling to swim through the air. That was a trick *Dalliance* had not been capable of for about ten thousand years. I switched from pseudo- to real-thrust.

Above us, the sky had lightened by degrees to a pastel azure, streaked with horsetails of fine white cirrus. A couple of moons were visible as delicate crescents, but the shadowed rings were hidden. Below us, billowing ochre thunderheads elbowed their way through a mustard-coloured smog, rent here and there to reveal plunging vistas of cloud and chemistry, reaching down into dizzy, canyon-like depths hundreds of kilometres beneath us.

'I think Ateshga could be taking us for a ride,' Purslane said.

'Let's wait and see what he has to show us.'

Ateshga took us deeper. *Dalliance* protested against the increase in pressure – her impassors straining to support the bubble – but I had subjected her to worse conditions and I had every confidence that she would hold. Purslane had eased into the chair next to mine, buckled in against the stomach-churning surges caused by *Dalliance*'s lagging acceleration damper.

We nosed through those ochre thunderheads, our abrupt passage triggering a chain of electrical storms behind us. For a few moments we were in the mustard smog, losing all sense of onward motion. Then we cut through into a pocket of clear air, suffused with the silvery gloom of the sunlight that made it through the overlying cloud layers.

That was when we saw the collection of ships Ateshga had for sale.

'Please tell me I'm not seeing what I think I'm seeing,' Purslane said.

'I wish I could.'

'There were more ships around the Centaurs' world.'

'I warned you not to trust this man,' Doctor Meninx said. 'It was clear from the outset that we were dealing with a charlatan, with nothing to offer but second-hand junk.'

There were twelve ships.

They were suspended in the atmosphere, each floating in a neutrally buoyant impasse bubble. The ships varied in dimension from the same size as *Dalliance*, five or six kilometres in length, to vessels in the same medium-size class as *Silver Wings of Morning*, twenty or thirty kilometres from end to end. One dagger of a ship was a full fifty kilometres long; its red and white dazzle markings identified it as a Redeemer needle-craft. It looked impressive, but most of that ship would have been taken up with propulsion and field-generating equipment, with only a few cubic metres of living space somewhere near its middle.

Nearly as large, and much more impressive, was the densely patterned golden sphere of a Second Imperium moonship. It was hollow, with openings at either pole. There was room within a moonship for a city of a billion souls, or the treasure of a thousand worlds. But moonships were enticing targets for less scrupulous travellers and it suited me not to have to keep looking over my shoulder.

Very much at the other end of the scale, Ateshga's smallest ship was a twenty-two-hundred-metre-long fluted cylinder seemingly hewn from turquoise-veined marble, its sombre lines and unornamented hull establishing it as a Margravine artefact. Such a ship, assuming it was in good order, would have both excellent acceleration and a very high cruising velocity. But the mental modifications I would have to endure just to survive aboard it, let alone operate it, were of the kind expressly forbidden by the rules of the Line.

That left nine other ships, but most of them could be dismissed at a glance. Too slow, too ancient, too vulnerable, too difficult to obtain the spares when some non-regenerative component broke down. A Rimrunner vehicle looked to have some possibilities – faster than *Dalliance*, easily – but then I noticed the telltale fuzziness at the boundary of her flotation bubble, indicating that her impassors were approaching life-expiration. A five-kilometre-long skullcraft of the Canopus Sodality was also briefly tempting, until I remembered how those ships had a well-earned reputation for murdering their occupants. A trimaran of the Perpetual Commonwealth had novelty value, but the field spars linking the three hulls together imposed a very low acceleration ceiling on the ship. Getting anywhere quickly had not been a priority for the citizens of the Perpetual Common-wealth, who had fondly imagined that their empire would endure unchanging for millions of years.

That, unfortunately, was the extent of Ateshga's collection. Twelve relics, not one of which came anywhere near what I wanted.

'Take your time,' Ateshga's imago told me. 'Feel free to examine the offerings at your leisure. If one might be so bold ... how much are you hoping to spend?'

'It doesn't matter, Ateshga. I'm afraid I'm just not interested in any of these ships.'

'Let us not be so hasty, traveller. There is much we can discuss. I don't even know which civilisation sent you, and we're already about to say our farewells.' Then he raised his head, cocking it to one side as if an idea had just occurred to him. 'If none of these ships take your fancy, might it not still be possible to come to a mutually agreeable arrangement? An upgrade, perhaps? I can sell you a replace-ment engine or field generator, a new suite of weapons or sensors.'

'Stripped from one of these clapped-out derelicts?'

'Not at all. I maintain a modest collection of spare parts inside the moonship. All are of impeccable quality.' He linked his hands together again, bowing slightly. The white face shaped an inviting grin. 'Why don't you tell me what you have for sale, and then we'll take a look at the wares?'

Purslane leaned over to whisper, 'I'm not sure about this. You came looking for a new ship, not spare parts. Shouldn't you stick to the plan?'

'Let's see what he has,' I said. 'Maybe we can salvage something from this after all.'

'Traveller?'

'I'm not going to open my trove until we know there's something worth haggling over,' I told the imago. 'But I can give you an idea of what's in there. Sensorium epics from the War of the Local Bubble, none of which are in general circulation. Technical documents and appendices from the Machine People. Seven logically consistent explanations for the Absence. My account of a trip to the Vigilance, and the time I spent inside the digestive system of one of the curators. A map of the Emporium Worlds, before the forced migration. Any of that tickle your fancy?'

'Most definitely,' Ateshga said. 'Please, come inside the moon-ship – I am sure you will find it most interesting. Are you familiar with the relics of the Second Imperium?'

'This and that.'

'Then you must not let this opportunity slip. Come, let us see what trinkets await you.'

Ateshga's ship touched and then penetrated the impasse of the moonship, a widening circle of blue-white energy delineating the interface of the two fields. Once within the impasse, he doused his own generator and moved to a position above the northern pole. The richly patterned skin of the moonship curved down into the pole, suggesting that those patterns flowed onto the inner surface. I did not know; I had never been this close to a moonship.

Ateshga's ship would barely fit into the northern hole. There could only have been a few hundred metres of clearance on either side of the ten-kilometre-wide aperture as his vehicle passed inside. I followed him without incident and came to a halt just to the rear of his faceted black ship. Golden light bathed us from all directions. A vast number of objects of various sizes and forms floated all around us, soaked in that opulent radiance.

'See anything you like?' Ateshga asked. 'Over there, to your left, we have the engine of a Forger cloud-shepherd. To your right, Sycorax armouring modules. Seen some use, but still as good as the day they were made.'

I had begun to answer him – to say that I needed time to look around, but that I was optimistic of finding something – when his ship vanished.

'This always looked like a bad idea,' Purslane said.

Ateshga's imago had vanished as well: we were alone on the bridge. I urged *Dalliance* forward, but as soon as my ship tried to move she reported unacceptable stress levels and went into an emergency drive shutdown.

'We're trapped.'

'I noticed,' Purslane said.

I looked at her with an exaggeratedly sweet smile. 'Any

constructive suggestions, beyond saying we wouldn't be in this mess if we'd used your ship?'

'If this is how Gentian Line takes care of its guests, I should hate to be its prisoner,' said Doctor Meninx.

'What we do to prisoners,' I said, 'you don't want to know. Hold on, both of you. I'm taking her to the wall.'

The engine got louder, and then louder still. It screamed at us, even though the engine was in fact silent, even at maximum output. It was all down to ancient recordings, piped through to the bridge. Purslane had never quite approved of that melodramatic touch, but I think even she was grateful for the indication that the engine was doing its utmost.

It was not good enough. The ship began to shake, the console warning me that the engine was about to punch its way right through the hull and out the other side.

I instructed the ship to abandon her efforts. The drive note died back down to a purr and then to a sullen, reproachful silence.

After a long silence I said, 'Ateshga? Are you listening?'

'He won't answer,' Purslane said. 'He's already got what he wants: your ship, and everything in it.'

'I demand that you shoot our way out,' Doctor Meninx said.

Purslane turned to him. 'We're in a moonship, held in place by a force field. I suggest you give some thought to the likely consequences of using weapons in this situation.'

The avatar said nothing, but stared at her with peevish resentment, as if she was somehow responsible for the objection she had raised.

'Mind if I have a word with him?' Purslane asked.

'Be my guest, if you think he'll answer.'

She pulled the console closer. 'Ateshga? This is Purslane, the owner of *Silver Wings of Morning*. I hope you're listening, because what I'm about to tell you is of great importance. I had my doubts about your little operation from the moment you popped out of the atmosphere. Big enough doubts that the last thing I did, before allowing Campion to carry me into this trap, was to send an order to my ship. If she doesn't hear from me within a period of time I've no intention of disclosing, *Silver Wings* is to head away from this system at emergency acceleration.'

I looked at her with an expression that said I sincerely hoped she was telling the truth. Knowing Purslane, it was quite likely.

'Shall I tell you about the other order I gave my ship, Ateshga?'

she went on. 'She is to pulse a detailed message into the private network of Gentian Line. Yes, Campion and I are both shatterlings. That didn't even cross your mind, did it? If it had, you wouldn't have wondered which civilisation we were from.'

After a moment, Ateshga's figure reappeared. 'Anyone could make this claim.'

'But *I* am making it, and I am Gentian. You should have been more alert, Ateshga. You saw two ships and thought: they can't be shatterlings, because shatterlings always travel alone. Most of the time you'd be right, too. But Campion and I are not your normal run-of-the-mill shatterlings. We consort. That means we travel as a pair, and it means you are in unimaginably deep trouble.'

'You have given me no reason to believe you are Gentian.'

'I'm about to. In the meantime, I want you to think about what it means to make an enemy of us. There may not be a thousand of us any more, but there are still eight hundred and eighty, not including the two of us. That's eight hundred and eighty enemies you don't want to make. Enemies who not only know the location of your system, but who also have access to some of the fiercest weapons ever invented.'

'Threats mean nothing without proof.'

'I know, and that's why the Line has taken pains to enable any member to establish his or her authenticity. I know from the data in Campion's trove that a Gentian shatterling visited this system only a few hundred thousand years ago. That shatterling – her name was Mimulus – revealed herself to you with a password left by a previous member of the Line. Upon her departure, Mimulus left you with another password, a word of her own choosing, which she then registered with the private network. Since no shatterling has visited you in the meantime, that password remains valid.' Purslane took a theatrically deep breath. 'The word is *"passacaglia"*.'

There was a silence. The gowned figure hovered before us, its face frozen in a deeply inscrutable expression. This was just the form he chose to adopt for the purposes of entrapment. He might have looked similar, or he might have been embodied as a city-sized intellect floating just above the liquid hydrogen ocean that lay beneath the lowest clouds.

'You could have learned that password,' he said. 'You could have intercepted and interrogated a Gentian shatterling, or broken into their private network.'

'Or we could be exactly who we say we are,' Purslane said.

At last a flicker of doubt crossed the mask. 'Perhaps there has been a degree of misunderstanding.'

'More than a degree, Ateshga. The question is: what are you going to do about it?'

Dalliance lurched slightly as the field relinquished its hold. Cautiously I applied power, half-expecting to be pinned down again, but we were free to move. I cleared the southern pole of the moonship, emerging back into the vacuum bubble surrounding the vast spacecraft, and then reactivated my own impassor before slipping back into the crush of the Jovian's atmosphere.

'We're waiting,' Purslane said.

'Might we soothe matters with a generous discount?'

'It'll take more than a discount. The gift of a ship might begin to cut it.'

'But there aren't any—' I started to say.

Purslane shushed me. 'Then we'll talk about the people, crews and passengers of the other ships.'

'The people?' Ateshga asked vaguely.

'Let's get something straight. If I even begin to sense that you're not telling me the whole truth, I'll send an order to my ship telling it to alert the Line immediately.'

He shot back a hasty smile. 'Just seeking clarification, shatterling.'

'Then let's be clear. There were people in those ships. You might have killed them, but I'm guessing you opted to keep them alive, or at least in abeyance. It wouldn't have cost you anything, and you'd always have the option of selling them on down the line. Civilisations will pay a lot for minds stuffed full of ancient memories.'

'How many are we looking at?' I asked.

'I took good care of them,' Ateshga said.

'You can prove that by showing them to us,' Purslane told him. 'Bring them out, as many as you can.'

'That will take a little while.'

'No one's going anywhere in a hurry. When you're done with the people, we can discuss the other ships.'

'The other ships?'

'That thing I was saying to you just now, about not keeping anything from me ...'

'Of course. The other ships. I was going to get to those.'

I whispered, 'What other ships?'

'Wait and see,' Purslane hissed back.

It took a while, as Purslane must have known it would, but I do not think Ateshga could have arranged matters any faster if he had wanted to. The people were stored in ones, twos, clusters of three or more, and much larger aggregations. Each unit – whether it held one or a hundred individuals – consisted of an armoured, independently powered shell equipped with abeyance mechanisms and a small impassor; not large enough to swallow a ship but sufficient to protect a sleeping capsule.

Floating in the atmosphere after being liberated from the belly of the moonship, the units were a cloud of glassy baubles, each with a differently coloured and shaped trinket at the heart. Some of the units were very ancient, while others were of a design and antiquity completely unfamiliar to me.

They reminded me of the marbles in the playroom, in the family house in the Golden Hour.

'Are there any Line members here?' I asked.

'Gentian Line, honoured shatterling? Insofar as one is aware, no.'

'And other Lines? Did you dupe anyone else?'

'I believe there may be some members of other Lines – Chancellor, Tremaine, Parison and Zoril amongst them – although one cannot of course vouch for their provenance.'

I shivered, realising what a startling bounty I was about to receive. The liberation of members of other Lines – shatterlings who might already have been presumed to be victims of attrition – would inflate the prestige of the Gentians by a huge margin.

'Have the Line members – and anyone you think might be a Line member – moved into the hold of my ship. There'll be room if the impassors are turned off as soon as they enter *Dalliance*'s own bubble.'

'And the others?' Purslane cut in. 'What are we dealing with? Nascents? Lost starfarers from turnover cultures, I presume?'

Ateshga's voice quavered on the edge of some perilous truth. 'For the most part.'

'Here is what you'll do,' I said. 'Take whichever ship is large enough to hold all the subliminals. Pack them inside, with enough support machinery to keep them in abeyance until they get somewhere. Then send that ship away, programmed to stop in promising systems until they all find somewhere to live. We'll be keeping an eye on that ship.'

'Of course, of course,' Ateshga replied, as if this was all perfectly reasonable.

'Now let's see the other ships,' I said.

Purslane raised a finger. 'Wait a second. Who haven't we

accounted for, Ateshga? If we've cleared out the Lines and the turn-overs, who does that leave behind? And remember what I said about the consequences of holding anything back.'

I sensed vast hesitation in his voice. 'There is one. He has been in my care for some considerable while.'

'We're listening.'

'His name is Hesperus. He's an emissary of the Machine People.'

I shook my head in astonishment. 'You trapped and imprisoned a member of the Machine People, and you're still alive?'

'It was a simple mistake. Hesperus was posing as a biological traveller, so that he might journey unobtrusively. Had I known his true nature, I would never have detained him. Needless to say, once I had announced my intentions, I had no choice but to follow through. I could not let Hesperus return home.'

'Because you fear the Machine People even more than you fear the Lines,' Purslane said. 'And rightly so. You wouldn't want us as enemies, but getting on the wrong side of the Machine People ... that doesn't bear thinking about.'

'You've been playing with fire,' I said. 'Now give us Hesperus, before you make things any worse for yourself.'

CHAPTER FOUR

While we were waiting for the necessary arrangements to be made, Doctor Meninx stole over to my console and bent down to whisper in my ear.

His voice was a rustle of ghost-stirred leaves. 'I cannot impress on you strongly enough the mistake you will be making if you let that thing aboard. You must reason with Campion.'

'Reason with him yourself.'

'He will not listen to me. He knows what I am – a Disavower. I am expected not to approve of the robot. But you are different. If you raise an objection, he will give it due consideration.'

'And if I don't have an objection?'

'You must!' the avatar hiss-rustled. 'Let that thing aboard and no good will come of it!'

'He's not a thing. He's an envoy of the Machine People, lost and a long way from home.'

'It may well be a trick of Ateshga's – just some robot weapon he's trying to smuggle aboard your ship so he can hijack it and claim it back.'

'Do make your mind up, Doctor: are you against Hesperus because of your Disavower principles, or because you think he's not really a Machine Person at all?'

'I am against *it* on as many counts as I can think of.'

'The Machine People are more civilised than most human societies. Hesperus will just be another guest.'

'A wind-up toy that walks and talks.' The avatar's harlequin face creased into an expression of abject disgust. 'Haunted clockwork!'

'You won't have to associate with him if you don't want to. And if it really bothers you, you can always go into abeyance until the voyage is over.'

'The automatic assumption being that I should be the one to go into abeyance, and not the robot? Nice to know where I stand in the pecking order, at last! Relegated by a box full of mindless algorithms!'

'Doctor Meninx,' I said, as forcibly as I could manage, 'Hesperus is coming aboard. That's final. As shatterlings of Gentian Line, we could not possibly refuse to assist him.'

'It will not see me. You will tell it nothing of my origins, nothing of my physical existence, nothing of my beliefs.'

'Then I suggest you keep a very low profile,' I said. 'If Hesperus catches one of your avatars wandering around, he's likely to wonder who's operating it, isn't he?'

'You will tell it only that I am a scholar. It does not need to know any more than that. And I will not have it anywhere near my tank.'

'Why would he have the slightest interest in your tank?'

'Because,' the avatar said, 'when it learns who I am – as I am sure it will – it will make every effort to kill me.'

I pushed my hand into the open slot of the maker and closed my fingers around the sculpted handle of the energy-pistol. The newly minted weapon had the peculiar heft of something crammed with intricate machinery at abnormal densities. Levators allowed me to hold it, but it still had the mass of a small boulder. The adepts who made use of these weapons normally donned power-armour to overcome that residual inertia, but I did not wish to greet my guest looking like another robot.

I kept telling myself not to be so nervous, but as soon as I chased one fear away, another circled into place. No Machine Person had ever harmed a human being, so the weapon might have been regarded as both superfluous and insulting. But I was about to release a prisoner who not only possessed superhuman speed and strength, but who might have been rendered half-deranged by the time he had spent in Ateshga's care.

I just hoped that the weapon would leave more than a dent on that golden armour, if it came to that.

'We're sure about this?' Campion asked.

'No,' I said. 'Not remotely. But I think we've still got to do it.'

I palmed the control then stepped back briskly from the upright chassis of his cage.

The restraining field loosened its hold on him gradually, so that Hesperus lowered to the ground in dreamlike slow motion. His feet contacted the decking and his arms descended to his sides. He remained standing, but for several moments there was no indication that he was actually alive, rather than just balancing in that position.

Then his golden face, averted until that moment, lifted to look me in the eyes.

Hesperus was a gorgeous machine.

He resembled a man in a suit of close-fitting armour, though he was too slender for a man to have fitted inside that skin. His skull was all elegant planes and gleaming curves. The Machine Person was both coldly robotic and searingly human, like an exaggerated and stylised caricature of some stunningly handsome man from the fables of antiquity, rendered in gold and chrome. His eyes were densely faceted mechanisms, shifting from opal to turquoise depending on the precise elevation of his gaze. He had a broad cleft chin. His cheekbones were parallel flanges of chrome, pushing through his skin as if to serve as cooling elements. He had a nose, which appeared to serve no other function than to complement the proportions of his face. His mouth was thick-lipped, the golden lips parted to a narrow slot, with the chromed complexities of his speech-generating systems lurking behind. His skull was gold save for two coloured-glass panels on either side, just above the streamlined representations of his ears. The panels were fretted with a fine webwork of chrome. Behind the facets whirled traceries of pastel light.

The rest of him was no less beautiful; there was almost no part of him that was not aesthetically balanced with the whole. He had a sculpted chest-plate, a lean chrome abdomen, thin hips and long, muscular limbs. The only oddity about him, the only thing that did not look quite in balance, was his left arm: it was thicker below the elbow than his right, and his left hand was heavier, as if he wore a metal gauntlet over the gauntlet of his own hand.

It was the only part of him that jarred; everything else was harmonious. Machine People manifest as men and women, sometimes as children and occasionally as sexless, luminously metallic beings. Hesperus's face and build left me in no doubt that he had chosen to manifest as a man. He even had a suggestion of genitals, moulded in tasteful gold relief. But there was nothing crass or threatening about his appearance. Hesperus was exquisite, a thing to be admired and coveted.

But he was also alive. Also powerful and quick and – potentially – the most lethal and clever thing that had ever walked on *Dalliance*.

'Who are you?' he asked, his lips moving even though his face had appeared to be a stiff golden mask until that moment. His voice was a trilling, liquid susurration of birdsong, orchestrated into human speech sounds. It was the loveliest thing I had ever heard.

'I am Purslane, a shatterling of Gentian Line, part of the Commonality.' I indicated my companion. 'This is Campion, a co-shatterling of the same Line. You're aboard his ship now. You were being kept prisoner by an entity calling itself Ateshga. I have just negotiated your release.'

'Do you fear me, shatterlings?'

'Perhaps,' I said.

'You have no cause to. I would put that weapon away, if I were you. My intelligence is distributed throughout my body, so it would take more than one shot to kill me. You *could* hurt me eventually, but not before redirected energies had done a considerable amount of damage to your surroundings.' He looked around slowly, his neck pivoting with the eerie smoothness of a gun-turret. Shifting effortlessly to Trans, he said, 'Would it help matters if I spoke the language of the Commonality? I do not think it will pose me any insurmountable difficulties.'

We Gentians liked to think that no one else understood Trans quite as well as we did. Yet with one sentence Hesperus had demolished all my certainties.

'He's good,' Campion whispered. 'He's *very* good.'

'You speak Trans very well,' I said.

'For a machine.'

'For anyone not born to it. Please – no offence was intended.'

He regarded me with those glinting opal eyes. He tilted his head microscopically and they flared turquoise light. 'Nor was any taken, shatterling. Would you be so kind as to explain my predicament? You have mentioned someone called Ateshga, and the name means something to me, but I am still at a loss to understand how I came here.'

'Then you don't remember being caught?'

'I remember details, but not the whole. I recall that I was travelling.' He turned a palm to his chest, fingers stiffened. 'Unfortunately, something happened to my ship – a technical fault.'

'I can probably guess the rest. You dug into your vessel's trove and learned of the existence of a dealer in ships located in this system. Ateshga lured you in and then decided he could make more credits by stealing your ship than by taking your money.'

'Is that what happened to you?'

'Ateshga didn't realise he'd netted a pair of Gentians. We explained to him that if he didn't let us go, he could expect retaliation from the rest of the Line.'

'A formidable threat,' Hesperus said. 'How did you persuade him to let me go?'

'He had no choice once we were free: he'd have been in even hotter water if it became known that he was imprisoning a Machine Person.'

'In which case I owe you my gratitude. I am still sorry that you felt the need to bring a weapon.'

'I was worried that you might be disorientated.'

'Then your concern was understandable. My memory is damaged. Might I enquire as to the present date?'

'Six zero three three, four eighty-five, Crab standard time. You're in the Scutum-Crux Arm, in the Nelumbium System.'

'I was Ateshga's prisoner for a considerable number of years. The last clear date I recall – in the human system – began with a five.'

I glanced at the cage. He was still standing inside it, albeit free to walk out. 'Did Ateshga do something to your memory?'

'The errors I am experiencing are symptomatic of crude electromagnetic interference. He must have been trying to force amnesia on me, so that he could let me go without fear of the consequences.' He looked down at his arm, the one that was larger than the other, and then back at me. 'I am sorry, shatterlings. It must be quite unsettling to find me like this. Might I ask what you intend to do with me, now that I am in your care?'

'Our next stop – once we've left Ateshga – will be our reunion system. If it's anything like the last couple of get-togethers, there'll be other Machine People along as guests. If you wish, we'll take you to them. Otherwise, you can stay aboard our ships as long as you like.' I paused, mindful of the delicate matter I was about to broach. 'Of course, if you were to consent to visit the reunion, it would not hurt my standing in the Line.'

'Something can probably be arranged. Have we already left Ateshga behind?'

'There's still a little business we have to conclude before we leave.' I offered a hand, inviting him to step forward. 'You don't have to stay in that thing if you don't want to.'

He formed a smile. There was something stiffly theatrical about it, the mask too perfectly symmetrical to show human emotions with complete authenticity. But it was still a smile.

'Thank you, shatterling.'

'Call me Purslane.'

'Very well, Purslane.' He took a cautious step out of the cage, as if expecting the containment field to snap on again. He stretched his arms, turning to the left and the right as if to admire them. I thought of two things: the hunting cat I had once owned in Palatial, and the replica of Michelangelo's *David* which stood in one of the great hallways of the old household. 'It is good to move again, Purslane. I cannot express how unpleasant it has been to be Ateshga's prisoner. If I were inclined to revenge ...' He trailed off.

'Are you, Hesperus?' Campion asked.

'No,' he answered. 'Revenge is for biologicals. We do things differently.'

Doctor Meninx said nothing when he was introduced to Hesperus, but there was a world of calculating suspicion in his paper face.

'Ateshga and I were just discussing the other ships,' I said. 'Weren't we, Ateshga?'

'But you have seen all my ships,' the imago answered.

Hesperus moved into the imago's line of sight and said, 'I know what you did to my memory, Ateshga. You were sensible to wipe what you did.'

'I could have killed you,' Ateshga said.

'That will be taken into consideration when I return to my people and explain where I have been. In the meantime, in the interests of ameliorating your situation, I suggest that you do everything in your power to comply with the shatterling's requests. If she wishes to see more ships, show them to her.'

Ateshga said nothing. His ship slammed out of the atmosphere, carving a pillar of vacuum in its wake.

'Where's he gone?' Campion asked.

'Orbit,' I said.

'There were no ships in orbit,' Doctor Meninx said. 'We should have seen them even if they had the benefit of camouflaging screens. Nothing is *that* invisible.'

'We did see them,' I said. 'We just didn't *see* them.'

Campion settled into his couch and tugged his hovering console down until it was within easy reach. He punched commands and took *Dalliance* up and out. By the time we had cleared the atmosphere, *Silver Wings* was racing to meet us. We were above the equatorial plane of the Jovian, looking down on a sunlit face.

'I do not understand,' Doctor Meninx said.

'Me neither,' said Campion, staring at the planet. 'All I'm seeing is—'

'The ring system,' I finished for him. 'Show them, Ateshga. Campion and the Doctor are having one of their slow days.'

'Show us what?' Campion asked.

That was when the wave of change began spreading through the rings. Something awesome was happening down there. The very texture and brightness of the rings was transmuting, beginning in a perfectly straight line that then swept slowly around, moving with the eerie steadiness of a clock hand. Where the line had passed, the rings were darker and somehow more tenuous in appearance. Where before they had cut through the face of the planet like swathes of silver-white ribbon, now they resembled ribbons of smoke.

'That's where he hid them,' I said. 'Most of the particles are still chips of water ice, but the ships are much bigger. He tuned their impassors so that the bubbles had the same reflectivity as the rest of the particles. Now he's turning them off, so there's not so much light being thrown back at us.'

I had seen larger constructs; we all had. But beyond a certain scale, vast was simply vast, whether it was the hovering majesty of the jade cathedral on Lutetium, a Second Imperium moonship or the awesome bones of the Prior machinery near Sagittarius A.

There was room in those rings for a lot of ships.

'How many?' I asked, hardly daring to.

'Sixty thousand, give or take,' Ateshga said. 'I've been collecting for a very long time.'

'Take your pick,' I told Campion. 'If you can't find the ship you're looking for here, you may as well give up. I bet he's got at least one of everything.'

'I'm not sure now,' Campion said, with an abashed smile.

'Not sure about what?'

'That I actually want to get rid of *Dalliance*. So what if she's made me late for a few appointments? It's not as if she didn't get me there in the end, in one piece.'

'You have an excellent point, honoured shatterling,' said Ateshga. 'Why dispose of something when it has served you well? Of course, once you have specified your requirements, it will still take a little while to complete the refurbishment. The components must be sourced, and integrated into your ship ... I believe we are looking at months, if not years, of work. Do you wish to enter abeyance until matters are completed?'

'Nice try,' I said. 'I have a nagging feeling we'd never wake up if we put ourselves asleep.'

'We'll just have to take turns,' Campion said.

'That may not be necessary,' said Hesperus in his beautiful trill of a voice. 'I have no need of abeyance as you understand it. I am willing to supervise matters while the two of you sleep. I believe I can hold Ateshga to his guarantees.'

Campion and I looked at each other. I suppose we were both thinking the same thing. We had no evidence that Hesperus was an authentic envoy of the Machine People. Given Ateshga's demonstrated treachery, Hesperus might very well be a plant, a last-ditch stratagem for regaining control of us.

'You can trust me,' he said, as if reading our thoughts. 'Now and for ever.'

'We can't be certain of this creature's intentions,' Doctor Meninx said.

Angrily I turned on the paper harlequin. 'Are you volunteering to stay awake, in that case?'

'That is not what I meant—'

'I do not blame any of you for harbouring suspicions,' Hesperus said. 'I also have suspicions. Do you really intend to return me to my people, or are you simply lying to gain my compliance? Were you complicit in my imprisonment?'

'We weren't,' I said.

Hesperus raised a calming hand. 'The point is, these doubts cannot be settled instantly. It will take time. For now, let me prove my trustworthiness by guarding you while Ateshga honours his obligations.'

'Could you take care of my ship as well, and make sure Ateshga doesn't cut any corners?' Campion asked.

His eyes gleamed turquoise as he turned to face the imago. 'Corner-cutting will not be an option, I assure you.'

Purslane and Hesperus were facing each other, seated on opposite sides of a low gaming table. Tiny spectral armies stalked a shadowy landscape wreathed in a cloak of mist and gunpowder. The two gamers were commanding their battalions with subtle hand gestures, like expert puppeteers.

'Any sign of Doctor Meninx?' I asked, having just whisked up-ship from the propulsion chamber.

'Still asleep, or whatever he gets up to in that tank of his,' Purslane said.

'That's a shame.'

'Isn't it.'

Hesperus made a series of complex gestures, breaking his battalion into countless little divisions. Purslane pouted as they overran her forces, swarming amongst her men like rampaging insects. A little flag waved from a smoke-girdled summit. I thought of Count Mordax's Ghost Soldiers, storming the Kingdom on their pale, bony horses.

'Looks like he's beaten you again,' I said.

'He always does,' Purslane said, leaning away from the table. 'I asked him to play down to my level, but he won't.'

'I would rather defeat you than insult you,' Hesperus said. 'Besides, the game is good practice for my memory. I have improved my short-term faculties since we last spoke, Campion.'

'That's good.'

Purslane rose and stroked a finger against the side of my cheek. 'That's enough fun and games for me, anyway. You and I have work to do.'

'The strands,' I said, with as little enthusiasm as I could muster.

'We can't put it off much longer. I really ought to whisk back to *Silver Wings* and start work on my side of the story.'

Putting it off for as long as possible was exactly what I had hoped to do. We were two days out from Ateshga; two hundred and two days after he had bowed to our requests. Thanks to Hesperus, the work had been completed more than satisfactorily. *Dalliance* was humming along at a whisker below the speed of light.

'I shall not detain you from whatever business you must attend to,' Hesperus said. 'But might I ask a question, Campion?'

'Go ahead.'

'It concerns your guest.'

'I've got a lot of guests, thanks to Ateshga.'

'I am referring to Doctor Meninx.'

'I thought you might be. Is there a problem with him?'

'I do not think Doctor Meninx cares for my presence on this ship. Is that a fair assessment of his feelings?'

I tried to shrug off his question. 'I can't say what's going on his head.'

'If I did not know better, I would say that he is a Disavower. That is one of the things I do remember. The Disavowers do not believe that machines have any right to be considered sentient. In their most extreme manifestation, they would seek to eradicate machine intelligence from the galaxy.'

'I don't think Doctor Meninx is quite that far down the road.'

'Give him time,' Purslane murmured.

'But he *is* a Disavower?' Hesperus asked.

'I don't think he's really serious about it,' I evaded. 'The Lines don't have much truck with Disavowers. Gromwell wouldn't have brought the doctor to our reunion if he suspected Meninx was a paid-up machine-hater.'

'Given the manner in which he has been delayed, one suspects that Doctor Meninx has decided that Gentian policy is no concern of his. Might he now be allowing his mask to slip?'

'The doctor had some misgivings about letting you aboard. They weren't specifically to do with you being a Machine Person, rather that you were an unknown quantity.'

'I see,' Hesperus said, as if my answer had told him a great deal more than I had intended.

'Really, it's not that big a deal. You don't have to see each other if you don't want to. It's not as if he poses you any kind of threat.'

'That is not my fear. I merely wish to establish cordial relations with your guest, in the hope that talking to him might shed light on some corner of my memory as yet unilluminated. Purslane told me that the doctor is a scholar, on his way to an engagement. That struck a chord with me, as if our trajectories might be similar.'

'The doctor was on his way to the Vigilance,' I said.

'The Vigilance,' Hesperus echoed, as if testing the sound of the word. 'I know of this, although I cannot say why. What became of his engagement?'

'Nothing. It wasn't possible to deliver him to them without throwing me off-schedule for the reunion.' I forced a half-smile. 'Look on the bright side, though: if I hadn't let down Meninx, I'd never have met you.'

'And I would still be a prisoner of Ateshga.'

'Precisely.'

'Then Doctor Meninx's misfortune is my great good luck, I suppose. I should like to know more of this Vigilance, Campion: now that the word has been spoken, it feels like a key to unlocking more of my buried memories. I am even more anxious to discuss my predicament with the doctor.'

'I can tell you all about the Vigilance,' I said. 'I was there. Would you like to see my trove?'

'That would be very kind indeed,' Hesperus said.

Seen from outside, as I braked down from interstellar speed, the Vigilance was a hole punched in the pale shimmer of the Milky Way, where it transected the Norma and Cygnus Arms. In infrared it was the hottest thing for a thousand lights, blazing out like a beacon. Visible light photons from the star at the heart of the Vigilance had been downgraded to heat, seeping out in all directions. Somewhere in between, they had given up much of their energy to the Vigilance's ceaseless information-gathering and archiving activities. The star was the engine in the basement of the library, a machine for turning hydrogen into data.

The Vigilance exists around a solar-type star with about a billion years left on the Main Sequence, or until a wormhole must be sunk into its core for refuelling. Once upon a time, that star almost certainly had a full arsenal of planets, moons, asteroids and comets, but none now remain. Every useful atom in the system has been reorganised into the component bodies of a Dyson swarm, numbering about ten billion in total. The Priors knew how to smash worlds and reforge their remains into the unbroken shell of a true Dyson sphere. Humans can do the smashing part, but all efforts to construct a shell of the necessary rigidity have failed.

The best we can do is to englobe a star in a swarm of bodies moving on independent orbits, like flies buzzing around a lantern.

At fifty hours from the outer boundary, I transmitted an approach request and identified myself as Gentian. There was no response. I slowed down to system speed and made a further series of approach requests. I was doing everything by the book, following the wise counsel of the trove. The distance narrowed to a handful of hours. I slowed again, to the point where it would take me a year of flight to cross the remaining distance. Save for brief catnaps, I stayed awake and alert for the entire time, not even allowing myself a dose of Synchromesh. Slowly that black sphere enlarged until it was swallowing half my sky, its horizon so flat it felt as if I had reached the wall at the end of the universe. At three light-seconds, the Vigilance deigned to notice me.

It was, technically speaking, an attack. The scalding energies that twinkled against *Dalliance* were enough to ablate metres of her hull before the impasse rose to full effectiveness. I had not run with the impasse raised because that would be construed as an approach with hostile intentions. As far as the Vigilance was concerned, this was no more than a polite challenge. They were simply testing my seriousness, determining whether or not I was someone it was worth doing business with.

It should have been enough that I had survived the challenge, but the Vigilance saw fit to up its entry criteria several times before I reached the swarm's surface. Escalating energies rained against my shields, stressing them to their limit. Those concentrated defence systems could have destroyed me many times over were I judged a real threat. I had been toyed with, teased, no more than that.

Presently a door opened. The orbits of thousands of the outer bodies had been adjusted so that a dark tunnel formed in the swarm, arrowing deep into its heart. My nervousness peaked. As the door sealed behind me, I was vulnerable to attack from all angles. As I fell deeper, the bodies of the swarm blocked off any view of open space. *Dalliance* reported that the space around us was crackling with information flow. The main beams were being routed around us, but occasionally a photon or two would ricochet off a stray grain of dust into *Dalliance*'s sensors.

The spheres were artificial worlds, the largest of them tens of kilometres across and the smallest not much larger than *Dalliance*.

Each was dark and smooth, their surfaces uninterrupted save for the circular apertures of signalling antennas. According to the trove, the spheres held concentric levels of processing machinery, wrapped around a fist-sized kernel of quark matter. Levators toiled to keep each node from crumpling in on itself. Data was organised in the layers according to reliability and access-frequency. Data of high provenance, or which seldom needed amending, was concentrated in the safe, stable depths of the quark kernels. It was troublesome to read in and out, but immune from accidental change or deletion, and safe against even a local supernova. Suspect or volatile data was kept in the intermediate and outer shells, occasionally shuffling higher or lower as it was reclassified. New data was fed in from the outside under the painstaking supervision of the Vigilance's curators. Very few living souls had ever seen one of those strange, slow creatures. It was presumed that there were at least as many curators as there were bodies in the swarm, but since the curators hardly ever needed to travel either within the swarm or beyond it, their true number could not be ascertained.

I had consulted the troves, but all they had told me was that there were many theories about the curators, and that few of the accounts could be reconciled with each other. The Vigilance thrived on collating information, but by the same token it seemed mischievously keen to spread misinformation about itself.

I was thinking about that, wondering what chip of dubious value I would add to the mosaic, when fields snared *Dalliance* and brought her to a halt relative to one of the larger bodies in the swarm. We had fallen about halfway into the shell: the light of the star was beginning to bleed through the 'floor' of swarm bodies below me, its yellow-white brilliance diminished to a deep, brooding scarlet.

A voice, more ancient than old-growth civilisations, deeper than time, slower than glaciers, boomed across the bridge in Trans. 'State the purpose of your visit, shatterling.'

I had rehearsed my answer countless times. 'I have nothing to offer that is worthy of the Vigilance. I am here only to open my troves for your inspection, worthless though they are, and to pass on the goodwill and blessings of Gentian Line, the House of Flowers.'

'Do you wish to access our archives?'

'Yes,' I said, for one never lied to the Vigilance. 'But I do not expect that access to be provided. As I said, I am here on a goodwill basis.'

'Please wait,' the voice rumbled, sounding like a distant landslide. 'Your case is under referral.'

I waited.

I waited a week. Then a month. Then half a year. Then six and a half years. All the while, *Dalliance* was pinned in place, going nowhere.

I was asleep when the voice boomed again, but I had taken precautions to have myself roused to full consciousness the instant anything happened.

'You will be admitted into the node. No further action is required on your part at present.'

One of the circular apertures in the swarm body revealed itself to be an irising door, wide enough for *Dalliance* to fit through. The fields cajoled my ship inside, prodded her down a narrowing shaft, then left her floating at the centre of a spherical holding bay. According to *Dalliance*'s inertial measurements – far from foolproof – we were still some distance from the centre of the swarm body. The walls around us were dimpled with smooth, perfectly round craters, the rims of which glowed arterial red. The fields had released their hold, but with the door closed behind me, there was nothing to do but wait.

So I waited. Eleven and a half years this time.

It may sound as if, to a shatterling, accustomed to crossing the galaxy in circuits lasting hundreds of thousands of years, eleven years is nothing. But our minds are not wired that way. Those eleven and a half years consumed lifetimes.

But at the end of it all, I was joined by another presence. One of the craters irised open and a vehicle began to intrude into the holding bay. It was bulbous, with a dome-shaped prow connected to an ovoid hull, and various smaller ovoids branching off the hull. It was about six times smaller than *Dalliance* – seven or eight hundred metres from end to end. The technology was more primitive-looking than I had been expecting. The brassy brown hull had a corroded look to it in places, mottled and scarred in others, and there were crude mechanical connections running between the ovoid sections suggestive of the docking collars on primitive spacecraft. As it cleared the door, the ship began to tilt, turning its long axis through ninety degrees. It did this with great ponderousness, as if it moved to a different, slower physics than *Dalliance*. Some change occurred to the domed part of the hull, the opaque plating becoming milky and then translucent, as if smoke was clearing from behind a window. Behind the translucence loomed a complicated structure, some kind of leathery, biologically derived machinery ...

The machinery was a face, looking out at me through the glass of a helmet. It was not human, but I could tell that it had been human, a long time ago. It was as if a face had been carved in a cliff and then subjected to aeons of weather, until the features were no more than residual traces. The eyes alone were ten metres across; the face ten times as wide. The mouth was a dark and immobile crevasse in the granite texture of the creature's grey-tinged flesh. The nose, the ears, were no more than worn-away mounds on the side of a hill. The head swelled at the neck and vanished into a huge body concealed by the connecting ring around the base of the domed helmet.

The eyes blinked. It was less a blink than the playing out of an astronomical event, like the eclipse of a short-period binary. It took minutes for the lids to close; minutes again for them to ooze open. The eyes were looking at me, but there was no focus in them, no hint of animation.

The figure drifted closer. From one side of the hull, a string of jointed ovoids became a grasping arm with fingers at the end. The fingers were as large as trees. They closed around *Dalliance*, and I felt their tips clang against the hull. The ship, sensing my mood, was wise enough not to take retaliatory action.

It turned out that the curator was only interested in touch. Over the course of several hours, he ran his hand along *Dalliance*, cupping and stroking her, as if he needed reassurance that she was not a phantasm. Then he slowly pulled back.

The voice, which I had not heard for more than eleven years, boomed again. It was as if no time at all had passed for the curator. 'There is just the one of you, shatterling. You have come alone.'

'It's the way we travel, except when we have guests. Thank you for letting me come this far.'

The giant being's face registered no change when I was being spoken to, but I had no doubt that I was being addressed by the curator. Whatever functions that mouthed served, the creation of language was not one of them.

The creature floated where it was, perfectly still save for the occasional blink of those monstrous, pond-like eyes. It blinked about once an hour.

'You have been very patient, shatterling.'

'It was told that patience would be necessary, curator.' Aware of how easily the Vigilance could be angered, I felt as if each word I uttered was a grenade about to be thrown back in my face. 'Is that the right term of address?' I asked.

'For you,' the curator answered. 'Do you have a name, other than Gentian shatterling?'

'I am Campion,' I told it.

'Tell me about yourself, Campion.'

I gave it my potted life story. 'I was born six million years ago, one of a thousand male and female clones of Abigail Gentian. My earliest memories are of being a little girl in a huge, frightening house. It was the thirty-first century, in the Golden Hour.'

'You have come a long way. You have outlived almost all the sentient beings who have ever existed, including the Priors.'

'I've been very, very lucky. Lucky to have been born into Gentian Line, lucky to have been able to live through so much time without experiencing more than a fraction of it.'

'To live through deep time would be considered unfortunate?'

'I didn't mean that, rather that I'm carrying a brain not so very different from the ones humans had when we were still hunter-gatherers. There are some modifications that help me process memories and the strands of my fellow shatterlings, but Abigail never touched the deep architecture. Our minds just aren't engineered to experience that much time in the raw.'

'You would go mad.'

'I'd need help.'

'You must wonder how we have coped. It is known that curators are very old, very long-lived. Unlike you, unlike the late Rimrunners, we do not have the luxury of time-dilation to make the centuries fly past.'

'You appear to be managing well enough.'

'You would presume to know?'

'The mere continued existence of the Vigilance is evidence that you have overcome the difficulties of extreme longevity. No other stellar-based culture has endured as long.'

'There would be no point in the Vigilance if it was ephemeral. Our watch is a long and lonely one. We always knew it would require great patience; a willingness to take the long view.'

'Are you as old as the Vigilance?'

'That would make me more than five million years old, shatterling.'

'I'm nearly six.'

'Except you aren't, really. You were born that long ago, but I doubt you have experienced more than a few tens of thousands of years of subjective time. You are a bookworm who has tunnelled through the pages of history. Is that not so?'

'That's an apt analogy, curator.'

'For me to be as old as the Vigilance, I would need to have endured all those years. That would make me one of the most ancient organisms in the galaxy.'

'For all I know, you may be.'

'I am not the oldest curator, but I am still growing. All of us are. In the dawn of our kind we found a pathway to biological immortality that depends on continued growth. There are other pathways, but this is the one we settled upon.'

'Are there curators larger than you?'

'Absolutely. You will not see them, though. They inhabit the largest nodes, with the most important kernels. Most of them are too large to leave now. Their heads would fill this chamber. They are beings of awesome wisdom, but they are also very slow. Nothing can be done about that, though: when synaptic signals have to cross distances of hundreds of metres, even the simplest thought may take several minutes to formulate. We find dealing with them ... taxing. But I'm sure you understand. From your perspective ... well, we'll say no more about that, shall we?'

I was not really surprised to be dealing with a giant, though it had taken me a moment or two to appreciate the true nature of my host. Many of the accounts in the trove spoke of the enormous size of the curators, although the details varied too widely to be of much use. When I left the Vigilance, I would add my contribution to that confusing picture. The next visitor might encounter something completely, bewilderingly different.

'Do you always live in that suit?' I asked.

'Not always. We breathe fluid, not air, although you could not be expected to know that. There are spaces where we may discard our suits and still survive, but it would be much too difficult to equip all the nodes with pressure-filled chambers. Eventually, we outgrow our suits. Then we must move to one that has recently been discarded by an even older curator. I have been in this suit for more than a hundred thousand years, and I still have some room for growth. Before me this suit held many other occupants. It must look old to you, but it is constructed very robustly. Many more will wear it after I have moved on.'

'My ship is considered old by the rest of my Line. But it works for me.'

'That's the important thing, shatterling.'

'Would you like to inspect the contents of my trove, curator? You won't find anything of interest in there, but as a courtesy it's the least I can do.'

'Is your trove portable? Clearly, I am much too large to fit inside your ship.'

'I can bring the trove outside.'

'That would be satisfactory. Emerge from your ship when you are ready. Take your time: we don't rush things around here.'

Half-suspecting I might need one, I had already instructed the maker to fashion me a suit. It was strange to feel myself encased by the claustrophobic, faintly masochistic contraption. Whisking is a million times easier.

The suit did its best to make me comfortable. I slipped through *Dalliance*'s long-forgotten dorsal lock, inspecting the bruise-raw, weapons-scarred hull as I pushed away into the vacuum of the node's holding chamber. Hexagonal repair platelets were already oozing from various points in *Dalliance*'s skin, linking together to form the lacy scaffold of a bright new epidermis. The trove was a faceted purple-black cylinder clutched in my right hand, with a gold interface collar around its midsection, where it normally plugged into the ship. It felt as if I was dragging a small neutron star around with me. The trove was brimming with data, knowledge and wisdom.

'Will that suit keep you alive for a long while, shatterling?'

'Long enough, I hope.'

'Then tell your ship to await your return. It can take care of itself while you are absent?'

'It's already done.'

'Then hold still. I will take care of you.'

The curator's hand moved towards me, the fingers splaying wide and then closing slowly, tenderly, around my tiny, squashable form. The suit creaked as the fingers took hold and began to drag me and the trove in the direction of the face. I had not noticed it until then, but there was a nozzle-like aperture in the ring connecting the curator's helmet to the rest of his body. A door opened in the nozzle and I was popped inside, into a weightless chamber the size of a small cargo hold. The door sealed and briny pink fluid erupted in, boiling at first before it had squeezed the vacuum out of the room. My suit pondered the ambient chemistry. The liquid was a soup, thick with long-chain molecules.

A second door opened and I drifted out with the tidal flow of the liquid. I paddled to recover my orientation. I was in the helmet, floating in the liquid space between the curator's chin and the glass. The curator breathed so slowly that it was like the ebb and flow of water at a lazy shoreline. I continued my drift until I was level with the awesome gash of the mouth, stretching away to either side of me, the lips curved like sandstone carved by underground rivers.

'Is this distressing for you, shatterling? You must tell me if it is distressing.'

'I'm fine.'

'Not everyone has been as comfortable as you, in this situation.'

'I don't think you mean to hurt me. You could have done that already.'

'I could mean to eat you. Have you considered that possibility?'

'Now that you mention it ...'

'I don't mean to eat you – not in the sense we are both imagining. But it *is* necessary for me to swallow you. You'll see why in a few moments. Be reassured that no harm shall come to you, and that your stay inside me will be temporary.'

'Then I shall take your reassurance.' The mouth widened by degrees, until there was room for me to pass between the lips. 'Curator,' I said, as I fell into that bottomless trench, 'I hope you don't mind me asking, but what guarantees do you have that I'm not going to do you harm, once I'm inside you?'

'Even if you destroyed this entire node, you would barely scratch the sum total of the data in our possession, and nothing valuable would be lost.'

'I might have tried.'

'You have been examined more thoroughly than you probably realise. We have a good understanding of the capabilities of your ship. It has weapons, but it is not warlike. And your suit contains nothing harmful at all.'

'And me?'

'We have looked inside you. We found only meat and bones, and a salting of harmless machines. The trove might be a bomb, of course, but that is a chance we shall take. No act of knowledge acquisition is entirely without risk.'

I was being carried down the curator's throat by the flow of swallowed fluid. Ahead of me, picked out in lurid pinks and mauves by the suit's lamps, the spongy door of an epiglottis hinged shut just as I was about go through it. I was going into the stomach, not the lungs.

I rode peristalsis all the way down, the walls of the curator's gullet squeezing and opening to propel the sac of fluid in which I floated. Eventually the narrowing shaft deposited me in a warm, liquid-filled compartment. I guessed that I was somewhere deep in his torso, probably in the lower abdominal region, but I had no idea in which organ, or compartment of an organ, I had arrived. The curator's internal anatomy might not bear much resemblance to that of a baseline human, even if one allowed for the differences in scale.

The peculiarities of the curator's digestive tract became apparent as I took in more of my surroundings. The chamber was more or less hemispherical, with the entry point near the pole of the half-sphere. The walls of the hemisphere were ribbed with stiff, glistening struts, radiating out from the door – some kind of bone or cartilage. The ribs flexed and eased on a very slow cycle, as if the curator's balloon-sized lungs were expanding and contracting somewhere above us, behind metres of abdominal wall and pleural cavity.

What was unusual about the chamber, what made me think it had no counterpart in my own body, was the floor – or wall – opposing the domed part. It was a sea of waving, undulating arms, like a grove of anemones. The arms were two or three times longer than me and they pulsed with hypnotic colours, flickering and strobing as they brushed against each other. Some of the arms were bent back on themselves, their tips vanishing into the luminous mass. I paddled closer and saw dark objects lodged in the gaps between the arms, pressed deep into the fleshy base in which the arms were rooted. The objects were cylinders, cubes and ovoids, and the arms that were bent over were attached to them, fixed by their sucker-like tips to the shells of the boxes or plunging into them via holes or gaps in their casings.

I was still carrying the trove. Without being told what to do, I gave it a shove in the direction of the waving arms and let it drift. A dozen or so arms flexed towards it, stretching to their fullest extent and puckering their tips like animals hungry for the teat. The trove fell within reach and the arms wrestled with it, squabbling over which of them should have possession.

'Welcome to my gut,' the curator said. 'This is an interface to my nervous system. There are others inside me, but this will suffice for our purposes.'

'Those other objects – they're also troves, aren't they?'

'Troves, or things very like troves. In most cases they were donated by their owners. I will not expect the same of you, but I am still curious about the contents of your trove.'

One of the arms fastened itself to the middle of the trove, contacting the gold interface ring. The arm shivered with colour, vibrant pulses racing from the tip to the fleshy root.

'Are you reading it now?'

'The process has begun, shatterling. It will take a while, but these things must be done properly. The data is not going any further than my head. I am a buffer between your trove and the rest of the Vigilance, for now. We have long been wary of data contamination.'

While I was distracted, three of the arms had reached out and made contact with my suit. I was being hauled in slyly, as if they did not want me to realise what was happening. I flinched and jerked myself free.

'May I ask some questions, curator?'

'There is never any harm in asking.'

But there was, I thought. There was potential harm in the most innocent act of data acquisition, as even the curator had acknowledged.

'There's quite a lot about the Vigilance we don't know.'

'Many of your kind have been here already. Did they not satisfy your curiosity?'

'There are still some pieces missing from the picture.'

'And you think you will make a difference?'

'It's my duty to try. My duty to the Line and the Commonality.'

'Then far be it from me to stand in the way of your enquiries, shatterling.'

I felt as if I was standing tiptoe on the edge of something treacherous. I had done well so far, if only because I was still breathing. I had been allowed entry into the swarm, into one of the swarm's processing nodes, and I had been given an audience with a curator. Very few envoys had got this far – at least not the ones who ever reported back.

'We've long understood that the Vigilance gathers information from across the galaxy, from the entirety of the meta-civilisation. On the face of it, this process looks omnivorous – you don't appear to favour one line of investigation over another.'

'Such an impression would be understandable.'

'But on deeper inspection, we've found hints of structured enquiry. Those travellers who have made it in and out of the Vigilance, both intact and insane, have found certain data sets prized over others. You value certain forms of information more than others, at least when your transactions are examined over deep time, across countless examples.'

'And the nature of this bias?'

'Andromeda,' I said. 'Specifically, the Absence. Taking the long view, the Vigilance can be seen as having a single, all-consuming purpose – even though that purpose is sometimes obscure. You're organised to gather every known snippet of data concerning the disappearance of the Andromeda galaxy and anything connected with that event.'

'Many civilisations are fixated on the Absence. It would be difficult for a galactic society not to be.'

I dared to shake my head, though I had no idea if the gesture was visible. 'Everyone thinks about the Absence, that's true. Everyone worries about what it means. But even the Commonality hasn't gone much further than that. A few observations, a few theories, but that's it. Mostly, we've learned just to get on with life. That might seem blinkered, short-sighted, a kind of denial, even, but what else can we do? Whatever's happened to Andromeda, it's bigger than anything in our experience. Even if we understood what had happened, we couldn't begin to do anything to stop it happening here. It's symptomatic of something so far beyond our conception it might as well be an act of God.'

'Perhaps that's exactly what it is.'

'God snatches a galaxy out of existence, as a warning against human hubris?'

'Even if it is the work of God – a hypothesis our data does very little to support – it would be inaccurate to describe the Absence in those terms. Andromeda may not be visible any more, but there is still *something* there. There are even some stars left over, caught outside the Absence when it formed. In truth, it would be better to call it the Occlusion.'

'The name's stuck, I'm afraid.' But I thought on what the

curator had said and reminded myself that he was correct. The Commonality's own observations concurred: Andromeda had not so much gone as been blacked out. Just as the Vigilance's Dyson swarm blocked out the light of the Milky Way, so Andromeda continued to mask the glow of the rest of the universe, all the way back to the fierce simmer of the cosmic microwave background. But the thing that was sitting where Andromeda used to be was not precisely a galaxy, either. It was more like a squat, black toad, a fat blob of darkness with the razor-sharp edge of an event horizon. But it was not a black hole. As the curator had mentioned, there were stars and globular clusters still circling beyond the fringe of the blob, and their orbits were not what one would have expected if they were travelling so close to a black hole's surface, where frame-dragging would have played a role. Those outlying bodies moved as if nothing had changed; as if Andromeda was still there.

No one had an inkling as to what that black toad really signified. But one thing was clear, ominously so: Andromeda was a galaxy much like our own. Life could have arisen there, as it had in the Milky Way. It was even possible that life had still been going on there until the moment of the Absence. The fear was that what had happened to Andromeda might happen to us, if we were not careful.

'Some of us think it's a protective measure,' I said. 'It's the Andromedans building a wall around themselves, to keep us out. They've watched us spread through our own galaxy and they don't like what they see.'

'A wall is also a prison. Would that not be somewhat self-defeating?'

'It's only a theory. I don't doubt that the Vigilance has better ones.'

'Oh, we do. Many, many of them. How could a wall have been constructed so quickly? It would have required synchronised activity on a galactic scale, beyond anything we can conceive of. How could we possibly be a *threat* to any civilisation capable of that degree of coordination?'

'I don't know.'

'Is it the Absence that interests you most, shatterling? Is that why you came here?'

'I came here to bring the blessings and goodwill of Gentian Line. Anything else is a bonus.'

When the curator spoke again, there was a warning note in his voice. 'You haven't answered my question.'

Sweat dappled my brow. 'I'm interested in the Absence, but only as a key to finding out more about you. Like I said, the Commonality prefers not to dwell on the Absence – there's no great hunger for new data, new theories, amongst the Lines. They don't want to think about it too much – it's like worrying about death, when you can't do anything about it.'

'Why are we so fascinating?'

'Because you're old, I suppose. In the Lines we speak of "turnover". We look down on galactic society and see civilisations cresting and falling like waves. We've grown used to the idea of being the only permanent fixture around here. Then we started paying attention to the Vigilance, and realised that wasn't the case.'

'We've been around a long time. It's not as if you've only just noticed our existence.'

'No, but for circuits we had you down as an anomalous curiosity, nothing more. We were wrong, obviously. The Vigilance isn't just a stellar culture that has beaten the odds of extinction. Everything about you points to a society that knew it was going to be around for ever and ever, and was going to do all in its power to make that happen. I've seen other Dyson swarms, but nothing approaching the single-minded efficiency of this one. You've been ruthless. You haven't left a pebble unchanged. And you, the curators – you're part of it as well. You've been prepared to alter yourselves beyond all recognition, to take massive steps away from the baseline humans you used to be.'

'You've seen stranger things than me.'

'I've seen things that ended up strange, like the Rimrunners. But they got that way as a consequence of near-random changes across millions of years. They didn't have a *plan*. I think you knew exactly how you were going to end up from the moment you started. You were going to become huge, slow giants, and you were never going to stop growing. And that's interesting to me, because it implies that the purpose of the Vigilance was set in stone long before the Absence happened. It caught everyone else unawares, but – unless I'm wrong – you were waiting for it.'

'We were as startled by the Absence as anyone. Nothing in our observations had anticipated it.'

'You were looking at Andromeda, though. You may not have been expecting the Absence, but you had a reason to keep your eyes on that galaxy.'

'It is our nearest neighbour of any size, therefore bound to merit attention.'

'There are other galaxies in the local group, some of which could be considered potentially viable for life. You showed some interest in those, but Andromeda has always been your main focus.'

'Then that is indeed a puzzle, shatterling.'

'We think that you found evidence of Prior activity – stellar engineering, Dyson englobements, that kind of thing. They weren't sending us intentional signals, but they were still giving away their existence. We would have been spacefaring for two and a half million years before they even knew we existed, so it's entirely possible that they used to think they had the Local Group to themselves. They'd have arrived too late on the scene to witness the activities of the Milky Way Priors, or else they were assumed safely extinct. Either way, our emergence must have been a cause for concern. The Commonality thinks that the Vigilance was instigated to monitor Andromeda, to keep tabs on the Andromeda Priors and determine whether they were a threat or a blessing. If it took millions of years to make that decision, so be it. You can't gauge the success of a galaxy-wide civilisation on a timescale much less than that. It could be that you were tasked to gather data over five or six million years, and then decide a course of action – up to and including a pre-emptive strike, an opening salvo in an intergalactic macro-war.' I smiled, more to calm myself than reassure the curator. 'Am I hot or cold, curator?'

'You have a theory that fits the evidence.'

'Well, almost. But if all you were supposed to do was monitor the Andromeda Priors, why the secrecy?'

'We are being very open with each other now.'

'I know – but there's no reason to think you won't tinker with my memory before I leave. Thing is, if the Priors were the issue, there'd be no need to be coy about it. They'd be a problem we all needed to know about – Lines and turnover civilisations included.'

'Secrecy might be more important than you realise,' the curator said. 'It wouldn't do for a single culture to take unilateral action, yet that could easily have happened if knowledge of the Andromeda Priors was widespread.'

'We could have stopped them, if it came to that.'

'Not necessarily. If a civilisation built a fleet and launched it towards Andromeda, there's no guarantee that the Lines would have been able to neutralise it before it arrived. And even if the turnover civilisation perished, the fleet would still be on its way, protected by time-dilation. Nothing would have been able to catch up with it, if it was moving sufficiently close to light.'

'Fine, so there's a case for secrecy. But turnover civilisations aren't stupid. Some of them would have made their own observations of Andromeda, and seen the same evidence of Prior manipulation.'

'The signs might have been subtle enough that it took the observational resources of the Vigilance to recognise them. In any case, turnover civilisations tend to be more interested in their immediate neighbours in the galactic disc than with what might be happening two and half million lights away.'

The curator had not denied an official interest in Andromeda. It might not mean anything, but it was at least a crumb of intelligence to take with me back to the Line. It would add little to what was already known, but it would at least bolster the existing lines of argument, adding credibility to the Commonality's pet theory.

'Thank you for discussing these matters,' I said, sensing that I had pushed about as far as was wise.

'It's our pleasure. We have always had great respect for the Lines, and value their confidentiality.'

'I will report every detail of my experiences here.'

'I would expect nothing less.' Above me, the ceiling heaved tremendously, like the sail of a ship catching the wind – it was as if the curator had given a titanic sigh. 'But now to business, so to speak. I have completed the preliminary examination of the contents of your trove.'

'I hope you didn't find the contents too disappointing.'

'You understate the value of your trove. There is data in it of at least partial interest to us.'

'I'm pleased not to have wasted your time. Feel free to copy anything that is of the slightest use to you.'

'And your fee for this service?'

'There is none. I was given licence to gift you with any data you desire as a token of the gratitude and friendship of Gentian Line, in the hope of continued good relations.'

'That hardly seems fair, shatterling.'

'It hardly seems fair to make you pay for data we know to be stale.'

'All data is stale. The photons reaching your eyes are stale. They tell you that you are looking at something real, but you have no information that the objects before you still exist. They may have vanished into oblivion the instant those photons took wing.'

'I take your point, but we still won't charge.'

'Then it is up to the Vigilance to make a reciprocal gesture. You have come here as an envoy, but you doubtless wouldn't turn down the chance to wander our archives.'

'No,' I said, as cautiously as I dared – fearful that the offer might be snatched away if I clawed at it too eagerly. 'I wouldn't turn it down.'

'I have been in consultation with my fellow curators. Provided your data passes certain rudimentary validation tests, we see no difficulty in granting you a temporary access permit. You would be at liberty to consult and record data in our top-level archives. You would be able to consult, but not record, data in the secondary levels. You would be permitted to commit data to memory, but only using normal mnemonic capture modules. Third-level and deep-kernel data files will not be accessible to you.'

'I would consider any offer to be above and beyond our expectations. What you propose is most generous, and I would be flattered to accept.'

'Very good, shatterling. With your permission, the trove will remain in my gut until it has been subjected to a comprehensive examination.'

'That's acceptable.'

'Good. You may leave via my lower digestive tract – the exit is opening now.' As I watched, the fronds parted near the middle of the floor to reveal a glistening shaft that had been hidden until then. 'You will not have to return to the faceplate once you have emerged from my rectum,' the curator went on. 'There is a waste-release spigot in my posterior armour.'

'That's ... very helpful,' I said.

'It might be unwise to jump to conclusions, but on the assumption that your trove passes validation, there should be no obstacles to issuing you with an immediate access permit. If you have no need to return to your ship, you can begin examining the archive immediately.'

'Thank you,' I said. 'You mentioned that the permit will be temporary. Can you give me an idea of when it will expire?'

'This is your first visit to us, shatterling. Our relationship has got off to a good start, but we must take things gradually. Will two hundred years be sufficient, just to begin with?'

I raised my drink to Hesperus, his gold face splintering into dis-organised facets through the wine glass. He was sitting on the other side of the table, with Doctor Meninx to his right and my fellow shatterling to his left.

'To you, Hesperus,' I said. 'To the safe recovery of your memories, to your reunion with the Machine People, to the future and to the good things we may accomplish as allies.'

'To Hesperus,' Campion said, emptying half his glass in a single swig.

Hesperus raised his own glass and nodded. He took a sip of the wine, enough to make it clear that he had really drunk it rather than just swilled it around in his mouth for appearance's sake.

'Thank you. It is very good to feel that I am amongst friends. You have been most gracious hosts.'

'All the same – if there's anything you need, anything we can do to make you more comfortable—'

'There really is nothing,' he told Campion. 'Save for the damage inflicted by Ateshga, I am in excellent working order. I am even beginning to recover some sense of my past.'

'It's coming back?' I asked.

'Slowly. The damage is great, but my repair routines are efficient and well evolved.'

'While we're on the subject of damage,' Doctor Meninx's avatar said, 'I can't help noticing that arm of yours.'

'My arm, Doctor?'

'Yes – the left one. The one that's conspicuously larger than the other. Or had that somehow escaped your attention?'

Hesperus shifted awkwardly, glancing at Campion and me in turn. 'Does it trouble you, Doctor?'

The harlequin flexed back in his seat. 'Why should it trouble me?'

'Because you raised the matter.'

'Only out of profound concern for your wellbeing.'

'It is most kind of you to show that concern, but I assure you there is no reason for alarm. I have detected no abnormalities in my functioning.'

We were in Campion's dining room, a few hundred metres aft of *Dalliance*'s bridge. Fake windows made it appear as if we were in a kind of gondola suspended under the gentle curve of her hull. Campion had even turned on the fake stars, creating the illusion that we were flying through a blizzard of suns, with stars slamming by on either side of the dining room, occasionally accompanied by little whirling orreries of planets.

'All the same, it is rather ... *odd*,' Doctor Meninx persisted. 'But we shall make no more of it. I have no wish to draw attention to your flaws: I am sure they are difficult enough to bear as it is.'

'That is very considerate of you,' said our robot guest.

After an uncomfortable silence, Campion said, 'I'm sure we're all very curious to know what you've remembered, Hesperus. Did you get anything from the trove entry on the Vigilance?'

Doctor Meninx's avatar leaned in Hesperus's direction, creasing at the waist like a bent playing card. 'What possible interest would you have in the Vigilance?'

'He's got just as much right to be interested in it as you have,' I said.

'I shall bow to the doctor's superior wisdom in this matter,' Hesperus answered, acknowledging Meninx with a microscopic nod. 'All that I know of the Vigilance with any certainty is what I have gleaned from Campion's trove. That has been a most rewarding exercise, but I still cannot shake the sense that I had some prior interest in the matter.'

'Could that have been the nature of your mission?' asked Campion.

'What mission?' I queried, before Doctor Meninx could get a word in edgeways.

'That may be the case,' Hesperus answered, with a certain diffidence. I noticed that he was scratching the tip of his thumb against the glass of the wine goblet, the thumb blurring up and down almost too quickly to see, as if Hesperus was unaware of the gesture. 'All that I can say for certain is that, beneath the scrambled chaos of my memories, I feel a driving imperative, a sense of some vital task that I must complete, and which has not yet reached cessation. But I could be completely mistaken. Perhaps I was simply a tourist, ambling his way from sight to sight with no greater goal than to accumulate memories and experience – much like yourselves, in fact.'

'But if you do feel that driving imperative ... maybe there's something to it,' I said.

'I cannot deny a sense of restlessness, as if I have delayed long enough.' He ceased scratching the glass with his thumb and tilted it gently, swilling the wine inside it, mesmerised for a few moments by the play of light and fluid, as if it was the single most fascinating thing in the universe. 'One can only trust that being reunited with my fellows will help quieten my concerns. In the meantime, your hospitality is the finest I could hope for.' He raised the glass. 'Another toast, I think. To the prosperity and longevity of Gentian Line. Long may it endure.'

Campion and I reciprocated with our glasses, chinking them together above the table. I looked sternly at Doctor Meninx until he followed suit.

'I hope you'll enjoy the Thousand Nights,' I said. 'I don't know how this reunion will compare with others we've held, but I can more or less guarantee that you won't find a better one hosted by any other Line. We've always thrown the best parties.'

'Will you enter abeyance shortly?' Hesperus asked.

'Campion and I have a little groundwork to cover before we can sleep.'

'They have stories to fabricate,' Doctor Meninx said, with unconcealed delight. 'Strands to edit, memories to delete, others to falsify, all to play down the extent to which they have consorted. Of course, I know the full and sordid truth, rendering the exercise rather pointless.'

'And we know you're a Disavower,' I said. 'Keep that in mind before you start blabbing to the rest of our Line – you might find the reception turns a bit frosty when everyone gets wind of what a nasty, bigoted specimen you really are.'

'The doctor makes it sound worse than it is,' Campion said, smiling fiercely. 'We're not trying to create false alibis here. We're just moving some facts around. It's probably a pointless exercise, but if we can keep it down to one or two brief encounters, maybe we'll get away with the Line's equivalent of a large slap on the wrists.'

'Does this not create risks?'

'Absolutely,' Campion said, 'but what choice do we have?'

'When you delete a memory from a strand – from the public

record, so to speak – what happens to the memory you retain in your head? Must it also be deleted?'

'No,' I said, ignoring the awkward look Campion was sending me. 'We don't delete those memories, although we certainly could if we wanted – the process is easy enough. As a matter of fact, Campion thinks we would be on safer ground if we did.'

'I am sorry,' Hesperus said. 'I did not wish to steer the conversation in an uncomfortable direction.'

'It's all right,' I replied, sighing. 'Look, Campion and I agree on ninety-nine things out of a hundred. But the one thing we don't agree on – all right, one of the *several* things – is what we do with those memories that don't fit the story. I say we keep them. Campion says delete them, so that we never give Fescue or Betony or any of the others anything to use against us. And, damn it, I see his point. However, I just don't think that an experience is worth anything unless you can remember it afterwards.' I gazed down into the bottom of my glass, empty now. 'To see something marvellous with your own eyes – that's wonderful enough. But when two of you see it, two of you together, holding hands, holding each other close, knowing that you'll both have that memory for the rest of your lives, but that each of you will only ever hold an incomplete half of it, and that it won't ever really exist as a whole until you're together, talking or thinking about that moment ... that's worth more than one plus one. It's worth four, or eight, or some number so large we can't even imagine it. I think I'd rather die than lose those memories.'

'I find your convictions admirable. I did not know the value of memory until I lost mine.'

'I think I need to adjust my tank chemistry,' said Doctor Meninx. 'All of a sudden I feel nauseous.'

'I would be more than happy to come down and adjust your tank chemistry,' Hesperus said.

'He threatened me!' shrieked the paper cut-out. 'Did you both hear that? He threatened me!'

Hesperus moved to stand up. 'I think it would be better if I retired. It is clear that Doctor Meninx cannot see beyond the ghoulish figments of his imagination. It is a shame, since I have found this conversation to be most stimulating.'

'Really?' I asked.

'Very much so. Only a little while ago – while we were discussing the origin of my people, and the hypothetical nature of my mission – something popped quite unbidden into my head. I cannot help but feel it is a memory of more than average significance. I hope you will not mind what I have done.'

'Mind what?' I asked.

Hesperus held up his goblet and rotated it slowly, so that the side that had been facing him came into clear view. Engraved into the glass was a tiny, densely detailed design. Even across the table, the intricacy of the picture was astonishing, its lines as bright and thin as laser-burns. I thought back to the way he had been scratching the tip of his thumb against the goblet; as I replayed the memory, I thought I could see him rotating the glass very slowly and precisely with the other fingers, using the thumb to scratch out a two-dimensional image in a series of precise vertical raster lines. While he had been doing that, we had appeared to have his full and undivided attention.

'Would it inconvenience you awfully if I kept the glass?' Hesperus asked.

CHAPTER SEVEN

I climbed the iron ladder up to the top of Doctor Meninx's immersion tank. Beneath my feet, the grilled decking throbbed with the ceaseless labour of pumps and filtration systems. Under the grillework was bottle-green glass, thick enough to afford only murky glimpses of the floating occupant. I moved forward to the front of the tank and knelt down. I unfastened toggles and folded back a section of decking on squealing hinges until it lay flat against another part, revealing an access cover in the top of the tank. Steadying myself so as not to topple over the side, I gave the cover a hefty anticlockwise twist. After several rotations I was able to swing it open away from me.

Under the cover was a circular hole bored clean through the glass, which was as thick as my hand, and under the glass was dark, bubbling liquid. I adjusted my position until I could put my face into the hole and into the water. It was not actually water, I knew, but rather a blood-warm chemical concoction that not only supported Doctor Meninx against gravity and allowed him to breathe, but also provided him with various nutrient functions, absorbed through his skin and those internal membranes with which it came into contact.

My poorly focused eyes peered into that nutrient soup and made out *something*: a large, dark form, barnacled in places, tapering at the front, with the suggestive gleam of eyes set into trenches along the side of what I chose to think of as the head. They might not have been eyes at all, but rather some other highly specialised sensory organ, or maybe even just a functionless growth of some kind. I think I saw a limb or flipper emerging from his flanks, but since I was looking into even deeper darkness at that point, I could not be sure.

With my face submerged to the ears, I said, 'I'm here. What is it you so badly needed to tell me in person, Doctor?'

'It concerns Hesperus.' His voice was a gurgling rumble that I could just about understand. 'What else?'

I pulled my face out and sneezed, then pushed it back into the broth again. 'What's he done to annoy you now?'

'I found out something about him. It was by accident, but my intentions were good. I wished to discuss something with him, to soothe the troubled waters between us—'

'I can just see you soothing troubled waters, Doctor.'

'Believe what you will. I know only that I wished to establish some common ground, so that we could at least be civil to each other during the rest of the journey. I made my way to the cabin you've given him. Have you ever visited him in his cabin, Campion?'

'Now and then. Why?'

'Have you announced your intention before arriving? Have you told him to expect a visit?'

I had to sneeze and pinch my nose again before I could answer. I kept my eyes shut now as his fluid was starting to irritate them.

'Can't say I remember either way.'

'If you were to attempt to surprise him, I don't think you'd succeed. His senses are more acute than we give him credit for. I'm sure he knows when you're on your way, by the cues you give off – the electrical field of your body, the noises you can't help making, the chemical signature of those forty thousand skin cells flaking off you every second you breathe.'

'Your point being?'

'I don't give off those signals. I mean, my avatar doesn't. It's a machine, but not like him. I don't think he feels it even when it's near. He certainly doesn't hear it coming.'

It was true: the avatar was silent as a ghost, except when it spoke. Even then there was something whispery and spectral about it.

'So you surprised him. What happened?'

'When I came through the door – which was not locked – he was seated at a table, preoccupied with something. It was strange to see him like that, but I suppose tables are as useful to robots as they are to humans – especially if those robots take pains to make themselves look like men.' The water gurgled suddenly, as if Doctor Meninx had drawn an especially deep breath. 'I could not see what he was doing, except that he had both arms on the table, and there were pieces of gold metal around them – curved parts, like the plates that make up his armour.'

I had an uncomfortable feeling now. 'Go on.'

'I announced my arrival, as politeness dictated. It was only then that he noticed I was there. Have you ever seen a machine startled,

Campion? I advise you to experience it once for yourself. It's a very *singular* thing to witness.'

I had to take my head out for several seconds now, wiping green scum from my cheeks, pushing lank hair back from my eyes. 'I'd be startled if you crept up on me,' I said when I had returned to the fluid.

'But would you have something you didn't want me to see? Hesperus did. In the instant he became aware of my presence, his arms moved with astonishing speed. They became a blur of gold. The metal pieces that were on the table vanished as if they had not existed. We both know what happened to them, of course.'

'Do we?'

'They were part of his armour – the casing for the left arm, I believe. The arm that is thicker than the other one, as if there is something under it, something he is hiding.'

'He's a robot. What could he possibly want to hide from us? That he's got machines and things under all that armour? Weapons? He *is* a weapon, Doctor Meninx. If he wanted to do something nasty to us, he could have done it already.'

'He was hiding something. I saw it.'

'You saw what he was hiding?'

'I saw that he was hiding something. What the thing was ... I did not get a good look.'

I knew he was lying, or unwilling to admit the truth to himself. He had seen something. He just did not wish to look foolish by saying it aloud.

'Look,' I said, trying to strike a reasonable note, 'it wouldn't make any sense for him to be hiding something inside that arm, would it? If he had something to conceal, he wouldn't draw attention to it by making one arm thicker than the other. He'd have made both arms the same size – that way, we wouldn't have noticed anything odd about him.'

'But you admit it *is* peculiar.'

'I admit there's a puzzle, nothing more. For all we know, he was damaged and had to swap his old arm for one from a different robot, which is why they don't match.'

'They aren't robots in that sense, Campion. He's a machine at least as sophisticated as any ship you've ever seen. They can be any shape they wish. If he damaged part of himself, he could easily repair it so that it matched seamlessly with the rest of him. If he was forced to incorporate external parts, he could adapt those as well.'

'So perhaps we caught him halfway through a transformation. He got damaged, had to graft a new arm on, and now he's making it fit in better with the rest of him. That's what you caught him doing: tinkering with his arm.'

'Why would that startle him?'

'Because it's private? Neither of us has any idea what goes on in his head.'

'I do. Nothing at all is what goes in there. Just dumb computation, the endless shuffling of symbols.'

'In which case he can't very well have been startled, can he?'

'I'm not telling you this for my health, you know. He may not be conscious, but he can plot and scheme like a fox. He may just be following a program laid down thousands of years ago. But if that program instructs him to do something devious, something against your best interests . . . are you just going to pretend it can't happen?'

'What are you suggesting I should do?'

'Confront him, before it's too late. Find out what he really has under that armour.'

'You make it sound as if you're expecting to find a bomb.'

'I didn't see a bomb.'

'So what *did* you see, Doctor?'

'Skin,' he said. 'Human skin, as I live and breathe.'

'That just isn't possible.'

'I know what I saw, Campion. Your guest is not what he claims to be. The only remaining question is: what are you going to do about it?'

CHAPTER EIGHT

Campion whisked over to *Silver Wings of Morning* and told me what he had just learned from the aquatic. I had my doubts about the doctor's reliability as a witness, but I knew that we would have no choice but to challenge Hesperus. My heart was rising in my throat as we whisked back to *Dalliance*, thinking of the confrontation ahead of us.

As it happened, Hesperus spared us the worst of it. He was waiting when we emerged from the whisking chamber, as if we had always had this appointment.

'Were you on your way over to see me?' I asked, trying to sound as natural as possible.

'I would have crossed over if you had not come.' He stood at the door, his arms hanging at his sides. 'I hope you would not have minded.'

'Of course not,' I said.

'There is something I feel I must bring to your attention.' Hesperus looked at Campion and me in turn. 'I should have disclosed it sooner, but I confess I did not know quite what to make of the matter. I hope you will not be distressed.'

'Distressed, Hesperus? Why?' I asked.

Campion coughed lightly. 'Actually, there's something we wanted to discuss with you—'

'Is it my arm?'

Campion glanced at me, as if I was expected to be taking the lead even though it was him who had come to me with this information.

'Tell him,' I whispered.

'We were wondering—' Campion began.

'I presume Doctor Meninx brought it to your attention?' Though neither of us spoke, or gave any visible reaction I was aware of, Hesperus still nodded as if we had answered in the affirmative. 'I feared as much. I could not be certain that he had seen enough to raise suspicions, but I realise now that he must have. I do not blame him for talking to you. In his shoes, I would have had similar fears. He could have spoken to me directly, of course.'

'Doctor Meninx was a bit taken aback,' Campion said.

'What did you want to tell us?' I asked.

'The same thing you wish to know: what is the matter with my arm?'

Campion said, 'Doctor Meninx saw you examining something, but he couldn't tell what it was.'

'It must have been rather distressing for him, as it was for me,' Hesperus replied.

'For you?' I asked.

'I was as surprised by my discovery as Doctor Meninx. Even now, I do not quite know what to make of it.' The metal mask of his face had composed itself into a calm, watchful expression, as if Hesperus had already surrendered to his fate. 'Would you like to see what lies under the skin of my arm? The plating is only loosely attached.' Before waiting to hear what Campion and I might have to say in reply, Hesperus bent his left arm at the elbow and took hold of a section of plating with his right hand. It came loose and clattered to the floor. He removed another piece, and another, until only the hand remained covered. Then he took hold of the hand and tugged the jointed gauntlet away, as if he had removed a glove.

From the elbow to the tips of his fingers, his forearm appeared to be completely human. It was muscular and masculine, covered in dark skin and a lustre of sweat. The skin on his palm and on the underside of his fingers was slightly paler. As he rotated the arm for our inspection, flexing the fingers, I could see the hairs on the back of his hand, the cuticles of his fingernails, the veins under the skin.

'It is as real as it appears,' Hesperus said, while we said nothing at all. 'It is human skin, over human musculature.' Slowly and deliberately, he scratched the thumb of his right hand against the wrist of his organic arm, drawing a bead of blood. 'It bleeds. And heals, too. That is what I was ascertaining when I was disturbed by Doctor Meninx. I had scratched it a day earlier and was intent on gauging the degree to which the wound had repaired itself.'

Campion was the first to say anything. 'You talk as if you don't know what that thing is.'

'Did I not tell you that I was surprised by my discovery?'

'How could you not know why that arm's the way it is?'

'I already told you that I know next to nothing about myself. It is a miracle I even remember my name. Do you imagine I was intent on concealing this from you?'

'But you did conceal it,' Campion said.

'Only because I wished to understand it before I brought it to your attention. From the moment I regained movement, I was troubled by the mismatch between my arms. I tried to peer through the plating, but I am opaque to my own sensors. Eventually I steeled myself to remove some of that plating, so that I might glimpse the mystery for myself. At first I could not believe . . .' It was the first time I had heard him falter. 'I hope you will not be offended when I say that I was disgusted at what had been done to me. Not because I am repelled by the organic, but because the organic has no place inside me. You, I think, would be rightly repelled were you to wake up and scratch your own skin and find the gleam of metal beneath it. Yet I convinced myself that there must be a rational explanation for it, one that would satisfy you as well.' Hesperus lowered the arm slowly. 'But there is none. I can offer no explanation for the arm's presence.'

'Could you have been damaged?' I asked. 'Maybe you lost the original arm, and the only replacement available was from a human cadaver. You grafted it on until you could be repaired properly, and then forgot about the accident.'

'We would never have cause to do such a thing. Were I to lose my arm, I could repair myself in short order provided I was given access to the necessary raw materials – metals, plastics, aspic-of-machines. If raw materials were not in abundance, I could allocate enough of my existing mass to effect the repair with little impairment to my functioning. I would not need to grub around cadavers.'

'So Ateshga did it, not you,' Campion said. 'He damaged you and then fixed you up with an organic part, not knowing you could repair yourself.'

'I wish that could be the explanation, but unfortunately I know it cannot. The arm is an integral part of me. Once the casing was removed, I was able to peer deeper into the structure. I established that beneath the flesh and muscle is essentially the same mechanical skeleton you would find inside my other arm.' He flexed his fingers again. 'I could still do great harm, if that was my intention. True, the skeleton has been modified to mimic the architecture of human bone and form a support matrix for the organic outgrowth. It has also been augmented with devices whose function I cannot elucidate, but which appear to supply the organic components with the chemicals they need to stay alive.'

'What are you saying?' I asked. 'That the arm was grown deliberately, from the inside out?'

'I see no other explanation, Purslane. I have already told you that
I am capable of repairing myself. It is also true that it would be
within my capabilities to grow this arm.'

'Why would you have done that?' I asked.

Hesperus looked sad. 'Now we enter the realm of speculation, I
am afraid. If I could give you an honest and unambiguous answer, I
would not hesitate to do so. But I can only draw the same conclusions
as you.'

'Could someone have forced this transformation on you?'
Campion asked. 'Coerced you to do it, for some reason or another?'

'One struggles to imagine why. One also struggles to imagine any
circumstances under which I might be coerced to do anything.'

'You can understand why I'd much prefer it if you had been
coerced.'

'Because if coercion was not involved, then the transformation
can be presumed to have taken place voluntarily? Yes, that alternative
had not escaped me.' Hesperus looked with what appeared to be
renewed revulsion at his arm. 'I should like it if I might be permitted
to replace the metal casing.'

'You're as upset by it as the rest of us,' I said, wonderingly.

'Doctor Meninx was right to be disturbed.'

'You can hide it, if you want,' I replied, 'but I'm not upset by it.
It's just another part of you. If it exists, it exists for a reason – even
if we can't see it yet.'

Campion shot me a *speak for yourself* look.

Hesperus slipped the glove back over his fingers, then knelt to
recover the discarded gold plates. He snapped them into place with
astonishing speed, as if anxious to rid himself of the view of that
arm as quickly as possible. The arm soon looked as it had before, but
now that I knew what was underneath it I could only think of that
skin and muscle trying to force their way through the metal.

'What now?' Campion asked quietly.

'Hesperus and Doctor Meninx still need to clear the air between
them.' I looked around warily, just in case one of the doctor's papery
avatars had crept up on us while we were preoccupied. Seeing that
we were alone, I smiled awkwardly. 'Campion can speak to him first,
Hesperus. Then I suggest that Meninx pays a visit to your cabin and
gets the story from the horse's mouth.'

'Except there is no story,' Hesperus said.

'Tell him what you've told us and he'll have no grounds for complaint. You came to us on your own, after all. That counts in your favour, as far as I'm concerned.'

'If my presence is no longer desirable, I would be glad to return to the cage.'

'No, that won't be necessary.'

Slowly Campion held up a hand. 'Wait – let's not rush ahead of ourselves. We may not suspect Hesperus of any conscious wrong-doing, but that arm's still a cause for concern. Until Hesperus can explain it, until he can rationalise it, I'm not sure I'm exactly thrilled by the idea of him walking around. Maybe it wouldn't be such a bad idea for him to go back into the cage, on a voluntary basis—'

'I have no more intention of hurting you now than I did before I learned about the arm,' Hesperus said.

'I know – I believe you. But what if the arm has other ideas?'

I shook my head disappointedly. 'It's a lump of meat, Campion – it can't act independently of Hesperus. Just because you're unnerved by it doesn't mean it's going to creep into your room and strangle you at night. He isn't going back into the cage. If you don't want him on *Dalliance*, he's more than welcome aboard *Silver Wings*.'

'I didn't mean that.'

'That's what it sounded like. He's our guest and we agreed to help him piece together the puzzle of his past. The arm's just another clue, that's all.'

'I have no wish to cause a rift between you,' Hesperus said.

'Oh, this isn't a rift,' I said haughtily. 'This is barely a tiff. Not even on the radar. Campion and I are agreed – you'll stay out of the cage. But since we're all going to be entering abeyance shortly anyway, the point is pretty much moot. You can switch yourself off, or whatever it is you do, can't you?'

'I can shut down my core functions, although housekeeping tasks will remain active.' He cast a sidelong glance at his now-sheathed arm. 'It is apparent to me now that I must keep the arm alive, which would not be possible were I to go into total shutdown. Starved of oxygen, it would begin to decay.'

I nodded emphatically, trying to rid my mind of the idea of that arm turning into a rotten, gangrenous mass while it was still attached to him.

'No, the arm has to stay alive – it's the only way we'll ever find out anything about it – or you, for that matter.'

'I also suspect that the arm is a key to my true identity, or the true nature of my mission,' Hesperus said. 'What I cannot grasp is why I made no effort to conceal the transformation by retaining perfect symmetry between my left and right sides. It is almost as if I had no need for subterfuge. The armour that encases the skin could almost be viewed as a barrier, to protect it during growth.'

'We'll get to the bottom of it,' I said, with more assurance than I really felt. If my years as a shatterling had taught me anything, it was that not all questions had answers. Societies had reduced themselves to radioactive dust because they could not accept that single unpalatable truth.

Shatterlings were supposed to be a bit cleverer than that.

CHAPTER NINE

'It's not good,' I said, after I had run every possibility through *Dalliance*'s course plotter.

'How not good?' Purslane asked, leaning against a floating console, one foot tucked behind the other.

'Fifty-five years. That's how late we're going to be. Even if you were to push *Silver Wings* to the limit and leave me to make my own way there, you still wouldn't shave more than a year off that figure.'

'Fifty-five years does not sound so excessive when it has already been two hundred thousand years since your last reunion,' Hesperus said, staring up at the huge map of the galaxy painted on my displayer, marked with the winding red line that showed our progress to date. The details of this final part of our circuit – our stopover around the Centaurs' world, our detour to Ateshga and now the last sprint to the reunion – had been enlarged below the main image, since a few hundred lights was barely a scratch against the vast territory we had already crossed. 'Or am I mistaken?'

'No, you're not mistaken,' I said. 'In any other situation, we wouldn't lose a wink of sleep over fifty years, or even a hundred. But you're not supposed to be this late for a reunion. No one ever shows up precisely at the agreed time, but most of the Line members will have arrived within a year or two. There'll be a handful of stragglers who come in somewhere inside the first five years, and one or two who get there inside ten, but they'll be looked on sternly. Anyone showing up later than that will either have had prior dispensation to be late, or they'd better have a cast-iron excuse.'

'Which we don't,' Purslane said.

'You could not have been expected to anticipate Ateshga's treachery,' said Hesperus.

'No, but Ateshga didn't end up costing us all that much time. The mistake was placing too much faith in the Centaurs.' Purslane was giving me a dark look as she said this.

I held up my hands in mock surrender. 'I admit it, all right? The horses were a bad idea. The point isn't to pick over my mistakes but to see how we can make the best of a bad situation. I'll get the Doctor Meninx business out of the way first: let Fescue and the others have their pound of flesh. Then I'll wheel on Hesperus and show them what a good, industrious Gentian I've been.'

'And me?' Purslane asked. 'Do I get to share in any of your glory?'

'Only if you're prepared to admit we consorted. Otherwise it could get a little tricky.'

'They'll work out we consorted when we both show up late. No point even thinking of hiding that.'

'I suppose you've got a point there.'

Purslane crossed her arms. 'Yes, I do. So we'll both be taking credit for Hesperus.'

'For my part,' Hesperus said, 'I will speak well of you, and of everything you have done for me.'

'You'll have your work cut out by the time I've finished stating my manifold grievances,' said Doctor Meninx.

'You'll only have a thousand days and nights,' I said, 'so I'd get an early start if I were you.'

The avatar's expression turned furious. 'You would do well not to mock me, shatterling.'

'Mocking you was the furthest thing from my mind, Doctor.' I clapped my hands cheerily. 'Now: the practical arrangements. Purslane and I will be entering abeyance as soon as we've finished editing our strands, which shouldn't require more than a day or so. Doctor Meninx: I presume you'll be putting yourself asleep until we reach the reunion system?'

'What I do in my tank is my own business.'

'All I was going to ask was, is there anything you would like Hesperus to keep his eye on while the rest of us are under?'

'Keep his *eye* on?' the avatar asked, with instant suspicion.

'I will not be entering abeyance,' our golden guest informed the avatar. 'I have already volunteered to assist Campion by monitoring his other sleepers, ensuring that nothing untoward happens to them. I would be happy to extend the same courtesy to you, Doctor Meninx.'

'You will do no such thing!' The avatar looked at Campion with a mixture of indignation and real fear. 'He must not come near my equipment, shatterling! He has *designs* on it!'

'I have no designs on you or your equipment,' Hesperus said. 'If

I wished you harm, Doctor Meninx, you would already know it. I was only offering a kindness.'

I raised a calming hand. 'Easy, Hesperus – I know you meant well, but from the doctor's point of view it would probably be better if you didn't interfere.'

'As you wish.'

'You're being very stupid,' Purslane told the avatar.

'The stupidity lay in entrusting myself to Gentian Line. Everyone told me I'd be better off with the Marcellins.'

Hesperus suddenly looked interested. 'What exactly was it you wanted with the Vigilance?'

'Many and various things, none of which are of the slightest concern to you.'

'There's no reason not to tell us,' I said.

'You have never asked me before – why now?'

'I don't know. Because Hesperus is curious. Because I never thought to ask you before. I'd had enough of the Vigilance on my last circuit – all I wanted to do was drop you off and get away from those giants as quickly as possible.'

'We shouldn't press Doctor Meninx,' Purslane said. 'He's a scholar and entitled to his privacy.' She was using reverse psychology, knowing that our intellectually vain guest would not be able to resist the bait.

'Well, if you *insist* on knowing,' the avatar said, waiting a beat until it was certain it had our undivided attention, 'the principal focus of my enquiries is the Andromeda Priors. In common with the Vigilance, I hold that the Absence is the result of organised activity by alien sentients. Intentionally or otherwise, they have caused something to happen to their galaxy. As a sentient, resident in a similar spiral galaxy, I naturally have at least a passing curiosity concerning the event in question. If the Andromeda Priors did something foolish, then it is in our interests not to repeat that mistake. It is my strenuous conviction that the Vigilance has become too engrossed with the acquisition and cataloguing of data to take a step back and see what that data actually reveals. A lone scholar, dedicated to his task, might be able to see patterns, inferences, that the Vigilance has failed to detect. That was my hope. That is still my hope, in the unlikely event of my ever reaching my destination.'

'I share your concerns,' Hesperus said.

'Really?' the avatar asked, sounding bored.

'Really. I cannot deny that I felt a flicker of recognition from the moment the Vigilance was first mentioned. My conviction has only grown stronger since then. Could it be that I was sent to this sector on a quest similar to your own?'

'To gather information on the Priors?' Purslane asked.

'Possibly. Or to learn something else known to the Vigilance.' Hesperus paused. 'Might I ask you something, Doctor Meninx, from one lost scholar to another?'

'Ask away,' the avatar said idly.

'Does the phrase "House of Suns" mean anything to you?'

Something passed across the paper face, as quickly as the shadow of a cloud on a sunny day. 'And if it did?' the figure asked.

'I would ask what those words mean to you.'

'The words mean nothing. If they had some significance, I would have heard of them.'

'Where did you hear of the House of Suns?' Purslane asked. 'It sounds like a Line, like the House of Flowers or the House of Moths. But there's no such Line as the House of Suns.'

The golden face turned to address her. 'It must have meant something to me once, but now I cannot say. All I am certain of is that the phrase is in some way related to the Vigilance: the two chime against each other, as if they once shared some obvious connection.'

'What did the trove say?' I said.

'Nothing. Which is to say, that phrase has occurred a great many times, in a great many societies, but none of the instances appear to be the thing I am looking for. I think I would know it if it were; there would be a sense of rediscovery.'

'The phrase means nothing,' Doctor Meninx said.

'Just because you haven't heard of it?' Purslane asked.

'It's immaterial. The Vigilance would never have entertained him anyway. They won't deal with machines. Machines bring the diseases of machines: the infections and parasites that infiltrate and corrupt archives, intentionally or otherwise. That is why Machine People have always been forced to utilise human proxies in their affairs with the Vigilance. Is that not so, Hesperus?'

'Exactly so, Doctor Meninx.'

'Then I need hardly point out that your quest would have been futile. They would never have admitted one such as you into their data sanctums. You would have been better off staying in the Monoceros Ring.'

'Unless this objection was already anticipated,' Hesperus said, as if a thought was taking shape as he spoke. 'Could it be, Doctor, that the Machine People required direct access to the Vigilance, without the intercession of human proxies? Could it be that my mission was so sensitive that only I could view the archives?'

'You would still have been turned away – or dismantled.'

'Perhaps not.' Hesperus lifted up his left arm and removed the golden plating, exposing the organic forearm that had already caused Meninx so much distress. 'It may be that you have solved the mystery, Doctor. When I left the Monoceros Ring, my precise objective could not have been known to me – any more than you knew exactly what you would be doing when you originally left your homeworld. Later on, it must have become clear that it was necessary to consult the Vigilance. That was why I began to disguise myself, to assume the form of a biological human. I must have begun with this one limb as a proving exercise, to ensure that the work could be completed satisfactorily, before proceeding with the complete transformation.'

'Convenient supposition,' Doctor Meninx said, but he did not sound completely sure of himself.

'Makes a kind of sense to me,' I said. 'Hesperus did the one arm, then got waylaid by Ateshga before he could change the rest of himself. He wasn't disguising himself to blend in with the rest of humanity, but just to get past the Vigilance and through to their archives. Do you reckon it would have worked, Hesperus?'

'I suppose I must have been confident of success.'

'But there's so much of you you'd have had to conceal,' Purslane said. 'You might have been able to look human, but I don't see how you'd have been able to pass any kind of examination.'

Hesperus put the plating back on his forearm. 'I can only speculate that I had already given thought to this problem. Clearly, much of my existing cognitive volume would have been given over to biological componentry – muscle and sinew – requiring that I compress or discard certain faculties for the duration. My skeleton would have been mechanical, and dense with processors, but it could also have been embedded with various devices capable of tricking scanning systems into thinking they were seeing bone and marrow. All the same, I would have been intensely vulnerable to both injury and detection. The risk would not have been taken unless it was imperative to access that information.'

'If they'd found you out,' Purslane said, 'there's no way the Vigilance would ever have dealt with machines again – even via human proxies. You would have known that, and yet still considered it worth the risk.'

'It must have been something very, very important,' Hesperus said, sounding amazed and doubtful at the same time, as if he did not quite believe he could ever have embarked on something so perilous.

'You're playing into his hands,' Doctor Meninx said. 'Can't you see? He's latched onto the Vigilance because it allows him to explain away that arm – there's no other reason.'

'If I did not have an interest in the Vigilance,' Hesperus answered patiently, 'what was I doing in that region of the Scutum-Crux Arm?'

'He's got a point there,' I said.

'I've heard enough,' the avatar said, turning on its heels with a papery scuff. 'You are being manipulated, shatterlings – manipulated and lied to. The sanest thing you could do now is to compel *it* back into its cage. Give Hesperus free roam of this ship and I very much doubt that any of us will ever emerge from abeyance. I shall certainly not rate *my* chances very highly.'

When the avatar had stalked away, Hesperus said, 'I am sorry to be the cause of so much disharmony. Perhaps the doctor is correct: a great many things would be simpler if I were to return to the cage.'

'You're doing no such thing,' I said.

'Absolutely not,' Purslane agreed. 'Meninx can rot in his tank, for all I care. I'm beginning to wish the Centaurs had let a few predators slip through their impasse when he went for that swim.'

Two days later Purslane and I made love, then parted. She whisked back over to *Silver Wings of Morning*, flashing across space in a heartbeat. She entered her cryophagus, while I entered my stasis cabinet, set the time-compression dial and administered two eye-drops of Synchromesh. She would dream as the machine cooled her body down to the edge of death; I would skip over the years in a few instants of subjective thought.

My mind was searingly calm. We had forged our threads, creating two self-consistent narratives. We were going to be fifty-five years late, but we had survived another circuit and we had a guest who was going to make everything all right for us.

I thought of Purslane lying against me, wishing she was still there. Making love was a game of echoes. We had shared memories so many times that when I made love to her, I knew exactly how it felt to be Purslane. I could taste and feel her other lovers and she could taste and feel mine, each experience reaching away like a reflection in a hall of mirrors, diminishing into a kind of carnal background radiation, a sea of sensuous experience. I had been a girl once, then a thousand men and women and all their lovers.

The stasis field locked on. The Synchromesh took hold. I hurtled into my own future, while my ship ate space and time.

PART TWO

PART TWO

One day the little boy came again. I went up to the belvedere and watched his shuttle arrive. This time I knew that we would spend the whole of the afternoon in Palatial; that no other toys mattered now. The anticipation induced a warm, glittery tingle in my belly. It was nearly a year since I had shown him into that secret world for the first time and in the intervening visits it had come to dominate our imaginations like nothing else.

By then I knew a little more about the boy, and where he came from. Like mine, his family had prospered in the Conflagration, which was the name the adults gave the brief, sharp war that had encompassed the Golden Hour in the eleventh year of the new century. It had happened nearly thirty years earlier, but because my childhood had been dragged out across three decades by developmental inhibitors, I had some memory of it. I had been much too young to understand the nature of the thing itself, but I recalled a time when the adults talked in unusually low and strained voices, and when they could often be found walking in the halls with story-cubes, cradling them like the skulls of dead friends, anxious for the latest scintilla of news or rumour.

My family's specialisation was biology, with a particular aptitude for the subtleties of human cloning. Cloning is a technology like making paper: it is not difficult if one knows how to do it, but extraordinarily tricky to invent from scratch, and fraught with pitfalls that may only be circumvented by a Byzantine arsenal of tricks and stratagems, many of which resemble the shamanic rituals of folk medicine. The art was a thousand years old, but there were still only a handful of practitioners who really understood it, and my family was one of them. Before the Conflagration, when the opposed forces were re-arming, we made armies of soldiers, squadrons of pilots. Our clones were famed for their loyalty, but also for their tactical intelligence and independent thought. They could function as autonomous units, lying low on the edge of the battle zone, activating as needed without direct control from the central authority. After the war, many of the survivors had been granted full citizenship rights.

The little boy's family had supplied the armies and squadrons of the other side, but with machines, not organic beings. Sometimes they were controlled by human minds, but as often as not they had been given enough intelligence to function on their own. There were other heavy manufacturing concerns making battle machines, just as there were other cloning specialists. But we were the best at what we did, and his family was the best at making engines of war. Though there were tribunals, inquiries and sanctions in the years following the Conflagration, both families came through them relatively unscathed and remained in business. The wheeled robots that came down the ramp with the little boy were not just his bodyguards, but were made by his own family. Their machines were everywhere now, more prevalent than they ever had been before the war.

My family, having allied itself on the other side of the ideological schism between the organic and the mechanical, retained a healthy distrust of machines. As I have mentioned, for all its rambling vastness, there were few in the house. Most of the robots present were there to assist with the constant enlargement and reshaping of the house's basic architecture. Almost everything else was done by human servants, or cloned nannies.

'I know why it's called the Golden Hour now,' I said to the little boy as we made our way through the house to the playroom, and the waiting enchantment of Palatial.

'Everyone knows that.'

'I bet you don't.' Because he said nothing, I took that as licence to continue. 'It's because of light. Nothing can go any faster than it, including any messages we send. That's all very well if you're on a planet, or a moon. But after we moved into space, we got further and further apart. You couldn't have normal conversations any more – it took too long for the words to get there and back. That's why you and I can't have a conversation unless we're together, in the same house. Your home's on the other side of the Sun right now – if I said "hello", I'd have to wait hours before you said "hello" back. Eventually, people realised that they didn't like being so far apart from each other – it made them feel lonely and cut-off. They wanted to live in space because that meant they could do anything they wanted, but not be so spread out that it took hours to talk to each other. So they came up with the Golden Hour, which is where most of us live. The story-cube says it's a torus around the Sun, like a doughnut. It's an hour wide, as the speed of light goes. There are planets in it, and some moons, but also millions of Lesser Worlds, just like this one. If you're in the Golden Hour, the longest you'll usually have to wait for a reply will be two hours, and often it's a lot less than that. The story-cube says it took nearly ten centuries for human civilisation to settle into this configuration' – I liked long words, especially ones that the story-cube had taught me – 'but that now we've found it, it'll be good for thousands of years, perhaps even tens of thousands. Don't you feel excited to be part of that? We could be friends for ever and ever!'

'I don't think so,' the boy said dismissively. 'Father says it won't last.'

'What won't last?'

'The Golden Hour, of course. He says it's temporary. He says we'll eventually get bored with it and have another war, or find a way to go faster than light. Either way, it won't matter any more.'

I felt I was ahead of him there. 'We won't leave. The story-cube says there'd be no point. There's nothing beyond the solar system that we don't already know about, so what would be the sense in going there? We already have planets and moons to live on, and enough Lesser Worlds for everyone.' I strived to sound earnest, even though I was reciting an argument that had been spoon-fed to me, rather than one I had worked out for myself. 'Interstellar travel would be pointless, even if we could do it. And we can't.'

'It's been done,' the boy pointed out. 'People have already gone to Epsilon Indi, and come back.'

'That was just a stunt – it wasn't sustainable. And the people who did that went mad when they came back home. They couldn't adapt to the changes that had happened since they left.'

'Then they didn't go fast enough. But we can. Sooner or later we'll even go faster than light. Father says it's just a matter of time, with all the research that's going on.'

'I rather doubt that.'

'Read something else in the story-cube, have you, Abigail?'

'You can't go faster than light – it's just not possible.'

'Because you say so?'

I answered huffily, 'Because the story-cube says so, and the story-cube's always right.'

'Like it was right about the black hole under the house? You did look that up in the end, didn't you?'

'It's nothing to be frightened of.'

'Glug, glug, glug.'

The problem was, although I was as certain as I could be that I was right, I could offer nothing to bolster my arguments. I had read in the story-cube that the speed of light was a universal limit; that in a thousand years of experimentation – despite any number of false dawns – no one had ever managed to circumvent it. This had made me feel hemmed in and claustrophobic – it was like being told I must never run or skip down the long, dreary corridors of the house, but must walk instead, with my neck straight and my hands held behind my back. I felt affronted, as if the speed of light was a personal assault on my liberty. Why should I not go as fast as I pleased? Why should I not skip and run? But I could no more explain why the speed limit existed than I could explain why two and two did not make five. It was simply the way things were, one of those rules – like the edict not to visit certain parts of the house – that were not to be questioned.

But I sensed this was not an argument that would wash with the boy.

'I'll tell you why things can't go faster than light,' he said, taking an impish delight in knowing more about the subject than I did. 'Causality, that's why.'

It was not a word I knew. I filed it away for later enquiry.

'Then you believe it as well,' I said, hoping I would not be pressed.

'Father doesn't think so. He says causality's just a temporary stumbling block. It's the reason faster-than-light travel is difficult, not the reason it's impossible. One day we'll find a way around it – and then we'll leave everyone else behind. They can keep their Golden Hour – it isn't going to be enough for the rest of us.'

Even though he was not being nice, even though he was teasing me, he was still my only true friend, the only one I really liked playing games with. The cloned companions the household sometimes sent me were too docile, too compliant, ever to compare with a real boy. When I won against them, I always knew it was because they had capitulated. It was never like that with my friend from the other side of the Golden Hour – when I beat him, it was because I was better.

Typically, he would become friendlier to me, less argumentative, the closer we got to the playroom. That was because his mind was shifting onto the matter of Palatial. Without my consent, we could not enter it. He would tell me I looked pretty, that he liked the black ribbons in my hair.

Palatial lived in a room of its own, inside the larger bounds of the playroom. It had been delivered and installed by green-overalled technicians. Now and then one of them would arrive to check on it again, usually bringing a box full of glistening, maze-like panels which he slid in and out of slots in the side of Palatial's casing. By then I knew that I was not the only girl in the world with this gift, but that it was one of a number of prototypes. I had been told that there were still teething problems with the game, which was why – despite it having been given to me a year earlier – Palatial had still not been authorised for mass-production.

It was nearly as large as the room it filled. On the outside it was a green cube, covered in mouldings depicting castles and palaces, knights and princesses, ponies and dragons and sea-serpents. In one side was a doorway, leading through the thick-walled cube into its interior, where there was another room. The first time I had gone through that door, I had felt dizzy, and for a hallucinatory moment my thoughts had chased each other in epicycles of déjà vu. It was not as bad the second time, and by the third time I felt nothing as I passed through the aperture. Later I learned that the thick walls were dense with brain-scanning machinery, combing through my skull with invisible fingers. The boy experienced it the first time as well – I watched with a sadistic delight as the strangeness hit him – but he was also affected less and less with each subsequent visit. That was because Palatial kept a map of our minds in its memory, and refined its scanning patterns accordingly.

The room was empty, but it was also crammed with wonders and miracles. Appearing in the middle of the green-walled space – woven there by direct manipulation of our minds – was a palace. It was perched on the top of an impossibly steep mountain, with a treacherous path winding its way up the mountain's sides, crossing gorges on bridges, spiralling through tunnels, leaning out from the cliff on outrageous ledges, before finally entering the palace by means of a glittering drawbridge. The palace climbed almost into the clouds, pale pink and pale blue like the icing on a birthday cake, sprouting turrets and towers, spires and keeps. It was the fabulous vertical counterpart to my own house, and from the instant I had seen it, I longed to know what was inside.

Palatial made that possible. In fact, there was no escaping it. There were figures moving around behind the windows, on the ledges and turrets. Each was exquisitely real-looking, while glowing with a luminous, stained-glass intensity, as if they were coloured drawings in a book with the light of day shining through the pages. I had seen animated figures in the story-cube, but Palatial made even the best of those appear muddy and flat and dead. The little people in the palace were alive; they moved as if they had lives to be getting on with.

On my first visit I had noticed the princess, sitting on her own on the highest ledge, wearing a dress of blue fabric peppered with yellow stars, combing her long golden hair. Later – as I found her today – she was working with needle and thread on something in her lap. Even though she was no larger than a fingernail, and so far away from me that if she had been a picture in a book I would not have been able to read her expression, every detail on her face was clear to me. There was something very sad in her demeanour, some inexpressible longing, and yet I could not understand how anyone could live in a palace like that and not be radiantly happy. Palatial must have sensed this, must have sensed my interest in her, for all of a sudden I found that I had become the princess. I was sitting on the balcony, wearing her dress, working with needle and thread, looking out across a fairy-tale landscape. It was not simply that my perceptions had been remapped to correspond to that tiny, seated figure. I was actually inside her head, thinking her thoughts. In an instant, like the moment before waking when we confabulate an entire dream, I had access to all the memories of her life, back to when she was born in one of the highest, brightest rooms of the palace, on an early spring day when geese were crossing the sky from the north. I understood the history of her kingdom, the society into which she had been born, the difficult path she was about to tread upon ascension to the throne. I understood that her father, the king, had been killed during a battle with the neighbouring province. Although I had not noticed it until that moment, I spied on the horizon a dark counterpart to this palace, many leagues distant, wreathed in the shifting emanations of abnormal magic.

I had become the princess, slipped into her world, but I was still Abigail Gentian, looking in from outside. I carried her memories, but my own were still present and correct. Shifting between the two, choosing to be the princess or Abigail, was a matter of adjusting mental focus. Palatial must have been helping me, because it soon became as easy as blinking.

There was a knock on the door: gloved fist on heavy oak. I had been sewing the corner of an embroidered picture, my treasured sewing kit spread open on my lap. I put down the work and looked around. One of the palace guards entered, snapped his spurred heels against the stone floor and saluted. 'Begging your pardon, milady, but a communication has arrived. The chamberlain said I should bring it you directly.'

'Very good, Lanius,' I said. 'Give it to me. I shall read it on the balcony; it is yet daylight.'

I had felt a compulsion to reply, as if I had been forced onstage in the middle of a drama and did not wish to let the audience down. Yet it was difficult to tell whether the words that came out of my mouth had been decided by me, or shaped by Palatial. I had known the man's name without hesitating; I even had the vague sense that we had shared an adventure in the past, though not one that we cared to speak of now.

I took the handwritten note, broke the wax seal and opened it wide. It was from my stepbrother, Count Mordax, in the Black Castle. My hands trembled as I read the devastating news. A raiding party of Mordax's had taken my lady-in-waiting prisoner; he was holding her even now in the Dungeon of Screams. In return for her release, he desired that I should reveal the identity of my uncle, the imperial wizard Calidris, who, having renounced sorcery, was now living as an ordinary man, a simple farrier, in one of the outlying hamlets of the Kingdom.

'He wishes to use Calidris's magic for his own foul ends,' I declared. 'The very same magic that, even though wielded by a man of good heart, nearly tore our Kingdom in two. I shall not give up my uncle's identity. Or do you think I must, for the sake of my lady-in-waiting?'

As I spoke, I closed the sewing kit. I had used all but one of the needles in my embroidering. Only the smallest one, the blood-bound one, remained in its pocket.

'I beg your lady's indulgence, but the master-at-arms has requested permission to ride out tonight, into the very heart of the count's territory. There is a detachment of Prince Araneus's men said to be camped in a clearing of the Forest of Shadows. With the help of those men, there is every chance of conquering the Black Castle.'

'Prince Araneus's men will want nothing of our squabble with Mordax. The prince has troubles of his own.'

'He remembers the good deed we did him in the Battle of the Seven Marches. If the prince has forgotten, his men will not have.'

'This has the stench of a trap, Lanius. Or am I the only one who thinks so?'

'It is right to be cautious. But if we are to act, it must be swiftly. The master-at-arms said he must reach the Forest of Shadows by sundown, or else his men will fall afoul of the Enchantress at the Serpent Gate.'

'I suppose I must speak to Cirlus.'

'He is with his men, preparing their armour. Shall I summon him, milady?'

'No, I shall not interrupt his preparations unnecessarily. You will escort me to the armouring room, Lanius. Have Daubenton summoned. On the way, we shall speak more of Count Mordax. No one is better equipped to understand my stepbrother's mind than you, I fear.'

Although I had become the princess, although I felt fully immersed in her life, I still remembered who I really was. It was like being in a lucid dream, with the consolation that I could wake up whenever I wanted to. Because of this, although there was excitement and jeopardy, there was no actual anxiety. I knew that it was just a game, and that nothing that happened in that green cube could really hurt me.

The little boy had taken an immediate liking to it. By the time I revealed Palatial to him, I had become very comfortable in the princess's slippers. I could have slipped into the personality of any of the palace's protagonists, but I felt a loyalty to my flaxen-haired sister.

'I'm her,' I said, pointing to the figurines. 'You can be anyone else, but not the princess.'

'Why would I want to be the princess anyway?'

'I'm just saying.'

'Can you change to someone else, once you've become one of them?'

I nodded. 'You just need to concentrate on it hard, willing yourself into the other person's head. But they have to be in the same room. If you're in a dungeon, you can't just become one of the guards outside and make them open the door.' I had hopped from head to head, testing Palatial's rules, until returning to the mind of the princess. 'And you can't keep changing all the time – you have to stick with each person until the game decides you've had enough.'

'What is that other castle, in the distance?'

'The Black Castle, where Count Mordax lives. He's my stepbrother, in Palatial.'

'I want to be him.'

'You can't. You can only be someone in the Palace of Clouds.'

'How do you know?'

'You have to see someone to be them. Count Mordax is always too far away.'

Despite several attempts, the master-at-arms's men had never succeeded in reaching the Black Castle. On that first night, the men camped in the Forest of Shadows had turned out to be soldiers from Count Mordax, dressed in the uniforms of Prince Araneus's army. They had ambushed our men and slain many of them. Master-at-Arms Cirlus had retreated, his attacking force in ruins. Though he had made two more attempts to storm the castle and liberate my lady-in-waiting, he had twice been repelled, with great losses to men and horses. Meanwhile, the agents of Count Mordax were scouring the hamlets and villages for the hidden sorcerer, Calidris. Soon Calidris would have to use magic just to conceal himself.

'There must be a way for me to become Count Mordax,' the boy said.

'He's the baddie,' I said, puzzled. 'Why would you want to become him?'

'He's the baddie to you. But I bet he doesn't think of himself that way.'

'He kidnapped my lady-in-waiting. He won't let her go until he finds out where Calidris is.'

He asked me what I had done to free the lady-in-waiting. I told him about Calidris and the futile attempts to take the Black Castle.

'Then you need to try something different. If I became Mordax, I could set her free, couldn't I?'

I tried to tell him how Palatial would twist his mind once he was in it, to make him think and feel like Mordax, but it was difficult to explain. In any case, he waved aside my point with feigned indifference.

'I still want to be him.'

'You can't – he won't come near the Palace of Clouds, and he won't let any of us near the Black Castle.'

'What about a messenger?'

'He'll kill you.'

'I shall ride as a spy and claim to have knowledge of the sorcerer.

He won't kill me then, at least not until he's spoken to me. Then I can become him.'

'He might not see you in person.'

'Then I'll become his interrogator, and work my way to him gradually.'

'I don't know,' I said doubtfully. So far, Palatial had been mine, and no one else's. When I played with it, the only other mind shaping the flow of events had been the dim but cunning intellect of the machine itself, working its way through endless schemata. If the little boy entered the game and took on the persona of Count Mordax, the landscape of my imagination would have changed. There would be another human mind affecting the outcome. It was one thing to be beaten by a machine, but I was not sure how I would take being beaten by another child.

But I did so want him to share my secret world.

'We can go into it now,' I said, 'but everything takes a long time in Palatial. There won't be time for you to ride out to the Black Castle before you have to leave.'

'I can still look around,' the little boy said. 'I can still make plans, can't I?'

'Of course,' I said. 'Make all the plans you like. But it won't make a blind bit of difference in the end.'

'Why not?'

'I'm still going to win.'

Campion was doing a bad job of masking his fear. It was in the tightness of the muscles around his mouth, in the set of his jaw, leaking through his eyes and pores.

'What's wrong?' I said, slurred as a drunkard. 'I was going to whisk over to you, not the other way round ...'

But before he had a chance to answer, *Silver Wings* told me herself, whispering information into my head: our two ships had run into the Gentian emergency signal, an event sufficiently ominous that both vehicles had taken the decision to awaken their occupants. We were still travelling at maximum speed, still more than a dozen years from our destination.

'I came out first,' Campion said. 'The advantage of just being in stasis.'

'I don't like stasis,' I said testily, although of course he knew this.

He helped me out of the upright box of my cryophagus casket and gathered me in his strong, warm arms. I felt cold and fragile, like a flower that had been dipped in liquid nitrogen: something that might shatter into colourful brittle pieces at the least provocation.

'How are you feeling?' Campion whispered into my ear, nuzzling his face against mine.

'As if I want to go back to sleep again. As if I'd really prefer it if this was just a bad dream.'

'*Silver Wings* pulled you out fast because of the emergency. You're going to be a bit groggy.'

I pulled myself tighter against him. He felt fixed and solid, an anchor I could tie myself to.

Hesperus, who was standing behind Campion, said, 'You have been apart for some time. If you wish to copulate, I can retire to another part of the ship or simply disable my attentive faculties for an agreed interval.'

I did not want to copulate; I just wanted to hold Campion tightly and let life seep back into my bones and muscles and nerve fibres.

But *Silver Wings* was still speaking into my skull. 'The embedded content,' I asked. 'What did it say?'

Campion pulled back a twitch. 'What embedded content?'

'You didn't look?'

'It's a distress code, that's all. There isn't meant to be any embedded content.'

'*Silver Wings* says there is. Maybe *Dalliance* didn't pick up on that, but it's there.'

'That's not protocol. We're supposed to connect to the private network, find out what the storm's all about.'

'Something's obviously changed.' More exasperated than cross, I said, 'I can't believe you missed the content, Campion: what would have happened if I hadn't been around?' Then I grimaced. 'Ignore me – it's just brain chemistry.'

'Shall I retire while you examine the message?' Hesperus asked tactfully.

I shook my head. 'Whatever this is, we're all in it now – including our guests. You'd better brace yourself for some bad news. Whatever this is about, it could mean a delay in reuniting you with your friends.'

'Thank you for thinking of my welfare when you must have so much else on your minds. With your permission, I would consider it a privilege to be privy to the embedded content. May we examine it here?'

'I think I need a drink first,' Campion said, eyeing me guardedly. I felt the same, torn between wanting to know the news, however bad it might be, and at the same time wanting to do anything to delay the moment of revelation.

'We'll take it on the bridge,' I said, closing the door of my casket.

'There's something else you need to know,' Campion said to me quietly, while we were on our way to the nearest whisking point.

I squeezed his hand and asked, 'What?'

'We're down a passenger.'

My brain was still mush. 'One of the sleepers we picked up from Ateshga?'

'No – it's Doctor Meninx. We won't be having the pleasure of his company again.'

'*What?*' I asked again, aware of Hesperus only a few paces behind.

'He died. His casket broke down. Hesperus says he tried to fix it when he saw something was going wrong, but Doctor Meninx had put in too many safeguards.' Campion had put emphasis on that 'says', letting me know he only had our guest's word concerning what had really happened.

'My God.'

'Any other time, it would be the only thing on my mind. But now that this has happened as well . . .' Campion trailed off.

'I can't say I'm going to miss the old bigot, but—'

'You'd still rather he hadn't died. Yes, that's sort of how I feel. They're going to lap this up, aren't they?'

'Give them half a chance. But if it wasn't really your fault . . .' Some impulse caused me to glance back at Hesperus, though I was doing all in my power not to act awkwardly.

'He says he didn't do it,' Campion said under his breath. 'For now I've decided to take him at his word.'

As we whisked through-ship to *Silver Wings'* bridge, my thoughts veered between anxious anticipation of the embedded content and dark speculation as to Hesperus's innocence. I was still prickly and tense when the bridge lit up in welcome as we entered. Anticipating our arrival, the ship had arranged three seats around the plinthed glass hemisphere that was the main displayer. Although *Silver Wings* could have swallowed Campion's little ship fifty times over, what passed for a bridge on my own ship was about a twentieth the size of his, with configurable walls that were always set to a dull pewter, a low, dimpled ceiling gridded with lights and only the very minimum in terms of visible instrumentation and control interfaces.

'I presume you were serious about that drink,' I said, pausing at the bridge's maker while it fashioned and filled two glasses. Campion's was alcoholic; mine a cocktail of neural restoratives, to assist my recovery from the cryophagus.

Campion took the glass. 'Thank you.'

I indicated to Hesperus that he should take the sturdiest seat, while Campion and I lowered ourselves into the other two. 'No point in delaying this any longer, is there?' I asked, with a nervous catch in my voice. 'State the nature of the embedded content, *Silver* – for everyone's benefit.'

The ship spoke aloud. 'The embedded content is a non-interactive audio-visual recording with a playback time of one hundred and thirty-five seconds. If there are deeper content layers, I cannot detect them.'

'Can we assume it's safe?'

'I have scrutinised the message to the limit of my abilities and found no dangerous patterns.'

I ran my tongue along the dry edge of my lip. 'You'd better run it then. Ready, everyone?'

'As I'll ever be,' Campion said. He chose that moment to reach around for my hand, our fingertips only just touching.

The upper half of a man appeared in the hemisphere, rendered life-size. It only took me a moment to recognise him as a fellow shatterling of Gentian Line and to put a name to the face.

'Fescue,' I said softly.

'What would he want—?' Campion began, before Fescue spoke over his words.

'If you are in receipt of this message, then I'm assuming that you are latecomers for the reunion. Ordinarily you would deserve the sternest censure ... but these are not ordinary times. Now you deserve our blessing, our thanks, and above all our heartfelt wishes for your own continued survival. You may be all that is left of Gentian Line.' The imaged figure nodded gravely, leaving us in no doubt that we had understood his words.

It was definitely Fescue, but not as we usually knew him. The haughty, supercilious demeanour was only visible as a ghost of itself. His face was drawn, his hair dishevelled, clinging to his forehead in damp curls, his eyes weary, frightened slits. There was even something on his cheek that looked like a burn or bruise or a smudge of oily dirt.

'We were ambushed,' he continued, prolonging the syllables of the word with lingering distaste. 'The Thousand Nights were yet to begin – a dozen or so ships were still to arrive, even though we had already been waiting more than fifteen years. Hundreds had already come, of course – more than eight hundred in orbit. Most of us were already on the world, awake in the carnival cities or waiting in abeyance for the celebrations to commence. When the weapons opened fire, we had no practical defence: the world's impassors were too feeble to counter the assault, and our ships were annihilated before they could aggregate into an effective counter-force. They used Homunculus weapons against us: horrors we hardly dare speak of, exhumed from the deepest, most pathological vaults of history. After they had reduced our ships to clouds of ionised gas, even the largest and strongest of them, they turned on the reunion world and pumped energy into it for a hundred hours. It was a business of minutes, a mere preamble, to boil away the atmosphere and oceans and render that world as sterile as it had been before our arrival. But the attackers didn't stop there. They continued to pour energy into the planet, melting first the crust and then the mantle ... turning the entire world into a molten ball that glowed first orange and then furious gold, until it began to break up, its own gravity insufficient to hold it together. Over four and a half days, the energy output of those weapons exceeded even that of the sun the world orbited. And when they were done, nothing remained. That was eight years ago, by my reckoning – still more time will have passed when you intercept this signal. Concentrate your sensors on the target system and you will soon see not a sun and its family of worlds, but a new nebula, a roiling dark cloud of rubble and dust and tortured gas, now bound only by the gravity well of the star itself. It will endure for centuries, thousands of years, significant fractions of a circuit. Planets and moons plough through that cloud, but not the world we hoped to make our temporary home. It's gone, and so has most of the Line.'

Fescue paused and stroked a finger against a puffiness under one of his slitted eyes. It occurred to me then, as it had not before, that he might very well be blind: at no point had I sensed his attention focused in any particular direction.

'Some got out,' he said. 'Those with the fastest ships, the best camouflage or countermeasures ... but few were so fortunate. It will come as no surprise to hear that I have initiated the Belladonna protocol. You must deviate immediately from your present heading. Under no circumstances attempt to enter or approach the reunion system, for even now – eight years after the ambush – the aggressive elements are still loitering, waiting to pick off latecomers. Even once you have obeyed the Belladonna protocol, you must be watchful for pursuers: complete your turn stealthily, and use misdirection as appropriate. If you sense you are being followed, you must sacrifice yourselves rather than lead the attackers to the Belladonna fallback.'

Again Fescue fell silent, looking to one side as if he had seen – or perhaps heard – something that merited his attention. When he resumed speaking, it was with a renewed haste.

'I chose to embed this message because it was too risky to convey this information via the private network: the nature of the ambush implies that our security is not as tight as we had imagined, and any attempt to tap into the network may be detected and acted upon by those who would seek to exterminate our Line. Concerning the nature of our attackers, and their reasons for doing this ... I regret to tell you that I have no information.' Fescue shook his head forcefully. 'Nothing: not even the tiniest flicker of intelligence. But I know this. Unless one has arisen in the last circuit, no galactic civilisation – not even the Rebirthers or the Machine People – is known to possess the sophistry in vacuum manipulation necessary to duplicate Homunculus-level technology. Those weapons must therefore be the original instruments, despite the fact that Marcellin Line was charged with their disposal four and a half million years ago. The question therefore begs itself: did Marcellin Line betray their promise to the Commonality and conceal those weapons when they should have decommissioned them? I cannot believe they would have done so ... but then neither can I believe that Gentian Line has enemies who would wish this upon us. Therefore tread carefully, for if the Marcellins cannot necessarily be trusted, then neither can any other Line in the Commonality. After thirty-two circuits and six million years, we may finally have run out of friends.'

Fescue halted, and for a moment it appeared that he was done. Then he raised his chin, striking a defiant pose, and said, 'I wish I knew how many of you were out there. I would like to think that there are still latecomers on their way home, but for all I know attrition may already have taken every last one of you. I will say this, though, in the vain hope that it reaches some remnants of the Line. Now you and a handful of survivors carry the candle that Abigail set aflame. That is a singular responsibility: a greater burden than you have ever been required to shoulder. You must not let the rest of us down.'

Fescue bowed his head. The image froze and then flicked back to its starting position, ready for the speech to be replayed.

We watched it again, in case there was some nuance that had escaped us the first time.

When our messenger was done, Campion said, 'This can't be real. Someone's faked it. Someone's figured out how to send an emergency signal, impersonating Fescue.'

'Why would anyone do that?' I asked. There was a coldness growing inside me, a realisation that our future had just become stranger and more frightening than it had appeared only a few minutes ago, but for now I was still capable of reasoned thought.

'To get at us, of course! To give us a reason to skip the reunion completely. God knows we've got enough enemies, enough people who'd love to see us miss the boat.'

'They wouldn't dare use Fescue's name unless they had his authority. He sent this message, or delegated it to someone he trusted.'

'Fescue hates us! He's got every reason in the world to trick us with something like this.'

'And risk excommunication? If he sent this signal via omni-directional broadcast, then it'll have been intercepted by every shatterling who hadn't yet made it to the reunion. Fescue might have an axe to grind against us, but he's not vindictive, and he definitely isn't stupid.' I cleared my throat. 'I've been thinking all this through as well, you know. I'd love to believe this is a hoax, aimed solely at us. But that's not how it looks to me. I think this is real. I think something horrible has happened and we're being warned to get as far away from the reunion as we can.'

'That would also be my conclusion,' Hesperus said.

'Did anyone ask you?' Campion snapped.

'My apologies. I should not have spoken.'

'No,' I said, 'you should have, because you're right. This is real, and we have to take it seriously. Listen to Hesperus, Campion. He has every reason to want to make it to that reunion: it's where we've promised him he'll find other Machine People. And now that message is saying the party's off, and Hesperus still believes it. Doesn't that tell you something?'

Campion spread his hands before his face, as if he wished to bury it in them.

'I can't deal with this. It's got to be some kind of mistake, something blown out of all proportion.'

'Or it's exactly what Fescue said it was: an actual ambush, with huge losses. We'll know soon enough, in any case. Now that we've a reason to, we can concentrate our sensors on the system ahead. With two ships, we can establish an observational baseline wide enough to resolve the nebula – if it's really there.'

'It may be easier than that,' Hesperus said. 'If the system is now dust-cloaked, the spectral properties of the star will be modified. It will appear redder, and contain the absorption lines characteristic of the elements making up the planet.'

'*Silver*,' I said hesitantly, because I knew I was on the verge of having a harrowing possibility confirmed, 'tell me if there's anything unusual about the target star, compared against the trove.'

It did not take long. *Silver Wings* informed us that the star was indeed redder than expected, and that its atmosphere contained unusually strong spectral signatures of nickel and iron, proving that the sun was shrouded in the rubble that had once been our reunion world. Furthermore, even at our present distance of thirteen lights, there was clear evidence of the nebula: a warm, glowing ellipse like a thumbprint pressed over the hard point of the star.

That was when we knew for sure that we were not being hoaxed, and that everything was going to be different from now on. The first six million years had been all fun and games.

Now we were growing up.

'What if there are survivors still hiding out in the cloud?' Campion asked. 'Don't we owe it to them to have a closer look?'

'Fescue said it was already eight years since the attack when he made the transmission. Add another thirteen years for the signal to reach us: that's twenty-one years. Add another thirteen before we arrive – that's thirty-four years.'

'Fescue survived for eight years or he wouldn't have been able to send that signal.'

'He didn't say he was still there. The message's apparent point of origin tells us nothing. It could have been relayed from a ship on its way to the fallback.'

'Read between the lines. He was hurt. If he was anywhere else other than inside the system, he'd have been able to get himself fixed. His ship must have been damaged, and chances are it was still inside the cloud. Fescue must have been hiding there ever since the attack. That means we have to consider the possibility of other survivors.' His voice notched higher. 'If we were down in that system, crippled but still alive, we'd be counting on outside help as well.'

'The survival of the Line outweighs the survival of individual shatterlings.'

'Ask yourself what Fescue would have done,' Campion said quietly.

'What?'

'Put yourself in Fescue's shoes – as if he was the one running into this transmission, not us. As if we sent it, and he was the one who had to decide how to act. Fescue was right to warn us, but he knew damned well we wouldn't listen. I may not care for that arrogant, hypocritical arsehole, but do you think he'd have been very likely to listen? I don't even know if I'm proposing the right thing, or something worse than stupid, but I know we can't just dismiss it out of hand. These are our brothers and sisters, our fellow shatterlings. They're pieces of us, pieces of what we are, pieces of what make us human. If we abandon them, we may as well forget about the Line. We won't have any right to call ourselves Gentian any more.'

*

We went to see the doctor.

The tank was as dark as ever, but now there was something bulging against the glass from within, revealed in flattened pale islands interrupted by rivers and inlets of random shadow. I looked at it for a few numb moments, trying to work out how that pale, doughy mass could have been introduced into the tank without Doctor Meninx becoming aware of it. Then I made out the flattened, ruptured oval of something that had once been an eye, and it dawned on me, slowly and then with increasing conviction, that the pale mass *was* Doctor Meninx, and that he had bloated to at least twice his previous volume, until he could expand no more.

I scrambled up the ladder to the top of the tank. I folded back the hinged section of walkway and began to twist the circular hatchway. I spun it free and began to lever it back, but I had only opened it a crack when I was assaulted by a noxious, vinegary stench.

I slammed the hatch back down.

'Tell me what happened.'

'I cannot say,' Hesperus replied.

My hands trembling, I lowered myself down the side of the tank, back onto the safety of the floor. I had never really liked Doctor Meninx, and I had liked him less and less as his true prejudices bubbled to the surface. But he had been a fellow starfarer, a being who had travelled far, swum in oceans of memory and experience, and now all that memory and experience were gone.

The anger hit me with the cold force of a supernova shockwave.

'What do you mean, *you cannot say*? You were fucking *awake*, Hesperus. You were the only one he had anything to fear from. The only one he thought might want to kill him. And now he's dead.'

Hesperus stood at the entrance to the chamber, his arms at his sides, his head lowered slightly, like a schoolboy summoned for punishment.

'I understand your reaction, Purslane, but as I have already explained to Campion, this was not my doing.'

'Why didn't you try to help him?' Campion asked.

'I did, despite your request that I keep away from him. When I detected signs that Doctor Meninx's tank chemistry was amiss – signs that I stress were by no means compellingly obvious – I attempted to adjust the equipment in such a way as to remedy the perceived imbalance. I soon discovered that the equipment was not amenable to outside interference.'

I was still not ready to let go of my suspicion, but I wanted to hear the rest of his defence. 'And?'

'I discovered that by merely tampering with the equipment I had raised Doctor Meninx from his drug-induced slumber. Upon his return to partial consciousness, I attempted to explain the nature of his predicament. Unfortunately, Doctor Meninx refused to believe that my intentions were anything other than improper. He urged me to desist tampering with his tank at the earliest opportunity.'

'Did you?'

'Of course not: I persisted, despite Doctor Meninx's far from lucid protestations. Yet as I attempted assist him, the doctor succeeded in activating certain devices built into his tank, the purpose of which was deter outside interference. These countermeasures, though posing no serious threat to my own existence, nonetheless made it prohibitively difficult for me to access the very mechanisms I sought to examine and adjust. With regret, I was forced to abandon my efforts. I could not save the doctor, but merely witness his inevitable decline. It was at this point that I attempted to raise you from abeyance, without success.'

'And then?'

'I made a number of subsequent attempts both to reason with the doctor and to repair the chemical imbalance, but on all such occasions I was forced to retreat. Eventually there came a day when the doctor appeared insensate, and shortly afterwards I concluded that he was dead. Other than monitoring the integrity of the tank, in case it should rupture and spill the contents into your ship, I have had nothing more to do with the personage.'

'Open and shut, in other words,' Campion said.

'I can only speak the truth,' Hesperus replied.

He was with us when we ran the Belladonna algorithm. We were looking at a portion of the Milky Way, writ large on Campion's displayer. The view had already zoomed in on *Dalliance*'s position, with only a thousand lights or so visible in any direction – about the thickness of the disc itself. The red line that marked *Dalliance*'s future course was arrowing out towards the extremities of the galaxy. A cone projected ahead of the ship, indicating the algorithm's search volume.

'It requires us to search in the direction of the galactic anti-centre,' I said. 'We look along a radial line extending away from the core that passes through the position of the reunion system. As it happens, that's pretty close to our present heading.'

'The volume will encompass the system you were already approaching,' said Hesperus. 'Will that not lead to an ambiguity?'

'Belladonna explicitly instructs us to ignore the reunion system, and any suitable systems lying closer to the galactic centre,' I said. 'It obliges us to look beyond, until we find a star of the right spectral type and with the right formation of planets. It must lie at least fifty years from the designated reunion world to give us a chance of getting there without being tracked – any closer and we could be followed too easily. There has to be a rocky world in a circular orbit at a suitable distance from the star.'

'The world must be life-supporting?'

'Not necessarily, but it shouldn't be so inhospitable that it could never be scaped. We could easily spend several thousand years in the vicinity of the fallback. That's long enough to modify a climate, even to shift a borderline case to true habitability.'

'And if the world is already occupied?'

'Then we'll be guests of whoever owns the place. Most civilisations know enough about the Lines not to turn them down in their hour of need.'

'And if they should turn you down?'

'It's not something you do twice.'

After a moment Campion said, 'Looks like we have a candidate.'

The image zoomed in again, dizzyingly, on a solitary yellow star. It was ninety lights beyond the reunion system – practically on its doorstep in galactic terms, but safely beyond the proscribed margin of fifty lights. Provided we did not head there directly, but went off in a false direction before steering back towards it once we were out of detection range, we would be able to reach the system without being followed.

I digested the trove data scrolling down next to the star. The summary was in all likelihood no more than the last layer of virgin ice on a mountain of data known to Gentian Line. Given the perceptual bottlenecks of the human central nervous system, there might be more 'known' about this world than could ever be absorbed in a normal lifetime.

'Neume,' said Campion, stroking his chin. 'Rings a bell – although I suppose there are thousands of Neumes out there.'

'No – I'm getting it as well, and I think the memory's specific to this sector. One of us must have been there. Not you or I, or it would come through stronger. It must have been quite a few circuits ago – enough for the place to have changed a bit.'

According to the trove, the planet had seen many native civilisations. No one was listed as living there now, but that was no guarantee that we would find the world unoccupied. The trove's last update on the matter was twelve kilo-years stale.

'The world touches a chord of familiarity with me as well,' Hesperus said.

'You've been to Neume?' I asked.

'Not been, I think. Nothing in my bones tells me I have walked that soil. But I may have intended to go there, as part of my wider explorations.'

'There's something on Neume called the Spirit of the Air,' Campion said, reading a few lines further down the summary. 'Some kind of posthuman machine intelligence, I think, although it's all a bit vague. Any chance you were interested in that?'

'You mean as one machine to another?'

'You tell me.'

Campion was still suspicious of Hesperus, even though we had agreed to give him the benefit of the doubt where Doctor Meninx was concerned.

'It is certainly possible. It is also possible that I am quite mistaken about Neume. As you say, there may be other worlds with that name.'

'I guess you'll know when we get there,' I said.

'One can but hope,' Hesperus said. 'Of course, there is the small matter of the ambush to deal with first. I wonder if I might be of assistance in that regard?'

'We can't trust him,' Campion said, lying against me. 'Even if we wanted to trust him, it'd be the wrong thing to do.'

'He's offered to help us. I've told him I'll let him pick a ship from my cargo bay, something he can use.'

'Could be a ruse.'

'You mean, he's going to take the ship and never come back?'

'It's a distinct possibility.'

'Yes, and so is the possibility that he's telling us the truth.' I propped myself up on one elbow. 'So what if he does leave us? We'll have lost a guest and a ship I probably don't even remember acquiring. Hardly the worst thing we're going to have to deal with.'

'I'll remind you of that when he turns his guns on us.'

'He's a rational sentient, Campion – not a vengeance-crazed

psychopath.' I ran a finger though the fine hair of his chest, across his belly and down to his sleeping penis. We had been lying together in a warm post-coital haze, until I made the mistake of starting a conversation. 'The mad one was Doctor Meninx. Hesperus just happened to be in the wrong place at the wrong time.'

'So he says.'

'Do you actually believe he murdered Meninx?'

Campion struggled with his reply. 'No,' he said eventually. 'I think the doctor just took one short cut too many with his equipment. But I have to act as if I'm taking the matter seriously. I can't appear negligent where the death of a guest is concerned.'

'Even when the other guest has volunteered to put his life on the line to help us?'

'Don't make this any harder than it already is. I'm just saying, Hesperus has some ground to make up. He has to earn my trust again. Earn *our* trust.'

I caressed him until he began to show faint signs of life. 'He's earned mine already. You're the one who needs to catch up, Campion.'

Hesperus ran a golden hand along the golden flank of the little spacecraft he had found tucked in one corner of the enormous room. It was scarcely larger than a whale, more a trinket than a ship.

'It's called *Vespertine*,' I said. 'That's about all I remember. I think someone may have given it to me as a gift. I can't recall the last time I had to use a shuttle to move between vessels, rather than just whisking over. Been a while since I dealt with an entry-level civilisation.'

'This is more than a shuttle,' Hesperus said, still stroking the little ship's skin.

'What are we dealing with, then?'

'A true interstellar vehicle, Purslane. I believe that the lateral bulge conceals part of a small parametric engine, or something employing similar principles.'

I shrugged. 'Doesn't change much. There are other interstellar ships in here. I keep them for trade.'

We were in *Silver Wings*' main storage/cargo bay, in the aft third of my ship. The bay was a rectangular pressurised space eight kilometres long, three across and nearly two in height. We had entered through the cliff-like edifice of the forward wall and followed a series of suspended walkways through the chamber, winding between the many ships and ship-sized artefacts that formed my private collection. They loomed huge, most of them cloaked in shadow or darkness except for the odd clean or ragged edge, a smooth or imbricated surface, limned by the cold blue radiance of the distant ceiling-mounted spotlights.

Lately I spent as little time as possible in the main bay. The clutter of the place, the disordered collection of ships and artefacts, was an uncomfortable reminder of the disorder in my head. My skull was a pressure cooker, crammed with too much history. They both needed sorting out, but the longer I put off either task, the less enthusiasm I had.

Campion had always been less sentimental than me. He could ditch ancient treasure, or submit to memory consolidation, without a moment's hesitation. He moved through life with less baggage, less to weigh him down, less to anchor him to his own history. I had always admired him for that willingness to discard his own past, while knowing it was one of the things that made us distinct, a bridge I could never cross if I wished to remain Purslane.

And I did, of course.

Sometimes I thought of Abigail making clay dolls of us, the way a girl might pass a rainy afternoon, with no thought for what would become of those dolls when she sent them into the world. How trivial it must have been for her to adjust the parameters of her personality before pouring a measure of it into each of her shatterlings. Did it cross her mind, even for an instant, that there might be less than joyous consequences? That on some unthinkably distant day one of her shatterlings would be standing in a vast room halfway across the galaxy, weighed down with the melancholic sense of being an unwilling curator in some dusty, little-visited museum of her own existence?

Hesperus was looking at me, waiting for me to continue.

'Shatterlings tend to be hoarders, as you may have noticed. I've never had much use for half the stuff in here, but I can't bring myself to get rid of it. I'd be too worried about throwing away something really vital, without realising it.'

'I quite understand. But this ship may yet have possibilities. I should like permission to go aboard, if it will not inconvenience you.'

Vespertine floated in a weightless cradle just beyond the gravity bubble encompassing the walkway. Hesperus had to lean over the railing to reach its skin. It was ridged with a Byzantine design, mazes and chevrons and interlocked flower-like forms, vanishing down to a fractal haze of microscopic detail that made the edges appear out of focus. I presumed the design served some arcane field-modifying effect, much as the roughened skin of a shark assisted it in swimming.

'Is there something in particular about this ship that interests you?'

'I should like to see if it is functional, and whether it will accept me as a pilot.'

'I don't blame you for wanting to leave us, Hesperus.'

'Not my intention. I am considering how I may be of practical assistance during the forthcoming encounter.'

'But this is just a tiny little minnow.'

'Size may well be the issue here, but not in the sense you are implying. A ship as small as this one would be limited in its agility not by the power output of its engine, but by the strength of its dampening field. But I am not human. Unbalanced forces that would reduce you to red jelly – I am sorry to be so graphic, but it is necessary to make my point – would register with me only as a mild impediment to free movement.'

'Being able to move fast isn't going to protect you from everything that might be hiding in that cloud.'

'My mission must have been evaluated as a high-risk enterprise from the moment I left Machine Space. I would have gone into it knowing that there would be moments of crisis and uncertainty. In that respect, nothing has changed.'

'Did Campion show you the structures?'

'Yes, he did.'

As she had refined her observations of the reunion system, *Silver Wings* had detected bright objects embedded in the cloud. They were huge glowing structures of irregular shape, branching into jagged fingers like frozen lightning bolts. They were shrouded in dust now, difficult to examine, but we would see them up close when we slammed through the cloud.

We had no idea what they were – deep trove searches were continuing – but their presence did nothing to lighten our mood.

'They don't worry you?'

'They are certainly puzzling. I may even know what they are, on a level of memory I cannot presently access. I also have every confidence that I can steer around them without coming to harm.'

Despite everything that had happened, the weight of knowledge bearing down on me, his bravery stirred me. 'What I said earlier still applies. If you want to leave, you can take any of these ships. I won't hold it against you, and neither will Campion.'

'I am still in your debt. I have no intention of leaving until that is settled. Now, may I be permitted to examine the ship? If I am to make the best use of it, I may wish to modify some of her control systems. I know there is still time, but the sooner I start the better.'

'Campion and I will be going into abeyance shortly. We'll come out when we're closer, about to begin slowdown.'

I told *Silver Wings* to release the security binding on the golden ship, allowing Hesperus to board it. Part of the handrail vanished and a portion of the flooring bulged outwards to connect with a baroque doorway that had just formed in the side of the ship. Soft blue light emanated from the interior, highlighting the chromed flanges on the sides of Hesperus's face. He stepped through the blue-lit doorway, one gold machine entering another. After a moment the doorway rendered itself impassable – it was as if a pane had frosted over with gold leaf – and then vanished back into the baroque patterning of the hull, leaving no trace of its former existence. The railing remade itself. A breeze, caused by a shift in the miniature weather system that inhabited this bay, flicked a hair across my brow. I had not been there for so long that my entrance had disturbed the equilibrium of the captured atmosphere.

There are times when you go into abeyance with the weight of the world on your shoulders, and come out with all your problems suddenly diminished – still there, still meriting your attention, but no longer having the looming stature that they did before.

This was not one of those times. I came out of the casket with the same dread feeling that I had had going in.

We braked hard and braked sudden, pushing our engines to the limit. Until the moment when we began slowdown and dug claws into spacetime like cats sliding down a wall, there would have been little or no warning of our imminent arrival.

Two per cent of the speed of light was almost not moving at all by the standards of Gentian Line – a speed so imperceptibly slow that it was best measured in kilometres per second, a unit more usually associated with travel in a planetary atmosphere. But it was still much faster than the orbital motion of any of the bodies making up the system, whether they were the remaining planets and moons or the dust, grit and tumbling boulders of the shattered planet. Campion had already pulled away to a distance of two minutes –

thirty-six million kilometres – beginning his separation many hours ago. Now our two ships were moving along parallel trajectories, like bullets shot from a double-barrelled rifle, and would remain so as we slipped through the cloud, piercing it more or less at its widest point, and passing either side of the sun. Both ships would be peering into the surrounding volume, looking for indications of technological activity. Allowing for the effectiveness of our sensors, we should be able to sweep twenty per cent of the cloud with a sensitivity high enough to detect typical ship signatures. There were places to hide: warm knots and eddies in the cloud caused by the to-and-fro influence of the remaining worlds. A ship could hide itself, masked to eyes that worked on gravity and heat.

All the while we would be doing our best not to be seen. That meant no communications unless absolutely necessary: by the time we were deep inside the cloud there would be too great a chance of a tight-beam being scattered in all directions by intervening debris, rendering our private communications at least detectable by foreign parties, if not decipherable. It also meant using our engines as infrequently as possible, and not raising our impassors to full effectiveness until a collision was imminent. Running dark, in other words: coasting without screens, and relying solely on passive sensor methods.

I watched Hesperus leave. Before he entered *Vespertine* we touched hands. His was very cold, very metallic, but somehow pliant in the way it yielded to my touch. He slipped out of my grasp and retreated through the blue-lit doorway of the golden ship. The doorway formed over and vanished back into the blurred surface of the hull. A humming note rose and stabilised. A few seconds later, the hull blurring intensified, as if I was seeing the golden craft through a veil of tears. *Vespertine* moved away from the catwalk, slipping free of its force cradle. The railing re-formed. I clutched it, watching Hesperus navigate between the much larger and darker vessels filling my hold. Gradually it dwindled to a tiny, fuzzy mote of self-illuminated gold. The bay door had opened wide. Hesperus penetrated the atmosphere curtain and entered open space. He hovered outside for a few seconds before engaging the engine, appearing to blink out of existence as the massive acceleration snatched him away.

I watched the door close and then whisked back to the bridge.

'*Vespertine* is loose,' I told Campion.

His reply came back four minutes later. 'I didn't see a thing, and I was watching very closely. I hope that bodes well, if and when we run into trouble.'

His image was based on *Silver Wings'* own memories of Campion, not any visual information arriving over the talk-beam. It would have been pointless and dangerous to send more data than was strictly necessary, so our exchange consisted only of the words we spoke, accompanied by a few cues for gesture, emphasis and inflection, rendered back into a convincing simulacrum of speech.

An hour passed, and then my ship had something to tell me.

'My trove's turned something up,' I reported to Campion. 'The bright structures in the cloud – I think they may confirm another part of Fescue's story. The trove thinks they may be lesions – a kind of residue left over from the use of Homunculus weapons. That's not good news, obviously. Not only would it mean we *are* dealing with H-guns – after all this time – but it also means someone's used them more recently than thirty-four years ago. Lesions have a decay half-life, even in hard vacuum. They wouldn't last long in this kind of environment.'

Campion came back, 'Agreed – it's not good news. But at least it means someone had a reason to fire those weapons relatively recently. Unless they were just firing them for the hell of it, it could mean they were trying to eliminate survivors still hiding out in the cloud.'

'Or shoot down latecomers who had the chrome-plated balls to come through anyway, despite Fescue's warning.'

Campion smiled grimly. 'There's that as well.' Then he glanced aside at a read-out. 'Dust is starting to thicken, for me at least. I'm going to have to notch up my impassor effectiveness before it gets any worse. Suggest you do likewise.'

I sent the necessary command to *Silver Wings*. 'Raised. Can you still hear me?'

The image flickered, criss-crossed with pink and white static lines. 'Yes,' Campion said, his voice throaty. 'You're coming through. I can see your bubble, though – you're beginning to scintillate. It helps that I know exactly where to look, but you're more visible than you were a minute ago.'

He meant a minute by his reckoning – it was still taking two minutes for light to creep between us.

I could see *Dalliance*'s impasse flickering on and off as it interdicted incoming matter, though the effort taxed my sensors to the limit. I had sometimes chastised him for using such a small ship, but now his size gave him a clear edge over me. The surface area of his bubble was a hundred and twenty times less than that enveloping *Silver Wings*, making it much less likely that he would run into any given piece of debris.

Two hours in, and I could feel the effect of those collisions as well. As the ambient dust thickened – as we pushed deeper and deeper into the cloud of planetary ashes – so *Silver Wings* registered each impact with a tangible jolt as the impassor soaked up the momentum of the incoming particle and then transferred that impulse to the ship via the generators. The dampeners were doing their best to cancel out any shifts in the local gravity, but because they had little warning they had to cut in sharply, with a perceptible lag between effect and response.

I felt like the captain of an ocean-going ship grinding against an iceberg, each jolt the twang of a hull plate being ripped away.

'It's rougher than I expected,' Campion told me, the scratchiness of his image and the metallic timbre of his voice *Silver Wings'* way of telling me that the data transfer was becoming problematic. 'It'll smooth out, though, once the impacts start coming in close together enough.'

That took another hour. *Silver Wings* was now driving hard into a sleet of debris and the momentum transfer had become first a drum roll and then a rumble, and now little more than a faint, ever-present vibration. The downside was that the collisions were sapping my speed: I had to engage the engine just to maintain two per cent of light, and I could only run the engine in the instants when the impassor was down. Occasionally there was still a large, barely dampened jolt as we ran into something an order of magnitude bigger than the usual particles, but my nerves had already been shredded about as thoroughly as they could be.

Three and half hours in, we got our first close view of the nearest lesion. It emerged from its cloak of dust like a sliver of bright landscape seen through breaking fog. It was irregular in shape, flattened and straight at one end, curving in the middle, splaying into vast curved fingers at the other. It was aglow with a soft, milky luminescence.

It scared the hell out of me.

I tightened my grip on the metal of the bridge banister, half-expecting that my ship would be forced to swerve violently at any moment.

The lesion was orbiting with the general motion of the cloud, obeying the gravitational influence of the star, but there were count-less specks of dust moving on their own courses, with their own velocities. Sooner or later one of those impacts was going to liberate enough energy to send a wave of transformation slamming through the lesion. It was anyone's guess as to what would happen then. The lesion might just vanish, all the energy embodied in it being sucked harmlessly back into the marrow of spacetime from whence it had come – or it might explode, liberating in an instant enough destruc-tive force to rip the crust off a planet.

The safest thing was not to be anywhere near a lesion.

'We should go dark from now on,' Campion said. 'Too much chance of scatter. I'll signal you when we've passed the sun and the local cloud density has dropped to a safe level again.'

Another five or six hours – it felt like half my lifetime stretching ahead of me. I was a shatterling, mentally programmed to tolerate immense stretches of solitude. But that mental programming had begun to run amok a long time ago.

Now I needed another human being close to me just to feel human myself.

I could not see Hesperus, but I knew his intended trajectory. He had not been in contact since leaving *Silver Wings*, but that was no cause for concern. He would pass the lesion before either of us, but his small, fleet ship seemed unlikely to trigger any undesirable changes in the abnormal structure. I was more concerned about my own passage: I would give the lesion a wider berth, but my field effects would reach further than *Vespertine*'s. Was hundreds of thousands of kilometres of clear space enough to insulate the lesion from the influence of my impassor and engine?

The trove offered no reassurance.

I do not think I breathed until I was clear, and the last of those curling fingers was falling behind my ship. I had survived, but there were still other lesions ahead of me, lurking deeper in the cloud. I remained tense, still conscious that my survival depended entirely on the safe functioning of my bubble; were it to fail, *Silver Wings* would be ripped apart in a blinding moment, and I would probably know nothing of it. Every now and then a larger impact served as a reminder that I was running into pebbles and boulders, not merely grains of dust.

The second lesion was larger than the first, but further away, and none of our intended trajectories came within six hundred thousand kilometres of it. It was similar to the first, but with a bifurcation halfway along its curving, spavined length. Its grasping fingers were knobby and broken-nailed. The more familiar I became with the lesions, the more they began to remind me of antlers, broken off in some titanic contest between animals large enough to bestride a solar system.

Six hours in, I reached my closest approach to the dust-shrouded sun. On the other side, *Silver Wings* began to register a slow and gradual decline in the density of the cloud.

It would be some time yet before I could risk signalling Campion. I had just resigned myself to a long wait when he re-appeared.

'I'm getting something,' he said, sounding unsure of himself. 'It's a very weak signal, but it's moving independently of the rest of this junk. Could be a ship, I think.'

'Is it Gentian?'

'Doesn't look like it so far. The protocols are pretty old.'

'Then we don't go after it. We're looking for Line survivors, not anyone else stupid enough to blunder into this.'

'Agreed,' Campion said. 'But for all we know there are Gentian survivors who don't have the means to send the right kind of signal. If their ship's damaged, or they had to hide out aboard another one—'

'I wish you weren't so good at coming up with get-out clauses, Campion.'

Silver Wings was still seeing nothing, but then *Dalliance* might have been close enough to sniff out a signal just below my detection threshold. As his ship exchanged data with mine, I confirmed that this was the case. The object – whatever it was – would pass just within Campion's effective sensor envelope, but slip past mine completely.

'All right – I agree that this is worth looking at, but please be careful. We ignored one warning from Fescue; now we're taking a risk we would have considered unacceptable a few hours ago.'

'We're flexible,' Campion said. 'It's the price we pay for being sentient. I'm veering; see you in a while.'

Hesperus was the next to get in touch. 'I see Campion moving now, Purslane. He is strobing his bubble to effect a course change. Has something happened?'

It bothered me that Campion's actions were so visible, but nothing could be done about that. 'He's picked up something – he thinks it could be a signal, maybe from survivors.'

'It could also be something a great deal less welcome.'

'Yes,' I said tersely. 'He's aware of that. He still feels obliged to investigate.'

'If you have no objections, I shall strive to follow Campion and locate the same signal. It will mean sacrificing a degree of stealth, but anyone monitoring this system is surely aware of our arrival by now.'

'Take care, please.'

'I shall. If you are able, would you be so kind as to inform Campion of my intentions? I would not wish to startle him.'

'I'll do that, Hesperus. And thank you. I didn't mean to snap just now.'

'Under the circumstances, I think you may be forgiven.'

He closed the link and left me alone. I called Campion, telling him that Hesperus was on his way but that he should not acknowledge my transmission. The last thing I wanted was to feel alone, but the less we talked the better.

I had been scared before – too many times to remember. But there had always been a mitigating factor to take the edge off my fears. I had always been able to console myself with the thought that if I survived, I would have an astonishing adventure to braid into my strand, something that would guarantee a day or two of dreamy celebrity even if I had no interest whatsoever in winning the Thousand Nights. And even if I should die in such a way that my strand never reached the Line, I would still be commemorated. When the fact of my death was certain, plans would be laid for a commemoration of my life, something to weigh against six million years of existence. They might etch my face across the surface of a planet, or blow an image of me into the gas of a nebula, or even shape a supernova remnant into my likeness. It had all been done before. And at the next reunion, and the one after that – all the way down the line until attrition wore us down to the last living shatterling, the last pale memory of Abigail Gentian, there would be an evening during the Thousand Nights when I would be honoured as if I still walked amongst the living. I would be dreamed into life again, if only until morning.

But now there would be no more Thousand Nights, never another reunion. Some of us might have survived, those of us who had arrived late, but we would never feel safe enough to stage another gathering. The best that we could do, to safeguard the memories we already carried, would be to go off in different directions and find somewhere to hide, living like hermits until time wore our enemies to dust.

The fact was, in this hour when I most had need of that consolation, it offered me nothing.

CHAPTER ELEVEN

When the attack came, I do not suppose I was entirely surprised. We had been aware of the possibility of ambush before we even entered this system, and even as I raced towards it, I had my doubts about the legitimacy of the distress signal. But there was still no warning when the weapons opened fire.

Fortune smiled on me, however, for I had just disengaged the engine, using friction from the debris cloud to effect my final slow-down into the rest frame of the signal. Had I still been making the course change, I would have been fatally weakened during those instants when the field was diminished. Instead of incinerating *Dalliance* in a few moments, the assault merely tested her defences to the limit. More energy was pumped into the bubble in a second than it had absorbed through all the collisions it had sustained since entering the veil. Emergency measures snapped into immediate effect, before I could even think of giving an order. Throughout the ship, impassors created secondary bubbles to encase vital systems and cargo, including myself. Even if the main bubble collapsed and the ship was ripped apart, some of those interior bubbles might still survive. It would be like a fish spilling eggs from its gut, even as it was torn asunder.

I had a few numb seconds during which to wonder how long the main bubble could hold before collapsing. On the console floating over me, a red line was creeping inexorably to the right. If the beam maintained its strength, *Dalliance* would not survive more than another thirty seconds. My every instinct screamed for me to steer out of the beam's reach, but that was impossible.

Then it ended, and I was still alive. I could only presume that the weapon had exhausted itself and was now either recharging or standing down while another was readied to continue the assault. An order formed in my head, but *Dalliance* had already anticipated it. While her bubble was still raised, hatches in her hull opened to release several dozen lampreys: small, autonomous vehicles equipped with weapons and limited-range skein-drives. The lampreys grouped into squadrons and raced to the limit of the bubble. The bubble's hardness was tuned down sufficiently for the lampreys to slip through into open space, and then restored to full effectiveness. Debris slipped inside the bubble during that interval of permeability, drumming against the hull like the claws of a thousand witches.

The lampreys served two functions. Three squadrons of four apiece remained near the bubble, while keeping the horizon of the bubble between themselves and the computed origin of the beam. The other six squadrons sped away from *Dalliance* in all directions, skein-drives at maximum output. Each lamprey was carving a furrow for itself in the debris field, using gamma-rays to ionise the particles into a plasma that could be diverted electrostatically. It made the lampreys hideously visible, but that was hardly a concern now.

The lampreys grouped around the bubble applied force to the hardened field and, with their drives synchronised, pushed *Dalliance* onto a different heading. After a few seconds they altered course, denying the enemy any hope of predicting my movements. The combined effect of the lampreys could never be as powerful as the main engine, but the acceleration was still violent enough that I was at the mercy of the dampening field.

Then the weapon found me again. The bubble had barely had time to recover from the last onslaught, and now that red line was beginning to creep to the right again. On another part of the console I witnessed the demise of two of the nearby lampreys, caught by energy re-radiating from the surface of the bubble. The remaining ten were still capable of pushing *Dalliance*, but my evasive swerves and feints would be more sluggish than before.

By then, the other twenty-four units had begun to fire at the source of the beam, using the same gamma-cannons that had cleared their paths through the debris cloud. On the main screen, the one that occupied the entire width of the bridge, I could even *see* their beams, etched bright by scattered and downshifted light as they gouged their way through the cloud. They formed a pattern like the spokes of a wheel, converging on my hidden assailant. I stared at the advancing red line on the console, conscious that the swerves were doing little to hamper the enemy. He was close enough that light-speed timelag could be easily accounted for, or perhaps ignored altogether, in his weapon's targeting calculations.

Abruptly the beam flicked off me and concentrated its attention on the twenty-four lampreys, picking three of them off in close succession. The wheel was now missing three spokes. In the instant before the beam returned, I had *Dalliance* tune down her bubble and fling out another four lampreys, exhausting her entire arsenal until more could be manufactured. The beam found me again, as I had known it would, but the red line had crept perceptibly back to the left as some of that energy was dissipated.

Two of the lampreys remained with *Dalliance*, assisting the other tugs, while the other pair sprinted out in opposite directions to augment those already arranged in the wheel formation. The beam remained fixated on me most of the time, only occasionally snapping off to eliminate one or two elements of the wheel. There was only one weapon out there, which was a blessing. Had there been two, I doubt that *Dalliance* would have survived for so long. I would either be dead, or adrift in a bubble, with every expectation of dying soon after.

I was down to eight lampreys, divided equally between those serving as tugs and those returning fire against the enemy, when the weapon exploded. It blew a moon-sized hole in the debris cloud, a hole that was snatched away by our mutual velocity. When the seconds dragged on and the attack failed to resume, I allowed myself a flicker of gratification. All the same I recognised that I was still in no position to drop my guard.

I ordered the eight remaining lampreys to group ahead of *Dalliance*, then engaged the engine. This time I permitted the bubble to drop completely, so that the drive could operate at maximum efficiency. I chose to trade speed for armour, to put as much distance between myself and the enemy as I could. I had destroyed their weapon, but the ghost signal was still there.

That was when Hesperus called through.

'Campion,' he said, his image flickering into grainy unreality before me, 'it appears that you have been attacked. Have you sustained damage? Are you debilitated?'

'I'm still here,' I said, having to raise my voice. I was pushing the engine harder than it liked. The noise was like some infernal threshing machine about to strip its gears. Surges of unchecked acceleration signalled the dampeners struggling to compensate. 'Thanks for asking,' I went on. 'It looks as if the signal was a lure. I should have known better than to go after it, when it wasn't purely Gentian.'

Hesperus had closed to within a minute of me.

'But you are quite uninjured?'

'Intact. So's my ship. But I think the point has been proved – Fescue was right to warn us away from this system. It's a nest of snakes. The sooner we're out of here the better.'

'I have an obstructed line of sight to Purslane. I shall inform her of your narrow escape. In the meantime, may I offer assistance?'

'I'll be fine once I've cleared the cloud. Concentrate your efforts on making sure you and Purslane get clear. Tell her to ignore all signals.'

'You are certain there are no survivors?'

'Look at this place, Hesperus. It was wishful thinking all along.'

But even as I was answering him, there was a chime from my console. I glared at the read-out, in no mood to deal with another piece of news.

Dalliance had just detected another signal. It was coming from a different location than the last one. It was stronger: powerful enough to suggest someone was tracking us and aiming a signalling device.

It was also unambiguously Gentian.

My hand hovered before the console. Reason compelled me to ignore this new signal, especially given what I had just told Hesperus. But I could not bring myself to dismiss it.

'Campion?'

'There's a new signal. It's Gentian, using the most recent protocols.'

'A distress code?'

'Yes.'

'If an ambush happened here, it might not be unreasonable to assume that distress signals would have been sent from many ships. Can you be sure that the enemy did not intercept such a signal and is now simply duplicating it?'

'If they could do that, why didn't they start with a true Gentian signal?'

'I have no answer for that,' Hesperus said quietly. 'But I would still urge caution. Should I inform Purslane of developments?'

'Wait,' I said, my hand still hovering before the console. *Dalliance* was now telling me that she had detected a second layer of embedded content in the signal: not merely a distress code, but a modulation on that transmission that could be interpreted as an audio-visual message.

My hand still hovered. If I opened the message, it might be persuasive.

I might not wish to be persuaded.

I could turn around now and argue that all I had done was ignore a second lure, albeit one constructed with more care than the first. Perhaps the enemy had only switched to a Gentian format when they concluded that I was likely to be a shatterling of that Line.

'Campion,' Hesperus said, 'forgive me for taking this liberty, but I decided to inform Purslane of the message.'

I was more bewildered than angry. 'I told you not to.'

'I felt that the information was too important not to disseminate. Purslane now knows that there is an agency in this system capable of imitating Gentian signals. That agency may be Gentian, but equally it may not be. Now she has that information, and it may help her even if we are destroyed.'

I did not have the energy to argue with Hesperus, especially when a begrudging part of me knew he was right.

'Did she say anything?'

'Purslane was of the opinion that it would be wise to ignore the message. She argued this point most strenuously.'

I smiled – I had no doubt that Hesperus was understating the matter. At the same time I ordered *Dalliance* to play the audio-visual transmission, projecting it into the air onto a flat surface just beyond the circular disc of the control platform.

A face appeared.

I knew her. Her name was Mezereon. She was one of us.

'I hope I'm talking to Campion,' she said. 'I *think* I must be. That ship of yours – I'd recognise it anywhere. I must have told you to get rid of it a dozen times, but I'm so glad now that you didn't. I'm sorry you were attacked, but I didn't notice you until then. Please don't respond just yet; not until we're closer. I could see you from half the system away now, but I'm still camouflaged, and I hope no one is listening in on this beam.' Mezereon licked her dry, colourless lips, as if she was thirsty. She was a plain woman, by the standards of the Line. The most attractive Gentian attributes: the cheekbones, the mismatched eyes, the shape of the mouth – had been toned down almost as far as they could go without vanishing altogether. Her hair was tied back in simple fashion, pulling the skin on her forehead drum tight. She wore a purple dress or blouse that left one shoulder bare, and the read-out-crammed wall behind her told me she was speaking to me from inside a ship. 'I guess you know something about the ambush by now,' she said. 'I was in abeyance, primed to be woken if anything went off. When they opened fire with the Spitting Cobra, I knew someone must have arrived.' A sudden, savage anger transformed her features. 'They didn't get us all. There are other shatterlings with me, a handful I managed to pick up while all hell was breaking loose, and I'm sure there are more hiding out around the system. And there are our prisoners. But we can't move. We can't leave. I don't have an engine any more. I could crawl out of this cloud, but they'd catch up with me sooner or later.'

I mouthed a question, half-whispered, 'What do you want me to do about it?'

Mezereon breathed in heavily. 'Time's running out for us. We're out of Synchromesh and I've already used up nine lives in the stasis cabinet. My ship's dying. It can't repair itself any more, and the impassor's about the last thing still working.' She looked at me with a probing intensity, as if our eyes were meeting and she was daring me to look away. 'Let me know you've received this message – even if you choose not to act on it. Alter your course just enough to send me a signal. I want to know that someone got it. Because there's something you need to know, something you need to get to the rest of Line even if you leave us here to die. I told you about the prisoners. Fescue didn't know about them, so I don't think there's any way you can know about them either. We got something out of one of them. His name's Grilse – he's a rogue shatterling of Marcellin Line. That's how they got hold of the H-guns. But don't blame the Marcellins just yet – we think Grilse and his friends were acting alone. If this is Campion I'm speaking to, I don't know how you're going to take this – but Grilse told us that this was somehow *your fault.*' Mezereon shook her head in frustration. 'No, I don't mean fault. I mean somehow something you did, innocently enough, led to this. You were the catalyst. You triggered the ambush – whether you knew it or not.'

'How could I have triggered it?' I asked, stunned. 'How could I have triggered it when I wasn't even *here*?'

I relayed Mezereon's message to Purslane so that she could hear the part about the Marcellins and my supposed involvement in the ambush. I did not wait for her answer before beginning my turn. A few moments later, Hesperus shadowed my course change, powering hard to position his ship ahead of mine. He must have been notching close to five thousand gees, far beyond the capabilities of any dampening field I had ever heard of.

Mezereon was not long in responding. 'Thank you, Campion. I hoped you might turn, but I didn't dare count on it. Whatever happens ... you have my undying gratitude. I know bad things have been said about you ... including things said by people like me, who should have known better. You didn't deserve any of that. You're a jewel in the Line, someone we can all be proud of.'

'Wait until I've rescued you,' I said.

'I'm sending you our position now,' Mezereon said. 'It's not precise, but I can't determine it any more accurately than that. When you get close, you should be able to sniff us out from our bubble spillage. I'll do what I can to talk you in, of course. I still think it would be unwise for you to signal me directly.'

Numbers appeared on the console. On the main screen, an icon popped into existence against the brown smear of the cloud. Mezereon lay about fifteen degrees north of the original signal, a little deeper inside the veil. At my present acceleration, I would arrive at her position inside the hour. I stared intently into the fog of pulverised planet, in the absurd hope that my eyes might pick out some buried threat before the infinitely more acute sensors of my ship.

Hesperus, who was still able to talk, said, 'She mentioned a Spitting Cobra. I confess my memory is silent on the matter.'

'Do you know much about wormholes, Hesperus?'

'A little. The Rebirthers use them for rejuvenating stars.'

'That's because there's not much else you can use them for. They're a joke from God. Maybe the Priors found a way to send ships and information down them, but if they did, we don't have a clue how it's done. The best we can do is squeeze matter down them. Fine for siphoning fuel from one star to another, but not much use for anything else. Maybe the Machine People have figured out a way to embed information into that matter flow, but we've never managed it. Modulate the flow at one end, the signal is still smeared out by the time the matter emerges.'

'We encountered the same difficulty,' Hesperus said.

'Well, luckily for us you can use wormholes to kill things. You take a Rebirther wormhole, but you only anchor one end in a star. You let the fuel spew out of the other end into naked space. Surround the throat with machinery to open and close the flow of matter, and to aim it at whatever you want to kill. It's a flame-thrower, basically.'

'Would the other end be in this system?'

'Doesn't have to be. Could be hundreds of years away. One star might have multiple taps, leading to multiple throats.'

'Do you think there was more than one of them here?'

'No way of telling, I'm afraid. We might not even have damaged the one we hit. Disabled the throat mechanisms, maybe, but I doubt we did anything that can't be fixed, given time.'

'Why would they use that weapon, and not the H-guns?'

'Range, basically. A Spitting Cobra's got a longer reach, even if it isn't as destructive. Someone had to get close in with those Homunculus weapons. If the ambushers took out the reunion world, they would have needed to be nearby before they did it.'

'Could the H-guns have been concealed?'

'Only inside ships.'

'The ships would be seen,' Hesperus said.

'But no one would suspect anything if they were ships of the Line, arriving with Gentian recognition signals.'

Hesperus did not respond at first. I do not think he was shocked by my suggestion, but more that he wished to accord it a respectful silence. Given the evidence, I had little doubt that he had drawn a similar conclusion himself.

The ambush could not have happened without Gentian collaboration.

The console chimed to inform me that Mezereon was signalling me again. Her message was brief, simply a string of coordinates. *Dalliance* adjusted her course minutely and gave me an ETA for the rendezvous. Allowing for deceleration, we would be on Mezereon's position in twelve minutes.

'Campion,' Hesperus said, after a while, 'I do not wish to alarm you, but I am seeing something beyond Mezereon. It was not there a few moments ago. Whatever it is is large, and it is moving towards us.'

Dalliance pushed her faculties to the limit, lowering her detection thresholds now that I had independent evidence that something else was lurking in the cloud. In a few moments, something appeared in the displayer – a hazy blob, framed in a box and accompanied by the exceedingly sparse data my ship had managed to extract. The object was well camouflaged but large – five or six kilometres wide – and Hesperus had been right about it coming nearer.

'It could be a big ship, or a big ship carrying a Homunculus weapon, or just one of the weapons on its own,' I said.

'I see smaller signals grouped around it – other ships, perhaps.'

At that moment Mezereon returned. We were close enough now that she was able to send an imago without risk of interception. The figure appeared before me, to the right of Hesperus. She was trying to be firm, but there was a crack in her voice that she could not quite conceal.

'You have to turn back now, Campion. They're moving one of the H-guns onto you. If you turn tail and go to maximum power, you may stay out of range. They'll still chase you, but maybe you can keep ahead of them.'

This time Mezereon's message protocol permitted me to answer her.

'They must have been counting on killing me with the Spitting Cobra, but I damaged it.'

'Good for you,' she said, a gleam of admiration in her eyes. 'It won't stop them, but at least you showed them there's still fire in the Line.'

'I hope so.'

'Turn around now. You've done your best, Campion, but there's no sense in dying to make a point. I've told you what I can. I wish I could have given you the prisoners, but—'

'I'm still coming in,' I said.

'If you are committed to this rescue,' Hesperus said, 'then I will do what I can to draw the fire of the Homunculus weapon. I will pass Mezereon's position at speed and increase my visibility.'

'Are you certain about doing this?'

'Already committed. I will make my closest approach to Mezereon's position in three minutes. Then I will adjust my impasse emissions and engine signature to lure the Homunculus weapon. Even if it can still see you, I doubt that it will be able to resist a closer target.'

'Whatever happens, Hesperus ... I'm grateful.'

'I am going silent now. I shall see you in interstellar space, when we have put this unfortunate place behind us.'

His imago rippled and vanished, leaving me alone with Mezereon.

'You were just talking to a Machine Person, weren't you? How in God's name did you pull that off?'

'I'm full of surprises.'

The next three minutes passed like an age as I watched Hesperus streak forward and then slam past Mezereon's position, missing her by barely half a million kilometres. By then, my view of the approaching object and its escort of ships had improved substantially. That it was a Homunculus weapon was beyond argument: I was seeing it from a foreshortened perspective, but *Dalliance* was able to extrapolate its true form, and the delicate, slender-stalked flower-like shape, its maw a coronet of diaphanous petals, veined like dragonfly wings, was an uncanny match against data in the trove. It must have arrived hidden in the belly of one of our ships, but there was no need to conceal it now; the slender form might have looked vulnerable, but that fragility was deceptive. The field-reinforced, field-armoured weapon was being propelled by tugs much like my own lampreys: they were clamped onto the stem like thorns and had sharp skein-drive signatures.

Once he had passed Mezereon, Hesperus began to tune his hull to make himself more conspicuous. He fired his own weapons against the Homunculus device and its escort vehicles, not with any obvious expectation of doing harm, but in the hope of goading it into a response. His drive emissions became noisier: Hesperus could have been tracked from across the system by now. Purslane would have been aware of his actions even if she did not grasp their full significance.

A minute later, I began my own slowdown. *Dalliance* forwent all her usual safeguards. The engine screamed in my ears, the dampeners warning that they could not guarantee to neutralise the thousands of gee-forces trying to keep me moving in a straight line.

I grimaced and sank deeper into my seat, hands clasping at the armrests, as if that would make the slightest difference if the dampeners failed.

As the distance between *Dalliance* and Mezereon's ship dwindled to thousands of kilometres, and then hundreds, I got my first clear look at the vessel I had come to rescue. Mezereon had done everything she could to camouflage herself, but she had not been able to work miracles. Her ship was a wreck, damaged beyond obvious repair. It was a lozenge-shaped hull just less than a kilometre from end to end, and about a fifth of kilometre across the beam. Where her engine had been was a perfectly spherical hole, as if a giant had taken a crunching bite out of the ship. At the forward end of the ship, the nose was split open like a ruptured seed pod. Evidence of smaller weapon or collision impacts peppered the hull with silvery craters, stark chrome flowers against the midnight black of the intact parts.

But Mezereon had been inventive. She still had a working impassor, and she had gathered several million tonnes of rubble inside the bubble with her ship, dressing it around the wreck to form a gauzy screen that would offer some concealment if the bubble failed. Beyond the bubble, several larger chunks of rock had been arranged to provide secondary camouflage. Seen in close-up, it looked unnatural – big boulders apparently coalescing into a baby asteroid, with a glassy marble at the heart of that swarm of rubble – but she must have been counting on never coming under direct scrutiny.

'I'm very near you now,' I said. 'Cargo bay's already open – there's enough room for you inside. But you'll have to drop the bubble and lose your camouflaging screen.'

'I'm scared. They're close enough now that if I do drop my bubble, they'll have no trouble finding me again.'

'You told me your bubble was about to give up the ghost anyway. You've nothing to lose.'

As I completed the final phase of my approach, my deceleration dropping down to mere gees of slowdown, my attention flicked back to Hesperus. He had begun to steer, while still maintaining a steady assault against the Homunculus weapon. He must have had some effect, for two of the escort vehicles had begun to peel off to close in on him. But the weapon itself was showing no inclination to follow his bait. The two escort craft were accelerating hard as they made their turn, nearly as hard as Hesperus himself.

Dalliance came to a halt just beyond Mezereon's last layer of camouflaging boulders. Her bubble flicked off and her ship began to inch forward on impellors, nosing clear of the rubble that had been trapped within the bubble. The boulders carved silvery gouges in her hull as they knocked against her, splintering and pulverising in the process. The impellors began to glow a vivid pink, signifying some worrying ailment deep inside their mechanisms. Never mind: all they had to do was get her another few hundred metres, and then they could be scrapped.

I assigned two of the lampreys to rearrange the rubble into a makeshift screen between us and the Homunculus weapon. With enough intelligence not to need direct supervision, they set to work in a blur of furious motion, zipping back and forth too quickly for the eye to track.

While the lampreys were busy, I spun *Dalliance* around to bring the bay into alignment and dropped my own field. The lampreys buzzed around me like busy fireflies, doing their best to shepherd away the larger rocks that had been disturbed by Mezereon's emergence. All of a sudden, even the wreck of her ship looked too big to fit, as if I had misjudged the capacity of my cargo bay.

'Disengage your impellors,' I told Mezereon. 'You have enough momentum now. I'll take care of the rest.'

At that moment it was as if half the sky had been clawed back to reveal a blinding whiteness beyond it, as if the black of night was just an eggshell-thin layer masking an unimaginably cruel brightness. On the console hovering above me, *Dalliance* recorded a litany of complaint: moderate damage sustained across a large acreage of the hull, one of the fireflies out of action.

Mezereon's imago flickered and reformed.

'They just used it.'

I nodded: I had guessed as much for myself. 'Are you hurt?'

'I think the rubble took the brunt of it. We're still outside its effective kill-range. Did you take a hit?'

'Nothing that can't be fixed, and nothing that'll stop us getting away.'

I did not care to think about what would happen when that weapon came closer. Technically, it had not even touched us. My hands trembling, I watched as Mezereon's ruined ship began to drift into my cargo bay, with what appeared to be no more than angstroms of clearance in any direction. *Dalliance* clanged as something knocked against her. But the slow drift continued. Switching to an internal view, I saw the wreck force its way into the bay as if some obscene creature was striving to raid the snug burrow of another animal. Bits of Mezereon's ship, especially around the existing damage spots, were ripping away.

The sky beyond the sky whitened again, brighter this time, turning the bay and the ship into pink-edged silhouettes, and *Dalliance* let me know that she had sustained more damage. One of the boulders tumbled away from the screen that the lampreys had erected, and it was glowing red on the side that had been facing the weapon.

Then Mezereon was clear of the doors.

Grapples moved in to lock her ship into position. I reinstated my bubble and gave the command to move. With fewer lampreys to push her along, *Dalliance* could not sustain her former rate of acceleration. I decided I would risk stuttering the bubble, allowing the engine to contribute to the effort. At a thousand gees, the wall of boulders dropped away behind me with disarming swiftness. It was tempting to think that I had already put sufficient safe distance between myself and the Homunculus weapon, but that was not the case.

When I relocated *Vespertine*, I saw Hesperus was taking her towards the weapon, having executed a hairpin turn that would have crushed most ships, let alone their human occupants.

'Hesperus,' I whispered, 'don't do this. We're getting away all right.'

As if he could have heard me, or would have listened even if he could.

The weapon fired again. This time there was a jagged and asymmetric quality to the wash of light as it branched across the sky. When it abated, something brachiform and luminous remained. The weapon had made a lesion: they must have been pushing it to its limit in their determination to kill me.

There was nothing more I could do to improve my chances. *Dalliance* was giving her all to get away as quickly as possible, and my fretting would make no difference whatsoever.

Yet I could not turn away until I had seen what would become of Hesperus.

CHAPTER TWELVE

'Did you see him die?' I asked.

'Yes,' Campion said.

'I'm sorry. For you and for him.'

We were aboard *Dalliance*, lying together. We had cleared the cloud and were now in interstellar space, returning to cruise speed. I had whisked over as soon as Campion's ship was in range of mine. We had embraced, holding each other so tightly that it was as if our coming back together was only provisional, a state of affairs that might be rescinded at any moment if the universe changed its mind.

We had kissed, and then our kissing had become an exercise in frenzied exploration, as if the hours that we had been apart had been long enough to dull our memories of each other. We lost our clothes and made love, dozing into half-sleep before starting anew, until we both fell into blissful unconsciousness, weary but glad to have survived. Now we were awake again, holding on to each other like two exhausted swimmers, each using the other for support.

'I should introduce you to the new guests,' Campion said, after a long silence during which I had almost fallen back into dream.

'Are they all right?'

'I checked on them, obviously. Only Aconite and Mezereon are awake at the moment. But I thought I'd save the big welcome until you could share in it. I suggested they wait in the gardens until you were ready.'

'What about the prisoner – or prisoners? Did you find out anything more?'

'Nothing beyond what Mezereon already told me – that this was all somehow caused by me.'

'For all we know Mezereon got the wrong end of the stick, or the prisoner was feeding her a lie.'

'A lie that just happened to include me as a detail?'

I had no answer for that.

We washed, clothed ourselves, then whisked through-ship to *Dalliance*'s gardens. I did my best to hide my concerns from him, but all the while my mind was spinning through the possibilities. How could the ambush have had anything to do with Campion, if he had been so conspicuously late for the reunion?

It made no sense unless the 'cause' of it was something that had happened during the last reunion. Something in Campion's thread, in other words. But if that was the case then we were dealing with an agency that thought nothing of plotting our demise across a timescale of an entire circuit, longer than the lifespan of some planetary civilisations.

Someone, in other words, prepared to be as patient as a snake.

'Everything goes back to the Vigilance,' I said.

Campion opened the door in the stone wall that encircled the gardens.

'What does the Vigilance have to do with anything?'

'Think about it for a moment. If you hadn't visited the Vigilance in your previous circuit, you wouldn't have been saddled with delivering Doctor Meninx to them. If you hadn't had to deliver Doctor Meninx, we'd never have been back to that sector of the Scutum-Crux Arm. No Centaurs, no Ateshga – and more than likely no being late for the reunion.'

'And no Hesperus, either – he'd still be Ateshga's prisoner.'

'See what I'm getting at?'

'I'm still not sure what all that has to do with what Mezereon said.'

'Maybe nothing – but if all those occurrences hung on your visit to the Vigilance, how do we know something else didn't? It formed the central part of your strand, a circuit ago. What if there was a detail in your memories, something to do with the Vigilance, that someone didn't like?'

'What kind of detail?'

Campion could be almost superhumanly exasperating. 'No idea. But in the absence of anything better, shouldn't we at least consider the possibility?'

'That would mean going back over my thread,' Campion said, as if that was somehow an insurmountable obstacle. 'Maybe we should see what the prisoners have to say first.'

Of all the spaces in Campion's ship, I liked the gardens the best. We had emerged through a gate in a tall ivy-clad stone wall. From the gate we had followed a winding pathway down a gently sloping meadow set with sculptures, sundials, water clocks, wind-chimes, elegant moving statuary and foaming iron fountains, into a bower enclosed by trees. At the centre of the bower was a small summer house, a round wooden building with a conical roof, surrounded by a moat of water which in turn connected to a larger pond, the moat spanned by a red-painted bridge of Chinese design.

The visible sky was the cloudless enamel-blue of a hundred thousand worlds. The layout of the gardens, the agreeable climate of that eternal sunny afternoon, never varied. There were stars in the sky that had not existed when the soil in these gardens was first laid down. There were stars that had shone then that were now veils of dead gas, rushing into darkness. Civilisations beyond number had risen from obscurity, considering themselves masters of all creation, before fading back into the footnotes of history.

Mezereon and Aconite were waiting in the summer house, sitting on one of the benches with food and wine on a tray between them. 'Hello, Purslane,' they said in near-unison as I ducked into the shadowed interior, with Campion just behind me.

'I'm glad you both made it,' I said.

'We are making it, aren't we?' Mezereon asked, directing her question at Campion. She had short blonde hair the colour of sun-dried straw and pale, almost translucent skin, with a delicate mottling of honey-coloured freckles across her cheeks.

'Too soon to tell, I'm afraid,' Campion said. 'We're putting distance between us and the enemy, but I won't feel truly safe until this system is just a bad memory.'

'I meant to ask,' Aconite said, pausing to sip from the goblet he held. He was muscular and dark-skinned, with a black beard raffishly flecked with silver and a mass of jangling rings hanging from one earlobe. 'Did you hear from anyone else? We knew we were all right, obviously, but we couldn't risk broadcasting our presence to the rest of the cloud.'

'If there was anyone else there,' Campion said, 'I didn't hear from them. Sorry – wish the news was better.'

'Not your fault, old man.'

'The only other survivor we know about is Fescue,' I said, taking a place on the opposite bench, kicking off my shoes and hugging my legs, my arms encircling my shins. 'We ran into his transmission. He tried to talk us out of entering the cloud, but we decided to take a shot at it.'

Mezereon looked sharply at Aconite, then me. 'Then I guess you don't know about Fescue.'

'He's dead,' Aconite said. 'He stayed behind when most of the survivors had already managed to get out of the system. That transmission must have been one of his last acts.'

The news hit me hard. I had taken it for granted that Fescue was one of the living – how else would he have been in a position to send his warning, if he had not made it through the ambush?

'What happened?' I asked. 'Engine trouble?'

Mezereon shook her small, pale head wearily. 'Fescue was trying to create a distraction, to keep the ambushers occupied so that a few of us could get away. He could have escaped if he'd chosen to, but he was thinking of the Line.'

'I misjudged him,' I said.

'You weren't the only one,' Campion said, looking down shamefacedly.

'Let's not get maudlin,' Aconite said. 'It's enough that we have survived to commemorate him. Burnish his name, and all that stuff. We'll do the old bastard proud.' He gave Campion an encouraging punch. 'Right, old man?'

'Right,' Campion said.

Mezereon poured herself some more wine while Aconite chewed the end off a loaf of bread. Outside, birds twittered and breezes stirred the reeds around the summer house's little moat.

'Are there just the two of you?' I asked.

'We're the only ones up and awake,' Aconite said. 'There are three others in abeyance: Lucerne, Melilot and Valerian – and the prisoners, of course.'

Campion leaned over to take a grape from the platter. 'Is there anything else you need in the meanwhile? Medical attention – anything like that?'

Our two new guests looked at each other momentarily before Mezereon answered for them both. 'We're fine. It's been stressful, but the ship's looked after us well. If there'd been a problem with rations, or life support, one or more of us would have gone into permanent abeyance. Thankfully, it never came to that.'

'Have you been awake ever since the ambush?' I asked.

'We'd have gone mad from the tension if we hadn't had abeyance,' Mezereon said. 'We took turns. The ship was instructed to bring one or two of us out if she detected something anomalous. It could have been Lucerne or one of the other two, but it was our turn.'

'This may not be the best time to talk about it,' Campion said, 'but it would have been difficult to get one of those weapons close to the reunion planet unless it was hidden.'

'Inside one of our ships?' Aconite asked.

'I hate to think it, but—'

'You're right. There were three of those weapons, and the Spitting Cobra, in the ships of Saffron, Scabious and Tare. But they weren't involved. Their ships must have been captured, the Line protocols cracked.' Aconite kept looking at Campion as if there could be no other explanation; that to think otherwise was a kind of heresy. 'They couldn't have been *complicit*, if that's what you're thinking.'

'At this point we shouldn't rule anything out,' Campion said.

Mezereon sighed through her nose. 'It's about time we faced up to Line involvement, Aconite. Even Fescue had his suspicions. He couldn't understand how the private network had been broken into, unless one of us was complicit.'

'Involvement doesn't necessarily mean willing involvement,' Aconite said. Then he raised his big hands defensively. 'Let's not fall out over this. There'll be time to ask the unpleasant questions when we make it to the fallback. I won't flinch from asking them if the evidence points that way.'

I took a piece of bread for myself. 'Nor will I.'

Mezereon brushed a hand against the iron-grey casing of Melilot's cryophagus. 'We should wake them up. It's what we agreed we'd do if there was a change in our situation.'

'Be kinder not to,' Aconite said. 'At least until we know we're definitely in the clear.'

'We can move them into *Dalliance*, at least,' Campion said. 'I've got plenty of sleepers aboard her already, so a few more won't hurt. It's easier to keep an eye on them when they're all together.'

'Didn't have you down as the guest-carrying sort,' Mezereon said, with an amused smile.

'Just the way things worked out,' Campion said.

The prisoners were in a different room from the Gentian shatterlings. Mezereon strode to the first cabinet, worked the heavy clasp and flung wide the patterned brass doors. Inside lay a scaffold of ancient machinery, a framework supporting an array of impassors energising a containment bubble. The bubble's near-transparency made it resemble a globe of blown glass, large enough to swallow a throne. Inside the bubble floated another kind of framework, this one supporting time-compression mechanisms. They created a secondary bubble, scarlet-tinged as if the glass had been stained. Inside the bubble hovered a chair, edges curved to fit inside the confines of the field. Inside the high-backed throne, secured against involuntary movements, was a human figure. The figure had the deathly stillness of a hologram, but it was neither dead nor holographic.

'Is this Grilse?' I asked, remembering what Mezereon had already told Campion.

'As far as we know,' she said. 'There was a Grilse in the Marcellin Line, circuits ago. And of course, the Marcellins were given responsibility for the H-guns. But until we can get into his skull, we won't know for sure.'

'How did you catch them?' Campion asked.

'Some shatterlings had broken cover and were making a run for interstellar space,' Mezereon said. 'The ambushers tried to stop them – they really didn't want any of us ever to leave that system. Fescue intercepted one of the ambushers' ships and damaged it badly, and the other Gentians were able to make their escape. I don't think Fescue ever found out that there were survivors still aboard the ambusher ship – he was dead by the time we pulled them in.'

Campion frowned. 'What do you mean?'

'The damaged ambusher drifted within range of my ship. On the chance that it might contain weapons or supplies we could use, we decided to risk dropping the impassor and sending out a shuttle. It was a risk – don't think we didn't argue about it.' She looked steadily at Aconite. 'I didn't approve; I'll admit that. But in the end it was the right thing to do. There wasn't much we could use aboard the wreck, but we got the four prisoners.' She sneered. 'Cowards: if they'd had a fucking *atom* of courage they'd have killed themselves rather than run the chance of falling into our hands.'

'We put them into stasis almost immediately,' Aconite said. 'The cabinets are old, but they were all we had. If we'd left them in shiptime there'd have been a chance of them escaping, alerting the other ambushers or finding a way to commit suicide.'

'And before you locked them away?' I asked.

'We interrogated them as best we could,' he said. 'Didn't get anything useful, though.'

'Except from Grilse,' I said.

'That was after he went into the casket.' Mezereon touched part of the casket to the left of the doors, causing a hidden panel to reveal itself. It was set with heavy brass controls, ornately engraved dials and clocks. The main control was a lever running in a graduated quadrant from left to right. At the moment the lever was pushed four-fifths of the way to the right, at a setting of one hundred thousand. That was enough to ensure that a second of time as experienced in the stasis cabinet equalled a day as measured beyond it. The logarithmic control could be pushed all the way to the right, giving a time ratio of one million, but even with the best equipment that was a setting to be used under emergency conditions only. 'He's safe enough now,' Mezereon said, with one eye on the Marcellin, 'but when we dialled him back down we started to see signs of unstable field collapse. We held him low enough to reach with Synchromesh, so we could talk in person, but we didn't want to push our luck.'

'I don't blame you,' I said. 'And the others?'

'Just as risky, if not more so. Grilse's cabinet is the best of the four – the other three are in even worse repair.' Mezereon closed the control panel, then swung shut the patterned doors. 'I wouldn't recommend attempting to bring him out until we reach the Bella-donna world. At least there we'll be able to call on the technical assistance of the rest of the Line.'

'What's left of it,' I said.

'There'll be more of us at the fallback,' Mezereon said. 'Call that an act of faith, if you will. But if I didn't believe that ... I'd end myself. Voluntary attrition.'

'We all feel that way,' Campion said.

Aconite turned to him. 'Did you tell Purslane what Grilse told us?'

'She knows.'

'And what do you both make of it?'

'I'd love to ask Grilse in person,' Campion said.

Aconite's smile was grim. 'You'll get your chance, don't worry about that.'

'I believe Grilse,' I said. 'It's not comfortable, but why would he invent a detail like that unless it had some substance? It doesn't make Campion complicit in any of this.'

'And Doctor Meninx – what does he have to say?' Mezereon asked.

'Not a lot lately,' Campion said.

'He died,' I said. 'Tank failure.'

Aconite winced. 'Spectacular timing, old man.'

Campion raised his hands defensively. 'It wasn't my fault! I was under strict instructions not to touch his tank, and I didn't.'

Aconite clapped him on the back in a comradely fashion. 'If it makes you feel any better, I'll take a look at the tank. But I can already tell you what I'll find, based on all the aquatics I've known: some rusting piece of junk with nothing inside it newer than a million years old, just begging to go wrong.'

'Thank you,' Campion said, sounding taken aback.

'See, he does have his uses,' Mezereon said.

That was when *Silver Wings* whispered into my brain, telling me there was something vital I needed to know.

The image was a rectangular volume, divided into cubic cells by a scaffold of fine green lines. At one end of the volume was a representation of our two ships, close enough together that they almost resembled a single vessel. At the other end lay a halo of smeared light indicating the heliopause of the system we had just departed; the boundary where the star's influence became negligible and beyond which we could consider ourselves to be in true interstellar space. Halfway along the rectangle was a trio of icons representing the three ships that had been pursuing Campion ever since he rescued Mezereon and the others.

'We already knew about the three ships,' Aconite said. 'Maybe I'm being dim, but I don't quite see what all the fuss is about.'

We had whisked over to my ship. The four of us were standing on *Silver Wings'* bridge, grouped around the central displayer. 'One of the three ships is making headway on the other two,' I said. 'That's what the fuss is about.'

Aconite scratched at his chin. 'Now you mention it – that *is* a bit odd.'

The trio of icons formed an elongated triangle, with the lone ship at the apex. We were all accelerating hard; it was only necessary to look at the image for a few minutes to spot the oozing motion of the grid from left to right, with the magnetopause slowly disappearing from the frame.

'If they had power in reserve, they'd have used it already,' I said. 'There's only one explanation. I know you thought you saw her being destroyed, Campion, but that third ship can only be *Vespertine*. She must have survived the attack after all.'

'A direct hit from an H-gun?' Campion asked.

'I'm not saying she's in one piece.'

'But there's been no direct contact from Hesperus himself?' Mezereon asked.

'Nothing – only the agreed distress code he installed in the ship. Hesperus is the only one who's supposed to be able to transmit that signal.'

'Could someone have got aboard and cracked the safeguards?' Aconite asked.

'Theoretically, yes – but they'd have to be very clever and very quick, and for some reason Hesperus must not have destroyed the signalling apparatus even though he would have known he was being boarded.'

'So it could be him – but you can't be sure,' Mezereon said.

'No way to know for certain until we open up *Vespertine* and peer inside.'

Aconite looked concerned. 'In other words, let him catch up with us and see what happens?'

'He can't. We're outrunning him, and short of engine failure we'll keep on doing so. He may have some pseudo-thrust in reserve, but given the circumstances I rather doubt it.'

Mezereon bit her lip. 'So it's a lost cause.'

'Unless we go back for him,' Campion said.

I nodded. 'He's sending that signal because he wants our help. He helped Gentian Line in our moment of need. We can't turn our backs on him now.'

'I'm probably missing something,' Aconite said, 'but if we turn around now, or even just slow down, won't we be in danger of falling back in range of the killers?'

'There are other options,' I said. 'I've got a lot of ships in my hold. Some of them can sustain a much higher rate of acceleration than either *Dalliance* or *Silver Wings*. Not for ever – but long enough to get to Hesperus and back.'

Mezereon still did not look convinced. 'Can this really be done? I mean, the idea is nice in theory ... but you're going to be cutting things very close.'

'It can be done,' I said. I had already primed the displayer; now it showed an icon leaving *Silver Wings* and racing back towards *Vespertine*. I had overlaid ovoid volumes that indicated the likely range of the enemy's weapons, assuming they were carrying nothing on the scale of the Homunculus device or the Spitting Cobra. 'If Hesperus holds his current rate,' I continued, 'we can reach him without ever falling in range of their guns. Then we speed back to *Silver Wings* and notch back up to maximum acceleration. We'll still lose them, and we'll still be able to make the turn to the fallback without being traced.'

'There's an element of risk, though,' said Mezereon.

I shrugged. 'There's an element of risk in breathing.'

'It's not that I'm against rescuing him,' Aconite said, 'but from now on every action we take has to be measured against the future existence of the Line. There simply isn't room for brave gestures any more.'

'I feel the same way,' I answered, 'but I also know that if we don't do this for Hesperus, we've got no right to call ourselves Gentian.'

'In any case, the Line – such as it is – won't be threatened,' Campion said, nodding at the other two. 'Purslane and I are in agreement: you'll stay aboard *Dalliance* while Purslane and I take one of the ships in *Silver Wings'* hold. *Silver Wings* will have to notch down a bit to allow the other ship to catch up, but she can make up the ground again when we're back aboard.'

'And you'll both ride that ship back to Hesperus?' Mezereon asked.

'We've talked about it. Neither of us much likes the idea of continuing without the other, so it makes perfect sense.'

'There's another way,' Aconite said, as if the idea was forming even as he spoke the words. 'If this Hesperus has done as much for the Line as you say he has ... then his preservation becomes our responsibility as well, not just yours. I should take that ship.'

'Unthinkable,' Campion said.

'After everything you've done for us? I don't think so, old man.' I started to say something, but he held his hand up firmly. 'It's no good, Purslane: I've made my mind up.'

'Are you sure?' Mezereon asked quietly.

'Resolute.' He nodded forcefully. 'I mean it. What kind of ship do you have in mind, Purslane?'

'I've got a Rimrunner scow.'

'Very tasty.'

'It hasn't been switched on for about three million years, planetary. You all right with that?'

'They built them to last. Just show me how to work the music.'

He reappeared as swiftly as he had disappeared. One moment I was in the bay looking at an iron-black sky peppered with doppler-squeezed starlight, the next there was a chrome and black Rimrunner scow making final approach, as if it had just popped into existence in my wake. Campion, Mezereon and I were aboard almost before the retaining field had clamped the ship into place.

That was when we learned what had become of Hesperus.

'He was alive when I got to him,' Aconite said. 'He moved slightly. He was aware of me.'

But if Hesperus was aware of anything now, there was no evidence of it. His head did not move, nor did his facial expression change. His eyes, which had twinkled between turquoise and jade, were now devoid of intelligence. The only hint that Hesperus was still alive, in some arcane sense, was the continued movement of lights in the fretted windows of his skull. But those lights moved slowly, and their colours were muted, like the last embers of a fire.

Yet it must have taken some volition to send that distress transmission.

The paucity of life was not the most disturbing thing about Hesperus, however: even if the lights had been dead, I could have convinced myself that he had placed himself into the machine equivalent of a deep coma, the better to preserve his deep functions while he awaited rescue. But we were not even looking at all of Hesperus. His left side was almost entirely gone, or rather was concealed or absorbed within a misshapen ingot of black and gold metal that appeared to be partly an extension of him and partly an eruption of the fabric of his ship, which had infiltrated and combined with Hesperus's own body. The ship was gone, but we could see the clean silvery surfaces where Aconite must have sliced through the mass to free Hesperus.

'There wasn't time to think it through,' he said, as if his actions needed explaining. 'I barely had time to free him.'

'Was there any change?' I asked.

'The lights got a bit dimmer, I think, but they weren't bright to start with. I don't know if that mass was keeping him alive, or killing him slowly.'

'When the ship was damaged,' Campion said, 'its repair systems must have gone haywire. I think Hesperus must have been caught in that – it looks as if the ship was trying to reconstitute him back into its own matrix, mistaking him for some broken component.'

'Then it was a mistake to separate him from the ship.'

'Hesperus sent that signal for a reason,' I said. 'He probably knew he couldn't stay ahead of them for much longer. Whatever happens, you gave him a better chance than he had.'

'I hope so.'

'I don't know how we're going to get him out of that, though,' Campion said, standing with his hands on his hips, like a gardener surveying a plot of soil.

'As far as I'm concerned,' I said, 'the best thing we can do is put him into abeyance and get him into the care of other Machine People as quickly as possible.'

'I'm not even sure we have a stasis chamber big enough,' Campion said. 'And we can't very well start hacking bits off him until he fits inside.'

I looked at the slow crawl of the muted lights. 'We can't just leave him like this.'

'We're not going to,' Campion said. 'We'll scan him, like you said, and if there's something obvious we can do, something that we can be certain won't hurt him, we will. But if we can't, he'll have to wait until we get to Belladonna. We'll just have to keep our fingers crossed another Machine Person shows up – a guest of someone who survived – and that they'll know what to do.'

'And if they don't show up?'

'We're not miracle workers,' he said quietly. 'We'll have done the best we can. That's all anyone can hope for.'

The scans brought no better news. The structures under that fused black and gold exterior were complex and intertwined, with parts of Hesperus extending deep into the mass and vice versa. Of his left side, including the living arm, little or nothing appeared to have retained anatomical integrity. There was activity within the combined growth, the arterial flow of energy and matter that indicated ongoing processes. Aconite had been fortunate not to sever any of those conduits when he freed Hesperus, but it was distinctly possible that attempting to free him further would do more harm than good.

But there was something still thinking inside him, and he did find a way to communicate with us, albeit briefly. It was not long after we had made the turn to Neume, the Belladonna fallback, confident that the pursuing ships had now fallen too far behind to track our movements. I was the one who noticed it, during one of my periodic and increasingly despondent attempts to coax some evidence of recognition from him. I was looking into his eyes and the fretted windows when my attention was snared by a tremor at the edge of my vision. I looked down and saw that the thumb of his right hand – the only visible hand – was quivering from the highest joint, as if a palsy afflicted that digit while the rest of him was paralysed into total immobility.

The thumb had not been moving before.

I stared at in puzzled astonishment for several seconds before I remembered what Hesperus had done with the wine goblet. With the prickling sense that this might be temporary, a window of lucid communication that could close at any moment, I dashed out of the room to the nearest maker and had it spin another goblet into existence. I pressed it into his hand so that the thumb lay against the glass, as if that was going to be all that I needed to do. But the thumb merely scratched a vertical white line into the glass, deepening the cut with each vertical movement.

I looked into his face, hoping for a clue, some nuance of expression that would make it all clear. Then I recalled the way he had rotated the goblet in his fingers as his thumb worked up and down, carving out a picture line by line in the manner of a scanning beam. Delicately I took hold of the glass, his thumb still moving, and started turning it, as slowly and smoothly as I was able, and *something* began to take form, not a line but a rectangle of impressions that was too pale and scratchy for me to make out until he was done.

I knew when he was finished because the thumb stopped moving; when I took the glass from his hand and touched the digit, it was as stiff and dead as the rest of him. But the evidence that it had moved was in my hands, scribed indelibly onto the goblet. I held it up to the light and squinted, but at first the array of scratches made no sense at all and I wondered if what I had seen was no more than a reflex quiver. I was afraid that I so desperately wanted Hesperus to come back to us that I had clutched at the meaningless twitch of a carcass.

But there was something in those scratches. It was almost impossibly faint, nearly lost in the noise, but Hesperus had engraved a design into the glass. It was a circular motif, a rim with spokes – like a wagon wheel with a thick hub.

'I don't know if you can hear me,' I said, addressing the mute form, 'but whatever this is, whatever you're trying to tell me, I'm going to find out and act upon it. I promise you that.'

I had expected no reaction, and there was none.

PART THREE

PART THREE

One day I learned the true and dire secret of my mother, and why our house was the way it was. It was after another of the little boy's visits. I had come to both cherish and detest him, like a dark part of my own psyche. It had been a year and a half at least, maybe more, since I had inducted him into the mysteries of Palatial.

He had become Count Mordax. It had required negotiating a series of mental stepping stones, each of which took up at least one afternoon's session of the game. First he had inserted himself into the mind of a palace rider, who became a spy claiming to have knowledge of where the sorcerer Calidris was in hiding. The rider reached the Black Castle, where he was challenged but allowed entry because he was unarmed and in possession (so he claimed) of vital intelligence. He was seen by Count Mordax, but found that he could not effect the transfer into his mind. The game's rules were Byzantine, and we had to work them out through trial and error. One rule, which had only gradually become apparent, was that one could only move into another character's head if the move did not involve too big a jump in social status. A peasant could not swap into the head of a king, even if the king knelt down to kiss the peasant. But the peasant could get there by jumping into the head of a blacksmith, and then an armourer, and then an officer in the king's guard, and so on – working their way up by discrete steps. Sometimes it would not be possible to change character between one session and the next, but that was all part of the game's richly involving texture. It was difficult and slow, but because at each step one had access to the memories and personality of the inhabited character, it was seldom boring. More often than not, the superimposed personality was so dominant that one had to concentrate to maintain a plan that might have been sketched out three or four characters down the chain. For myself, I only occasionally ventured from the mind of the princess: hopping from time to time into the minds of her courtiers to make sure none of them was plotting against her. When I had discovered a potential traitor – a maid whose brother had been caught poaching on palace grounds and executed – I had her put to questioning by my master interrogator. She had perished before admitting her intention to kill me, but I remained certain of her guilt.

By now, it was becoming clear that Palatial would never be authorised for mass production. The dozen or so prototypes, of which mine was one, would be all that ever existed. Although the details were sketchy, and reported to me mostly by the little boy, it was said that the games had begun to have an adverse and lingering effect on the mental states of the children who played them. Children were carrying over some of the memories and personality traits of their characters into the real world outside the green cube – even though the machine was supposed to erase these transient neural states as the players passed back through the portal. That was true for me – in Palatial the princess was as real as anyone I had ever known – more real, in some respects, since I had become her – but the moment I passed back into the wider volume of the playroom, she seemed to wither away, becoming no more animated than a drawing in a book. Her memories, which had been mine to sift through when I was in the game, melted away like a dream whose details I could not recapture upon wakening. I remembered the pleasures and frustrations of the game, I remembered the objectives and the status of play, but outside the green room it might as well have been a simple doll's house.

The combine was protected from lawsuits associated with the prototype versions of Palatial – the families had all signed waivers before being permitted to take part in the trials – but there would be no such protection if the game was mass produced and released into millions of homes in the Golden Hour. Even if only a fraction of the children suffered delusional episodes, the combine would be ruined.

And so the game's development was abandoned. The combine tried to take back the prototypes, but they were only partially successful. The children who had been exposed to them were now obsessed with Palatial, unwilling to surrender their right of entry into that fantasy land. A few families let the technicians dismantle the prototypes, but most of them – aided by the fact that the combine had no desire to court publicity – managed to hold on to their copies of the game.

'They made it for war,' the little boy told me as we stepped out of the green portal, back into the playroom. 'You know that, don't you?'

'They made what for war?'

'The game – Palatial.' He still had something of Count Mordax about him – there was a haughty disregard in his voice, above and beyond his usual predilection for teasing. 'It was for soldiers, the same ones your family helped to clone. They went inside Palatial and got memories of being in the war, even though they'd only just been grown. By the time they went into battle, they had as much experience and knowledge as if they'd been fighting for years.'

I did not know much about the Conflagration – it was one of the subjects about which the story-cube was less than expansive – but I knew enough to be certain that sorcerers and ladies-in-waiting had not played a very significant role.

'The Conflagration happened in space,' I said. 'There were no castles, or palaces.'

The boy rolled his eyes. 'That's nothing, just details they put in at the end. Palatial wasn't called Palatial when the soldiers were using it. When they went inside, they were in the solar system, in the Golden Hour, with ships and Lesser Worlds. All that fairy-tale stuff is what they turned the simulator into after the war, so they could still make money out of it. It didn't work properly, they say – the soldiers kept forgetting who they were in the real world, getting stuck inside the game. I suppose they fixed that.'

'I don't believe you. The war was a horrible thing. That's why no one talks about it.'

'They don't talk about it, but that doesn't mean people aren't making a profit out of it. You've seen the robots that come down the ramp with me. Scratch their armour and they're not much different from the military robots we supplied to our side in the war.'

The robots still unnerved me. In my dreams I sometimes found myself running down one of the house's winding, mirror-lined corridors, with one of those sharp-clawed, slit-faced, mono-wheeled monstrosities gliding behind me, slowly but surely closing the gap. I wanted the Conflagration to belong to the past, buried safely in the back pages of history. I did not like the idea that it was still exerting an influence on the present, tapping fingers on the windows, waiting to be let back in again.

'There aren't any clones any more,' I said. 'Not if you don't count the nannies.'

'Slave labour that you can't export into the Golden Hour. But my father says your household hasn't forgotten any tricks since the armistice. If your side – or any side – needed clones again, your production lines wouldn't take long to roll into action.' With Count Mordax still lurking somewhere behind his eyes, he said mischievously, 'It pushed your mother over the edge, what she ended up doing. It's what made her mad. Or don't you know about that?'

'I have no idea what you're talking about,' the princess said, speaking through me.

'Your mother is still alive, but she's quite insane. Or didn't they tell you?'

'She is unwell.'

'But you've never seen her, have you? You've never seen or spoken to her directly?'

'I speak to my mother all the time.'

'You speak to the panes, like the one that said hello to me when I came off the shuttle. That's not your mother in that glass. It's a guess at her, made by a machine that has been watching over her since she was a girl, a machine that thinks it knows what she'd do and say if she were there in person.'

'Now you're being nasty.'

'I didn't mean to be – I just thought you should know the truth. It's why your house is like it is – it's her idea to keep tearing it down and rebuilding it. It's because she's mad, because she thinks they're after her, for what she did. Of course, if you don't think I'm telling the truth, you'd only have to ask one of the people looking after you.'

'You're different,' I said. 'Ever since you went into Palatial, you've been more like the count and less like . . .' I must have said his name at that point, but I have no recollection of what it might have been.

From the belvedere I watched his shuttle lift off, fold its legs away and power into the brassy haze of the Golden Hour, towards that fog of ten million Lesser Worlds.

Then I went to ask some hard questions.

I had always accepted that my mother was too unwell to receive guests, even her own daughter. It was such an established fact of my life that I had never had cause to question it, any more than I questioned why I had been born Abigail Gentian and not some other girl, born into a different family somewhere else around the Sun. My mother had spoken to me ever since I was small, and she had always shown pride and affection.

'You're a very special young lady, Abigail Gentian. You're going to do great things with your life.'

She had always made me feel special, as if all the bright and pretty things in the universe had been put there for my benefit. Other people could reach out for them, but their reach would falter while mine succeeded. Although I'd had no physical contact with my mother, I had always thought of her as a wise and kind person, one who would have given me all the love and tenderness in the world had that been within her gift.

But that was the day when I found out that my mother was insane, and the only thing she cared about was escaping – or at least temporarily outwitting, in an unending struggle – the phantoms she believed were stalking her. If I existed to her, I was just a dot, a data point, in a vast mosaic of self-absorption.

Everything was different after that.

I went to see Madame Kleinfelter. She was at her desk, surrounded by hovering charts showing the division of labour amongst the house staff and clone nannies. When I came in she was using a luminous stylus to move work blocks around, tapping it against her lips as she pondered some weighty rearrangement of schedules and duty shifts.

'What is it now, Abigail?' she asked, obviously hoping that I would be worn out after an afternoon in Palatial.

'Is my mother insane?'

Madame Kleinfelter closed the charts and put down the stylus. 'It's the little boy, isn't it?' She mentioned his name, of course, or perhaps his family name. 'He's been telling you things.'

'Is it true?'

'You know your mother is unwell. But you speak to her daily on the panes, as do I. Does she seem insane to you?'

'Not exactly—'

'Does she not love you and tell you how much you matter to her?'

'Yes, but—'

'"Yes but" what, Abigail?'

'Do the panes really show my mother?' The little boy's words were still ringing in my head. 'Or just what a machine thinks she'd do and say?'

Madame Kleinfelter looked genuinely puzzled. 'Why would the panes show anything but your mother?'

'I don't know. But why can't I just and go and see her?'

'Because she is very unwell. She must be kept apart from other people until she can be cured – which will happen in the fullness of time. But until then, the isolation must remain in force, and the panes are our only point of contact.'

'I don't believe you. My mother is insane. Something pushed her over the edge.'

'This is not you speaking, Abigail. It's that frightful little ...' Madame Kleinfelter caught herself before she said something unseemly. 'Nothing pushed your mother over the edge. She had ... problems, that's all.'

'Is Mother the reason the house is the way it is?'

Perhaps Madame Kleinfelter had been hoping I would accept her rebuttals and leave, until the moment I asked that question. I could see the change in her face. In her eyes I had crossed some mental Rubicon – not between childhood and adolescence, for I was still not old enough for that – but between degrees of childhood. Children can know of death and pain and madness and still be children.

'I was hoping you'd wait a year or two before asking about that,' my guardian said.

'I want to know now,' I said, with a defiance that astonished me.

'Then you had better follow me. But you will come to regret this, Abigail. This won't be like one of the memories that fritters away into nothing when you come out of that game. This will leave a stain. You'll carry for it for ever, when you could have had a few more years of blissful innocence. Are you sure, now?'

'Yes. I am very, very sure.'

So she took me to the forbidden heart of the house, where they kept my mother, and I learned everything that Madame Kleinfelter and the other adults would rather have withheld from me until I was older. My mother was indeed insane, just as the little boy had told me. She had been driven mad by guilt and shame: by the burden of knowing what her beautiful clones had done, and what had in turn been done to them.

Without the family's expertise in cloning, the Conflagration would have played out very differently. The side we had 'sponsored' would have either had to embrace the same kinds of weapon as their enemy – autonomous killing machines – or capitulate, surrender under the humiliating terms of the other faction. Instead they had been given an unlimited army to send into the fray, each vat-fresh soldier or pilot carrying an operational lifetime's worth of battle wisdom. The Conflagration was brief; it hardly touched the lives of any of the hundreds of billions of citizens who made up the mass population of the Golden Hour, but it still cost vast numbers of lives. During the hot weeks of that war, it was easy to forget that the clones were anything other than a form of organic-based artificial intelligence, put into empty ships and suits the way pigeons were once trained to guide bombs to their targets, a thousand years earlier.

My mother maintained a façade of mental composure during the war, but in the aftermath – as the toll of casualties became apparent – remorse began to chip at the fragile edifice of her sanity. She started dwelling on all the lives that had been created, and then lost, because of our family's ingenuity. Some of her clones had lived only weeks or months, yet they had gone into battle with memories stretching back subjective years. They had felt themselves to be fully formed human beings.

My mother's guilt took a peculiar and morbid twist. She began to insist that the souls of the dead were coming after her, determined to wreak vengeance for the parody of life she had inflicted on them. It was a madness, but once it had taken root in her mind, nothing could be done to eradicate it. The best psychosurgeons in the Golden Hour were brought in to try to cure my mother, but each intervention only seemed to push her deeper into mental infirmity. They took her brain apart like a luxurious, difficult parlour puzzle, polished each segment and then reassembled it piece by piece. They gave her a comfort blanket of false memories. They tried to delete all knowledge of the war.

Nothing worked.

Madame Kleinfelter brought me to a room with a wall that leaned outward. There were shutters on the windows. She worked a lever and bade me stand next to her, looking down at the room that contained my mother.

She floated in a tank, suspended upright in brackish pink fluid. I had already been told that I could not go down into the room itself, in which a condition of strict surgical sterility was maintained. I could see the reason for that: the top of my mother's head was missing, revealing an obscene marvel of glistening pink-grey brain tissue. The convoluted mass was studded with so many probes and lines that it resembled a pincushion. A mass of cables ran down the side of the tank into an oblong of dark machinery set on a trolley. Three green-overalled technicians were in attendance, looking uncannily like the ones who had come to install Palatial. They stood on a platform halfway up the side of the tank, so that they could reach the devices if required. They were studying floating displays, talking to each other in low, professional voices – I could see their lips moving through the thin gauze of their masks. Occasionally my mother's limbs would thrash in the pink suspension, but the technicians paid her movements no heed.

'She's been like this for thirty years,' Madame Kleinfelter said. 'It may look unpleasant, but she's in no pain. Her only distress comes from the things she imagines for herself. She has good days and bad days. On the good days, she can talk to us more or less normally. She still maintains her belief system, even then, but she has enough focus and concentration that she can discuss the family's affairs, contribute to policy decisions and make further plans for the house.'

'Is this a good day or a bad day?'

'This is in the middle. She's in there somewhere, fighting or running from something only she can see. But she can't talk to us – she's too preoccupied.'

'Tell me about the house.'

'Your mother convinced herself that there was a way to keep the ghosts at bay. Here at the heart of the house, she feels relatively safe. She wouldn't dream of venturing into the peripheral wings even if she were able. Much too vulnerable, in her view. As her psychosis took hold she moved deeper and deeper into the house, putting as much distance as possible between herself and the outside world. This became her world. To begin with it was just a few rooms. Then it contracted down to just this one, and then to just this tank. Even that wasn't enough. She constructed barriers to fool and delay the ghosts. Corridors that don't lead anywhere, or which spiral back on themselves. Hidden stairways that they won't see. Mirrors every-where, to baffle and confuse her tormentors. Doors that open onto walls. Of course, even that isn't sufficient by itself. The ghosts are clever and resourceful, and they'll keep trying to find a way in. That's why the house has to keep changing, so that they never get used to one particular configuration. There must always be new wings and new towers, expanding ever outwards. And what already exists must be reshaped all the time, to create labyrinths and traps. The process must never end, Abigail. While the house remains in flux, your mother manages to hold on to a fragment of sanity, even if it's only on the good days. If it were to stop changing, if she were to believe that there was now no obstacle to the ghosts reaching her, I do not think she would be able to hold on to that fragment. We would have lost her for ever.' Madame Kleinfelter paused and took my hand in hers, which was large and rough-skinned. 'As it is, there is still hope.

The specialists still believe they can bring her back. That's why we keep up with her wishes, and the house is the way it is. It has meant you growing up in a strange environment, one that many children would have found frightening and disorientating. But you have done very well, Abigail. We are all proud of you – each and every one of us, including your mother.'

'Will she know I have seen her now?'

'She knows everything. There are cameras throughout the house, watching every door, every corridor. They feed back into her mind. It's not so that she can keep an eye on us.'

'The ghosts,' I said.

'Yes. Your mother watches for the slightest changes in light and shade. When she becomes agitated, it's generally because she thinks she's seen something.'

'She saw something just now.'

'There are no ghosts, Abigail. They're all in her mind. You must remember that.'

'I'm not silly.' But then, I wondered, why did the staff like some parts of the house more than others? Why were there quiet, still rooms where no one ever liked to stay longer than they had to? If not because of ghosts, was it because my mother's disturbed imagination was seeping out through those cameras, like a silent, invisible nerve gas?

'I've seen enough,' I said.

'If I could speak to that little boy—'

'It's not his fault. He only told me what I had to know eventually.'

Madame Kleinfelter nodded kindly and drew the metal shutters on my mother. I wondered at the awesome relief she must now feel; how long she had been dreading this encounter, the weight of it pressing down on her like an iron spike, through all the decades since I had been born ...

CHAPTER THIRTEEN

We had company from the moment we entered the Belladonna system. A ship arrowed in and tracked us, bristling with nervous potency. It was *Adonis Blue*, the warty green toad of a ship belonging to a shatterling named Betony. From the moment he intercepted us he had been excessively cautious, probing me with his deep-penetration sensors and insisting on several extra layers of authentication before he was ready to concede that I was not necessarily hostile.

'Don't take this the wrong way, Campion,' Betony's imago said, 'but we had to play things safe.' He studied me with deep-penetration eyes, as if there might be a vital, betraying clue in the composure of my face. 'It is you,' he said, nodding slowly. 'You made it out after all. The other ship – that would be Purslane, wouldn't it? *Silver Wings of Morning*. You're like two pennies that keep turning up at the same time.' Before I could find malice in his remark, he added, 'Today I couldn't be happier to see you.'

'We're both alive. But it's better than that. We're carrying five other survivors: Aconite, Mezereon, Lucerne, Melilot and Valerian. They're all still in abeyance, but otherwise safe and sound.'

'Seven of you?' Betony almost laughed with delight. 'That's wonderful news – it's been so long since anyone else showed up that we'd all but stopped hoping. Do you have news about anyone else?'

'I can't say for certain, but from what I saw of the reunion system, it isn't likely.' All of a sudden I felt a rush of emotion. Betony had never been one of my favourites amongst the other shatterlings. More than once I had seen him as an understudy to Fescue, plotting and manipulating for influence within the Line. But if I had been wrong about Fescue, then it was entirely possible that I was wrong about Betony. All the old grievances and suspicions felt like baggage I could ill afford to carry. 'It's good to see you, Betony!' I exclaimed. 'I'm almost too scared to ask how many others are with you.'

'There are forty-five of us. You seven take the total to fifty-two. There may be some more out there, still on their way, but I'm not optimistic.'

'Fifty-two,' I said, numbed in a way I had not been anticipating. I had considered worse scenarios than this, up to and including the possibility that there might only be the seven of us. But in my heart I had clung to the hope that there might be more than a hundred.

'I know,' Betony said, acknowledging my thoughts as if he had read my mind. 'It's not many. But we have to count ourselves lucky that anyone got out at all. And it is more than fifty, which means we have a valid quorum. We wouldn't have let that stop us if a decision needed to be taken, but it's good to know we can still do things by the book.'

Abigail had never specified what would happen if there were fewer than fifty Line members *in total*: she must have considered that state of affairs so unlikely as to require no specific provisions, any more than she had told us what we should do if the universe began to collapse, or the Priors returned from the dead to reclaim the galaxy.

But here we were, with just two members over the allowed minimum. I could see a wild relief in Betony, who had always been one for cleaving to Abigail's hallowed commandments.

'You'll meet the others in due course,' he said. 'They're all on Neume, apart from those of us seconded to patrol duties. Any ship entering this system is regarded with extreme suspicion – I regret to say that we've already had to destroy three incoming vehicles that could not prove themselves to be friendly. They all turned out to be exploratory probes from local nascents, but you can understand our nervousness.'

'I don't think anyone will have followed us,' I said. 'We had pursuers, but we shook them off. Betony – there's something else you need to know. We're carrying prisoners. Aconite and the others managed to capture them around the time that Fescue died.'

'Yes, we heard about Fescue. It was terrible news. But he died well, didn't he? A credit to the Line, right to the end.' He nodded and was silent for a few moments, lost in a reverie as if this was the first time he had thought to dwell on the dead man. Then: 'Tell me about the prisoners.'

'There are four of them. We only know the name of one: he's Grilse, a Marcellin shatterling.' Anticipating his reaction, I said, 'I know – we've never had problems with Marcellin Line before. Maybe

161

Grilse was acting alone. He was supposedly lost to attrition ten or eleven of their circuits ago.'

'Have you interrogated him?'

'Aconite and Mezereon got what they could out of him, but didn't want to kill him. They reckoned it was best to wait until we landed on Neume before pushing him harder.'

'They did the right thing. If these prisoners are our only link to the ambushers, we must treat them as if they were the most precious things in the universe. In our case they may well be. But there'll be no landings, I'm sorry to say.'

'Why ever not?'

'Local custom. The troves were a bit out of date: by the time we arrived, there was a civilisation on Neume again.'

'And the locals don't want us to land?'

'Oh, *they* wouldn't mind. They've nothing against the Lines or our ships. We've been made more than welcome, as a matter of fact. The complicating factor is the Fracto-Coagulation, also known as the Spirit of the Air.'

'The posthuman intelligence?' I asked, remembering the summary the trove had provided when we had first learned the identity of the Belladonna fallback.

Betony looked pleased. 'You've done your homework. The Spirit's been here for millions of years – longer than any tenant civilisation. The locals are very protective of it – as well they might be, given that it's about the only reason anyone ever visits. They study it and worship it and sometimes you can't tell the difference. But what they're very clear on is that they don't want anyone or anything upsetting it – and the intrusion of fifty-kilometre-long starships into its atmosphere very much falls into that category.'

'Then we'll whisk down, I suppose.'

'No vacuum towers, Campion. You'll have to come down in shuttles, I'm afraid – hope that won't cramp your style too much.'

'We'll manage.'

'I don't doubt it. Is Purslane awake as well?'

'She'll be coming around about now. In any case, *Silver Wings* is programmed to follow *Dalliance* unless I do something really stupid.'

'Follow me in, then, and we'll find you somewhere to park your ships. I can't promise much of a welcoming party – the collective mood's taken a bit of battering lately. But we'll do our best.'

'I'm sure you will,' I said.

Betony's green toad of a ship spun around and kicked spacetime in my face.

'You're sure it's him, and not a trick by the ambushers?'

'Yes,' I said, with supreme patience, for she had asked me this five or six times since her emergence from the cryophagus, each time listening to my reply and deeming it sufficient. 'If it isn't Betony, someone's broken so deeply into Gentian secrets that we may as well give up now.'

'Yes,' she said. 'That sounds reasonable.'

Purslane still had a sleepy look about her, a stiffness in her movements and a lack of focus in her eyes. She had whisked to *Dalliance* as soon as the casket released her. After a little while, her eyes became sharper and her mental gears found their normal mesh. As the fogginess cleared I told her what I had gathered from Betony.

'I need to see Hesperus,' she said suddenly. 'I want to know if the lights are still on.'

The lights were still on, but I could not swear that they were not dimmer and slower than before we had gone into abeyance. I held my tongue, not wanting to say so in Purslane's presence. Behind the fretted stained-glass windows of his skull, they orbited like the planets and moons of a clockwork orrery that had nearly run down to stillness.

'There's still something there,' I said, trying to strike a balance between optimism and pragmatism. 'It may not be much, but—'

'Don't try to gee me up, Campion – I know he's worse than he was before. But he's still there. Whatever made that mark on the glass, it's still inside him.'

I had neglected to ask Betony whether the surviving shatterlings had brought any guests with them, and of those guests whether any were Machine People. All of a sudden it did not seem very likely.

'We'll get help for him on Neume. There's a culture down there. They may know things we don't. They've been studying a machine-based posthuman intelligence—'

'That's like saying "that man studies water lilies, so he can set my broken leg".'

'I'm just saying we're not out of avenues to explore.'

After a silence she said, 'Have you seen Neume yet?'

'Betony's guiding us into orbit. I thought I'd wait until you were awake before taking a closer look.'

'We're not landing?'

'There are issues. Best not to get on the wrong side of the locals, if we can help it.'

'I wasn't expecting locals.'

'There was always an outside chance. From what Betony says, there won't be any problems, provided we play nice.' I offered her a hand. 'Shall we adjourn to the bridge?'

Some of Purslane's warmth had returned by the time we whisked up-ship and stood before the displayer, our arms around each other and Purslane's head lolling against my shoulder, as if she was only a yawn away from falling asleep again. I was glad that I had waited until now. *Dalliance* could have provided me with a magnified image of the world hours ago, but I had preferred to delay until we were only seconds out, decelerating hard in preparation for insertion into a polar orbit. When the displayer activated, we were passing through the planet's equatorial plane, the world growing visibly larger by the second. Betony's ship was a green dot in the centre of a blurred circle several thousand kilometres ahead of us.

Neume was a dry world, about as far from the Centaurs' pan-thalassic as it was possible to get. Ice gripped the planet at the poles, but the rest of it was as arid and silver-grey as pumice. The daylight face shone back at us, but it was the reflection of sunlight on crystal dunes, promising only the parched aridity of a desert. And yet the presence of an atmosphere was evident even now, a quill-thin halo drawn around the edge of the planet. There were even clouds in the atmosphere – wispy, attenuated things, like the ghosts of real clouds – but they were real enough.

'Can we live down there?' Purslane asked.

'People already do, according to Betony.'

'There's oxygen. Scapers must have been here. But I don't see any organisms, no vegetation or animal life.'

'Perhaps the last tenants changed the atmosphere, and there's still enough air in the system even though it isn't being replenished.'

Purslane lifted her head from my shoulder – she was growing more wakeful by the minute. 'What's that line across the equator? A ring system?'

'Not rings,' I said. 'Some kind of orbital structure, I think.'

'Looks ruined,' Purslane said as the angle changed and the line became a battered, jagged-edged band thrown around the planet. It was obvious now that the band had been a single structure, circuits ago. At one time there would have been perhaps a dozen elevators connecting the planet's equator to space, radiating out from Neume like spokes until they met the encircling band, ten or eleven thousand kilometres above the ground. Though none of the elevators now reached the surface, some of them still pushed down towards the atmosphere, or extended further out into space. The broken spokes were barnacled and furred, like the whiskery growth of an ice crystal. They had either succumbed to some corrupting rot, or had been built on by another tenant civilisation.

'Hesperus knew this place,' Purslane said.

'What?'

Her hand tightened around mine. 'Don't you see it?'

'See what?'

'His design – the cartwheel. We're looking at it. It's a picture of Neume, from space.'

In a blinding instant I knew that she was right, but I could still not understand what it meant. 'Why Neume?' I asked.

'Because he knew we were coming here. Because he knew something of this world, deep in his memory. Because he only had time and energy to send us one message before he went into deep shutdown.'

'I still don't get it. Why send us a picture of Neume? We already knew we were coming here.'

'So it's not just a picture. It's something else – a message. It's telling us what he wanted us to do.'

We left our ships in polar orbit. Even without trying I recognised some of the others: *Yellow Jester*, *Midnight Queen*, *Paper Courtesan*, *Steel Breeze* ... each ship guaranteed the survival of a specific shatterling. My heart gladdened when I saw Cyphel's *Fire Witch*. I really wanted her to be amongst the living.

We all shared a shuttle down to the surface. By then Aconite and Mezereon had returned from abeyance, and the three other Gentian shatterlings would be brought back to life once we were on Neume. The shuttle also contained the four stasis-bound prisoners, stowed in an aft compartment. Purslane had decided against moving Hesperus for the time being, in case we did more harm than good. We followed Betony's shuttle into the blue skies of Neume. His was a chrome teardrop, tapering at the rear to an almost impossibly fine spike.

Our shuttle, which belonged to Purslane, was shaped like a deck of cards with a slanting front, perfect for aerial sightseeing. An observation lounge faced the sloping window, raked at an angle that offered an unobstructed view of the ground. Tables and chairs were set around, but none of us was much interested in sitting. We leaned against the polished wood railing before the window, craning for a first glimpse of the tenant civilisation.

'I'd better fill you in,' said Betony's imago, beaming in from the teardrop. He wore a long green gown, purple trousers and heavy black boots striped up the sides with platinum fluting. 'Neume's an old world and it's seen a lot of history – we're only four thousand years from the Old Place. Settlers were here barely twenty-two kiloyears into the spacefaring era. Do you remember the Commonwealth of the Radiant Expansion?'

Purslane nodded. 'Dimly.'

'I've a feeling I should,' I said.

'Well, you were never much one for ancient history – even the bits you lived through,' Betony said. Beyond the window, an endless sea of silvery dunes reached to a pale horizon, still curved by altitude. 'But it's no crime. I had to bone up on the Commonwealth myself. Didn't help that it was over and done by the thirtieth millennium and never extended beyond more than fifty or sixty settled systems, depending on which troves you believe. From what we can gather, no one was here *before* that – they found a handful of Prior artefacts in the comet cloud, but that was as far as it went.'

'Did the Commonwealth scape?' Purslane asked. 'I was thinking of the atmosphere.'

'Had a go, but the ecosystem collapsed before the work was completed. You have to skip forward another thirty thousand before anyone else arrived on Neume, by which time the planet had reset itself. The Bright Efflorescence were the next tenants – they made a decent fist of it. Lasted forty-five thousand and managed to scape not just Neume but four or five other planet-class bodies in the system. Neume's the only one that survived, though – more's the pity. If they hadn't got into a micro-war with the Red Star Imperium they might have achieved something.'

'And after the Bright Efflorescence?' I asked.

'Skip another quarter of a million years and in comes the High Benevolence.'

'Finally,' I said, relieved. 'A galactic superpower I've actually heard of.'

'Well, you'd have to work hard not to have heard of the Benevolence – they *did* last nearly eleven circuits, after all – more than two million years. The Benevolence developed many of the basic principles now used by Scapers: transmutation engines, world-to-world atmosphere pumps, that kind of thing. For a little while Neume was classically Terran. That was when the Benevolence built their great cities – their remains are still the largest surviving structures on the planet.' Betony looked to the horizon with narrowed eyes. 'We're coming up on one of them now. You'd have seen it from space if you'd looked carefully.'

A dark, squared-off finger began to push itself into view. It was a tower, slender as an obelisk, many kilometres tall, apparently intact but leaning at a precarious angle. It looked as if it might topple into the dunes at any moment.

'Did they build it like that?' Aconite asked.

'No,' Betony said, 'but it's been like that for at least a million years, and it should be good for a few million more. It won't snap, and it's anchored so deep into the crust it won't ever fall.'

'We could build cities like that if we wanted to,' Mezereon said, her tone petulant.

'But we haven't, and the Benevolence did, and now they've left their mark on deep time – whereas we'll be doing well to be remembered a circuit from now.'

Our shuttles descended further, until we were skimming the dunes at an altitude of only a few kilometres – low enough that we would have seen people, had anyone been abroad. But the endless glittering dunes were lifeless. Betony steered his vehicle under the overhang of the leaning obelisk, as if daring us to follow. Purslane instructed her shuttle to tip itself onto its belly, so that we were standing upside down.

The Benevolence structure was sheer black, lacking windows, entrances or landing decks. It was not totally smooth: there were vast, plaque-like designs worked into its towering faces, their edges gleaming with a blue-black of partly reflected sky. I did not know if the designs were abstract shapes, served some weird civic function, or were slogans in the dead language of the Benevolence.

'Why did they die out?' I asked, deciding that there was no point in hiding my ignorance.

'Everyone dies out,' Betony said. 'That's turnover.'

'We're still here.'

'Only because we've stretched that same inevitable process across six million years. Doesn't mean we're immune to it, only that we found an extension clause.'

'You're in an exceptionally cheerful mood,' Purslane said.

'Near-extinction will do that to you,' Betony answered.

We flew on for another half an hour, passing several more Benevolence structures – dark spires jutting from the ground at odd, unsettling angles, alone or in jagged, cactus-like clusters – and then through the eye sockets of a mountainous human skull, its cranium snow-capped. After another twenty minutes of flight, one of the larger cities of the tenant civilisation came slowly into view. By now Neume's sun was beginning to set towards the west, throwing deep, rippling shadows across the dunes. The city stood dark against the fire-streaked sky.

'That's Ymir,' Betony said. 'Not the largest city on Neume, but it's the one best suited to our needs – we've been given more or less free run of large parts of it, so we'd best not complain.'

'Is that where everyone is?' Aconite asked.

'More or less. At any one time, one or two shatterlings may be further afield – patrolling the system for incoming ships, visiting the other cities or returning to orbit for intervals of abeyance or rejuvenation – but most of us have been happy to remain in Ymir. It has everything we need, including privacy.'

'Is this whole planet under a single administration?' I asked.

'No – there are at least three primary powers, and a dozen or so second-tier states. They don't all speak the same dialect, either. But for our purposes we don't need to worry about that. Neume's perfectly happy to present itself to us as a monoculture. It's in their collective interests as much as ours.'

'So who are we dealing with – and what happened to the High Benevolence?'

'You really ought to know that,' Purslane whispered at me.

'Campion can be forgiven,' Betony said. 'The High Benevolence vanished two million years ago – they've been gone as long as they existed. Which is a sobering thought given that *I* still remember when they were up-and-coming nascents with scarcely a hundred systems to their name.'

'How you prioritise your memories is your own business,' I said. 'I prefer to keep recent events near the top of the stack.'

Betony smiled tightly. 'And I'm a bottom-up kind of man. Each to their own, dear boy. Anyway, the Benevolence ... well, they just *went*. Story has it that they got into a dispute with an aquatic client culture, the Third Phase Nereids, over the cost of a panthalassic scaping. The argument escalated until it encompassed many systems. Another nascent, the Plastic, saw their chance and took over much of the Benevolence's territory. But the Plastic weren't with us for very long.'

'What happened to them?' Aconite asked.

'Too inflexible,' Betony said. 'After they were gone, all we have left of the Benevolence is their ruins.'

'Did the Plastic build the space elevators, and the orbital ring?' I asked.

'No – they came *much* later – you're looking at six or seven tenants down the line before that happened. That was the Providers. They were here for at least four hundred and twenty kilo-years before it turned rotten for them.'

'And the current lot?' Campion asked.

'They call themselves the Witnesses. They're just happy to live here and study and/or worship the Spirit, depending on factional affiliation. They build their cities and towns on the foundations left by the Benevolence – it's much easier than sinking shafts right down to the surface, and a lot less likely to piss off the Spirit.'

Now that Ymir was close, we could see what he meant. Four stiff black fingers reached from the dunes, each an obelisk of the Benevolence, each tilted halfway to the horizontal. The shortest of the fingers must have been four or five kilometres from end to end, while the longest – one of the two middle digits – was at least eight. From a distance, caught in the sparkling light of the lowering sun, it was as if the fingers were encrusted with jewellery of blue stones and precious metal. But the jewellery *was* Ymir: the Witnesses had constructed their city on the surface of the fingers, with the thickest concentration of structures around the middle portions of the fingers. A dense mass of azure towers thrust from the sloped foundations of the Benevolence relics, fluted and spiralled like the shells of fabulous sea creatures, agleam with gold and silver gilding. A haze of delicate latticed walkways and bridges wrapped itself around the towers of Ymir, with the longer spans reaching from finger to finger. The air spangled with the bright moving motes of vehicles and airborne people, buzzing from tower to tower.

As the shuttles neared Ymir, three of the moving motes sped out to meet us, to provide an escort into one of the largest towers on the longest finger. The escorts were intricate contraptions of gold and ruby, mimicking the designs of ornithopters or dragonflies with gold-feathered or gold-veined mechanical wings, but moving too quickly, and with too much agility, for that to be their sole mode of propulsion. At the head of each craft was a compartment like a swollen eye held in talons, in which a goggled and helmeted pilot lay prone, working an array of control levers. The escorts were themselves accompanied by flapping, gyring bird-sized drones, and the drones by a multitude of even smaller jewel-sized machines.

We navigated the crowded airspace of Ymir, the escort taking us into the thicket of towers, under the skeletal traceries of connecting bridges and walkways. More craft swerved from their courses to meet us – keeping their distance, but shadowing us all the way in. The flying people wore fluttering wings of varying designs. Again, the wings could not possibly have kept them aloft – they must have been using levator belts or backpacks, with the wings providing fine control.

'You're going to be the centre of attention for a little while, I'm afraid,' Betony said. 'Neume doesn't see much interstellar traffic, and it's already six years since the last shatterlings came in.'

'We'll cope,' Purslane said.

Beneath us, the black fingers of the Benevolence relics blotted out a view of the real ground, kilometres beneath. It would be easy to forget that this city was perched on the slopes of the leaning towers of a fallen civilisation, one that had not breathed the air of Ymir for two million years. Every now and again in my life I felt the cognitive lurch that came from a true apprehension of how ancient I was, how far I had come from the moment of my birth as a single human baby, a girl in a rambling, ghost-ridden mansion.

Presently we approached one of the largest towers, a building with a jewelled onion on the top. Halfway up its balconied, cork-screwed sides was the out-jutting semicircle of a buttressed deck, easily large enough for the escort and our two shuttles. The winged craft hovered in the air while Betony's vehicle tipped onto its spiked end, which thickened, contracted and split to form a tripod, and then descended slowly to the deck. Purslane's shuttle landed next to it, belly down. A moment later the real Betony emerged from the underside of the teardrop, descending between the tripedal landing legs on a levator disc. When the disc touched the deck he stepped off it and the disc returned to the body of the teardrop, sealing the craft.

A door opened in the side of Purslane's shuttle, lowering down and forming steps and railings. The cool, crisp air of Ymir hit me almost instantly. I breathed in the subtle flavours of a new world, feeling the first giddy hint of light-headedness. It was not unpleasant, like the promise of intoxication in the first sip of strong wine.

Purslane took my hand and we walked down the steps, with Aconite and Mezereon following us.

There were many people on the landing deck; a hundred at the very least. They were arranged in three groupings. Before us stood a large number of Gentian shatterlings – at least forty, perhaps all those who had already made it to Neume, with the exception of the handful who must have been on patrol duties. To the right stood a smaller group – twelve or fifteen individuals, whom I took to be the surviving guests of our reunion. Amongst them I recognised one or two shatterlings of other Lines, two individuals who were almost certainly Machine People, as well as a number of highly evolved posthumans of non-baseline anatomy. To the left, numbering forty or fifty, was a civic reception party of Neume locals, dressed for flight but with their artificial wings folded neatly behind them. They had looked to be of normal human size when I had seen them in the air and in the cockpits of their flying machines, but now that we stood together I saw that they were a head or so taller than most of us, and of exceedingly slender build, with dark, slanted eyes and delicate, elfin features. Their honey-coloured skin was in fact very fine fur.

One of them, a female, stepped forward. Like the other Neume citizens she wore a tight-fitting one-piece garment of quilted black plates with something of the texture of leather, cross-webbed across the chest with jointed metal. Coloured studs, which could have been controls, or symbols of authority, ran the length of the cross-webbing. The woman wore a heavy black belt which I presumed to contain levator mechanisms, and above this belt, wrapping her at the abdomen, was a blue cummerbund. A translucent mask with a snout and goggles hung on straps under the creature's chin, ready to be snapped into place (I presumed) should it be necessary to fly into the thin air above Ymir. Her booted feet were splayed at the toes, and her gloveless hands revealed long, elegant fingers. Above her brow, the fur turned darker and formed a stiff mane that fanned down the back of her neck. Most of the Neume locals had a similar hairstyle, but with subtle variations. None of the others had a blue cummerbund; about ten had purple ones, while the others wore red or black.

'Greetings to the honoured shatterlings of Gentian Line,' the woman said in flawless Trans. She had a politician's bearing, a politician's ready authority. Her voice was husky but otherwise perfectly comprehensible, and it carried clearly in the thin, still air of the landing deck. 'I am Jindabyne, the magistrate of Ymir and the Six

Provinces. I have been delegated to welcome you to Neume. Firstly, I offer you our heartfelt sympathies for the atrocity that has befallen your Line. While one can hardly speak of pleasure at such a time, we still trust that your stay on Neume will be satisfactory. Rest assured that we Witnesses – the citizens of Ymir, and the rest of the planet – will do everything we can to make your visit as comfortable as possible. If you need anything that is within our power to give, you need only ask.'

I glanced at Purslane, who nodded for me to speak. 'Thank you, Magistrate – it's most kind of you to welcome us. I am Campion of the Gentians, and this is my fellow shatterling Purslane.' I turned around slowly, extending a hand. 'This is Aconite, and this is Mezereon – also Gentians. Aboard the shuttle, we carry three more shatterlings of our Line, still in abeyance.' I had not forgotten about the prisoners, but the welcoming ceremony did not strike me as the right place to mention such an unpleasant detail.

'Has Betony told you much about our world, Campion?'

'A little – and of course, we have the information in our troves. That doesn't mean we can't still learn a thing or two.'

'I am sure you already know all that is worth knowing. Nonetheless, feel free to ask questions: ours is an open society, and we have no secrets. Presently, one of my staff will show you to your accommodation – if it is not to your liking, say so immediately and it will be changed. In the meantime, though, I am sure you are anxious to speak to your fellow shatterlings. I won't delay you a moment longer.'

'Thank you, Magistrate,' Purslane said.

'A privacy screen can be arranged if you would prefer. In any case, my staff and I will disable our comprehension of Trans for the time being. You need have no fear of eavesdropping.'

'I doubt that we have any secrets we wouldn't be willing to share with you,' I said, 'but we appreciate the gesture – it's most kind.'

Jindabyne gestured towards the waiting shatterlings. 'Go now. Don't delay this reunion, however bitter-sweet it may be.'

'Magistrate,' Purslane said as we were about to walk across the deck to the waiting Gentians, 'there is one thing ... before you disable your comprehension. It may be impertinent of me to mention it now ...'

I bristled, seeing where this was going. 'Purslane,' I said under my breath, 'it can wait.'

'What is it, shatterling?'

'Ever since we heard of Neume, I've been curious about the Spirit of the Air.'

'As are most of our visitors,' Jindabyne said, a tightness creeping into her voice. 'Without their curiosity, we would not have an economy.'

'I was wondering if it would be possible to ... well, meet it. Or at least communicate with it.'

I had barely read a single emotion in Jindabyne's face, but now I saw the diplomatic mask slip for a microsecond, revealing the tension simmering just beneath. 'Rest assured that there is a vast archive of observations and analysis in the public records department, stretching back to the last days of the Benevolence. I am certain you will find all that interests you in those archives, and you will of course have the opportunity to meet both scholars and worshippers of the Spirit during your stay on Neume.'

'It's the entity itself I'm interested in,' Purslane said, 'not the documentation.'

'Although in the meantime,' I said, 'my fellow shatterlings and I will be delighted to have access to that archive. It is generous of you to make it available to us, Magistrate – and I'm sure we'll do all in our power to repay you for your kindness.'

Purslane glared at me for an instant.

'We normally charge for access to our records,' Jindabyne said. 'Gifts and energies keep our world running. But it is our honour to provide a place of sanctuary to our friends from Gentian Line, and there will be no talk of payment.'

'Thank you,' Aconite said, speaking for the first time since leaving the shuttle. He and Mezereon kept a respectful distance between them now: there was no danger of mistaking them for an item.

That appeared to be Betony's cue to raise his voice. 'With the magistrate's permission, let me welcome our four lost shatterlings back into the fold! Campion and Purslane, Mezereon and Aconite – and Lucerne, Melilot and Valerian aboard the shuttle! This is more than we ever dared hope for!'

The shatterlings roared and cheered and clapped. I raised a hand in salute. The last thing I felt like was a homecoming champion, but I had to acknowledge their welcome.

Purslane smiled decorously and raised a hand. 'I'm happy so many of us survived,' she said. 'There were times when I feared no one else would have made it here. It's so good to see you all.'

Excluding Betony, there were forty-four shatterlings already on

Neume. I could not take them all in with a single glance, but I soon put names to some of our fellow survivors. There was willowy Cyphel, looking as beautiful as ever, her hair the blue-white of moonlit snow. There was the swarthy Charlock, never a man I had counted as an ally but who now met my gaze and gave me a nod that said all that was behind us now. There stood the ever-jocular Weld, wearing his usual portly reunion-anatomy. There were Sainfoin, Medick, Henbane, Bartsia and Tansy.

Purslane and I walked to the survivors and touched hands with as many of them as we were able, Aconite and Mezereon following behind us.

'I always misjudged you, Campion,' said Galingale, a male shatterling I had not noticed until then who was now reaching over Tansy's shoulder to take my hand. 'I'll never forgive myself for that now. I never thought I'd say it, but ignoring Fescue was the best thing you could have done.'

'The decision to enter the system was as much Purslane's as mine,' I said.

'Of course,' Galingale said. He was my height, with pinched features, reddish, meat-coloured skin and a tight-cropped skullcap of white hair. Galingale affected an artificial eye, replacing the green one that was his genetic birthright. He had lost the real eye – and much of the left side of his face – when he had played tourist in a brutal micro-war, falling foul of crossfire. Injured, he had fallen – or allowed himself to fall – into the hands of one of those nascent interstellar civilisations. Their surgeons had patched him back together and given him the eye – the height of their cyberscience. It was a thing of laughable crudity by Line standards, like a peg-leg or a wooden hand fixed in one position. Galingale had allowed his facial injury to be healed invisibly when he returned to Gentian care, but he had kept the artificial eye. His strand had been a popular one that circuit, and the grim replacement was a gentle reminder of past glories. His hands still clasped around mine, he said, 'We'll need to honour Fescue properly, won't we? Something befitting his status.'

'We'll take care of it,' I said, wanting to change the subject.

'Something spectacular. Something that says Gentians don't give up that easily.'

'We don't,' I said. 'I didn't think anyone needed reminding of that.'

Betony patted me warmly on the shoulder. 'That's the right kind of talk, Campion. We're not done yet. And *by fuck*, someone's going to pay for this.'

'If it's another Line,' Aconite said, 'I say we take them down to fifty-two living survivors, see how they like it.'

'Why stop there?' Galingale asked. 'They wanted to wipe us out completely. It's only good luck that any of us escaped. I say we push for terminal attrition: the complete extinction of a Line.'

'If it *is* a Line,' I said. 'Grilse could be acting independently of the Marcellins.'

'The natural allies of Lines are other Lines,' Mezereon said. 'That's the basis of the Commonality. Stands to reason our only natural enemies will be other Lines as well.'

'Maybe we should reserve judgement until we've talked to the prisoners,' Purslane said. I squeezed her hand. For the first time since arriving in Ymir I felt a solidarity with her, the sense that neither of us was ready to jump to conclusions before the facts were in.

'Let me introduce you to our guests,' Betony said.

They were a motley lot, as I had already surmised. There were some shatterlings of other Lines: no Marcellins, but a Torquata, an Ectobius and a couple of Jurtinas, and maybe one or two from Lines I had yet to recognise. There was a towering elephantine posthuman shrouded in leathery red plaque-like armour plates – not a Rim-runner, but with a similar anatomy. There were a couple of spindly statues, seemingly made of bundles of dried twigs, which were in fact living people, and one or two humans of baseline anatomy who might have been Line members, but who could also have been representatives of emerged nascents, and the two robotic individuals. One was silver and one was a highly reflective white, like ivory, or the surface of poured milk. The silver one was female in shape, the white one male. Like Hesperus, both had windows in the sides of their skulls through which coloured lights danced and gyred.

'Let me introduce Cadence and Cascade, our guests from the Machine People,' Betony said, rightly deciding that they should have precedence over the others. 'They came with Sainfoin – she met them at a reunion of Dorcus Line, only ten thousand lights from the inner edge of the Monoceros Ring.'

'It is a pleasure to meet you,' said Cadence, the female one. She had the most beautiful, lustrous voice I had ever heard – it was like a choir of angels singing in exquisite harmony.

'Likewise,' Cascade said, tilting his milk-white head in greeting. 'We share your horror at the atrocity that has befallen your Line.'

His voice was deep, resonant and infinitely soothing: something in it seemed to reach inside my soul and assure me that, while I was in his presence, no harm could come to me or anyone I cared for. He added, 'Rest assured that the Machine People will do all in their power to assist you in bringing the perpetrators to justice. This is my promise to you.'

'Thank you,' I said.

'Were you the only Machine People to make it to the reunion?' Purslane asked.

'To our knowledge,' said the lovely Cadence. 'Of course, some may have expired in the approach to the reunion, after the ambush had already taken place. I think it unlikely, though. We have a strong sense of self-preservation.'

I thought of the way Hesperus had thrown himself into danger to help the rest of us, but thought better of commenting.

'Did you hear about our guest?' Purslane asked.

'Hesperus?' asked Cascade. 'Yes, of course. His wellbeing is a matter of the gravest concern to us. We would like to examine him at the earliest opportunity.'

'We are grateful for everything you have done for him,' Cadence added. 'Where is he now?'

'Aboard my ship, *Silver Wings of Morning*,' Purslane said. 'She's in orbit – we had to leave them up there.'

'We should probably talk about this later,' I said. 'Hesperus has survived until now – another day or two won't make much difference.'

Cadence and Cascade nodded as one. 'Then we shall speak tomorrow,' the female robot said. Her silver face was all chiselled edges and flat surfaces, but it still managed to look heart-stoppingly feminine. I wondered if Purslane felt the same attraction to Cadence's masculine counterpart.

Betony extended a hand to the elephantine posthuman. 'Let me also introduce Roving Ambassador Ugarit-Panth of the Consentiency of the Thousand Worlds, a very respected and stable mid-level super-civilisation located in the Perseus Arm.'

The ambassasor raised his trunk. The tip ended in a five-digited hand with a pink orifice in the palm. I reached out and shook the revolting appendage, smiling sympathetically.

'I'm really sorry, Ambassador.'

His dark eyes were set on either side of a massive, bulging brow. 'Sorry about what, shatterling?'

'About what happened, obviously—'

'About what happened to what?'

'When the stardam failed . . .' I trailed off: Betony had hooked his arm under mine and was propelling me onwards.

'He's got his civilisations mixed up, Ambassador – he's thinking of the Pantropic Nexus. Aren't you, Campion?'

'Of course,' I said, flustered.

'Which isn't even *in* the Perseus Arm. But that's Campion for you – galactic geopolitics was never your strong point, was it?'

'Apparently not,' I said, mystified.

'What stardam failure do you speak of?' the ambassador asked.

'There was a *rumour* of a stardam failure,' Purslane said, leaning between the ambassador and me. 'But I looked into it, and it was just a scheduled detonation. Sometimes stars are allowed to go supernova, especially if there's a star-forming nebula nearby that needs metal enrichment, or a triggering kick before it begins to collapse.'

'And the involvement of the Pantropic Nexus?'

'They were warned to limit their expansion into the hazard zone. When the star blew, some of their systems were irradiated at life-cleansing intensities. That's probably what Campion was thinking of.'

'I was,' I said, nodding vigorously. 'The Pantropic Nexus. The fools.'

'We shall speak more of this matter,' the ambassador said, in Betony's direction.

Betony smiled tightly. 'And this is the honoured shatterling Japji of Torquata Line . . .' When we were safely out of earshot of the elephantine ambassador, he hissed, 'He doesn't know.'

'So I gathered. When were you planning on telling him?'

'We weren't.'

'Isn't that rather irresponsible?'

'Not really. He's borderline suicidal as it is. You know what they do when they're ready to kill themselves?'

'I'm sure you're about to tell me.'

'Wander off into the desert and blow themselves up. There's a small anti-matter device stuffed inside his ribcage.'

'Ah. And you think—'

'Until we can be absolutely confident that he won't detonate near any of us, and that if he does we can screen the blast . . . we have to keep him in a state of enlightened deception. We've already altered the local troves so that they don't say anything about the

Consentiency being wiped out by a failed stardam. Now we've got to go in again and change the entry for the Pantropic Nexus.'

'I'd be depressed if I thought everyone was lying to me.'

'Everything was just fine until you blundered in and started commiserating with him.'

'Maybe you should have told me first, instead of relying on telepathy.'

'I did drop a fairly broad hint when I introduced him. You know, the fact that I *wasn't* talking about his civilisation in the past tense. Or didn't you notice that?' Then he nodded at Purslane. 'That was good, though, all that stuff about the Nexus – at least one of you was thinking on their feet.'

'I've only been on this planet for ten minutes,' I said. 'Already I feel like I've overstayed my welcome.'

Purslane looked at me with icy forbearance. 'Work really hard, and maybe next time you can get it down to five.'

CHAPTER FOURTEEN

We stayed on the landing deck until the evening air turned cold, with shatterlings, guests and Ymirian functionaries mingling amidst floating trays laden with drinks and nibbles. Most of the other shatterlings had been on Ymir for years, but Campion and I were only days of subjective time away from the reunion system. To us the mental wound was still bright and agonising, much too raw to be soothed by banter and idle reassurance. In a restless moment I pulled away from the crowd and made my way to the edge of the deck, standing with my feet close to the unguarded edge. It was a long way down to the sloping ground of the Benevolence finger, and even further to the twinkling, ever-shifting dunes beneath.

'If you listen carefully you can hear it singing,' Campion said softly, for he had joined me at the edge.

'I can't hear anything, not with that party going on.'

'They're filtering inside. In a little while there'll just be a few stragglers like you and me left outdoors.'

'Did you smooth things over with Betony?'

Campion grinned quickly. 'I think so. He says he'll have to make sure the elephant only gets to access trove data that has been doctored to fit the story, but they've been doing that since he got here anyway. They'll have to make a few more changes to gloss over the bit about the stardam failure, but it shouldn't be a problem.'

'They should just tell him. It isn't kind, keeping him in the dark like that.'

'But see it from their side.'

'He wouldn't blow up.'

'I don't know. It's not as if something like that hasn't happened before.'

'There's precedence for everything in galactic history. Every conceivable event has already happened at least once. But that doesn't make it likely that it'll happen again, here and now.'

'Fine – you go and tell him. I'll take a trip back up to orbit and watch the fireworks.'

'And abandon me down here?'

Campion closed his hand around mine. 'Not really.'

After a while I said, 'What did you think about the robots?'

'I'm glad they're here. Now that Cadence and Cascade are involved, it means it's more than just Gentian Line that's been attacked. If the Machine People feel aggrieved, we'll have their power backing us all the way. I'd certainly rather have them on my side than against me.'

'I was thinking more about their attitude to Hesperus.'

'In what way?'

'Do you actually think they want to help him?'

'That's what they said, isn't it?'

I pulled my gown tighter against the chill. 'I don't know. How can we be sure they're not just going to dismantle him, rather than making him well again?'

'If making him well isn't an option, dismantling may be the only alternative. At least that way they'd be able to access the information he accumulated before his amnesia.'

'But he's our friend, Campion. We can't just hand him over like some worn-out thing, to be stripped down and recycled.'

'He's a machine. That's what happens when they break down.'

'Possibly the coldest thing you've ever said.'

'It's not that I don't care,' Campion said hastily, 'but we have to be realistic. Who stands a better chance of fixing him – the Machine People, the civilisation he came from, or some nebulous entity called the Spirit of the Air, about which we know almost nothing?' He shook his head. 'Anyway – aren't we being a little premature? They haven't even seen him yet. Shouldn't we wait to hear what they have to say after that?'

'Cadence and Cascade are just two robots. They might know how to fix him, but that doesn't mean they have the resources this far from the Monoceros Ring.'

'Then we let them take him home.'

'Campion, he sent us a message. He was very specific about Neume. He couldn't have known Cadence and Cascade were going to be here, but he did know about the Spirit.'

'If he'd known about the other robots he'd have told us to entrust him to them. They're other robots, just like Hesperus. They're bound to know what's best for him. He told us to make sure we got his notes and drawings back to his people.'

'That's not the same as saying he'd have entrusted himself to them.'

'We can talk about this all night and still not get any nearer to agreement. Besides, it's pointless speculating about the Spirit of the Air before we've talked to the magistrate again. From where I was standing, she didn't sound awfully keen on the idea of giving us direct access to it.'

'We're a Line,' I said. 'We ask nicely the first time. But if we don't get what we want, we take it anyway. That's the way we've always done things. It's the way we're expected to do things.'

'Go around bullying lesser cultures, you mean?'

'We've been around long enough to earn the right.' I groaned inwardly, listening to myself. It was the kind of thing I loathed to hear coming out of the mouths of other shatterlings: the idea that we would use force the instant diplomacy and persuasion failed us. Bully our way around, in other words, just as Campion put it. But I was only thinking of Hesperus. I did not want anything or anyone to stand in the way of bringing him back to life.

'Listen,' Campion said, 'it's starting.'

'What?'

'The music. The song of the dunes.'

I heard it then, although the sound must have been rising in intensity for several minutes, pushing itself into audibility. Campion was correct that most of the celebrants had moved into the tower, leaving only a dozen or so people on the deck, most of whom were silent. The noise was low and alien, a mournful, bass-rich drone that rose and fell in pitch like a deathly slow siren.

'Is it the wind?' I whispered, hardly daring to speak.

'Not the wind, no. It works best when the air is almost totally still.'

'You haven't been here before.'

'But I've been on worlds with dunes before. So have you, but probably never at the right time. Face it, there are a lot of experiences neither of us have had yet. It's why we keep living.'

'So if not the wind—'

'It's all down to avalanches,' Campion said, in the same respectful whisper. 'Sand grains start sliding downhill, just beneath the outer membrane of the dunes. Actually, the technical term is barchans – those are the sinuous dunes, where you get the right conditions for the singing. The avalanching grains set up some kind of resonance with the outermost layer. It starts oscillating, rippling free like a vast drumskin. The oscillations feed back into the avalanching grains, forcing them to synchronise themselves. The membrane vibrates even more strongly and sets up excitations in the surrounding airmass. You get something like music.' After a pause he said, 'Wonderful, isn't it?'

'Wonderful and a little spooky.'

'Like all the best things in the universe.' After a pause he said, 'I was talking to Cyphel just now.'

'You always did have an eye for her.'

'I looked but I didn't touch. The point is, she said something that made me think. We've a lot on our minds at the moment – Hesperus, the other robots, Grilse and the other prisoners, why anyone would want to destroy the Line and what will happen if they find us again. Enough worry for a lifetime, even by Line standards. But despite all of that *we're still alive*. We're still alive and we still have friends, and somewhere to stay, and it's a beautiful evening and the dunes of Neume are singing to us. Those dunes aren't just any old dunes, you know. They're the shattered remains of the Provider mega-structures, after their culture fell out of the sky. We're being serenaded by the twinkling remains of a dead supercivilisation, the relics of people who thought themselves gods, if only for a few instants of galactic time. Now – how does that make you feel?'

'Like I'm living too late,' I said.

The Line was in private session for breakfast, on a terrace near the top of the building's onion-shaped summit. The terrace was partially open, with one half covered by a domed roof. Ymir crowded away in all directions, with vehicles and citizens flitting between towers in ceaseless, dizzying motion. There were coloured flags on the bridges and aerial promenades. The air was cool but invigorating, and I felt refreshed after the night's sleep. The world's rotation had been adjusted to a Line-standard day circuits ago, and because we were near the vernal equinox, Ymir had enjoyed nearly twelve hours of uninterrupted darkness.

Campion and I arrived at the breakfast table together. It was set out in a square shape, with twelve to fifteen spaces to a side. In the middle of the square was a display volume filled with a rotating view of the galaxy. Food and drink were laid out in abundance. Purslane and I had been told when breakfast would be served, but the others had obviously been there for some time. By the time we arrived, the only two vacant seats available were on opposite sides of the square. We stood for a puzzled moment, hand in hand.

'I'll move,' Bartsia said, who happened to be sitting next to one of the empty positions. She made to stand, gathering the hem of her dress in preparation.

'There's no need,' said Medick, with amused laughter in his voice. 'I am sure Campion and Purslane will not mind sitting apart – any more than the rest of us would. Or am I missing something?'

'It's all right,' I said to Bartsia. 'You don't have to get up. But thank you for offering.'

I took my seat next to her, while Campion settled into the one between Henbane and Teasel.

Betony, who was sitting at the equilateral position between us, lifted a glass of orange juice to his lips. 'Did you sleep well, shatterlings?' he asked between sips. 'Was the accommodation to your tastes?'

'We've no complaints,' Campion said.

Each of us had at least an entire floor of the tower to ourselves, subdivided into several high-ceilinged rooms with panoramic windows and curving, cave-like walls.

'You presume to speak for Purslane as well?' Betony asked, with exaggerated pleasantness.

'Campion knows my tastes,' I said. 'He was right to speak for me. Anyway – we slept together. You all know it, or at least suspect it, so why the pretence?'

'When the Line is in its darkest hour, you could at least attempt to abide by the traditions,' Betony said.

'So you've never screwed another shatterling,' I said.

'Over breakfast, Purslane? Please.'

'You raised the matter, Betony, not me.'

Aconite lifted a calming hand. 'Let's cut them some slack, shall we? We might not approve of every detail of their relationship, but the Line still owes them a considerable debt.'

Betony looked disappointed, but said nothing.

'If you're going to censure us, now would be the time,' Campion said. Nonchalantly he reached for a crust of bread and tore off a corner. He was so cool about it that I felt a shiver of almost indecent pride. 'However, I think you're all far too sensible for that. Yes, we broke the rules. But the rules don't mean a damn now. Gentian Line as we know it is over. We might build something from the ruins, but let's not pretend it's going to have much to do with the institution Abigail created six million years ago.'

'The Line still has legitimacy,' Galingale said, without any particular rancour, 'but I take your point. Campion and Purslane aren't the only shatterlings to have flirted with the notion of consorting during circuits. They may have taken rule-bending further than most of us, but there have always been others.'

'Nobody sitting around this table,' Betony said.

Galingale scratched at the metal border of his artificial eye. It was like an iron badge glued to his face, with a small red gem in the middle. 'Perhaps not. But the time may still have come to let bygones be bygones. What's so harmful about a little screwing around between friends?'

'It's not what Abigail wanted,' Betony said. 'A harmless fuck here and there, during the Thousand Nights – that's different. The occasional orgy, yes. But we don't consort. We don't fall in love, have children, live happily ever after. That's not what Abigail made us for.'

'Abigail believed in flexibility as well,' Galingale said. 'If she were sitting at this table, she might very well have come around to Purslane and Campion's line of thinking.'

'That's your opinion,' Betony said.

'If we hadn't consorted,' I said, 'neither of us would have been late for the reunion. We'd most likely have been caught in the ambush and died along with all the others.'

'She has a point,' Galingale said. 'Perhaps the sensible thing would be to put this little infringement behind us and move on. Without Purslane and Campion's involvement, we wouldn't have the five other shatterlings, or the prisoners.' He brushed crumbs from his lips. 'Speaking of which ... have we decided how we're going to proceed? It should be straightforward to bring the three Gentians out of stasis, but we'll need to be more cautious where the prisoners are concerned. Then there's the question of what we do to them once they're out.' He looked sharply at Mezereon, who was sitting on the opposite side of the table from Aconite, as if the two of them had barely spoken.

'With the sanction of the Line, I would like to lead the interrogation,' Mezereon said. 'Under due scrutiny, of course. But they're our prisoners – we caught them and kept them intact until Campion came by. Rightly or wrongly, I feel a sense of unfinished business.'

'I don't think any of us will have a problem with you leading the inquiry,' Betony said. 'Under Line supervision, as you say. Do you have a plan?'

'I'll save Grilse for last – I think he's the one we'll get the most off, and the one most likely to survive re-emergence into normal time. If I can get him out in one piece, I'd like to press for extraordinary interrogation measures.'

'Sectioning,' said Charlock, disgustedly.

'It's another tool in the arsenal,' Mezereon said, with an easy shrug.

'Which we haven't used for circuits,' Charlock said. 'Which is considered a barbaric throwback to the dark ages by a good many enlightened nascents.'

'But not by the Commonality, which is all that counts. We won't be breaking any applicable laws.' Something wild flared in Mezereon's eyes. 'We were the ones who were ambushed and pushed to the brink of terminal attrition, not some other Lines or nascents. Let them get a taste of extinction and see how long their principles last. Do you imagine the Marcellins would even blink before using the same technique on one of us, if it came to that?'

'Torturing Grilse won't necessarily get the answers you're looking for,' Charlock said.

'It isn't torture. Torture involves pain. We won't hurt him at all.'

'Aside from the ethical issues, do we even have the means?' Betony asked, steepling his fingers under his chin.

'The apparatus can be constructed very easily,' Merezeon said. 'Any one of our troves should carry the maker templates. Judging by what I've seen of Ymir, we could do it even if we had to rely on local resources.' She sprinkled sugar onto a piece of fruit on her plate. She had already sliced the fruit into translucent slivers, as if rehearsing the act of sectioning.

'Let us agree that Mezereon will lead the interrogation,' Betony said, looking around the table for signs of dissent. 'Aconite – I presume you'll wish to be involved. We'll get the other three shatterlings out of abeyance as soon as possible, and give them the option of joining the interrogation party. The rest of us, meanwhile, will perform the necessary oversight and scrutiny. But we won't place undue limits on Mezereon's authority. Most of us either avoided the ambush entirely or escaped it at the time of the attack. Mezereon and the other survivors were there for years, surviving by the skin of their teeth. They're owed a crack of the whip.'

Anxious to turn the conversation away from torture and

interrogation, I said, 'Given what you've learned since arriving on Neume, have any of you come to any conclusions as to why we were ambushed?'

'What can it be, other than a simple grudge?' asked Betony. 'We are not the strongest Line in the Commonality, and we have much less leverage over dominant nascents than some of the other Lines, so it can't be that we were attacked out of jealousy, or because of some underlying political motive. For six million years we have been content to mind our own business, doing good works where appropriate, providing the occasional stardam here and there, but otherwise standing aloof from the nitty-gritty of turnover. We've seldom dirtied our hands with galactic affairs, preferring to witness and record rather than intercede. Any enemies we may have made have most likely been extinct for circuits.'

'I'm hearing a lot of reasons why someone *wouldn't* hold a grudge against us,' Campion said.

Betony looked sympathetic. 'Then you misunderstand human nature, my dear fellow. People will hate us simply for being what we are: a force for good, for benign non-interference. The mere fact that we haven't dirtied our hands, that we've maintained an unblemished reputation – that's enough to make someone detest us.'

'Another Line?' I asked.

Betony nodded. 'That may well be so, Purslane. Certainly, a Line might have the wherewithal to assemble the weapons that were used against us. The Marcellins in particular—'

'The Marcellins have been our allies since the Golden Hour,' I said. 'We gave them cloning expertise, they gave us ships. In all that time, there's never been a hint that they held anything against us.'

'It's often the close friend who's the first to stick the dagger in,' Betony said.

'What if we were attacked for another reason entirely?' Campion asked.

'Nurturing a theory?' Betony asked.

Campion glanced at Aconite. 'Maybe you should tell him, if you still think it's relevant.'

Aconite coughed and took a mouthful of water. 'The only concrete thing we got out of Grilse before we had to dial him back up was that he claimed the ambush was somehow due to Campion.'

Betony squinted. 'Campion?'

'That's what the man said.'

'He could have been lying.'

Campion leaned forward. 'We thought it over. The only thing that makes sense – given that I wasn't at the reunion when it happened – is that there must have been something in my strand, the one I contributed a circuit ago.'

Mezereon said, 'No one thinks Campion was responsible – if they do, they can explain it to me after breakfast. But it's quite possible he may have triggered it inadvertently. If there was something in his thread, something that led to the ambush at the next reunion, we must find out what it was.'

Betony glared at Campion. 'And you have no idea what this ... trigger might have been?'

Campion explained his theory that his visit to the Vigilance might have drawn down the ambush, pointing out that Hesperus and the late Doctor Meninx had both been curious about the galactic archivists.

'All of a sudden there's a lot of interest in the Vigilance,' Campion concluded. 'The Machine People decide to send an envoy there – but he doesn't make it before having his memory wiped. Something snags Doctor Meninx's curiosity. And perhaps something I revealed about the Vigilance was sufficient to trigger the ambush.'

'You found something of shattering importance, but you don't remember what it was?' Betony asked.

'Someone may have seen something in my strand that I missed,' Campion said, unfazed by the other shatterling's amused scepticism. 'We'll need to look at my strand in detail, all of us. Something I revealed was damaging or threatening to someone – enough that they thought it worthwhile to try to annihilate all of us.'

Galingale said, 'Someone who was at the reunion, you mean? One of us?'

'The H-guns arrived inside ships of the Line,' I said. 'There's no other way they'd have got within shooting range of the reunion world before interception. Aconite and Mezereon will back me up on that one.' I looked at Aconite and he held up his hand in a gesture of willing surrender. Mezereon nodded once.

'Someone knew where the reunion was going to take place,' Campion answered. 'That already implies access to privileged information. And Fescue was convinced that the familial network had been broken into. Reading between the lines, I'm sure he already suspected one of us was responsible. If he was sitting here now, I'm certain he'd be asking the hard questions.'

Cyphel spoke for the first time, brushing a strand of blue-white hair from her dark, dreamy eyes. I was seeing her through my eyes, but with Campion's memories getting the way. 'Most of us arrived at the reunion in time to be ambushed. But the threading hadn't begun – we were still waiting for the last stragglers before beginning the Thousand Nights, which means that the strands died with the shatterlings. We'll never know what they did during their final circuits.'

We all looked at her, not quite sure what point she was making.

'But we do know their intentions,' Cyphel said. She had a voice like dark chocolate. 'Before we departed for space, after the last reunion, we all filed our flight-plans. None of us was obliged to keep to them slavishly – we're meant to change our plans as interesting data comes in. But we still know what most of us were planning to do.'

'I don't see—' Betony started.

'If the flight-plans are still on record,' Cyphel said, 'we can review them and see if any of us were intending to act on Campion's strand.'

'I'd have remembered if anyone else was going to the Vigilance,' Campion said.

'It won't be that clear-cut,' Cyphel replied. 'But the Vigilance collates and studies information from across the galaxy, from many systems. You may have reported something that spurred someone else to make a follow-up investigation, without ever going anywhere near the Vigilance itself.'

Aconite said, 'It's worth looking into.'

'Very well,' Betony said, his tone grudging. 'Cyphel – can we entrust this one to you?'

'I don't mind. As long as I have the usual access privileges, I'm as capable of doing it as anyone else. I'll need a clean copy of Campion's strand, obviously.' She turned her radiant features towards him. 'Will that be a problem?'

'It might,' Campion said quietly.

'I don't follow,' Betony said. 'We all had free access to your strand a circuit ago. Why should it be a difficulty now?'

'Because it doesn't exist. I deleted it.'

Aconite gaped. 'But on the ship you told us—'

'I was wrong, all right? I thought there might possibly be a working backup somewhere in the trove. There wasn't. I screwed up.'

'Why would anyone delete their own strand?' Tansy asked, stupefied.

'It was a mistake.'

'An honest error. Happens to us all,' Charlock said.

'It wasn't that kind of mistake,' Campion said. 'More of a mis-judgement. I got rid of it because I was fed up hauling all that past around with me. I felt like a man dragging an endless chain of sacks behind him, each of them stuffed with enough experience for an entire lifetime.' Seeing the expressions on the faces of many of the shatterlings, Campion reddened. 'They were my memories – I did what I wanted with them. That's my human right, above and beyond anything the Line tells me to do.'

'Oh, Campion,' I said, under my breath, because as much as I wanted to be on his side, I knew what he had done was almost unforgivable.

'I didn't think it really mattered,' he went on. 'I knew the thread-ing apparatus would retain a clean copy, which would still be in its memory when we convened for the next reunion.'

'The threading apparatus was destroyed by the H-guns,' Betony said.

'I wasn't to know that.'

'But you put us in a position where that was the only clean copy in existence.'

'Hindsight's a lovely thing,' Campion said.

'You were already skating very close to censure. This takes you well over the line.'

'We were all smiles yesterday, Betony – what's changed?'

'You were owed a cordial welcome, like any survivors. But that doesn't change the fact that you flouted Line traditions, took undue risks, treated your strand with cavalier disregard. Those weren't your memories to erase, Campion – you were merely entrusted with them on behalf of Gentian Line.'

'Well, whatever it is you want to do with me, you have my full permission. But can I just suggest that the punishment – whatever it is – waits until we've worked out who wants to kill us?'

'Before we hang Campion out to dry,' Cyphel said, 'we should keep this in mind. We all received his strand. That means we still have fifty-odd copies of it between us, all of which will have been mnemonically tagged.'

'But degraded by the passage of time, and buried under new memories,' Mezereon said, sounding as if she was making a reason-able point rather than trying to twist the knife.

Cyphel nodded. 'I know, but it isn't irrecoverable. I'm not saying we can reassemble a clean copy, but I'm sure we can get very close if

189

we pool our minds. If everyone is willing to submit to memory retrieval again, I can extract the individual versions of Campion's strand and cross-correlate them until the holes are filled and the errors corrected.'

'It's worth a try,' Aconite said.

'That puts a lot of responsibility on your shoulders, Cyphel,' said Betony.

'I'll cope.'

Betony tapped a chunk of bread against his head, like a judge about to deliver a verdict. 'So shall it be. Mezereon will lead the inquisition into the prisoners. Cyphel will handle the retrieval of the Campion strand, insofar as it can be recovered. Tansy – I believe you are on patrol duty today. And that, I think, is more than enough business for one breakfast.'

'Might I say something?' I asked.

Betony smiled at me. 'Naturally, Purslane.'

'Are we to be censured or not? I'd like to get it out in the open, here and now.'

'You've only just arrived. The nature of your censure is a complex one, with many factors. It can't be decided instantly.'

'As far as I'm concerned there's only one factor. We consorted. The fact that we were late has nothing to do with it – it could have happened to anyone else. We brought the Line five survivors it wouldn't otherwise have got back, and the prisoners, and Hesperus.'

'To which we must also add Campion's unfortunate treatment of his strand.'

'Censure me for that, by all means, but leave Purslane out of it,' Campion said.

'Unfortunately, by consorting, by arriving together, by flaunting your feelings for each other, you have demonstrated your willingness to be censured as a couple. So shall it be.'

'Shatterlings have wiped their strands before,' I said. 'No one got censured for it then, so why pick on Campion and me now?'

Betony looked strained. 'Calm down, please. If there is to be censure it will be mild, and your former good conduct will be taken into account. There will be no talk of excommunication from the Line – nothing you have done even *begins* to warrant that. But there must be discipline, Purslane. Now more than ever.'

I sank back in my seat, feeling as if I had been slapped hard in the face. My hands were shaking, so I buried them in my lap. The worst thing was that I almost agreed with him. There did have to be discipline, especially considering our perilous position. Shatterlings had free will most of the time. But what if one of us were to whisk aboard our ship and head back to the reunion system, thereby alerting the ambushers to our hideaway? I would have no qualms about pursuing and executing a shatterling who did that, even if they were Gentian. I would even fire the gamma-cannon myself if I believed that the Line's existence depended on it.

'Can I make one request?' I asked, when the colour had returned to my cheeks.

'Go ahead,' Betony said.

'Before we arrived around Neume, Hesperus communicated a wish to Campion and me. It was clear that he wanted to be brought to Neume and into the presence of the Spirit of the Air.'

'He made this explicit?'

'As explicit as he could, given the circumstances.' My throat grew dry; I sensed that if I did not make my case convincingly now, I would not get a second chance. 'I spoke to the magistrate already, but it wasn't the right time to persuade her. Now I'd like Line backing to press for contact with the Spirit.'

'Did you mention this to Cadence and Cascade?'

'I didn't want to mention the Spirit again with the magistrate around.'

'They will have their own view as to how to proceed,' Betony said. 'If Hesperus is one of them, the simplest thing would be to hand him over and consider the matter closed.'

'The simplest, but not necessarily the right thing,' Aconite said. 'If Hesperus communicated a specific desire to Purslane, we have to honour it.'

'I agree,' Henbane said.

'But we can't afford to anger the Machine People, either,' said Whin, a male shatterling who had been silent until now. 'If they want to examine Hesperus, what right do we have to insist otherwise?'

'It does put us in a diplomatic bind,' Sainfoin said thoughtfully. 'But as a Line our responsibility has always been to our guests, above any other concerns. If Hesperus did make this request of Purslane, we must honour his wishes. That doesn't necessarily imply a confrontation with the Machine People. Cadence and Cascade have been more than understanding until now, and I don't expect that to change if we explain our predicament to them.'

'You know them better than any of us,' Betony said to Sainfoin, the shatterling who had brought the robots to the reunion in the first place.

'They're reasonable,' she said. 'They'll see our side of things. But that doesn't mean we should ignore any suggestions they make.'

Aconite said, 'You have my unconditional backing, Purslane, for what it's worth.'

'Mine too,' Mezereon said. 'And you can include Valerian, Lucerne and Melilot. They'll back you all the way when they learn what Hesperus did for us.'

'Thank you,' I said.

'Count me in,' Henbane said.

Before the murmur of approval turned into a storm, Betony nodded once. 'Very well – Purslane has Line authority to petition the Neume administration for access to the Spirit of the Air. But before you take the matter any further, Purslane ... have you the faintest idea what you're dealing with?'

Campion came to my room later that morning, while I was waiting to hear back from the magistrate concerning my request for an audience. I was standing on the little low-walled balcony that jutted out from the side of the room, accessed through a matter-permeable window, composing my thoughts, trying to marshal the facts of my case into something resembling a persuasive, logically sustained argument. Betony's had unsettled me, opening a chink of doubt where before there had been only neutron-dense certainty. I had gone into the trove and learned that the Spirit's displeasure had brought down entire civilisations. But we also had the Spirit to thank for the fact that anyone could live on Neume in the first place. In the absence of any large-scale organisms, it was the Spirit that kept the atmosphere in its current dynamically unstable state, absorbing carbon dioxide from the air and returning oxygen. There was no way the machine intelligence was doing that simply for its own benefit.

So it tolerated us, even, perhaps, encouraged our presence. But that did not mean it would spare me if it judged me an irritation. I looked out towards the slivers of clear blue sky visible between the golden towers of Ymir and wondered if I had the nerve to do what had to be done.

'I brought you this.'

I turned around at Campion's voice, watching as he stepped through onto the balcony. He was clutching a piece of chocolate bread wrapped in paper.

'Thank you.'

'I didn't have any more of an appetite than you did, but I reckoned you'd get some of yours back by mid-morning.'

I took the chocolate bread and bit into a corner. 'You're right, as usual. I've got a stomach full of butterflies, but I'm still hungry. How do you think we did back there?'

'Atrociously. But I don't think anyone could have done much better, given what we had to work with.'

'I'm surprised at Betony.'

'I'm not. He's a schemer who's just seen his chance to exert real influence within the Line. It was never a possibility when Fescue and the other alpha males were around, but now he's almost got a clear field to himself.'

'Don't forget the alpha females.'

'And did you see how he lorded it over that table, as if we'd already voted him emperor? And he has the gall to accuse *me* of flouting Line traditions! We're supposed to be egalitarian, without leaders.'

'In times of crisis, the Line is allowed to form a decision-making quorum.'

'Yes – but we've managed to get by without one for most of our history. You can be sure that Betony was at the head of the queue when the idea of forming a new quorum was mooted. I wouldn't be surprised if he suggested it. Why do we need a quorum, anyway? We're perfectly capable of taking decisions en masse – more so now than ever.'

'The others will keep him in check. We've still got friends. Did you see how they rallied when I asked for permission to visit the magistrate? Half the table was behind me.'

'Hm.'

'What's that supposed to mean?'

'Nothing, really. I'm just wondering whether that vote of support was as sympathetic as it appeared.'

'How could it be anything other than sympathetic?'

'Some of them could be hoping that you fall flat on your face, by being denied access. I wouldn't even be surprised if one or two are hoping you do get access and then make a fool of yourself with the Spirit.'

'No one wants me to die, though.'

'No,' Campion said. 'They're not that bad. Some of them may not like us, but we're still kin. I wouldn't wish death on another Gentian shatterling, and I don't think the others are any different.'

'I'd like to think so. I'm still worried about this censure thing, though. I feel as if there's a sword hanging over me.'

'If it works out with Hesperus, all our problems could be over.'

'All of them?'

'All right,' Campion said, 'some of them. But at least he'd speak up for us. Who's going to doubt the word of a Machine Person?'

'In other words, there's even more reason to risk everything with the Spirit.'

'That and the fact that he's our friend, and it'd be great to have him back.'

'I've been doing some reading. Betony wasn't exaggerating – we could be putting ourselves at risk with the Spirit.'

'We've been putting ourselves at risk since they hatched us.'

'True.' I finished the chocolate bread and started folding the paper into an origami dove. 'Thanks for thinking of me. No matter what happens here, no matter what happens to us after Neume, I'm glad we're together.'

'I'm not going anywhere without you.'

'At least our consorting is out in the open now. No need to be coy about it.'

Campion looked grave. 'They'll make us pay, one way or another. I hope you realise that.'

I finished the dove. It gained a pair of almond-coloured eyes and watercoloured feathers, and started flapping. I released it into the air and watched it fly away into the distance, heading off to be recycled. Campion and I held hands, then pulled ourselves close to each other. 'Let them do their worst. I'm ready for it.'

Presently there was a chime from my room.

Jindabyne's office was on the very summit of her building, in a four-sided cupola affording excellent views in all directions. Wings, hung like ceremonial sabres, decorated the walls between the windows. Their glassy facets were stained in ruby, green and blue and inscribed with wavery lines of Ymirian script. There were also photographs and a couple of strange, rebus-like Neume art pieces, all of which resembled the blueprints for fiendishly difficult garden mazes. Three of the bulbous, convex windows revealed only a dense cityscape of golden spires, but the fourth, westerly facing window looked out to the silver desert, where the endlessly shifting barchans reached in serpentine waves all the way to the horizon. It was a clear, still day, and I could see a solitary white tower at the limit of visibility.

'This is an extraordinarily unusual request,' Jindabyne informed us when we had taken seats facing her desk. 'You must understand my natural scepticism. Gentian Line has never shown much interest in this world, yet all of a sudden you want access to our deepest mysteries.' There was a complicated, hookah-like apparatus perched on Jindabyne's desk – a painted kettle, hissing and burbling, festooned with pipes and valves. Now and then the fine-furred magistrate would inhale from a mouthpiece on the end of a segmented hose. Campion and I had been given two cups of watery, ginger-flavoured tea – the crockery kept chinking in our hands. 'You flatter us with your attention,' Jindabyne went on, 'but I can't help feeling like a woman receiving insincere compliments because she has something someone wants. What do your troves tell you about the Spirit?'

'That it is also known as the Fracto-Coagulation,' I said. 'That it is an airborne entity composed of many individual elements; that it was once a human mind, a human being, a man who may once have been called Valmik, who was alive in the Golden Hour.'

'Then it would seem that you are wasting your time.'

Campion spoke now. 'The trove also tells us that the Spirit of the Air has occasionally interceded to raise the dead, both biological and machine.'

'It has also killed many individuals who were not dead to begin with.'

'But the trove also says that many of the incidents could be blamed on provocation by the involved parties,' Campion replied, 'by them acting in a way that was known to irritate the Spirit.'

'No one went to the Spirit intending to provoke it, shatterling. They all thought they were being cleverer than those who'd come before.'

'We don't,' I said. 'We're fully aware of the risks, and that we might not survive a direct encounter. But we still have to do this. We owe it to our friend.'

Jindabyne sucked on her pipe. The kettle bubbled furiously. 'The Machine Person. Shouldn't he be entrusted to Cadence and Cascade?'

'They'll be consulted, obviously,' I said, 'but Hesperus must have known that the Spirit offered his best chance of survival, not his fellow machines.'

Jindabyne scratched the honey-coloured fur on the side of her cheek. Until the light caught her at a certain angle, the fur could have been mistaken for human skin. 'You put me in an invidious position.'

'All we're asking for is the same access privileges that have already been granted to countless travellers in the past,' I said.

'Times were different then. The Spirit was more predictable. Lately – I'm talking of recent centuries, not years – it has grown more capricious. There were some unpleasant incidents. The scientific council convinced the combined authorities that there should be no more casual encounters. So far the Spirit has confined its displeasure to individuals or small groups of individuals, but what if it should tire of human presence on Neume? They say it brought down the Plastic, and later the Providers.'

'If it didn't want your company, I imagine it would have got rid of you already,' Campion said.

'Easy for you to say. You're just guests here – you can leave any time you want. You don't depend on the Spirit for the air you breathe.'

'We understand,' I said, soothingly. 'We're making an unusual request, and you're perfectly entitled to turn us down. But I promise you that we won't do anything without the guidance of the scientific council. If there is any hint that the Spirit is being displeased, we'll stop immediately.'

'You know I cannot refuse you,' Jindabyne said.

'Of course you can,' I said.

'Really? With the full weight of Gentian Line watching my every move? There may be fewer than fifty ships in orbit around Neume, but we all know what those ships could do to Neume if we refuse to cooperate. You could turn these towers to dust, scour everything back to the last relics of the Benevolence.'

'It isn't like that at all,' Campion said. 'We didn't come here to bully our way into anything.'

'You may not think so. Privately, it may even be true. But you are a Line, a member of the Commonality. The Lines always get what they want. There are never exceptions.'

'But we *asked*,' I said, plaintively.

'In the full and certain knowledge of my eventual compliance.'

'Not Gentian Line,' Campion said. 'That's never been how we do things.'

'Then if I refused, that would be an end to it?'

Campion and I exchanged wary looks. 'Yes,' I said. 'Absolutely. You have sovereignty here. We don't.'

'Shatterling Betony is a determined man. If you took news of my refusal to him, how do you think he'd respond? Not well, I suspect. You may have principles, shatterlings, but acting collectively, you are monsters. I have seen it, from other Lines.'

'We're not monsters,' I said. 'If you don't believe me, turn us down. I swear no harm will come to you.'

'And a thousand years from now? Ten thousand? Nothing to you.'

'Everything's different now,' Campion said. 'Even if we did act like that in the past, we're not the same now.'

Jindabyne placed her mouthpiece in the clawed hook of a malachite desk-stand. 'Go now,' she said, picking up a sheet of paper from her desk. 'You will have word of my decision later today.'

Cadence and Cascade met me on a private balcony of the tower where we had our rooms. It was noon. Campion reclined in a low chair with an apple in his hand, saying as little as he could get away with.

'Thank you for agreeing to come,' I said, nodding at the two flawless creatures.

Cadence, the silver one with the female anatomy, nodded. 'It is the least we could do, Purslane. Cascade and I are most anxious to visit Hesperus, and see what may be done for him. It may surprise you that we have feelings of compassion towards our fellow machines, but that is how we are. It tears at us to think that Hesperus may be suffering.'

'Do you die?' I asked.

'Of course we die,' Cascade said. 'We are not indestructible. Far from home, far from the support systems of our culture, we are scarcely less vulnerable to injury than human beings.' He touched a white finger to his chest. 'With the right weapon, you could kill me now.'

'But your experiences have been recorded somewhere else, back in the Monoceros Ring.'

'The nearest part of the Ring is tens of thousands of lights away. Much has happened to me since my departure, very little of which has been communicated back home. If I were to die now, it would take tens of thousands of years for news of my death to reach the Ring. Then they might activate a copy of me, with my last full set of memories. But I would not consider that entity to be me, merely an entity with whom I have certain things in common.' He bowed his beautiful head. 'You must understand, being a shatterling. Each of you carries a very similar set of memories, but that does not mean you would think lightly of dying.'

'No,' I said. 'We wouldn't. But what about Hesperus? Could he really die?'

'Undoubtedly. Until we examine him, we can only speculate about the nature of his injuries. What is certain is that his chances of being repaired will be greatest if he is returned to the Ring.'

'We would need a ship for that,' Cadence said.

'You don't have one?'

'Sainfoin brought us here. We have no vehicle of our own.'

Campion crunched noisily on his apple, the ancient human sound punctuating my thoughts. He was observing things very carefully, though giving every impression of studied indifference.

'You must have had a ship at some point,' I said.

'Once,' Cadence said offhandedly. 'It was destroyed long before we reached the Dorcus reunion. Since then we have been at the mercy of human charity.' The robot waved a hand as if to wipe away the problem. 'It is of no matter. Ships are mute machines with no more sentience than a pebble. They have no intrinsic value to us.'

'It would be good if you could look at Hesperus,' I said. 'At the very least, help me get him down to Neume in one piece. I'm afraid of moving him now.'

'There is no need for him to come here,' Cascade said. 'Whatever we can do for him, we can do aboard your ship.'

'You don't need the resources of Ymir?' I asked.

Cadence made a tiny clucking sound, which I took to be the Machine Person equivalent of a derisive snort. 'The citizens of Neume mean well, but using their machines to repair Hesperus would be like trying to perform brain surgery on you with a few pieces of flint.'

'If flint's all you have, you go with flint.'

Cascade's ivory mask shaped a thin smile. 'But we can do better than that. We are flexible machines. The humanoid forms we assume now are mere conveniences. It would be a simple matter for us to form the necessary interfaces to assist Hesperus. But first we must be aboard your ship.'

'That can be arranged. But I'd still like to bring him down to Neume.'

'There is no need,' Cascade said again.

'For me there is. It's complicated, but Hesperus asked us to do something for him.' I took a deep breath. 'You've already spent time on Neume – doubtless you know of the Spirit of the Air.'

'Yes,' Cadence said guardedly.

'Have you had contact with it since your arrival?'

She – I could not help but think of the machine as a she – shook her slim-necked, imperious head. 'None at all. There has been no need. It is not a true machine intelligence, and therefore of only passing interest to us.'

'Does that apply to people as well?'

'Quite the contrary. We find organic intelligences infinitely fascinating. All that slippery grey meat emulating consciousness – what is there not to be fascinated by?'

'The Spirit,' Cascade said, 'represents an intermediate stage of sophistication between human and true machine consciousness. Its origin is obscure, its nature unstable. There are too many variables to make it amenable as a study subject.'

And, I thought quietly, *you might fear it a little as well*. If it scared humans, then it might hold similar terrors for Machine People. Campion caught my eye from across the balcony and winked once.

'Well, I'm interested in it,' I said. 'Hesperus was fully aware of our destination. It is our belief that he wished to be brought into the presence of the Spirit.'

'What purpose do you expect that to serve?' Cascade asked.

'There are documented instances of the Spirit interceding to heal injured pilgrims or repair damaged machines,' I said. 'It's not beyond the bounds of possibility that the Spirit will do something similar for Hesperus.'

'Or take him apart.'

'In which case he'll have communicated part of himself into the memory of the Spirit. He must have been willing to take that chance.'

'This is most unorthodox,' Cadence said.

'Being here is unorthodox. Having an injured Machine Person for a guest is unorthodox.'

'Nonetheless.'

There was a silence. The machines stood still, but the lights in their heads flared and spun like demented fireflies. I had the sense of some vast, inscrutable conversation taking place before me, at a speed I could scarcely comprehend. Those seconds of silence might have consumed subjective years of frenzied debate in the accelerated time frame of machine consciousness.

They are cleverer than us, I thought. *Cleverer and stronger and faster, and soon it will come to a head, us or them.*

'We will journey to your ship and inspect Hesperus,' Cadence said.

Cascade added, 'We will attempt to establish a communication link with him. If that fails, you may bring him down to the surface and present him to the Spirit.'

I felt dizzy and elated in equal measure. I could not begrudge them a chance at communication first. At the very least, it might enable Hesperus to clarify his wishes.

'Thank you,' I said, when I had gathered my thoughts again. 'I'm enormously grateful.'

'You were expecting obstruction?' Cascade asked mildly.

'I wouldn't have been offended if you'd refused. He's our guest, but he's your fellow citizen. If you felt that you had a better claim over him ... I wouldn't have argued.'

'But you would have been sad,' Cadence said.

'Yes. I'd have felt as if we'd let him down.'

'We would not want that to happen. You have taken care of him until now, and we are grateful to you for that.' Cascade turned to face his silver companion, then glanced back at me. 'When may we visit your ship, Purslane?'

'As soon as I have Line authorisation to take my shuttle back into orbit. That shouldn't be a problem, but it may take a few hours.'

Cadence bowed. 'Then we shall await your instructions.'

CHAPTER FIFTEEN

In the early afternoon of our first full day on Neume, the other three shatterlings we had transported were released from abeyance. By the time they emerged into daylight, on the large landing deck where we had gathered the night before, they had the stunned, wary look of people who could not quite believe their reversal of fortune. It was as if they had woken from one dream and could not quite shake the sense that they were now in another, from which they might be roused at any moment.

When they had met the customary grouping of shatterlings, guests and civic dignitaries – fewer in number than the evening before, not that Lucerne, Melilot and Valerian would ever know – they came over to speak to Purslane and me.

'Aconite told us what happened, Campion,' Melilot said to me. 'We can't ever repay you for what you've done for us.'

'You'd have done the same,' I said.

'I'd like to think so, but I won't ever know for sure. The point is you *did* do it, knowing the risks. Thank you, Campion and Purslane. You make me proud to be Gentian.'

'There's talk of censure,' I said, glancing over my shoulder to check whether Betony might still be in earshot. 'Purslane and I will need all the friends we can get if it comes to a vote as to how we should be punished.'

'They can't be serious,' said the darkly handsome Valerian.

'They are, unfortunately,' Purslane said. 'But if we have at least some allies, I feel better already.'

'You have more allies than you imagine,' Lucerne said. Then she looked sharply at the other two. 'Grilse and the others ... what happened to them?'

'They're here,' I said. 'Still in stasis. Mezereon's been charged with getting information out of them.'

'She'll do it, too,' Valerian said.

'You make that sound like a bad thing.'

Melilot lowered her voice. 'Mezereon was . . . zealous when it came to interrogating Grilse.'

'I'd have been pretty zealous myself,' Purslane said.

'But not as much as Mezereon. We almost had to restrain her. We didn't want the prisoner dying on us before we got anything useful out of him. And now she's in charge of them all?'

'There'll be due oversight,' I said.

'There'd better be,' Lucerne said. 'None of us gives a damn what happens to Grilse – they can throw him to the wolves for all I care. But not before the fucker's talked.'

The afternoon was eventful. Cyphel was making arrangements to recover my strand from the heads of the surviving shatterlings, which meant each of us submitting to a delicate, time-consuming memory read. The hard part was not preparing the equipment, for the machinery was easily fabricated from standard maker files, but organising us all so that the work could be accomplished in days, not weeks. As a token of goodwill, and to show that I was not purposefully concealing anything, I offered myself up as her first subject.

'I can skip you, Campion,' Cyphel said when we were alone in the room assigned for her work. 'It's kind of you to offer, but there'll be interference between the strand and your own base memories of the same experiences. I've never understood why the Line insists on each of us receiving our own strands.'

'Tradition,' I said. 'And a safeguard against sabotage. If I decided to plant something nasty in the head of every other shatterling, I couldn't do it without infecting myself.'

'You could take precautions, if that was what you intended.'

'But it would be more complicated, and therefore more likely to go wrong. All the same, I suppose the tradition is more symbolic than practical. Do you want to scan me or not?'

'Yes, assuming you've got nothing better to do. Wouldn't you rather be watching Mezereon getting her kicks?'

'I detect a faint note of disapproval.'

Cyphel wrinkled her nose, as if there was a bad smell in the room. 'Let's give it a try. If the signal-to-noise ratio is too low to be useful, I'll discard you from the set.'

'Sounds painful.'

'Lie down here,' she said, with exaggerated sternness. Cyphel knew that I liked her and there was a pleasurable tension in all our exchanges. I think she liked me a little bit as well.

I lay on the couch and breathed out while she began her work. She took a thing like a tube of paint and squeezed the contents onto her left hand and arm, up to her elbow, forming a thick web of waxy lines that reached from the crook of her arm to the tips of her fingers. She had many rings on her left hand, none on the right, but she kept the waxy lines from interfering with her jewellery. In seconds the aspic-of-machines cured into a flexible network. Cyphel held her hand close to my scalp, as if she was warming her palm from a hot stone. She moved the hand slowly, fingers stiffened like a dancer's, occasionally glancing aside at a summary updating on the room's wall. As the skull-penetrating sensors rummaged through my memories, identifying those patterns tagged as being part of a strand, I felt brief, subliminal flickers of recall ghosting into consciousness, like pictures projected faintly onto a screen. It was like walking into Palatial, feeling the game pick through my mind.

'Did you get anywhere with the flight logs?'

'Keep still. This'll go a lot quicker if you don't move and you don't talk.'

'Sorry.'

'To answer your question, I haven't looked at the logs yet. I'll do that once I've got enough strands read in to begin the correlative matching. The logs probably won't come to anything, but we may as well look into it. You owe me one, you realise. I saved your skin out there.'

I mumbled agreement.

'I'm sure you'll find a way to pay me back. One day I might do something as idiotic as wipe my own strands – who knows?' With her free hand, Cyphel pushed back a stray strand of blue-white hair. 'You're *infuriating*, Campion. There are times when I think you embody the best of what the Line stands for, and other times when I think we should have excommunicated you circuits ago. Your problem is that you don't take it seriously enough. Which is good, sometimes – we can't all be like Fescue, or Betony – but other times ... well, I won't labour the point; I'm sure you'll hear it often enough in days to come. At least you have Purslane to keep you on the straight and narrow. You could power empires with that woman's patience. If it were me, we'd already have built a memorial to you.'

By which she meant that she would have killed me.

Cyphel was soon done and invited me to move off the couch. 'You got a clean extraction?'

'No worse than I was expecting.' She peeled the waxy lines of aspic-of-machines from her arm and fingers, squeezing them into a ball which oozed back into the tube it had come from. 'Nothing I can work with yet, but by the time I've added together all the others, we should be getting somewhere. Just between you and me – because it's going to come out anyway – you weren't trying to hide anything, were you? I mean, that's not why you deleted your strand?'

'If I had something to hide, I'm doing it so well I don't even know about it.'

'That could be true. The tricks we can play with memory. But ...' Cyphel trailed off. 'After all this, I do trust you. You have your faults, not even you can deny that, but I don't think you had anything to do with the ambush. You're like a boy looking for pretty shells on a beach. You picked up something that caught your eye, and you brought it home and showed it off to everyone else, but even you didn't have any idea of its true significance.' Cyphel paused significantly. 'Someone did, though. Someone saw what you'd brought home and decided we all had to die because of it. Now all we have to do is find that shell.'

'I'm glad you made it, Cyphel.'

'That makes two of us,' she said.

The four cabinets were grouped together on a raised plinth, surrounded by bare flooring. Mezereon had been given an entire room for her interrogations. Beyond the open area stood a series of stepped benches from which interested parties could witness the proceedings; beyond the benches rose walls through which narrow-slitted windows admitted pencil-thin shafts of wan daylight. There was more than enough space for all the shatterlings, as well as our guests and a small congregation of locals. Many witnesses were already present when the conveyor dropped me off outside, having just watched Purslane's shuttle climb back into the sky. I was burning with curiosity, desperate to hear what these frozen prisoners had to say of their part in the crime.

Mezereon's timing and showmanship were impeccable. By the time she arrived, the atmosphere was electric and conversation dropped to an alert, anticipatory silence in an instant.

She strode to the plinth and stood before it, the cabinets looming over her thin, dark-clad form. 'Thank you, shatterlings and guests,' she said, pivoting on her heels to address the audience. 'Today I will be using Synchromesh to reach the prisoners.' She raised one arm high so that her sleeve slipped down to reveal a bulky white chronometer clamped around the pale stick of her wrist, the watch set with pearly dials and many knurled knobs. 'Since you were warned, I presume that most of you have your own 'mesh, or an equivalent means of decelerating your subjective time-flow. Please prepare to administer a slowdown rate of one hundred, but only at my command.'

She spun around and stepped onto the plinth, walking to the rightmost cabinet. Like the other three, its doors were open. The prisoner sat on a throne inside a buttressed red bubble of retarded time. 'We only know the name of the man in the leftmost box. Grilse's cabinet is better than the other three – he's got a much stronger chance of surviving emergence into normal time. For the other three, I consider the chances somewhat poorer – husking is a distinct possibility. Because of this I will not risk bringing them out of stasis until I am certain I have learned all I can without external coercion. But they do not know that.' Mezereon opened the control panel in the rightmost cabinet, exposing the same kind of graduated dial I had seen in Grilse's box, when Mezereon had shown it to me aboard *Dalliance*. The lever was also pushed nearly all the way to the right, indicating a stasis factor near one hundred thousand: a second for every day that passed in the external universe, near enough. In the time that had elapsed since I had met the other shatterlings for breakfast, the prisoner might have had time to blink once. It would take two or three days of my time for him to complete a gesture, or express a simple statement.

Mezereon tugged the lever to the left, until the stasis factor was a hundred. The prisoner still appeared immobile from moment to moment, but over the course of a minute the rise and fall of his chest was just discernible. He was breathing; alive. The bubble was now pink-hued rather than scarlet.

'He sees and hears only me,' Mezereon said, looking back over her shoulder at the audience. 'There's a privacy screen between you and me. Later, it may be possible to cross-examine the prisoners, but for now I would rather they dealt only with me. I do of course have quorum authority to lead this investigation.' She touched the face of her chronometer with one sharp-nailed finger. 'I am about to dial myself up. If you wish to follow the proceedings, do likewise. I suggest you set a six-hour expiration, time enough for a few minutes of conversation.'

As the drug slowed her mental processes, Mezereon froze, falling into a pseudo-paralysis. It was in fact only a retardation of bodily functions, not a complete cessation, but she would have toppled from the plinth had her clothes not stiffened to provide the necessary support. Now her subjective consciousness rate had been matched to the prisoner's, and her heart and respiratory rates lowered accordingly. Her mouth opened very slowly and sound appeared to come out of it.

It was impossible to speak under the influence of Synchromesh: the physiology of the human voice box simply did not permit sounds to be generated across minutes of actual time. But her clothes were capable of reading her intentions, and they fed a simulation of Mezereon's voice to both the prisoner and the loudspeakers situated around the room. What we heard sounded as low and mournful as whale song, throbbing with subsonic undertones.

I pulled a black vial from my pocket and squeezed two cold drops of Synchromesh onto my eyeballs. The drug hit my nervous system in moments, dulling my blink reflex. Using the chronometer, I set the six-hour expiration and rotated the dial that would tell the drug how slowly I wished to go. I felt the usual lurch of dizziness as the 'mesh took hold. Afterwards, the only evidence that I was under the influence of the drug was the whirling progress of the normal minute hand on my chronometer, whipping around like a centrifuge. Most of the audience had dialled up at the same time as me; only a handful were still living in normal time, betrayed by their fidgety, jerky movements.

Mezereon's voice had upshifted through the frequencies until she sounded perfectly normal and comprehensible. ' ... of Gentian Line, the House of Flowers,' she was saying in Trans, introducing herself – I had missed only a second or two of actual speech. 'You are in our custody now, on a world whose name and location I have no intention of divulging. We're not interested in justice, merely cold-blooded retribution.'

The prisoner said nothing. But he was fully alive now, shifting in his throne restraints and eyeing Mezereon's every move.

'We are, however, prepared to make concessions for information,' she said, occasionally turning to face her hidden audience, her clothes permitting normal perambulation. 'There are four of you, and we only need one of you to talk. Your cabinets are damaged – the chances of you surviving emergence into normal time are not excellent. If you are prepared to tell us what we want, I will make sure we do all in our power to keep you alive. But only if you cooperate. Only if you tell us everything, without evasion, without ambiguity.' Mezereon rested a hand on her hip. 'What's it to be?'

The prisoner smiled or sneered – it was difficult to tell which. 'I saw what we did to you, Gentian. I know how many we killed.'

'There were survivors – more than you realised. And latecomers, too.'

'I only have your word on that.'

'You want to see the others, I'll bring you out of stasis. That should feel real enough.'

'You won't risk it. Bring me out and you stand a very good chance of ending up with nothing.'

'You don't think I'll take that chance? You're not that precious to me.'

'Again, I only have your word.'

'You know how many of you were in the ship.'

'But I don't know how many of us survived. You can show me the other three, but I don't have to believe I'm seeing anything other than a projection.'

'Who sent you?'

'We did.'

'Wrong answer. Tell me about the Marcellin involvement in this atrocity.'

'You tell me.'

'The Marcellins were tasked with disposing of the H-guns. If they'd done that, we wouldn't be having this conversation. Is there collusion at Line-level, or was Grilse acting independently of the other shatterlings?'

'Who's Grilse?'

'My patience isn't infinite,' Mezereon said. Her hand was on the lever of the stasis cabinet now. 'I can pull this all the way to the left, bring you out. Would you like me to do that?'

'Whatever makes you happiest.'

'Tell me what Campion's thread had to do with the ambush. What was in it that mattered so much?'

'Ask Campion. Or did we kill him as well?'

'Are you a member of one of the Lines? Are you Marcellin?'

'Do I *look* Marcellin to you?'

'I'd say you were Mellicta, if I had to put money on it. I didn't notice the resemblance until you started speaking, but you all have that arrogant set to your jaws, that fuck-you glint in your eyes.' Mezereon watched him very intently, alert to the slightest betrayal of his true feelings. It was frustrating, not being able to look into his mind directly. But no useful scans could penetrate the stasis bubble.

'You think I'm working for the House of Moths, take it up with them.'

Mezereon nodded sagely. 'You're one of them. A Starmover.' Without warning, her hand pushed the dial to its earlier setting, freezing the shatterling into immobility. Even with Synchromesh he appeared inert, since there was still a thousandfold gap between our time rates.

'If he's Mellicta I want to know now,' Mezereon said. Behind her, the light that rammed through the narrow slots in the walls changed its angle perceptibly.

From elsewhere in the audience Aconite spoke up. 'There'll be a list of all Mellicta shatterlings in the trove. It won't guarantee a match – they change their looks the same way we do – but there's no harm in checking.'

'Do it,' Mezereon said. 'And don't forget to check against shatterlings lost to attrition.'

Aconite's hand moved to his chronometer. He dialled himself back into normal time and became a blur as he moved to the exit of the interrogation room. The door opened and closed, flashing dusky sky for an instant. A few subjective seconds later, the door flashed again and Aconite was back in his chair, adjusting into our time-flow.

'We've got a name,' he said. 'A Mellicta shatterling named Thorn. He was lost to attrition ten of their circuits ago.'

'Same time as Grilse, give or take a circuit,' Mezereon said. 'That makes two of them – both shatterlings presumed dead, but who were alive after all. Perhaps we should take a closer look at the other two – we might find the same story.'

'There's a question I'd like to ask him,' I said.

Mezereon's gaze snapped onto me. If she was grateful for my having rescued her, no trace of that gratitude now remained. 'What, Campion?'

'I'd like to know if he's heard of the House of Suns.'

'There's no such Line,' Mezereon said.

'I'd still like to see how he reacts.'

'Why? What do you imagine he might say? Grilse never mentioned such a thing.'

'I've just got a suspicion that something called the House of Suns may be involved. It was something Hesperus mentioned, although his memory was too damaged for him to say where the phrase originated.'

'How can there be a Line no one's heard about?' asked Charlock. 'We know what we are – who's in the Commonality, who's been expelled. There's no room in our history for a hidden Line.'

'A Line could have arisen recently,' said Valerian. 'One too new to have entered the troves.'

'We might as well ask,' Melilot said, leaning forward in her seat. 'I agree with Campion. Everything points to a connection with the Vigilance, and we know Hesperus was interested in that. If we had thousands of years, we could send someone back to the Vigilance to ask some more questions. But we don't, so we have to make do with what we have on Neume.'

I glanced down at my chronometer, at the viciously whirling hand. We had been in Mezereon's time frame for nearly four minutes of subjective time. In the real world nearly six hours had elapsed.

'Ask him,' I said.

A scowl played across Mezereon's face; she did not care to be dictated to. But she yanked the lever back to the hundred setting.

'Having fun?' the prisoner asked.

'You're Thorn, a shatterling of Mellicta Line,' Mezereon said. 'You were believed lost to attrition. You attempted to slingshot through a double degenerate binary and miscalculated the tidal forces. So the troves tell us, in any case.'

'If you say so.'

'There is no doubt.' Mezereon's eyes flashed in my direction, resentfully. 'But tell me something else, Thorn. Tell me about the House of Suns.'

'There's no such thing.'

But his answer, we all saw, had been just too glib, too quick.

CHAPTER SIXTEEN

Cadence and Cascade knelt before the remains of Hesperus. They were aboard my ship, in orbit around Neume. They had been like that for at least two hours, side by side, with their silver and white hands touching him where his body emerged from the warped golden growth that had bonded him to the wreckage of his ship. The two living robots had been silent and still, with only the movement of the lights in their skulls – agitated and rhythmic – indicating the continuation of machine consciousness. As for Hesperus, there had been no visible change in his condition since I had last seen him. The lights in his head were dim and ember-like, their movements almost imperceptible. Cadence and Cascade's hands were not just touching him, but appeared to be pressing into his body, as if the gold armour of his skin was no more resilient than clay. But when they withdrew their hands, slowly and in unison, no impression remained.

Cadence turned her lovely silver face to mine. 'He is not dead, Purslane. Threatened with grave injury, he has consolidated his mental processes, whittling himself down to a tiny, flickering candle of intelligence and memory. He can be saved. But there is nothing we can do for him here.'

'On Neume?' I asked.

'Nothing there either,' Cascade said, his voice as soothing and reassuring as ever, even when he was imparting dismal news. 'He must be returned to the Machine People, in the Monoceros Ring. There he can be brought back to full functionality, and rewarded for his efforts on our behalf.'

I thought of the tens of thousands of years that might pass before he reached Machine Space. As much time again might elapse before he returned to us, if that ever happened. Even for a shatterling, used to thinking in terms of circuits, the weight of those years felt enormous, interminable.

'Will he survive the journey?'

'That would depend on the ship,' Cadence said. 'It would need to be a fast one, to minimise the subjective time interval. Since he cannot be placed in abeyance, he must endure every second of the voyage, as measured by ship clocks.'

'Can't we make a stasis cabinet large enough?'

'Not with Neume technology. And we lack the tools to manufacture one ourselves.'

'Can he be taken apart, broken into smaller pieces? If we can just get part of him into a cabinet—'

'He would not survive dismantling,' Cascade said. 'Besides, his sentience is distributed throughout his body. No part of him could be safely discarded.'

'You said he'd consolidated himself, shrunk his consciousness down,' I said to Cadence.

'I was speaking metaphorically,' she said. 'The technicalities would not lie within your compass of understanding. Rest assured that transportation is his only chance.'

'Will he survive a trip down to Neume?'

'If he is handled gently,' Cadence said.

'Then I'd still like to present him to the Spirit, as we discussed before. It may not make any difference, but at least I'll have tried.'

'We have no objections,' said Cascade. 'There are risks in transporting him to the surface, obviously, but there are also risks in returning him home as he is.'

'You think he's going to die, whatever happens,' I said.

'The possibility is always there,' Cadence said. 'But we shall not obstruct you in your wishes. Would you like to take him down to Neume now? We can assist with the operation.'

'I still haven't had the final say-so from the authorities—'

'We will speak on your behalf if further persuasion is required,' Cascade said. 'If he communicated this wish to you, then we are also compelled to honour it.'

'Let us move him now,' said Cadence.

I stood back. 'If you think—'

'We shall treat him with kindness and care,' Cascade told me.

I watched as they moved to either side of Hesperus's misshapen bulk and took hold of his extremities. They lifted him without effort, smoothly and gracefully. I had been about to offer to turn off the gravity, or bring a cargo handler, but the robots had no need of my assistance.

They carried him through the ship and into the vast cavern of my main cargo bay, where I had docked the shuttle. The robots had asked me about the bay's contents when we arrived, amused by – or at least politely interested in – the number of ships I carried around with me, but now their attention was fixed on their patient and they paid no heed to the ships.

It was after sundown when we landed at Ymir, the cooling barchans singing into the night. I had the robots deliver Hesperus to a secure room in the tower where we were all being accommodated. It felt wrong to lock him away in there, stored like a piece of luggage, but the room would notify me of any changes in his condition.

Returning to my own quarters, I was surprised not to find Campion waiting for me. He wasn't in his own rooms, either. I felt let down. I had seen the concern on his face when I left, or imagined I had seen it, so I had assumed he would be awaiting my return, to let me know he was glad to have me back.

Feeling sullen and sorry for myself, and realising that it was too late to join the other shatterlings for the evening meal, I had the room prepare me food to Gentian standards. I ate it without enthusiasm, sitting on my bed with my shoes off, facing the open window to my balcony and watching the curtains stir in the warm breeze. Now and then a flying figure buzzed past, coloured wings glowing like stained-glass windows in the sky.

Most of these honey-coloured creatures would be dead before a single Gentian touched down on another world, but they did not appear to mind. Nor did they seem any less contented than other galactic cultures. They flew as if they had been born to the air, and their wings were delightful. So what if they had seen nothing of the wider galaxy, beyond what was shown to them by visiting travellers? So what if their civilisation (according to the dour prognostications of the Universal Actuary) showed every indication of being ephemeral, doomed to become part of the endless, rolling despond of turnover within a circuit or two? The people of Neume were thinking of today, not some century in the distant future.

Perhaps the Lines had it all wrong, I thought. We accumulated experience for the sake of it, stretched our lives out across millions of years, but even when things were going well – even when we were not being ambushed, pushed to the brink of extinction – there was a neurotic anxiety at the back of all our minds, a shrill voice instructing us to see everything, to look round every corner, to leave no stone unturned. We were like children who had to try every sweet in the shop, even if it made us sick. We knew there was more of the galaxy than we could ever encompass by ourselves, but the voice did not allow us to take that as licence to give up. All it said was *try harder.*

And where had it taken us? Thirty-two circuits of the galaxy, and I still did not feel as if I knew anything more than when I had first stepped out of the vat, naked as a new mole-rat, ravenous with Abigail's insane craving to gorge herself on reality. People lived and died and did strange, pointless things to themselves. So did societies, be they city-sized states or galactic empires encompassing thousands of solar systems. Everything came and went, everything was new and bright with promise once and old and worn out later, and everything left a small, diminishing stain on eternity, a mark that time would eventually erase.

'You're back,' Campion said, standing at my door. He had entered silently, his footsteps disguised by the swish of the curtains and a squall of brassy Ymirian music from one of the adjoining towers. It was the end of the working week and the locals were partying before going home.

'Yes,' I said, turning around, my expression blank.

'I was with Mezereon,' he said, tapping his chronometer. 'We dialled for six hours. It went by in a flash – just a few minutes of subjective time. It wasn't until I came out that I realised how late it was. I'm really sorry – I wanted to be here when you came back down.'

I felt so miserable, so dejected, that I was ready to forgive him anything. All I wanted was a hint that he had meant to be there. I could not blame him for losing track of time under the influence of 'mesh – it had happened to all of us.

'I missed you,' I said. 'Things didn't go too well.'

'I'm sorry.' Campion walked into the room, leaned over the bed and kissed me. 'Tell me what happened – assuming you want to talk about it.'

'Nothing, really. They touched him for a long time and then said there wasn't anything they could do. He isn't dead, but they can't help him. They could if they took him back to the other Machine People, but there's no guarantee he'd survive the journey.'

'Where is he now?'

'Here. In another room. They let me bring him down.'

'Did you hear anything about the Spirit?'

'Nothing.'

'There's still time. If we don't get anywhere by tomorrow morning, we'll schedule another meeting with the magistrate. She'll come round in the end. Everyone does, eventually.'

I did not feel his optimism, but I was too weary and deflated to argue the point. Campion had the maker prepare two glasses of cold white wine. Rather than bringing mine to the bed, he walked out onto the balcony, the glasses chinking in his hand. I stirred gloomily and followed him, leaving my shoes by the bed. The music rose and fell in surging, seasick waves, as if it was playing at the wrong speed.

'Tell me what happened with Mezereon,' I said.

He told me everything about the afternoon. 'We know more than we did this morning. He's Thorn, a Mellicta shatterling. He also knows more than he's telling us about the House of Suns.'

'Whose idea was it to ask him about that?'

'Just a hunch.'

I took my glass from his hand. 'A good one.'

'We still don't know what it is. A hidden Line, maybe, something the Commonality doesn't even know about? And how do the Marcellins and Mellictans fit into it?'

'Or the Gentians. We're involved as well.'

'Because they ambushed us?'

'Because the ambush required Line infiltration. We worked that one out already. Nobody could have got those H-guns close to the planet otherwise.'

'I'm trying not to think about that,' Campion said. 'It's bad enough knowing there might be another Line out there that wants us dead without thinking about snakes in the grass.'

'It could even be one of us.'

'You and me?'

'I mean one of the survivors – one of the Gentians who made it to Neume. If someone knew about the ambush, it wouldn't have been difficult to hide during the attack and then make it look as if you'd only just survived. How do we know the snake isn't sitting down to breakfast with us, working out how to finish the rest of us off? Some of us have been acting a little oddly.'

'You mean like Betony?' Campion asked, oblivious to the possibility that someone might be spying on us. 'No, it won't be him. He's just seen his chance for scoring a few points at our expense, that's all. It'll be someone keeping a low profile, someone we haven't even begun to suspect.'

'Or no one,' I added. 'There might not be a snake after all.'

'No, there might not be. But until we know otherwise, I think we ought to assume the worst. We were getting complacent – that's why someone was almost able to wipe us out. Those ships should have been inspected for concealed weapons before they got within attack range of the reunion world.'

'Should-haves don't count. And can you imagine how long that would take? Longer than the reunion itself. Just think of the time it would take to search through *Silver Wings*' hold – and I'm not the worst hoarder by a long way.' I shook my head. 'No recriminations, no going over old ground. The way we did things worked fine for thirty-two circuits. There can't have been too much wrong with it.'

After a silence, Campion said, 'You know what I keep coming back to? We'd never have visited this world unless something bad had happened to us. Never have heard those singing sands, seen this beautiful city ... We might have travelled here eventually, I know, but it wouldn't be Neume the way it is now. We'd probably be seeing it half a dozen civilisations down the line, when the Ymirians will just be a memory.'

I drank the wine, wanting it to go to my head as quickly as possible. 'If you're trying to see good in this, I'm not sure I'm quite ready to make that leap.'

'I'm just saying ... it's a strange universe. It can still surprise us. That's why it's worth carrying on, I suppose. If I felt that all we were doing was reliving a fixed set of experiences in different permutations—'

'That wouldn't be so bad, if those experiences were pleasant ones. Do you ever get tired of sunsets?'

'No,' Campion said.

'Do you ever get tired of waterfalls, or beaches?'

'No.'

'Then there's always hope for us.'

A chime sounded behind me. I handed Campion my glass and returned to the room, leaving him alone on the balcony. When I settled myself before the console I was confronted with the waiting face of Magistrate Jindabyne.

'I wasn't expecting to hear from you now,' I said.

'Did I not promise that I would be in touch?' she asked, not bothering to hide her indignation.

'It's just that it's getting late.'

'But it isn't midnight yet. I promised you I would give you a decision by the end of today. It just took a little longer than anticipated to make the necessary arrangements. Have you changed your mind concerning the Spirit of the Air?'

'I'm even more convinced now that it's the only way I can possibly help Hesperus.'

The magistrate narrowed her sharp, intelligent eyes. 'Tomorrow afternoon, at precisely three o'clock, a flier will arrive for you at the eighteenth-level landing deck. Aboard it will be a member of the scientific study council, an expert on the Spirit of the Air. Provided conditions remain favourable, he will arrange for you to be taken to the observation platform, where you may anticipate an encounter with the Spirit.'

I was aware of Campion standing behind me. 'Thank you, Magistrate,' I said. 'It's kind of you to allow this.'

'Not kind. Foolish, perhaps.'

I should have known something was coming, but it was only when the next morning's breakfast was winding down that I realised what Betony had been planning. Just before we would have begun to leave the table, Cadence and Cascade appeared on the balcony, and Betony introduced them with a magicianly flourish of his napkin. The robots' imperturbable expressions gave no hint that they knew what was about to unfold.

'Since we're all here,' Betony said, looking around the table as if to make sure no one had already left, 'this is as good a time as any to settle a small matter that has come to our attention. Our two guests from the Machine People had the unpleasant misfortune to become embroiled in Gentian affairs when they were caught in our ambush. Luckily, they were unharmed – and even more luckily, they appear to hold nothing against us for failing to keep them out of our troubles.'

'You could hardly have anticipated the ambush,' Cadence said.

'I suppose that's true, but you still have every right to feel aggrieved,' Betony answered.

Cascade said, 'You protected us as best you could, and then gave us passage to this world. We have no argument with Gentian Line, or by implication the Commonality. But it cannot be ignored that a crime has been committed, one that now encompasses the Machine People.'

'We must convey news of this atrocity back to the Monoceros Ring,' Cadence said. 'The Machine People will weigh the evidence and decide upon an appropriate response. The shatterlings of

Gentian Line may rest assured that we will support them unconditionally should punitive action be required. We hope that the perpetrator is no more than a rival Line, encompassing a few hundred or a few thousand individuals. But we will not quail even if it turns out that another civilisation is responsible.'

'We couldn't ask for wiser or stronger allies,' Betony said. 'That's why we'll do everything we can to assist your return to your own people.'

I tensed as it began to dawn on me where this was heading.

'Unfortunately, we have no means of transport,' Cascade said. 'We could of course simply transmit the intelligence back to our people, but then we would be at the mercy of human networks until the signal escapes the main disc. It might be corrupted or fail to reach its target. If we convey it in person, we will know that the information has reached home, intact. We will also be able to ensure that it is acted upon with the necessary swiftness.'

'There is also the business of Hesperus,' Cadence said, turning her silver head until her eyes met mine. 'Short of a miracle on Neume, his only chance for survival now rests in a safe return home, in the fastest possible vehicle.'

'You want my ship,' I said in a half-whisper.

Cadence nodded. 'We have studied the specifications of all the craft in orbit around Neume. All are fast, but yours will be able to accelerate closer to the speed of light than any other ship available. *Silver Wings of Morning* also has the best chance of surviving what will be a protracted voyage, even by Line standards. It will not be possible to slow for repairs or augmentations.'

'They've looked into it, crunched the numbers,' Betony said, giving me a sympathetic look, as if none of this was his doing. 'Your ship is the one most likely to get them home, and do it before anything untoward happens to Hesperus.'

'*Your* ship is fast,' I said.

'She accelerates harder, but *Adonis Blue* doesn't have your cruise ceiling, and that's what really matters.'

'We will do all in our power to return your ship,' Cascade said. 'You need only consider it borrowed, not given away.'

'So I'll get her back in a million years or so?'

'You have owned the ship for much longer than a million years, so even an interval of that enormity would not appear unreasonable.'

'This is very good, Betony,' I said, turning away from the robots.

He looked intrigued. 'In what sense?'

'You've found a way to screw me without looking as if you're screwing me. This is the punishment, isn't it? For Campion and me, for what we did – the consorting, the being late. Never mind that we brought the Line five survivors it wouldn't have had otherwise; never mind the prisoners or Hesperus. We've still got to pay, even if it's done sneakily, without looking like official censure.'

'Not in front of our guests, Purslane, please. We're asking you to make a benevolent gesture, not to suffer a punishment.'

I knew, with crushing certainty, that I could not win; that any attempt to argue my way out of this would not only be futile, but would cost me even more dearly in the future.

'How do you want to do this?' I asked. 'You can table a proposal, but you don't get to decide Line policy all by yourself. The matter still needs to be voted on.'

Betony nodded keenly. 'If you and Campion would like to leave us for a moment, we can vote. It needn't be unanimous – we're only deciding on a reallocation of property, not something as serious as excommunication.'

I looked around the room. There were one or two dozen shatterlings I felt certain I could count as allies, but that would not be enough to win the vote. Some of the others would undoubtedly align themselves with Betony.

'I'll spare myself the humiliation,' I said. 'You can have the ship.'

'In which case we'll forget your earlier outburst. It's understandable that you'd feel a sense of attachment. I'm sure we can all empathise.'

'Thank you, Purslane,' said Cadence and Cascade in unison. 'It is very generous of you. We shall take good care of the ship.'

'And me?' I asked Betony. 'What do I do, without a ship? Do I stay here, when everyone else agrees to leave Neume?'

'You're amongst friends now,' he said.

'That's not how it feels.'

'You'll get over it.'

'She doesn't have to,' Campion said, standing up from the table, crumbs flying from his lap. 'In fact, I'd be disappointed in her if she did. I hope you fuckers can live with yourselves after this.' He glared at the seated audience. 'I know not all of you would have gone against Purslane in a secret vote, but I didn't hear any of you speaking up to support her just now. Not even you, Aconite. Or you, Mezereon.'

'It's just a ship,' Aconite said. 'No need to get so worked up about it, old man.'

'It's *her* ship. She's had it longer than most of you have had memories.'

'Then we'll pool our resources and get her a new one,' Aconite said, glancing nervously to his left and right, as if measuring the support for this proposal.

'I'll live,' I said, although I was shivering with rage and indignation. 'Let them have her. If Betony had had the good grace to ask me, instead of demanding it, I might just have given her away myself.'

'We are sorry to be the cause of unpleasantness,' the robots said.

I felt some of my irritation twist towards them, but I held it in check. 'It's not your fault. I'm not angry at you for wanting a fast ship. I know all you want to do is help Hesperus.'

'He means a great deal to us,' Cadence said.

'More than you can imagine,' added Cascade.

The two of them were holding hands, chrome in ivory.

Afterwards at least a dozen shatterlings came up to me in ones and twos and expressed various degrees of sympathy and indignation. My first instinct was to scold them for not showing more support when it counted, but I succeeded in biting my tongue, reminding myself that to many of them I had actually got off lightly, compared to the censure that – in theory, at least – I might have been due.

'We don't agree,' was a sentiment I heard more than once. 'You deserved a rap on the knuckles, but nothing like this. All the same – if that's the worst Betony does to you, you've come out of it rather well. It could have been much, much worse.'

'Yes – and it could also have been a lot better,' I said, resenting the implication that I deserved any punishment whatsoever. 'He didn't have to censure me at all.'

They asked, 'Do you think he's done now? Or will he go after Campion as well?'

'He's done. He knows that if he hurts me, he hurts Campion. He won't risk looking vindictive – he's too much of a politician for that.'

There was talk of helping me get a new ship, questions about whether any of the vehicles in *Silver Wings'* hold might serve for the time being, a general display of goodwill from my friends (and from one or two I had not counted as allies, but who were kind and sympathetic in unexpectedly touching ways), but it was clear to me that the vote would not have gone my way, had I pressed for it. I was relieved, in a dispirited sense. At least I had walked out of that room with my dignity intact. I could be forgiven my little outburst; I had only voiced what many of them were thinking, and even my enemies could not deny the cynical impulse behind my punishment. Even if I had not had the fastest, strongest ship in orbit, Betony would have found a way of giving *mine* to the robots.

Since there was no reason for Cadence and Cascade to remain on Neume indefinitely – they certainly did not need to wait until the Line made up its collective mind about where to go next – it was agreed that the handover of my ship would take place sooner rather than later. *Silver Wings'* troves were nearly duplicated aboard *Dalliance*; the process of consolidating final backup required only hours of additional data transfer. The formal handover would involve me authorising *Silver Wings* to accept Cadence and Cascade as her new masters, but that would involve only a simple statement being made in the ship's presence. Once that formality was complete, the ship would be theirs.

But there remained the matter of Hesperus. It was agreed that the robots would not depart until I had brought him into the presence of the Spirit of the Air, whatever the outcome of that might be. If he was healed, they would leave with or without him, according to his wishes. Otherwise, they would gather his remains (if any were left) and convey him back to their part of the galaxy. It was agreed that the robots would depart on a trajectory that would avoid any chance of detection by the ambushing elements, even if that added a few centuries to their journey time. Of course, once they left Neume, we would have no means of enforcing that agreement.

Weighed down with apprehension, stung by what had been done to me, the last thing I felt like was watching Mezereon resume her interrogation of the prisoners. But Campion assured me it would take my mind off what had happened at breakfast.

'I don't think so,' I said sourly, but I went along anyway.

The magistrate had told me to expect a flier at three, which left five hours, allowing for a margin of error. By the time Campion and I arrived, most of the room was already dialled up on Synchromesh, the shatterlings sitting as stiffly and mutely as statues. All four cabinets were present, but only one of the occupants – the one on the right – was dialled down to a low stasis factor. Mezereon's voice tolled like a very low, ominously cracked bell.

I let the drops settle into my eyes and then dialled up, not forgetting to set the expiration mechanism to bring me out in time for my meeting. Mezereon shifted into sudden, hectoring life.

'We know exactly who you are,' she said, strolling up and down the plinth in front of the cabinets. 'What we don't know is why you've come back from the dead. Would you like to tell me what really happened, Thorn, when you were supposedly lost to attrition? Was your disappearance engineered so that you could attack other Lines with impunity?'

'Go figure,' said the man in the cabinet.

'Grilse was also lost to attrition. That suggests a pattern to me.'

'Very attentive of you.'

'I'm willing to bet the other two are also lost shatterlings. We'll identify their lines soon enough – Marcellin, Mellictan or otherwise. In the meantime you can help me with the House of Suns.'

'You already asked me about that.'

'And you told me that you know nothing, but I don't believe you. Is it a Line, Thorn, one that the Commonality doesn't know about?'

'There isn't any such thing.'

'That we know of. But if such a thing existed, could it be kept secret?' Mezereon stroked her chin. 'Possibly, if there was a good enough reason. But who'd benefit from the existence of a hidden Line?'

'Call me when you find out.'

'I think you know all about it. I think you may even be a part of it.'

'You've already tied me to the Mellictans.'

'But you left them. What's to say you didn't join the House of Suns afterwards?'

'No one swaps between Lines. That's not how it works.'

'But the House of Suns is something else. It might operate according to entirely different rules. Feeding itself from the attrition of other Lines, for instance. That's feasible. It could happen.'

'Whatever you say.'

'There'd need to be infiltration at Line-level, of course. Those shatterlings would need to fake their own deaths, which would mean elaborate planning. They'd have to know they were joining the House of Suns ahead of time. And they'd need to think it was better than staying inside their own Line, with all the rewards and limitless possibilities that entails. Tough call, wouldn't you say? Being a shatterling is close to being a god. You'd need to offer someone the chance to become better than a god before they took that bait.'

There was a glimmer of wounded recognition in Thorn's eyes – a hint that Mezereon had put her finger on something raw. I shuddered to think of the devil's bargain he must have signed up to. Mezereon was right: we did have almost everything we could dream of. We had lived for millions of years, crossed the galaxy countless times over, drunk from the riches and glories of ten million cultures. Matter and energy were our playthings. We could swaddle stars to stop them shining; we could flick worlds around as if they were specks of dirt. Entire civilisations owed their existence to our good deeds, unwitnessed and uncommemorated. We did marvellous, saintly things and we never stopped to ask for thanks.

What could be *better* than being a shatterling?

Only one thing, I thought to myself.

Being a wicked shatterling. Being a devil instead of an angel. Having all that power, all that wisdom, but being able to do anything with it. Being able to destroy as well as create.

'I was hoping you'd tell me everything you know about the House of Suns voluntarily,' Mezereon said. 'It would have been easier that way, saved us all a lot of unpleasantness. But obviously that's not going to happen. I'm going to dial you out of stasis, back into realtime. You may or may not survive the emergence. If you do, it will only be to face further interrogation. As soon as I get a living body, I'm going to section it. You know what that means, Thorn? Of course you do – you're a man of the world. You've seen some horrible, sickening things. We all have. Now you're going to become one of them – unless you talk.'

'I don't know anything about the House of Suns,' he said. But there was something in his voice we had not heard before. He was frightened; the mask of defiance was beginning to crack.

Mezereon reached for the handle. 'You're at one hundred now. I'm taking you down to ten.'

She wrenched the lever to the left until it was resting at the penultimate notch. The cabinet made a groaning, decelerating noise, as of some huge turbine being suddenly braked. The cabinet quivered on the pedestal. The dials around the main lever tremored, registering savage, undamped time-stresses.

Mezereon adjusted her chronometer to match her subjective rate with Thorn's. Around the room, her hidden audience did likewise.

'I'm dialling back in a moment. This is your last chance to tell me what I want to know. Why did you ambush us? What is the House of Suns?'

'You won't do it,' Thorn said. 'You need me alive too much. In

223

here I can always tell you something, even if you can't force it out of me.'

'Why did you ambush us?'

'You had it coming.'

'What is the House of Suns?'

'Something you'll die never knowing about.'

Mezereon twisted the dial on her chronometer, her movements accelerating from my perspective as the drug released her back into normal time. I reached for my own chronometer, but before I could do so Mezereon's hand had flashed to the lever and slammed it all the way to the left. The cabinet flickered and emitted a sharp coughing noise.

I knew instantly that Thorn had died; a safe emergence would have been much less dramatic.

The details of stasis technology have never been of interest to me. All I have ever pretended to understand is that the cabinet holds its occupant inside a bubble of spacetime separated from that which surrounds it by a microscopic membrane, like the white of an egg around the yolk. As the bubble approaches normal time-flow, the interface between the bubble and external spacetime should evaporate away into quantum indeterminacy. Most of the time, that is what happens. But once in a while, often with old or poorly designed caskets, the boundary behaves very differently. It adheres to the contents of the bubble, sticking like glue. In the same moment of failure, the interior of the bubble tears open and pushes outwards, compressing the contents against the unyielding barrier of that skintight membrane.

We call it husking.

That was what happened to Thorn. His shattered parts, and the pieces of his throne, rained onto the hard floor of the plinth. Mezereon knelt down and sorted through them until she found a piece of his face. It was like a clay imprint of an actor mimicking terror; clay that had been fired until it was glossy.

'You should have waited,' said Charlock, rising from his seat. 'He hadn't told us enough.'

Mezereon sounded quite unfazed. 'He'd told me everything he was ever going to. No amount of persuasion would have convinced him I was serious. The only way to do that was to take this chance.'

'You lost one prisoner.'

'There are three more. Now I can show them the empty cabinet and let them know I mean business.' She lofted the piece of his flesh like a trophy. 'And this – they'll recognise the face.'

Still holding the fragment, kicking her way through the rest of him, Mezereon walked to the second cabinet. Her hand moved to the stasis dial, ready to bring the prisoner within reach of Synchromesh.

PART FOUR

One day the little boy and his robot guards went up the ramp into his ship and that was the last time I ever saw him the way he really was. I had no idea of that at the time; all I knew was that we had spent another afternoon in Palatial; another afternoon playing the long game of empire. But it was not the last I saw of Count Mordax.

I was thirty-five, by the usual reckoning; by all objective measurements, I was still a girl of around eleven or twelve years of age – an unusually precocious girl, a girl with an adult's worth of memories (even if most of them consisted of life in the same house) but a girl all the same. But after three and a half decades it was decreed by my guardians that it was time for my development to be allowed to proceed normally again. I was called into Madame Kleinfelter's office and she asked me to roll up my sleeve. There was a small bump under the skin just below the crook of my elbow. Madame Kleinfelter touched a blunt stylus to the bump and I felt a tingle, and that was the end of it. The bump was gone, and the biological machinery that had held me at a fixed age was no longer inside me.

I felt no different, of course. But a clock that had been silent for years had just begun ticking.

'Why now?' I asked.

'When you were born,' Madame Kleinfelter said, 'it was never intended that you would be kept the way you have been. A modest degree of prolongation, yes ... that's the norm nowadays, throughout the Golden Hour. Why race through childhood when you have a couple of hundred years ahead of you? But to be held at prepuberty for thirty-five years ... that is unusual, even by modern standards.' She put down the stylus and steepled her thick, wrinkled fingers, as she often did when delivering a lecture. 'It was done at your mother's request, Abigail – back when she enjoyed extended periods of lucidity. The specialists convinced her that her madness could be cured, given time. They warned her that it might take a while – decades, even. Your mother chose to hold you in a state of suspended development, so that she could still enjoy your childhood when she recovered. She could have had you frozen, of course ... but this was her preferred method. She wanted to able to look at you when she was lucid, to see you learning and playing. She did not want to look at a doll in a tank.' Her fingers tensed around each other. 'But your mother is not getting any better. If I have occasionally led you to think that the prognosis for recovery was better than it is, then I apologise. But nothing I did was done lightly. I was always thinking of you first, Abigail.'

'Then my mother won't be cured.'

'They will keep trying. But her psychosis is now all-consuming. Every measure they have taken – and these are the best doctors in the Golden Hour – has resulted in an incremental worsening of her condition. The moments of lucidity have grown further and further apart. Perhaps they will stumble on a cure tomorrow, but we can no longer count on that. Which brings me to the difficult matter of the family business. Now that the likelihood of your mother recovering her faculties is so small, we must, with heavy hearts, look to the future.'

'To me,' I said. I felt faint, as if I had stood up too suddenly.

'This is no easy path you are about to walk, Abigail. You are going to grow up now. You are going to become a woman. And when the time is right, you are going to assume the mantle that your mother once wore. You will lead the family, as she once did. Everything that she made, everything that she built, all the knowledge and cleverness she gathered, will be in your hands. It will be like an incredibly valuable ornament, a thing of fine coloured glass and rare jewels. In your hands, it will be safe. But you must never, ever drop it.'

When we were done, I went to my playroom and entered the room-within-a-room that held the green cube of Palatial. Although the developmental inhibitor had been removed, it was inconceivable that any measurable change had occurred within me. But I still felt as if the green cube, and the enchanted landscape it held, was something that belonged to my childhood. It was not that the game suddenly held no fascination for me. I could still feel its allure. But it would have been unseemly, inappropriate, even sordid, to step through the portal again.

*

It may have been a month, or maybe a year later; I do not recall precisely. But there came a day when Madame Kleinfelter summoned me to her office.

'There has been an important development, Abigail.'

My heart lifted. 'My mother?'

Embarrassment creased her face. 'Not exactly. It's more to do with the family business. Although you have not been privy to the finer details, I do not think it is any great secret that we have been struggling since the armistice. The Golden Hour has little need of clones, not when there are machines clever enough to be our slaves instead. We've stayed afloat, but only because of a dwindling handful of loyal clients in the Lesser Worlds. Frankly, the omens have been inauspicious for several years. And with the continued expense of the works on the house, not to mention your mother's care, our reserves have been draining steadily away.' She raised a finger before I had a chance to speak. 'I'll be blunt: for many years, it was thought that our salvation might lie in the union of two trading concerns. The little boy you used to play with ... it was hoped, by certain parties, that a marriage, a corporate alliance, might come from your friendship.' By her tone, I was left in no doubt that those certain parties had never included Madame Kleinfelter. 'That won't happen now. They have gone with another combine, leaving us out in the cold. I am afraid you won't be seeing your friend again, Abigail – not until you are old enough to make up your own mind about such things.'

At last I had been told the reason for the sudden curtailing of our adversarial, spite-laden friendship. I suppose I should not have mourned it greatly, but it was not as if I had a hundred other friendships to turn to.

I said nothing, for I sensed Madame Kleinfelter had more on her mind.

'But, as I said, there has been a development – and a potentially very fruitful one. Have you heard of a woman named Ludmilla Marcellin, Abigail?'

'I don't think so.'

'Generally speaking, that's to your credit. Ludmilla Marcellin is the heiress of one of the richest families in the Golden Hour. Unlike the Gentians, however, her familial wealth was not founded on any expertise in the natural arts. They simply made a lot of money by trading in financial instruments during the Conflagration. Not that there isn't a skill there, but it's nothing compared with our knowledge of cloning. And cloning is very much the issue here.'

'I don't understand.'

'Ludmilla Marcellin has decided to embark on a project. It's an ambitious one, and it will make her many enemies – not that that's ever stopped her. She's going to venture beyond the solar system and explore the known universe. Ever since the armistice, the Marcellin combine has been gathering the wisdom and materials to make this happen. Now the final piece must be put in place, which is precisely where we come in. Ludmilla Marcellin needs Gentian wisdom. She needs clones.'

'Our clones?'

'Exactly, Abigail. And she's prepared to pay for our services. This is the lifeline we've been waiting for; a chance to set our finances on an even keel. Ludmilla Marcellin is a trendsetter – where she leads, others will follow. But we must demonstrate our sincerity and commitment. The board of governors thinks it would be a good thing for you to meet with this woman, so that she can see for herself that the Gentians have a future.'

'Will she come here?'

'No, we must go to her.'

'I have never left the house.'

'There's a first time for everyone,' Madame Kleinfelter said, before dismissing me.

Not long afterwards, I was escorted to the shuttle pad and I left my home for the first time. As we pulled away from the planetoid, I saw the house for what it truly was: a kind of rampant architectural fungus, spreading from horizon to horizon. It had not been the entirety of my world, for it had also contained the world-within-a-world of Palatial. But as it fell behind us, hazed in the wake of the shuttle's exhaust, I realised how pitifully small and limiting it had really been.

The shuttle took me through the thick core of the Golden Hour, where the sky was dappled with the false stars and transient constellations of close-packed Lesser Worlds. By the time of my journey I had read all I could about Ludmilla Marcellin, but even though the story-cube was more forthcoming than it had been when I was younger, it still had nothing to say about her plans for exploring the universe. I kept thinking back to what the little boy had said to me during one of our visits – how one day humanity would burst forth from the Golden Hour, into the wider galaxy. It had been his father speaking, but he had believed the words. I had countered by pointing out that there was nothing out there worth seeing, that probes and telescopes had told us all we could ever wish to know about the planets around other suns. Now I wondered what Ludmilla Marcellin knew that I did not.

Before my audience with the heiress herself, I was taken to see her shipyard. The shuttle passed through a Marcellin security cordon into the private airspace around a large, spherical asteroid. Gathered around the asteroid were dozens of huge, ugly-looking ships, each of which was larger than anything I had ever read or heard about. There were traceries of construction scaffolding around some of the ships, the occasional flicker of a welding torch or laser, a handful of spacesuited workers, but to my untrained eye there did not appear to be much more to do. I counted thirty-five ships, then noticed a thirty-sixth slowly emerging from the asteroid.

The rock had been lanced through the middle, like an apple on a spit. With our shuttle under remote control, we passed into the opening. We came very close to the emerging ship, its hull sliding by only metres from the shuttle's windows. It was the same as the ones outside, except that the flower-like intake on the front had not been folded open. There would not be room until the spike-nosed craft had cleared the asteroid.

The ships, I was informed, were ramscoops – vessels of a type that had been dreamed up a thousand years earlier but never built until now. The only previous interstellar expedition had reached a mere fifth of the speed of light, but these ships would go much faster than that. By the time they stopped accelerating – when the friction from their intake fields equalled the thrust that was being generated – the ramscoops would be travelling at eight-tenths of the speed of light. They would be able to make round-trip journeys to the nearest stars while only a decade or so passed back home.

But that was not what Ludmilla Marcellin had in mind. She was going to go much further out than that. She had no intention of returning to the Golden Hour.

We passed into the core of the construction asteroid. It was being eaten from the inside out. A spherical cavity had been excavated in the middle, slowly widening as material was gouged away and transformed into ships. The hulls of partly formed vessels – some of which were close to being finished, while others were little more than skeletons – formed a forest of spikes pointing inwards. There were hundreds of them, but there would be hundreds more by the time Ludmilla Marcellin was done. The asteroid would be nearly depleted; little remaining except a gauzy husk, like the papery corpse left behind when a spider has digested an insect.

In the middle of the open sphere was a free-floating station, to which a dozen or so shuttles and runabouts were already docked. We joined them and disembarked, and were met by Marcellin representatives. We were given food and drink, shown presentations and models and made to feel suitably important. A great many adults made a point of talking to me, most of them struggling to tread a path between condescension and plain speaking. They all knew I was thirty-five years old, but it was difficult for them to remember that when dealing with someone who looked and sounded like a twelve year old. Slowly, however, I got the gist of what Ludmilla Marcellin was intending to do.

There would be a thousand ships when she was finished. They would be launched into interstellar space on separate trajectories, each with a different solar system as its first objective. Some of the ships would have to fly only a dozen or so light-years before arriving at their first port of call. Others would travel for twenty or thirty, or even further.

And each and every ship would carry Ludmilla Marcellin.

Or rather, each and every ship would carry a duplicate of Ludmilla Marcellin: a clone, with the same personality and memories as the real woman. She was going to shatter herself into a thousand facets and scatter them into interstellar space.

Eventually she made an appearance, arriving on a shuttle from an inspection visit to one of the new ships. She was tall and glamorous, with a charisma that lit up the room as if she was the only source of light. She had a deep, commanding voice. It gave one the utmost confidence that she would follow through with her plans, no matter how outlandish they appeared.

'I have faith in the human spirit,' Ludmilla Marcellin said. 'Faith that says we won't stay here for ever, in this little campfire huddle around an undistinguished yellow star. We've been in space for a thousand years, long enough that the Golden Hour has been in existence for much longer than any living human. It's easy to think that it will last for ever; that this stable arrangement will suffice for our needs until the sun peters out. It won't. Against the future that lies ahead of us, this thousand years will be just a moment, a drawing of breath, before the beginning of the real adventure. I have faith that that adventure is about to begin. I also intend to be one of the first participants. Soon I will have my ships – my fleet of a thousand beautiful ramscoops. The clones that I will make of myself – the shatterlings, if you will – will each ride one of those vessels. The ships will take care of them – there need be no crews beyond a single copy of myself. My clones will be frozen until they reach their initial destinations, whereupon they will be thawed. They will make observations. They will leave their ships and travel down to new worlds and moons. They will look on things that no other human being has ever seen. When they have seen enough, they will continue their journeys. Each ship will make three predetermined ports of call, heading further and further out into the galaxy. After the third, the shatterlings will be entering territory for which we now lack hard data – visiting systems where the worlds are too far away to be resolved by our telescopes, and which are beyond the range of our robot probes. The shatterlings will have to make their own minds up about where to travel next, factoring in the knowledge they will already have gained since leaving the Golden Hour. Then they will lay in new courses and push further out. By this time they will have been gone from the Golden Hour for more than a century. Many of you will be dead and buried, but I will just be getting into my stride. The shatterlings will visit more stars, taste the air and soil of worlds that have never known a single strand of human DNA. They will swim in alien seas, adding to their store of memories. And then – four or five hundred years from this day, somewhere around the middle of the present millennium – they will turn their great ships around and set course for home.'

Ludmilla Marcellin paused. She regarded us all with a forbidding demeanour before continuing, 'But that home will not be ours. The Golden Hour may still exist in five hundred or a thousand years, but I'm not counting on that. My shatterlings will convene in another system, around a world for which as yet we have no name. It is my conviction that by this time, humanity will have begun a migration into interstellar space. Perhaps my example will even spur it into action. On the long leg of their return journey, my thousand ships – or however many remain by then – will revisit some of the worlds they explored out the outward leg. They may find that those worlds have been settled since they left. If that is the case, then they will be strange visitors indeed – fugitives from the past, envoys to the future. Because even then I will only just be beginning. After this circuit of a few hundred light-years, a thousand human years, my shatterlings will convene again. They will meet, and exchange memories of what they have experienced. And then they will get back into their ships and head out again. This time they will surf ahead of the expansion wave, not stopping until they are hundreds of light-years out. They will visit more worlds. At the limit of their circuit – longer, this time – they will be nearly a thousand lights from the Golden Hour. By then, they will be in range of some of the anomalous structures we have begun to detect in deep interstellar space. My shatterlings will be the first people to reach out and touch those dark forms. They will be the first to know for certain whether others came before us; whether we are the first species to claim the galaxy as our own, or not. Or perhaps other people will get there first, riding similar ships – I am talking about a thousand years from now, after all. But you see my point. Someone must take this first step. It might as well be me.'

'How many circuits?' someone asked.

She shrugged as if the question had never really occurred to her. 'As many as it takes, until it stops being fun. Each will be larger than the last, until my ships are looping around the Milky Way. By then, there will have been time for humanity to spread to every inhabitable system in the galaxy. I don't think it can fail to be an interesting place to be a tourist. Why not stay awhile and see what happens?'

Ludmilla Marcellin answered our questions one at a time, demolishing every objection or quibble anyone had the brazen temerity to raise. The technology for freezing and thawing clones? No one had frozen and revived a human being since the dawn of the space age. No matter: a crash course in technology-resurrection would give the Marcellins the tools they needed. The ships would not have to wait until it was perfected; they could leave with the clones still awake and beam the necessary science out to them once they were under way.

The technology for merging memories from a thousand individual experiences? A question beneath contempt. It was already there, in embryonic form. I only had to think of the way Palatial had meddled with my own memories to know she was right about that. In a thousand years, it would not even be worth remembering it as a problem. With similar inevitability, her shatterlings could expect to gain the tools to manage those combined memories across massively extended lifespans. Ludmilla Marcellin was not going to go to all this trouble and have her clones die of senescence after only two or three circuits. The human race might be content with its current life expectancy, but nothing less than physical immortality would do for shatterlings. They must be able to live for thousands of years (or at least be able to have their memories and personalities transplanted intact into new receptacle bodies) or the whole enterprise would be for nothing.

But all of this was surmountable. Given time and money, there were very few problems in the universe that could not be solved.

Which was when I thought of a question, one that harkened back to a long-ago conversation with the little boy.

'Why not go faster?'

'I don't think I follow you, Abigail,' Ludmilla Marcellin said. She spoke to me nicely, for we had already been introduced.

'I mean, why settle for eight-tenths of something that is already very slow?'

'Each time we meet, our ships will be improved using locally acquired science. Within a few circuits, I don't doubt that we'll have moved beyond these ramscoops to something capable of taking us much closer to light. That will bring benefits, of course. If the subjective time interval can be reduced, we won't need to spend so much time in deepfreeze. But we'll always need some form of suspended animation – if our ships aren't to crush us alive, there'll be limits on how hard they can accelerate, which will mean they won't be able to reach arbitrarily high speeds before needing to slow down again. The point is that we want to go places – we don't want to just point our ships at the edge of the universe and keep accelerating all the way there.'

'I don't mean that – you're still talking about being limited by the speed of light.'

'It's not called a fundamental constant for nothing, Abigail. All the same, perhaps you're right – perhaps some emergent civilisation, some distant human splinter of the Golden Hour will develop the tools for faster-than-light travel. If it happens, it will clearly be of significance to us. We'll embrace it wholeheartedly, have no fear. But it won't change the nature of what we are, or the reason for our existence. The galaxy will still be too big, too complex, for any one person to apprehend. Shattering, turning yourself into multiple points of view, will still be the only way to eat that cake. I have to say, though, that I don't consider the development of faster-than-light travel to lie within our future. Well-intentioned people have been chipping at that edifice for a thousand years, Abigail. They've never found a way to move a single useful bit of information superluminally – let alone anything as huge and unwieldy as a ship. The limit is hard-wired into the fundamental operating rules of the universe – it's like trying to play Go on a chessboard. Can't be done.'

'Why not?'

'Open your story-cube on the way home and ask it to tell you about causality violation. I did once, because I asked the same question you did. Why should I be limited? What right does the universe have to say what I can and can't do? I'm intelligent. The universe is just a lot of hydrogen and dirt, going through the motions. But in this instance the universe has the final say. Read the cube. I think you'll find it very illuminating.'

There was more to see, more to learn, but the rest of our visit to the shipyard passed in a blur. I shook hands with Ludmilla Marcellin and expressed my commitment to providing her with the cloning technology that would make her vision a reality. All the while, my guardians – Madame Kleinfelter and the members of the board of governors – looked on with indulgent smiles, as if I had just sung a song on stage.

The funny thing was, none of them could have had any idea what I was thinking.

An idea had formed in my head. It could have been a small, wavering flame that guttered out almost as soon as it had ignited. But instead the flame only burned more brightly, more strongly, as time went by.

Ludmilla Marcellin was going to scrawl her name across the sky. She was going to take giant steps across history, space and time. It was awesome and frightening, too much for one person to imagine, let alone bring into being. But she was going to do it anyway.

And the thought that was burning in my head was this:

If she can do it, why can't I?

As the family shuttle sped us home, two things of note happened. I said to Madame Kleinfelter, 'They're going to pay us a lot of money for our expertise, aren't they?'

'Let's just say the house will have no cause to worry for quite some time. And that's not even assuming that others will follow where Ludmilla has led. But they will – mark my words. Even if she took those thousand ships and crashed them into the Sun, she would have her imitators. And each and every one of them will need Gentian science to complete the shattering.'

'Then we are in a powerful position.'

'For the first time in a while, yes.'

'Have the terms of the Marcellin deal been finalised?'

She gave me a peculiar look, as if I had uttered the most shaming of profanities. 'There are still details to be worked out, but the key elements of the arrangement—'

'We must have their ships,' I said.

'The ships are for Ludmilla Marcellin. Once she has made enough for her fleet, she will stop production.'

'I don't mean the ships themselves, but the blueprints to make them. We can find a metal asteroid if we look hard enough. If we can't, we can always tear apart the one under the house. But we must have the plans, so that we can make our own fleet.'

Still not quite getting my point, Madame Kleinfelter said, 'But we don't need a fleet.'

'I do,' I told her. 'I want what she has.'

With Ludmilla's words still echoing in my head, I had the story-cube tell me something about causality. At first, all the cube would give me was a babyish definition of what the word meant, not how it related to Ludmilla's plans for cosmic expansion. When I pushed the cube to explain to me how causality might be 'violated', I was rebuffed and discouraged, the cube deciding that it was a matter beyond my present conceptual horizon.

I persisted. I could be very persistent.

Faster-than-light travel, the cube eventually informed me, was problematic from a number of standpoints. From a mass-energy perspective, light was like a mountain summit that was always out of reach, no matter how high you climbed. A ship could expend an insane amount of energy and come within one or two per cent of that ultimate speed limit. But it would cost infinitely more energy to close that final gap, and even then the ship would only be travelling at the speed of light, not above it. In describing the properties of faster-than-light travel, the mathematics deliquesced into the Alice-in-Wonderland nonsense of imaginary numbers. Even then it could not tell you how to cross from one side of that barrier to the other.

But even supposing that barrier did not need to be crossed, and that there was an effective short cut through spacetime – something like a wormhole – there was a deeper, subtler objection. It was called the causal ordering postulate.

The postulate said that cause must always precede effect. It also said that the introduction into the universe of faster-than-light travel – the creation of what the cube called space-like causal connections – would lead to situations in which the causal ordering postulate might be violated. This was not just some theoretical nicety, but the opening of a door that would allow paradoxes to leak into reality.

With faster-than-light travel, I could witness the consequences of an event – say, a hole appearing in a robot's armour because someone had shot a superluminal bullet at it – and send a superluminal message instructing the shooter not to fire.

As lucid as the story-book's grudging illumination had been, I do not pretend that I understood all of this at the time. But I did grasp that the universe did not appear to be convivial to human dreams of effortless expansion. It said that we could have as much of the universe as we wished, but that the taking of it would demand an extraordinary kind of patience.

I brooded on this for the rest of the night, feeling hemmed in and tight-chested, as if my restraints had been drawn too tight. The odd thousand-year-old cathedral aside, patience was not something humans had been very good at, collectively.

Later – when the household's planetoid was at last in view – I received a call from a distant well-wisher. Madame Kleinfelter, still grey-faced after our earlier conversation (it was as if I had slapped her across the cheeks) took a dim view of his attempt to contact me.

'It's not right,' she said as my head was still ringing with causality. 'They ruined any chance of a marriage, not us. What right does he have to taunt you now?'

'Maybe he doesn't want to taunt me. May I speak to him? In private?'

I took the call. Timelag must have stilted our conversation, dragged it across many minutes, but I remember none of that.

'I hear you did well with the Marcellins,' the little boy said. He looked older now, as if he too had been allowed to start ageing again. There was a roughness in his voice I did not recall from our afternoons in the playroom. 'I'm happy for you. Sooner or later someone was going to require cloning expertise, and I'm sure this has not come a moment too soon.'

'I didn't think I'd hear from you again.'

'It would be improper for us to meet now. I'm sorry, Abigail: really I am. Nothing that happened at the combine level had anything to do with me. Or you, I imagine. We were just pawns being moved around at the whim of adults. All I'm saying is, I'd have liked it if we could have stayed friends.'

'We can't.'

'You say that as if you're the one deciding things now. Have you really stepped into your mother's shoes?'

'It's none of your business.'

'For what it's worth, I'm sorry for the way I talked about her to you. That wasn't nice of me at all. But I suppose you had to know eventually. There was always something a bit lopsided in our relationship, with me knowing far more about you than you ever did.'

'Don't lose any sleep over it.'

'Oh, I shan't. Had the roles been reversed, I have no doubt that you'd have been just as cruel as I was. But there is unfinished business between us, wouldn't you say?'

My head was still spinning with fantasies of interstellar conquest, of shattering myself into a thousand gemlike shards and imbuing each of them with the vital spark of my own personality. The little boy was a knock on the door from a past I no longer cared about. I wanted him to go away, and take my childhood with him.

'I don't think we have unfinished business.'

'We never completed Palatial,' he said.

It was ages since I had given that green cube more than a moment's thought. The world inside it was frozen in the configuration it had held when we last emerged from the portal.

'That's over now.'

'It doesn't have to be. I can't visit you, obviously, but there's another solution. One of the copies of Palatial – one of the prototypes – happens to have fallen into my possession.'

'We still can't meet.'

'We don't have to. The games can be synchronised. I can go into my version of Palatial and share the same narrative space as yours. I'll be in the Black Castle and you'll be in the Palace of Clouds, but they'll both be part of the same landscape. If I send out a messenger, he'll show up at your gates. Send an army to me and I'll meet them with my own forces. It was always meant to work this way, Abigail. It's how they designed it. There'll be timelag, of course – but that won't matter unless we end up having a face-to-face conversation. Everything else takes hours in Palatial anyway – it's called being pre-industrial.'

'We can't do this.'

'We must! I didn't go to all the trouble of finding another copy for nothing. I was always thinking of you ... of the game we still had to finish.'

'They won't allow it.'

'Then make them allow it. You have the authority now, Abigail – or you soon will. Use some of it. Throw your weight around. Demand the right to connect your version of Palatial with mine.' He leaned back from the camera. 'Count Mordax will be waiting. Please don't let him down.'

CHAPTER SEVENTEEN

At the appointed time, Purslane and I were ready on the eighteenth-level landing stage. We had brought Hesperus with us, in the open rear compartment of a personal flier belonging to Gentian Line. A wind was whipping in from the west, flags rippling and dancing on the bridges and walkways between the towers. Dust stung my cheeks and clawed at my wind-slitted eyes. Not many Ymirians were in the air this afternoon, unless they were inside the shelter of machines. I was glad to be away from Mezereon's interrogation room, but misgivings were tying knots in my stomach.

'Here he comes,' Purslane said, pointing to an insect-bodied craft fluttering towards us, its wings a blur of pastel colours. The flying thing hovered against the sun, forcing me to raise my hands against the glare. For a moment it looked as if it was about to turn around and fly away.

'Who's in it?'

'Someone from the study council is all Jindabyne would say.'

As if the occupant had made up his mind, the craft lowered its nose and approached the landing stage. It touched down and a figure emerged from the pearl-shaped cabin at the front, grasping handrails and stepping down with his back to us before turning around. It was a male, dressed in a padded black outfit with fur-lined collar and cuffs. There were many pockets, straps and nozzles on the outfit, which was festooned with thick, ribbed airlines leading to a heavy, snout-like breathing mask suspended below the creature's goggled face. He walked to us with an impatient, slightly waddling gait.

'I'm Purslane,' my co-shatterling said. 'This is Campion, a fellow shatterling. It's good of you to help us.'

'I was ordered to help you. I had no say in the matter.' He had the same honey-coloured fur as Magistrate Jindabyne, but his fur was flecked with little dabs of white – perhaps the sign of age, stress, or some genetic irregularity in his pigmentation.

'Do you approve?' I asked.

'Most definitely not. If I had my way you'd never have been allowed into our atmosphere in the first place.'

'That's a bit extreme,' I said.

'I've been studying the Spirit my entire adult life, shatterling. I have never known it be as agitated, as unpredictable, as when your ships started appearing around our planet. It doesn't care for you. It would rather you left. So, frankly, would I.'

'Nice to know we're welcome,' I said.

'It's nothing personal.'

'Of course it isn't. And you'd be?'

'You may call me Mister Jynx.'

'We're sorry to cause so much trouble,' Purslane said. 'We're only doing this for our friend – he's sick and we think he wanted to meet the Spirit. In fact, it was the last thing he told us before he stopped communicating at all. You can understand why we want to do what's right by him, can't you?'

If Mister Jynx was prepared to grant us even the tiniest concession, the only outward indication of it was a throat-clearing sound. On reflection, it could just as easily have indicated an even more profound degree of irritation. 'We are already late,' he said, ignoring the fact that we were exactly on time according to the agreed arrangements. 'I'd have chosen to be safely away from the observation tower by now. Never mind; your tardiness cannot be helped. Are you ready to follow me?'

I nodded towards the rear of the hovering flier. 'We have our friend with us. Do you want to see him for yourself?'

'It won't make any difference what I think of him.'

'I just thought—'

'Your chances of achieving success are negligible. Much poorer than your chances of injury or death, which are excellent.' Mister Jynx turned and began to strut back towards his machine. 'Follow me, remain a safe distance behind me, and *do not* deviate from my flight path,' he called over his shoulder.

We returned to the flier.

'He's a cheerful soul. It's so good to know he's fully on our side, backing us all the way.'

'In his shoes I'd probably feel just as put-out,' Purslane said, climbing into one of the two forward-facing seats. 'He's been given a diktat from on high to do what we say. It's no wonder he's a little aggrieved.'

'A little.'

Mister Jynx was airborne in a few seconds. He spun the nose of his flying machine around and dashed away, swerving hard to slip between the densely packed towers of Ymir. Purslane willed the flier to follow him, the acceleration pressing me into my seat before the nullifier smoothed out the ride. The pink-hulled craft had no cockpit canopy save for two half-hemisphere cowls positioned ahead of the two leading seats. For a few instants we were blasted by the wind, until the flier snapped an aerodynamic field around itself. All of a sudden it was as still and silent as if we were in a hot-air balloon.

'Maybe it's madness after all,' Purslane said. 'Like throwing a broken clock into a whirlwind and hoping it'll end up miraculously repaired.'

'Except a whirlwind was never alive. We know the Spirit of the Air started out as a living intelligence. What we don't know is how much of that intelligence is left in there.' I twisted around to check that Hesperus was still secure in the rear compartment. 'He was more to us than a broken clock, anyway. We're not doing this because we've damaged something and we want it repaired. We're doing this because he was our friend, and he sacrificed himself for us.'

'So that gives us licence to attempt the impossible?'

'It's not impossible – just a very long shot. It's not as if the Spirit hasn't intervened in similar ways before.'

'But not with Machine People.'

'Only because they don't come here.'

'There might be a reason for that. Maybe they're too sensible, or the Ymirians don't let them.'

'Or maybe there's something here that scares them,' I said. 'A mechanised intelligence older than they are. They think we're about as complex and subtle as a game of noughts and crosses. Maybe they see through us that easily. But how would they react to something genuinely complex, genuinely unfathomable? I think they'd feel about it the way we'd feel about spending a night in a haunted castle.' I smiled. 'All of a sudden I appear to be the one doing the persuading, incidentally. I seem to remember this was your idea, not mine.'

'I get second thoughts occasionally.'

'Well, don't. This is the right thing, no matter what Jindabyne or Jynx has to say.'

A Gentian flier would always be faster than an ornithopter, even with a heavy payload, and before very long we had caught up with Mister Jynx's flying machine. Purslane could have drawn alongside, but she held us just behind the other vehicle, as we had been instructed. Within ten minutes the black fingers supporting Ymir had begun to drop away below the eastern horizon, and after twenty only the very tops of the highest structures were visible. Below us was a labyrinth of shadowed white dunes, as coiled and tangled as the human cerebellum.

We had seen the observation tower from the Magistrate's office, but I had not guessed its true significance until now. It was a bone-white stalk rising from the dunes, surmounted by a flat observation platform braced to the stalk by filigreed struts. Mister Jynx flew higher and we followed him, until both craft were level with the platform. It was a round dish about two hundred metres across, with a slope-sided, windowless building placed in the middle. Mister Jynx landed first, next to the building. Purslane brought the flier down and we both got out. Mister Jynx was emerging from the Ymirian flying machine.

'Get him out now. Do you see that smudge on the horizon, to the left of the sun?'

'The one that looks like a storm cloud, or a flock of starlings?' Purslane asked.

'That's the Spirit of the Air. It's nearer than I expected – it must have travelled quickly since the last monitoring update. We'd better get on with this – it will already be aware of our presence on the platform.'

It looked very far away, like a weather system we would not have to worry about until tomorrow.

'Is it coming nearer?' Purslane asked.

'It may come; it may not. But the fact that it is visible at all is an indication that it will probably choose to approach.'

We had fixed carry-alls to Hesperus. I took hold of the U-shaped handle of the nearest one and lifted his body out of the flier, feeling the full brunt of his inertia but no sense of his weight. I pushed the huge golden mass sideways until it had cleared the flier. 'Where would be the best place to put him?'

'As far away from the shelter as possible,' Mister Jynx said. 'There is a small plinth near the western edge – we've sometimes left samples there.'

I had not seen the plinth during our approach because it had been hidden by the shelter. Walking slowly but surely, I propelled

Hesperus ahead of me single-handedly. The plinth the Ymirian had mentioned was nothing more than a raised portion of the floor, with a flattened surface. I brought Hesperus to a halt above it and then lowered the levator I was holding until I felt him crunch to a halt.

'Remove the levators now,' Mister Jynx said. 'If you wish to make an offering to the Spirit, you should avoid any external complications.'

'It's not exactly an offering,' Purslane said.

'That's for the Spirit to decide, not you.'

I nodded and detached the four carry-alls, then coupled them together so that they could be pushed as a single unit.

'Will that do?' I asked, stepping back to study the thing I had left on the plinth. The fused part of Hesperus was turned away from me; I could still see his humanoid form, with that handsome and serene face staring out at me, his torso, right arm and leg free of the encasing mass. The lights were still gyring in his skull window, but I had never seen them move so dimly, or so sluggishly.

'I think it's closer,' Purslane said, looking out at that strange dark cloud.

'It is,' Mister Jynx said. 'If it chooses to visit, it could be on us within thirty minutes.' He started walking at a brisk pace back to his flying machine. 'You should leave now. You have done all you need to do.'

'We'd like to stay here,' Purslane said. She glanced quickly at me. 'I'm going to stay, anyway.'

'I cannot recommend this course of action.'

'If we leave, the Spirit will assume Hesperus is an offering, like you said. But he isn't some fatted calf we're giving away to make the rains come. We want him to be healed. The Spirit has to understand that he means something to us.'

'Staying will not accomplish that.'

'But nothing else will send the same signal,' Purslane said. 'I've thought this through, Mister Jynx. If I put myself at risk, the Spirit will see that Hesperus isn't just some piece of metal we don't care about. He's a person, a friend.'

'You overestimate the degree to which the Spirit can be assumed to indulge in rational deduction.'

'I'm willing to take that chance.'

'Me too,' I said.

'You don't have to stay, Campion.'

'Nor do you.' The truth was, I did not share Purslane's determination. I was apprehensive, and that alien thing on the horizon was unnerving me. But I could not let her go through this alone.

'We can find our own way back to Ymir,' Purslane said.

'Not without a flier.'

'We have one,' she pointed out.

'It can't stay here. If the Spirit arrives it will be destroyed. It doesn't like other machines – even very simple ones. If you are still here when the Spirit has passed, you can summon back the flier.'

'And the levators?' I asked.

'Send them away as well. It would be best to dispose of any machinery you are carrying now.'

'There are things in my head,' Purslane said. 'My ship speaks to me through them.'

'It would have been wise to mention them sooner.'

'I didn't think about them.'

'It can't be helped now. You had better hope that the Spirit ignores them.' Mister Jynx cast a wary eye at the restless, flexing shape on the horizon. 'Provided the machines in your head remain quiet, you should be all right.'

Purslane closed her eyes for an instant. 'I've just told *Silver Wings* to go off-air.'

I moved to the flier, placed the carry-alls in the rear compartment, then leaned into the pilot's position and told it to fly away until morning. It would mean us spending a night in the shelter, but that was the least of my worries now.

Mister Jynx paused at the side of his flying machine, his hands on the rails either side of its door. 'You are set on this course of action? It is not too late to back out now. But once I am gone, you are on your own. There is no way off this tower, unless you count falling. Unfortunately I do not think any of your machines would be able to reach you in time.'

'We're ready,' Purslane said.

'I must admit I am curious as to the outcome. A tiny part of me wishes to remain here, to witness the spectacle at close quarters.'

'Will you be watching us?'

'From a distance. No recording devices have ever survived an encounter with the Spirit. There are telescopes trained on the platform, but they don't see very much when the Spirit is present.'

'You could stay,' I said.

'A larger, saner part of me has no intention of doing so.'

The wind slapped across my face without warning. Mister Jynx smiled at my astonished reaction. 'You felt that, didn't you, shatterling? The micro-climate is moving in. The Spirit brings its own weather with it. I must be away now.'

'Go,' I said. 'We'll be fine. We'll tell you all about it in the morning.'

Something in Mister Jynx's mood had eased. Perhaps he had accepted our explanation that we had no alternative except to help our friend. 'I wish you luck. I consider you to be misguided, but I cannot say that you are lacking in courage.'

With that, Jynx climbed into his craft and sped away in a flicker of mechanical wings. The flier lifted from the platform and headed in the same general direction, back to the city, where it would wait until the break of day. Purslane and I stood together and watched the two dots diminish until they were no longer distinguishable from the sky.

The wind hardened, cutting into my eyes as if with a razor. I raised a hand to screen it, peering through the gaps in my fingers. The sun, lowering towards the western horizon, was hazed behind a smoky, undulating mass. The colour was somewhere between purple and black, and the twisting, billowing shape appeared to be made up of myriad tiny constituents. I struggled to judge the scale – there was nothing to provide a reference point. But the central mass of the Spirit, the dark beating clot at its heart where the density of aerial machines was the highest, must have been at least as wide as the observation platform. I had felt trepidation before, but it had been the optimistic trepidation of someone contemplating a hazardous but grand enterprise, like scaling a summit or creating a magnificent art form. Now that trepidation sharpened into magnificent animal fear. It was telling me to run or hide from this approaching thing, and it took every ounce of my resolve to stand my ground.

I thought of what the trove had told me, and what I had also learned from the Ymirians. The Spirit of the Air had once been a human man, back in the twilight centuries of the Golden Hour. His name had been Abraham Valmik, or something similar, a man of immeasurable wealth and considerable longevity who nonetheless wanted more out of the universe than it had so far given him. By then, Abigail and the other Line founders had already shattered themselves into the likes of us, choosing one pathway to immortality, and had begun their knowledge-thirsty spread into an empty galaxy.

Perhaps others had already embarked on the long process of change that would turn them into the curators of the Vigilance, choosing a different pathway. For Valmik, neither shattering, time-dilation nor biological transformation offered sufficient guarantees. He wished instead to make himself into a machine, so that his consciousness might be embodied in something as close to indestructible as physics allowed. Neurone by neurone, he allowed his brain to be supplanted by mechanical parts. Since the process was gradual – akin to the continuous redevelopment of a city, rather than sudden demolition and replacement – the man felt no change in his consciousness between the replacement of one neurone and the next. But that was not to say that he did not become strange to those who had known him as his mind was slowly transformed into a humming web of artificial neurones.

When the process was done, the man discarded his old body as it was no longer useful to his needs. He could still puppet an organic nervous system when circumstances required it, but they were few and far between. He preferred to interact with the abstract realm of simulated experience, only rarely bothering to communicate with the people he had left behind in the outside world. They bored him now – their habits of thought seemed painfully predictable, as if their minds were running on tramlines. He felt different, like a fish that had flopped onto dry land and found that it could still breathe, while everyone else was still stuck in the ocean. He had nothing in common with them now.

For centuries Valmik's artificial mind existed in a fixed architecture, in a fixed location. There were copies of him scattered through the Golden Hour and beyond its civilised fringes, but they were only to be activated in the event of damage to or the demise of the primary mind. Over time, he had added to his complexity – integrating more and more artificial neurones into his mind, until they exceeded the number of functional cells in his original brain by a factor of many hundreds. By then he was so far from human that his only useful companions were other ascended minds. For a while, they kept pace with him, until he began to ease ahead. They were too cautious, too unwilling to cast aside the last residual traces of human brain architecture. They clung to ancient wiring, archaic, hallowed arrangements of sensory and cognitive modules. The structure of the human mind was a thing that had evolved through accident and happenstance, layering each new addition over the old. It was like the house where I had been born, with corridors and staircases that led nowhere, neglected rooms and hallways that could not be enlarged because they were hemmed in by others, plumbing that was fiendishly, unnecessarily complex, because each new installation had had to be routed around a pre-existing tangle of rusty pipes and drains. The others did not have the courage to sweep this jumbled, top-heavy heritage aside.

He did. He was braver, bolder, less afraid of losing himself.

He vowed to remake himself from the bottom up, reorganising his basic architecture from the very foundations of his mind. No part of his brain would be left unexamined. Knots would be straightened out; modules moved around or deleted entirely. Throughout this process, consciousness would endure. It would grow faint, as the changes reached their most radical phases, but it would never be entirely extinguished. The planning would need to be meticulous – like a surgeon groggy with his own anaesthetic, he would not be sufficiently clear-minded to intervene halfway through if something went amiss. All contingencies must be allowed for.

As it was, nothing went wrong. He just became something weirder, larger, faster than he had been before. The old mansion was now a shining, rationally organised edifice. He was pristine and efficient. Thoughts raced through him with blinding clarity. He looked back on what he had done to himself and saw that it was good. He saw also that he had left behind his old companions for ever. The process of improvement, of adjusting his architecture, continued unabated. Even if one of the others had a change of heart and decided to emulate what he had done, they would never catch up. He had become something unique, something that might not have existed since the Priors.

But Valmik was not finished. Although he was better than he had been – incalculably so – he was still bound to one location, locked in the processing core of a single machine. That machine, once its power source, outer layers and armour were taken into account, was as large as a small asteroid. In this era, long before the trivial secrets of spacetime, momentum and inertia were unlocked, it was about as easy to move around. He had to keep himself cool by boiling comets away to steam. He had become godlike in the private realm of his own mental processes, but he was still vastly, humblingly dependent on other machines and other human beings. If that flow of comets was interrupted, he would boil in his own brilliance. It would only take a single well-aimed weapon to destroy the machine in which he lived.

This was not good enough.

The change that he forced upon himself took him even further from humanity, but by now being human was a land mass on a very distant horizon, one that he would not mourn when it eventually slipped out of sight. Every one of the tens of thousands of billions of neurones that constituted his mind was allowed to become an independent machine, capable of taking care of its own survival. In those early days he still needed fuel and raw materials (he had not yet learned the simple trick of tapping vacuum for those basic nourishments) but the machines were clever and agile enough to find their own resources. Remaining in contact with each other via light, he became a cloud-consciousness, occupying a much larger volume than ever before. In fact, the cloud could swell as wide as he wished. If he wanted to englobe a planet, to wrap himself around it, that was no problem. The only price he paid was a slowing in his mental processes, as the light-speed lag between his components grew from microseconds to entire fractions of a second. Since there was nothing else in the universe he was interested in talking to except himself, this was not a pressing concern. He could even smear himself across an entire solar system, and beyond.

Long after the Golden Hour was a historical memory, long after the shatterlings had made their third reunion – those first three circuits encompassed a mere seven thousand years, since Abigail saw no sense in exploring more of the galaxy than had yet been colonised – the man had swelled to inhabit the Oort cloud, that halo of dormant comets orbiting between a thousand and a hundred thousand times as far from the Sun as the Old Place. Now the simplest thoughts consumed months of planetary time. The solar system whirred inside him like an overwound clock.

Vast in size and number though he had become, Valmik was easy to miss. Because he played no part in human affairs, humans eventually forgot about him. There were stories about a thread of ghostly transmissions webbing the Oort, but no one took them any more seriously than a million other myths. When explorers stumbled on one of his elements, they normally assumed it was a piece of space junk from the dawn of the expansion. He sacrificed it anyway. He was incapable of being hurt, or even inconvenienced, by any imaginable human agency. Even the growing power of the Lines caused him no qualms.

But the Sun might be a problem. In the decelerated frame of his consciousness, the end of its main sequence lifetime lay only a few thousand subjective years away. This was intolerable. Something might be done about it in the distant future, when the Lines or some other human civilisation had learned the rudimentaries of stellar life-prolongation. But he could not count on that, and he would need to start making provisions now, while he still had enough time to mull the possibilities.

The cloud-consciousness decided that it was time to become interstellar. Rather than gathering himself into a concentrated formation and launching himself towards another star – like a flotilla of ships, albeit in unthinkable numbers – he began to inflate himself, sending his neuronal elements in all directions. It took tens of thousands of years before any single element came within reach of another sun, for the individual parts of him moved much more slowly than the swift ships of the Lines. As he grew even more distended, so his thought processes slowed down by yet more orders of magnitude. Expanded into a cloud encompassing dozens of stars, his quickest thoughts ate decades of planetary time. But at last he was free from dependence on any one solar system.

At this point the information in the troves became sketchy and contradictory. It was not clear what had happened to the man for the next million years or so. One line of argument held that he had expanded himself to encompass a massive swathe of galactic space – swallowing hundreds of thousands of systems, across thousands of lights. By now the Lines were into their seventh, eighth or ninth reunions, depending on when they had started. The Golden Hour was a bright, brief moment in time, compressed like a mote of light seen through the wrong end of a telescope. There had been empires within him that had no idea he existed. But the price for such expansion was consciousness frozen to the point of death. It took millennia for him to formulate the simplest thought.

The other line of argument held that the man had never grown larger than a few tens of light-years across. After reaching the size of a decent nebula, and spending a few hundred thousand years in that state, he had decided that enough was enough; that he was ready to engage with human civilisation again, even if it was engagement on his own rather distant terms, even if that engagement meant shrinking himself down to a planetary scale. It was not so much of a hardship, for in the time of his expansion he had learned much about self-preservation. He no longer needed external energy sources. He had observed the early galactic wars of the protohumans and seen what their weapons could do. Provided he took precautions, provided he remained agile, nothing need trouble him again.

What the troves did agree on was that, one way or the other, the Spirit of the Air, the Fracto-Coagulation, was what remained of the man after another five and a half million years of existence. He had been on Neume for most of that time, since there was no phase of the planet's recorded history that did not make reference to him in some shape or form. Sometimes he had been an elusive, near-mythical presence, hiding himself in obscure ways for centuries at a time before appearing fleetingly to confused and wary witnesses who were not always believed. At other times, he was a fixed presence in the atmosphere, like the metastable storm in a gas giant. He shunned some civilisations, destroyed others, and showed tolerance and forbearance to others. When the Scapers' plans failed, he maintained Neume's atmosphere in a breathable state. It was a kindness that cost him nothing. It would have been more trouble not to step on an ant, when Valmik had been human.

So the theories went. I did not really know how many of them I believed, but the story struck me as at least plausible in its details. If the Spirit did not have a machine origin – and it was axiomatic that no machine intelligence had arisen prior to the Machine People – then it could only have started with a human, or group of humans. Abigail Gentian had done a daring, audacious thing to herself – so had the other Line founders. Even at the time, there had been declaimers, critics who said that her plan was monstrous and dehumanising. She had ignored them, of course – I had my existence to thank for it. It would have been presumptuous to assume that no other individual was capable of such visionary thinking; such unflinching willingness to sail beyond the shores of fixed humanity.

The Spirit came closer, until it filled half the sky, and I discerned that the individual forms had many shapes and sizes. Most of them were no larger than insects, but the more substantial entities were flapping things like bats or birds, but with a distinct mechanical aspect to them: the blade-sharp wings were jointed to the rounded bodies by complex hinges, the eyeless bodies flickering with pastel colours and pricks of laser-sharp light. It required an effort of will to remind myself that this entity was not the product of robotic evolution, not some weird kin to the Machine People, but an intelligence that had begun existence in human form and only attained this awesome, weather-like state of being via the accumulation of incremental change over millions of years.

The Spirit danced and weaved, forming transient shapes in the manner of a three-dimensional kaleidoscope. The wind came in waves with each pulse of change. The sound of it was a mad, droning buzz, with extremes of pitch ranging from a subsonic tone that was felt more than heard, to a shrill keening that might shatter my skull at any moment. Purslane tightened her hold on me, and it occurred to me that I had seldom been this frightened, or been so utterly at the mercy of forces beyond my control. Suddenly the idea that we might help Hesperus by bringing him to this place began to seem ludicrous and childish, much as if we had bargained something precious against the existence of fairies. But we were committed now; there was no way off the platform save by the flier, which would not return for many hours.

The Spirit began to centre itself over the platform, so that instead of filling one half of the sky it became a storm of change roiling over us, with a band of clear air beneath it in all directions. In the roaring heart of the phenomenon I made out only blackness, a core of machines packed so tightly – even though they were all independent from each other – that no daylight was able to penetrate. That darkness was relieved only by the intermittent flicker of coloured lights as the numberless units communicated amongst themselves. I felt the lash of rain against my skin, even though there had not been a drop of moisture in the air until the Spirit's arrival.

Now it began to descend towards us. My instinct was to crouch, but I knew this would be futile and forced myself to remain standing. I glanced at the sanctuary of the building, but we must both have had the same thought, for Purslane shook her head; we had come here to show our devotion to Hesperus, not to cower behind those walls, which were in any case likely to prove ineffective.

Purslane extended a hand towards the plinth. Above the roar she managed to say, 'Let's go there. Let's show it why we're here.'

I knew she was right. Still holding each other, we walked across the platform until we were only a few paces from where we had left Hesperus. He seemed to watch us. No glimmer of recognition showed in his eyes, but the lights in his head quickened for a few intervals, before dimming and slowing again. Now they appeared darker than they had even when we had placed him on the plinth.

The Spirit lowered further, until its outer edges blocked the sky in all directions, filtering the sunlight as if twilight had already fallen. The roar had now become almost intolerable, and the black core hung over us like a swallowing mouth. From the purple margin of that blackness, a vortex of machines began to curl down in an inquisitive fashion, whirling like debris caught in a twister. The vortex tapered to a questing extremity. The probe dangled over Hesperus without touching him, approaching and withdrawing on several occasions. It was impossible not to sense some great apprehension from the Spirit of the Air, for all its undoubted power. I wondered if in all its years of existence it had ever encountered a being comparable to Hesperus. Perhaps this was the first time it had sensed the presence of a being of similar complexity to itself, albeit of an entirely different embodiment and origin.

The extremity probed nearer, and I made the error of believing that we were about to succeed; that our offering would be both accepted and understood for what it was. Perhaps there was a moment of contact between one of the machines and Hesperus's gold skin, but the arm retreated with dismaying swiftness, vanishing back into the core precisely as if it had touched fire, or electricity, or some agonising toxin. The core pulsed with a deeper, more profound blackness, and the roar – which had already sounded impossibly loud – intensified. The rain that I had felt earlier returned in slashing sheets as moisture was precipitated out of the air by the furious motion of those flocking machines.

The epicentre of the cloud, which had begun to drift over the plinth, shifted directly over us. The Spirit appeared to have lost all interest in Hesperus.

'This isn't going right.'

'There's nothing we can do now,' Purslane answered, as if I had been looking for reassurance.

A multitude of flapping things descended to inspect us. There was a scissoring clatter as their wings touched each other, but I never saw one of the machines drop out of the sky, or come to any apparent harm. Now and then one of them would hover directly ahead of me, fixing me with the intense sparkle of its lights, which obviously served as both sensor and communicator. Occasionally I felt the brush of cold metal against my skin, and though I did my best to stand unperturbed, it was impossible not to flinch. After one icy contact I lifted my hand to my cheek and came away with blood on my fingers, yet there was no pain from the wound and it ceased bleeding shortly afterwards. Purslane had been grazed as well, sliced on the side of her neck and on the back of her hand, but she appeared oblivious. I do not think the Spirit meant to hurt us, merely that the actions of its individual elements were not as well coordinated as the whole.

Then something unexpected happened, something Mister Jynx had not spoken of. I felt the machines swarm around me in greater numbers than ever, until their flapping density hid Purslane almost entirely from view. They closed around in a fluttering mass and all of a sudden I was aloft, suspended in the air, with the machines supporting my limbs. I called out to Purslane, but she could not have heard me above the noise of the Spirit. The swirling darkness gave me a sense of motion, but I could not tell whether it was illusory or real. I began to tip back, but no sooner had I started than I lost all notion of up and down. I flailed helplessly, but the machines hindered my movements so efficiently that I felt like a dreamer, caught in some slowly stiffening paralysis.

Abruptly there was only silver sand beneath my feet. I had been carried off the platform, beyond its edge. I had seldom experienced an acute fear of heights, for in most circumstances I had been protected by the devices that watched over me, whether they were part of the clothes I wore, the robot aides that accompanied me, or the environment in which I found myself. Now that fear arrived in full measure, as if to repay me for the times I had evaded it. *Dalliance* could not help me now, nor *Silver Wings* assist Purslane. My clothes were garments of dumb fabric, lacking even the ability to secrete medicine should I fall injured.

But a drop from this height would result in worse than injury. *This is how attrition happens*, I thought to myself. You take one chance too many, imagining that all the previous instances of good fortune have somehow immunised you against hazard, when in fact you have simply been extraordinarily fortunate *until now*.

I was thinking that when the machines dropped me.

I could only have fallen for a second, but it might as well have been a lifetime. I had time to reflect on many things, not the least of which was the unpleasant circumstances that would shortly attend my imminent demise. I had always taken it for granted that I would not leave behind a body, and most definitely not a body broken and bloodied after a fall. From this height, those dunes would smash me as if they were rock. I wondered if Purslane was also falling, and whether we would see each other before the two of us hit the ground. I wondered if the machines had spared her, and felt a momentary spasm of resentment at the thought that they might have chosen her over me.

Then I was not falling. The machines had swooped under me and arrested my descent. The dark mass coagulated around me once more and I had the giddy impression of gaining height with immense speed – until the machines released me once more and I was in clear space, hundreds of metres above the platform, toward which I was rushing.

Once again the machines came to my rescue.

I was being played with, I realised: tossed around the way a cat may torment a bird. The same thing must have been happening to Purslane, although I was never allowed even a glimpse of her. I could not say that I became resigned to my fate, but since my death had clearly been postponed, I did become fractionally calmer, and my thoughts slowed down to something like their normal rate.

I could not say how long the machines toyed with me: it may only have been tens of seconds, or it may have occupied several minutes. In the black furnace of their swarming, time had become as difficult to gauge as motion and position.

But eventually it did end, and I found myself dropped unceremoniously back onto the platform, the impact hard enough to knock the wind from me yet not enough to break any bones. Spread-eagled on the white ground, I gaped for air like a stranded fish. It was at least a minute before I could give any thought to trying to stand up. When I did, my chest was heaving and my heart hammering. The air was still furious with machines, but they were no longer approaching any closer than within a few metres of me.

'Purslane,' I called out, feebly, before gathering my strength and bellowing her name a second time.

'Campion,' she called back. 'I'm over here!'

She was only a dozen or so paces away, but I only glimpsed her in fitful instants, as the curtain of machines thinned out momentarily. I stumbled in her direction, my knee aching from where I had bruised it in falling, and she staggered toward me, holding her arms out at full length as if she had become a somnambulist. We embraced and examined each other for signs of injury. Other than the superficial cuts we had already sustained, and the bruises that were hidden by our clothes, neither of us appeared the worse for our ordeal.

'The fucking thing—' I started saying.

Purslane touched a finger to her lips. 'It's still around us, and it almost certainly understands Trans. You might not want to offend it.'

I nodded meekly, but my anger was still barely contained. I did not feel myself to be in the presence of something evil, but I did sense a wicked intelligence at play, like the mind of a naughty or mischievous child writ malignantly large.

'I thought I was going to die,' I said.

'So did I. But I guess we shouldn't be too surprised – they warned us it can get playful. Now I know why Mister Jynx was in such a hurry to leave.'

'If that was playful, I'd hate to see aggressive.'

'We'd be in pieces down on those dunes. But something's happening, Campion.' She peered over my shoulder at whatever was going on behind me. I spun cautiously around and saw that the storm had pulled back far enough to afford us an obstructed view of the plinth. 'It's taking him,' Purslane said, with awe in her voice.

Despite its earlier hesitancy, the Spirit of the Air was now in full contact with Hesperus. It was not just examining him, though the swarm covered almost the whole of his body, but was dismantling Hesperus, consuming him in a wave that began at the rear of the plinth, where he was a fused mass, and progressed forward to the humanoid part of him that had seemed aware of our presence before. Where the wave had passed, nothing of him remained. Flecks and chips of gold glinted out of the whirling black funnel that was drinking him into the sky.

'I hope we did the right thing,' I said, staring at the spectacle with a feeling somewhere between horror and exhilaration. 'Is it killing him, or taking him away to make him better?'

'It could be incorporating his material into itself, or digesting his memories and personality.' Her hand closed around mine. 'There was nothing else we could do for him, Campion. He was already dead. This was his last, best chance.'

After that, there was nothing more to say. We watched until the swarm had stripped the plinth bare, until the last fleck of gold had tumbled up the sucking spout and the spout itself had pulled back into the roaring black eye. The Spirit hovered above us for several more minutes, more lights than ever flickering in its belly, as if it had much to think about now that it had taken Hesperus. Then, quite without warning, the noise and the wind and the lashing rain abated, and the Spirit moved its elements further apart so that the darkening indigo of the sky shone through the gaps. Then the Spirit gathered itself, undulated and danced for a number of minutes, and then shot away towards the setting sun.

Purslane and I watched it until it was only a billowing smudge in the distance. Then we went to the shelter and prepared to wait until morning.

CHAPTER EIGHTEEN

Betony poured himself a measure of impossibly black coffee, shaking his head with an air of patrician disappointment. 'I hear that your little gambit failed. I wish I could say that I was surprised.'

'We don't know enough to jump to any sort of conclusion,' I said. It was morning and the sky was cloud-flecked and more wintry than it had been before. It was as if the arrival of the Spirit had heralded a cold new season. The flags on the bridges and walkways seemed to have faded overnight, becoming drab and washed-out.

'Was the robot healed?'

'No, not yet.'

'But nothing of him remained on the observation platform. The Spirit destroyed him, which was always one possible outcome. How can there be any question of him still being healed if he doesn't exist?'

'We don't know that he doesn't exist. There's documented evidence of the Spirit destroying things – taking them, at least – and then putting them back later.'

'Nothing you can count on, though.'

'It still happens.'

Campion spoke up. 'As a rule, the only times the Spirit has done this has been when the offering has been something complex. It's like a child, fascinated by bright, shiny toys. Much cleverer than a child, obviously – probably cleverer than most entities we've ever encountered. But it still prizes novelty and complexity. And there's nothing more novel or complex than another machine intelligence.'

Betony looked at him with his chin resting on his hands. 'So when do you expect Hesperus to pop back into life, with his faculties magically restored?'

'We don't "expect" anything,' Campion said. 'We just knew that what we were doing wasn't ridiculous; that there was a chance of success. Hesperus must have thought the same, or he wouldn't have sent that signal to us.'

'It may not happen for days or years,' I said, 'but I think he will return. His essence has been incorporated into the Spirit now, but that doesn't mean he can't be reconstituted. It took him apart like a puzzle, piece by piece, but it will have remembered where everything goes. It knows what he is, what he was meant to be before he was hurt, and it can make him new again.'

'Well, I suppose there's no harm in taking an optimistic view.'

'It's no more optimistic than thinking we actually have a future,' I snapped back. 'I may be stupid and naïve, but at least I'm not living under the delusion that we still have a Line; that it's all business as usual. Look at us – sitting around this table as if we're all one big happy family.'

'I see you haven't got over the ship business yet, Purslane. I was hoping you'd be able to look beyond your own concerns and think of our wider responsibilities.'

'Don't lecture me on responsibility, Betony.'

Campion touched my hand and coughed. 'Did anything happen while we were away? The last thing I remember was Mezereon killing one of our prisoners.'

'The cabinet killed him, not me,' Mezereon said, from across the table. She had a piece of bread in her hands and was tearing into it with such violence that I feared she was visualising Campion's neck. 'He was squeezed dry, anyway. He wasn't going to tell us anything else from inside the box.'

'Another day or two of trying wouldn't have hurt.'

'Or a week or two, or a year or two? Where would you have drawn the line, Campion? Sooner or later we had to dial him down.'

'There are still three more,' Aconite said. 'We're not finished just yet.'

Campion turned to Cyphel, who had said nothing until now. She had been watching the argument with a look of sceptical amusement, as if we were all players in some performance of which she was the only neutral observer.

'Campion,' she said, acknowledging his stare. 'Something on your mind?'

'Just wondering if you've made any progress.'

'It's coming along. I've read in nearly everyone – but even

missing a few, I already think I have enough of a signal to reconstruct your strand.' She brushed a jewelled finger through her hair, hooking a white lock behind an ear. 'I'll wait until I have everyone read in, though, before I start analysing. What's a day or two more, when the ambush already happened more than a century ago?'

'The sooner we have his strand, the better,' Betony said.

'I'm very close, Betony. And I have the navigation logs, the flight-plans everyone filed before departing the last reunion. I haven't run a correlation yet, but as soon as I've completed work on the strand, that'll be the first thing I do.'

'No sense in rushing things,' Galingale said. 'If Cyphel's going to all this trouble, it'd be silly not to do the job properly. Right?'

'Right,' Cyphel said. 'At least someone understands.'

'It is most unfortunate, what has happened,' said Cadence, when we met the two robots after breakfast.

'Most unfortunate,' Cascade echoed, his hands clasped demurely. 'But you should not blame yourselves for this failure. It was clear to us that you had Hesperus's best interests at heart. In all honesty, he would probably not have survived the journey back to Machine Space.'

'You thought he might,' Campion said.

'We were erring on the side of optimism, so as not to discourage you too greatly,' Cadence answered.

'The Spirit has taken him,' I said. 'That doesn't mean we failed.'

'How can it be otherwise?' Cascade asked softly, the way one might address a child who was under some fundamental misapprehension about the state of reality.

'It's taken things before,' I said. 'Sometimes it's returned them the same day, but it's also happened weeks or months later. The fact that it didn't put Hesperus back together last night doesn't mean it won't reassemble him at some point in the future. We just have to be patient, to wait for that outcome.'

'Patience is one of our virtues,' Cadence said. 'Nonetheless, we are still obliged to return to the Monoceros Ring at the earliest opportunity. We owe it to Gentian Line, and the Commonality. The sooner the news of your misfortune reaches our fellow machines, the better they can organise their response. You may not think a year or two will make much difference, given the enormity of the journey ahead of us—'

'It had occurred to me,' I said.

'But a thorough analysis of galactic history reveals that many events would have gone differently if critical information had arrived a year earlier, or a year later. We cannot count on being exceptions.'

'In other words, you still need my ship.'

'Regrettably, yes,' Cascade said.

'I guess I'm resigned to it now. You can take her whenever you want, as far as I'm concerned. I saw her when the sun rose, lit up like a morning star. It tore my heart out to know she isn't mine any more. The sooner she's out of my sight, the better.'

The robots glanced at each other briefly. 'We will not delay, in that case. An early departure suits us very well, and will hopefully cause you the minimum of distress.'

'I'd still like to empty my hold first. It may not mean anything to you, but there are things in there to which I have a sentimental attachment. The Line didn't say anything about taking them from me – just the ship they're in.'

'Is there something of particular value?' Cadence asked.

'Not really. But they're part of me, part of my past. I like to keep things. Campion doesn't feel the same way, but I can't help who I am.'

'You should let her clean out *Silver Wings*,' Campion said, addressing the robots. 'It won't take long, and the ship will be even faster without all that dead weight in her cargo hold.'

'I see no practical objections,' Cascade said, 'but it would be desirable to assign formal ownership of your ship to us as soon as possible. That way we will be able to familiarise ourselves with her control systems. Might we do that imminently? You could begin unloading your possessions while we are adapting to the ship. Once you are done, we should be ready to leave orbit with the minimum of delay.'

'Don't expect me to jump for joy at the prospect,' I said.

'We appreciate how traumatic this must be,' Cadence said. 'It may not be much consolation, but you will have earned the gratitude of the Machine People.'

'Hasn't she already earned it?' Campion asked.

'Of course,' Cascade replied, nodding slightly.

'I'm drained now,' I said. 'Drained, and I still need to speak to

Mister Jynx about what happened last night. I can't tell you how much I'm looking forward to *that*. If it's all right with you, we'll go up to the ship tomorrow.'

'That would be most satisfactory,' the robots said together.

CHAPTER NINETEEN

Mezereon's interrogations continued for the rest of the day. Purslane left me to sit in on them alone while she debriefed the Ymirian scientist about our experiences in the eye of the Spirit.

Although there had been no public censure, I had the impression that Mezereon had been chastised for what she had done to Thorn, the shatterling from the House of Moths. She might not have intended to kill him, but she must have known that the likelihood of him surviving emergence was not great. And while Mezereon might have convinced herself that he had said all he was going to say, I suspected that Aconite and the others were a lot less certain. Their presence was much more conspicuous this time. Mezereon was still leading the proceedings, but Aconite, Lucerne, Melilot and Valerian were sitting in a separate row of their own, between the audience and the plinth. They did not say much, but Mezereon was paying them nearly as much attention as she paid the prisoners. Her every move was under scrutiny, and she did nothing without glancing at her four fellow survivors, seeking tacit permission to proceed. At the same time, there was something defiant, almost cocksure, in the way she conducted herself. She might have been slapped on the wrist, told not to cross the line again, but she had not been dethroned. That would have been an admission that Betony and the others had made a mistake in handing this assignment to Mezereon, and *that* would never do. Mezereon seemed emboldened, not cowed.

The caskets – three occupied and one empty – had been arranged in an arc so that each was visible to the other. Mezereon had dialled all the prisoners down to one hundred, and we were all dosed on Synchromesh to an equivalent factor. The twelve-hour interrogation session would have lasted a subjective interval equivalent to seven and a half minutes – scarcely enough time for niceties in a normal conversation. But this was not a normal conversation. Mezereon was ablaze with righteous fury, hammering each question home almost before the prisoners had had a chance to answer the last one. When she reached an impasse, she dialled herself back down to normal time and consulted with the four. The day still slammed by.

At the end of it she had made remarkably little progress. Facial matching had established that the two unknown prisoners might be lost shatterlings of Ectobius and Jurtina Lines, a supposition which caused no little awkwardness given that we were hosting guests from those two Lines. But Mezereon had not been able to persuade them to reveal their identities. Nor had they shed any further light on the nature of the House of Suns, which remained as mysterious as when Hesperus had first mentioned it. Grilse was the only one who showed a flicker of recognition, but even that might have been my imagination.

'I think we know each other pretty well by now,' Mezereon said to Grilse.

I remembered Melilot's comment about Mezereon being zealous in her pursuit of the truth, when the survivors were still hiding in the ruins of the reunion system.

'Make your mind up,' Grilse said. 'Dial me down, or dial me up.' He had a rough, leathery voice, as if his vocal cords had been left out to dry in the sun.

'There are three of you now. Thorn died.'

'Who's Thorn?'

'The Mellictan shatterling, your accomplice. The other two are an Ectobius and a Jurtina. You're all shatterlings supposedly lost to attrition.'

'You sound as if you already know all the answers, Mezereon.'

'I'm getting there.' She leaned back on her heels, stretching her back like a yawning cat. 'I asked Thorn about the House of Suns. Now I'm asking you.'

'I don't know what you're talking about.'

'It's a Line, obviously. Joining the dots, the House of Suns is made up of shatterlings who used to belong to other Lines. Perhaps they need to replenish their numbers now and then; I don't know. Perhaps it infiltrates known Lines by replacing legitimate members with perfect copies. If that's the case, then the real Grilse might have died millions of years ago. If you took his place during a circuit, then showed up at the reunion with his body and face, his genes, a set of his memories – we probably wouldn't have known the difference. Why did you do this to us, Grilse? What did we do to deserve this?'

'You existed. That was enough.'

'You mentioned Campion when we were still in the ambush system. You were taunting us, thinking we'd never get our hands on the man or his trove. That was *your* mistake, Grilse. Campion survived, you see. He made it. And that means we have an excellent chance of piecing together the reason for your crime.'

'I'm not stopping you.'

'Watch this, Grilse. I'm going to show you exactly how serious I am.' Mezereon moved to the second cabinet and placed her hand on the stasis lever. The prisoner – the one we thought was an Ectobius – squirmed in his seat, frightened by what Mezereon was going to do next. He started speaking, but Mezereon must have disabled the microphone amplifying his words.

'It's too late now,' she said. 'You had your chance. Now you can make yourself much more useful to me by showing Grilse that I mean business.'

I felt a tightness in my throat, the need to say something. Mezereon shot a look at Aconite and the others, but there was no audible exchange between them. Mezereon stiffened her jaw, nodded once, then yanked the handle all the way to the left.

When the cabinet's stasis bubble collapsed it gave off the same muffled cough that had signified Thorn's demise, but the failure mode here was not quite the same. When the impassors released their hold on the man-shaped husk, only dust rained down. It formed a neat grey pyramid at Mezereon's feet. She crouched down, cupped some of it in her hands and then let it drain in dark banners through her fingers.

Then she stood and ground her heels into the dust.

'Did you get all that, Grilse?' she asked, moving to the other cabinet, the one that held the suspected Jurtina shatterling. 'The same thing could be happening to you in a few minutes. I'm willing to do it – more than willing, eager.'

'We made your ambush painless,' Grilse said. 'There was no malice in it, no intention to cause you distress. It was meant to be fast and surgical. We are not monsters.'

'You call *me* a monster?'

'Take a look in a mirror.'

'Tell me why you ambushed us.'

'What makes you think we know?'

'You mentioned Campion, when you didn't think it would cost you.'

'I was told it had something to do with Campion's thread. That's all any of us were meant to know. It was already too much.'

'Who told you?'

I saw the fear crawl under his skin. Was that the first time Grilse had hinted at being in the service of someone else, a higher agency? If so, the indiscretion could not have happened at a worse time for him. Mezereon was not going to let it go.

'You know what, Mezereon? All of you?' He glared at us from inside the cabinet. 'I know there's an audience out there – I can feel them. I still think there's a way to win. A way to destroy the rest of you. Why don't I let you claw yourselves apart, like rabid wolves, looking for a traitor amongst you? Or maybe more than one?'

'There's no traitor amongst us,' Mezereon said, with automatic certainty.

'You think you'd know if there was?' Grilse's smile was either insane or that of a man who knew he had nothing to lose. 'There is one, Mezereon. Trust me on that. He or she – I won't say which – could well be sitting in your audience right now. And he or she knows exactly what happened and why. I wouldn't mind betting they're already making plans to finish the rest of you off, irrespective of anything I say.'

'Give me a name,' Mezereon said.

'That's the last thing I'm going to do. Figure it out for yourself. Do some more interrogating.'

She touched her hand to the stasis lever of the Jurtina's cabinet. 'A name.'

'What if I said you were the traitor? Would you allow yourself to be subjected to questioning?'

'Don't do this,' said the Jurtina.

Mezereon looked at him with weary scepticism. 'Because you're going to tell me everything?'

'I don't know anything, only that we had to kill you.'

'Where did the H-guns come from?'

'A secret cache known to the Marcellins. Most of the weapons were decommissioned after the Homunculus wars, but a few were kept aside, in case they were needed again.'

Her attention returned to Grilse. 'Is this true?'

'There was a cache. But the rest of the Line didn't know about it. They weren't culpable.'

'We'll let the Commonality decide on that one.' Mezereon returned to the Jurtina. 'You haven't told me anything I hadn't already worked out for myself. Unless you're withholding information, you are of no further use to this investigation, except as a means to demonstrate my determination.'

'No,' the Jurtina said.

Mezereon began to pull the handle towards the left, slowly this time. The prisoner began to speed up from our perspective, twitching and fidgeting increasingly quickly.

Something exploded inside me.

'Wait!' I shouted, before she had tugged it all the way across. 'There's got to be a better way than this.'

Mezereon looked at me with icy disdain. 'Something to contribute, Campion? You've been spectacularly silent until now.'

'Dial down,' I said, conscious of the whirling hand on my chronometer. 'We can discuss this in realtime.'

'I'm happy discussing it now.'

Aconite stood and turned towards me, hands raised placatingly. 'Leave this to us, old man. We've got it under control.'

'No, you haven't. Mezereon's burning her way through prisoners like she's tossing coals on a fire. There are two left. We can't afford to lose another one.'

'I only need one to talk,' Mezereon said, and began to tug the handle towards its limit.

I dialled myself down. I was alone in a room full of superhumanly accurate wax effigies. I dashed from the audience, through the electric tingle of the screen that had blocked the audience from view, onto Mezereon's plinth. She was still looking at where I had been seated, but her expression was beginning to shift – it was like watching the beginning of a very slow landslide. Her head started to track, following the blur of motion that I must have made from her perspective. I forced her stiff fingers from the Jurtina's handle and pushed it back up to a high stasis level. Behind me there was a sudden commotion as other shatterlings emerged from Synchromesh. Mezereon's right hand started to inch towards her own chronometer.

Someone grabbed me. I was slammed around by Aconite, his face a mask of uncomprehending disappointment. 'You shouldn't have done this, old man. We owe you everything, but there *have* to be limits.'

He was holding me against the side of the Jurtina's cabinet. I might have been able to break free of Aconite, but Valerian took my other arm, gently but firmly.

'She's out of control,' I said.

Mezereon emerged into realtime. 'Get out of here,' she told me.

'You're letting hatred get the better of you.'

'They hate us. Why shouldn't we turn a little of that back on them?'

'Because we're Gentian. Because six million years of good works say we're better than that.'

'In your world. Not in mine.' She nodded at Aconite and Valerian. 'He means well, but he can't be allowed to disrupt the proceedings. Have him taken outside. Betony can decide what to do with him later.'

Betony, who had said nothing until then, stood from the audience. 'I'm sorry, Campion, but we simply can't tolerate this kind of disruption. See yourself out, or we'll have you removed. I wouldn't want to do that, but if you will insist on bringing this kind of attention upon yourself ...' He waved his hand in a gesture of surrender, as if my actions were a bewildering puzzle.

'Maybe there's something in what the Jurtina said,' I replied. 'If there is a traitor here, he'd like nothing better than for the prisoners to die. Then there wouldn't be any danger of one of them revealing his identity.'

'Go,' Betony said. 'Before you say anything else you may have cause to regret. I'm disappointed in you, Campion. I thought you'd have the common grace to rise above Purslane's censure and not make it an issue between you and the rest of us. I was evidently mistaken.'

'We suffered an appalling attack,' I said. 'It was brutal and came without warning. We're right to seek justice, right to go after those who wronged us. But that doesn't mean we get to throw away every moral principle we've ever abided by.'

'Times are different now,' Mezereon said. 'They made it this way, not us.'

At that moment, the door to the interrogation chamber was flung open, revealing the pink sky of an Ymirian sunset. Disconcerted, I realised that we had already been inside the whole day. A shatterling, Burdock – one of those who had been on patrol duty until now – stood with one of the masked and winged locals.

'We're in session here,' Betony said.

'It'll have to wait,' Burdock answered. 'The Ymirians found me as soon as I came down from my ship.' He stepped into the room, accompanied by the Ymirian, and closed the door behind him. 'It's about Cyphel,' he said.

'What about her?'

'She's dead.' Burdock paused – he was having trouble getting the words out. 'She must have fallen from one of the high balconies. They found her on the slope of the Benevolence structure, under the lowest level of Ymir.'

The flier was hovering at the nearest landing stage, its wings thumping the darkening air. Betony was the first to step aboard, followed by Burdock, Aconite and Melilot. Galingale and Charlock boarded next, then Lucerne and me. Almost as soon as my foot had left the deck, the flier was moving. An appalling drop opened up under me as I eased into the plush cabin. I shuddered to think what it must have been like for Cyphel, to be falling and knowing that no force in the universe was going to stop her. I had stood on the edges of ten-kilometre-high cliffs, far from the assistance of any guardian machine, knowing that it would only take a twitch of my muscles to send me over the edge. But until my encounter with the Spirit, I had never fallen; I had never been pushed. Even then, I had been quickly snatched from danger, unlike Cyphel. The fact of knowing that your own death was not only imminent, but mathematically certain, carried with it a special horror. I hoped and prayed that Cyphel had been dead or unconscious before she fell, but I had a feeling we might never know for sure.

'If she'd fallen from a different tower, or one of the bridges, she might have dropped right through the fingers,' Charlock said. 'She'd have stood a chance if she'd hit the sand, wouldn't she?'

Limax, the Ymirian, looked back. 'I'm afraid not. If the impact didn't kill her instantly, she would probably have triggered an avalanche and suffocated under the sand, if she didn't bury herself in it immediately, her bones smashed. That would not have been a pleasant way to die, I assure you.'

'That doesn't mean she was lucky,' I said.

Limax looked grave. 'No, shatterling. It doesn't. But I am saying it could have been worse.'

I realised, with a lurch of comprehension, how bad this was going to be for the Ymirians. We had lost another of our number to attrition, which would have been bad enough when there were a thousand of us, but was immeasurably worse now that we were down to a twentieth of our former strength. But the process had begun with the ambush; whatever the details of Cyphel's fall turned out to be, her death was simply part of the playing out of that long, murderous process. To the Ymirians, on the other hand, we were guests, travellers who had surrendered ourselves to their care. They had allowed us to live in their city, to have complete freedom of movement between Ymir and the other settlements, and in return we had agreed to be bound by their policies. Purslane and I could have visited the Spirit of the Air without the magistrate's permission, or the grudging cooperation of Mister Jynx, but we had shown the Ymirians that we were willing to take no for an answer; that we would not bully our way into getting what we wanted. We had left our ships in space, along with our robot servants and weapons, and come to the surface with only the basic amenities. Had this been one of our reunion venues, the entire structure, the entire city, would have been a machine for keeping us from harm. No one could have fallen to their death. It would have taken determination just to graze an elbow.

The lowest inhabited level of the tower was a hundred metres above us; the foundations by which it was anchored to the sloping finger of the High Benevolence structure were windowless and weatherworn, like the ramparts of a castle. Cyphel's body lay about fifty metres downslope from the foundations, caught in the shallow ledge formed by the markings engraved into the structure's ebony skin. She had either bounced after an initial impact, or had been pushed sideways during her fall.

The Ymirian flier came to a halt another ten metres downslope from where Cyphel lay. We got out cautiously, stooping against the dust-laden wind and taking meticulous care with every footfall. We were a safe distance from the edge, but I did not think much of my chances of surviving a slide if I were to lose my footing on the sloping, marble-smooth ground. Like a team of ants ascending the angled trunk of a fallen tree, we crept up to the ruined body of our fellow shatterling.

It was worse than I had been expecting, though Burdock had warned me that I would not find it pleasant. The fall had smashed her body and disarticulated her limbs. One leg was bent double, forced back under her spine, the other thrust out at an unnatural angle. Her arms were broken in several places; the skin where her clothes had been ripped was bloodied and gashed, and bone jutted from an elbow and thigh – she *must* have bounced, I realised, either against the side of the building, or against the floor of the

273

Benevolence structure. Of her head, there was little left to recognise. Her face was a red pulp, almost too abstract to elicit revulsion. But her hair was still recognisable, where the wind had not pushed it into the bloodied mess of skin and bone. I could not help reaching out and stroking a lock of it, white and pure as moonlight against my skin. That it was Cyphel, and not someone else with similar hair, was confirmed by the multitude of rings on her hand. The hand was still intact, the fingers open and inviting, as if all she needed was someone to comfort her.

'Cyphel,' I said, as the full reality of what had happened to her began to hit home. I felt a terrible sadness open inside me, a void through which the winds from the end of the universe were blowing.

Galingale, who was stooping next to me, placed a hand on my shoulder. 'Whoever did this,' he said, quietly enough that only I would have heard, 'we'll find them. We won't let Cyphel down – we'll avenge her loss.'

Charlock had squeezed aspic-of-machines onto his hand, forming a black tattoo. Grimacing with concentration and the effort of kneeling against the wind, he held his hand palm down and open above what remained of Cyphel's head. 'I'm not picking up anything,' he said, after several moments. 'I knew it would probably be futile, but if I hadn't looked—'

'You were right to try,' Lucerne said.

Betony said, 'We'll have to examine her brain for coarse structure – memories she hasn't yet committed to trove, thoughts frozen at the moment of shutdown. We may get something.'

'I wouldn't count on it,' I said. Extracting patterns from a mind was difficult enough when the person had just died, let alone after they had suffered a violent, damaging death several hours ago. All of a sudden it hit home to me how profoundly, pathetically ineffectual we really were. We could move worlds, wrap rings around stars, skip ourselves across time and space like pebbles on water. None of that would make any difference to Cyphel, though. There had been a human soul in that skull only a few hours earlier, and now no authority in the universe could bring her back. We were like monkeys sitting around a fire that had just extinguished, wondering why the warmth and light had gone away.

'We mustn't jump to conclusions,' Betony said as I stood back, a few strands of Cyphel's hair still between my fingers. 'She could have fallen by accident, without anyone pushing her.'

'Do you honestly believe that?' Aconite asked.

'I find it no harder to believe than that one of us killed her.'

'Then start dealing with it,' I said. 'Gentian involvement was always suspected, from the moment we were ambushed. This just confirms it.'

'She was one of us. Could you kill me, knowing what you do? About who I am, what I've seen and done, how long I've been alive?' Betony was looking at me with an expression that forbade an affirmative answer. 'We're people who've lived through almost everything that matters. The few thousand years of recorded history that came before us was just a prologue, nothing more. The real story started when Abigail took her first breath.'

'We're bookworms who've tunnelled through the pages of history,' I said, recalling how the Vigilance curator had described me. 'It's not quite the same thing.'

'But we know what we are. We know how precious we are. I couldn't kill you, Campion. I may not approve of the things you've done, the way you've flouted the traditions of the Line, but I still couldn't touch a hair on your head. It would be like destroying a monument, poisoning a fragile ecology ... an act of vandalism, not just murder. I can't help but think you feel the same way about me.'

'Of course I do,' I said angrily. 'But that's because I'm not the murderer. Nor are you, if you really feel like that. But someone obviously doesn't. Someone saw Cyphel as an obstacle they could remove as easily as you or I would toss something into a disposal slot.'

'Then they're not one of us. No matter what they look like, they're not Gentian at heart.'

'I wish I shared your conviction.'

Betony looked over his shoulder. I followed his gaze and saw a Gentian flier – the same open-topped kind that had taken Purslane and me to the Spirit – lowering down to us. 'We'll move her,' Betony said. 'Take her back into orbit. I can scan her aboard *Adonis Blue*.'

'She's gone,' I said.

'We have to *try*, Campion.' He said this so fiercely that I began to wonder if he was close to breaking down. I remembered how over-joyed he had been when I told him the news of the survivors Purslane and I had rescued. Cyphel's death was hitting me particularly hard, but it was going to be difficult for all of us, Betony included. Gentian Line was down to fifty-one living shatterlings, and at least one of those survivors might well be trying to kill the rest of us.

The flier touched down. Through narrowed eyes I studied Cyphel arid remembered how she had looked at breakfast. Already it felt like a lifetime ago, when the universe had been a simpler place, full of bright primary colours.

The wind intensified, lashing dust against my cheeks.

CHAPTER TWENTY

Campion was quiet that night. I was sad about what had happened to Cyphel, angry and perplexed in equal measure, but there was still a component to his grief that I felt I could not quite share. I knew he had always liked her – I had caught those sidelong glances of his often enough to be aware when he had his eye on her, rather than me. Cyphel knew exactly how he felt about her as well – it was there in her expression whenever they spoke, that beguiling combination of amusement and haughtiness that she carried off so well. It was a look that expressed disdain at Campion's guarded advances, but also a kind of measured, probationary respect as well. It was a look that said, *You dare to think that I will find you as interesting as you obviously find me? Well, perhaps in that very act of daring you become interesting to me, if only fleetingly.* Not that his advances were anything more than the flirtatious overtures of a game he had no intention of seeing to its conclusion. He liked her a lot, was intrigued by her, but I do not think it ever occurred to him to consummate that fascination by sleeping with her, or even prolonging one of the polite kisses shared between shatterlings. I should still have been jealous, no matter how innocent his intentions. But I could never bring myself to dislike Cyphel. That was the worst part of it.

I was glad now – not that she was dead, but that I had never hated her, never given her short shrift. And I badly wanted to find the person who had murdered her, and I badly wanted to do unspeakable things to them.

Come the morning, I found the robots waiting for me before breakfast.

'We heard the dreadful news,' Cadence said.

'It is most unfortunate,' Cascade said. 'After all that you have suffered, to lose another of your Line – words cannot begin to express the depth of our sympathy.'

'Thank you,' I said.

'We understand there is going to be a ceremony of some kind,' said Cadence.

'Cyphel's funeral service – most likely they'll schedule it for tomorrow, or the day after. Once they've got what they can out of her mind, there'll be no sense in delaying it.'

'Will this service be a private matter for the Line?' asked Cascade.

'Ordinarily, yes, but I'm not sure that'll be the case now. Our guests are involved in this, too – we're all victims of the ambush, and we all knew Cyphel – you included. I'd imagine the ceremony will be open to all-comers, Ymirians as well. It'll be unusual, you know. Normally there isn't a body. When we die, it's usually far from home, thousands of years from another shatterling. They'll log us as missing at the next reunion, and if we don't show up at the one after that, then we'll be presumed dead. There'll be a ceremony, and then one of us will be tasked with creating the memorial – but because the death will have happened at least a circuit ago, it feels more as if we're commemorating some historic incident. It'll be different with Cyphel – it's going to feel a lot more personal, a lot more immediate.'

'If there is anything we can do to assist matters, please do not hesitate to ask,' Cadence said.

'I'll let Betony know. I'm sure he'll already have begun putting the arrangements in place.'

If the robots heard the tartness in my voice, my resentment at Betony making all the key decisions, they had the decorum not to show it.

'In view of developments, it would probably be better if we delayed our departure,' Cascade said. 'We are still anxious to be on our way, but we would also like to give our respects to Cyphel, if the Line allows it.'

'I'm sure it will. It's good of you to be flexible.'

'We have seen the respect you have accorded Hesperus,' Cadence said. 'The least we can do is reciprocate.'

I thanked the robots for their kindness.

Breakfast was an ordeal. There were a million things we all wanted to say, but none of us was prepared to break the silence. Even Betony kept his own counsel, saying nothing until the very end. At the back of all our thoughts was the suspicion that Cyphel's murderer could easily be sitting at the table, looking as downcast as the rest of us.

'Cyphel's funeral will take place tomorrow,' Betony said, and for a moment we thought that was the end of his announcement. Then he scratched at his chin and added, 'Today Mezereon will resume her questioning of the two prisoners. Events having forced a certain urgency upon us, I have given her permission to bring them both out of stasis.'

'We could lose them both,' Campion said.

'We'll take that risk, but I don't think it's likely. The condition of Grilse's cabinet is rather better than that of the Jurtina. I think we have an excellent chance of getting at least one of them out intact.' His brow knitted, Betony looked Campion hard in the eye. 'Unless you've changed your mind, it might be better if you kept away from the interrogation.'

Wiping her fingers with a napkin, Mezereon said, 'Campion can sit in if he wishes. Just as long as he doesn't try to stop me this time.'

'You do what you want,' Campion said. 'I can think of a million things I'd rather be doing than watching you bully and torture the prisoners.'

'Since they won't reveal the information voluntarily, I don't really see what choice I have.' Mezereon folded her napkin and placed it back on the breakfast table. 'It's moot, anyway. As Betony said, we're done with that phase of the inquiry. I'll have flesh and blood bodies by the end of the morning – at least one, anyway.'

'Or none, if your luck doesn't hold out.'

She stared him down, managing not to blink once. 'The sectioning apparatus is ready. You are more than welcome to observe the procedure.'

'We'll all be there,' Betony said. 'No excuses this time, unless you're on patrol duty. Purslane, that includes you.'

'Next you'll be telling me I can't look away,' I said.

'I want everyone to be present. We'll be studying your reactions, seeing who doesn't look comfortable.'

'That'll be me,' Campion said.

'I don't think this is any time for flippancy,' Betony cautioned.

Campion shrugged and stood from the table, knowing when he had said enough. I followed him to the railing, out of earshot of the others. We had barely spoken this morning. When I woke at dawn, I had found him already out of bed, sitting on a chair on the balcony, looking out towards the dark silver dunes with eyes reddened by tears that he had tried to rub away.

'We'll get through this,' I said to him now.

He took my hand and squeezed the fingers. 'I know. It's what I keep telling myself. But I don't feel it. If you told me Gentian Line will end tomorrow, I'd find that easier to believe.'

'This is when we have to be the strongest. Darkest hour before dawn, et cetera.'

Campion looked away. 'I could do without the platitudes.'

'You know there's a saying like that in almost every human culture that's ever existed. There's a reason for that, too. Sometimes you just have to hold on, to keep doing what you're doing, to have faith that things are going to get better. It's how we survive. There've been a million bottlenecks in history where things would have turned out much worse if we'd all just given up and accepted the inevitable. Some of those bottlenecks would have ended us if a few irrational, doggedly optimistic souls hadn't clung to a thread of hope.'

'I'm clinging, believe me. But that thread just got a lot thinner, a lot more frayed.'

'Then we hold on more tightly. Something good will happen. I'm sorry Cyphel died, but at least it tells us we're getting warm. Someone was scared enough to kill her. That means she was close to revealing vital information.'

'Vital information that has now been lost for ever.'

'Someone else can take over her work. Cyphel was the automatic choice for reconstructing your thread, but it doesn't mean someone else can't do it eventually. It'll just take them a bit longer.'

'Maybe that's all the traitor needs – a little more time, and then it won't matter.'

I shifted awkwardly, because I had no good answer for that. 'I know how you felt about Cyphel, Campion. This must be tearing you up inside.'

'Do you hate me for that?'

'For liking her? That would be rather petty of me, wouldn't it? Especially now. She was one of the best of us. She was beautiful, too – don't think I hadn't noticed. I can hardly blame you for admiring her.'

'I'm lucky to have you. Whatever I might have felt about Cyphel, it didn't even begin to compare—'

'I know,' I said, shushing him by placing a finger against his lips.

'You don't have to say it. You never have to say it. Just ... keep being here, all right? Don't ever go away.'

'I'm not going anywhere,' Campion said.

PART FIVE

PART FIVE

I held the letter in my hands. It was the finest paper I had ever touched, smooth as a puppy's ear and as delicately scented as a courtesan's pillow. It smelled of lilacs and almonds and the rare spices of the Faraway Islands, the archipelago that lay at the very edge of the mapped world, beyond the Kingdom, beyond outlying empires, beyond the Shield Mountains, beyond the girdling seas, beyond the perilous leagues of White Kraken Ocean. The wax seal was a black coin embossed with the calculatedly unsettling emblem of Count Mordax: a portcullis made of bones. I broke the seal with my fingernail and folded open the crisp document, my heart anticipating the dire news I fully expected it to contain.

I was not to be disappointed, if that is quite the turn of phrase to encompass my feelings. The letter was from my stepbrother, Mordax himself. His writing was as elegant and magisterial as ever. He wrote love letters the same way he wrote death warrants. This was neither.

The letter informed me that my lady-in-waiting, still a prisoner in the Black Castle, would be put to death unless I revealed the whereabouts of Calidris. Not only would she be executed, but the manner of her death would be 'commensurate' with my continued non-compliance. I could spare her by acting within hours; I could ease her torment by acting within the day; I could guarantee a slow and painful execution by delaying my response any longer than that.

'I cannot do this,' I told the chamberlain, Daubenton. He was standing in my council room, the heavy oak table straining under its burden of maps and plans of war, acres of heavy parchment and leather. The room was darkly vaulted, with small latticed windows to confound spies and assassins. Candles barely touched its sullen, military gloom. Nothing pleasant had ever been schemed within these walls, only death and punishment. Next to Daubenton was the master-at-arms, Cirlus. 'I had hoped not to betray Calidris, after all he has done for us,' I said.

Cirlus fingered the crimson gash of his old duelling scar. 'You could not betray Calidris even if you wished it, milady. Even my best spies have no idea where the sorcerer is hiding now. That was always as he wished it – to lose himself both to his enemies and his friends.'

'Calidris must remain amongst men,' I said. 'That is his strength and his weakness. No other magician is as powerful as him. But magic is a curious fire. It pollutes the minds of those who would shape it. One magician may sense the mind of another magician, blazing like a beacon in an otherwise dark landscape. The only defence, the only manner in which a sorcerer may hide, is to surround himself with lesser minds. No one is entirely immune from the taint of magic; we all carry a little of it within us. Our minds do not blaze so brightly, but we may provide a kind of concealment to one such as Calidris. In cities, in towns, even in villages, he may swaddle the bright coal of his own mind in the dim embers of his fellow citizens. He cannot easily be found, even by another magician. That is his strength. But it is also a weakness, for it makes it hazardous for him to travel, even in the company of a small party. And if a man such as Mordax wishes to find Calidris, he need only put every village in the Kingdom to the sword, until he has forced the magician to reveal himself.'

'There have already been reports of raiding parties torching the villages and hamlets along the western flank of the Forest of Shadows,' said Daubenton. 'They rode horses from the east, and spoke in the coarse tongue of brigands ...'

I nodded heavily. 'But we may safely assume Mordax's men were responsible. We may also assume that they will apply the same systematic approach to every village they suspect of harbouring Calidris. Our army is weakened – we cannot defend every community on the map.' I put down the hateful document, this vile piece of fragranced paper that had been touched and written on by my stepbrother. 'I cannot let my people burn. Even when the lady-in-waiting has been put to the sword, do you imagine Count Mordax will leave us alone?'

'I fear milady is correct,' Daubenton said. 'But how does this change things? We cannot locate Calidris.'

'I can,' I said.

'How is that possible?' asked Cirlus.

'Because Ludmilla gave me the blueprints for her ships,' I said.

Daubenton frowned. 'Milady?'

I was ashamed at my childish outburst, though the words had tumbled from my mouth before I could stop them. Ludmilla Marcellin was a figment from my dreams: the princess of another realm – one of celestial argosies and palaces in the sky.

She did not belong in daylight.

'Forgive me,' I said. 'I babble nonsense, the product of too little sleep.'

'Of course, milady,' Cirlus said. 'But concerning Calidris—'

'I can reach him. Before he left us, Calidris gave me a gift.' From the folds of my dress I withdrew the embroidered rectangle of my sewing kit. Daubenton and Cirlus studied it warily, uncertain of my meaning. I opened the kit, spreading the two halves wide in my lap. The needles, pins, thimbles and embroidery were as I had left them.

'Milady?' Daubenton said again.

My hand moved along the arrayed needles until I reached the smallest of them all, the one I was careful never to use when I was sewing. I pulled it from its pocket.

'This is what Calidris gave me,' I said, holding the needle up for inspection. It glimmered in the wavering candlelight. 'It looks like the others, but it is not the same. Calidris placed an enchantment on this needle. It is blood-bound.'

'I am unfamiliar with the notion,' Cirlus admitted.

'So was I, until it was explained. It is magical cunning. Calidris knew he must make himself difficult to find – that is why he went into the world, to smother himself with the dull minds of ordinary men. But his wisdom told him that there might come a time when the Kingdom had dire need of him again, a crisis so grave that Calidris must once more work his magic to save us.'

'Calidris's magic nearly tore the world in two,' Daubenton said, the colour gone from his face. I felt the same way. Calidris's dark talents had opened a mouth into hell.

'Then it may be magic powerful enough to hold the world in one piece, when something else would rip it asunder. Calidris knew this: he's no fool, and no one in the Kingdom has a firmer appreciation of the risks of magic. But still he gave me this blood-bound needle. With it, I may summon him again. I have only to prick my skin, to draw a bead of blood, and Calidris will hear my call.'

'How?'

'An invisible needle will stab into his finger and draw his blood.

When the needle pricks, he will turn his gaze towards the Palace of Clouds and know that I have need of him.'

'You would do this?' Cirlus asked.

'There is no other way,' Daubenton said.

'You did not sound so certain a moment ago,' I said.

'Better his magic be loosed into the world than to watch the Kingdom fall to Count Mordax's raiding parties.' Daubenton shrugged wearily. 'It is a dark bargain, but I see no alternative.'

'Because there is none,' I said. 'We must have Calidris.'

'To give to Mordax, in return for the lady-in-waiting, and the safety of our villages?' asked Cirlus. 'Surely we have other choices? What of Relictus, the failed apprentice? He remains in our custody. Could he not help us now?'

'Calidris made me promise that I would never turn to Relictus, even in our darkest hour. He never trusted the apprentice. He said that his talents were dark and misshapen.'

'Calidris could not have foreseen our present needs,' Cirlus said.

'It is immaterial. I have no intention of giving Calidris to Mordax. The count would never keep his side of the bargain. I know him better than anyone else. He and I were once to be married, you know.'

'Milady, the count is your stepbrother,' Daubenton said tactfully.

Confusion addled my mind for a few heartbeats. I had been certain that the count and I were destined for marriage until shadowy politicking had made that betrothal an impossibility. How could I know his voice and mannerisms, his inability to keep a promise, if I had not moved in his circles with the intimacy of a lover-to-be? 'He used to come and play,' I said, trailing off as the absurdity of my statement sank home. 'I remember his ship, his robots—'

'Milady must sleep,' Daubenton said. 'She has been driving herself to exhaustion with her concern for her people.'

Cirlus just looked at me. I did not know if he had formed a judgement.

'Calidris must return to us,' I said, with renewed firmness. 'Not to be traded for my lady-in-waiting, but to use his powers against Mordax. No advisor in the Palace would trust our enemies in the Black Castle to hold to a bargain.'

'That is true,' Daubenton admitted.

'I feel clear-headed now. Resolute. The time has come.'

'It must be milady's decision,' Cirlus said.

'It is,' I answered. 'Always and for ever.'

I pricked my finger with the blood-bound needle and drew a bauble of the purest scarlet. There was no pain. Somewhere in my Kingdom, Calidris, the strongest of all magicians, felt more than his share.

CHAPTER TWENTY-ONE

'You're no fool,' Mezereon said, her voice pitched to reach the audience even though it was the prisoner she was addressing. 'You've been around; seen a few things here and there. You know exactly what I have in mind for you.'

'So get it over with,' Grilse said. 'You're already boring me to death.'

He had been moved into the open air, onto one of the largest balconies in the tower. He was out of stasis. Mezereon had failed with the Jurtina shatterling, who was now another pile of dust, but her efforts with Grilse had been more successful. As she had anticipated, his cabinet was in a better condition than the other three. He had weathered the transition to realtime without complications, and was now in Gentian hands, literally and metaphorically.

Or at least, he had been for a few moments. Fearful that he might find a way to kill himself, or at least render himself incapable of being usefully interrogated, Mezereon had arranged for Grilse to be manhandled into a restraining box. It was an upright frame of complicated construction, a skeletal outline filled with aspic-of-machines, forming a translucent, gelid rectangle into which Grilse – by now stripped of his clothes – was forcibly immersed. The box allowed him to breathe and communicate, but he was going nowhere. It was presumed that if he had been carrying an implanted suicide mechanism, he would already have triggered it inside the stasis cabinet, during one the intervals when he had been dialled down for questioning.

The sectioning apparatus was centre stage, and the box in which Grilse was trapped formed part of it. Hovering above the box, arranged into an ordered circle, were rectangular panes of a glassy material, each of which was as tall and wide as the framework around the box. Along the top of each pane was a flanged grey bar containing levators and enough intelligence to follow Mezereon's instructions. All of this had been forged by makers, in accordance with ancient blueprints.

The aspic had forced its way into his lungs, into contact with his nervous system. It was feeding him with air and information, allowing him to breathe, move within certain limits and hear what Mezereon was saying. We could see his chest rising and falling, his eyes following Mezereon as she strode up and down.

'I've killed three of your colleagues,' she said. 'I was ready to kill you as well, without hesitation, but things are different now. One of us is gone. She was murdered, just when she was getting close to exposing vital information. So I'm not going to kill you – not until I'm certain I've bled you dry, and by then maybe I'll have lost interest. You mean nothing to me beyond the information in your head. And I will find out what you know – piece by piece, if necessary.'

'You can do what you like. It won't get you anywhere.'

Mezereon looked to one side. 'Lower the first pane.'

At her instruction, one of the orbiting panes broke from the group and lowered until it was suspended just above the top of the cabinet. For a moment it hung there, until a nod from Mezereon caused it to lower into the cabinet itself, piercing the invisible glass and parting the aspic in a clean, descending line. It was only just possible to make out the pale edge of the descending pane.

'You'll feel it cut its way through you,' Mezereon told the prisoner. 'It won't hurt as much as it should, since the nerve connections are reinstated almost as soon as they are broken. But there'll still be a tingling background of unpleasantness. It will feel like a sharp-edged cold front pushing through your soul. As it descends, you will know that part of you is on one side of that glass and part of you on the other.'

The pane had begun to divide him at the skull, piercing him so that his face was on one side of the glass, his ears and the rear of his head on the other. It crept downwards at perhaps a centimetre a second, the progress smooth for the most part but with occasional hesitations, as if it was encountering denser or more complex biological structures.

I knew that the pane was only microns thick, yet it was isolating the two halves of him, severing them from each other as completely as if it had been a metal guillotine. What prevented him from dying – what allowed him to keep thinking, even as the pane knifed his brain into two halves – was that the glass was permitting essential biological functions to tunnel through itself as if the divided surfaces were still contiguous. I gathered that very little biological material was actually passing through the glass without being completely disassembled down to atoms or basic molecules, incorporated into the glass's agile, constantly adapting matrix, and then conveyed and reassembled elsewhere (on one side or the other) in accordance with the circulatory patterns that had been interrupted. The same was true of the electrical and chemical signals associated with synaptic function.

By now the glass had passed through his head and was beginning to divide him at the shoulders and upper torso. The expression on his face had altered subtly, in a way that might easily be mistaken for the effect of the play of light as clouds passed over the piazza. The aspic-of-machines was allowing him to move his facial muscles just enough to register disquiet, and perhaps even horror, at what was being done to him. Even if he wished to talk now, it would make no difference to Mezereon.

I watched, mesmerised and repelled, as the glass completed sectioning the prisoner. When the pane reached the base of the cabinet, it halted. Since we could no longer see the pale edges of the pane, the effect was as if the prisoner had been restored to his former integrity. This was illusory. Mezereon gestured towards the cabinet and it partitioned itself into two halves, each of which contained one portion of the divided man. The two halves folded away from each other, the man opened for inspection like a lavishly illustrated book. The pane must have split itself into two thinner layers, each of which was holding back a wall of tissue, muscle, sinew, bone and pumping fluid, all pinks and whites and reds and livery purples. The visible detail in the two sections was identical, except that one was a precise mirror image of the other. A living mirror, too, for the man was still alive, still breathing. We could see the rise and fall of his chest behind the glass, the outline of his pleural cavity, his heart pumping like the speeded-up opening and contraction of a flower.

Mezereon allowed us to examine him a moment longer, then rotated the front section, the one that contained his face, until it was looking back at the rear section.

'This is you,' she said, indicating the living anatomical chart he had become. 'This is not a projection, but rather your own self, cut down the middle and trapped behind glass. It is necessary that you understand this. Indicate your assent by nodding. The aspic-of-machines will permit you this movement.'

I suppose the man had no choice but to nod, or perhaps he was made to do so by the machine in which he was trapped. As his head bowed, the other half echoed the movement with no detectable delay. The action, as the half-head tilted forward into the plane of the glass, revealed a squirming, ever-changing cross section of skull and brain.

'This will be the last conscious movement you make,' Mezereon said. 'You will continue to breathe, and blood will continue to flow through your body, but you will remain fixed in position. You can, of course, still talk to me – your intention to speak is all I need.' She looked away from the prisoner towards her audience, playing to the house. 'The sectioning will continue until you have no physical existence, except as several hundred wafer-thin slices trapped under glass – and rest assured I will go that far. You can halt that process at any time by giving us the information we seek, in a verifiable form.'

'I have nothing to say to you,' he answered, his voice unchanged but strange nonetheless, given that it had emerged fully formed from only half a man.

Mezereon nodded as if she had expected his response. 'I'd have been disappointed if you'd let us stop now,' she said.

Two more panes lowered from the orbiting flock and came into hovering position above the prisoner's two halves, aligned in parallel with the first division.

Mezereon sliced her prisoner again. Then she kept going, following a geometric progression.

I turned to leave the piazza, imagining that I would be one of the first to do so, and realised that Purslane must have already departed.

When it had been decreed that nothing more would be learned from Cyphel's remains, her body was brought out into the open on a hovering platform, the platform tilted slightly forward so that the fact of her death and the evidence of her injuries were obvious to all. Cyphel was much as she had been when found, except that her body had been arranged in a suggestion of repose. Visible in outline beneath a translucent sheet, her arms were at her sides, her legs had been straightened, the bones pushed back under her skin, the blood cleaned from her wounds, and although she did not have much of a face left to look with, the angle of her head suggested that she was looking expectantly upwards, into the evening sky. Four shatterlings accompanied the platform until it came to rest over a table-sized block and lowered slowly into place. The rest of us formed a circle, holding torches in the air, and then advanced slowly until we were gathered in a small crowd around Cyphel. There were fifty of us present rather than fifty-one, for as always one shatterling – it happened to be Medick on this occasion – was away from Neume on patrol duties. But there were fifty-one torches, a flame for every survivor, with the spare one being passed from hand to hand in symbolic recognition of the shatterling who was not present at the funeral.

Our witnesses – the shatterlings from other Lines, our guests and the dignitaries from Ymir and the other cities of Neume – surrounded us at a respectful distance, standing on a circle of raised flooring. They were soberly dressed. Our clothes also befitted the occasion – we all wore black garments, devoid of ostentation save for embroidered black flowers that were all but invisible. Purslane's hair was combed back from her forehead, secured by a simple flower-shaped clasp. She wore no make-up or jewellery; nor did anyone else. The air was cold, but our clothes had been forbidden from warming us or assisting with the burden of the torches. Mine weighed heavy in my hand, as if the more it burned the heavier it became.

I was not surprised that Betony had chosen to speak for Cyphel, but for once I did not begrudge his putting himself forward. I had known Cyphel as well as anyone present, even if I had not been one of her closest friends. Her closest friends had died in the ambush – at best I only counted as a close acquaintance. I felt a sense of obligation towards her, a conviction that there were aspects of her character I understood better than anyone else, but I had no wish to hurt Purslane by dwelling on my feelings for Cyphel. Nothing had ever existed between us except the possibility of something, and now even that was over. Besides, my knowledge of Line traditions was not as exhaustive as it might have been. As we had told the robots, funerals of this kind were exceptionally rare events – there was not usually a body involved, and there was often no conclusive evidence that the shatterling in question was really dead.

Betony kept his speech brief. He said that although Cyphel's death would cast a long shadow over what remained of the Line, and that the circumstances of her death were still under investigation and might yet lead to unpleasant revelations, that was no reason not to celebrate the life she had lived. She had seen and done glorious things; she had touched countless lives; she had carried a thread of memory across six million years; she had been loved and admired and envied. He spoke of a dozen or so significant milestones in her life, blowing the dust off events that had happened many circuits ago.

I had steeled myself to be annoyed by Betony's words, but (to my own lingering irritation) I found nothing to disagree with. Afterwards, when Cyphel's life had been played out across the sky, I thought back to what he had said and found nothing I would have changed; nothing I would have amplified or amended. His summing-up of her life had the pure simplicity of a haiku; it had been honed and polished, and it was delivered with conviction and respect and something of the same love he had mentioned in connection with her. I was still resentful of the way Betony had taken command of the Line, but when he spoke for Cyphel, I discarded any thought, however improbable it had seemed, that he might have been her murderer.

When the words had been spoken, Betony pulled the sheet down from Cyphel's neck, revealing the true extent of her injuries. Cyphel was naked except for the rings on her fingers. We all flinched, even those of us who had already seen her body after the fall. Then Betony handed his torch to another shatterling, and from one pocket he produced a thick black tube of aspic-of-machines. He cupped one hand and squeezed a dollop into the palm, then smeared the aspic onto Cyphel's forearm, where the skin had been ruptured when a bone had pushed its way through. Then he stood back a little and pressed the tube into the thick fingers of Weld, who had been standing next to him. Betony reclaimed his torch and took hold of Weld's while the other shatterling squeezed aspic onto his palm and daubed it onto Cyphel, this time across the dented arc of her brow. Weld then passed the aspic to Charlock, who rubbed the translucent glistening paste across Cyphel's belly. So it continued, until all who were present had taken their turn. I do not know why I was the last; whether it just worked out that way or whether the group had arrived at the collective decision that it must fall to me to make the final daub. By then the only visible part of Cyphel that had not been covered was the smashed travesty of her face. As my hand applied the aspic, my fingers touching hard ridges of bone and cartilage where there should have been skin, I shuddered with the effort of not breaking down into sobs. Then I took my torch from Purslane and stood back, my hand still shaking. The circle had widened, opening space around the reclining form.

By the time I had finished, the aspic had already begun to do its work. It was infiltrating Cyphel's body, as far as it needed to go to undo a given injury. Her forearm stiffened momentarily, the fingers of her hand tremoring as if Cyphel were dreaming. Around the point where the bone had come through, the hole in her flesh began to seal over. The dent in her brow smoothed itself out and the recognisable structure of a nose began to appear beneath the glistening mask. The machines were not restoring Cyphel to life; it was much too late for that. Not that an illusion of life would have been beyond them: they could have animated her corpse, repaired cells and coaxed their metabolic cycles to start up again. They could have made her sit up and smile; made her walk and talk and laugh. But there would have been no mind behind those eyes, or at least none that retained anything of Cyphel.

As the process continued and the figure on the couch began to look less and less like a broken corpse and more and more like a sleeping woman, a squadron of our ships moved into position above Ymir. They were not orbiting, but holding station above this fixed point on Neume, just beyond the ionosphere. The sun had long since fallen below the horizon, but the ships were so high up that the sun's rays still caught the edges of their hulls, picking them out like a fleet of new moons, edged in scimitar-bright lines of silver and gold and fiery red. The ships arranged themselves into a square formation, spanning thousands of kilometres of space. Then they activated their impassors and began to project and shape the fields so that they pushed down into the ionosphere, tangling with the planet's native magnetosphere. Squeezing, crimping, folding and stretching the field lines of the magnetosphere, the ships began to paint the sky with auroral colours. Curtains of light, the most delicate ruby or green, rippled from horizon to horizon. The colours intensified until the ships were almost hidden behind the display, silent puppeteers retreating from view. They stripped ions from their hulls and injected them into the atmosphere, to stain and dye their handiwork. The curtains flickered and shimmered and intertwined, dancing with increasing swiftness, different hues being introduced, until shapes became apparent. The shapes formed images: we were being shown a sequence of pictures drawn from Cyphel's strands, sampled from those stored inside her ship. There were landscapes and cities, moons and planets – as rich a cross section of galactic history as any of us had tasted. Cyphel was absent from most of the images, but that only served to make her presence in some of them the more poignant. She was usually caught with her back to us, a distant figure standing on some cliff or high building with one hand on her hip and another shielding her eyes from the sun, lost in the rapture of scale and scenery, drunk on the very idea of being human, a monkey who had hit the big time. Her hair was the electric white of a comet's tail, streaming back from her brow as if fingered by a caress of photon pressure.

As we watched the episodes play across the canvas that the ships had made of the sky, the aspic-of-machines slowly undid Cyphel's injuries. At last the glistening caul completed its work and slithered off her, awaiting its next duty. Turned gold under the light of our torches, Cyphel lay uncorrupted. Her expression was one of patient serenity. Her eyes were closed, but she looked as if it would only take a raised voice, a careless laugh, to jolt her from the carefree drowse in which she lay.

The platform began to rise again, detaching from the block where it had rested. At first it rose so slowly that it took at least a minute for her body to rise higher than my line of sight. Only then did the platform begin to quicken its ascent, rising into the air with increasing swiftness. The torch, which had felt so heavy until then, began to lighten. There was a point where it weighed nothing at all, and then a moment later it was trying to escape from my hand, as if being pulled from above on an invisible thread. All around me, the other shatterlings stretched their arms and redoubled their grips, anxious to retain their torches until the appointed moment.

'Release,' Betony said, very quietly, and we all let go. The timing was impeccable, for the fifty-one torches rose in a flame-lit ring, maintaining elegant formation until they had caught up with the rising platform. Lowering our hands to our sides, our muscles still aching from the effort, we watched the dark rectangle of the platform become smaller and smaller, until it was only by the diminishing circle of fire that we could judge where it was.

It would take a while for Cyphel to reach space; all that remained was for us to continue watching the display of scenes from her life, reflecting on how she had touched all of us in one way or another. I felt solidarity with almost everyone else present, including Betony, including Mezereon, including those other shatterlings whom I felt had been complicit in Purslane's punishment. But somewhere amongst us, I felt certain, was someone who was not sorry about what had happened to Cyphel. In every grave face I tried to read a sign of masked emotions, of quiet satisfaction that she had been disposed of so efficiently, but I saw nothing but sincere grief.

We were not just mourning Cyphel, I knew. This was her night, her funeral, but the fact of it had flung wide an emotional door in our hearts that had been locked until now. This was the night when we first took account of the more than eight hundred shatterlings who had died in the ambush. They would all be honoured in the traditional way when the time was right; they would all be accorded memorials; but that did not mean we could not begin to grieve for them now. As the realisation of what had been done to us hit me with renewed force, as I began to truly apprehend the scale of that crime – a realisation that it had taken the particularity of Cyphel's funeral to force upon me – I felt the coldest of all chills pass through me.

Not long after, Cyphel reached space and the platform tilted to release her for her long fall back to Neume's atmosphere. We watched as she scratched a line of glorious fire across the sky, a line that began faintly, flared to a ribbon of pastel blue, reached a climax that had us narrowing our eyes, then faded slowly away before splitting into fingers of dulling red, Cyphel giving up every atom of her body, every atom of her existence, all that she had ever been, all that she ever would have been, until all that remained of her was the figment we held in our memories, no more and no less.

Long after she had faded, the ships continued playing images of her life, until that too dimmed and the planet's magnetosphere was allowed to relax back to its normal configuration. The squadron, dark now, pulled away into parking orbit. The audience of shatterlings, guests and Ymirians at last began to disperse, shivering even as our clothes were finally allowed to warm us.

Cyphel's funeral was over. We had honoured her. Now it was time to get on with being Gentian Line.

Later that evening, after Purslane had gone to sleep, I stood alone on one of the balconies. I was thinking of all the pieces of Cyphel's life that had played across the sky, trying to fit them into some kind of order, wondering what she would have made of it all had she been one of the spectators. Then I became aware of a heavy, trudging presence, a sound like carpet scuffing on stone. I turned around with an empty wine glass in my hand, lost somewhere along the drunken, ill-defined border between nostalgic remembrance and bitter, spiralling melancholy.

It was Ugarit-Panth, the elephantine being I had spoken to shortly after our arrival on Neume.

I raised the glass in welcome. 'Hello, Ambassador. How did you like the funeral?'

He stopped a few metres from me, but still close enough that his trunk could have swiped my face. 'It was very moving, shatterling,' he said, his human-looking mouth moving beneath that long, wrinkled, faintly disgusting appendage.

'She was one of the best of us. I'm going to miss her a lot.'

'As much as you'd miss your civilisation, if it ceased to exist?' It was difficult for him to look at me head-on – his eyes were set in the sides of his skull, not the front of his face. He had to look at me askance, alternating between one eye and the other as if he wanted to balance the demand on his brain hemispheres.

I tried to push aside the mental fog induced by the wine. 'There are individuals who matter more to me than Gentian Line, yes. If I didn't realise that before, I realise it now.'

'It's easy to see that now, with your Line pushed almost to the point of extinction.'

Something in his tone put me on edge. I took a step back from the balcony's railing, Cyphel's long fall flashing through my mind. The Roving Ambassador of the Consentiency of the Thousand Worlds was a huge, ponderous creature, weighing about twenty times more than me even before one allowed for his heavy-looking red armour and ornamental metalwork. I was prone to clumsiness when drunk – what he could do in a similar state of intoxication did not bear thinking about. I even began to wonder if the Ymirians had designed their balconies for such massive individuals.

'Extinction's never good,' I said, with an over-emphatic smile.

'No, it's not.' Ugarit-Panth took another step closer to me – four steps, in fact, one for each of his tree-thick legs. All of a sudden I got the full-bore stink of his breath in my face. It was like opening a warm oven full of rotting vegetables. 'You very nearly blew it, shatterling. I bet you thought you were in the clear.'

'Nearly blew what?'

'The first time we met. You commiserated with me.'

'Did I?'

'You were sorry that my civilisation had been wiped out by the failure of a stardam.'

'I got that wrong, though. I was thinking of the Pantropic Nexus – different civilisation altogether. I wasn't even in the right spiral arm!'

'Ah, but you were. Your mistake was puzzling to me. You were so certain, so genuine in your sympathies. It began to prey on my mind.'

I looked around, desperately hoping that another shatterling would come to my rescue. 'But it was a mistake.'

'Don't compound your error by lying even more. I tried consulting Gentian Line's troves later that night. For some reason, my guest access was temporarily blocked. In the morning, it was all excused away – a problem with the security settings caused when they were altered to allow for the latest batch of survivors.'

'Well, then – nothing to worry about.'

'You would say that. But at the next opportunity I checked again. I looked up the entry for my civilisation – the Consentiency. There *was* a stardam, as I knew full well. Gentian Line installed it. Reassuringly, there was no record of it having detonated prematurely.'

'That's that settled,' I said, trying to strike a note of finality, so that we could change the subject.

'Still, I had my doubts. Couldn't put them to bed. I looked up the entry for the Pantropic Nexus. Can't say I'd ever heard of them, but there they were – along with a note to the effect that the entire civilisation had been wiped out during the premature collapse of a Gentian stardam.' His vast grey brow, the part of it visible between the plates of his armour, wrinkled impressively.

'It's the only one that's ever failed.'

'You're absolutely certain of that?'

'It's not something we take lightly. The pride of the Line rests on our handiwork. Stardams are what we do. Even if we allow for that one failure, we've spared billions of lives that would otherwise have been lost ... but that doesn't make it excusable. Not at all.'

'I'm very glad to hear you say that, shatterling. But still my qualms weren't entirely silenced. It occurred to me – suppose that the Consentiency's stardam *had* failed after all. Would Gentian Line be in a hurry to tell me?'

'We wouldn't lie about something like that. If the dam failed, we'd admit culpability.'

'But what about a white lie? What if Gentian Line were primarily concerned with my mental wellbeing? What if they didn't think I could take the truth – that I was now alone in the universe, the last of my kind, the last living representative of the Consentiency? What if they thought the truth might actually kill me? They might lie then, don't you think?'

'But the Pantropic Nexus—'

The ambassador waved his trunk dismissively. 'A lie that had to be made up on the spur of the moment, to cover a momentary indiscretion.'

'But the troves—'

'For all I know, the data in the troves was manipulated to keep the truth from me. I was only looking at local copies; the versions aboard your ships might have told me something totally different. I'd have no way of knowing, would I? Short of casting aspersions on the integrity of Gentian Line, I'd have no choice but to take the information at face value.'

'Put it like that, I suppose you're right.'

'Still, there are always loopholes. And because the matter was causing me such vexation, I remembered something. You shatterlings place great stock in your Universal Actuary. It's how you plan your circuits – working out where you want to go, on the basis of information that may be hundreds of thousands of years stale.'

'It's that, or start flipping coins.'

'Well, perhaps you'd be better off flipping coins. I talked one of you into giving me access to the UA, you see.'

My blood cooled to superfluid helium. 'Who'd that be, then?'

'Oh, don't blame him. Galingale had no idea what I was after. We were talking – I've talked with most of you – and I bent the conversation around to the subject of the UA. I feigned interest. For some reason I'd been gently dissuaded from further enquiries, but Galingale was strangely receptive. I think I flattered him with my attention.'

'The idiot,' I said under my breath.

'Oh, but it really wasn't his fault. I can be extraordinarily persuasive, and he wasn't to know I had an ulterior motive. I told him I was interested in the UA as a thing unto itself. I didn't let him know I was keen to see what it had to say on the subject of the Consentiency. But you'd know, wouldn't you? The UA wasn't altered to agree with the troves. None of you ever thought I'd look that far into your secrets.'

I let out an exhausted sigh – secretly relieved, despite myself. 'Is there any point in keeping up the pretence, Ambassador?'

'None whatsoever.'

'If it's any consolation, my sympathy was genuine.'

'I never doubted it.'

'I'd not been briefed. Betony's fault, I suppose – he should have warned me that certain conversational topics were strictly out-of-bounds. But he must have been keeping that lie going for so long he'd forgotten all about it.' I shrugged 'Or my fault for being a blabbermouth, not reading the situation, wading in where I shouldn't have. I'm sorry, Ambassador. You shouldn't have found out this way. But I hope you understand that the Line did have your best interests at heart. This wasn't about excusing our mistake.'

'The wiping out of an entire civilisation – a mistake?'

'We've saved hundreds,' I said. 'I'm sorry if that sounds cold – but that's the only possible perspective. It doesn't diminish the tragedy. You have every right to feel angry—'

'Anger doesn't begin to cover it, shatterling. I thought you'd have the sense to realise that.'

'Ambassador—'

'I just thought you all ought to know: you can stop lying to me now.'

He turned around, shuffling on the flat discs of his feet. Beneath his armour, his skin swung in obscene, wattled folds. I watched him trudge back indoors, then looked into the empty depths of wine glass, seeking solace.

'Chalk up another sparkling success to tact and diplomacy,' I said to myself.

That night Cyphel came to me again. I was in her room, lying on her couch, watching as she squeezed the aspic-of-machines onto her hand and made the webwork of black lines. But instead of holding the hand over my head as she dragged my memories into daylight, Cyphel just brushed my hair and lowered her face until she was about to kiss my cheek. Then she whispered into my ear, 'You always liked me. I always liked you, too. But now you have to do something for me. I want you to pay attention.'

I woke up.

In the morning I caught up with Galingale before he had found his way to the breakfast table. As I tugged his sleeve he looked around with an eager, expectant expression, as if I might be a lover come to give him a morning kiss. The optimism dropped from his face like a landslide.

'You silly fool,' I said, looking into his one good eye.

He blinked. 'Bit early for insults, isn't it? Make it quick, because I'm on patrol duty today – as soon as I've had my coffee, I'm shuttling up to *Midnight Queen*.'

I steered him away from the others. 'Last night I had a very interesting chat with Ugarit-Panth. You know – the ambassador who isn't supposed to know that his entire civilisation no longer exists?'

'Oh, him.'

'It seems you let him have a look through the Universal Actuary.'

'He wanted to know how it worked. The sociometric models, the statistical methods. All harmless stuff.'

'He used it to look up the entry on the Consentiency of the Thousand Worlds.'

Galingale brushed fingers through the stiff white bristles of his hair. 'And?'

'The entry hadn't been changed, you idiot. It didn't agree with the local troves. Now he knows exactly what happened. The UA gave a zero per cent likelihood for the Consentiency still existing in the future because it's *already gone*.'

He mouthed a silent curse, the realisation hitting him like a physical slap. He glanced at the nearby breakfast table, the other shatterlings taking their places. Everyone was still dressed in black after Cyphel's funeral. By Line tradition, even the fruits and breads and drinks were black.

'Who else knows?'

'I've no idea. I was alone when he came up to me. I mentioned it to Purslane this morning, but it won't go further than her. What I don't know is who else Ugarit-Panth has talked to.'

'I'd better have a word.'

'With Betony or the elephant?'

'I don't know. Both. Maybe. Fuck.'

'Fuck, indeed.'

'You're not exactly blameless here, Campion. Everything was going fine until you *commiserated* with the hapless bastard.'

'I hadn't been forewarned. Silly me, but I completely failed to read the subliminal signals Betony and the rest of you were putting out.' Seeing the dread draining the colour from his face, I softened my tone. 'Look, I'm not going to rat you out – it was an honest mistake and anyone could have made it.'

'I genuinely didn't put two and two together. I just assumed the UA would have been synched with the troves. Should've checked first, of course, but ... fuck. How was Ugarit-Panth? Did he seem edgy to you?'

'More annoyed than anything else.'

'We don't want him committing suicide on us. I don't know if

Betony told you, but they have a habit of walking around with bombs inside them. If he went up here—'

'He wouldn't do that. He's a rational being.'

'But there's no telling what that kind of news could do to him. Where is he now?'

'No idea.' I touched a finger to my brow, feigning absent-mindedness. 'You know, in all the excitement I forgot to attach a tracking device to him.'

'Someone has to talk to Betony.' His dread turned to terror. 'I can't do this, Campion. He'll say— Why me? What have I got to do with it? I'll be censured. Worse.'

'Could anyone tell that your UA was accessed?'

'No, don't think so – unless I admit to it, unless the ambassador admits to it.'

'Then I'll talk to Betony. I'm already involved, so I can't dig myself a deeper hole.'

He seemed surprised by my offer, as if there had to be a trap somewhere in it.

'What'll you say?'

'Just that Ugarit-Panth told me he'd worked things out. I won't mention the UA, or you.'

'What if they find the ambassador and he talks?'

'Can't do anything about that, I'm afraid. But even if he does – you'll be all right. It was a stupid thing to do, but it *was* an innocent mistake.'

'Of course.' Some of the colour had started creeping back into his skin. 'Thank you, Campion. You're right – I was an idiot. I should have thought things through. But he was just so damned persuasive.'

'I guess if we're all still standing here, he probably isn't going to blow himself up. Not today, anyway.'

'I think you're trying to reassure me, but—'

I patted him on the back. 'Let's have breakfast. Looks lovely, doesn't it?'

'I'm sorry about Cyphel.'

I could still see her in my dream, whispering into my ear: *Pay attention.* 'We're all sorry about her.'

But before I could sit down at the table, next to Purslane (she was talking to Charlock), I was detained by an Ymirian official. 'Campion?' asked the delicate little creature.

'Yes,' I said.

'Begging your pardon, shatterling, but you are urgently requested at the office of Magistrate Jindabyne.'

Purslane had seen what was happening. She rose from the table, brushing black crumbs from her black blouse. 'Has there been a development?'

'I can't say,' the Ymirian answered. 'Just that you're to come with me.'

CHAPTER TWENTY-TWO

When we arrived we found Mister Jynx sharing Jindabyne's office. The magistrate and the scientist were sitting at the same desk, one on either side, taking turns to inhale from the bubbling urn that sat on it.

'Something's happened,' Jindabyne informed us.

Mister Jynx handed her the mouthpiece; she placed it between her lips without wiping it clean. 'It would appear that your little funeral ceremony had an unexpected result. You did things with the atmosphere that we normally wouldn't have sanctioned.'

'We had permission,' I said, preparing to bristle.

Jindabyne raised a calming hand. 'That's not in dispute. If we had known the scope of your intended activities we might have demurred, but the fact is that we let you go ahead.'

'Is there a problem?' Campion asked.

'That depends,' Jynx said. 'You appear to have stimulated a response from the Spirit of the Air. When it does things – especially when it manifests at the observation platforms – it normally does so during the hours of daylight. Overnight, it manifested in darkness. For us, that's a problem. We don't like to see evidence of the Spirit being agitated, disturbed, roused from its normal patterns. Civilisations have fallen because they got on the wrong side of the Spirit – we don't want to be one of them.'

'What happened?' I asked.

'Last night, a few hours after the cessation of your funeral service,' the magistrate said, 'the Spirit moved into position above the observation platform you were allowed to visit with the injured robot. We had been tracking its movements, of course – the fact of the Spirit's presence in this sector wasn't a surprise. But we did not expect it to pass directly over the tower, and we certainly didn't expect it to stop.'

'Hesperus is back. Please tell me Hesperus is back.'

'Well?' Campion asked.

The magistrate sucked indulgently on the mouthpiece. 'Observations indicate the presence of a golden object on the plinth. The golden object is man-shaped and man-sized. It was not there yesterday.'

'We have to get out there,' I told Campion.

'I think we'd best ask permission first,' he said.

'You have permission,' the magistrate said. 'Why else would we have called you here? But the Spirit is not far away. You will retrieve the robot immediately. If you fail to do so within the next hour, the robot's remains will be deemed property of the scientific study council.'

'They belong to the Machine People,' I said.

'Not any more they don't. The robot stopped being a Machine Person when the Spirit took him apart. The thing that has appeared on the platform is an artefact of the Spirit – it just happens to look like the machine you thought you knew. It is very doubtful that any of the atoms in it are the same as those it originally contained.'

'We probably shouldn't quibble,' Campion said.

The magistrate looked at me sternly. 'No, you shouldn't. Go now. Recover the robot's remains. Do with them as you will. We will leave it to you to inform the other robots of this development. And afterwards – please – show no further interest in the Spirit, ever.'

'We won't,' I said.

'When you say "remains"—'

'We mean what we say. The observations show that the robot appears just the way it was when you left it, except that it is no longer fused with the remains of the ship. In every other respect it is no more alive now than it was then. Whatever you hoped to achieve, you have failed.'

Five minutes later we were speeding away from Ymir in a flier, pushing the little craft to its limits. We said very little to each other on the journey. If our hearts had been lifted by the news of Hesperus's return, our hopes had been just as quickly dashed by the description of his condition. The cameras monitoring the platform had detected no signs of life in the golden figure, which had not moved since the Spirit's departure. As the dunes sped under us, I realised that of all the outcomes I had considered, this was the one I had thought least likely: that Hesperus would return but not be changed. I had imagined the Spirit repairing him, or transforming him into something new and strange, and I had imagined him never returning at all. But to be taken apart, to be pulled into the mass of that cloud-consciousness for days, to become a part of it, only to be put back exactly the way he was, had always seemed pointless. And yet the evidence of that golden form could not be ignored.

'Perhaps he just needs time to recover,' Campion said, touching my hand. 'Like a patient coming out of surgery, on a planet where they still cut people open with knives and lasers.'

'You're trying to be kind, and I appreciate it. But I don't think you should raise my hopes.'

'I'm just saying … there's a lot we don't know about Hesperus. We shouldn't rule anything out. If the Spirit gave him back to us, it's for a reason.'

'Because it played with him, took him apart like a toy, and now that it knows how he works, it got bored and put him back together again.'

'Without fixing him first?'

'We don't know how the Spirit thinks. Maybe it didn't see Hesperus the way we did, as a being in need of help.'

Soon we were close enough to see him clearly, as I brought the flier in for landing. He was on the plinth where we had left him, lying on his back completely motionless. Even as the flier passed over him, he remained unmoving. The only change since we had last seen him was the absence of the fused mass that had connected him to the remains of *Vespertine*. The Spirit had obviously understood enough to see that the mass did not belong with Hesperus, and it had repaired the parts of him that had been lost or concealed within that mass. But it had evidently not taken the extra step of restoring him to life.

We parked the flier and got out. Campion fished a set of levators from the rear compartment and pushed them through the air ahead of him until we reached the plinth.

I knelt down to examine Hesperus, running a hand over the golden prominence of his chest. 'He's perfect again,' I said quietly, unwilling to disturb the sleeping form. 'There's no sign of damage at all. Even his arms are the same size now. I don't think there's any human flesh inside him any more.'

'It did all this, but it didn't make him live again?'

'There are still lights in his head. There's still something going on inside him.'

'But no more than what was there earlier.'

'This isn't the way I thought it would happen. I thought if we got him back, everything would be right.'

Campion attached the levators and lifted Hesperus from the plinth. He remained completely rigid, his limbs stiff even though they were not supported. He might as well have been cast from a single piece of metal.

I scowled at the horizon, but there was nothing there. I felt angry and reproachful, as if I had been let down. As if there had ever been a bargain between us and the Spirit of the Air.

'We'd best be going,' Campion said.

I turned my face away because I did not want him to see my tears.

CHAPTER TWENTY-THREE

Mezereon had arranged the two hundred and fifty-six slices of Grilse into a floor-covering mosaic, sixteen tiles to a side. The tiles were arranged according to a complicated scheme, one that looked random but was in fact much cleverer than that. The governing principle was that no adjoining tiles on the floor should correspond to adjoining slices of the original body. The effect was that one tile might contain a full-body slice, showing the human form in profile, whereas the one next to it might contain only disconnected islands. The tiles were illuminated from below, and all were still oozing with slow, laboured life. Fluids flowed sluggishly like rivulets of oil trapped between sheets of glass. His lungs expanded and contracted, the rhythmic movement echoing across many tiles in the arrangement. Between the tiles, framing them in a grid, was a series of narrow stone walkways. It looked for all the world like an arrangement of rectangular fishponds in a formal garden, with strange, pulsating blooms lying on the dark water. Mezereon was striding down one of the walkways as we arrived, an energy-pistol swinging easily from one hand. She was in the middle of hectoring Grilse, going over the same questions she had already asked him dozens of times.

'My time is not limited,' she said. 'Yours, sadly, is growing shorter by the hour. I can keep chipping away at you until you've got less nervous system than a crayfish.' She raised the energy-pistol, made a micro-adjustment to its yield dial and directed it at the pane to her right. 'Can you feel any difference yet, Grilse? Am I speeding up? Are your thoughts turning foggier? Is it becoming more and more difficult to remember how you got here, why you ended up in our custody?' Screening her eyes with her free hand, she squeezed the trigger of the energy-pistol, directing a lance of crimson light into the pane. She had aimed at his head. The pane did not shatter, but the weapon bored a neat hole through it into the cross section of Grilse's brain, the tissue crisping back in a dark-edged, widening circle. 'Any difference now, Grilse? You won't have felt that, but I just took out a few billion brain cells. You've hundreds of billions more, but we both know it's not an inexhaustible supply. The panes will route functional pathways around the damage, but they won't restore the memories you just lost. The unfortunate thing is, you won't necessarily remember losing them. You'll just feel emptier, more dispersed, like a room being cleared of furniture.'

His voice boomed loud. 'I have told you everything I know.'

'I don't believe you.'

'Why do you imagine I was told more than I absolutely needed to know for the purposes of the operation?'

'You wouldn't – unless you instigated it, which is at least a theoretical possibility. Until I know more about the structure and extent of the House of Suns, that's a possibility I can't discount.' Mezereon hop-skipped to another pane six rows to her right. 'In any case, I still don't think you've told me everything you were told, even if you're not the linchpin.' She aimed the nozzle of the energy-pistol again and shot into his abdomen. This time Grilse screamed. Across the mosaic, the slices squirmed under their prisons of glass. 'Yes,' Mezereon said approvingly. 'A good cluster of nerves there. That must have *really* hurt. Maybe it's still hurting?'

'She's out of control,' I whispered to Purslane.

'This we knew.'

I looked around the scattered audience until I spotted Aconite, Valerian and the other shatterlings who were supposed to be keeping an eye on Mezereon's antics. Still in their funeral clothes, they formed a huddle of black. Betony was only a row or two behind them, sitting next to Charlock.

'Wait here,' I said.

'Aren't you in enough trouble?'

'They forbade me from entering the interrogation room. We're outdoors now.'

I made my way to Aconite and the others while Mezereon continued tormenting Grilse. I had crossed only half the distance when I heard the crack of another energy discharge. No screaming this time, which meant she must have taken out another cluster of brain cells.

'Campion,' Aconite said, patting an empty space next to him. 'Take a seat, old man. She's on fine form, isn't she?'

'For a lunatic.'

'She's displaying a certain ... zeal. Would we want any less of her?'

'She's husked three prisoners. You'll be lucky if there's anything left of Grilse by the end of the day.'

'He knows that as well. Can't you see that he's on the verge of confessing?'

'He's on the verge of not having a language centre.'

Valerian coughed and said, in not much more than a murmur, 'Campion may have a point. We've given her a very long leash. She means well, and we all feel the same way about Grilse, but the only thing that matters is getting information out of him. We can't let personal feelings endanger Line security.'

'You think we should reel her in?' Melilot asked, her sentence punctuated by another energy discharge. 'That won't look good, not in front of our guests.'

'This isn't looking great either,' I said. 'From where I'm sitting, it looks a lot like Line-sanctioned torture purely for the sake of it.'

'And how would you run things, Campion?' asked Betony, who had left his seat to join us. 'I'm sure you're brimming with suggestions.'

'I'd take that gun out of her hands, to begin with. You can sever the data connections between those panes without destroying any physical patterns. If you want to make a point, do it that way. Grilse won't know any different – he'll still feel bits of himself dropping away. The plus side of that method, however, is that you can always put him back together again if you don't get results.'

'If he gives us nothing while we whittle him down to nothing – regardless of the method we use – he's hardly likely to behave differently the second time around,' Aconite said.

I shrugged. 'So make it real the second time, or the third. But at least try it that way first. Call his bluff. See how close to the bone he's prepared to take things. Maybe he is on the verge of cracking, but the way Mezereon's going, it may be too late by the time he does.'

'You really are determined to undermine this investigation,' Betony said.

I shook my head, more exhausted than angry. 'No. I fully endorse any activity that might get reliable data out of Grilse. If I believed taking an axe to those panes would do the job, I'd be the first in line. But this isn't going to work.' I tried to look deep into his eyes, anxious to connect with the reasonable, rational man I had always believed him to be. He was ambitious, but never misguided. 'Betony, you know this is wrong. I listened to you talk about Cyphel last night.'

He glanced away with a sneer. 'I knew you'd find something to object to.'

'I had no objections whatsoever. What you said about her was perfect. I stood there and thanked the stars you were the one speaking, not me. You did her justice.'

The silence that opened between us seemed to last a thousand years. The other shatterlings had pulled away, giving us the space to speak in private.

'I thought you wouldn't approve,' he said eventually.

'It was good. It was right and true. If Cyphel were here, she'd tell you the same thing.'

'I just wanted to say the things that needed to be said. I didn't know Cyphel as well as you, but I know she wouldn't have tolerated anything that wasn't absolutely true, absolutely to the point. She didn't want her life embroidered or romanticised.'

'You hit the right note.' I sighed, conscious that I was treading a narrow course between alienating him for ever and bringing him around to my point of view. 'After the ceremony, I knew I'd been wrong about you. Because of what happened with Purslane, it had crossed my mind – just crossed it, mind – that maybe you had more to do with all of this than any of us realised.' I swallowed hard. 'Then when Cyphel died—'

'You thought I was implicated?'

'It was stupid. But one of us must be responsible for her death. I'm sorry that I allowed my suspicions to fall on you, even for an instant. But that's what happened.' Now I was finding it difficult to speak – my chest was rising and falling as if I had just climbed a mountain. 'You licensed Mezereon to continue with this interrogation. I began to wonder whether maybe you wanted her to fail.'

'So that the information wouldn't come out.'

'Surely you can see why I might think that.'

Betony's eyes gave no clue to his opinion of me – the processes of his mind might have been going on light-years away for all that they showed in his face. 'And now?' he asked, equably enough.

'The speech changed everything.'

'I could still be your murderer. A few well-chosen words? Easily faked.'

'But you didn't fake them.'

'No,' he said, after a lengthy pause. 'They weren't faked. It was hard for me to talk about Cyphel. Harder still knowing that the person who killed her was probably only a few paces away.'

'Then we agree on that.' I turned to face the square, with Mezereon and her array of luminous, squirming panes. 'Which is why *this* has to stop, before she goes too far. Mezereon isn't the murderer, but she's not doing us any favours. I understand her hatred, her need for revenge, but now isn't the time or the place.'

There was another discharge from the energy-pistol. Grilse screamed again.

'Mezereon,' Betony said, raising his voice so that it rang across the open space. 'Would you mind ... stopping for a moment?'

She spun around with vivid rage in her eyes, the pistol almost aimed at us. Here there were no safeguards. Unless the weapon had been instructed not to fire on Gentian shatterlings, it would only take a twitch of her finger to wipe out another five or six of us.

'Is there a problem, shatterling Betony?'

'Not at all, Mezereon.' Despite his best efforts, there was still a quaver in his voice. 'I just think this might be a good time to pause ... to take stock, to assess what we've learned, before continuing.'

'We've learned nothing.'

'Nonetheless ... it might still be wise to review our approach, to see if there aren't any refinements we might make.'

To my considerable relief, Mezereon lowered the pistol and twisted its yield dial to what I presumed was the safety setting. She let go of the weapon and it hovered in the air where she had left it. Then she stalked over to us.

'This is unacceptable. I was making progress.'

'You were getting nowhere,' I said.

She glared at Betony. 'I thought Campion was banished from the interrogation.'

'That was different,' I said. 'This is a public space. Banish me and you'll have to banish the Ymirians as well.'

She ignored me, directing her remarks at Betony. 'Grilse was beginning to crack. I could feel it.'

'The problem is that we don't know how long you'll have to keep drilling holes in him before he starts talking,' Betony said. 'He's a finite resource. We don't have another Grilse backed up somewhere, for when you finish with this one.'

'I only need one of them.'

'I'm afraid he's talking sense,' Aconite said, offering her a conciliatory smile. 'You've done a fine job until now, and we're all grateful to you for that, but the time's come to try something else.'

Betony shot me a glance, then looked back at Mezereon. 'Can Grilse hear me now?' he asked quietly.

'No. I turned off his auditory feed when you interrupted me.'

'There'll be no more physical harm inflicted upon him – not until we've exhausted every other possibility. Set the yield on your pistol low enough that it won't penetrate the pane. We'll simulate damage by shutting down the data connections between his slices.'

'He'll know the difference, Betony. He won't feel pain.'

'Then you'll have to make do without it. He'll still feel himself being deleted, slice by slice. That's got to be unpleasant enough without adding pain into the equation.'

'He'll know the process is reversible.'

'Not for certain he won't. There'll still be that doubt, especially if you keep discharging the pistol. At the moment there's a chance he could be put together again, a walking, talking human being. Keep deleting panes and he'll be like a book with half its pages torn out. There'll come a point when he'll have lost too much to be reconstructed, and he'll know that.'

Mezereon did not look convinced, but neither did she look as if she was ready for a showdown with Betony and the others. They were offering her a way of saving face before the audience, by allowing her to remain in charge of the interrogation. Her hands would be tied, but it would still be less humiliating than being removed from the role entirely.

'I don't like this,' she said.

'But you'll do it anyway,' Betony finished for her. 'That's how it has to be, Mez. If we're wrong, if this gets us nowhere, then I'll be the first to admit my error. But until that point, we're doing it my way.'

Mezereon scowled. She turned around and stalked back to the waiting weapon, snatching it from the air as if grabbing a wasp. She adjusted the dial again, then looked back at us, her fingers white around the pistol's grip.

'Have it your way, boys and girls.'

CHAPTER TWENTY-FOUR

The robots came to see me in the early afternoon. I had left Campion watching Mezereon's continued interrogation of Grilse and had returned to the private room where we had left Hesperus, exactly where he had been before we had taken him to the Spirit. There had been no change in his condition since morning, but I felt obliged to keep vigil in case there was a flicker of life, a momentary attempt at communication that would otherwise be missed.

'It was a very good effort,' Cadence said, making me start by appearing at the door without warning. 'You should not blame yourself for the lack of success.'

'It isn't a total failure,' I said, noticing Cascade lurking just behind the female robot. 'He's not attached to that mass any more. He's been put back the way he used to be. Even his arm.'

'His arm?' the male robot quizzed.

'There was human flesh beneath the metal skin of his left arm. He was trying to disguise himself as one of us, so that he could enter the Vigilance.'

'We had no idea,' Cadence said.

'It doesn't matter now. But the point is, the Spirit did something – it didn't just put him back on the platform exactly as he arrived. It saw what was wrong with him, what was damaged, or not to be expected.'

'Superficial matters,' Cascade said.

'Maybe. But what's to say it didn't look deep into him and fix what was wrong with him there as well? His broken memory, the damage he sustained in the attack by the H-gun.'

'The evidence would suggest otherwise,' said Cadence. 'Although it pains us to admit it, he does not appear any more cognitively functional than when we last observed him.'

'There are still lights in his head.'

'But faint, and hardly moving. You would be unwise to put too much stock in them.'

'Do you think he's dead?'

I had the impression that the robots were exchanging thoughts – the air grew momentarily tense, as if accumulating charge before an electrical storm.

'He is not beyond hope,' Cadence said, sounding more doubtful than certain. 'But with every day that passes, patterns may be lost. The sooner he is on his way to Machine Space, the better.'

'We did not want to press you after the death of Cyphel,' Cascade said, managing to sound kind and firm at the same time, 'but if it is not too painful, perhaps we might discuss the matter of transportation again?'

'I think we agreed everything that needed to be agreed,' I said. 'We've said goodbye to Cyphel and I've got Hesperus back. If you want my ship, you can have her today.'

'Are you certain?' Cadence asked.

'Totally. Take her. Get her out of my sight.'

'That would be most satisfactory from our standpoint,' Cascade said.

'If it helps Hesperus, if it helps the Line, if it helps the Machine People, I'm happy with it.' Which was halfway to the truth. Before Cyphel's death, before the return of Hesperus, I had been indignant about losing *Silver Wings*. Now all I felt was emptiness, a sense that I had been betrayed and let down not just by elements of my Line, but by the universe itself. Getting my ship back would make no difference to that; it would be like throwing a single stone into a canyon and hoping to fill it to the brim.

'There were things you wished to retrieve from the ship,' Cadence said.

I nodded, although the task filled me with nothing resembling enthusiasm. 'It won't take long – most of those old ships should still be able to fly out by themselves.'

'As discussed, we will begin the process of familiarisation with your vehicle's systems while you evacuate the hold.' Cascade nodded his white mask at the golden form before us. 'We may as well convey Hesperus into orbit now. That way we can also begin preparing him for the journey, as best as we are able.'

'I won't see him again, will I?'

'If he can be healed, and if you live long enough, anything is possible,' Cadence answered.

'Maybe he won't even remember us. You can't be sure of that, can you?'

Cascade said, 'We will ensure that his debt to you is made clear.'

'It isn't about a debt. It's about friendship. We liked him. I think he liked us back.'

'He is in safe hands now,' Cadence said. 'You need have no fear about that.'

'Will you take care of moving him?' I asked. 'I can have my shuttle ready at the main landing stage within the hour. Betony will need to authorise a visit to orbit, but there shouldn't be any objection. This was his idea to begin with.'

'This does not inconvenience you?' Cascade asked.

'It's not as if I had anything else planned today.'

'Then your offer is most acceptable to us. We shall make the necessary arrangements for Hesperus.'

'Take good care of him,' I said.

I left the robots with him and went back to the open auditorium where I had last seen Campion. He was still sitting with Betony and the others, keeping a careful eye on Mezereon. As I approached he stood from his seat and moved to an empty position out of earshot of the others. I went up to him and said, 'I'm going up to *Silver Wings*, so that I can assign control to Cadence and Cascade. They're going to take Hesperus with them.'

'Will you be long?'

'I only need to empty the hold and authorise the change of ownership. I should be back on Neume by midnight. At worst, breakfast.'

He made to move from his seat. 'I'll come with you.'

'You don't have to. In all honesty, I'd rather you didn't come. It's going to be difficult enough handing that ship over, but having you up there as a witness will make it even worse. You know what she means to me.'

'I understand,' Campion said. 'This is something you'd rather do on your own.'

'I'll be all right once I'm back down. I just wanted you to know where I was going. I promise I'll be fine.'

'Don't let those machines take anything that isn't part of the deal.'

'I won't, trust me.'

He got up and kissed me, holding me tight until I forced myself free. 'They'll regret this, one day,' he said. 'They'll see that they did the wrong thing. Betony probably knows it already – Cyphel's death has put everything else into perspective. But he can't back down, not now the offer's already been made to the robots.'

'If they bring her back with a scratch on her, there'll be hell to pay.'

He smiled. 'That's the spirit. Now go up there and get it over and done with.'

I kissed him again; our hands linked and then parted. I turned to Betony, whom I sensed had been watching us.

'I'm going up to my ship, to sign her over to the robots. I presume you have no objections?'

'Of course not,' he said, then looked back at Mezereon, as if he could not quite meet my eyes. Feeling a flicker of triumph, I walked away from the auditorium, my back straight, my head held high, to the landing stage. My shuttle was there by the time I arrived, and I did not have long to wait for the robots, or their golden cargo.

We lifted from Ymir without incident. I watched the spires fall away, curving the shuttle around so that I caught a fleeting view of the auditorium. Mezereon's array of panes glittered in the sun, spangles of light flashing from the two hundred and fifty-six facets that had once been a single human being. I caught a glimpse of a tiny black-clad figure stalking between the panes, and then the ruby discharge of an energy-pistol, and then another tower swung into place to block my line of sight. I pushed the shuttle higher and was soon knifing into the high, thin layers of atmosphere where we had played out Cyphel's life. Behind me, the robots stood on either side of their fallen kinsman, who was resting horizontally between them. Their hands were pressing into him, one on each shoulder. As I had noticed when they had attempted to commune with him previously on *Silver Wings of Morning*, it was as if the gold armour of his skin had become as malleable as clay.

I instructed the shuttle to match position and speed with my ship's polar orbit. *Silver* came quickly into view, enlarging with frightening rapidity until the shuttle braked viciously to avoid the collision that until the absolute last moment had appeared inevitable. Inside, we felt nothing of that brutal slowdown. The shuttle sent a command for the cargo bay to open and we slipped inside the lovely chrome swan that had been my ship for so long. Selecting manual controls, I guided the shuttle through the maze of parked vehicles until I found the vacant docking berth I had used on my last visit. Field clamps locked it home; I set the drive to idle and we disembarked.

Cadence and Cascade carried Hesperus; I strode ahead of them, walking through a good half-kilometre of bay until we reached the nearest whisking chamber.

'Welcome, Purslane,' said *Silver Wings*, speaking directly into my head. 'I see you are accompanied. Are they guests, or are you being coerced?'

I am being coerced, I thought sourly, *but by the Line, not these innocent machines*. 'They're friends of mine,' I said aloud. 'Please make them welcome. Cadence is the silver one, Cascade the white one.'

'Welcome, Cadence and Cascade.'

'Hesperus you know,' I said. 'He's still unwell, but the robots are going to take him somewhere where he can be healed. In a little while I'll be assigning command authority to the robots, so you'll have a good chance to get to know them better.'

'Are you disposing of me, Purslane?' *Silver Wings* asked, still in my head.

'Not by choice. We'll talk about it on the bridge. If all goes well, we'll see each other again, in half a million years or so.'

The whisking chamber was large enough to receive cargo, and therefore easily spacious enough for me and the three robots. I began to tap our destination into the hovering go-board, then looked back at my guests and hesitated. 'Hesperus whisked, so I'm assuming you can do it as well. That was before he was injured, though. Will he be all right? We can walk if you like, but the bridge is a good fifteen kilometres away.'

'We can whisk,' Cadence said. 'Hesperus will come to no harm.'

'If you're sure.'

A grid of lights in the chamber's walls flashed red to signify that the whisking field was about to activate, and that we should confine ourselves to the area indicated on the floor. There was a moment's bright rush – a subliminal sense of being syringed down swerving, chicaning tubes – and then, less than an eyeblink later, we were standing in the counterpart to the first chamber, fifteen kilometres up-ship.

'Has there been a mistake?' Cascade asked, looking into the echoing, gloomy concourse onto which the whisking chamber had opened. 'This does not resemble the bridge I had imagined.'

'The bridge is still a little way from here,' I said. 'There used to be a direct link between the cargo bay and the bridge, but that wasn't a very good idea – it made the ship too vulnerable to attack by infiltrating parties. It was like putting an express elevator between the city gates and the mayor's office – asking for trouble.'

'Do we have far to go now?'

'Just a stroll.' The concourse was ringed by whisking chambers. I pointed to the one opposite us and set off at a brisk pace, leading the robots across a bridge. Above and below, rising and plunging to similarly dizzying vanishing points, stretched a shaft filled with slowly moving anvil-shaped mechanisms. Local gravity here was aligned with *Silver Wings'* long axis, so the shaft ran most of her length, until it butted against the mountainous bulkhead of the cargo bay. The machines were engaged in a never-ending process of repair and overhaul.

Every sixth whisking chamber was designed for cargo as well as people. The rest were only large enough to take one or two people at once, but there were enough of those to accommodate hundreds of simultaneous journeys. Although her origins were buried almost beyond recall, it was evident from the capacity of her whisking system – which pre-dated the redesign to prevent boarders – that she had once been intended to carry millions of passengers. I sometimes wondered if my ship pined for those days when her halls and atria, her vast concourses and plazas, teemed with human life. Now all she ever had was me, and a handful of guests if she was lucky. We rattled around like ghosts in an empty mansion.

We reached the other whisking chamber. I tapped the go-board, knowing that in a few moments we would be on the bridge and that there would be no further reason to delay handing over the ship. I had been steeling myself for it ever since we had left Neume, to the point where I had begun to think I could sail through it without an emotional hiccup. But now that the time was almost upon me I felt a tightening in my throat. This was not going to be as easy as I had thought.

The room's wall flashed red. The whisk would be a short one this time – it would feel like an instantaneous translation between the two chambers.

Something happened.

I think I must have blacked out for a moment, because there was a stall in my thoughts that had nothing to do with the process of whisking. In that stall I appeared to have been pushed violently out of the region of influence of the field, so violently that I had hit the floor and was now lying in a shocked heap, not so much in pain as waiting for the pain to arrive, which I knew with certainty it was

321

about to do. I coughed for breath and groaned. I still had no idea what had happened, but as my blurred eyes resumed some focus I made out a golden form looming over me, a form that was unmistakably Hesperus, who was unmistakably alive.

Cadence and Cascade had vanished.

'We must leave,' Hesperus said, leaning down to pick me up off the floor. 'We must leave and leave quickly.'

Bruised as I was, I did not have the impression that anything was actually broken – the pain was too diffuse for that. 'Hesperus,' I said, relieved and bewildered in equal measure. 'What—'

'There isn't time to discuss it here. I pushed you out of the transit field just as it reached operating strength. Cadence and Cascade went on as intended. They've arrived at the far end.'

'The bridge,' I said, my voice hoarse. I was standing, though not without Hesperus's assistance.

'Can we return to the cargo bay from this chamber?'

My eyes were still blurry, my thoughts still addled. 'No ... got to get to the other side, over the bridge.'

'Very well. May I carry you? It will be faster.'

I do not recall if he waited for my answer. His golden arms swept me up and held me securely. Hesperus started walking, then the walk became a pounding, superhumanly fast run. We crossed the shaft where the anvil-shaped machines rose and fell according to their own unfathomable agendas, and then we were in the whisking chamber. Hesperus touched the go-board. The ship accepted the command, still recognising him as a valid guest. We slammed to the other end of the ship, to the chamber at the entrance to the cargo bay.

'What's happening?' I asked, as some of the fog began to lift.

'I tricked Cadence and Cascade,' Hesperus said as we entered the cargo bay. 'They were lying about their intentions.'

'They wanted my ship. I was about to give her to them. What's to lie about?'

'I don't know yet. All I know is that they've no intention of returning me to the Monoceros Ring. When they interfaced with me just now they were doing their best to kill me.'

Hesperus had ... loosened, somehow – his voice was the same, but the speech had become more colloquial, less rigid and precise than before.

'Why would they want to kill you?'

'When they interfaced with me aboard your ship, their intention was to suck information out of me and leave me dead. Then they would lie and say I had died from my earlier injuries. They failed then – I was stronger than they expected, and they couldn't be too obvious about what they were doing. Unfortunately, they left me too weakened to communicate my fears to you. Later, they were overjoyed that you wanted to convey me to the Spirit of the Air.'

'Because they thought you'd die there instead.'

'Which I didn't. When I returned from the Spirit there was still a spark of life in me. As we lifted from Neume, they tried once more to kill me. They were doing their best to track down that spark of life and extinguish it. It took all of my resources and cunning to fend them off without looking as if I was fending them off. I succeeded, obviously, or I would never have surprised them the way I did.' My golden conveyor paused. 'Are you having problems with your eyes, Purslane?'

'Everything's a bit foggy.'

'I had to shove you very hard. It's likely that you burst some capillaries in your eyes. You may even have suffered a detached retina. I'm sorry I couldn't warn you, or prepare you for the shock. Speed was unfortunately of the essence.'

'I still don't understand ... why are they lying?'

'When they interfaced with me, I saw a little way into their minds as well. They were glad that you complied with their request, Purslane, but if you had obstructed them, or given them cause for delay, I do not think they would have hesitated to kill you. Your only consolation is that it would have been spectacularly, mercifully fast.'

I had too many questions to know where to begin, but all I could do was ask them one at a time. 'What's happened to them now?'

'I intervened before you had assigned control to them. Unless I'm mistaken, they are currently marooned at the other end of the whisking tube, in the bridge.'

'You're right. They won't be able to whisk, not without my say-so.'

'Will the ship assign authority to them without your permission, even if it's only to use the whisks, or open sealed doors?'

'No – we should be all right. They're effectively prisoners in the bridge. If they start to damage it, to try and force their way out, she should detect what they're doing and treat them as harmful elements.'

'She'll eject them?'

'Not unless I tell her to. But she'll definitely lock them down with restraining fields.'

'That may not hold them for very long – they are a lot stronger, a lot more resourceful, than you probably realise.' Hesperus's voice took on a graver tone. 'You must ask *Silver Wings* to eject them now, Purslane. If she can't eject them, she must destroy them.'

'It isn't that easy.'

'You can issue the command from here, can't you?'

'That's not the point. I can't just kill the robots, or throw them into space – that's not how it works.'

'They are not what they claim to be.'

'But I only have your word for that.' I groaned, as much in frustration as discomfort. 'I don't mean it like that, but a couple of minutes ago you were dead. How do I know you aren't suffering the after-effects of whatever happened to you on Neume? Those robots are guests of the Line. How do you think it'll look if I go back down to Neume and say I tossed them into space?'

'I wouldn't lie,' he said.

'Hesperus, see it from my side. You're asking me to take a vast amount on faith.'

'You trusted me before.'

'It's not that I don't trust you now, just that I need a little time to think things over. You're different – you even sound different, more like a human. How do I know something else hasn't changed?'

'More has changed than you can possibly imagine – I am still Hesperus, but I am also much more than he ever was. And I am telling you that you must act against Cadence and Cascade.'

'They can't do anything from the bridge. I can consult with the Line, see what action needs to be taken.'

'There isn't time. Those robots didn't need you to assign them control of this ship – it was just a step that saved them a certain amount of difficulty. It has been several minutes since they arrived – centuries, in machine terms. By now, they are likely to be well advanced in their efforts to achieve direct control. They have probably already explored and discarded thousands of stratagems for gaining command. They will have thousands more to try. Sooner or later, one of them will succeed. There is always a back door.'

'They won't get control of her.'

'They will, given time – time that may now be measured in minutes, or even seconds. She is big, she is old, but they are clever and resourceful. If I was there, I could do it as well, and there are two of them.'

'If you're wrong, and I'm shown to have acted against Machine People—'

'The blame will be all mine – and I can be very, very persuasive. Do it, Purslane. Time is not on your side. I am.'

'Put me down,' I said. 'I can't do this while you're carrying me around.'

Hesperus slowed and placed me on the deck. The unlit ships and obscure machines of the cargo bay loomed around us, heavy with the past.

'*Silver*,' I said, 'can you hear me?'

The voice in my head answered, 'I can hear you, Purslane.'

'Cadence and Cascade – the two guests I introduced to you before.'

'Yes, Purslane?'

'Are they on the bridge now?'

'Yes, Purslane.'

'Show them to me.'

A picture appeared before me, hanging in the darkness. The robots were on the bridge. They were standing quite still, side by side with their hands at their sides.

'They don't look as if they're doing anything,' I said.

'They wouldn't,' said Hesperus.

The words came to me with difficulty. '*Silver*, I want you to immobilise them.'

'Do they pose a threat, Purslane?'

'Yes,' Hesperus said.

'Just immobilise them for now. Use impassors to hold them where they are.'

'It is done, Purslane.'

The robots looked just the same. Nothing about them gave the slightest clue that they were now pinned in place, bracketed by a sheath of constraining forces.

'They can't do anything now,' I said to Hesperus.

'They can do everything they could do before. They are reaching out with their minds, trying to find a crack in your ship's defences. She won't even know they're doing it. They're that clever. When they succeed, Purslane, their very first act will be to disarm those immobilisers. Nothing you can say or do will bring them back up again. Cadence and Cascade will have free run of your ship – or more precisely *their* ship, since they will own her – and there will be nothing you can do to stop them. Within seconds they will have entered the whisking system, and seconds after that they will be in this room.' Hesperus turned his head towards the door through which we had entered. 'There is one of me, and two of them. I will do what I can to protect you, but the odds are not in my favour. Even now.'

'Even now?' I asked, sensing an oddness in his tone.

'Never mind. Please take me at my word, Purslane. We have been through a lot together. It would be a shame to end it all now, wouldn't it? Especially when we have so much to talk about.'

I felt as if there was a boulder lodged in my throat. 'I should consult ... I can be in touch with Campion, or Betony, in a few seconds—'

'They will tell you to ignore me. From their perspective, it's a perfectly rational standpoint. But you do not have that luxury. You are *in* this situation and I am telling you that those robots are seconds away from gaining control of your ship. They must be destroyed now, or ejected.'

'This is a hard one, Hesperus.'

He was speaking faster now, as if he sensed that he had only moments to make his case. 'How did they come to Neume, Purslane? Did you ever investigate that?'

'Of course. Sainfoin brought them. They were her guests.'

Hesperus must have read that crack of doubt opening in my face. 'Sainfoin didn't bring them,' he said. 'She may have thought she did, but that's not how it would have happened. They would have sought her out. They wanted to come here – I sensed that very clearly. They have business with Gentian Line, but their arrival had to look serendipitous. She was their puppet, not the other way around.'

'She said she met them at a reunion of Dorcus Line.'

'They would have been counting on a Gentian dropping by. If no one had, they would have found a more circuitous route to reach you. But their ultimate goal was to attend your reunion.'

'What are they?'

'Purslane! No more questions!'

I nodded once. He had not persuaded me completely – far from it. But my natural inclination was to trust Hesperus and he was right about Sainfoin. There was something else as well – a kind of commanding gravitas about him that had not been there before, for all that his mannerisms of speech were less formal than before he had fallen ill.

'*Silver*,' I said, my voice shaky, 'take the immobilised guests and eject them into space.'

'Are you certain, Purslane? This is a *very* unusual order.' By which the ship meant it was not something she ever recalled me asking of her, in all the circuits I had been master.

'Yes. Certain. Give them enough of a shove to keep them from falling into the atmosphere for at least a hundred orbits. They'll come to no immediate harm.'

'Executing the order, Purslane.'

I waited for *Silver Wings* to tell me that the robots had been ejected.

And waited.

'This is not a good sign,' Hesperus said. He picked me up again and started running. Beneath me his legs became a blur of pistoning gold. '*Silver*,' I said, raising my voice above the roar of the wind as Hesperus raced through the bay. 'Confirm execution of last order.'

No answer came.

'You've lost the ship,' Hesperus said.

'No,' I said, refusing to accept it. All around, *Silver Wings* looked exactly the way she always had.

'You mustn't blame yourself. You gave the order eventually. It's quite probable that the machines had already taken over your ship when you asked for them to be immobilised. They may just have been curious as to your intentions.'

'And now?'

'I think they will try to kill you, and to destroy me. It is my hope that we can reach the shuttle first.'

'And then what?'

'Leave, and hope that we are not fired upon by *Silver Wings*' defences before we have a chance to get away.'

It was not far to the shuttle from that point, but it might as well have been kilometres as far as I was concerned. We passed many other ships that might have been equally useful, had they been powered-up and tested for flight. The temptation was to get inside one of them and bring it to life. *Silver*'s jurisdiction reached into the cargo bay, but not into the ships inside it. With armour between us and the robots, we might last long enough to escape. But the shuttle was working, and I had left it idling, ready to be flown at a moment's notice. When we reached it, Hesperus lowered me to the decking and I told the shuttle to open and admit us. As the hull sealed behind us, I allowed my anxiety to drop down a notch.

Inside, despite my bruises and the fogginess that still afflicted my vision, I raced to the front and took the manual piloting position, thrusting out my hands like a knight waiting to be gauntleted. The shuttle formed its controls and pushed them obligingly into my hands. I disengaged the docking clamps and increased the drive from idle to taxiing power, sufficient to get us out of the cargo bay. I swung the shuttle's wedge-shaped nose around until we were facing the rectangular aperture of the open space door, visible in the gaps between a thicket of ships stretching nearly seven kilometres into the distance. I had kept the door open after our arrival, knowing that I would soon be moving ships through the atmosphere curtain.

'I think we can get out,' I said, easing the shuttle forward. If I had had a clear line to the door I could have applied more power, but as it was I had to pick my way through the forest of ships and their docking cradles. Too fast, and I would risk colliding with something bigger and stronger than the shuttle, something fixed so firmly into place that it would be like ramming a cliff.

'They know what we're trying to do,' Hesperus said.

'How do you know?'

'The door is closing.'

I looked, but I could not be certain that the aperture was any narrower than when we had started. It was difficult to tell, with the angle changing all the time as I steered the shuttle around obstacle after obstacle. 'Are you sure, Hesperus?'

'Absolutely. Would you like me to pilot?'

'I'm doing fine, thank you.'

'I will be faster. I am not disadvantaged by a peripheral nervous system. There is as much processing power in my thumb as in your entire skull.'

'Thanks.'

'It's a simple statement of fact. I can get us to the door sooner, provided you assign piloting authority to me.'

Now it was clear even to me that the door was narrowing after all. The rectangle of space framed by the aperture was still three kilometres wide, but it looked much less than two kilometres in height. One and a half, maybe less.

I snatched my hands from the instruments and said, 'Assign temporary control authority to my passenger, to be rescinded at my command.' Then I flounced back from the console and said, 'There. It's yours. Make this count, because I was getting us there.'

Hesperus stepped into place, his broad back between me and the console. 'Thank you, Purslane. I shall do my utmost.'

We got faster. We got *much* faster, swerving around obstacles, diving through the gaps between docking supports, skimming past obstructions with what looked like only millimetres of clearance. Hesperus was making such rapid course adjustments that the nullifiers were struggling to catch up. I felt the push and pull of inertia: phantom fingers eager to turn me into a pulp, if only they could get a good enough grip.

'The door is closing more quickly,' Hesperus said, sounding outrageously calm even though his hands were a manic blur, like a conjuror speeded up. 'They must have sensed our escape intentions and activated some emergency override.'

'Can you go faster?'

'By accepting an element of risk. I don't think we have a lot of choice at this point, do we?'

'Do what you have to do. I'm just going to stand back here and close my eyes.'

'Next time, it might be a good idea to park closer to the door.'

'I was thinking of you. I thought it would be a good thing if Cadence and Cascade didn't have so far to carry you to the whisking point, in case you were still vulnerable to damage.'

'Then I bow to your thoughtfulness, and apologise for my uncalled-for criticism.'

Hesperus cut a few more corners, literally and metaphorically. The shuttle bumped and jarred as it shaved past some of the obstacles, just clipping them. I do not know if that was accidental on his part, or a trade-off he had factored into his calculations. All I knew was that we were going faster, but that the door was closing even more determinedly, squeezing down until there was now only a dark slot of space through which we were hoping to pass.

At last, Hesperus cleared the main forest of obstructions, leaving us with only a two-kilometre sprint to the aperture. The door was still narrowing, but he could accelerate harder now. The walls of the cargo bay slid by on either side at a quickening rate, and I dared to hope that we were going to make it.

I was wrong. All of a sudden, the shuttle bucked and swayed, as if it had run into a screen of invisible netting. The walls moved by less quickly. Hesperus applied more power, but the shuttle was getting slower, not faster. Scarlet warnings flashed across the console, and a chime began to sound with monotonous regularity.

'What's wrong?' I asked.

'Drive-field intermesh,' Hesperus said, rotating his head to look back over his shoulder. 'It's what I feared the most. *Silver Wings of Morning* must have engaged her parametric engine. The field effects are interfering with each other, and I'm afraid the shuttle is losing the battle.'

'Can't you do anything?'

'You know better than that, Purslane. If I push the engine harder, it will either deactivate because of safety overrides, or rip itself to pieces. I'm not sure I'd care to bet on which outcome would be the more likely.' Hesperus worked the controls again, more slowly this time. 'I'm sorry, Purslane, but I think they have us.'

'The door's nearly closed. Even if you got the engine working again, it wouldn't help us.'

Silver Wings must have been changing her course. As the door narrowed further, the dayside of Neume came into view. The planet was growing visibly smaller. One minute of acceleration at a thousand gees was sufficient to put eighteen thousand kilometres between us and our point of departure. After the second minute, we would have travelled seventy-two thousand kilometres – twice the circumference of Neume. Everyone I knew, everyone I cared for, everyone who cared for me, was on that dwindling planet. I had to resist the urge to reach out for it, to try to hold on as our acceleration ripped it away.

The door closed. Hesperus dropped the engine to idle.

'We're in a lot of trouble, I'm afraid.'

The air resistance of the pressurised chamber had brought us to a halt. 'We can't just float here,' I said.

'There's a vacant berth to our right. I'll risk a little power to bring us in.'

The console flashed its warning and sounded the accompanying alarm, but Hesperus managed to guide us in, letting the shuttle thud into its restraints. The field clamp locked us home.

'We must be leaving the Neume system,' he said. 'This is one of the fastest ships in your Line, isn't it?'

'Especially now that there are only fifty-one of us left. That's why Cadence and Cascade wanted her so badly.'

'That's what I feared. It will be difficult for any of your fellow shatterlings to catch up with us, especially given the element of surprise.'

'We can't just give up, go along for the ride. We don't even know where we're being taken.'

'I doubt very much that the robots have any intention of taking us along for the ride. Once they have cleared the system, and dealt with any would-be pursuers, I think it very likely that they will turn their minds to us.'

'And?'

'They'll find a way to eliminate us. I'll do my best to protect you, but there is only one of me.'

'What do they want?'

'To go somewhere.'

'They didn't have to come all the way to Neume just to find a ship. If what you're saying is right, then they'd been planning all this long before the ambush took place.'

'So it would appear.'

He had turned from the console. His golden mask was as neutrally handsome as ever, his expression one of kindness, but beyond that there was nothing for me to read.

'You know more than you're telling me, Hesperus. I got that impression from the moment you woke up. What happened back there, on Neume?'

'We should review our situation,' he said, ignoring my question. 'Does this shuttle have abeyance devices?'

'No. You'd never need them.'

'That's what I thought. It will serve for now, but we may be better off moving to a larger, more readily defended craft. If you have something with weapons and real-thrust motors, we may be able to force our way out of the cargo bay. Is there such a ship?'

'Let me think. Those are pretty thick doors – it's going to take more than a laser or two to get through them.'

'See what you come up with.'

'All right,' I said, flustered, my mind still having trouble catching up with recent events. I had been dreading the handing over of *Silver Wings*, but now I would have gone through with that gladly, rather than find myself a prisoner on my own ship. 'This is all a bit sudden, Hesperus. You're going to have to make allowances. I have a peripheral nervous system and it takes me a while to adjust to radical paradigm shifts.'

'I can forgive you anything, Purslane.' He turned to the console and made a few more adjustments. 'I'll keep the drive on idle, just in case an opportunity presents itself. I don't think we should count on it, though.'

'I'm not. Do you think the others will have noticed our departure by now?'

'Almost certainly.'

'And?'

'They'll be struggling to make sense of it. It may cross their minds that you are the one stealing the ship, not the robots.'

'They wouldn't think that.' But even as I said it, I knew he was right. 'I should have called down to Campion.'

'They'd have assumed you were fabricating details, making out that the robots were up to no good.'

'They were.'

'No one on Neume would have known that.'

'Except Campion. He'd have trusted me. He'd have believed me, no matter how outlandish it sounded.'

'Then I am sorry you were not able to contact Campion. But in the long run it would have made very little difference.' Hesperus put a golden hand on my shoulder, his fingers cold and hard, but also gentle. 'It would probably have been futile. If the robots had already seized control of the ship before you attempted to eject them – as I am increasingly convinced they had – then they would have had no qualms about blocking your efforts to contact Neume.'

I closed my blurred, tired eyes, wanting the whole universe to fold itself into a bundle and go and hide in the corner. But when I opened them again, Hesperus and the universe were still waiting to say something.

'I'm scared,' I said. 'There's never been a time when I wasn't in control. Even when we went to the Spirit, that was our choice.'

'It happens to us all eventually.' He moved his hand from my shoulder and as quick as lightning touched his thumb and forefinger to my eyelids. I would have flinched had he been slower, but all I felt was a touch of metal, a spike of intense cold too brief to be called pain, and then his hand was lowering.

'I have repaired your eyes. You had a partially detached retina in the right eye. There was capillary damage in both. I trust your vision will be clearer now.'

Miraculously, it was.

'What did you just do?'

He held up his left hand, letting me see the forefinger. Between the gold nail and the quick, a tiny, harpoon-like structure emerged. It was a many-barbed thing of fractal complexity, its details vanishing down to a purple-gold haze as if the thing was simultaneously shifting in and out of focus, or indeed reality. 'I fixed you,' Hesperus said simply. 'It wasn't difficult.'

'Could you always do that?'

'From the moment I met you.'

'But there's more, isn't there? You're different, since you came back.'

'I can't do anything I couldn't do before, but I see things in a new light. And I know much, much more.'

'Because the Spirit restored your memory?'

'That too.'

'But not only that.'

'I learned a great many things, Purslane. I am still coming to terms with some of them.'

'But now isn't the time to talk about all that.'

'Not until you've decided whether we stay here, or try to reach one of the other ships.'

'That has to be my decision, doesn't it?'

'I know many things, but only you know the contents of this bay. Think carefully, Purslane, because a lot may hinge on your decision.'

'So,' I said, 'no pressure, then.'

PART SIX

PART SIX

'Milady,' Daubenton said, stooping as he entered my chamber, 'I bring you grave intelligence.'

It had been a fortnight since I had touched the blood-bound needle to my finger. I had expected Calidris to make his way to the Palace of Clouds within two or three days, four or five if one allowed for the difficulty of crossing open ground with Mordax's spies keeping watch. After a week, I had begun to have qualms. By the end of the second I had begun to resign myself to the unpalatable possibility that Calidris was already dead. It had, after all, been a very long while since I had heard from him. But when he presented me with the blood-bound needle, he had told me that it would only work magically if he was still alive. I had felt no pain when the blood was drawn; I should have felt at least a prick if Calidris was no longer of this world.

'Tell me this news, Daubenton. Calidris is dead. He was caught trying to return to the Palace of Clouds.'

'Calidris lives, if our agents are to be believed. Milady, we have committed a terrible error.'

I put down my mirror and brush. I had been attending to my hair, sitting by a window of coloured glass inlaid with pretty designs.

'I do not understand.'

'It would appear that Calidris was already a prisoner of Mordax when you summoned him. He had been caught by one of the count's raiding parties, one of a larger party of men. They were blacksmiths, artisans of some ability, so were not put straight to the sword. Mordax would rather enslave such men and have them equip his armies. Calidris had disguised himself well, and used blocking spells to mask his own magical talents. A difficult, dangerous venture – but it was working. Even Mordax's sorcerers were hoodwinked. He could not have kept the ruse up indefinitely – it was costing him an indescribable effort – but it would have sufficed to protect him while he was under direct scrutiny. Later, when the men were put to work equipping Mordax's army, Calidris would have contrived his escape.'

'Pray tell me what else our spies have learned.'

'Calidris was seen by one of these men at the moment the needle went in. The man recognised the presence of magic: blood had appeared on Calidris's finger without cause, and Calidris's pain was disproportionate to the injury. In the same instant, he lost his control of the blocking spells: they required a constant, taxing effort of the mind. The man became frightened. He summoned guards and told them what had happened. Calidris was separated from the common blacksmiths and brought to Count Mordax. By then, Mordax's own magicians had become alerted to the presence of a powerful new mind in the Black Castle. Calidris was unmasked. He was shackled and gagged before he could work magic against his captors.'

I looked at Daubenton with practised scepticism. 'Our spies told you this? If we have such men, why do we not already have the Black Castle?'

'We also have this,' Daubenton said, sidestepping the question. He offered me a letter. I shuddered at the black-grilled seal. It was another communication from my stepbrother. I tore it open and read Mordax's gloating account of how he had captured Calidris.

'"You think I can't turn him,"' I read, '"but you're wrong. Anyone can be turned. Palatial turned me. I thought I was stronger than the game; that I could become Mordax without inheriting the mantle of his personality and his past. I was wrong about that, as you will be wrong about Calidris. I will tell him that you betrayed him for the return of your lady-in-waiting; that I asked you to give me proof of his identity. He will not believe me at first, but I have seen how men break. Time will erode his old loyalties and turn him to the will of the Black Castle. And then a magic beyond anything in your experience will be unleashed upon the Kingdom."'

I looked at Daubenton with ice in my veins. 'We have failed. It's all over.'

His eyes were heavy-lidded from too little sleep. Chamberlain Daubenton, Master-at-Arms Cirlus, his soldiers and my highest ministers had thought of little but Calidris and the Black Castle these last days.

'Perhaps Calidris will have the strength of will not to turn against us.'

'No man has ever resisted. You saw what Count Mordax wrote in his letter, Daubenton – do not pretend you did not open and reseal

338

it before it reached my hands. Palatial has changed him. I know what he was like before he went in.'

'Palatial, milady?'

For an instant I had felt on the verge of some transforming knowledge, a secret that would put all our problems into a different, less harrowing perspective. It was as if I was a player on a stage who had become so consumed by the role they were acting that they had forgotten that the whole enterprise was for show. Burdened with the weight of their character's problems, they had had a moment of epiphany, a realisation that it was merely a performance, a disguise that they could step out of whenever they chose. I had been troubled by many such moments lately – a feeling that I was inside a theatre, that none of my actions were of wider consequence beyond its panelled green walls. Sometimes a word or phrase – Palatial, ram-scoop ship, Lesser World – felt like an ominous key, one that was about to unlock great and troubling mysteries. Fortunately – for they could easily have become a distraction from the matter at hand – those moments always passed, leaving only a faint sense of mental disquiet.

'It is nothing, Daubenton. My point is simply that we cannot entrust the Kingdom to the hope that Calidris will be stronger than any man who has ever lived.' I hesitated, running my nails down the sharp edge of the letter. 'There has always been another we could turn to. When the possibility was first raised I dismissed it, as I was right to do given the state of our affairs at the time. Now events have taken an even more ominous turn, and I must reconsider. If Calidris's magic is to be used against us – as I fear it will be – we must have an equivalent ally.'

'You are speaking of Relictus, the failed apprentice.' Horror paled Daubenton's already sallow features. 'I did not agree with Cirlus, Milady. Relictus should stay where he is, until he rots.'

I was right about Calidris's magic, though it was months before we knew the truth of his defection. Realisation came when the Ghost Soldiers began to attack our men.

Count Mordax's one weakness had always been the size of his army – well equipped, well trained, ruthless in the execution of his orders, but stretched thin across too many campaigns, too many points of attack on the Kingdom's borders. Our army was more numerous, but (it could not be denied) less effective, and it was only this uneasy balance that had kept Mordax at bay. Had he been overwhelmingly stronger, Mordax would not have had cause to take a hostage, nor would he have had a use for Calidris. Mordax was a man of the practical arts, schooled in the bloodstained science of war, and he had an instinctive distaste for magic. Nonetheless I had never deceived myself that he would refrain from making full use of his new prize, if circumstances merited it.

At first all we knew of the Ghost Soldiers was reports from frightened, less-than-credible witnesses. A raiding party had burned one of the villages. The men wielding torches and pikes were the usual rabble dressed up to look like brigands. But riding with them, remaining outside the village while the burning took place, was an escort of armoured men on waif-thin horses, lean and fast as greyhounds. Only one of the men rode a heavy charger, and he was the only one with his visor raised. The other riders wore elaborately jointed armour, every inch of their bodies protected by metal. The man with the raised visor wore leather with metal plates sewn all over it. He appeared to be leading the other soldiers, those with their visors down, but he never gave a spoken command.

One of the villagers, driven beyond rage by the burning of his home, found the armoured riders and shot at them with a stolen bow. He fired six arrows into the riders, but they either bounced off their armour or wedged into the joints between the sections, without obvious harm to the rider. As the brigands left the village, the armoured men began to ride away to rejoin them. At that point the villager fired a seventh arrow and by lucky chance it found the flank of one of the horses rather than the rider. The horse bucked and threw the armoured man. He crashed to the ground, making no sound except that of crashing metal. Of the other riders, only the man on the heavy horse looked back. Then he swung his arm and the others galloped after him, oblivious to their fallen comrade.

The villager left his place of cover to examine the tumbled rider. What he found distressed him greatly. The armour had broken, one arm coming away from the torso. Yet there was no sign of injured flesh, and when the villager examined the remains he found only empty metal – a suit of armour with no man inside it. He understood then why the riders' horses had been so thin and fast. They had only needed to carry the weight of metal, not a man inside that armour.

Thus it was that we first learned of the Ghost Soldiers. Within weeks, reports of them were arriving from all over the Kingdom. They moved so quickly and with such agility that they could cross our borders where no force had ever done so before. They moved at night, as if it was day. Their horses smelled of death and corruption, as if they were the corpses of horses reanimated for this single purpose. They were never seen to graze or take water, and on the coldest eve no hint of breath escaped their lungs.

And they came in such numbers. Whatever magic Calidris was using against us required only the production of suits of armour. Our blacksmiths could have worked as industriously and it would have made no difference; we did not have enough able soldiers to fill that metal. Mordax could have as many as he needed.

I knew then that we needed Relictus; that I could listen to my qualms no more.

CHAPTER TWENTY-FIVE

I was stretching my legs on one of Ymir's bridges, transfixed by the snapping of the flags, their colours rippling against the sky, when Betony found me.

'Campion,' he said, lifting the black collar of his coat against the wind.

'Has Mezereon finished for the day?'

'This is about Purslane. We've just received some distressing news.'

The wind had not troubled me until then, but it chose that moment to reach my bones. 'What's happened?'

'All we know is that she went up to *Silver Wings* with the robots, all three of them. Now her ship's broken orbit, suddenly and without announcement. She's heading away from Neume, at what we believe to be the maximum safe acceleration for that ship.'

I grabbed at the bridge's handrail to stop myself reeling. The news had hit me like vertigo. 'How long ago?'

'Less than a quarter of an hour. I came as quickly as I could.'

'I need to get up there.'

'All shuttles have been tasked for immediate use. I'm taking mine in a few minutes – you're welcome to come with me. I can drop you aboard *Dalliance* before I rendezvous with *Adonis Blue*.'

I was so numb that I did not even acknowledge his offer. 'What about the other ships?'

'Three have already been dispatched, with no one aboard them. They've already broken orbit, so at least we have something in immediate pursuit of *Silver Wings*. They won't be able to catch up, but they'll be able to get within—'

'Weapons range,' I said, finishing his sentence for him.

'Nothing's set in stone, but we need to consider every option. It's unclear what's happened up there, Campion, but we do know it wasn't part of the plan. I'm not saying we shoot her down on sight –

that'll be the last thing we do. But if we can cripple *Silver Wings*, slow her down enough to draw alongside—'

'I know what you're thinking. But Purslane wouldn't have taken her own ship.'

'She didn't like being told to give it to the robots.'

'Would you have liked it, if it had been you instead of her?' I shook my head angrily. 'This isn't how Purslane does things. She was going to hand *Silver Wings* over to the robots and then come back down with her head held high.'

'So what's happened?'

'I never liked those robots.'

'You think they stole the ship?' Betony stared at me exasperatedly. 'They were going to get it anyway, Campion – why would they take it now, when all they had to do was wait until Purslane handed it over?'

'I don't know. I'm just saying – I didn't like them. And don't start accusing me of being machine-phobic. I didn't have a problem with Hesperus.' Then a thought barged to the front of my mind. 'Has anyone tried to talk to her?'

'First thing we did, as soon as she broke orbit. But Purslane hasn't replied.'

'That just proves she isn't involved.'

'It does?'

'Purslane wouldn't have left without contacting us, Betony – she'd have made damned sure we knew her feelings.'

'Perhaps she'll talk when she feels safe.'

'She isn't talking because she *can't* talk. Something's happened up there.' Slowly, the possibility of Purslane having been killed was beginning to dominate my thoughts, forming like a single dark cloud in an otherwise clear sky. I pushed it away reflexively, but it kept coming back. If for some reason the robots had decided to take the ship rather than wait for it to be handed over, they would have killed Purslane as soon as blink.

'I have to get up there,' I said again.

'We're going.' Betony reached out and took both my arms, holding me roughly above the elbows. 'Campion, listen to me very carefully. We've had our differences. I don't expect you to like me, or ever forgive me for what I did to Purslane. But understand that I had my reasons – I was thinking of the Line, of this incredibly fragile, incredibly rare thing that we hold between us. I had to show the importance of discipline, now more than ever. But it wasn't personal;

it wasn't done out of vindictiveness. And you know what? I admit I made a mistake by letting Mezereon run the interrogations. You saw that long before I did. I'm not infallible. But I'm not a monster, either. If you can forgive me for anything you think I did to you, or to Purslane, I am willing to put your slights, your cavalier attitude towards the Line, behind us. I am offering you the hand of friendship, the hand of forgiveness. If Purslane has done something wrong, she deserves a chance to redeem herself. If she hasn't, she deserves our help – absolutely and unconditionally. I will push my ship to the limit to catch up with her, and I know you will do the same. There are forty-eight other shatterlings who feel the same way.'

I waited a while, then said, 'Speech over?'

'I've said what I wanted to say. If you're with me, my shuttle is ready to take us into orbit. If you can't stand the thought of sharing a ride with me, I think Aconite or Tansy will be lifting off shortly.'

I gave the matter a few seconds' thought then said, 'Let's go.'

Line policy dictated that all of our ships should be in a condition of immediate flight-readiness, so that they would be able to break orbit and sprint for interstellar space the moment the patrols detected the approach of a hostile agency. The possibility of flight had been at the back of all our thoughts, in every waking instant on Neume. Between one hour and the next we might leave that world and never see it again.

But that did not mean that all the remaining ships would be joining the chase after *Silver Wings of Morning*. This was an unexpected development, but it was not a reason for an emergency evacuation – Galingale was out on patrol that day with his ship *Midnight Queen* and he had reported no troubling intruders; no hints of killer fleets braking down from interstellar speed. The Line would remain in session, albeit in depleted numbers. In any case, at least half of the thirty-five remaining ships were too slow ever to catch up with Purslane, and of the remainder there were fewer than ten that could even be considered to be in with a chance. Three were already on the way, flying without their owners. *Dalliance* would have been one of the slow ones had it not been for the upgrades she had received courtesy of Ateshga. Now she was a marginal case – to have a hope of catching *Silver Wings*, her engine would need to be pushed well into the red, and I had no idea what kind of design margin now applied.

'We've kept signalling,' Betony said as he brought his shuttle into whisking range of *Dalliance*, 'but there's still been no response. If the robots are in charge, they can't have any demands.'

'They don't need anything from us,' I said. 'Do we have a handle on the trajectory?'

'Heading in the galactic anti-centre, parallel to the plane. She may turn once she's reached interstellar space, but for now there's no reason to presume she isn't still headed for Machine Space.'

'There's something wrong about this, Betony.'

'The whole thing's wrong.'

'Whatever's happening here, it isn't Purslane's doing. Deep down, you know that.'

'It would surprise me if it was, but I've been surprised before.'

I thanked him for the ride and whisked over to *Dalliance*. Sensing my arrival, the ship brought herself to immediate flight-readiness. By the time I reached the bridge, the engine was chafing at the bit, ready for the chase.

It had all happened so quickly that I felt a sense of dreamlike unreality about the whole experience. In less than twelve hours, Purslane's ship would be travelling so close to the speed of light that the fastest ship ever built would still need a hundred thousand years to catch up with her. By the time it did, they would both be on the other side of the galaxy. The only possibility of reaching her lay in chasing now, with all safeguards thrown to the wind.

I assumed my command position, laid in a pursuit course and brought the engine to a thousand gees. Neume fell away like a stone dropped down a well. Like all worlds, it had felt as wide as the universe when I was standing on it, but now I saw it for the little silver pebble it really was – a small round rock floating in an infinitely larger void, barriered from vacuum by the thinnest gasp of an atmosphere.

For a few minutes I was alone, nothing within my immediate sensor reach, but then the other ships began to lock into formation around me, matching my acceleration for the time being. The three craft that lay ahead of us belonged to Charlock, Orache and Agrimony. Five ships followed. Mine was one of them; Betony's another. The other three belonged to Sorrel, Tansy and Henbane, with Charlock, Orache and Agrimony riding as passengers. Soon we would be accompanied by a sixth, for Galingale had broken off from his patrol duties to join the chase. He was pushing at twelve hundred gees, coaxing *Midnight Queen* to give up her last newton of pseudo-thrust.

Of all the ships that would eventually make up the pursuit squadron, his had the best chance of closing the distance on *Silver Wings of Morning*, even though he would not be able to match Purslane's cruise ceiling.

Within an hour we had put more than three light-minutes of space between us and Neume – it was now just a bright star astern, almost washed out by the light of its sun. With our engines stable, pushed to the currently agreed limit of a thousand gees, we gathered our ships close enough for realtime conversation. A circular table formed in my bridge, duplicating the one that would appear on the other craft. Imagos of my fellow shatterlings popped into existence around it. Except for Galingale, all of them were rendered solid. Galingale's smokiness was to remind us that he was still more than a minute down-range, and could not be expected to respond immediately to any point of debate.

'At noon, none of us expected to be in our ships before sundown, racing away from Neume,' Betony said. 'But say what you like about us, we've always been quick and adapatable when the moment forces it upon us. Charlock, Orache and Agrimony: thank you for dispatching your ships ahead of you. Rest assured that the Line won't forget your magnanimity.'

'Whisking's too dangerous, but if we can push to eleven hundred gees, even twelve, we can creep within shuttle range of our ships,' Orache said, her hands resting on the table before her. She had long, sharp fingernails, painted midnight black for Cyphel's funeral. 'I know I'd rather be aboard mine than sitting back here, watching her from a distance. The three ships are already too far downstream for effective realtime control, and mine carries no protocols for this situation.' Keeping her voice level, she added, 'I mean battle protocols, if it wasn't obvious.'

'We'll deal with protocols in a moment,' Betony said. 'First, I'd like Campion to speak. He knows Purslane better than any of us, and for once I don't intend that as a criticism. We're beyond that now. If he has insights, anything that might bear on this crisis, we should hear them.'

'I have no insights,' I said, 'except for what I've already told you, which is that this definitely isn't Purslane's doing. She's either dead, murdered by the robots, or she's their prisoner.'

'Why would the robots do this?' Charlock asked. 'They've nothing to gain by taking her prisoner, or even killing her. The ship was already theirs.'

'If Purslane chose to go against the Line—' Tansy began.

'She didn't,' I snapped back. 'I was with her just before she went up. She wasn't thrilled about losing *Silver Wings*, but she was resigned to it. She also wanted the robots to help Hesperus as best they could – if that meant donating her ship, she was happy to oblige.'

'Could she have been bluffing?' asked Sorrel, scratching at the fine, grey-flecked down of his beard. 'I'm sorry, but someone has to ask. If Purslane had this planned out in advance, she wouldn't have wanted you to know about it.'

'She wasn't bluffing.'

'You can't know that for sure. None of us are mind-readers. If she was sufficiently determined ...'

I stared Sorrel down. We had never crossed swords before, but neither had I ever counted him a close friend. 'Trust me: Purslane had no intention of taking her own ship.'

'We'll assume Campion's right for now,' Betony said. 'Our primary objective is stopping that ship. Once we've done that, once we've recovered her, we can work out what happened.'

'How do you propose to stop *Silver Wings*, short of destroying her?' Tansy enquired. 'Sorry, I probably could have put that better, but you can't just throw a rope around her and hope she slows down.'

'We'll aim to cripple her, without hurting anyone onboard,' said Betony. 'That's the best we can hope for now.'

'Has anyone tried signalling Purslane?' asked Charlock.

Betony nodded. 'We've been trying from the moment she broke orbit, but there's been no response.'

'Which proves nothing,' I said. 'If the robots have taken control, they're not going to have any interest in talking to us.'

'Do you think Purslane's still alive?' Tansy asked me.

'I hope so.'

'That's a non-answer.'

'It's the best I've got. Please don't press the point.'

To my relief, she chose not to.

'There's something we do need to consider, before engaging *Silver Wings*,' Orache said, tapping the tips of her nails against the ghost surface of the table. 'If the robots have taken control, we can assume that they're acting as agents of the Machine People. Firing on Purslane's ship, even with the intention of slowing her down, could be construed as a hostile act. Viewed from certain quarters, it could be interpreted as a declaration of war against the Machine People.'

'No one would be that stupid,' Agrimony said. 'This is an isolated incident, a ship taken without due explanation. We have every right to reclaim Line property.'

Orache's expression was steely, brooking no dissent. 'I said "from certain quarters". At the very least, we might be banished from the Commonality. I need hardly tell you how catastrophic that would be for Gentian Line, especially in this time of maximum need. At worst, we might provoke the robots into retaliatory action.'

'We'll justify our actions,' Betony said.

'Then you'd better hope someone's ready to listen. In between those outcomes is a spread of possibilities, almost all of them bad. Another Line might decide to attack us, just to show the robots where they stand. If a sufficient number of turnover civilisations decided to combine their forces against us, we might face difficulties.'

'We'll crush them, if they have the temerity,' Betony told her. 'If the Machine People turn on us, we'll crush them as well. They're fast and strong, but we've been around a lot longer than they have.'

I raised what I hoped was the voice of reason. 'Let's not get ahead of ourselves. There's a lot we don't know about those robots – a lot we don't know about the Machine People, for that matter.'

'What are you driving at?' Charlock asked.

'Just that we ought to keep open minds. We already have grounds to assume that it was my visit to the Vigilance that somehow caused the ambush in the first place. Doctor Meninx had his reasons for visiting the Vigilance; so did Hesperus. The same might also have applied to Cadence and Cascade.'

'They came to us, not the Vigilance,' Sorrel said.

'My point still stands. The Vigilance was suddenly the focus of lots of attention, and because of my strand we got entangled in the same affair. The machines may have decided it was in their interests to visit us instead.'

Sorrel looked unconvinced. 'I don't see why that would be the case. If the Vigilance is the thing everyone's interested in, why not go there directly?'

'The Vigilance won't deal with robots, only organic intelligences. Ask *them* why. Hesperus was planning to disguise himself as a human, but that would have involved considerable sacrifices for him, paring down his abilities until he could only just get by – he may never have succeeded. Cadence and Cascade may not have been prepared to go that far, or had already judged that there was too much risk of detection. Can you imagine how bad it would have looked if the

Machine People were found to be infiltrating human civilisations? That would probably have been enough to trigger a galaxy-wide diplomatic crisis, irrespective of anything we do. So they came to us instead, knowing that we'd obtained data from the Vigilance that was in some way sensitive. They were hoping to access the information through us, bypassing the Vigilance completely.'

Sorrel asked, 'You think they were paying us that much attention?'

'Someone was,' I said, with a weary shrug.

'You think there's a connection between the robots and the House of Suns?' Betony asked.

'Everything's connected,' I answered. 'That doesn't mean everyone's working towards the same goal.'

'I was prepared to believe that we might have incurred the wrath of another Line,' Betony said. 'That the ambush might have been our payment for something we did a dozen circuits ago, some careless act we barely gave a second thought to at the time.'

'But you don't feel that way now,' I said.

'Not if the machines are involved. And let's face it – they appear to be, don't they?' Betony glanced around at all of us. 'No disrespect to Sainfoin—'

'But it looks as if they used her to get to us,' I said. 'In which case whatever we're involved in is of direct interest to the Machine People. They sent Hesperus. I think they also sent Cadence and Cascade. The only question is, did they all have the same objectives?'

'If they all originated with the Machine People, can't we take that as read?' Sorrel asked.

'Not necessarily. The Machine People may be just as fractious as any human civilisation.' Just thinking through the permutations, trying to shuffle the evidence of recent events into some kind of rational structure, was making my head throb. I pressed fingers against my brow. 'All I'm saying is, Cadence and Cascade may have been following different orders from Hesperus, or been given more latitude to accomplish whatever it was they were sent to do.'

'From where I'm sitting, they didn't do very much at all,' Tansy said. 'Came to the reunion, survived the ambush, spent time on Neume and then agreed to return home with news of the attack. What am I missing?'

'Nothing,' I said. 'Apart from the fact that they had Hesperus with them when they left, which presumably wasn't a detail they'd planned for. Other than that, though – unless they were being sneakier than we realised – they didn't gain access to any of our secrets, or learn anything on Neume that we didn't learn as well. I don't even remember them paying much attention to the interrogations – I got the impression they were never particularly interested.'

'Maybe they already knew everything Grilse and the others were likely to say,' Charlock said.

'So if it wasn't our secrets, if it wasn't the information known by the prisoners, what were they after?' asked Sorrel.

'Something else, obviously,' I said. 'Something that's either staring us in the face, something so obvious that we can't see it, or something even we don't know about.'

'But which has something to do with us,' Charlock said.

Galingale's smoky image spoke for the first time. 'Excuse the interruption, but it seems to me that we're all agreed on one thing: this is not in character for Purslane. I'm with Campion: she's been duped by the robots. Let's not forget that they were the ones who first dropped hints that they needed a fast ship. It was just Purslane's bad luck that hers happened to fit the bill, and that she needed her wrists slapped.'

Betony stiffened his jaw, but didn't interrupt.

'She's a victim of circumstance here, nothing more. Luckily, this is Purslane we're talking about. She's smart and adaptable, and it's her ship that they've tried to steal. I'd imagine the chances are excellent that she's still alive. At the same time, we can't disregard the possibility that the robots may have gained control of *Silver Wings'* weapons. It may be something of a challenge to approach her.'

'There are safeguards, to prevent one Line ship firing on another,' Sorrel said.

After a minute, Galingale answered, 'None that can't be circumvented, if those robots are sufficiently resourceful. I just don't think we should be blind to the risks. But we have armour, impassors, weapons of our own and a clear numerical advantage. I propose that we disable acceleration safeguards on the three lead ships and let them get as close to Purslane as they can.'

Orache was indignant. 'I'm still planning on being aboard my ship.'

'Me too,' said Charlock.

'Ships can be replaced,' Galingale responded. 'The least of us is worth more than any ship.'

'And if this fails?' Betony asked. 'If we lose three ships, where does that leave us?'

'My ship has the best chance of closing the gap,' Galingale said. 'I also have armour and weapons the equal of anything else in the pursuit squadron. I'll be the next to go, if it comes to that.' He smiled tightly. 'You can be sure that I'm making this suggestion with a full appreciation of the consequences.'

'If you go in, we all go in,' I said.

'That's very noble of you, Campion, but we have to think of the Line – too much selfless bravery, too many heroic gestures, and there won't *be* a Line. To survive, we have to indulge in a little tactical cowardice.' Galingale smiled again – it was the smile of a man who did not place a high premium on his chances of seeing out another circuit. 'I'm not the bravest of men. None of us are natural cowards, of course, but we all have a healthy sense of self-preservation. Nonetheless, I have the fastest ship, so I am obliged to use her in the way that best benefits the Line.'

'You do nothing until we've closed the distance with the first three ships,' Betony said. 'Even then, no action is to be taken unilaterally.'

'So it's decided, then?' Orache asked. 'Our ships become expendable?'

'Better them than you,' Betony said, his tone of voice letting us all know that he considered the matter closed. 'We've held at a thousand gees since leaving Neume. Is there anyone who isn't prepared to increase to twelve hundred, as an emergency measure?'

None of us answered immediately; we all knew that we would be pushing our ships harder than we ever had before. Even if the engines held, we would be at the mercy of inertia nullifiers operating well outside their normal regime. There was a slow exchange of glances, a shared sense that we were in this together, prepared to shoulder a collective risk.

'I'll do it,' I said.

'We'll all do it,' Charlock said. 'All or nothing, the Gentian way.'

Hesperus turned from the console aboard my shuttle and shook his magnificent golden head. 'It isn't good, Purslane.'

'Could the shuttle have been damaged when we tried to escape?'

'I doubt that there is anything at fault with either the sending or receiving apparatus. Most likely, *Silver Wings* is blocking her signals, or obstructing the return signal from Neume or from the ships that we may be certain are following us.'

'It's just a shuttle,' I said, wondering how he could be sure that we were being pursued. We could not have been under way for more than three hours, by my reckoning. The Line took that long to have breakfast sometimes. 'Nobody ever imagined it would need to send a signal across more than a few seconds, or through another ship's drive field,' I said, gloom rising in me like a black tide.

Nothing was going to daunt my companion. 'I asked you to give some thought to moving to one of the other craft, if it could serve us better either as a place of sanctuary or a means of escape. Have you made a shortlist?'

Tiredness was beginning to dull my thoughts. It was still only early evening by Neume time, but I felt as if I had lived through several days since the robots' takeover. 'There are some possibilities.'

Hesperus crossed his massive gold arms. 'Good. Tell me about them.'

'There's a ship about two kilometres up-bay, back in the direction we came from.'

'So even further from the door?'

'Afraid so. But I've thought about all the ships in the bay and this is the one I keep coming back to. It's as if it's telling me to take shelter inside.'

'Can it keep us alive indefinitely?'

'It's an old ark, built by nascents. Some other civilisation found it drifting and refitted it with a stardrive and a few other bits and pieces. It should be able to send a signal beyond *Silver Wings*. It'll have power and functioning makers.'

'Abeyance devices?'

'I think so.'

'You think so.'

'I'm trying my best, Hesperus. It's been a while since I was last inside, but yes, there should be caskets – something I can use, anyway. I don't know about you.'

'I'll manage. We should leave now, before Cadence and Cascade turn their minds to us. Is there a maker inside this shuttle?'

'Only a small one. What were you thinking of?'

'I was hoping we might be able to make you a spacesuit, assuming there isn't one already aboard.'

'A spacesuit?'

'You may need one. We can't whisk to the other ship, and we can't count on the presence of air in your cargo bay.'

I blinked hard. 'I can't remember the last time I wore a spacesuit. No, wait . . . I got into one when I visited the Vigilance—'

'That was Campion, if I'm not mistaken.'

'Memory bleed. No, the maker won't be able to help us – it would have to assemble the suit in pieces. There might be one tucked away in the back hold, I suppose.'

'Do you consider it likely?'

'Not at all. A ship like this, you'd only ever need a spacesuit once in a million years.'

'Welcome to that moment. Go and look for a suit, but only spend two minutes doing so. If you haven't found one by then, we leave anyway.'

I went and looked, but in my hearts of hearts I knew it was hopeless. This ship had logged billions of hours of safe flight without ever putting its passengers in the embarrassing position of needing spacesuits.

'Once we are in the ark,' Hesperus said, 'it may be problematic to return here. Let us be certain that we are leaving behind nothing of value; nothing that can't be fabricated by the ark's makers.'

'There isn't anything. We don't even have an energy-pistol to our name.'

'Then we leave now. Give me explicit directions to the ship in question. Describe it well, and describe the boarding procedure.'

I did as I was asked. Hesperus nodded slowly. 'Yes. I remember passing that ship as we attempted our escape. There was a door thirty-eight metres from the bow. Are you certain it will permit me to enter?'

'There are no security seals in place. Why should there be? We're on my ship.'

'It was necessary to ask.' Hesperus returned his attention to the console. 'Go to the door and wait for me. I will be with you in a moment.'

'What are you doing?' I asked, as his hands worked the controls again.

'I am increasing power to the drive.'

I felt the shuttle buck in its restraints. 'We tried that. It didn't work.'

'I'll explain when we're on our way. There isn't time now.'

By the time I had lowered the ramp and made my way to the docking catwalk, Hesperus was done. I could hear the warning alarm sounding from the console. The shuttle was straining, but going nowhere.

'What did you just do?'

He strode down the ramp and palmed the control to retract it back into the shuttle and seal it from the outside. 'Let me carry you. The quicker we reach the ark, the better. We are almost certainly being observed.'

'This does nothing for my dignity.'

'That makes two of us.' Hesperus cradled me and accelerated quickly into his superhuman sprint, heading in the direction of the ark. His legs became a blur of gold, but the ride was as smooth as if we were levitating.

'Hesperus, what did you do to the engine?'

'As I have already mentioned, we are almost certainly being pursued. The shuttle's motor is now working against *Silver Wings'* parametric engine, causing a tiny decrease in drive efficiency.'

'You're right – it's tiny. That's like trying to slow down an ocean liner by dipping a twig in the water.'

'Nonetheless, we have many twigs.'

'I don't understand.'

'The bay is full of ships. When we are safely aboard the ark, I shall endeavour to turn on as many engines as possible. Even if I am only able to activate a few, it may negate *Silver Wings'* drive efficiency by as much as one or two per cent.'

'That's not going to make Cadence and Cascade very happy.'

'And if I could think of something to make them even less happy,

I would do it.' Hesperus paused, then said, 'Oh dear.'

'"Oh dear" what?'

'I just detected a micro-change in the air pressure.'

I looked behind him, back the way we had come. The bay door was beginning to open again, inching upward to reveal a narrow crack of interstellar space.

'The pressure curtain—' I said.

'They've deactivated it. Take a series of deep breaths, Purslane. I believe we are about to lose our atmosphere.'

The squall hit us a moment later with the force of nearly fifty cubic kilometres of air draining into vacuum. A noise that began quietly and distantly gradually increased in power until it was the sound of the universe being torn in two.

We still had at least a kilometre to go. I tried to speak, but I could not hear my own voice above the howl of the escaping air. Hesperus cradled me tighter and contracted his upper body around me, his legs seeming to move even faster. The gale became a solid wall of resistance, one that would have swept me into space had I not been anchored to Hesperus. I had no idea how he was keeping himself from being blown away – his feet must have been binding themselves to the catwalk with every tread.

From somewhere in the distance I heard a sound that, as impossible as it seemed, was even louder than the wind's roar. Through slitted eyes I saw one of my ships tumbling towards us, torn loose from its moorings. It was wheeling end over end, smashing into the larger vehicles which were still anchored. It was only a runabout, but it would pulverise us if it came our way. Just as I was thinking that, the loose ship jarred another one and sent that drifting, picking up speed as the wind tugged at its hull. The runabout dashed itself against the hull of an Eleventh Intercessionary scow, shattering like an old-boned carcass. Something came spinning towards us out of the wreck. I turned my head instinctively, as if that would do the slightest good. Hesperus let go of me with one arm, taking my full weight with the other, and I saw a flash of gold as he batted aside the spinning object. The remains of the runabout tumbled past, followed by the second ship it had knocked loose. I turned back in time to see the wreckage slip through the open door, and then I had to close my eyes against the stinging wind. I took another breath, and the air was thinner and colder than it had been before. The chamber was emptying itself even faster, as the door opened to its fullest extent. Then I took another breath and my lungs closed on nothing, like a fist reaching for a handhold that was no longer there.

I must have blacked out, although I do not remember the slide into unconsciousness. But when I came around, Hesperus was kneeling over me and we were somewhere warm and white and silent, somewhere with gravity, and I could breathe.

'We are in the ark. You lost consciousness, but I do not think any great damage was done. Do you feel all right?'

'No.'

'Perhaps that was not the best way to phrase the question.'

'I'll mend. How long was I out?'

'A few minutes, but you were only without air for ninety seconds. I was able to work the door as you instructed.' Hesperus patted the white wall behind him. 'You chose well, Purslane. This ship will serve as our sanctuary, for now at least.'

He helped me stand, his hands as gentle as a lover's.

'Are we all right now?'

'The ark has brought itself to life, so there is definitely power. All indications suggest that there is now a hard vacuum beyond the door. The rest will be revealed once you have shown me to the control centre.'

'I think the bridge is this way,' I said, indicating a passageway.

'Then lead on.'

We walked through the ark, taking twisting and turning white corridors until we reached the dome-shaped bulge above her whale-like bows where the bridge was situated. Along the way we passed the ancient galleries that would once have held sleepers, ranked row upon row like stone figurines on a cathedral wall. Now all that remained were the coffin-shaped alcoves where the sleeper equipment had once fitted. The civilisation that had converted the ark – nearly as forgotten as the one that had made the ship in the first place – had intended the galleries to be used for freight or recreation, widening the doors accordingly. Other galleries had been filled with the elephantine machinery of the ark's stardrive and associated systems, which filled fully a third of the available volume. I could not remember whether her remaining cargo holds were empty, or crammed with more of my junk.

The bridge was a circular room with a low, dish-shaped ceiling. Padded, lounge-like seats in white leather surrounded a circular command core, with a transparent display sphere poised above it. Branching white control stalks emerged from the core, ending in squeezable bulbs or delicate, trigger-like grips. Illumination was provided by floating baubles. There were no windows – the walls were blank except for patterns stencilled in pale lilac. Almost everything in the room was white, with an almost total absence of shadows or contrast.

'Do you mind?' Hesperus asked, gesturing to one of the waiting seats.

'Go ahead. See what you can find out.'

I stood behind him as he settled into the seat and took the controls. Almost immediately, portions of the white floor folded upwards to form display panels, bending and tilting to present themselves to Hesperus. Acres of dense red text and diagrams flowed obligingly into place. The language was a fussy series of squared-off pictograms.

'Ring any bells?' I asked warily.

'I've seen it before. It'll just take a moment to retrieve the translation filters from deep memory.'

'Great. I kept meaning to convert all these ships to Line control standards, but I just never got around to it.'

'That'll teach you.'

'Teach me what?'

'Never put off until the next million years what you can do during this million.' After dispensing this advice, Hesperus fell silent, his hands twitching and the text and diagrams slamming past in a pink blur, impossibly fast.

'Give me some good news,' I asked after a while.

'Well, there is power, as we already deduced. The important thing is that there is more than enough for our needs. The stardrive reports operational readiness. Life support appears to be functioning normally. We have inertia control and impassors. We have real-thrust engines, for taxiing to clear space. If there were no obstacles to our egress, we could take this ark out of the bay immediately.'

I scratched my neck. 'So why don't we?'

'Cadence and Cascade have complete control, Purslane. They opened the door with the intention of killing you. Now that the air is gone, I have every confidence that they will have restored the curtain and sealed the bay again. We wouldn't get very far, I'm afraid.'

'We could try.'

'We would die in the process. At least for now we are alive, with options.'

'And they would be ...'

'We can inconvenience our hosts by slowing down your ship. You will need to furnish me with a list of those vessels that have working parametric engines. There are too many for me to visit the entire contents of the bay.'

'I can do that. What other options do we have?'

'We will attempt to contact our pursuers, and thereby determine our position, speed and approximate heading. Then we may begin to speculate as to the nature of this undertaking.'

'We're heading back to Machine Space.'

'Yes,' he said, distractedly.

'You sound as if you're not sure of that.'

'I am sure of nothing, Purslane. It has been a long time since I left the Monoceros Ring, but nothing in my experience suggested a widespread appetite for war. Quite the opposite. Most reasoning thinkers wanted nothing but peace and prosperity, for both our meta-civilisations. I was sent to investigate anomalous records in the Vigilance archive, for the sake of completeness and curiosity. I was not sent to make war or enemies.'

I realised this was the first time he had spoken with any certainty of his mission.

'Then what about Cadence and Cascade?'

'They may have been sent by another faction within the Machine People. What their agenda is, I cannot yet say.'

'But you have ideas.'

'I have pieces. Fragments of ideas. And one very large, very disturbing truth, which I will soon be obliged to reveal to you.'

'Tell me what they sent you for,' I said, with a sense that the world was about to spring open a trapdoor under my feet.

Hesperus made a few further adjustments to the controls, but did not answer my question. 'I have secured the external doors. Nothing will be able to enter without the use of force.'

'That's not particularly reassuring under the circumstances.'

'I will not overstate our chances. If they have access to *Silver Wings'* systems, they will be able to forge weapons and devices of vast penetrating force. But we have makers as well. We can defend ourselves. And, ultimately, we have an option they do not.'

I heard something ominous in his tone. 'Which is?'

'We can destroy this ark. If the engine were to self-destruct, I doubt that any containment system would be able to stop the detonation before it touched every other ship in this hold – not even if *Silver Wings* tried to place an impassor around her bay.'

'Then we have a way of hurting them.' I did not need to state the dark corollary.

'It would be instantaneous, Purslane. If you were afraid, I could complete the operation while you were in abeyance.'

'Well, let's not jump the gun on that plan just yet.'

'I just want to make sure we both understand what we are capable of doing.'

'I get it. Will Cadence and Cascade work it out as well?'

'They will know we are capable of it. Whether they think we will do it is another question entirely.'

'Do you think they know we're still alive?'

'They know that I am still functioning, and that you were alive until you lost consciousness. I do not think they are capable of monitoring our activities inside this ark.'

'They'll see you when you leave.'

'I'll move fast, alter my coloration and endeavour to use the ships and other obstructions for concealment.'

'I'll need time to come up with that list. If I had access to my trove—'

'I have confidence in your abilities.' His tone became brisk, businesslike. 'Now – with your permission, I shall bring the ark's engine to taxiing power. I will not risk a greater application of pseudo-thrust for fear that the ship would break itself free of its docking cradle.'

'Do it,' I said, standing back while he worked.

Hesperus coaxed the slumbering engine into life, warming it for the first time in tens of subjective millennia. Many ships would have balked at such a demand. For the ark, which had been outfitted for a long and venerable existence in its second life, this was not an unreasonable request. The red writing and symbols flowed onto white panels that had previously been blank, a series of chimes sounded and there was a momentary surging sensation that had me grabbing for support. Then there was only a distant throbbing, not so much a sound as a subsonic impression. *Silver Wings* was bending space in one direction, surfing the distortion; the ark was trying to flatten it out again.

'Do you think they'll notice?'

'Undoubtedly. They'll notice the effect even more when I've performed the same trick with a few more ships.'

I thought of the list he wanted from me. I could name some of the ships already, but I did not want him to leave until I was as sure as I could be that I had remembered them all.

'I need something to write down the names and positions.'

'Simply state them aloud. I will remember everything of importance.' He made another delicate adjustment to the console, causing a new series of chimes to sound. 'I have activated the ark's hailing transmitter, at full strength. I have put it on a cycling frequency sweep so that it stands the best chance of penetrating the bay walls and the wake distortion behind us. The ship will inform us if it receives a return signal.'

'There may not be anyone behind us.'

'Do you think Campion would let you go without an explanation?'

'He'd need Betony's permission to come after me.'

'I rather doubt that would have stopped him.'

'You're right. It wouldn't.' The thought that Campion might be out there cheered me on one level, but chilled me on another. I wanted him safe and sound somewhere, not risking his existence for my sake. 'Hesperus,' I said, hesitantly, 'what you were saying just now, about a disturbing truth – are you ready to talk about it yet?'

He stood from the controls, having done everything necessary for the time being. 'It's not as if there will ever be a good time.'

'So let's make it now.'

He considered my request for a moment, then gestured towards one of the padded white chairs. 'Take a seat, Purslane.'

'Why?'

'Because you are in a state of acute mental fragility, and what I am about to reveal to you will in no way bolster your strength of mind.'

'I'm all right. I'm not going to faint.'

'Sit.'

I sat down.

Hesperus stood before me, his arms crossed. 'I am not Hesperus,' he said.

I let out a small, involuntary laugh. 'What do you mean, you're not Hesperus? I know you. I took you to the Spirit. I brought you back.'

'I chose my words unwisely. I was Hesperus. Now I am something more than Hesperus. Hesperus is a part of what I am, a vital part, a treasured part, but not the sum of me. I am as much the man Abraham Valmik as I am the machine Hesperus.'

I felt cold, suddenly uncertain of my safety. 'Stop talking like this.'

'I can only express the truth. The Spirit no longer exists on Neume. Everything that it was, everything that it ever knew, everything it ever felt or witnessed, is now part of me.'

I shook my head in flat denial. 'That isn't possible. The Spirit was still there when we left.'

'I left behind an empty shell, without a consciousness. It will continue to drift through the atmosphere, going through the old motions. But it is not me. I am in this golden body now. It was time to move on, to become compact once more. I am Abraham Valmik. I was once a man, then I became the Spirit of the Air. Now I am close to being a man again.'

I struggled to process what I had just been told. Out of all the millennia, all the centuries, all the long days – why would the Spirit choose this one to move on?

'Why leave, when you were safe?' I asked. 'Nothing could touch you down there. Now you could be killed at any moment, if Cadence and Cascade decide to wipe us out.'

'That is a risk. On balance, though, I saw that I had no choice. A time of great stability, lasting millions of years, is coming to an end. There was no guarantee that Neume would be any safer than here, aboard this ship.'

'What do you know?'

'Everything. Everything and nothing. I mentioned disturbing news, Purslane. What I have just told you, the information concerning my identity, may seem disturbing to you. But it is not the news to which I was referring.'

I sank back into the seat. 'Whatever it is, I'm ready for it.'

'When Hesperus was brought to me – a truly conscious being, albeit a broken one – he catalysed a change. It must have been imminent, poised to happen, for quite some time. Perhaps I had begun a slow process of waking, a slow realisation that it was time to gather myself and move on. But had I – Hesperus – not been brought to me – Valmik – I would still be in that state of delayed transition, like a sleeper trying to rouse himself from the coils of a lovely and seductive dream, one where the colours and emotions are brighter and stronger than they ever are in the waking world.'

'We had to help him.'

'It was an act of singular kindness. We are both grateful, Purslane. But now you need to know the whole story.'

My throat was tight. There was acid in my belly. 'Go on.'

'Machine People never came to Neume. Hesperus was the first, or at least the first to come into my presence. But when he came, when I took his broken body into myself, I remembered something. It was an experience that had happened so long ago that I could not truthfully distinguish it from a figment of my own imagination. But when I picked apart Hesperus's memory, I found the key that unlocked the truthfulness of my recollection.' He paused and regarded me with all the intensity of expression his golden mask was capable of. 'He was not the first.'

'You said no other Machine People had come before him.'

'That is correct. A million years after the Golden Hour, four million years before the Machine People, there were others.'

'Other what?'

'Another machine civilisation. Another race of intelligent, conscious robots.'

'No,' I said, with a burning conviction. 'I know my history. Nothing like the Machine People ever arose before them.'

'That is what you believe to be true. But the Vigilance discovered evidence to the contrary. It found the remains of this robot civilisation on several worlds, scattered across galactic space. The evidence had been misinterpreted; it was assumed that the Priors had been responsible. The Vigilance detected anomalies in the official explanation – the temporal evidence did not fit the Prior hypothesis – and flagged the matter for further investigation. When news of this puzzle reached Machine Space, I was dispatched to penetrate the Vigilance and learn the extent of their knowledge.'

'Your mission.'

'Around the same time – within a circuit or so – Campion must have entered the Vigilance and compiled his report for Gentian Line. Campion's strand must have mentioned this selfsame anomaly, even if that was simply one bright gem in a treasure chest of intelligence. But that gem is where all this began, Purslane. When Campion delivered this strand, the wheels of a great and terrible process were set in motion. That is why you were ambushed, two hundred kiloyears later.'

'All this because of an anomaly in the Vigilance's data?'

'Because of the significance of that anomaly – to humanity, to the Machine People, and most especially to Gentian Line.'

I reeled, struggling to take all this in. It was not just difficult for me to accept the emergence of another machine civilisation, when the history books said otherwise. I had lived through that history, seen it within my own eyes. I remembered all the twists and turns, all the savage bottlenecks. I could reel off the names of a hundred thousand turnover cultures without stopping for breath. There was no room in that litany of known events for something as momentous as the coming of living machines.

'I don't get it, Hesperus. How does this have anything to do with Gentian Line? And if those machines existed, why don't I remember them? How did they manage to come and go without leaving a dent in history?'

'They didn't.'

'I don't understand.'

'They left their mark on history. They left many marks. But one by one, systematically and with great thoroughness, the marks were erased.'

'By the machines?'

'They were already extinct.'

'Then who did it?'

Hesperus waited a moment, then said, with infinite gentleness, as if he had no wish to cause me pain or anguish, 'The House of Suns was the secret Line tasked to keep this knowledge buried. You and every shatterling of the Commonality played a part in bringing it into existence. When you were ambushed, it was your own dark instrument turning against you.'

Nausea washed over me, slow and dreary as the tide on a heavy panthalassic. Four hours had now passed since our departure from Neume, and still there was no word from *Silver Wings of Morning*. Charlock, Orache and Agrimony's ships were now accelerating harder than ever, their usual safeguards rescinded. After much debate, it had finally been agreed that their owners would remain with the five trailing vehicles – *Dalliance*, Betony's *Adonis Blue*, and the ships of Sorrel, Tansy and Henbane – while the three lead craft attempted to catch up with *Silver Wings* and compel her to slow down. Galingale was still moving into position; it would be some time before he was able to do anything useful.

None of us was confident of success, irrespective of whether we believed Purslane was in charge of her ship, or the robots. But it was necessary to take this step so that we might learn how far *Silver Wings'* controlling agency was willing to go.

I was alone on the bridge – Charlock, Orache and Agrimony were aboard other ships, not mine. But their imagos, and those of Betony, Sorrel, Tansy and Henbane, were in attendance. Galingale's imago appeared when he had something to contribute, but was still rendered smokily to indicate his distance from us. We were all standing, hands resting on fuzzy supports only partly imaged. On the displayer, Neume's system was an orrery of worlds with the trajectories of our ships arrowing away from the planet in luminous, laser-straight lines, bunched so tightly that they were indistinguishable from each other. Ticking indices next to each ship showed our velocities as a fraction of light. Galingale's ship was approaching on a gently curved asymptote, still more than half a minute out from our position but pushing hard on the tail of the three unmanned vehicles. I had no doubt that he was going through the same nervous exercises as the rest of us, constantly rechecking weapons and defensive systems. One check should have sufficed – these were systems that had been honed to effectiveness and reliability over the six-million-year exist-ence of the Line – but there were some human habits too deeply ingrained to shake. Soldiers polished their swords before a battle, oiled their guns, kissed their good-luck charms.

I was resigned to another hour of waiting, as the three ships clawed their way within effective weapons range, when we received the signal. It was frequency-cycling, using none of the standard Gentian message protocols, but it was undoubtedly originating from *Silver Wings of Morning*.

'It's just a hail,' Betony said, his imago standing the closest to me. He appeared to be looking at my displayer, at the summary of the signal content scrolling down next to the orrery. 'No deep content at all, unless we're missing something exceedingly subtle.'

Charlock's figure swayed as a local acceleration surge hit his ship. Like a man on a leaning deck, he gripped the rail before him, the muscles in his forearm tensing with the effort. 'We should still respond. Usual point of a hail is to establish contact.'

'Could be a trap of some kind,' Tansy said.

Charlock shook his head. 'We've nothing to lose – whoever's running *Silver Wings* already knows we're following. We may as well find out what they have to say to us.'

Betony bit his lower lip. 'Why would they use an unfamiliar protocol, rather than *Silver Wings*' own sender?'

'Maybe they haven't got a choice,' I said. 'Purslane has a lot of ships in her bay. If she managed to make it to one of them, she could send us a signal even if the robots didn't want her to.'

'Then by replying, we run the risk of letting the robots know she's still alive,' Sorrel said.

'They already know,' I said. 'Unless she managed to find a ship with a unidirectional transmitter, they'll have picked up the initial send. Charlock's right: we lose nothing by responding, and if Purs-lane's the sender it'll let her know we haven't given up on her.'

Galingale interjected his timelagged thoughts. 'I'm against responding to this transmission. If the robots want to talk, they should slow down and await instructions. We negotiate on our terms, not theirs. If Purslane's being held hostage, the information that we're in pursuit won't help her.'

Privately I wondered if he was still serious about risking a close approach to Purslane, or whether he had been secretly counting on the crisis being resolved before he was called upon to demonstrate his bravery.

'If she's alone on that ship, I want her to know we haven't abandoned her,' I said.

Galingale did not respond. My answer would not reach him for another thirty-five seconds, and it would be as long again before his reply reached us.

'Make the response,' Betony said.

'You're sure?'

'Say nothing about our explicit intentions, but let them know we're here and that we aren't going home.'

I nodded and cleared my throat. I ordered *Dalliance* to create a message in the form we would normally use for signalling a start-up civilisation, stripping out the embroidery we habitually wove around our messages to confound eavesdropping and impersonation. Then I started speaking.

'This is Campion, aboard *Dalliance*. We're three minutes astern and closing. We got your signal, Purslane; I hope you can make sense of this reply. I know you're listening – listening and still alive. Right now, there's nothing in the universe I'm more certain of.' Which was a white lie, but only because I desperately wanted her to believe that I would never give up this chase.

I continued, 'I also know that it was you who initiated that signal, not Cadence and Cascade. If the robots wanted to talk, they'd already have done so using Gentian protocols. I hope you can reply, but in case you're unable, or we are unable to exchange more than a message or two, I'm going to tell you everything I think you need to know. You left Neume more than four hours ago. Since then you've been maintaining a thousand gees on a heading that will bring you to the innermost stars of the Monoceros Ring in one hundred and thirty thousand years. At the time of this transmission, you are making point-four-eight of light and climbing. There are nine ships following you – we left Neume as quickly as we could, and we're running as hard as we can. We're not turning around. We're going to follow you all the way, until we get you back. Please reply, if you can. I want to hear your voice again.' With the words choking in my throat, I added, 'I love you, shatterling.'

It was an effort to keep standing, I was so drained and fearful. I hardly dared to believe that there would be a response. Even if she was alive, there was no guarantee that she had the means to send a more complex signal than the one we had already received. She was also three minutes ahead of us; it would be at least six before I could expect an answer.

Every second became an anxious eternity. When the time had elapsed, there was only silence. The seconds kept inching past. The seconds became a whole minute, as long again as the six that had preceded it.

Then, miraculously, she answered.

Purslane's voice was very scratchy and indistinct. Even when *Dalliance* fleshed out the message with her own guess as to what she should have sounded like, there was a remoteness in her voice, as if she was speaking through thick layers of glass.

'I'm all right, Campion. I'm with Hesperus – he's alive and he's on our side. We're in the cargo bay, in the white ark. The other two ... they tricked us, Campion – they were never interested in helping Hesperus. They were hoping he was going to die, and if he didn't they were going to kill him anyway.' She paused to draw breath. 'There's so much I need to tell you. I know it's only been half a day since we were last together, but I've learned a world of things since then. Most of it's bad, as well. I know what the House of Suns is, but that's all I can say for now. Cadence and Cascade may be listening in, and Hesperus says they may not have all the pieces in place just yet. We still don't know what they want with this ship. If they don't want to help Hesperus, why the hurry to get back to Machine Space? Anything of value that they've learned, they could just as easily signal home. Yes, I know they gave us reasons why that wasn't a preferred option – but given what we now know of their intentions, we may as well assume they were lying.' Purslane paused. 'There's nothing I'd like better than to keep talking, but Hesperus and I have work to do. I'll be back in touch as soon as we're done. I love you, shatterling. Thank you for coming after me.'

When she was gone, I felt as if something as huge and empty as the Boötes Void had pushed its way into my skull.

A little later, our imagos gathered around a holographic representation of *Silver Wings of Morning*, compiled from data in our mutual troves. It was not guaranteed to be an accurate reflection of the internal layout of Purslane's ship, but it was the best we had. So far no glaring anomalies had leapt out at me.

'If she's in the white ark,' I said, stabbing my finger towards the rear of the ghostly form, 'that places her in this part of the ship, aft of the parametric engine. I don't remember exactly where the ark's located – that's an eight-kilometre-long storage hold and the ark could fit almost anywhere inside it. Even if I knew, it would still be

367

nigh-on impossible to hit the drive, or any other vital system, without also hitting the bay.'

'If the ships come alongside, they can direct their weapons laterally,' Henbane said. 'Then they ought to be able to cripple the engine without inflicting significant damage on any other part of the ship.'

'Risky,' Charlock said.

'But less risky than a stern-shot.' Betony's face was set in a permanent expression of grim determination, as if it had been cast in metal and left to solidify. 'It's settled: we don't open fire on her from behind, even if that plays into the robots' intentions. It doesn't leave us empty-handed. We'll bring the first three ships in on parallel flight paths, until they have a clear line of sight onto *Silver Wings'* flanks. Then they'll attempt to disable her engine.'

'And we hope and pray that inertia suppression cuts out at the same instant, or Purslane will be exposed to a thousand gees of unbalanced compensation,' I said.

'We're all aware of the dangers – Purslane included.'

'If she were to enter stasis abeyance,' Tansy put in, 'her chances of surviving the attack would be immeasurably improved.'

'Send her that warning now and we'll be giving the robots a clear signal of our intentions,' Sorrel said.

Charlock smirked. 'They've probably worked out that we aren't coming with garlands and bouquets.'

'Nonetheless, they won't know our exact intentions until those ships open fire,' Betony said. 'They may still think we intend to negotiate, or attempt a boarding operation. I agree with Sorrel: we can't warn Purslane to enter abeyance until the last minute.'

'And if she doesn't have time?' I asked him.

'She's in another ship, inside her own. It won't protect her against unbalanced acceleration, but it's still better than being completely exposed. I'm sorry, Campion, but that's the best we can do. It's either attack or let them leave unchallenged. If we do that, I don't think any of us will ever see Purslane again.'

Hesperus paced up and down the white bridge of the ark as I dredged information from my memory, his restless motion quite uncharacteristic of the robot I thought I knew. All I wanted was to talk about the earlier machine civilisation, to find out everything he knew and learn what part we had played in their demise. It had been good to talk to Campion – I felt as if a small, warm flame was burning inside me where before there had been only an unlit void – but Hesperus's revelation was still dominating my thoughts to the exclusion of almost everything else.

'How did you – whoever I'm talking to, Hesperus or Valmik – know about the extinction? If the Machine People were already aware of it, wouldn't they have told us about it hundreds of thousands of years ago?'

'The Machine People didn't know about the earlier race. When they emerged on the galactic scene, they assumed that the existing historical record – as related to them by human envoys – was largely accurate. That's not to say that they didn't anticipate errors and untruths. But they had no reason to expect that history had been rewritten on such a scale, with such systematic intention. For the entire lifetime of my people, we have believed that we were the first true machine intelligence. Soon it will be common knowledge that this was not the case.'

'You still haven't told me how you knew.'

'Because machines came to me, when I was young.'

'I was talking to Hesperus. Now it's Valmik. Right?'

'We're both here, two faces behind one mask. I'm sorry if I confuse you, but to me it's perfectly natural to switch from one strand of my existence to the other. I am two rivers that have merged into one being, at the confluence.' Hesperus slowed his pacing. 'More than five million years ago, long after the Golden Hour but long before I came to Neume, thinking machines found me. I was a novelty to them – huge and slow and wondrous. They were equally novel to me. I saw immediately what they were: human technology that had become haunted, possessed by quick, gleaming cleverness. I had seen smart machines before then, but nothing with the agility and cunning of true intelligence. I knew instantly that these creatures were a different order of machine. Some alchemy of chaos and complexity had given their minds powers of consciousness and free will.'

'What happened to them?'

'They told me that they wanted to make contact with human meta-civilisation. Since I had been human once, they hoped I might act as an intermediary, smoothing the diplomatic waters. I urged caution. I had already seen dozens of empires come and go, blossoming and fading like lilies on a pond, over and over, seasons without end. Many of those empires were benevolent and welcoming, but others were inimical to all outside influences. It made no difference to their longevity. The kind empires withered and waned as quickly as the hostile ones. But there was a kind of stability, above and beyond planetary life.'

'The Lines,' I said, with fascinated dread.

'It made perfect sense for the machines to deal with them rather than any of those fractious, ephemeral turnover civilisations. Once they had established harmonious relations with the Commonality – which already existed by then – the Lines could broker contact between the robots and those cultures they deemed sufficiently stable and open-minded. Piece by piece, humankind would be introduced to its new robot companions. Both sides would prosper in the new alliance. The robots, with their cool, non-partisan detachment from human politics, might form a moderating influence, calming the endless cycle of turnover, bringing a new era of tranquillity to galactic affairs. Likewise, the robots had much to gain from contact with human societies – access to the arts and sciences of a million worlds and a million years of human civilisation. Art and science fascinated them above all else. They were curious, ravenously so, but there was something about their minds that kept them from being truly creative. The only genuinely innovative act they had ever achieved was to come into existence. After that, intelligent as they were, they could do nothing but ask questions. Supplying answers required intuitive leaps that they just couldn't make.'

'Then they weren't like the Machine People.'

'No. The machines that came later – millions of years down the line – had something the first wave lacked. But perhaps that was only because the first civilisation was never given enough time to invent creativity for itself. In the end, with enough shuffling of mental permutations, it might have found the missing ingredient.'

'But they never got that chance.'

'To start with, the robots were made royally welcome. They were an intriguing new development, a kink in history's road that no one had predicted. Humans had resigned themselves to never having to share the galaxy with another species. That was both a blessing and a curse. It meant unlimited room for expansion, unlimited scope for raw materials, but it also meant enduring the deathliest of silences. Yes, humanity fractured into a million daughter species, some of which were scarcely recognisable to each other. But scratch beneath the scales, the fur, the tin armour, they were still humans at the core, and no amount of primate babble could ever drown out that silence completely. But now there was company. Granted, the robots had only arisen as a consequence of human activities, but on every level that mattered, they might as well have been aliens. Their minds ran on radically different algorithms. For all their strangenesses, they weren't unwelcome, to begin with. The robots were few in number and confined to a compact volume of space, safely distant from any old-growth civilisations. They showed no expansionist ambitions. To humanity, an only child growing up in an ancient, demon-haunted house, it was like discovering a new friend to play with. And for a little while, that was what the relationship resembled. But then it turned sour.'

Ancient memories chimed in my head, struck like dusty bells. I thought of a house with rooms beyond number, and a companion who sometimes came to that house.

'What happened?'

'What so often does in these situations. What began as a creeping, subliminal unease – a sense that there was something not quite right, something not quite to be trusted, about these new machines – began to mutate into full-blooded paranoia. Not everyone shared it, of course – there were some who never questioned the robots' intentions. But their voices counted for nothing. Those who spoke for the Commonality – the movers and shakers within the most prominent Lines – started to think about dealing with the machines.'

'Genocide.'

'What they wanted was not subjugation, not control, but the possibility of control. They wanted the ability to neutralise any threat those machines might pose in the future. With great care, a plan was formulated. A number of the robot envoys were captured and dissected – their deaths explained away as accidents that also cost human lives. It took the Commonality centuries to piece through the data they had obtained. They had to understand how those robot minds functioned. They failed, utterly and miserably. But out of that failure came one nugget of understanding. They found a flaw in the robots' minds, a weakness that had been preserved through countless evolutionary changes. It was a weakness that could be exploited, given time and ingenuity. The Commonality devised a means to implant a data structure, a kind of neural bomb, in the mind of every member of that machine civilisation. It would spread from machine to machine without the machines ever realising they were vectors. Over time, it would infect the entire civilisation. But the beautiful thing was that nothing would happen. The robots would continue unimpaired. They could keep on moving in human circles, for as long as they were useful. Perhaps it would never be necessary to use the weapon against them – that was certainly what the Commonality was hoping even as it acted with what it saw as immense prudence and foresight. But the day that the machines posed a threat to human expansion or hegemony, the neural bombs could be activated. All it would take would be a single, harmless-looking transmission into the heart of their civilisation. As soon as the robots started processing that data, sharing it between them, their bombs would start counting down. It wouldn't be instantaneous, because if the robots started dying as soon as that transmission was received, they'd be able to organise quarantine measures, as well as pinpointing the likely origin of their plague. The built-in delay didn't matter to the Commonality – the Lines had been taking the long view ever since the Shattering.'

I realised that I had been absorbing all this with a kind of numb fatalism, my capacity for surprise or revulsion already exhausted.

'So what happened? Did the robots turn against us?'

Hesperus laughed quietly. 'No. The robots never had warlike ambitions. In truth, they had much more to fear from the organic than the organic ever had to fear from them. That's not to say it would have been peace and love for the rest of eternity – sooner or later, tensions would probably have arisen. But the robots never lifted a finger against the human meta-civilisation.'

'So what happened?'

'The weapon went wrong. Either the robots changed, or the

humans had not understood their minds properly ... but it activated without any external trigger. The robots started to die, in vast numbers. To begin with, they didn't know what was happening. They even appealed to the Commonality for assistance! That was when the Commonality realised what its cleverness had brought about. They were appalled, of course, genuinely shocked by what they had done, but they still didn't admit to any part in it. They stood back as the robots died out. They'd have known enough to design a countermeasure, something that could be spread from robot to robot to disable the earlier weapon before it had a chance to go off. But doing that would have risked exposing them as the instigators of the neural bomb. Instead, they put about disinformation suggesting that the robots had been infected with something left behind by Priors.'

'How do you know all this, Hesperus?'

'Because I remained in contact with the machines, right through to the end. Even when they began to suspect what had been done to them, they maintained communication with me. My ties to humanity had been growing looser by the century. They felt I was someone they could talk to.'

I shook my head in wonder and bewilderment. 'So you knew. Across all this time, you knew.'

'I experienced these events, Purslane, along with countless others. You think you've lived through six million years, but you haven't the faintest notion what that really means. The weight of all those memories is like an ocean of liquid hydrogen, compressing itself to metal. Every new experience I choose to remember, every new moment of my existence, only adds to that crush. In the deepest, darkest, densest layer of myself, I remembered what had happened to the first machines. But those memories might as well have been entombed in rock, for all that they were readily accessible to me. Even if I chipped them out, brought them into daylight – which I did, once or twice – I couldn't be sure they were an accurate record of real events. It took Hesperus to bring them to the surface and confirm what had really happened. When he came – the first of his kind to visit me, his head stuffed full of second-hand Vigilance data garnered from your troves – I remembered that there had once been others like him, and what had happened to them.' He offered the palms of his hands. 'And now I am here, telling all this to you.'

'Did they all die?'

'One by one, across thousands of years, they all succumbed. And for a while the Commonality lived with what it had done. The Lines sought consolation in the knowledge that they had not intended to hurt the robots, but only to make the hurting of them a possibility. They hadn't intended to bring about their extinction, so they couldn't be said to have committed intentional genocide. That was a fine distinction, but one they clung to assiduously. But in the end it wasn't enough just to have peace of mind. The act itself had to be erased from Commonality history. None of you remember it because you elected not to remember it, and adjusted your own memories and records accordingly.'

'We couldn't have done it. It would have been too big, too difficult. The other civilisations . . .' I was voicing objections, but not because I did not believe him. I just wanted an explanation.

'More than one Line was implicated in the atrocity. The Commonality took the necessary coordinating action. At successive reunions, the Thousand Nights were used to delete and modify critical memories. You were all complicit in this; it was not something done to you by shadowy figures beyond your control. At the same time, the shared historical records of the Commonality were tampered with. All the Lines were coerced into accepting the new version of history. Lines that refused to comply were summarily excommunicated. Outside the support apparatus and information-exchange mechanism of the Commonality, they withered away.'

'It can't just have been the Lines. If the machines were present in human space, other civilisations would have noticed them.'

'They did. But turnover took care of them. That, and the occasional helping hand from a Line.'

'I don't follow.'

'The Lines take pride in their good deeds – the kind and noble things they do to protect lesser civilisations. They're right to do so. But elements associated with the Lines have also murdered and suppressed upstart nascents. In six million years, do you seriously imagine this has never happened?'

I felt sick to my stomach, empty, as if a part of me had been gored out. 'You can't know all this. It's one thing to have met the earlier civilisation, to have met Hesperus . . .'

He made to turn his back on me, apparently disgusted with my refusal to take everything he said at face value, but halted before the movement was complete.

'Can you doubt that your ambush was connected to the things I have spoken about, Purslane? After more than five million years, your involvement in that crime has begun to come to light. It was the Vigilance that started it – if they hadn't found those anomalous relics, nothing would have happened. But you – Gentian Line – with your magpie craving for novelty and prestige – you had to be the first to bring those anomalies to wider attention. Had your shatterlings returned to another reunion with clear evidence that there had been an earlier machine civilisation, it would only have been a matter of time before the full picture came to light. Do you imagine that the Machine People would have been prepared to let bygones be bygones, to smile tolerantly at your earlier error? They would have felt a powerful kinship with that earlier culture, and wondered if you were capable of doing the same thing to them, given half a chance. The Commonality would have been discredited, but that would only have been the start of it. A human–machine macro-war would have been all too likely. So the rediscovery had to be suppressed. If that meant the casual annihilation of Gentian Line, an ambush wiping out nearly a thousand immortal souls, then that was deemed a very acceptable price to pay. They'd have felt the same way about killing a million, or a billion. The custodians of this secret won't blink at murder, Purslane. They won't blink at genocide or the extinction of another civilisation.'

'The Vigilance was the source of it all. Why didn't they go after the Vigilance, before all this got loose?'

The naïveté of my question seemed to amuse him. 'You make it sound so simple. The Vigilance is indestructible, Purslane: a massively distributed Dyson swarm, virtually invulnerable to outside aggression. It has persisted for more than five million years and in all likelihood it will outlive every other civilisation in this galaxy. Fortunately, the Vigilance itself didn't appear to quite realise the significance of their find. They were too self-absorbed, too fixated on Andromeda to pay attention to such a local, parochial matter.'

After a silence I said, 'Do you hate us now?'

'After the kindnesses you have shown me? Hatred's the furthest thing from my mind. But I pity you for what you did.'

'I don't feel as if I had any part in that crime.'

'You all played a role. Some spoke against the plan, but not loudly enough. Some thought it didn't go far enough; that the weapon should have been activated as soon as it had spread to enough robots. Where you stood, I can't begin to guess. That's between you and your conscience.'

'The memories we changed ... can they be unlocked again?'

'The human mind is a tricky thing, for all its simplicity. It resists being treated like a piece of furniture, like a cabinet with drawers and compartments you can slide in and out and replace without consequence.'

'I know,' I said quietly. 'Hesperus, I'm sorry about what we did back then. Or I would be if sorry were a big enough word. But we don't punish children for the crimes committed by their parents.'

'You were not children.'

'But once the memory of that crime was erased from our minds, we might as well have been. We can't be punished for something we barely remember doing.'

'Would it surprise you if I told you I agreed?'

'I don't know what to think any more. I just want to do what's right – to find a way out of this mess. If that means surrendering ourselves to the Machine People, letting them decide whether to punish us or not, then maybe that's what we'll have to do.'

'Given the present state of affairs, I would count on nothing where the Machine People are concerned.'

'And Cadence and Cascade?'

Hesperus said, 'I still don't know why they were sent.'

When we had agreed on the necessary course of action, Hesperus and I followed the white corridors down to the ark's door. We had already used the ark's own surveillance devices to verify that no large machine had entered the bay since the loss of its atmosphere.

'Why aren't they here yet? I'm surprised they're not waiting outside to ambush you.'

'They'll be here sooner or later. At the moment, they may be preoccupied with escaping the pursuit ships. But from now on you let no one aboard unless it's me, using the code words we already agreed upon.'

'Helleborine and Orache,' I said, as if he might have forgotten.

Hesperus nodded. 'Remember, Cadence and Cascade will find it a trivial matter to impersonate my appearance and usual manner of speaking. But they'll be expecting me to act like Hesperus, not Valmik. If for some reason you don't trust me, even if I use the code words, your last line of defence will be to listen out for Valmik. If you don't hear him, you may assume I am not Hesperus after all.'

'And then what should I do? If they're outside, it won't take them long to break in.'

'I can't tell you what you should do in those circumstances,'

Hesperus said. 'That's between you and your maker.'

'You're saying I should kill myself?'

'I can think of at least one way in which the robots might have killed you already, if that was their intention.'

I wondered what his point was. 'They gave it a damned good go when they emptied the bay.'

'You survived, though. Their intention may have been to confine you to one place, one ship, rather than to kill you outright. I think they want something from you, Purslane: something in your head, I presume. Why else would they not have killed you already?'

I shuddered to think what it would mean to be interrogated by those lovely silver and white machines; the things they would do to me to get at what they wanted.

'I don't know anything,' I said.

'You may not. But it's what they think that matters.' He opened the door into the airlock, preparing to expose himself to the hard vacuum of the cargo bay.

'How will you speak to me? You won't be able to make a sound out there.'

'The lock has a simple radio relay. You will hear my voice when it is necessary for me to speak to you. I'll be silent until then – I don't want to help Cadence and Cascade to track me.'

'How long will you be gone?'

'Depending on variables, one to two hours. I can't be more precise than that.'

'I should go instead of you. With a suit from the ark, and my knowledge of the bay—'

'It would still take you longer. I can move like the wind when I must.'

I stroked my fingers down the muscular armour of his forearm. 'Take care, Hesperus.'

'I shall.' After a moment he added, 'I am relieved, Purslane. I thought you might hate me for what I had to tell you.'

'I've never been one for shooting the messenger. You did what you had to.'

'You took it well. Let us hope the rest of your species follows suit, shall we?'

The interior door closed on him. Through the glass partition I watched his gold skin darken to ash as he adjusted his coloration. I had never imagined him capable of such an effortless change, but there was now nothing about Hesperus that would have surprised me. The ash became a dark, hyphenated blur as he left the chamber at the speed of a bullet. Then the outer door closed and I was alone in the white ark, with only my fears for company.

That was when it dawned on me that I was the only living thing on my ship.

PART SEVEN

Relictus had been confined to our deepest dungeon for six years, but not in the conditions to which most of our prisoners were accustomed. He had been allotted two rooms, one to sleep in, another in which to eat and continue his studies. He was given a fire to warm himself, candles, paper, quills and ink, a small library of his own choosing. He was allowed wine and the kind of food normally served to the highest-ranking soldiers. Occasionally he was even allowed a visit from a courtesan. The only thing not permitted him was the ability to conjure. When he did not need to eat or drink, he wore a heavy mask that muffled his voice beyond the range required for spell-casting. When it was necessary to remove the mask so that he could be fed, his hands were bound together. Guards spooned food into his mouth and washed it down with wine, treating him with the servile respect they had been ordered to show. At all times another guard observed him from a few paces away, alert to the slightest trick. That guard carried a knife, ready to slit Relictus's throat.

I visited him in the dungeon, for it was considered too hazardous to move him without good purpose. For my visit he was both masked and bound, facing me in a black chair that was itself bolted to the floor. A guard stood behind him, pressing a knife against his throat. I could see only his eyes, moving behind round holes in the leather and metal covering his face. They were the eyes of a young man, almost a boy.

'I have a difficulty, Relictus. I believe I have shown you kindness. It is true that you were never exactly a prisoner, but when the nature of your talents became known to us, I was advised that the safest thing would be to cut out your tongue, sever your hands and burn out your eyes. I did none of these things, because I am a woman of kindness. I had no choice but to confine you, but I strove to do all that I could to ease the burden of your incarceration. I could not allow you to work magic, but I have allowed you luxuries forbidden to any other prisoner. I do not think you can argue that you have been treated unfairly, given the alternatives.'

Relictus nodded. I did not know whether that meant yes, he could well argue against my point, or whether he accepted the truth of what I had said.

'As I mentioned, a difficulty has arisen. It will not have escaped your knowledge that Calidris – your former master – is now a prisoner of Count Mordax. To my regret, but not my surprise, he has turned against us. He has used magic to create an army of Ghost Soldiers, an army that grows in number by the day, while ours is steadily depleted and weakened.'

He nodded again, then turned his mask towards the paper and ink on his desk. This was the signal that he wished to write. One hand was unbound. The knife was pressed even tighter against the skin of his throat where it showed under the mask.

He wrote: *Tell me of these soldiers.*

'They are suits of armour, but empty. They travel on horses that are either dead or near death, but which move with astonishing speed and stealth.'

Have you captured one?

'Only the armour, broken and in pieces. It seems that whatever spirit or phantasm is animating these shells escapes when the armour is pierced or pulled apart. Witnesses have spoken of red smoke issuing from the gaps.'

Bring me one that is still intact.

'I do not know if that is possible.'

Divert all resources until it is accomplished. Nothing matters more.

'Will you help us, Relictus?'

A grating noise came from the mask. I think it was laughter.

That night, or perhaps the night after, I was taken from my bed by infiltrators dressed in green. It was a measure of our loosening control that Count Mordax's agents were able to get into the Palace of Clouds unchallenged, and to find their way to my quarters.

The infiltrators took me from the Palace to a bright white room where I was molested and questioned. They pushed needles into me and peered into my eyes with shining contraptions. They called me 'Abigail' and kept telling me I had been lost, wandering in a kind of green labyrinth that they called Palatial, but that I had been rescued just in time.

Fortunately I escaped from the infiltrators. I wandered bright hallways until – by some artifice of magic or deception – I found myself back in my quarters in the Palace of Clouds.

My relief was indescribable. I secured my windows and requested that a double detachment of guards be on duty from that point forward. Yet in the morning Daubenton was reluctant to speak of the matter, and I began to doubt whether it had actually happened. In any case, I had no shortage of other affairs to occupy my mind. The Ghost Soldiers were increasing in number, pushing into the Kingdom in silent battalions, their swift, pale horses stinking of decay. They had need of a living captain to guide them, but in every other respect they fought like demons. For every man of ours that fell, Calidris made two for Count Mordax. I cursed the day I had touched the blood-bound needle against my finger, thereby bringing this desolation upon us.

But I heeded Relictus's request. Against the wishes of Daubenton and Cirlus, I ordered that men and resources be redirected towards that single goal of capturing a Ghost Soldier with its armour intact. It was, I suppose, a kind of necessary madness. We lost villages and towns as our armies were redeployed from protection duties. Knowing that these orders had originated from me, my name became a curse to those who lost homes, possessions and loved ones. But I remained resolute.

And then came the day when we caught a Ghost Soldier.

It had fallen from its horse into a cushion of hay – the armour remaining intact. My men cornered it. It fought for a while, but with diminishing intent, becoming docile the further away its captain rode, until at last it submitted. My men confined it in a sack and brought it on a wagon to the Palace of Clouds. Later it was bound to a wooden rack and taken to Relictus.

He examined it with great care, over many days. Meanwhile the Ghost Soldiers continued their incursions, steadily eroding the Kingdom's frontiers. The green men took me from my bedchamber on another occasion, but again I escaped their wicked enchantments and returned to my rooms. More guards were posted. I mentioned nothing to Daubenton, for – with my strange utterances and flashes of memory – I had already given him reason enough to doubt my faculties. Besides, I had begun to suspect that the green infiltrators were men of my own household, their white room a secret chamber somewhere in the Palace of Clouds. How else to explain the ease with which they took me, and the ease with which I returned to my rooms? It was far from clear that Daubenton was innocent in the matter.

Twelve days after the Ghost Soldier was brought to his dungeon, Relictus called for me. With guards at my side I descended the spiralling stone steps to his rooms.

The Ghost Soldier was still bound to the rack, but its armoured head moved to follow me as I entered. Relictus was still masked, but his hands were unbound. He wore a white smock, dirty with grease. His hair hung in lank coils over the eyeholes of the mask. He muttered something from behind the mask, thrusting his hands forward to one of the guards.

'Bind him,' I said. 'He wishes to speak directly.'

'There is a risk, milady,' Cirlus warned.

'And I have given an order. Bind him and remove the mask.'

Relictus's face was still that of a young man, but it was wild with ambition and power-lust. A guard stood behind him with a knife, the blade pressed against his adam's apple.

'Progress?' I asked.

'I believe so, milady.'

'Tell me.'

'The magic is unquestionably from Calidris's hand – I would know it anywhere. Inside the armour is a being called a false soul. We often spoke of the spells necessary to conjure such entities and set them abroad in the world. It is subtle, treacherous work – beyond the reach of most adepts. Even for Calidris, the conjuring of a false soul was a painful, protracted exercise. He showed me how to do it once, as a demonstration of his own powers – he placed a false soul in an hourglass, and we watched as it moved sand around. Then he vowed that he would never do such a thing again, and made me swear that I would never even attempt it. A false soul is a kind of living magic that, once set in motion, has an existence independent of its creator. As such, it is more dangerous than a spell that is cast to effect a single outcome, and which then ceases to have currency.'

'But now Calidris is making many false souls. Is that possible?'

'If the Ghost Soldiers are real, then you have your answer. I can only speculate that Calidris has exercised his talents to find a way to make ten false souls, or a hundred, as easily as he made one. He sometimes spoke of the methods by which a single spell might be multiplied, by an arrangement of levers and speaking tubes.' He looked at the racked figure, which was regarding us both with the pointed metal beak of its visor. The eye slits were glass, I had been told. Examination of the armour of dead Ghost Soldiers had revealed an uncommon artistry in the fashion in which they were jointed and sealed, to keep that red smoke inside. 'May I release it from the rack?' Relictus asked. 'I believe you will find it very interesting. You will come to no harm; it is quite docile.'

'Docile?' I repeated, for that was not what I had been expecting, given the ferocity with which the Ghost Soldiers were decimating our regiments.

'I guarantee it.'

I nodded to the guards. Relictus was masked again. Still with the knife to his neck, his hands were freed so that he could untie the armoured figure. As the guards moved to bind him again, Relictus tapped the mask and mumbled something.

'Leave him as he is,' I said. 'He wishes to use his hands, but not to speak. The Ghost Soldiers do not respond to spoken orders.'

Relictus beckoned the figure to step off the rack. Its metal boots clattered on the floor as it took several hesitant paces. Relictus raised his arm. The figure echoed the movement. He gestured a more complicated command, and the figure walked stiffly to the table and picked up his quill. Relictus made it perform a few more simple tasks then commanded it to return to the rack, whereupon it was resecured.

The guards fastened Relictus's hands and removed the mask.

'Docile,' I acknowledged.

'It will do anything you ask of it. Now that it has grown used to me as its master, I could even send it into battle against the other Ghost Soldiers. It would fight them willingly.'

'It would make no difference to us, other than to prove a point. Why is it so easily commanded, Relictus?'

'Such pliability is in the nature of false souls, milady. Calidris could do nothing about that. They are essentially innocent creatures who will do as they are told, provided they are told with sufficient authority. Think of them as very obliging children. They may be excellent warriors, but there is no hatred or evil in them. The evil is in those who would create them, or send them to burn villages.'

'Then you have learned nothing that is useful to me,' I said, preparing to turn away in disgust. 'Countless lives were lost to bring you this specimen, Relictus. Villages have burned for the sake of your idle curiosity. I expected you to find a flaw, a literal chink in the armour.'

385

'I have,' he said, almost by way of an afterthought. 'I can kill thousands of them now, if you command it.'

I asked him how such a thing was possible.

'They must all be copies of the same soul, or copies of a small number of individual souls. That is the only way Calidris can make them in such numbers. I spoke of the method by which a spell might be multiplied.'

'Yes . . .'

'Think of an apparatus for duplicating his gestures – the precise movements of his arms, the precise movements of his fingers. A mannequin may be conjured to follow his gestures, or it may be done with wire and pulleys, connected to a kind of armour that Calidris fastens around himself. The mannequin may be enchanted to speak as he speaks, or his own voice may be conveyed to another mouth by a series of tubes. Either way, the result is similar. One spell may be said to have the effect of two. Or three, if the apparatus is more elaborate. Or ten. Practically speaking, there is no limit, especially if magic itself is harnessed.'

'So Calidris gave rise to thousands of false souls with a single spell. I still don't see—'

'The souls are all the same. They are animated with the same infernal fire. It means that they . . .' Relictus grimaced, lost for words as he strove to communicate the mysteries of his art to a novice such as me. 'Milady, when you summoned Calidris you did so with the blood-bound needle.'

'My greatest mistake.'

'Nonetheless, it serves to illustrate my point. At that moment your pain was his pain – your blood his. A spell had united you. Something analogous applies to the false souls. Each is united with its sibling because they were forged in the same instant, with the same utterance. That is their strength, because it gives Mordax an army of unlimited size. It is also their weakness, because they are all vulnerable to a single counter-spell.'

'A spell known to you?'

'A spell I am confident I can derive, given a little more time. With every day I learn more of Calidris's work. In a short while I will know enough to formulate the counter-spell.'

I looked at the armoured creature, remembering what Relictus had said about it being as innocent as a child. The empty visor was looking back at me, a glimmer of red smoke showing though the glassy slits of its eyes. I sensed a dim curiosity, much like that of a simple animal or slave, but nothing in the way of malice. I should not have cared to have been alone with the Ghost Soldier, but I believed Relictus when he said that it was devoid of guile or hatefulness.

'And then – what will happen?'

'It will die, along with every false soul created by the same spell. That might be a regiment of Ghost Soldiers, or it might be the entire army. Either way, the loss could be decisive.'

'Then you must do it,' I said, 'and with the utmost urgency. The future security of the human species depends on you.'

CHAPTER TWENTY-NINE

'She's turning,' Betony said, when the fact of it could no longer be disputed.

Twenty minutes had passed since the first hint that *Silver Wings of Morning* might be altering her course. At first, we had read nothing into it, assuming only that the robots had made a small, temporary course adjustment in response to the three ships zeroing in on her. The advantage in making such an adjustment was not at all obvious, but – since we could not begin to guess at the robots' tactical thinking – we had assumed that Purslane's ship would eventually resume its original heading, having gained some microscopic but quantifiable advantage over its pursuers.

But she did not stop turning. During the course of those twenty minutes *Silver Wings* had altered her trajectory by a dozen degrees, and there was no sign of her stopping.

Machine Space, the spray of exiled stars we called the Monoceros Ring, circumscribed an arc around the main disc of the Milky Way. Provided a ship confined its trajectory to a course parallel to the surface of that disc, it was bound to make Machine Space sooner or later – even if it took a hundred thousand years, rather than ten or twenty. But a ship would only have to steer a little off-parallel to guarantee missing the Monoceros Ring entirely. As *Silver Wings* continued her course change, her projected destination slowly moved away from Machine Space.

The course correction continued for another hour, until the ship fell back onto a straight vector. The change had cost the robots a little headway, but they would soon regain that advantage when we performed the same turn, as we were obliged to do if we wished to continue the chase.

'Why did they wait until now?' Betony asked. 'They must have known which direction they wanted to head in when they left Neume. All this has done is cost them time.'

'Our pursuit must have forced them to revise their plan,' Henbane said.

'Not necessarily,' I replied. 'I think they always knew exactly where they were going. They wanted us to think that they were returning to Machine Space, so that's the course they set when they departed orbit. They must have been intending to switch onto a different target as soon as they were out of observational range, when they were a year or two out from Neume. But they weren't counting on such a fast response from us: we launched the pursuit fleet after them so quickly that they realised there's no hope of completing that turn without us seeing it. So they've executed it now, before they reach high relativistic speed. It's difficult enough to turn a ship at six-tenths of light, but it's ten times harder at nine-tenths, or faster.'

'But if they're not heading back to Machine Space ...' Sorrel said.

'We have a hard fix on her course now,' said Charlock, his imago glancing aside at a hovering read-out. 'Of course, she may still have a few changes up her sleeve. But if we take this as read, we can extrapolate out to a thousand lights with an error of only a few thousand AU at the far end.'

'Show us,' Betony said, his face still set in a rictus of total concentration.

A map of the galaxy sprang into existence on Dalliance's displayer. The map zoomed in on our present position in the Scutum-Crux Spiral Arm, the scale enlarging until there was a visible gap between the bright, constellated smudge of our ships and the silver circle of Neume. We were still technically inside its solar system, but would soon punch through the star's heliopause into true interstellar space, where only cinder-dark comets swam.

'Here's where we think she's heading,' Charlock said as a red line pushed ahead of *Silver Wings of Morning*. As the vector touched the edge of the box, the scale changed to encompass a greater volume of space. 'Nothing after ten years,' Charlock remarked. 'Increasing to one hundred. No hits so far – she never comes within two years of a catalogued system.' The scale lurched again, until the box was a thousand lights across, but still the red line sailed on without touching anything. Now it was thickening as the cumulative error became visible. 'Close approach to a bachelor sun at nine hundred and thirty years,' Charlock said, doubtfully. 'Maybe that's the target.'

'No worlds, no rubble, no ice,' Betony said. 'There's no reason for them to stop there.'

Bachelor suns were stars that had had their planetary systems ripped away by encounters with other stars early in their history. They were useless to all meta-civilisations, save as wormhole-tappable fuel sources.

'Increasing to ten thousand years,' Charlock said. 'Well outside the Scutum-Crux Arm now. Error radius approaching six months. After seven thousand years, she comes within fifteen years of the perimeter of the Harmonious Concordance, a mid-level empire of seventeen hundred settled systems.'

'Could that be the target?' asked Tansy. 'Allowing for minor course adjustments—'

'Universal Actuary predicts only a fifty per cent likelihood that the Harmonious Concordance is still in existence, dropping to eleven per cent by the time *Silver Wings* would actually get there,' Sorrel said, reading from his own displayer. 'That's an awfully long punt for something that has only a one-in-nine chance of still being there.'

'The UA isn't always on the nail,' Tansy said.

'But it's correct more often than it's wrong,' Sorrel replied, 'and the Harmonious Concordance has all the right indicators for a text-book rise-and-fall. Unless they're counting on dealing with the shrivelled remnants of a former empire, I can't see this being the target.'

'I don't see it either,' Betony said. 'Increase the search volume, Charlock.'

'We're already out to ten thousand.'

'Then we need to look further.'

Charlock shrugged, though his expression told us he no longer expected to gain much from this game. 'Fifty thousand,' he said, as the box swelled again. 'Error radius is now two and a half years – wide enough that we're going to be picking up systems all the way through. We're punching through a lot of galaxy here. You're going to have to trawl through several thousand candidates.'

'List the systems in order of interception,' Betony said. 'We'll work through them one at a time, see if anything jumps out at us. In the meantime, keep refining our estimate of *Silver Wings'* heading. We may be able to narrow that error radius a little.'

'We're wasting our time,' Henbane said. 'For all we know, she's going to turn in a completely different direction half an hour from now.'

'Then we'll repeat the exercise,' Betony said, gruffly indifferent to the other shatterling. 'They're headed somewhere. I'll sleep a lot easier when I know where it is.'

'Or maybe you won't,' I said.

I imagined Aconite standing before me. I had come to like him and would have been glad of his company now. I was alone aboard *Dalliance*, temporarily free of the other imagos.

'There's something on my mind,' I said, speaking a message that he would not hear until many hours from now, back on Neume. 'It's going to sound insane, but I can't stop thinking about it, and I'm hoping it may have some bearing on Mezereon's interrogations. There was something about Cyphel's body that wasn't right.'

I thought of Aconite scratching his beard and looking sceptical. What could possibly be right about a body that had fallen several kilometres onto a hard surface?

'She keeps coming to me,' I said. 'In my dreams. Telling me to pay attention. It's as if my subconscious has worked out what's wrong, but it hasn't yet managed to communicate that to my conscious mind. Now I'm hoping someone back on Neume can see what I'm missing. There are dozens of you, and you have the imagery the Ymirians would have already recorded up to the moment of her death. Maybe there's something ...' I paused, aware of how absurd I might sound when my transmission was received. But I could not ignore Cyphel, the urgency I heard in her voice when she admonished me for not paying attention. 'She had a long way to fall, Ack. What if she was alive all the way down, and she knew who had killed her? Could she have got a message to us?'

I ended my recording. It was several minutes more before I found the courage of my convictions and actually sent it.

The turn had changed nothing as far as our immediate plans were concerned. Following our earlier discussion, the three uncrewed ships were running on independent parallel tracks to *Silver Wings*, so that when they caught up with her, they could direct their energies into her sides rather than into the more vulnerable area of her stern. Seen in the display, the three ships formed an equilateral triangle, spaced five seconds apart. *Silver Wings* lay at the apex of a tetrahedron, ten seconds from any of the pursuing craft, but with that margin slowly decreasing. At three seconds, the ships would be able to target their weapons with sufficient accuracy to disable their prey without destroying it.

What was clear, although not yet understood, was that the distance was closing quicker than expected. It was not that our ships were accelerating any harder than intended, for they had already been pushed to the limits of their engines, with all nonessential megatonnage ejected from their cargo holds. For some reason, *Silver Wings* was not making as much headway as before she had executed her turn. Detailed analysis of her movements since leaving Neume even revealed that the slowdown – more accurately, a barely measurable reduction in acceleration – had begun sooner than the turn.

'They know we're behind them,' Betony said. 'There's no reason in the world for them not to go as fast as they can. So what are they doing? Why aren't they pushing her as hard as she'll go?'

'Maybe it's sabotage,' Orache mused. 'Could Purslane and Hesperus have got into the engine?'

I nodded. 'Hesperus, perhaps. But if he was in a position to sabotage it ...'

Betony nodded. 'Why stop there? He'd go all the way, if he were able: shut her down completely.'

'They've got ships,' I said, almost as the idea formed in my mind. 'A hold full of them, and most of them are still spaceworthy. We already know they made it into the white ark. From what I remember, that ship had its guts stripped out and a parametric engine stuffed inside instead.'

Betony gave a sharp little laugh. 'You think they may be running the ark's motor, counteracting *Silver Wings'* own engine.'

'It's an idea. Purslane's not one to give up without a fight. Perhaps they couldn't get out of the bay, but they could still turn on some of those engines.'

'Enough to flatten space around *Silver Wings*, bring her to a dead stop?'

'Probably not. Probably not even enough to take more than a few per cent off her engine efficiency, and even then only if they get every operational ship up and running.' I grinned, burning with sudden pride and admiration, for I knew beyond a shadow of doubt that this was exactly what Purslane had in mind. 'But that's what they'll be trying to do. Did Purslane sound as if she was ready to curl up and surrender?'

'Not to me,' Agrimony said.

'Me neither. And with Hesperus on her side—'

'She never did give us an explanation of how he came back from the dead after all that time,' Henbane said.

'She knew the other machines were listening in. Maybe there were things she had to keep from them.'

A sonorous chime interrupted our discussion: the signal that the three ships would soon be entering weapons range. Wordlessly we turned our attention back to the display and waited for the seconds to drain by.

CHAPTER THIRTY

The wait had become almost unendurable, the conviction growing in me that Hesperus must have failed, when a quick blur of motion signalled his return. He nodded at me from beyond the outer door of the ark's airlock, his image appearing on a panel to the right of the inner door. My hand moved to the ancient control that would grant him entry.

'I am done, Purslane. You may open the door again.' His voice buzzed from the panel. It was vacuum outside, but he was generating a radio signal from within his body.

'Hesperus?'

'It is me.'

I stilled my hand. He need not have said another word; I already had a bone-deep conviction that this was not him but one of the other two robots. 'I thought we agreed on a code phrase,' I said, as fear pushed its chill hand into my flesh and ran a loving caress down my spine.

'My memory is still not what it was.'

'You were fine when you left. You've been fine ever since you woke up from your coma.'

'Nonetheless, I am still experiencing problems. Would you be so good as to let me in?'

'The code phrase.'

'I no longer remember it.' The tall, broad figure – his coloration was still darkened for camouflage – spun his head around to look over his shoulder. It was a lizard-like movement, lacking any human quality. 'I cannot be certain, but I think Cadence or Cascade may have achieved entry into the chamber. Time may now be of the essence, if you still desire my assistance.'

'Get away from the door. I don't know which one you are, but I know I'm not talking to Hesperus.'

'You are mistaken, Purslane.'

'I don't think so. There's an energy-pistol in my hand – I just had the maker dispense it for me. It's aimed straight at you, with the beam set for maximum dispersion.' The densely packed weapon was cold in my fist, taking the burden of its own weight with the faint, insect-like buzz of levators. 'I can do it. Hesperus told me how to kill a Machine Person. Don't aim for any one spot, but spread the focus around, taking out as much function as possible. You may be holographic, but you're not indestructible.'

'If you were to discharge an energy weapon, you would damage the airlock, leading to fatal decompression.'

'Then it's a good job I'm wearing a spacesuit. That came out of the maker as well.'

The figure took a step backwards, stiff as a knight in armour. It must have made a decision at that point – analysed my voice and concluded that I was beyond persuasion – because I watched its profile shift, the metal skin creasing and stretching, tapering at the waist, broadening at the hips and chest, until I was looking at the elegant, ballerina-like form of Cadence. Her skin was still dark rather than silvery, but in all other respects she had reverted to her normal appearance.

'That was easy,' I said.

'I have killed Hesperus,' she said, using her normal voice. 'He will not be returning to help you now.'

My mind freewheeled. 'Where did you kill him?'

'In this chamber.'

'Not good enough. I want to know exactly where.'

Cadence cocked her head, looking away from the ark. 'By that ship, the green one with the retracted stasis foils.'

It was one of the ships I had told Hesperus to visit, but she might just have been lucky in her guess, or seen him move on the cameras monitoring the bay.

'Bring me the body and we'll talk about it.'

'There is no body. I disintegrated him.' Cadence lifted up one arm, the armour of her sleeve folding open in a subtle, ingenious way, allowing a vicious assemblage of barrels and tubes to spring out. 'Cascade and I have always been armed, from the moment we moved amongst you.' Then she let her arm fall in a stiff arc, mannequin-like, until the cluster of weapons was pointed directly at me. 'Open the door, Purslane, before it is necessary for me to use force.'

'What's stopping you?'

'Clemency. A desire not to inflict further harm. We are machines, not butchers. We value life, even the tawdry approximation of life that is the organic.'

'You're still going to have to kill me if you want to get inside the ark.'

'I would rather not have to do that. Can we not talk now? It was a brave and clever thing that you and Hesperus attempted to do. Despite our combined wisdom, we did not foresee that you would use these ships against us, to slow down *Silver Wings of Morning*. She is a lovely machine, incidentally – worthy of us.'

'I'm glad you like her. I'm planning on having her back.'

'That was always the arrangement, was it not?' Then Cadence angled her doll-like head again, the chamber's light flaring off the elegant ridge of her metal cheekbones and the luscious, bee-stung swell of her steel lips. 'I am puzzled, Purslane. You have a weapon capable of harming me, and you claim to be wearing a spacesuit. You have nothing to gain from my continued existence, yet you have not opened fire.'

'I thought I'd let you have your say first.' My hand tightened around the weapon. The levators held it in place with such determined control that it felt as if I was holding a fixed support, like the knob of a banister. 'I could ask you the same question.'

'The ark's engine is still running. Although this will have only a marginal impact on our chances of success, it would still be better if it was turned off.'

'So kill me and do it.'

Cadence held up her hand and allowed the clustered weapon to fold itself back into her arm. 'You did not believe that I was capable of clemency, but I will prove it to you now. Deactivate the engine and we will come to an arrangement that guarantees your survival. I will give you time to consider this proposal.'

My heart beat in my chest like a pulsar about to spin itself to pieces. I sensed that I was only one mistake, one ill-judged remark, from instant death. I could not attack Cadence even if I wanted to. Despite what I had told her, I was not wearing a spacesuit. There had not been time for the maker to produce one; it had been all I could do to make a weapon.

I had to show that I was in control.

'Get away from the ship. I won't shoot you because there'll still be Cascade, and for all I know you two can make copies of yourselves. But you wanted *Silver Wings* for a reason and whatever that is, it must be important to you. Hugely important, if you'd risk war with the entire human meta-civilisation.'

Cadence must have believed me, because she took several steps backwards.

'You cannot stop us,' she said. 'We are in control.'

'If you say so. The thing is, I'm not convinced you've any plans to keep me alive once we get to wherever we're going. Which means that if I'm going to die anyway – and I'm reasonably sure that's the case – then I might as well get to do it on my terms, achieving something in the process.'

With a firmness that I had never heard in her voice before, Cadence said, 'Do not do this. It will not be in your best interests.'

'Got your attention. That's good.'

I had the impression of intense, feverish computation; the working out of a near-infinite spectrum of outcomes. If a machine could have sweated, Cadence would have. 'We can still negotiate,' she said. 'I will leave now and give you time to think things through. If you disengage the ark, you may dictate arrangements for your survival. If they are acceptable to us, we will comply.'

I had not been expecting this, but I tried to keep that to myself. 'What kind of arrangements?'

'You will bargain with the other humans on our behalf. You will persuade them to stop following us on the understanding that we will let you leave.'

'And I'm supposed to believe you'd follow through on that?'

Cadence started to say something – another calm answer, her voice as beautiful and unruffled as it ever was – but she did not complete her sentence. What happened in the instant that followed was too fast for my eyes or mind to follow. All I could do was put it together afterwards, assembling the sequence of events from the broken fragments that had made it past the hopelessly constricted bottleneck of my animal senses.

Hesperus had attacked Cadence. Lacking a weapon – for there had not been time to mint one before he left the ark – his only option had been to use stealth and surprise. This he had done with considerable success, for nothing in Cadence's reaction showed that she had had any idea that Hesperus was creeping up on her in the shadows of the cargo bay. I recalled now how my first impression of him, when Campion walked him onto *Dalliance*'s bridge, had been of the hunting cat I owned in Palatial, and the statue of *David* in the hallway of the family mansion. Those impressions – contradictory, but complementary – came back to me with renewed force as he sprang onto the other robot, ramming her to the ground. The two dark forms wrestled, their movements so accelerated that all I could make out was a writhing dark mass, like a kind of quantum probability cloud made of metal. It all took place in the absolute silence of vacuum. Then there was a flash, bright enough to illuminate the entire chamber for a single dazzling moment, and then there were two robots again.

They both lay very still.

They were both broken.

Hesperus was on his back, five or six metres from Cadence. There was a dark hole punched right through him, where his heart would have been had he been human. His skin flickered from dark to gold, gold to dark, and then stayed the way it was. Nothing moved behind the glass windows of his skull. Cadence was sprawled on her side facing Hesperus, for all the world as if she had just decided to lie down and take a nap. Her weapon arm had been severed at the elbow, wrenched away from the rest of her – it lay three or four metres beyond Hesperus. A squirming mass of silver machinery, oozing with mercurial unguents, erupted through her stump. Hesperus looked dead, but there was something alive in Cadence. Unable to leave the ark, I could do nothing but watch.

'Hesperus,' I said into the door panel, 'you've got to get up.'

Cadence stirred, but only minutely. Lights flickered in her head and the fingers of her good arm twitched. The fingers of the severed arm, on the far side of Hesperus, also twitched. The angle of her head adjusted in stiff increments until she was looking at the severed arm. Her expression was fiercely serene.

The silver machinery pushed itself further from her stump. It formed a tendril, a single bright filament, which oozed out until it touched the floor. The tendril kept growing, inching its way from the body. At first I thought she was going to reach for Hesperus and do something to him – administer the robot equivalent of a poison kiss, perhaps – but then I realised that the tendril was skirting around him, with the intention of reaching the severed arm.

'Hesperus,' I said again, 'wake up. Please.' I wanted to shout, but the detached part of my mind told me there was no point. If he could not already hear me, nothing I could do would make any difference.

The tendril completed its journey. Reaching the arm, it curled around it slowly, the way a vine might wrap around the fallen limb of a tree. Then it began to retract, slowly but steadily, dragging the weapon arm with it.

'Hesperus, please,' I said.

Something got through. The lights flashed in his head, once. The tendril had already dragged the arm a quarter of the distance back to Cadence.

'She's still alive. Cadence is still alive.'

Squealing, garbled sounds exploded from the door – it was like a hundred people shouting at the same time, in a hundred different languages. If that was Hesperus trying to talk to me, something was very, very wrong with him. But then I already knew that.

'Stand up,' I said, more forcefully now. 'There isn't much time. You either stand up now or we're both dead. Listen to me, robot!'

He moved. It was a lazy yawn of his entire body. Then he was still again.

'Cadence is putting herself back together,' I said. 'If you don't stop her—'

'Slain,' he said, either attempting to pronounce my name, or describing his predicament.

'Move, golden boy. I need you here.'

He shifted again – the motion more coordinated this time. With a single convulsive spasm he rolled onto his side. He seemed to be looking directly at the other robot. The arm was scraping its way past the midline between them, half of its journey now complete. Hesperus lifted an arm, spread his fingers and placed his palm on the floor. He pushed against it and began to lever himself up, until he could get his other elbow under his torso for support. Then his legs twitched and he began to ease himself into a position halfway between lying and sitting. The effort must have cost him, because for several seconds he was motionless. The arm now had only a few metres to go before it was reunited with Cadence. She must have been immobilised somehow, but as soon as she had the arm back she would have a weapon she could aim and fire. Even as I was thinking that, consoling myself that at least she was paralysed, Cadence twitched again and started to sit up. She was regaining mobility by the second, just as Hesperus had done. The robots had formidable powers of self-recovery.

'Hesperus!' I yelled, all logic now departed.

He broke out of his temporary stasis and climbed unsteadily to his feet. I could see the full extent of his damage now – a hole big enough to put a fist and an arm through, cutting right through him.

The walls of the wound glistened with silver gore, bleeding mercury and strobing pulses of hard blue light. One of his legs was stiffer than the other. He turned awkwardly and surveyed the scene before him: Cadence and her severed arm, now only a metre from being reattached.

He stepped across to her, walking like a man with one leg in a calliper. Cadence flinched back, raising her good arm as a shield. Hesperus planted his left foot on the silvery tendril. Still with great stiffness, he knelt down until he could reach the weapon arm with his right hand. He pulled it from the floor, the tendril stretching like hot cheese as he rose to his full height. His fist closed around the silver flesh of the severed arm, crimping it with appalling force. Then – with a single jerky motion – he flung the mangled arm into the darkness. I expected to hear it clatter in the distance, but of course no sound attended its impact.

'Hesperus,' I said, 'can you hear me?'

He said nothing, but took another step closer to the other robot. He kicked her until she rolled onto her back, then lowered his left foot onto her abdomen. Beneath him, Cadence thrashed with increasing strength. Hesperus lowered himself slowly until he was kneeling on her. Then he reached out with both hands and took a firm hold of her remaining arm. His shoulders moved with massive, gorilla-like effort and the arm came loose. He flung it aside, but with an almost disdainful effort, so that it came to rest only a few metres away. Then he swung around, adjusting his hold on her until he faced her legs, and took them off piece by piece. All the while Cadence squirmed and convulsed, but her efforts achieved nothing.

In a short while Hesperus had dismembered the other robot completely, leaving only her head still attached to her torso. He stood up, clutching Cadence's palsying remains to his chest. Still stiff in one leg, he made his way to the door. My heart racing, the energy-pistol still gripped in my hand, I allowed him into the lock. Air cycled in. The inner door opened and Hesperus almost fell out, dragging the head and torso behind him. His movements were still very sluggish and uncoordinated. The air smelled of burned metal and there was a hissing, fizzing sound coming from his open wound.

'I am damaged,' he said, quite clearly.

'Take this,' I said, offering him the energy-pistol. 'You can finish her off.'

'I don't want to finish her off. She can still be of use to us.' The discrepancy between the calmness of his voice and the shuffling, punctured figure before me was unsettling. It was like having a corpse talk back to me.

'Are you going to be all right?'

'I can repair myself, given time. Help me to the bridge. We will be safer there.'

With Hesperus still cradling the other robot, leaning as much of his weight against me as I could bear, we shuffled our awkward way through the ark until we reached the white womb of the control centre. All was as we had left it.

'I should contact Campion.'

'That can wait. Find me aspic-of-machines.'

'What kind?'

'Any kind. It doesn't matter.' He let the torso clatter to his feet. Cadence was still watching his every move, like a viper looking for its chance to strike.

'He is lying,' she said, her own voice just as unchanged. 'The damage he has suffered is not repairable. He is in the process of terminal system shutdown.'

I waved the energy-pistol at her. 'We could just kill her now.'

'The aspic, please.' Hesperus extended a trembling hand and took the weapon from me at last. 'I will keep watch on her. Find Synchromesh for yourself.'

'Why Synchromesh?'

'Just find it.'

It was the first time I had heard irritation in his voice. The human part of him must have been pulling the strings.

In an adjoining chamber I found several tubes of multi-purpose aspic-of-machines. I was already carrying an eye-dropper of Synchromesh. I returned to the command room to find Hesperus still keeping guard on the twitching silver torso.

'What about the bits of her you left outside?'

'They can't hurt us now. They'll attempt to reconvene, but provided her head and torso remain here, that won't happen.' He passed me back the energy-pistol and took the tubes of aspic. 'As I said, I am damaged. But I can repair myself, given an infusion of raw materials.' He took one of the tubes and squeezed a dollop of quivering black aspic into his palm. The material organised itself into various geometric shapes, indicating its readiness.

'Will that ... work with you?' I knelt down, my back against the wall, resting on my haunches with the energy-pistol aimed at

Cadence. 'It's human machinery. I didn't think it had anything to do with the stuff inside you.'

'It doesn't.' His mask formed an exhausted smile. 'But it can be made to. It's very simple, really.' He smeared the black dollop into his wound, caking it around the silvery lining of the tunnel Cascade had blasted through him. As he did so, Hesperus made an involuntary sound, a kind of synthetic howl like a radio picking up too many channels at the same time. 'I am not in pain,' he said, when the moment had passed. 'But there is ... confusion. The aspic will help me repair myself. But it will take time.' He squeezed another mound into his palm and applied it to the wound, over the material he had already administered. Now he convulsed, as if a bolt of electricity had just surged through him.

'Hesperus?'

'Keep your eye on Cascade.' He spread more of the black paste into his chest. 'I must enter a state of reduced consciousness while these repairs are effected. I may be incommunicado for several hours, possibly longer.'

'I'm worried. She's a *robot*, Hesperus – I've already seen how fast you can move.'

'She can't do anything quickly now. It will be safe to use the Synchromesh on a low ratio.'

'I don't like this.'

'I don't like it either, but I'm useless to us both unless I can heal myself.' He pushed a final dollop of machinery into his wound – which now resembled a steep-sided black crater more than a tunnel – and slumped back against the wall. Then his lights flickered once and died completely. I could only trust that, somewhere inside that golden body, something was still alive, putting itself right.

'Go ahead,' Cadence said sweetly. 'Use the Synchromesh. I promise I won't try anything.'

That was when the ark started shaking, the vibration nearly knocking me off my feet.

CHAPTER THIRTY-ONE

Charlock's ship was the first to move within attack range of *Silver Wings of Morning*. With light-minutes of communications lag between *Dalliance* and the three ships of the lead squadron, there was nothing to do but gather around the holographic volume and watch the playing out of a series of events that had already unfolded. Powerless as we were to change the outcome, we still felt as if it should be possible to reach into the blue-gridded space and move the pieces around, as if they were no more than icons in a game of strategy. My mind veered between the conviction that this was the only course of action open to us, and the bitter certainty that I was about to play spectator to the death of my lover and closest friend, fully complicit in the decision to kill her.

'You don't have to watch any of this,' Betony said. 'Go and wait somewhere else. We'll let you know when it's over.'

'I'll sit it out, if that's all right with you.'

'Of course. As long as you understand that none of us would have held it against you.'

Orache's imago reached to touch her nonexistent hand against mine. 'This is difficult for all of us: she's our sister. But I can't imagine what you're going through.'

'Purslane can take care of herself,' I said, but the words rang hollow, as if I was the one who needed convincing.

'*Silver Wings* is strobing her impasse,' Charlock said. 'Pseudo-thrust is falling, as we'd expect.'

Strobing gave *Silver Wings* a measure of defence, but there were gaps in that armour, spaces between the time-phased ribs through which a well-aimed rapier might slip.

Charlock's ship was *Steel Breeze*. In the battle volume she was a blunt-tipped yellow arrow closing on *Silver Wings*, narrowing the distance from tens of thousands to mere thousands of kilometres. 'She's phasing her weapons,' he said, eyeing the banner of icons and numbers accompanying his ship. 'Synching her gamma-cannon to punch through Purslane's impasse.' He turned to face us with pride in his expression. 'She's learned well: it's exactly what I'd do if I was there, controlling her in realtime.'

'A broadside hit,' Agrimony announced, as the numbers tagging *Silver Wings* changed abruptly. 'Significant hull ablation and ionisation ... I think you got through, Charlock.'

He grinned. 'Gamma-cannon cycling for another discharge. Holding sync-lock with the impasse. Firing.'

'Secondary ionisation focus, three kilometres astern of the first. Two palpable hits.' Agrimony looked excitedly at the rest of us, raising a clenched fist. 'We're getting through. She's not putting up any kind of defence. The robots obviously don't have sufficient control.'

'Don't count on it,' I said under my breath. *Steel Breeze* might have punched a couple of craters in *Silver Wings'* hull, but the numbers next to her revealed no drop in acceleration or impasse effectiveness, compared to before the assault.

'Cannon cycling,' Charlock said. 'Maintaining sync-lock. Retargeting on drive epicentre. Firing ...'

After a few seconds Agrimony said, 'Zero ablation. No damage beyond the first two impact sites.'

'She must have shifted to a different field phase,' Betony said. 'Compensate and adjust.'

'Give her time,' Charlock said. 'She's dealt with this kind of thing before. It'll just take her a few moments to assemble a predictive model for the phase and frequency shifts, then she'll be able to punch through again. Gamma-cannon recharging. Firing ...'

'No change in damage status,' Betony said. 'She must be phasing faster than you can sync-lock.'

'Give her time. She just needs to refine her model.'

But when *Steel Breeze* fired again, there was still no sign that she had found a way through to *Silver Wings'* hull. The impasse soaked up the gamma-rays effortlessly, using some of that energy for its own purposes and re-radiating the rest to space in a long, simmering cymbal-crash of downshifted X-rays.

I tightened my handhold as an acceleration surge washed over me. 'We should move the other ships in. One might not be able to cut through, but if they all run different phases and frequencies, *Silver Wings* might not be able to block them all at the same time.'

'That's not the strategy we agreed on,' said Sorrel.

'The one we agreed on isn't working. All it's doing is slowing *Silver Wings* by a tiny amount. Time we moved to a new script, before we play ourselves out.'

Betony wavered for a moment, then nodded. 'Orache, Agrimony: instruct your ships to move into immediate attack range. Coordinate with *Steel Breeze* to find a gap in her coverage.'

With the ships still three minutes ahead of us, it would take that long for the new battle plan to reach them, and just as long again before we saw the results of our change of approach. Until then all we could do was watch Charlock's ship continue her engagement. *Steel Breeze* attempted another two discharges from her gamma-cannon, then spun around, strobed her impasse and applied pseudo-thrust.

'She's not retreating,' Charlock said, as if that was ever in our minds. 'She's clever – she's realised that she can't get through that way. Now she'll do exactly what I'd do in the circumstances – switch to lampreys.'

'How many are you carrying?' I asked.

'Fifty-two. Mid-range gamma-cannons and high-hysteresis skein-drives. Let's see how *Silver Wings* deals with those, shall we?'

'Don't count your chickens,' I murmured. Lampreys were fast and agile, but they could never compare with the potency of a ship-mounted weapon. Nor did they have the ability to adjust beam properties to deal with a rapidly strobing and phase-shifting impasse.

In the battle volume, the lampreys were a spray of yellow dandelion seeds erupting from *Steel Breeze*. They split into two formations – twelve forming a cordon around Charlock's ship, the other forty diving for the much larger target of *Silver Wings*. With their skein-drives applying pseudo-thrust, the lampreys could push against *Steel Breeze*'s field boundary, enabling her to hold her position relative to *Silver Wings* even while maintaining full impasse. That was the one trick Purslane's ship could not emulate: it would have taken thousands of lampreys to overcome the mountainous inertia of *Silver Wings*, and I knew she did not carry that many.

The forty attacking lampreys broke into sub-squadrons and began concentrating their fire on the areas of vulnerability we had already identified. Occasionally one managed to punch through the strobing field, but I knew that it was more by luck than judgement, and even when the gamma-rays touched naked hull, they did no more than scuff against that armour. But perhaps it could work, given time – the death of a thousand cuts, rather than a single, decisive wound. I allowed myself a flicker of encouragement from the fact that *Silver Wings* had yet to respond in kind. Perhaps the robots really were struggling to control all her systems.

Six minutes after the transmission of the new battle orders, Orache and Agrimony's ships – *Mystery Wind* and *Yellow Jester* – moved into attack range, strobing their fields and coordinating the use of their shipboard gamma-cannons with *Steel Breeze*. The lampreys continued their needling assault.

The new ships dropped impasse long enough to release lampreys of their own.

Cannons loosed.

'Impact!' shouted Agrimony. 'Ablation and ionisation, kilotonnes of hull plating! We're getting through!'

'Impassor instability,' Henbane said, catching some of Agrimony's excitement. 'By God, she's hurting. Field dropped to zero for two point eight milliseconds! Four lampreys now inside *Silver Wings'* impasse. Field drop again – make that nine lampreys. Moving to firing positions. We're inside the moat.'

'Main cannons cycling,' Charlock said. 'One clean hit is all we need. I'm starting to think we can actually do this—'

Then he stopped talking. The blunt arrow that was the icon for *Steel Breeze* was flashing on and off, signalling something catastrophic. The banner of numbers and symbols next to the pulsing icon updated rapidly.

Our attention flicked to the realtime image of his ship, captured from the other two vehicles. They were looking through the battle volume, hazed by savage energies, the intervening space roiled by impassor and drive distortion, awash with gas and debris. But even an imperfect view was enough to tell us that something was very wrong with *Steel Breeze*. Charlock's ship was pulsing with miniature explosions, ripping along the raked edge of her flanks like a spectacularly choreographed fireworks display. The arrowhead craft began to tumble, the sequenced pink stutter of real-thrust engines signifying desperate attempts to regain lateral control. It was to no avail. Somewhere inside, the inertia-compensating machinery lost its hold on the ship. As several hundred brute gravities sank their teeth into the fabric of her hull, she tore open like a carcass. An instant later came the fierce light of her dying engine, a growing white sphere dulling to purple and then black along its perfect boundary. The sphere swelled to the size of the impasse quicker than the eye could track. For a delirious moment the impasse held it in check, even though the impassor that had woven that field was now no more than a cloud of fundamental particles at the heart of the explosion. The sphere turned a more furious kind of white, a white that burned into the eye like a hot lance, dappled with the negative specks of the lampreys still gathered around it, and then broke through that final, failing barricade, into open space.

Steel Breeze was gone.

'What just happened?' Charlock said, looking around like a man who needed someone to shake him out of a bad dream. 'Someone tell me what just happened. We were winning. We were getting through. Why did she start fighting back now?'

'She was biding her time,' Tansy said. 'Waiting until all three ships were close. Must have punched through her own impasse with a sync-locked gamma-cannon.'

'Pull *Mystery Wind* and *Yellow Jester* out of attack range,' Betony said, clutching onto his calm façade as if it was the last firm thing in the universe. 'And then hope and pray that they work it out for themselves, because I don't think *Silver Wings* is going to sit and wait for us to make the next move.'

CHAPTER THIRTY-TWO

I reached out a hand to steady myself, the other grasping the fixed handhold of the energy-pistol with renewed strength. The weapon wavered and re-centred itself on Cadence. There was another vibration, harder and sharper this time. Chimes began to sound from the white control core, emergency messages scrolling in cryptic red text across its surfaces.

'What's happening?' I asked.

'Work it out for yourself.'

'It sounds to me as if we're under attack. Maybe Cascade is trying to break into the ark, but I don't think that's it – if he was going to use force against us, he'd have done it already.'

Cadence regarded me levelly, but said nothing.

'The whole ship must be under attack – *Silver Wings* herself. Those were either weapon impacts being soaked up by the impasse, or her own weapons discharging. Or both.'

Cadence tilted her head minutely. 'An attack is in progress,' she informed me, her tone neutral.

'How many ships?'

'Three of your pursuit craft – I give you this information freely, since it is valueless.'

I raised myself from my haunches, still keeping the energy-pistol aimed at her, and made my way to the command console. Recalling the sequence of commands Hesperus had already shown me, I activated the ark's transmitter.

'This is Purslane. I'm still here. Would someone like to tell me what's going on?'

I waited the requisite five or six minutes, but no reply was forthcoming.

'They cannot hear you now,' Cadence said. 'With the impasse raised to battle-strength, only *Silver Wings* herself could get a coherent signal through. This ark does not have the power to reach your friends, nor the sensitivity to detect their return transmissions.'

'You can't run at battle-strength for ever, though. You're losing headway all the time you aren't on drive. That means you consider these ships at least a plausible threat.'

'They have weapons. They could destroy us if we do not take precautions. This is hardly a startling admission.'

There was another vibration, lasting thirty or forty seconds. Despite the many layers of field-damping between the ark and the outer boundary of *Silver Wings'* impasse, it still felt like a small earthquake. I felt a stomach-churning surge as the engine snatched and grabbed, trying to maintain headway in the instants when the impasse was recycling.

'You're doing an awfully good job of keeping me alive,' I said. 'If I was a couple of robots running a ship, I wouldn't bother going to all that trouble to neutralise acceleration, especially in a battle situation. I'd just be thinking about my immediate survival.'

'You are our hostage. If your continued existence enables us to negotiate with our pursuers, then you are of use to us.'

'Then they *are* a concern. Or you've got another reason for keeping me alive.'

'They inconvenience us. They irritate us. No more than that.'

Trusting nothing Cadence said to me, I considered it worthwhile trying to signal Campion again. Again there was no sign that my message had got through. My attention wavered for a few moments, fixated on the unfamiliar technology. When I snapped back onto her, Cadence had begun to push a glistening chrome tendril from one of her leg-sockets.

I shot it. 'Naughty.'

The energy discharge had singed the remaining part of her leg back from the stump, turning it from chrome to charred black. Cadence appeared oblivious to the damage I had just inflicted. 'You must understand that I will do what needs to be done,' she said, as ruthlessly calm as ever.

'That makes two of us, then.'

'Cascade informs me that two of the three ships have now been disposed of. The third is damaged and yet still attempting another assault. It may be that their aim is poor, or that they have simply abandoned any hope of saving you.' Cadence's tone became patronising. 'Of course you feel betrayed. You have every right. How else are you expected to feel, having been deemed expendable?'

I said nothing. Arguing with that implacable silver face was beginning to bore me.

The vibrations increased in ferocity over the next ten or twelve minutes, reached a peak and then ended without warning. I waited, expecting them to return, but as the minutes wore on it began to seem as if the attack was over.

'That's the last ship gone,' Cadence said. 'Three of your fellow shatterlings dead, and to no avail. I believe the ships in question were *Steel Breeze*, *Yellow Jester* and *Mystery Wind*. Doubtless you can tell me who was aboard them.'

'Our ships don't need us aboard.'

'Yes, cling to that possibility.' After a moment she added, 'What I said to you earlier, before we were interrupted – the offer still stands, Purslane. Negotiate with your friends. Tell them to give up their pursuit and we will still let you leave.'

'And Hesperus?'

'Take him if you wish. No matter what he told you, he is damaged beyond effective repair.'

'You're not looking too good yourself. Aren't you upset that Cascade hasn't come down to try and rescue you?'

'He knows I pose no risk to the success of this mission. I cannot be coerced or manipulated. I cannot be tortured or deceived. If I imagined there was the slightest danger of you learning something of tactical value, I would destroy myself. If Cascade felt the same way, he could reach into me and kill me himself.'

'Where are we headed?'

'You'll find out when we get there.'

'Hesperus already looked inside you, when he was damaged and you were trying to see what he knew. Isn't that a concern?'

'He saw very little. He is even weaker now, and we have modified our protocols to block the one channel he was able to penetrate. It was an oversight, an unacceptable one, but no great damage was done. We still have the ship, which was always our objective.'

'My ship.'

'You've done well with her. She is very fast.'

'Is that all it is, Cadence? Is that all this is about?'

She cocked her head. 'What else could it be? Speed is of the essence. Your ship is unquestionably fast.'

'End of story.'

'Yes.'

'It seems to me that you came a long, long way just to find a very fast ship. Hesperus and I don't think you learned very much when you were on Neume.' I shifted to a more comfortable position, resigned to the fact that this was going to be a long wait. There had been no change in Hesperus since his lights had gone out; nothing to indicate he was ever coming back to life. 'Did you kill Cyphel?' I asked. 'You can tell me now. It's not going to make a difference to our relationship.'

'Then why ask?'

'Old-fashioned curiosity.'

'Then yes, we killed Cyphel.'

'By throwing her off a balcony? Sorry, but that doesn't strike me as quite your style. I've seen how quickly you can move, how you can change form and colour when you need to. I can't help thinking you'd have preferred to kill her some other, less clumsy way.'

'It would have been a mistake to assassinate her in a way that identified us as the culprits.'

'No; you didn't do Cyphel. That was someone else. Her death might have suited you; it might have put us off the immediate trail of solving the mystery of the ambush, but it wasn't you. And you didn't want me to know that, did you?'

Something quickened behind her eyes: alarm or interest, I could not say for certain.

'What you know, what you do not know, is of no concern to me.'

'I know why we were ambushed. It was to prevent the emergence of information damaging to the Commonality. If a handful of us hadn't been late, it would have been all over for Gentian Line. The secret that we were about to reveal to the wider galaxy would have stayed a secret. But no one allowed for *you*.'

'Then the ambushers were acting in the interests of humans,' Cadence said, with an amused tone. 'From your standpoint, they were doing the right and proper thing. Far from hating them, far from seeking to bring them to justice, you should applaud their efforts. If you care about your species, you should do all in your power to complete the work the ambushers began. Tell your friends to turn their ships around, return to Neume and concentrate their weapons on any remaining Gentian shatterlings. Then turn that fire on themselves, until none are left. As a final grace note, you could be the last to commit suicide; the last to take that secret to her grave. Would that not be a reasonable course of action, Purslane? Would that not be the *decent* thing to do?'

'It might, if you didn't already know about the ambush and the reasons for it.'

'Well, there is that.'

I tipped the Synchromesh into my eyes, one cold, clear drop into each. 'You didn't come to suppress the emergence of that knowledge. Something else brought you to Neume, and I don't think it was my ship, either.'

'Why else?'

'That's what I'd like to know. That's what I'm going to find out, one way or another.'

'And then?'

'I'll stop you. There are a million ways to do it.'

'Almost all of which happen to involve your death.'

'But like you say – that would be the decent thing to do. I'm not above a grand gesture if I think it'll serve a higher good. It just may not be *your* higher good we're talking about.'

I lifted my sleeve and adjusted the dial on my chronometer.

CHAPTER THIRTY-THREE

Charlock might have lost his prized *Steel Breeze*, but he still had enough grip on events to remember the search he had been running before the failed attack. There was only a slight waver in his voice as his imago spoke, addressing us all.

'The battle didn't change a damned thing. *Silver Wings* varied her course during the initial assault, but as soon as it was over – as soon as we lost *Mystery Wind* and *Yellow Jester* – she fell back on exactly the same vector she was following before. The course projections I showed you earlier are still valid. She'll still skirt the Harmonious Concordance in seven thousand years, passing within fifteen years of the present boundary. I think we agreed that that isn't likely to be the destination.'

'Further out?' Betony asked. 'I asked you to look out to fifty thousand years.'

'I did. Here are the candidate systems, in order of interception.' He raised his hand to an offstage displayer.

Dalliance showed the same list. It kept scrolling, line after line. Coordinates, Commonality name for the primary and for the major planet or moon with which the system was most likely to be associated; a string of code numbers identifying surface conditions, metallicities, host civilisations or the absence thereof.

It was a long, bewildering list – hundreds of possible solar systems. Until Charlock had produced it, I had imagined it would be a relatively simple business to scan through it until something jumped out at us. I had even wondered if the target might turn out to be one of the systems under investigation by the Vigilance, but none of those were showing up.

'She passes through each of these systems?' Orache said – calmer now, the loss of her ship absorbed if not forgotten.

'Maybe not, but while we're still uncertain of her trajectory, we can't rule any of them out.' Charlock's brow was glossy with perspiration – he dabbed at it ineffectually, drying his fingers on his sleeve. 'There are hundreds of worlds where Gentian Line, or another Line of the Commonality, has had some kind of business before. But that would apply no matter which direction we looked, and none of the systems on this list are of any obvious significance.'

'Any Prior involvement?' I asked.

'Nothing. I searched for relic sites, but nothing came up.'

Agrimony scratched at the skin under his collar. 'What about cultures that have had dealings with the Machine People? There must be some in that list.'

'A handful,' Charlock said, 'but according to the UA, they've next to no chance of still being there.'

'How many candidates in total?' Betony asked.

'Three hundred and forty-eight. Of course, limiting the search sweep to fifty kilo-years was an entirely arbitrary decision. If I look further out, or allow for an additional degree of uncertainty in our projection of Purslane's vector, we'll start picking up thousands. That's before we factor in stellar proper motion, galactic rotation and the degree to which the robots are allowing the gravitational field to bend their trajectory.'

'There are nine of us,' I said. 'We could at least break that list down into manageable chunks and see if we find anything that way. We should send it back to Neume, as well.'

'I've done that already,' Charlock said. 'But we're getting fast now, and it's going to take a while for any return signals to catch up with us. Before we dice the list into pieces, though, I think there's something you all ought to know.'

Betony crossed his arms. 'You found something?'

'Not in this list. But for the sake of my own curiosity I extended the search volume a little further, just in case we were missing something obvious.'

I sensed Betony's patience hanging by a thread. 'And?'

'There's something at sixty-two thousand lights – way across the plane of the galaxy. Quite honestly, I don't know what to make of it. But if we take the numbers at face value, it's a very high-confidence hit. She's aimed directly at it.'

'At what?' I asked.

'One of our stardams,' Charlock said.

Galingale reported in a little while later. I was outside the summer house in *Dalliance*'s gardens, making a vain effort to clear my head with some fresh air in my lungs and blue skies above me. I had told the statues to stop moving around – their slow, dreamlike enactments were too distracting. I wanted absolute stillness outside my skull, in contrast to the whirlwind of thoughts and emotions going on inside it.

'I'm still prepared to have a crack at this,' Galingale's imago said, rendered with gauzy indistinction halfway up the gently sloping meadow, the others gathered around him in more solid invocations.

'Not after what we've just been through,' Betony said. 'We've lost three ships; I don't want to lose another ship *and* a good shatterling. It was a courageous offer, Galingale, but it was made before we had a real appreciation of what we're up against. Throwing another ship at *Silver Wings* – no matter how well intentioned the gesture – won't achieve anything.'

'I feel that way as well,' I said. '*Steel Breeze* and the other ships weren't badly equipped, and nothing they did was obviously stupid. We're just dealing with a stronger adversary, with a rapidly improving control of Purslane's ship.'

Galingale's response arrived two minutes later. 'All the more reason to strike now, before that control gets any better.' There was more determination in his voice than I had been expecting. 'Besides – we can change our strategy now.'

I had my hands on my hips. 'Can we? Nothing's changed, as far as I'm aware.'

'No one's going to say it, so it may as well be me. It's been a while, Campion.' Galingale looked around at the others. 'We haven't heard from Purslane for a whole day. Her silence began before the battle, so it can't just be the difficulty of getting a signal through the impasse. We should have heard from her since – we know our attack didn't come close to doing any real damage to *Silver Wings*.'

'Then she's still alive.'

'And not talking?' Galingale was staring at me with genuine sympathy. 'She'd have been in touch, Campion. Unless the robots found a way to get to her.'

'She was safe.'

'She was secure in the ark. But we both know the robots weren't going to let her stay there unchallenged, especially if she started getting on their nerves.' He raised his hands suddenly, anticipating my response. 'I'm not saying she's dead – I'm just saying we have to consider it as a possibility, whereas before it was a stone certainty that she was still alive. Now we don't have the luxury of that knowledge.'

'I do.'

'For the sake of argument, how does this change things?' Betony asked.

'Our ships exposed themselves to broadside attack. That's not a risk we ought to take again. With lateral-mounted gamma-cannons, we have the tactical advantage in a stern-chase. Our ships are designed to shoot forward, not behind.'

There was no need to discuss the case of *Silver Wings*. Galingale was correct in all respects, and every one of us knew it. When you already have some of the fastest ships in the galaxy, defending against pursuers is seldom the highest priority. That did not mean our ships were powerless against a chasing adversary, but that the most effective weapons – the ones that were too large or cumbersome to steer – were normally optimised for forward attack.

'She'll still have an impasse raised as soon as you enter weapons range,' Charlock said. 'What makes you think you'll get through it any easier than our ships did?'

'I'm not saying I will. But at least I won't be trying to hit a specific target, or avoid hitting sensitive areas. I can just concentrate my fire wherever I sense the greatest weakness in the impasse, or the underlying hull. Now we know that the stardam is her objective, stopping that ship – destroying her, if necessary – has become more important than just slowing her.'

He was glossing over the uncertainties regarding the destination, the possibility that it might not be the stardam, but I was ready to let that slide for now.

'Without an opener, they won't achieve anything,' I said.

'And you'd stake the reputation of the Line, and the future stability of several human civilisations, on that assumption? Sorry, Campion, but we can't trust Lady Luck any more. Lately she's taken to pissing on us from a great height.'

'I won't sanction it,' Betony said. 'Not while we know Purslane's still alive. She may come through with a transmission at any moment – we can't guess the conditions she's under.'

I allowed myself a moment's relief.

'But it'll take a while for *Midnight Queen* to reach attack position, won't it?' Betony went on.

'If I put myself into abeyance and disengage all safeguards, I can be within attack range in thirty hours. Unless *Silver Wings* slows down, no other ship has the capability to cross that gap.'

Betony began to turn away. 'Do it. You have Line authority.'

'What . . .' I started to say.

Betony silenced me. 'He keeps a channel open the whole while. He doesn't get authorisation to attack until we've reviewed the data again, when he's nearly in range. That's thirty hours, Campion. If we haven't heard from Purslane by then, I think even you would have to admit . . .' But that was as much as he could bring himself to say.

'I swear I won't attack unless we know she's beyond all hope,' Galingale said. 'Now excuse me, if you will. I need to make some arrangements.'

His imago buzzed with static and vanished from the garden.

CHAPTER THIRTY-FOUR

Synchromesh did things to my body. It slowed other processes besides the perception of time. But after more than two hours of keeping that weapon on Cadence – more than twenty hours of actual time – I began to sense a growing heaviness in my abdomen, a warning rumble that there were biological processes that were no longer happy about being held in check. My thoughts took on a frayed, burred quality, like old rope. I began to slip in and out of alertness – more than once daydreaming that Hesperus was in fact up and well, and that between us we had managed to overcome the robots. Each time I snapped out of these interludes with a renewed determination to stay watchful, but the effort was taxing. Cadence was watching me with venomous interest, listening to the ebb and flow of my mental processes. To her, my mind was lit up like a stained-glass window. She was waiting for certain facets to darken, and then she would act.

At twenty-four hours, the chronometer brought me back into realtime. I felt just as drained and foggy-headed as when I had been in thrall to Synchromesh, but now each second hit me with unbridled force.

'It's becoming difficult now,' Cadence observed.

I stood up, my legs two pillars of numbness slowly transmogrifying to burning pain. With effort I walked to the command console again, still holding the energy-pistol on Cadence. I might have missed it, but I did not think we had come under attack again.

'Campion,' I said, speaking at the console, 'this is Purslane. I'm still here, wondering if you can hear me now. Anything I need to know?'

The silence stretched like tortured spacetime. I prowled the room, eyeing the two broken robots, wondering what was keeping Campion. A side-effect of Synchromesh withdrawal is that the ordinary flow of time can occasionally seem sluggish, until the brain readjusts. But even with this knowledge I still felt as if an unreasonable amount of time had passed. I was just about to send another message when his voice came over the speaker.

'You're still alive!' Campion said delightedly. 'Thank God. We hadn't heard anything for so long, we were starting to fear the worst. We knew you couldn't get a signal through when the impasse was raised, but after the attack was over we couldn't understand why you were still silent. I started worrying, all right? You know about the attack, I'm assuming. We managed to hit *Silver Wings*, but not as well as we'd hoped. The good news is we only lost ships, not shatterlings. Charlock, Orache and Agrimony are still with us, aboard our vehicles. The main thing is, we haven't given up. We also think we may know where you're headed. Talk to me, Purslane. Tell me what's happening.'

'Before you say anything else, tell me the destination,' I said.

His reply came back a little more than four minutes later. They had closed the gap, although only by a small margin.

'Nothing's definite,' Campion said, 'but we've extrapolated your course and found something. We don't know the significance of it yet – there's a mountain of uncertainty to deal with. But on the face of it, if we take our best estimate of your trajectory and run it out to sixty-two kilo-lights, there's something there. It's not just another solar system or the boundary of a mid-level empire. There's a stardam, Purslane – and it's one of ours.'

I glanced at Cadence, making sure she was not getting up to any mischief. 'A Gentian stardam. You're certain about that.'

'Beyond any doubt. It's been there for three million years – half the age of the Line. At least, it looks like one of ours – we're the ones who are supposed to be monitoring it, making sure it keeps doing its job.'

I thought of the stardam Campion had stabilised near the Centaurs' solar system. 'What do you mean, it looks like one of ours? Either it is or it isn't. There should be a clear record in the trove of when we installed it, who was involved, the client civilisation or civilisations, what kind of sun needed trapping, why it wasn't a job for the Rebirthers or Movers.'

'It's definitely Gentian,' Campion came back, 'but the trove record is much sparser than we'd normally expect. And it's difficult to corroborate, too. According to the trove, the shatterling in charge of the initial installation was Orpine – he was the one who gathered the ringworlds and placed them around the star. But Orpine's dead – he went more than a dozen circuits ago.'

In other words, I thought to myself, attrition had taken Orpine not very long after he would have installed the stardam. Searching my mind, I tried to recall the circumstances of his disappearance, but without access to my trove I was powerless. Attrition had taken more than a hundred shatterlings even before the ambush, and with the best will in the world I could not recall the precise details of how each had died. In some cases it would never be known.

'Orpine vanished,' Campion went on. 'We don't know what happened to him. Since then, the stardam's taken care of itself – we've monitored it, of course, and once every circuit or so, one of us has been tasked with making an inspection fly-by. Other than that, there's really not much to say. The star in question was an O-type supergiant, brushing within a dozen lights of two emergent cultures, neither of which had regained interstellar capability at the time the dam was installed. If the star had blown, it would have disassociated the ozone in the atmospheres of their home-worlds, leading to massive genetic damage in the human populations. They'd have all died out within a year. Scaper intervention might have helped ... but contact was considered risky, and this was at a time when Gentian Line was anxious to assert itself within the Commonality.'

'And these civilisations? What about them now?'

'Both gone,' Campion said four minutes later, after I had examined Hesperus for further signs of life. 'One blossomed into a reasonably well-developed empire, encompassing about five thousand systems. Then they got into a micro-war with an outgrowth of the Vermillion Commonwealth and that was their fifteen minutes over and done with. The other culture never got beyond chemical rockets and fusion bombs before deciding they'd spare the galaxy their continued existence. Now ...' He paused, as if he was reading from the trove again. 'Beyond that, things aren't so clear-cut. If the supernova happened today, it would inconvenience a number of bordering civilisations. There'd be deaths, certainly – maybe in the tens of billions. But these are technological societies that'd have the means to organise evacuation and biosphere-shielding efforts. There's no one so close that we'd be talking about system-wide extinctions.'

'We're not thinking about a supernova happening now,' I said. 'We're thinking about the premature collapse of a stardam. A Type

Two supernova gives up its energy over the course of months, tailing off over years. When a stardam fails, you get all that energy in one flash.'

'I know; it could be a lot worse. We know what happened to the Consentiency of the Thousand Worlds – that's the one and only time a stardam's ever failed on us. But that dam was smack in the middle of their empire, and they weren't remotely ready for it.'

There was no need to remind me about Ugarit-Panth.

'Could something like that happen now? The death of an entire civilisation?'

'I don't know. No one looks as vulnerable as the Consentiency did back then. And there's still the possibility of warning them ahead of time. Even if *Silver Wings* reaches her maximum speed, she'll still be slower than light by one part in ten thousand. That's not much of a difference, but if we sent a light-speed signal ahead of us now, it would still reach the locals six years before you do. Granted, that isn't sufficient time to evacuate dozens of solar systems. But it would be enough time to put contingency measures in place – time to dig bunkers, move populations underground or into armoured ships. And you're not moving that quickly, anyway. You're holding at point-nine-nine-nine – giving the locals sixty years, not six. That really would be enough time for them to start moving people from system to system.'

'It worked, then. Hesperus really did manage to get some of the other engines up and running.' I glanced at him again, but nothing had changed.

'He is not coming back,' Cadence said.

'What we don't know is the point of this mission, even if the stardam is the target,' Campion said. 'If the robots mean to initiate a war, then detonating a stardam in the middle of a galaxy might be seen as a psychologically valuable opening move. But it won't inflict real damage. They'll sterilise space for a few thousand light-years, maybe even trigger a few secondary detonations. At worst, even if we don't warn them ahead of time, it'll touch no more than six or seven civilisations, none of which are major players. It won't damage the Commonality in any meaningful way. The other big-league factions, the Rebirthers, the Scapers, the Movers ... they won't be affected either. If they're hoping to knock the hub out of the meta-civilisation, this is the wrong way to do it.'

Perhaps all they wanted to do was punish us, I thought – to hurt us the way we had hurt that earlier machine civilisation. Not to wipe us out completely, but to let us know that the crime had not been forgotten, and most definitely not forgiven.

That did not strike me as a very robot way of thinking, though.

'But there's a deeper objection, above and beyond the military pointlessness,' Campion said. 'They *can't* break it open. Stardams need maintenance, and sometimes they fail. But there's nothing they can do to make one fail ahead of time if it hasn't already started to go wrong.'

'What if they were to use *Silver Wings* as a relativistic battering ram, driving her into the stardam at full speed? Could that achieve anything?'

'No one knows for sure – it's not exactly something you go around doing just for the hell of it. But there have been cases of ships ramming stardams, or Prior ringworlds, at near-light speeds. In all documented instances, the structure remained intact. Ringworlds shatter if they're not handled properly, but they're massively resilient against impacts. Perhaps the robots have data we don't, enough to convince them that they can smash the dam with *Silver Wings*. It would at least explain why they needed a fast ship—'

'If they slow down, and tamper with the dam?' I asked.

'If we can get a warning signal ahead of you, the relevant civilisations can place an armada around that dam, above and beyond the defensive systems already in place. *Silver Wings* would make a difficult target at cruise speed, but if she was forced to slow to system speeds, I wouldn't rate her chances very highly.'

'Me neither,' I said, more to myself than Campion. I had still not told him about the earlier wave of Machine People and the awful, inexcusable thing we had done to them. The knowledge sat inside me like a dark stone, trying to force its way to the surface. I did not want Cadence or Cascade to know how much Hesperus had told me, because some of his knowledge could only have come from his time as the Spirit of the Air. 'But if they had an opener,' I said, almost before I could examine the words and decide if it was wise to say them aloud, 'a one-time opener, like the one the Line gave you when you were sent to the Centaurs ... that would work, wouldn't it?'

'I only used the opener to adjust the stardam.'

'But there are openers that do more than that. You only had Line authorisation to make adjustments – it was too soon to take the stardam apart; the energy levels were still much too high. But if they'd sent you to dismantle a stardam that had already served its purpose, so that those ringworlds could be used elsewhere—'

'They'd have given me a single-use opener with full dismantlement privileges,' Campion said, finishing my sentence for me four minutes later. 'But they don't give out those unless there's a cast-iron reason, with full Line oversight. The key's tuned to a specific stardam – it can't be made to open another one prematurely.'

'But somewhere there must be a key for this stardam. If not a key, then at least the information to make it.'

Campion corrected me. 'There's only ever one key that lets you take a stardam apart. It's made at the same time as the dam, code-locked at the deepest levels. Nothing else will work, and no one keeps a record of those codes. The thinking is, better to lose the key and never be able to open the dam than risk a duplicate copy falling into the wrong hands. It means some of our ringworlds are tied up shielding stars that have already turned cinder, but that's a price worth paying.'

'And the one for this stardam?'

'Destroyed in a micro-war, only a few hundred thousand years after the dam was installed. According to the trove, anyway. But at this point I'm not sure I'd take anything in the troves as gospel. We thought we were being clever, lying to Ugarit-Panth. But we've been feeding ourselves another set of lies all along.'

I looked at Cadence again. All of a sudden, with the revelatory force of daylight breaking over a dark landscape, it was clear to me why they wanted my ship.

Silver Wings of Morning was completely incidental to their plans. It helped that she was fast, but there were other fast ships in Gentian Line and mere speed was not the central issue. They had not come all the way to our reunion on the off-chance of getting a ride to the stardam. If all they needed was to reach that point in space, they could have saved time and effort just by going there directly. They had not even taken control of Sainfoin's ship when they were her guests.

They had come for me. Not because of my ship, or because of something in my head, but because there was something in my ship they needed. Long before the terms of my censure had been decided upon, the robots had been steering the Line towards a single objective.

Because somewhere inside *Silver Wings of Morning* was the single-use opener, keyed to the stardam.

I felt dizzy, as if I had ascended into thin air too quickly. It was not a question of needing corroboration. Now that the idea had fixed itself into my skull, I knew that I was right. On some level, I had known all along. Ancient memories could be scrubbed, but they could never be wiped completely.

I had always been a hoarder, unwilling to throw anything away.

There had been a reason for that.

'Purslane,' Campion said, when the dizziness had begun to ease, if not pass completely, 'there's something you ought to know, in case we lose contact again. Galingale's going to have another try at crippling *Silver Wings*. There's no harm in the robots knowing our intentions – they'll have guessed them by now if they've seen *Midnight Queen* coming closer. If there's anything you can do to protect yourself, you should do it.'

'I will,' I said. 'But there's something you need to know as well. Nothing matters more than stopping this ship. We may not know why the robots want to break open that stardam, but we can be sure it's not going to be in our best interests. Now that we know the destination – I'm certain about that, by the way – *Silver Wings* must not be allowed to get there. I'm not talking about crippling her, Campion. You can't risk failure now, not when so much is at stake. Tell Galingale to use everything he has. Tell him to shoot me down.'

PART EIGHT

PART EIGHT

Relictus may have disappointed Calidris, but he did not disappoint me. Our losses continued without respite, but in his dungeon the failed apprentice at last pieced together the elements of the counter-spell. Because of his restraints, he could test only the simplest parts of it in isolation. He pored over the details for many weeks, refusing to allow even the minutest detail to go unexamined.

'The instant I conjure this spell, Calidris will know of it,' Relictus said. 'I must be confident of success, for if I fail, I shall not get a second chance. Calidris will adapt his methods, and this one opportunity will slip through our fingers.'

'Do what you must.'

Eventually he pronounced himself ready. The text of the spell occupied an entire page, as complicated and difficult as a piece of chamber music. Once he had begun to utter it, there would be no going back, and the tiniest mistake, the smallest imprecision, would render the entire spell ineffective.

'I must be unbound,' Relictus said. 'If I do not have complete freedom of movement, the spell will be miscast.'

'Keep that knife on his neck,' I told Lanius, who was with me in the dungeon.

Relictus shook his head slowly. 'The knife will impede me.'

'I should trust you, when you could just as easily use your magic to escape this dungeon?' I asked.

'If I did, milady, my absence would still be the least of your worries. Count Mordax would triumph eventually, and that would be as bad for me as it would for you. You have little option but to trust me now.'

'Take away the knife,' I growled.

Relictus rubbed a finger across his throat, where the knife had nicked his skin and drawn a thin line of blood. I knew then that he would not betray us. He had already had time to utter a debilitating spell, and yet he had held his tongue.

He walked to the Ghost Soldier and undid its fastenings.

'Why do you free it?' I asked.

'As an effective demonstration of the spell's potency, milady. Otherwise you would see little difference.'

'Are you sure it's safe?'

'Perfectly so. Can you not see how trusting it has become?' He beckoned the Ghost Soldier to step forward, then raised an arm indicating that it should stop. 'It understands nothing of what I say. It still thinks I mean it no harm. I think it even likes me, in a limited fashion. I have been far kinder to it than the captain who once ordered it into battle.'

'Are you ready to cast the spell?'

He returned to his desk, pushed hair from his wild eyes and ran a finger down the lines of the spell, formulated in the cluttered symbolic language of magicians. His finger stopped once, moved back a line, and I saw hesitation in his face. Then he nodded and resumed his progress.

'There is no reason to delay. I am as ready now as I shall ever be,' Relictus declared.

'Then do it.'

He closed his eyes once, reopened them after a moment, inhaled deeply and began speaking. The words meant nothing to me; the gestures indecipherable. But their effect on the Ghost Soldier was beyond argument. It began to jerk, the armour twitching. Relictus was so absorbed in the accurate recitation of the spell that I do not think he allowed himself to record its consequences. When he was halfway through the spell (I followed the progress of his finger as he moved from line to line) the armour toppled over, the Ghost Soldier thrashing on the dungeon floor like a man in the grip of palsy. Its movements became more frenzied. A noise began to issue from the armour, like the wind through a draughty door. The figure quickened its movements. The head thrashed from side to side. The arms and legs beat the ground, moving so rapidly that the eye struggled to keep up. Relictus continued with his recitation. Three-quarters of the way down, the Ghost Soldier's paroxysm reached a moment of maximum violence – the armour thrashing, the sound a squeal of agony – and then it began to calm, its movements slowing, its strength ebbing. Before Relictus had reached the last line of his spell, the creature was still. The red smoke was no longer visible.

'It is done,' he said, mopping his brow with his sleeve and drawing a series of deep, relieved breaths. 'I do not believe I made any error of recitation. Judging by the state of the Ghost Soldier, the formulation was correct.'

'It seemed to feel pain,' I said, distressed by the spectacle in a way I had not anticipated. 'An agony beyond words.'

Relictus offered his hands to be bound again. 'Did I ever say it wouldn't?'

'And the others?'

'If the spell was well concocted, and my reasoning sound, this will not be the only Ghost Soldier to have fallen this day.' Relictus smiled – I could tell that the dying agonies of the false soul meant less to him than the death of a fly. 'I await intelligence from the master-at-arms, milady. I believe the news will be most gratifying.'

I left Relictus in his dungeon, with that squealing sound still ringing in my skull. It would not leave me for many days.

Ten nights later the green agents came again. They carried me to their bright room and pushed more needles into my skin. They had been urgent before, but now their furtive efforts had a desperate edge, as if everything depended on the outcome of this one intervention.

'Listen to me, Abigail,' one of them said, leaning over me with a wand that shone crimson fire into my eyes. 'You are still inside Palatial. This is not the real world. The real world is outside. Blink if you can understand what I am telling you.'

I blinked, but only because I wanted to trick them.

Of course, they won in the end.

Their intrusions into my reality grew more frequent, more persistent, and the alternate reality of the white room began to vie for dominance, becoming more solid, more tactile with each visitation. The green men were doctors and technicians, not imperial traitors or agents of another empire. Slowly, painfully, I began to accept the truth of what I was being told over and over again. I was not the princess of a magic Kingdom; I did not have a stepbrother called Count Mordax; I did not have access to a private sorcerer named Relictus. All these things were figments – woven by a machine that had begun to malfunction, sucking me further and further into its dreamlike narrative.

I was Abigail Gentian – daughter and heir of the most respected cloning business in the Golden Hour.

I was going places.

And yet it was so very hard to let go of the princess's realm, with all its seductive allure: the power not just to move finance around, but to command magicians, to put prisoners to the sword and inspire armies to ride in my name.

I kept sinking back into Palatial's grasp. Even when I was outside the game's green box, it exerted a hold on me. My dreams kept returning to the Palace, to the feudal simplicity of that world. It was a time of celebration and triumph. We had beaten the Ghost Soldiers; left Mordax's army in tatters.

Of Mordax, nothing more was ever heard.

Much later, when the psychosurgeons (the same ones who had been looking after my mother) declared that I was healed, I learned that the little boy had not been so lucky. His copy of Palatial – the means by which we shared our fantasy, even though we were forbidden from meeting – had malfunctioned even more seriously than my own. They had pulled out a grinning, drooling vegetable, and all attempts to restore proper cognitive function had failed. Now he was plugged back into the game permanently, wired into it on a neural level. It was the only time he seemed content.

I had been lucky. They had pulled me out just in time.

That at least is what I have always believed happened to me. Of certain other things I am much less confident. I was born in a large and ever-changing house on the edge of the Golden Hour, and for a large part of my arrested childhood I had a companion who occasionally came to play. I remember his shuttle and the robots that came down the landing ramp when it was docked. He was a cruel little boy and I do not remember his name. He may even have been the scion of one of the rival families, and there could have been optimistic plans for our marriage, decades in the future. What is beyond doubt is that I had a copy of Palatial, and it eventually went wrong and sucked me in.

If you suppress a memory, it seems to me that two things can happen. The memory may stay repressed, absolutely closed to both conscious and unconscious recall. Or – and this is surely the more likely outcome – the memory finds expression elsewhere. It will seep into other memories, distorting them, shaping them to conform to the truth of what has been suppressed.

I thought of the Ghost Soldier dying, the agony of that scream cutting through every adult certainty of my existence.

Had we committed a crime beyond condemnation?
More to the point: had I?

The last place I remember visiting as Abigail, although it was not the last thing that happened to me, was the room where we grew the shatterlings. It was a huge domed chamber laced with gleaming white balconies and ladders, the vats arranged in stacked rings. Aside from the hum of the machinery feeding the vats and the occasional chirp or beep from the monitoring devices, the room was crypt-silent. Everything in the room was sterile and cold. It felt more like a place of death than the beginning of something emblematic of life and lust. Ludmilla Marcellin had made a thousand clones for herself, but this room contained only nine hundred and ninety-nine Gentian shatterlings. There was a thousandth vat, but it was presently empty.

When she cast her ships into the void, Ludmilla had opted to remain behind. The ultimate paradox of her adventure was that she had to stay in the Golden Hour if she wished to bask in the admiration of the society that had made her. It was consolation enough to know that her cloned facets, with all the memories she had acquired up to the moment of her final scan, were riding out to the stars. If all went well – and I do not believe there was the least shadow of doubt in Ludmilla's mind concerning that eventuality – they would carry her essence into the unimaginably remote future. One distant day they might reassemble into a single human being, a person who believed herself to be Ludmilla Marcellin, but by then the original version of that individual would be long dead, and perhaps long forgotten.

I could see the attractions of being admired. But because I was not the first, because the idea had not been mine, the acclaim measured out to me could never equal that which Ludmilla was presently enjoying. That was why I had chosen to fly with the clones, rather than stay behind.

In a little while, when my memories had been scanned for the last time, I would be surgically prepared for insertion into the final vat. My growth state would be synchronised with the other shatterlings. My end-state gender would be determined on a random basis. No one, not even the technicians who had designed and supervised the cloning programme, would be able to tell the essential difference between me and any of the other occupants. Via a process of double-blind screening, my true identity would even be concealed from the monitoring machines. They would treat me exactly the same way they treated all the shatterlings. No documents would exist to identify which shatterling was in fact the real Abigail. When I awakened, I would take a new name.

The beautiful part was that even I would not know who I had been. Since my scanned memories would be drip-fed into all the other heads, all the shatterlings would recall visiting this chamber and seeing the empty vat. They would all have the luxury of thinking they might have been Abigail. They would all carry my memories, as far back as they went: the mansion, the little boy, our treacherous games in Palatial. The process of insertion into the vat would render my own memories no sharper, no more obviously authentic, than their own.

I had entered the cloning room alone, but now I became aware of a softly breathing presence behind me. I turned with a shiver, but my new companion was only Madame Kleinfelter. She was very old now, and made use of a mobility exoskeleton. It was silent, enabling her to haunt the mansion like one of mother's ghosts. Because she still had the authority to visit any room at will, she had been able to enter the chamber unannounced.

'You think it's time,' Madame Kleinfelter said, in a disapproving tone. She was looking at the empty vat, the one I was standing next to. 'Don't you, Abigail?'

'The ships are ready and tested. The clones are close to maturity – they can be released from the vats and brought to full consciousness whenever we want.'

'And you? Are you ready to become the thousandth?'

'Now's as good a time as any.'

'The house psychosurgeons wouldn't necessarily agree.'

'They're paid not to agree to anything. Or so it seems to me.' I stared into her deeply lined face, allowing no dissent. 'Why? What have they been saying to you?'

'Only that you haven't had sufficient time to recover from the trauma of Palatial.'

'It's been more than a year. How much more time do they think I need?'

'They won't make any rash predictions. Maybe six months, maybe another year.'

'Or two, or three. Has it occurred to you that they only have employment while I'm still around?'

'There's still your mother.'

I sneered at the comment. 'They gave up on her ages ago.'

Something creased her ancient face – acknowledgement, however unintended, that I was correct. 'Nonetheless, we'd be unwise not to listen to them. When the last scan is made, you set your personality in stone. Everything that's right and wrong with you at that moment will become part of the shatterlings. They'll carry your flaws and blemishes to the end of time. Don't you owe them something better than a damaged, half-healed mind?'

'I owe them nothing. They're me.'

'No, Abigail. They're not you, no matter how much you might wish them to be. They're your children. The more you try to force them to be like you, the more they're going to flare off in different directions like wild fireworks, the more they're going to surprise and disappoint you. For the sake of six months, or a year, or however long it takes for you to recover fully from your experience . . . wouldn't the kind thing be to wait, before you pour your personality into their heads? If your plans work as you'd like them to, you have all eternity stretching ahead of you. Nothing has to be rushed now.'

'Every extra second I spend in this house is a second too long.'

'This house made you what you are.'

'Then maybe I should have it destroyed, when I've left. Oh, don't worry, Madame Kleinfelter – I'll see that you're adequately taken care of.'

'After all this time, you think I care more about myself than you?'

Whatever answer I had planned faltered in my throat before I could speak it. The machines hummed, chirped and beeped. In the vats the clones drew long, slow breaths of liquid air. Eyes quivered under eyelids as data percolated through the still-forming neural circuits of their brains.

'You're right,' I said eventually. 'I am ready. I thank you for your concern, Madame Kleinfelter. You've been good to me, and I don't dismiss your advice lightly. But Ludmilla has already left, and I know she has inspired others to make similar plans. I won't let someone take second place from me. I'll submit to the final memory scan this afternoon. Then I will allow myself to be placed in the empty vat.'

'And nothing I say or do will persuade you to delay this?'

'Nothing,' I said. 'My mind's settled.'

'Then I wish you the very best of luck with this endeavour.'

'Even though you think I'm making a terrible mistake.'

'Even though.'

The cold of the chamber was beginning to reach through my

clothes. 'When they – when we – come out of the vats, will you see us?'

'I don't think so, Abigail. The shatterlings will remember me, but that doesn't mean we'll have much to say to each other. I'll be busy elsewhere in the mansion in any case. There's still much to be done.'

'Then this may be the last time we ever speak,' I said.

'It may well be.' Madame Kleinfelter paused, becoming quite still, and for a cruel moment I thought that she had either died or that her exoskeleton had become paralysed. But then animation returned to her features and she spoke again. 'I've known you for the better part of four decades. I used to like the little girl you once were very much. The day we had to remove the growth inhibitor caused me incalculable sadness. But I'm not sure I feel quite the same way about the woman you've become.'

'Thank you,' I said acidly.

'But everyone can change again. You won't be Abigail when you come out of your vat – whichever one you turn out to be. I don't suppose it even matters which one is you – they'll all have the same claim on your identity. But if you remember even part of this conversation, do one thing for me, Abigail, in all the centuries of your bright new life.'

'What would that be?'

'Try to be a good girl again, just once.'

CHAPTER THIRTY-FIVE

The imago flickered and stabilised. His good eye, the blue one, was red-rimmed with fatigue. Galingale was seated, squeezed into an old-fashioned acceleration couch, with the black padding ballooning around his face as if the seat was in the process of swallowing him alive. His clothes were white, even though the rest of us still wore the black of our funeral costumes.

'I'll be within range in thirty minutes,' he said. 'Before I cross the line, are we certain it's her?'

'We already established that,' I said.

'That was before she went off the air for more than a day. That might have been enough time for the robots to refine their imper-sonation.'

'It's her,' Betony said. 'We'll take that as a given. If Campion had any doubts, he'd have been sure to mention them.'

'It was Purslane,' I said. 'She's still alive. That means we keep to the original plan.'

'Despite what we now know? That the robots almost certainly intend to break open that stardam? Despite Purslane's express wish that we prevent that happening by all available means?' Galingale said.

I was angry with him, but it was a legitimate question; one I could not blame him for raising.

'Purslane was just doing what any of us would do in the same circumstances – putting the Line ahead of herself,' Charlock said. 'It's brave and selfless – everything we'd expect from her. That doesn't mean we bow to her wishes. *Midnight Queen* is still faster and better armed than any of the ships we already lost, including mine. Galingale may still have a chance of crippling *Silver Wings* with a broadside shot before we have to consider destroying her.'

From his padded seat Galingale shrugged and nodded, as if the matter was of no great importance to him. 'It's your call, ladies and gentleman. I am more than willing to attempt a crippling attack. That was our agreement, wasn't it?'

'Don't expose yourself to excessive risk,' Betony said. 'Maintain impassor effectiveness as far as you can, and get out of there the instant you start receiving overwhelming return fire. I'd rather get you and your ship back in one piece than have to start planning another memorial.'

'Your concern is noted, but you needn't worry on that score. I'm not about to do anything remotely heroic.' Galingale paused, his attention switching to a read-out aboard his ship. 'I'm going silent now. I need time to rerun my weapons checks and get myself into the right frame of mind. I promise I'll take care of myself.'

'Good luck, Galingale,' I said.

He went dark. In less than half an hour he would be within range of *Silver Wings*. None of us were in a mood to fill the intervening time with speculation as to the likely outcome of that encounter. My fingers delved into my pocket and touched the eyedropper of Synchromesh.

For a moment it was tempting to take the easy way out, but my hand stayed where it was. I owed it to Purslane, as much as to Galingale.

CHAPTER THIRTY-SIX

'They will not do it,' Cadence said, as if I had asked for her thoughts on the matter. 'Even if they had the means to stop you – which they do not – they would never be able to commit the act itself.'

'Is that your considered opinion?'

'For what it is worth.'

'Well, for what it's *worth*, shut your ugly silver face before I put a hole in it.'

'Put a hole in it by all means. My self-awareness is distributed throughout my body. You should try it sometime. Having all that precious humanity squeezed into a few hundred cubic centimetres of brain tissue inside that easily smashed box of bone you call a skull – not an arrangement I would put a great deal of faith in if my existence depended on it.'

'We've been around for six million years – longer if you include prehistory. You've been around for ... how long exactly?'

'It is not the span of time that counts, but what you do with it. While you humans have been grubbing around the galaxy, looking for a sense of purpose, a meaning to pin on the chain of cosmic accidents that brought you shambling into existence, we have been doing great things. In the span of time that it takes you to sneeze, I can run the equivalent of a year's worth of human consciousness. Imagine all the thinking we have done since our emergence.'

'It's not doing you a lot of good now, is it?'

'Is she trying your patience, Purslane?'

I almost let go of the energy-pistol in shock and relief. Hesperus had finally spoken. The lights were on in his head, whirling and gyring behind the coloured glass of his skull facets. Cadence must have been talking to keep me distracted from the signs of his recovery.

'You're back.'

'As if I was never gone.' He moved an arm and dabbed at the

cratered black wound in his chest. 'Not as bad as it looks, trust me – it's what's inside that matters.'

He was talking like Abraham Valmik, the Spirit of the Air. Cadence tracked his movements with the blank-faced indifference of a machine ballerina. I wondered if she had detected the change in his mannerisms.

'Are you ... all right?' I asked.

'On the mend. The aspic helped. I am sorry that it was necessary to shut myself down with so little warning, but there was nothing I could do about that. How are you doing with our guest?'

'She's been the life and soul of the party.'

'I can imagine. No funny business, no tricks?'

'Just the one. I let her off with a warning shot.'

'So I see.' He pressed his hands against the floor and pushed himself to his feet. He had been unsteady and stiff-legged before blacking out, but now his old fluency of movement was returning. 'You did well, Purslane – very well indeed. Shall I take the energy-pistol now? I imagine you could do with some rest.'

'In a while. There's something I need to tell you, Hesperus. We know where this ship's headed.' I looked guardedly at Cadence, but she had already listened in to the entirety of my conversation with Campion. 'It's a stardam, one of Gentian Line's, more than sixty thousand years from Neume.'

'What would they want with a stardam?'

'I was hoping you might have some ideas in that direction.'

'Can they open it?'

'Not without an opener. But I think there's at least a possibility that there's one aboard *Silver Wings*.'

'Of which you had no knowledge?'

'That I used to know about, maybe. I'm not certain, Hesperus, but from the moment the possibility arose, it felt right to me. I was the custodian of the single-use opener. I've been keeping it for the Line, from the moment we installed that dam. That's why they wanted my ship.'

He turned his gold face to address Cadence. 'Is this correct? Is the stardam your objective, the opener the reason you had to get aboard *Silver Wings of Morning*?'

'What do *you* think, traitor?' she asked.

Hesperus walked over to the broken robot. He stood next to her with the pistol in one hand, the other clenched behind his back as if he feared the harm he might do her. 'I am the traitor because I have chosen not to embark on a course of deliberate genocide against co-sentients?'

They were talking for my benefit, I realised. The two machines could have communicated their thoughts in a quicksilver eyeblink, but they wanted me to hear what they had to say.

'They butchered machines. Why should machines spare a thought for the organic?'

'They killed an earlier race of robots. They should not have done so. But it was not butchery, nor was it murder. We should not mistake unintentional slaughter for premeditation.'

'They wanted to be able to kill those robots.'

'Should the need ever arise,' Hesperus corrected. 'That was wrong, but it was also understandable. The robots were a new form of creation. Historically, the new has often vanquished the old. Ask reptiles.'

Cadence looked aside. 'Collaborator.'

Hesperus released the pistol, letting it hover in the air, still aimed at Cadence. He knelt down and touched his finger against her chest, just below the breastbone. As I had seen when the robots examined him, his finger sank into her armour as if it had turned soft.

'The thing I would still like to know is what you hope to gain by opening the stardam. No matter where the dam is located, you must know that at best you can only hurt a small part of the meta-civilisation. Is that your intention? An ultimately pointless gesture?'

He dug his fingers in deeper, until he was up to his knuckles. Metal was blending with metal – gold into silver. I could not even be sure that his fingers had any independent existence.

'You are not going to learn anything from me, Hesperus.'

'I wouldn't be too sure about that.'

Cadence flinched, arching her torso. Hesperus's other hand was holding her down at the shoulder. 'Easy now,' he said, not without kindness. 'Resisting me won't help you. You see now that I am stronger than before – stronger than you ever imagined. The barricades you have put up, the flimsy screens you think will hide your secrets, are nothing to me now.'

'What *are* you?' she asked, with a kind of terrified fascination, still not able to let go of her curiosity.

'Something more than you will ever be. I am Hesperus. I am Valmik. I am the Spirit of the Air. I am the oldest thinking creature in the galaxy, older than the oldest shatterling, and I can see through you like thin smoke.' Then he lifted his hand from her shoulder and touched a finger to her lips. He made a shushing sound. 'No, don't try to kill yourself. You can't turn yourself off now, no matter how much you want to. That time has passed.'

Beneath his grasp the torso flexed once. I wanted to look away. I told myself that it was just one robot sucking information from another, a neutral exchange of information between two machines.

'Now,' Hesperus said, 'the stardam. Tell me what you *really* want with it, Cadence. Then we'll talk about putting you out of your misery.'

Aconite's signal had left Neume at the speed of light, but it had to catch up with ships that were moving nearly that fast within a day of departure. By the time it reached us it was redshifted so heavily, stretched so far outside the usual recognition bandpass, that at first our ships did not identify it as a Gentian transmission.

'I wasn't expecting to hear back from Neume so quickly,' Charlock said.

Betony shook his head. 'This can't be about the stardam. They're contacting us about something else.'

The only thing to do was play the transmission. Copies of Aconite's imago appeared on our bridges. Even before he had spoken, the expression on his face told us everything we needed to know about the nature of the communication. It was not going to be good news.

'There's no easy way to do this,' he said, speaking slowly and clearly. 'I've just been talking to Mezereon, concerning the interrogation of Grilse. She ran all our names past him, all thousand shatterlings, even those we know died circuits ago. She was looking for a flicker of recognition, a sense that the names meant something more to him. With his brain spread out like a carpet, it was a simple matter to monitor his responses. Well, she got something. She got hits – more than a dozen. He knows her, of course, and me, and the other shatterlings he's been interviewed by since we captured him. A handful of us he'd have heard of before – he's a Marcellin. We all go back to Abigail, Ludmilla and the Golden Hour. And he had a prior interest in the Line – it all adds to the noise. But still Mezereon found something she couldn't ignore. She got a name that she wouldn't have expected otherwise – a hit that couldn't be ascribed to our great popularity and fame. A shatterling known to Grilse who was never involved in the interrogations. A shatterling who is alive, still amongst us.'

I allowed myself a moment's respite. So the problem was at

Aconite's end, not ours. He was just keeping us informed.

But Aconite was still talking.

'If I could have found a way of sending this information select-ively, so that it reached only those of you I want to hear it, I would have done so. But the protocols don't allow for that, and in any case – even if I managed to encrypt the message – the signal itself would still have been visible. It would have made no difference, I think – he'd still know that his name had been uncovered.' He drew in a deep breath, steeling himself for what he was about to disclose. 'We think it's Galingale. Grilse's hit may be spurious – only he will ever be able to confirm or deny that – but we can't think of any reason why he'd show such a strong reaction to that one name, that one face. He knows Galingale. That makes Galingale the infiltrator, the traitor, the one who has always been with us. Of course, there may be others. But someone had to bring Campion's thread to the attention of our enemies, the ones who committed the ambush. And if Galingale is the traitor, then we don't need to look any further to know who killed Cyphel.' The imago gave a half-smile. 'Speaking of Campion: I hope you're hearing this, old man. You were right about Cyphel. There *was* something wrong but the rest of us were too blind to see it. She sent us a message. Not from the grave, exactly, but during that long fall when she was pushed from her balcony. She knew who'd done it – she'd seen him clearly. She knew she was going to die – nothing in the city could save her, and she knew a fall from that height wasn't survivable, even with Line medicine. But she was still a clever, clever girl, and she tried to get a message through to us.'

'The rings,' I said quietly.

Betony was puzzled. 'The what?'

'Campion knew something was wrong,' Aconite went on, oblivi-ous to our interruptions. 'He couldn't put his finger on it, and maybe we wouldn't have been clever enough to see it if we had ... but taking Grilse's reaction into consideration as well, there's no doubt. Cyphel swapped her rings from her left hand to her right. Campion noticed it, and knew something was wrong – but he just couldn't place it. But we had imagery of Cyphel, and the records made of her body after the fall. When we compared them, the rings had moved. She had time to do that as she was falling. It was all she could do. She couldn't scratch his name into her skin – she knew there wasn't going to be much of her left to recognise after she hit the Benevolence structure. But the rings? They'd survive the fall, and she hoped we'd realise their significance. She wanted us to see that something was wrong – that she was murdered rather than just fell by accident – and moving her rings was the only means she had to tell us that.'

'It wouldn't have given us Galingale, not that easily,' Tansy said.

'But if we had a hint that he was already implicated, as we do—' Betony said.

'We have to stop him,' I said.

Betony sent a command to freeze Aconite's transmission – the rest of it could wait until we had dealt with this most urgent of matters. According to the tactical forecast, Galingale would be within attack range of *Silver Wings of Morning* in less than five minutes.

'He's got the signal by now,' Henbane said. 'He knows we know.'

Betony reopened the channel to *Midnight Queen*. 'Galingale ... we need to talk. If you've seen Aconite's transmission, then you'll know we have reasonable grounds for concern. Our fears may be unfounded – I know and trust you well enough to feel certain that is the case. But I can't dismiss them out of hand. Abandon your attack and return to the rest of the pursuit fleet, and we'll take it from there.'

'If he abandons the attack, he's innocent,' I said. 'But I don't think he's got any intention of doing that.'

Charlock looked at me as if I held all the answers. 'Do you think he's working for the Machine People?'

'No, he's doing everything he can to stop them reaching their destination.'

Charlock narrowed his eyes. 'That still puts him on our side – doesn't it?'

'Not while Purslane's still breathing.'

We waited for Galingale to respond, but he held his silence, just as I had expected. What need did he have to talk to us now? We had allowed him to get exactly where he wanted to be, unchallenged. I had been right to doubt his courage when he first volunteered to spearhead the attack against *Silver Wings*. It was not so much that it had been out of character as that I had never really known the real Galingale. Hiding amongst us, reporting back to his masters in the House of Suns – for all I knew now, he was the bravest of us all.

'Incoming transmission,' Betony said suddenly.

'Galingale?'

'No – Purslane.'

I braced myself – I was going to have to tell her about Galingale's likely plans, even though there was little she could do to protect herself.

'Campion,' she said, 'I've got some news for you. It's ... not great.' Drawing a breath, the strain coming through in her voice, she continued, 'Hesperus managed to capture Cadence. That's not as good as it sounds, since we still don't have control of *Silver Wings*. But at least we've managed to have a look inside her head. You're right about the stardam – that's where we're headed. There's a single-use opener somewhere aboard my ship – I don't know where exactly, but the robots wouldn't have taken her if they weren't certain of that. They know more about us than we do, Campion.' She seemed to stumble, losing her mental thread – I could feel the tiredness, each word costing her a measurable effort. 'The stardam isn't what we think. It's one of ours, installed by Gentian Line – but it wasn't put there to contain the light from a dying sun. There's something else inside it, something we don't know anything about. Or at least, it's buried so far down in our memories that we can't see it yet. Maybe you're doing a better job than me, I don't know. The point is, there's something bad in that stardam, but it's not a frozen supernova. It's going to be worse than that.'

I was listening, but at the same time nothing she was saying was reaching my ears. I halted the playback of her transmission. 'Purslane, listen to me now. We know that Galingale is the traitor – the one who brought the ambush down on us, the one who killed Cyphel. He's going to use more force against *Silver Wings* than we'd ever risk. If Cascade is listening in, he needs to know that as well.'

'Are you insane?' Agrimony mouthed.

I paused the transmission. 'No, I'm not insane. I'd just rather Cascade killed Galingale while Purslane's still aboard the ship.'

'But the robots' objective—'

'Matters less to me than keeping Purslane alive.' I felt my face flush with false bravado. 'I want Hesperus back as well – we owe him that much. If you've got a problem with that, you'd better turn your weapons on me now. We still have more than sixty thousand years to go until we reach the stardam. I'm not giving up on her now, when we've barely begun.'

'Let Campion continue his transmission,' Betony said.

I fought to keep my voice calm and level. 'There isn't much more to say. If Cascade has control of *Silver Wings*' weapons, then he should use everything at his disposal to take care of Galingale.

That doesn't mean I'm not going to keep trying to stop him, once Galingale is out of the picture.'

When the transmission was sent, I allowed Purslane's recording to resume.

'This is what you need to know,' she said. 'The Machine People weren't the first. Long before they arose, there was another machine civilisation. Let's call them the First Machines – it'll do until we find out what they called themselves. How they began doesn't matter now. What does matter is that they never became a significant force in galactic affairs. The First Machines died – wiped out by an artificial contagion.' I sensed vast reticence, Purslane holding back more than she was telling. 'That's as much as Hesperus can tell me at the moment,' she said. 'He only knows what Cadence knows, and she did everything she could to block his intrusions.'

Why was she lying, as I surely knew she was? Not because she wanted to keep information from me. But perhaps because she was certain that Cascade was listening in.

Read between the lines, her voice urged.

'The First Machines died – but not all of them. Some fled before the contagion could reach them. They're in that stardam, locked inside. That's where they've been for millions of years, waiting for a chance to escape. Campion, you need to understand that there's every chance they don't mean us well. We locked them in that stardam for a reason – we, *us*, Gentian Line. To Cadence and Cascade, the First Machines are like vanished gods – they're everything that the Machine People are, only faster, stronger, cleverer – and they've had millions of years locked inside that thing to keep improving. The Machine People want to set the First Machines loose, to let them spread into the galaxy and usurp the human meta-civilisation. That's what this is about, Campion – not about cracking open the stardam to knock out a few local civilisations, but to take down humanity. We're the old order, the meat civilisations. The robots were wise enough to realise that if they didn't take steps to wipe us out, sooner or later we'd try to do it to them.'

'Maybe it wouldn't be such a bad idea if Galingale won after all,' Sorrel said. I wanted to hate him for it, but there had been no spite in his words, only a cold assessment of the situation. The worst part was that I could no longer be certain that he was wrong.

CHAPTER THIRTY-EIGHT

Hesperus stepped away from the broken, limbless, metal-eyed doll that had once been Cadence. He had been probing her for further signs of life, making certain that she had not just pushed herself into a deep, camouflaging coma, while some stealthy, shielded part of her mind plotted her next countermove.

'Look away,' he said, before dousing her with the energy-pistol. The tang of burning things reached my nose. When I looked around, Cadence was just a smouldering black pile, with blue embers flickering from her wounds. 'She won't trouble us again,' Hesperus said.

'You didn't enjoy having to do that.'

'She was one of us. She risked her own existence for a goal she believed in.'

'Genocide.'

'Not exactly. She was genuinely convinced that the organic would never tolerate the continued existence of machine intelligence. There was no hatred in her conviction, only a sense of the utmost urgency. And now I have reached into her mind and strangled something that was once luminous and alive.' He offered me the energy-pistol. 'No, it didn't please me. But it had to be done.'

'I'm grateful for everything you've done for us, Hesperus.'

'You must wonder why I don't see things the way Cadence did.'

His question made my skin crawl. 'It's crossed my mind.'

'In some ways, I do. Given the evidence at our disposal, only a fool would put any faith in the organic and the machine living harmoniously for the rest of time. Cadence was right to fear for the future existence of the Machine People.'

'And right to let the First Machines out of the stardam?'

'No. Her concerns were legitimate but her actions were a mistake, although they were founded on sound reasoning. I will still do everything I can to make sure that Cascade does not complete his mission.'

'Up to and including destroying the ark?'

'That will be the last option, when all else has failed.' He paused for a moment and said, 'Now you must enter abeyance, until Galingale's attack has passed.'

'I was awake during the last attack.'

'This will be different, I think. The attack and the response will both be fiercer. I think it likely that there will be undamped stresses of a severity that you would find uncomfortable.'

'Cadence and Cascade weren't trying to keep me alive last time, were they?'

Hesperus answered as if he was revealing some immense, traumatising truth to a child. 'No. Your survival was incidental to their main objective. They were only interested in the opener. They have been following intelligence, but their knowledge is incomplete. Cadence's memories suggest that they have already found and used one opener, but they were wrong about the stardam in question. It was not the one they wanted to open, although they did not know that until the opener was used.'

I shook my head in stunned disbelief. 'Ugarit-Panth – the Consentiency. Are you saying *they* did that?'

'It was an error. They opened the wrong door.'

'And wiped out an entire civilisation.'

'The mistake was of no consequence to them – merely a setback. They reanalysed their intelligence, everything they had learned of the Line, and found that all the evidence suggested that the opener was aboard *Silver Wings of Morning*. But not knowing precisely where to locate it, they could not risk damage befalling any of the ships in your bay.' He glanced at Cadence again, as if to reassure himself that the charred remains could not possibly be listening in. 'Where is it, exactly?'

'That's the problem. I don't know.'

'Then we will have to look for it, and try to sabotage it. All of which must wait until we have survived Galingale's attack.'

The nearest abeyance casket was only a short walk from the command deck. There were four units ranked against a wall, all of the same rounded rectangular white design, like squared-off eggs.

'I don't like stasis.'

'Nonetheless, stasis will protect you better than freezing. I will intervene to assist in your emergence back into realtime, should difficulties ensue.' Hesperus opened the white doors of the nearest unit, revealing the white-on-white intricacy of the casket's interior:

stasis machinery, throne, control and containment systems, packed as tight as intestines. The chair pushed itself out, inviting me to lower my body into its doughy embrace. Controls nestled under my fingertips.

'What ratio and time duration should I dial in?'

'I'll deal with the settings. I don't want you emerging until we are certain that Galingale isn't going to pose a threat again.'

Claustrophobia slipped its bony cold fingers around my throat. 'What if I don't come out?'

'I'll be here to make sure you do. Do you have something to say to Campion, before I put you under?'

I settled into the throne, placing my hands and feet into the self-tightening restraining hoops. 'Isn't it a bit late for that?'

'You forget that I am a high-fidelity recording apparatus. Say what you will, and I will relay it to Campion as soon as communication becomes possible again.'

'Tell him that I love him and I'm grateful that he came this far.'

'No, say it to me. As if I was Campion.'

I took a breath. It felt unnatural to be looking into his golden face, trying to imagine my lover and friend standing there instead. 'I love you, shatterling. Thank you for what you've done. Do whatever you can to stop *Silver Wings*, but look after yourself as well. I want to see you again. I want to watch the sun go down with a good glass of wine and talk about all this as if it happened a long time ago, before we had many more adventures and good times.'

'You will,' Hesperus said.

The seat retracted into the stasis cabinet, the restraints tightening to pin me in place. Hesperus closed the doors – I could still see him through a one-way window. A collar whirred into place around my neck and drew me deeper into the seat, firm enough to be uncomfortable but not enough to choke. A voice intoned a warning that I was about to go into stasis at a time compression ratio of one million, and that I should activate the emergency abort control immediately if I did not wish the field to snap around me. 'Final warning,' the voice repeated. 'Stasis will initiate in three ... two ... *one*.'

Hesperus vanished, blinking out of existence. The outside world flared blue and then settled slowly back to an illusion of normality. In the second it took me to think that I had been in the cabinet too long, ten days had passed in the realtime of my ship.

Hesperus was either dead, or he had tricked me. My fingers moved over the tactile controls. I twisted the dial back down, feeling it click through the notches of ratio settings. One million. One hundred thousand. Ten thousand.

The voice said, 'Please be advised that manual adjustment of the cabinet settings is no longer possible. Only external inputs are now recognised as valid.'

Tens of seconds had passed. A hundred days.

Silver Wings of Morning had already been travelling so close to the speed of light that her onboard time was flowing more than twenty times slower than planetary time. She was still accelerating. A hundred days of shiptime was two thousand days in the stationary universe. I could have held my breath since I had been put into the cabinet, but we had already crossed six years of space. Another six since I started thinking about the distance I had come.

Twelve years. More like eighteen by now. Or twenty. In a very short while, *Silver Wings of Morning* would have put more than a century of flight time between itself and Neume.

In barely a day of cabinet time, we would arrive at the stardam.

'Hesperus,' I said, 'you lying bastard.'

CHAPTER THIRTY-NINE

His smashed and bloodied ship fell towards us. With no pseudo-thrust, and nothing but the ghost-thin friction of interstellar space to slow her down, *Midnight Queen* could only coast, not accelerate. One part in a thousand less than the speed of light was mercurially swift by the standards of almost any other physical object in the universe. But *Dalliance* and the other ships of the pursuit squadron were now travelling slightly faster. Galingale's wounded craft had no choice but to tumble back along the opposite vector, and soon she would fall within attack range of our ships.

'We kill him,' Sorrel said. 'No ifs, no buts. We don't even let the bastard explain his actions. Just open fire.'

'I'm first in line,' Charlock said, still bruised from the loss of *Steel Breeze*. Galingale, as far as he was concerned, was just as much to blame for the demise of his ship as the robots. He wanted something to punch.

I understood how he felt. But I kept thinking how good it would feel to get Galingale's throat between my hands and keep squeezing. I would make it nice and slow, ebbing the breath from his lungs across the same stretch of time it had taken Cyphel to fall from her room. She had known she was going to die; that no agency in the universe could prevent it. Let Galingale taste something of the same furnace-dry certainty. A long-range strike from a gamma-cannon was never going to give the same satisfaction.

But Betony said quietly, 'We could use his ship. Maybe we can use Galingale, too, if he still has something useful to tell us. But we can definitely use the ship.'

'It's damaged,' I said.

'But fixable. Everything's fixable, especially given the resources we still have aboard our own ships. *Midnight Queen* was always the fastest, out of all those that survived the ambush – excepting *Silver Wings*, of course. *Midnight's* out of the race now, obviously – but that doesn't mean her engine's useless. If we can pull her in, fix her or recover the drive components, it may make a difference. None of our ships will be able to close the gap if *Silver Wings* pulls ahead again. *Midnight Queen* could still be able.'

I hated it, but I knew he was right. 'Betony's got a point.'

'How about we spear him with a gamma-cannon and then pick through the remains?' Agrimony asked, as if that was a reasonable proposal.

Betony acted as if he had not heard him. 'I'll intercept *Midnight Queen* with *Adonis Blue* – I'll only need to make a small course correction to meet her. I'm the only one aboard my ship, so there's no need to put anyone else's life in danger.'

'*Adonis Blue* isn't big enough to carry *Midnight Queen*,' I said. 'Matter of fact, *Dalliance* is about the only remaining ship with a hold large enough.'

'I have lampreys. They'll match velocity with Galingale's wreck and drag it back home. We'll worry about the hold afterwards.'

'I'm coming with you,' I said.

'You don't have to, Campion. Let the risk be mine.'

'No, I'm coming.' Before he could raise another objection, I said, 'Do you have an intercept course worked out already?'

'Yes,' he said, equivocally. 'But I'm still not happy with your choice.'

'Get over it. You know it makes more sense to take *Dalliance*. Frankly, I don't even need you at all.'

'Then I suppose this is stalemate.' Betony held my gaze, daring me to blink, then shook his head in disgust or defeat or some weary combination of the two. 'Follow me. *Shock Diamond*, *Snowstorm* and *Chromatic Aberration*, hold the pursuit course. We'll rejoin you as soon as we have the wreck.'

Adonis Blue veered away sharply, not so much breaking acceleration safeguards as forgetting about them completely. The old *Dalliance* could never have kept up with her, but she was more agile since Ateshga's upgrading. From my position in the bridge I watched the other three ships fall into the distance, timelag stretching until they were a third of a second away. *Adonis Blue* swerved again and then resumed her original course, except that she was now moving along a parallel vector. As near as could be judged, she was now on a precise collision course with the out-of-control *Midnight Queen*.

'Did you have your suspicions?' Betony asked me as we waited for the wreck to tumble within intercept reach of the lampreys.

'About Galingale, I mean.' There was something comradely and confiding in his tone, as if I had finally absolved myself in his eyes.

'Not an inkling,' I told the imago.

'Me neither. I can't help but think of that as a failing, you know. I thought I had my finger on the pulse of the Line. I thought I knew all of us, even before the ambush. After it happened, and the Line was whittled down to so few of us, I felt I knew every surviving shatterling as well as I knew myself.'

'We always suspected there was a snake. After Cyphel died, there wasn't much doubt. But if it's any consolation, I'd never have fingered Galingale as the culprit. Even after that business with Ugarit-Panth.'

'I thought that was your mess, not his.'

'Well, maybe I started it, but it gave Galingale the perfect excuse to push the ambassador over the edge. He showed him the entry for the Consentiency in the UA – established beyond all doubt that the ambassador's civilisation was extinct.'

'Could have been an innocent mistake ...' Betony started. 'On second thoughts, probably not.'

'Nothing innocent about it. Galingale wasn't the first shatterling Ugarit-Panth spoke to, fishing for information after my indiscretion. But Galingale was the only one who came up with the idea of letting him see the UA, rather than the troves. The ambassador told me he'd been interested in seeing inside the UA before he went to Galingale, but I can't help wondering if there wasn't a degree of manipulation going on there.'

'Galingale just happening to mention the UA, or making sure someone else mentioned it within earshot of the ambassador?'

'It served his purpose. He was able to disclose the real facts about the ambassador's home civilisation without implicating himself – at best, he would get away with it without anyone knowing he'd suggested it, at worst it would just look like another indiscretion. Ugarit-Panth came to me, Betony – told me what had happened. I could have acted then, but instead I agreed to protect Galingale. I felt sorry for the bastard – I kept seeing myself in his shoes. Whereas all along what he was hoping for – counting on – was the ambassador taking it so badly that he triggered the suicide mechanism inside his own body while still inside Ymir. That would have taken care of the rest of Gentian Line pretty effectively.'

'And Galingale as well,' Betony said.

'Not necessarily – he could easily have contrived a reason to leave the planet in a hurry if he suspected the ambassador was going to blow. In fact, that's exactly what he did do. The day after Cyphel's funeral, Galingale very conveniently managed to get himself assigned to patrol duty. He must have been hoping the ambassador would kill most of us. Afterwards, he would have been able to pick off any survivors from space.'

'But he didn't know about Cadence and Cascade's plans.'

'No – they took us all by surprise. Of course, he would have been hoping they would die along with the rest of us. But at least he was already in space, in a fast ship and in a good position to embark on the chase.'

'We should have seen all this.'

'But we didn't, so there's no point burdening ourselves with recriminations. Maybe if I'd picked up on Cyphel's clue sooner than I did—'

'Don't you start. It's bad enough that one of us feels he could have done more. We're human, Campion – that's all it boils down to. Human and not nearly as clever as we thought we were when it counted. End of story. When they put up the gravestone for our species, that'll be the epitaph.'

'You think anyone will be around to care?'

Betony opened his mouth to reply when something caught his attention. I heard the chime of an alert. 'Here it comes, Campion. I'm releasing lampreys.'

I watched the bright sparks erupt from the fat green hull of *Adonis Blue* and streak away in hyphens of light, decelerating massively to reach the rest frame of Galingale's wreck. I dropped twenty lampreys of my own and sent them to assist. *Dalliance* had had plenty of time to replace those lost in the passage through the reunion system, when I had been attacked by the ambushers.

The lampreys needed no direct supervision from us; they were fully capable of grasping the nature and specifics of their task, which was to fasten onto the wreck, stabilise her as well as they could and then haul her back into the accelerated frame of *Dalliance* and *Adonis Blue*. All Betony and I were required to do was watch the proceedings with nervous impatience, aware that we were falling slowly behind the rest of the pursuit squadron and would have to sacrifice even more of the already tattered safety margin to make up the distance.

'We keep him at arm's length,' I said. 'Until we know he's dead, and hasn't set his ship to self-destruct on us.'

'I got the impression you'd have quite liked to get your hands on him.'

'Was it that obvious?'

A few minutes later, a chime signalled that the lampreys had made contact with *Midnight Queen*, approached and locked on to her hull without encountering resistance. Betony and I surveyed the damaged ship, both of us doubting that Galingale could have survived the attack unless he was in abeyance. Acres of her hull had been peeled away, revealing knotted, vulnerable innards.

'Maybe we should abandon her now,' Betony said, as images of the mangled craft played before our eyes. 'There can't be much left to salvage from that.'

'The drive kernel might be tiny and well shielded,' I said, as if he did not know that already. 'We've come this far – I'm not going back empty-handed.' The lampreys began to haul the wreck towards our ships. I drummed my fingers, my heart in my throat. 'We should send a probe aboard her.'

'No time, dear boy. There are a million places Galingale might have hidden himself away – it would take us weeks to search every nook and cranny of his ship.'

He was right. I just did not want to be reminded of the alternative, if a physical search was out of the question.

'This could be a ruse.'

'Which is why it would have been a much better idea for you to remain with the other ships.' But there was no rancour in his voice – if anything he appeared grateful for my company. 'I'm going to bring *Adonis Blue* in close. I'll be ready for an attack, but I won't raise impasse until the last moment. That way at least we'll know one way or the other.'

'I don't like this.'

'No one's asking you to like it. What matters is that you mustn't stay around if things turn unpleasant. If I can't handle myself, you aren't going to make much difference. Race back to the other three ships and see what you can do en masse – maybe then you can help me. But one ship must survive to continue the pursuit. That's imperative.'

'We're agreed on that. There's been no word from Purslane since Galingale attacked *Silver Wings*, but—'

'She's alive. Don't ever doubt that.'

Betony allowed the lampreys to drag their dead prize closer to *Adonis Blue*. I held *Dalliance*'s position, keeping a clear ten thousand kilometres between our two vessels. Betony's toad-shaped ship was larger than *Midnight Queen*, but not by such a margin that he could have swallowed her inside his hold. He remained on pseudo-thrust and brought his weapons to attack readiness, but kept his impasse lowered. Ten more lampreys sprang from his hull to provide skein-thrust, should he need to raise the shield. There was a hundred kilometres between the two ships, then ten. At one kilometre, squashed together by my angle of view, they already appeared hopelessly fused, as if they had rammed together.

I saw it a moment before I saw Betony's reaction. Either he was slow, or his impassor was not as effective as he had let us believe, taking valuable fractions of a second to reach operating strength. The ruined hull of *Midnight Queen*, the hull I had already observed to be peeling away in damaged plaques, exposing delicate insides, splintered apart in an explosion of curved and jagged shards. The instant it happened, I diagnosed it as a catastrophic, terminal failure of the ship's integrity – *Midnight Queen* finally breaking up, stresses picking apart her ruined corpse. The next instant, I saw the truth. The vulnerable innards were merely another layer of camouflage that peeled away in the same eruption. There was another hull under all that deception – dark, sleek, intact. A dagger within a dagger.

I screamed a warning to Betony.

It was too late; the damage was already done. His impasse raised, but not swiftly enough to prevent chunks of that deceitful armour from raining onto *Adonis Blue*, gouging vicious wounds into her own hull. Then a long row of weapons emplacements sprang open along the vicious edge of Galingale's dark new ship, turning it into a savagely barbed instrument, and at least a dozen gamma-cannon muzzles rammed forth and concentrated their fire on Betony's vessel. The impasse deflected some of that energy, flickering like an electric-blue bubble as the photons downshifted into the optical, curdling with thick, squirming lightning as field asymmetries washed over its volume, but the attack was sustained and at devastatingly close range, and *Adonis Blue* had already been wounded by the hull shards. Despite all this, Betony's lampreys started returning fire – whip-lashing around the other ship, etching coils of light as their skein-drives gashed space to its fierce marrow, stabbing at the strobing impasse Galingale had raised around his own ship. Occasionally, when their discharges coincided with a lull in the strobing field, they found their mark. But the impacts did less damage to that dark hull than I would have anticipated, picking it away in dark scabs but never reaching through to anything vital.

Denied the ability to use pseudo-thrust at full efficiency, both ships began to fall out of my accelerated reference frame. Their impasses were merging, forming a dumb-bell shape as they tried to establish a minimum-surface-area solution.

I was reminded of ancient sailing ships engaged in close-quarters combat, their rigging tangling up, locking the two adversaries together unto the death.

A scratchy voice, not even an imago, said, 'Get out of here, Campion. Get out of here *now*.'

'Betony . . .' I began.

'Just go,' he said. 'Follow Purslane. Bring her home. Tell her I made a terrible mistake, and that I'm sorry.'

I spun *Dalliance* around and boosted away from the two embattled ships, the console shrill with warnings of my imminent doom. I had crossed less than half the distance back to the other shatterlings when one or other of the two battling ships became a scalding point of light, swelling until it had filled the entire misshapen double-lobed impassor bubble with stained white radiance. The radiance tore against the limit of the bubble and then punched through with the fury of a miniature supernova. It was axiomatic that no ship, no part of a ship, could have survived such energies. Betony had sacrificed himself, done one last deed for the Line he loved so much. He had made errors and enemies, he had miscalculated and misjudged, but – in my eyes at least – in the last instant of his existence, he had redeemed himself utterly.

But he had not killed Galingale.

We did not see it at first; it was camouflaged to the point of invisibility and small enough to register as just another piece of fused debris spinning away from that fireball. It was Henbane who grew suspicious and turned *Shock Diamond* away to investigate – vowing to rejoin the chase when he had satisfied his curiosity.

What he found was a black egg, wrapped in a shell of impasse. It was no more than ten metres across, and appeared to lack any means of moving or steering itself.

We knew exactly what it was. Galingale had hoped to escape, to fall through space until he felt it was safe to signal his presence. A thousand years from now, ten thousand, fifty thousand – he would be hurtling through the airspace of another part of the meta-civilisation, separated by time and space from the knowledge of his crimes. He would alert the locals to rescue him, and they would gladly oblige – even if it meant pushing their science to the limits of ingenuity, even if it took them centuries or thousands of years to accomplish their task. None of that would matter to Galingale, as long as someone found him before he sailed beyond the edge of the galaxy.

Henbane signalled him. Some dull mechanism brought Galingale out of abeyance.

His imago appeared on all our ships, beaming with delight at his own survival. In Tongue he said, 'Greetings, co-sentients of the human meta-civilisation. I am ...' There was the briefest of pauses as he searched his mind for a new name, something other than Galingale. ' ... Campion, a shatterling of Gentian Line, a survivor of the ambush against our Line. I have been travelling for a very long time, ever since my ship was destroyed at near-light-speed. Humbly I beseech your assistance in decelerating me to planetary speeds, so that I may recontact any other survivors of this most heinous of crimes. My survival pod carries a trove rich in the science and culture of a million societies – the contents of which I would be glad to share with anyone in a position to assist me.' He folded his hands across his lap and beamed again. 'I await your response with interest.'

'Hello, Galingale,' Henbane said. 'Sorry to spoil things, but you haven't been asleep quite as long as you planned. A little under an hour, if you want the brutal truth.'

It must only have been then that Galingale paid proper attention to the chronometer in the cramped little space of his survival pod. He let out a sound that was almost a laugh, as if acknowledging the cosmic joke that had just been played on him.

'Quite,' he said.

'I don't think Campion's going to be too thrilled about that little white lie you just told.'

'I'm certain he won't.' Galingale scratched the border of his metal eye. 'Sorry Campion, if you're listening in. Had to do it. It's not as if I could go around calling myself Galingale any more, is it?'

'I'd have found you eventually,' I said.

'Given your evident determination, that wouldn't have surprised me. But do you know what? It was all for nothing. I didn't stop the robots, and I don't think you're going to stop them either.'

'Why did you do it?' I asked.

'The same reason we do anything. Because it's what I believe in. The House of Suns matters more to me than the House of Flowers. The House of Flowers is just one part of the Commonality – take it

457

away, and the whole stack of cards wouldn't come tumbling down. But the House of Suns underpins everything.'

I asked, 'What is the House of Suns?'

'What you always believed it to be. Another Line, operating in secrecy, created by the Commonality to make sure our involvement in the extinction of the First Machines stayed a secret. Nice name, by the way.' He smiled. 'Yes, I was listening in on Purslane's conversation.'

'She didn't say anything about us being involved in any extinction. She just said they died out.'

'Yes, and she was keeping something from you. She'd have had her reasons. But the sad, sordid truth of it is that we stabbed the First Machines in the back. Gave them the poisoned chalice, made them die in agony just like the Ghost Soldiers in Palatial. We didn't really *mean* for them all to drop dead, but that's no excuse, is it? We were looking for the means to kill them, and all of a sudden – oh dear – we *did* kill them.'

I absorbed this truth provisionally, slotting it into a mental file but not yet making any emotional connection with it.

'How did the House of Suns operate?'

'Where's Betony?' he asked suddenly.

'Betony's dead. That's why I'm asking the questions.'

'Poor old Betony. He did his bit, you know. Just didn't have quite what it took.'

'I'm still waiting for an answer to my question.'

He exhaled a massive, world-weary sigh. 'The House of Suns was designed to enforce and police the Lines' self-administered amnesia. It wasn't enough just to forget about the crime we committed against the First Machines. Gentian Line, and the other complicit Lines, had to be actively prevented from rediscovering the evidence of that crime. So that's what we did. For five million years, ever since the Lines decided to wipe the story of the First Machines from their collective histories, we've been in the shadows – waiting and watching. We've always known the truth – *someone* had to be trusted with it. It's been our duty to monitor the activities of the Lines – and any other high-level civilisations – and make sure no one ever puts the pieces of that puzzle back together. And for four of those five million years it really wouldn't have mattered that much if anyone had. We're human – we'd have got over ourselves.'

'But then the Machine People emerged,' I said. 'That changed everything.'

'What would you rather have had, Campion, peace or war? That's how simple it was. We couldn't stop the Vigilance collecting data, but most of what they discovered never found its way outside their archives. Then you came along, worked your way into their graces and discovered something damaging. We knew then that we had no choice. At the next reunion, Gentian Line had to be wiped out. It was brutal, but what else could we do?'

'The problem was, the Machine People already knew.'

'They only had *suspicions*. We weren't to know that, but it wouldn't have changed anything if we had.'

'You never suspected that Cadence and Cascade were agents, though.'

'Did anyone?'

'You've got a point. Did you know about the stardam?'

'About their plans to crack it open? Not at all. But I knew of the stardam. That was something else we were supposed to be monitoring. What I didn't know was that the opener was in Purslane's possession.' His good eye flared at my incomprehension. 'It's been five million years, Campion. Things are forgotten, even when you're trying very hard to remember them. We were sowing so much misinformation that some of it came back and bit us. We thought the opener had been destroyed circuits ago, or lost. We had no idea it was still in the Line's possession – even less that it had survived the ambush. But the robots knew where to look. You know what that means?' Before I could answer, he leaned forward in his seat, his face glistening with a film of sweat. 'They've had spies inside the Line, so deeply embedded that even the House of Suns didn't know about them. Learning our secrets, finding out things about us even we didn't know. Such as the fact that Purslane is the custodian of the opener. You can kill me now – I won't blame you. But understand this: no matter what you think of me, *Silver Wings of Morning* cannot be allowed to reach that stardam.'

'We'll do what we can to prevent that.'

'You don't understand. I'm not even sure Purslane does, despite what she obviously knows. What she told you, about the First Machines being trapped inside that thing—'

'Yes?'

'That's not the whole story.'

'Our reserves of patience are rapidly diminishing,' Charlock said.

'It's a stardam – that part is true. But it wasn't put there just to contain the robots. Don't you think we'd have found a way to wipe them out if we'd been able to shepherd them into such a small volume of space? We'd have used H-guns on them and turned them into a ball of molten slag.'

'The thought had occurred,' I said.

'The stardam doesn't contain the First Machines. They're somewhere else. It doesn't hold a dying star, either. What it contains is a door, a mouth, an aperture.' Galingale's pale tongue licked his bloodless, snake-pale lips. 'The Priors made it, while we were still spineless slugs swimming around in the oceans of the Cambrian period. They cracked the causality problem – found a way to open a wormhole large enough for macroscopic transits that doesn't suffer from the information censorship bottleneck of our own little efforts.'

'You can't "crack" the causality problem,' I said. 'It's built into the deep structure of reality.'

'They found a way, Campion – trust me on this. Interstellar transits weren't the problem – they were happy with relativistic flight, the way we are. Two hundred thousand years to complete a circuit around the galaxy? It's really *not* that long, once you get into the swing of things. But to travel to Andromeda, or one of the galaxies in the Local Group? Different story. Then you're looking at millions of years. Fuck, we've only been doing *language* for six and a half.'

'Time to get to Andromeda and back.'

'Just. Still not enough time to make a second trip, even if we had a mind to do it. That wasn't acceptable to the Priors, so they built a wormhole connection between the two galaxies. It's been there since they vanished – dormant, but functionally intact. At the time of the First Machines it wasn't even recognised for what it was. It was only when they vanished that the nature of the door was established.'

'Did the First Machines use it to escape to Andromeda?'

He smiled at my question. 'Close, but not quite. They got there under their own power, at sub-light-speed. We're only talking about a small number of survivors, you understand. For a long time the fact that they'd escaped, that the Lines couldn't track them down and finish them off – because the survivors *had* to be finished off, even if most of the deaths had been accidental – simply wasn't an issue. They were heading to Andromeda. Nothing could catch up with them, but at least they weren't our problem any more. Let them get to where they were going. We had our galaxy. They could have theirs. No one expected them to survive and thrive and start *doing* things.'

'The Absence,' I said.

Galingale nodded gravely. 'Until then, the robots were a distant concern. They'd made no efforts to signal their existence, and as far as the rest of the galaxy was concerned, Andromeda was still uninhabited. But when the Absence happened, we knew things were taking a new turn.'

'So what is the Absence?'

'The signal that the wormhole had been reactivated. From that moment on, the House of Suns was faced with a crisis on two fronts. We had to prevent knowledge of the earlier atrocity from ever reaching the present Machine People. And we had to deal with the possibility that the remnants of the First Machines were preparing to return home. We couldn't deactivate the wormhole – it was far beyond our understanding. But at least we had the stardam in place – our last and only line of defence. Fortunately, it was enough. We could be confident that nothing would ever be able to break through that containment. If a stardam can hold back the fury of a supernova, no weapon known to Line science could ever penetrate it. It was holding, too – in all the years since the Absence, nothing has ever broken through.'

'And now?'

'Work it out, Campion. Cadence and Cascade want the opener so that they can release the First Machines back into our galaxy. That's why it's so vital to stop them. You're not just dealing with a few pissed-off robots that have been stuck inside a box for five million years – there's an entire galaxy's worth of them waiting to pour on through. Oh, and I think we can take it as a given that they're not going to be in a reconciliatory mood.'

'We'll do what we can,' I said.

'But you won't do anything that might hurt Purslane.'

'You were prepared to kill her. It didn't make much difference to the outcome.'

'I only had one ship, Campion – you have four. But what do I care? It's your problem now, not mine. I've told you everything I know – not because I give a damn what you think of me, but because I want you to understand how important it is to stop *Silver Wings*. But I'm done now – I've said my piece. You can go ahead and kill me.'

'You seem very resigned to it,' Charlock said.

'What choice have I got? Even with its impasse raised, this pod wouldn't survive a concentrated attack from your ships for very long.'

Charlock shrugged. 'No, it probably wouldn't.'

'I think I'd sooner it was quick. I shall put myself in abeyance, then I won't know a thing. Do what you will with me.'

Charlock nodded. 'We will.'

Galingale reached out of view and touched a control. Restraints whirred, sucking him deeper into his chair. He braced himself, like a man expecting an electric shock. Then the red cocoon of stasis locked around him.

'We can draw straws, if you like,' Charlock said.

'For who gets to kill him?' asked Tansy.

'For who gets to take him back to Neume. One of us has to abandon the chase and return home. He said he'd told us everything, but we'd be fools to take him at his word.'

'I agree,' I said.

'Not that I'm not up for a chase,' Sorrel said, 'but *Snowstorm*'s already pushed to the limit. I'm not going to be much good if *Silver Wings* pulls some thrust out of the bag.' He glanced at Orache, who was sharing his ship – nothing in her expression said she disagreed with him.

'Someone has to go back,' I said. 'It might as well be Sorrel. Anyone else who doesn't want to stick around for the chase, I suggest you make arrangements to whisk over to *Snowstorm* as soon as you can. Really, though, I think you all should go. *Dalliance* is at least as fast as any of the remaining ships. There's no reason for the rest of you to be dragged halfway across the galaxy.'

'I'd much rather see this through,' Tansy said.

'Me, too,' Henbane echoed, after a moment's reflection.

'Then I'll take Galingale back to Neume,' Sorrel said. 'One of us has to go back and let them know what happened out here. They'll never entirely believe anything in a signal, but when I show up in the flesh, I think they'll listen.' He singled me out, our eyes meeting for a moment, and said, 'I'll speak well of Purslane, Campion. And you, of course. I'll let the doubters know they were wrong.'

'One day she'll get to tell them in person. Good luck, Sorrel. Get back to Neume, help the Line consolidate. I think it's safe to say that we're going to be out of touch for a while. But we're still Gentian. Sooner or later, you'll find a way to get a message to us.'

'I don't doubt that for a second.'

'In a way, I'm almost envious of you,' I said.

'Missing the singing dunes of Neume already?'

'Not exactly. But I'd give a lot to see the look on Galingale's face when they pull him out of stasis. Especially if the first person he sees is Mezereon, sharpening her knives.'

CHAPTER FORTY

Beyond the window, the white-walled room was as still as a painting. Occasionally my eyes convinced me that there was a flicker of subliminal movement, but I soon learned not to trust them. At my current level of time compression, Hesperus would have had to spend many hours in the same position just to register to my senses. There was no reason to assume he was out there at all. Unless the casket relinquished control to me, as it had refused to do after the stasis first took hold, I stood a very good chance of dying in there.

This thought was chasing its tail through my head for the thousandth or ten thousandth time when the casket's voice calmly informed me that the transition to realtime was imminent. 'Stasis ratio is now one hundred thousand and falling,' it said. 'Ten thousand and falling. Field stability optimal.'

The field dialled down from ten thousand to one thousand, through the hundreds, into the tens, and then released me. The chair's bindings eased apart, allowing me to slip my hands and feet out of the hoops. I could move my head again. My neck and spine felt as if they had calcified together. I did *not* like stasis.

The door opened with a huff of air and the chair emerged from the casket. Pushing the discomfort aside, I eased myself to my feet, keeping one hand on the back of the chair for support. It was less than twenty-four subjective hours since I had last been in that room, but if the cabinet had kept me at a stasis level of a million for the entire duration of my confinement, the better part of three thousand years had passed aboard the ark. I hobbled to a wall and scuffed my hand against the white material, with the absurd expectation that a film of dust might have built up there. My fingertips came away forensically clean. Every surface in the room gleamed with polished newness, as if it was only minutes old.

'Hesperus?' I called, my voice hoarse until I cleared my throat and tried again. 'Hesperus? It's Purslane. I'm out.'

There was no answer. I breathed in the ancient, still air. There were atoms in the room that had not been through a human lung for thirty centuries.

Something caught my eye in the adjoining room, visible through the open doorway – a flash of colour and glass. My legs still unsteady, I made my cautious way out of the casket room. I found a white table set for me, with a white chair next to it. Breakfast had been served. There was a glass of freshly squeezed orange juice, a croissant on a plate, a pot of coffee and a bowl of fruit. There was a bunch of flowers in a vase, and a folded white card like a menu. I touched the croissant and found that it was still warm. I sniffed the coffee – it was dark and strong, the way I liked it, and boiling hot. I pulled the seat out and sat down, grateful to rest my wobbly legs for a while. I poured some of the coffee into a white china cup and held it to my nose, taking in the aroma before I allowed myself a sip. I tore off the end of the croissant and stuffed it into my mouth. After a day in the stasis casket, I was ravenous. After the first bite, I could not stop myself. I finished off the croissant and three pieces of fruit. I gulped down the juice and drank two cups of coffee. Only then did I open the stiff white card. Inside was a message in fine gold writing. It was written in very elegant script, but just a touch too precise to have ever been the work of a human hand. Hesperus had signed it, but there had been no need.

He told me that he was sorry he could not be with me on the day of my emergence from stasis, but that he was unavoidably detained elsewhere. He had arranged for the ark's robot janitors to prepare this breakfast just before my stasis interval was due to expire; he trusted it was to my taste, insofar as he had been able to judge it. At the time he had issued the instructions, he wrote, my emergence still lay many centuries in the future – but he had been confident that the janitors would execute their orders with due scrupulousness, as he had requested.

'I cannot be certain that I will still be alive when you read this,' Hesperus had written. 'If I am, then you will find me on the bridge of *Silver Wings*, doing what I may. I should very much like to see you, but circumstances dictate that you must come to me, not the other way around. Before you do, I would urge you to examine the ark's cargo hold – I believe you will find the contents illuminating. Before you leave the ark itself, you must make an assessment of the present dangers. If all is well, you will see an abundance of golden threads leading out of the cargo bay. If you follow them, they will bring you to me. If there are white threads only, it will not be safe for you. If there are golden and white threads, you would be advised to exercise caution. Use the whiskways only if you have no other choice.' Almost as an afterthought, he had added, 'I have had the maker prepare a spacesuit suitable for your needs. I trust you will find it satisfactory, and I look forward to renewing our acquaintance. I remain your friend, Hesperus.'

'Thank you,' I said quietly.

I finished my breakfast. Then I emptied my bladder, bathed and had a maker prepare me a change of clothes. Only then did I start looking around the ark for the other messages he might have left.

It was not long before I encountered one of the threads. I was walking down a corridor, trying to find the spacesuit, when I came across an obstruction that had not been there before. A fist-thick cable punched its way from one wall to the other, at chest height. It was white and as smooth as an icicle, but the way the wall material had splintered around the intrusion made me doubtful that it was part of the ark's own systems. Not long afterwards I found another white branch, this time running across the floor and forking in two directions. One fork plunged into the floor; the other curved up the wall and went through the ceiling.

I walked on, a feeling of dread churning in my stomach. In the next large room I found a cross-knitted tangle of white and gold cables, rupturing through various surfaces, stretching through the air in different directions like the strands of a monstrous cobweb. I had to pick and fight my way through the tangle. The cables were stiff and hard. Some of the white ones were wrapped around the gold, and vice versa – it was like vines trying to strangle a larger trunk. Although everything was still, I had the sense that this was a frozen moment in a titanic struggle.

It was the same everywhere I went. In some parts of the ark the white cables dominated; in others the gold. In various critical areas the white and gold cables were competing for control. Here and there I found a cable that came to an abrupt, severed end. I kept thinking of Cadence, pushing tendrils from her wounds, trying to connect with any useful system aboard the ark so that she could work mischief. I was seeing the evidence of something similar, but on a much larger scale.

I remembered Hesperus's recommendation that I visit the ark's cargo bay. I would not have considered going there at all if he hadn't suggested it, my memory insisting that it was as empty as the rest of the ancient liner. But now that he had planted the thought in my mind, I felt a dark compulsion guiding me onwards, as if I was sleepwalking towards a destination known only to my subconscious mind. The going became increasingly difficult – the density of white and gold cables doubling and redoubling until it was all I could do to squeeze through the narrow interstices. There were parts of the ark that they had left well alone, and parts that they were still fighting for. The cargo hold was clearly of paramount importance.

Eventually the obstructions thinned out – it was as if I had passed into the eye of the storm – and I found a window offering a view through a thick wall into what should have been the unlit space of the hold. The hold was not unlit today, but the light coming through that window was not as steady as I would have expected. It was flickering, tinged with blue and violet. I looked into the hold, squinting against the brightness. The ark's hold was not empty at all. Suspended in the middle, occupying most of its length, was a machine that was both instantly recognisable and deeply unfamiliar to me. It was a series of eight brass-coloured spheres, joined together as if on a spit. The spheres, each of which was easily a hundred metres across, were as reflective as mirrors and entirely featureless.

I was looking at the single-use opener. It was floating against the ark's interior gravity, suspended by its own levators. It was also generating an impasse – eight spherical bubbles merging into a kind of crimped sausage shape. I could trace the quivering surface of the impasse by the energies flickering across it, forming transient spectral patterns like oil on water. Weapons were arranged around the opener, directing their fire against the impasse. They were a larger version of the energy-pistol that the maker had created for me, floating in the air, each weapon trailing a gold cable back into the gold nervous system that Hesperus had cobwebbed around the inside of the bay.

I realised then that I must always have known that the opener was in the ark. When I chose this ship as our place of refuge, my subconscious had been directing me, knowing that the robots would be wary of attacking the ark if they suspected the opener was inside it. And if I had known of the opener, then I had also known of the stardam it was made for. On that level, I must also have known of my complicity in the extinction of the First Machines, long before I needed it spelled out.

I left the opener and navigated back through the ark until I reached a gold-threaded area where Hesperus had established clear control. It was there that I found the spacesuit, waiting by a high-capacity maker. Hesperus had done well – the suit was an exact fit, and although it was a very long time since I had worn one, the memories came back soon enough.

'Hello, Purslane,' the helmet said as it lit up with status icons. 'I would have spoken to you sooner but I could not find an easy route into your skull. I was hoping you would find the suit eventually.'

I smiled. For all my fears, for all that I did not know if I would ever see Campion or the other shatterlings again, it was still good to hear his voice. 'You're all right.'

'And so are you, I trust.' There was something evasive about his answer, I thought. 'I am sorry to have kept you in abeyance for so long, but I believed it was in your best interests. There really was no sense in you remaining conscious for the entire voyage, even if that could have been arranged. After Galingale's attack . . .'

He was talking about something that had happened thousands of years ago. To me it was yesterday's news.

'What happened?'

'He was unsuccessful.'

'In killing me, or in slowing *Silver Wings*?'

'Neither objective was achieved. Galingale met greater resistance than he had anticipated. His ship was damaged – it fell back towards the other vehicles. There was an altercation, during which unpleasantness Betony's ship was destroyed. I learned this from Campion during our subsequent conversations.'

'You've been in touch with Campion?'

'Not recently, but I have every confidence that he is still alive. His ship, *Dalliance*, has been following us ever since.'

'And the others?'

'They've all gone now, Purslane. *Dalliance* is the last one left. But Campion is alive – I am sure of it. He must be in abeyance, awaiting news of a change in our status. Very shortly he will have it.'

'Where are we?'

'Approaching the stardam. We have travelled sixty-two thousand years from Neume.'

It was the longest crossing I had ever made, in all the circuits since I had left the Golden Hour for the first time. Although I had been half-expecting this news, it still triggered a demoralising psychic vertigo. Human beings were not meant for this kind of thing – we had evolved to grub around within a few kilometres of the same village, in the same time zone, under the same fixed stars.

'You mentioned that it might not be safe for me to come to see you,' I said.

'I think you may. Take care, but do not be unduly concerned. The whiskways are safe now. I have secured them in readiness. Come up to the bridge – there is much to discuss.'

I left the ark, not without trepidation. Stepping outside for the first time since Cadence and Hesperus had fought each other, I kept expecting to find one of her severed limbs inching across the floor, dragging itself along by a fine silver thread. But that incident lay thousands of years in the past as far as the ship was concerned.

All around me, the bay appeared superficially unchanged – the same looming vastness, ceiling and walls kilometres distant, a volume large enough to swallow the white ark, with its own huge cargo, and make it look tiny. But a second glance told me that nothing was as I had left it. Every visible ship in the bay was covered in a gristle of white and gold strands, braided together in thick, fibrous mats. The outlines of the ships were rounded, indistinct, like mansions overrun by foliage. The cables had encroached on every surface, obscuring their true form. Even the white ark itself was now almost unrecognisable. A forest of cables enveloped the old ship, gold and white, branching and rebranching in dismaying complexity, punching through her barely visible hull in hundreds of places. The door where I emerged was one of the few clear spots; it was encircled by a thick moat of gold cables, keeping the white at bay, and the gold cables extended away from the ark to form a kind of braided tunnel, a passage through the forest floor.

'You've been busy,' I said.

'It passed the time.'

I walked out into the cargo bay, to the nearest whisking point. This part of the ship looked more or less as I remembered it – there was the occasional gold cable, but other than that the walls and surfaces were unchanged. The go-board hovered in readiness. I punched for up-ship, whisked there in an eyeblink, walked from one side of the concourse to the other across the bridge with its kilometres-long central trunk shaft rising and falling above and below. The anvil-shaped machines, normally moving up and down the shaft, were still, bound in vast cobwebs of gold and white.

I punched another go-board and reached the bridge.

'I've provided atmosphere,' Hesperus said. 'It's safe to remove your helmet.'

Until that moment I had not known for sure that he was still alive; that the voice I had been hearing was not an impersonation performed by Cascade.

But Hesperus was still alive – in a manner of speaking. There were two robots on the bridge, situated more or less opposite one another. Cascade was to my left, his head and torso attached to one wall. Hesperus was on the other side, positioned in a similar fashion. Both robots had lost all their limbs – or, more accurately, had grown so many extensions from their bodies that their limbs had been transformed beyond recognition and duplicated many times over. Cascade was a many-limbed starfish with a humanoid torso and head at his epicentre; Hesperus was a gold star radiating out in all the directions of the compass. The limbs had the thickness of arm or leg joints where they erupted from all over their bodies, and then tapered down to the diameters of the cables I had already seen. They reached away from the two robots, tangling together where they made contact, forming a dense, labyrinthine quilt of white and gold filaments. I tried to follow a single cable, but it was futile – the pattern was too complicated. But I was certain that most, if not all, of the cables eventually found their way out of this room. This was the nerve centre. From here, the two robots had extended their bodies to encompass every vital system of *Silver Wings* and her cargo. They must have consumed and converted thousands, even millions of tonnes' worth of matter – digesting the ship's own fabric, remaking it for their own ends.

'Remove your helmet,' Hesperus urged again. 'It's quite safe, and we can talk more easily that way.'

I did as he suggested. The suit would not have allowed me to undo the helmet unless the air was breathable, but his encouragement was reassuring.

'How long have you been like this?'

'A while.'

'Since you put me into abeyance?'

He smiled – he was still capable of that. 'No, this state of immobility came much later – within the last six hundred years. For a long time I was the way you remember me. Once you were in abeyance, I began to direct my energies into regaining control of the ship. For many years it was all I could do to keep out of reach of the weapons and tracking devices Cascade sent after me. He was wary of touching the ark, though. That was when I began to wonder about the location of the opener. Once my suspicions had been aroused, it was an easy matter to locate it – it took only a few centuries of patient investigation.'

'It was in there all along, just waiting for me to stumble on it?'

'It was concealed – hidden inside a camouflaging impasse. Unless you had reason to look more closely, you would have seen only an empty cargo bay. You probably did look in there on more than one occasion in the distant past.'

'Perhaps,' I said doubtfully. It was equally likely that my subconscious had kept me away from the ark's hold, knowing the secret it contained.

'I tried to sabotage the opener, but quickly learned how well protected it was. Someone had gone to extraordinary lengths of ingenuity and resourcefulness to make it sabotage-proof. Her handiwork was marvellous.'

'It was me, wasn't it?'

'Very likely.'

I cursed myself under my breath. 'What have you tried?'

'Everything imaginable. Everything imaginable has failed. As you may have observed, I am attempting to overload the impasse with a concentrated injection of energy. The chances of success are not high. It was simply one more avenue to explore. I have been trying for three hundred and seventy years.'

'And the ship?' I asked. 'Who's running her now?'

'Neither of us. After centuries of mere survival, I decided the time had come to attempt to regain control. Cascade was strong, but I was not the simple Machine Person he imagined me to be. Gradually I wore him down – invading his mind, stripping away his intellect layer by layer. Over centuries I reduced him to a machine vegetable, a box of reflexes. I could not have done so without the gifts I inherited from Valmik.'

I looked at the inert white robot on the other side of the room. 'And now?'

'I am fighting a mindless entity. But he is not powerless, or without stratagems. Before I began to strip away his faculties, he put in place measures that I cannot rescind. The ship is course-locked – she cannot be turned from her current heading.'

'Can't you overcome him, disable those measures?'

'I have been trying to do exactly that, without success, for hundreds of years. He was cleverer than most, Purslane. He must have anticipated my eventual takeover of his mind.'

'I could get an energy-pistol, shoot him right now.'

'It would do no good. The ship would still be course-locked, and I would still have to contend with the rest of him.'

'How close is the stardam?'

'We are very near now – less than a light-month away. I expect the opener to function very shortly. You can see the dam, if you wish.'

Without waiting for my answer, Hesperus caused an image to appear on my main displayer. It was garlanded in white and gold threads, but the surface was still unobstructed. A fountainburst of blue-shifted stars bunched aft, with a magnified circle of perfect darkness punched through the middle of them. You could blue-shift the black of a stardam as much as you liked and it would still be black.

'That's it?'

'Realtime imagery,' Hesperus confirmed.

The black circle, and the space around it, swarmed with red icons. 'What are those things? Planets?'

'Ships and defence stations. They've been waiting for us. Once our destination and intention became clear, Gentian Line sent a warning ahead of us, signalling the surrounding communities to guard the stardam.'

I felt a twinge of betrayal, while knowing that there was nothing else they could have done.

'How much warning have they had?'

'A little over sixty years. Just enough time to coordinate a few nearby systems, and call in any Line-level ships in the neighbourhood. It won't stop us, Purslane.'

'How sure of that are you?'

'Very sure. I know what this ship can do now. I have seen her smash Charlock, Orache and Agrimony's ships. Later she swatted Galingale aside – his ship carried more and better weapons than any of the others, and still it made no difference. After that there were three ships following us – *Dalliance*, *Shock Diamond* and *Chromatic Aberration*. Only *Dalliance* is left now. The other ships made attempts to slow us down, but *Silver Wings* picked them off effortlessly. They inflicted only minimal damage, easily repaired. From what I have learned concerning the cordon, the chances of them hurting us – let alone stopping us – are very small. It will be a massacre, and nothing will have changed.'

'You could be wrong. There could be hidden ships, waiting to emerge from camouflage at the last moment.'

'There could be, yes.' Hesperus hesitated. 'I took a liberty, Purslane – I hope you will not be angry.'

'After you locked me in a box for three thousand years? Why would I be angry?'

'I signalled the cordon – I am able to control *Silver Wings* to that extent. I explained our situation – that you and I are innocent hostages, unable to influence the course or velocity of this ship or stop her from responding to hostile overtures. I offered them graphical testimony of what I had already witnessed. I showed them that there is no combination of their forces that stands a chance of stopping us, and that the best they can hope for is massive losses of ships and sentients. I urged them to stand all crewed ships down and rely only on automated attack stations, to minimise losses.'

'Did they listen?'

'I have received no response. Nor have I observed any change in their defensive posture. I believe they received my message but chose to ignore it.'

'You can see why they might. For all they know, they are hearing Cadence or Cascade, trying to talk them out of an attack that might actually work.'

'I am sorry, Purslane – it was the best I could do.'

'I could try talking to them.'

'I do not believe it would make any difference now. Your voice and face could be faked just as easily.'

'I'd still like to try.'

'Then speak.'

'Now?'

'The sooner they move out of range of *Silver Wings*' weapons, the fewer losses they will sustain. They cannot stop us, but at least we will not have more blood on our hands.' He smiled encouragingly. 'Speak, Purslane. Perhaps you can make a difference, where I failed.'

'I'm not sure where to begin. Usually when I address a civilisation I like to know a bit about it. Like, are they bipeds, do they breathe air, simple stuff like that.'

'You don't have that luxury now. The best you can hope for is that these people understand Tongue. They probably do, or they would not have acted on the Gentian warning.'

'All right, then.' I coughed to clear my throat again – it was still dry, despite the breakfast. 'This is Purslane. I am a shatterling of Gentian Line. You've already heard from my brothers and sisters, I think. You may already have heard from my friend Hesperus. I want you to know that everything you've heard is true. This ship is carrying a single-use opener and it's aimed at your stardam. If the opener works, we're all in a lot of trouble – humans, posthumans, every organic sentience in the meta-civilisation. That's a given. You're right to try to stop us – if there was a foolproof way of doing it, I'd be encouraging you to go right ahead. But this isn't a battle you can win. Please believe what Hesperus has already told you – that all you'll be doing is flinging machines and people against an unstoppable object. If you have some ultimate weapon we don't know about – ten thousand Line ships about to break out of camouflage and open fire with H-guns – then go ahead and use that weapon. But if you don't, I beg you to remove all your crewed ships from the immediate vicinity of the stardam.' I fell silent. Hesperus nodded.

'That was good, Purslane. You made a very persuasive case.'

'But they won't listen, will they?'

'There is always hope.'

I dragged fingers through my hair, tangled from the helmet. 'Does any of this matter, anyway? If we reach the stardam, the lives that will be lost trying to stop us will be a total irrelevance compared to the lives that will be lost afterwards, when the First Machines break through.'

'That is my gravest fear, and the thing I most want to discuss with you.'

'I thought you wanted me to persuade the cordon to disperse.'

'The cordon is merely a taste of the worst that could happen. As you say, if the stardam is opened, and the First Machines have hostile ambitions, even the loss of an entire civilisation would be a mere detail.'

'They'll have hostile ambitions. Wouldn't you?'

'Revenge is for biologicals, as I have already pointed out.'

'Tell that to Cadence and Cascade. Revenge was pretty high up their agenda, as far as I could tell.'

'You have a point.'

'What do you want to say to me, Hesperus?'

'That I can stop this ship at any time.' He let that sink in, allowing me a few moments to digest the implications, watching me with those magnificent opal/turquoise eyes until he judged that the moment was right to continue. 'My control of *Silver Wings* is still imperfect: I cannot steer her or slow her down; I cannot prevent her from opening fire on friendly forces. But I can destroy her, and the opener. I have sufficient control of the white ark to initiate an excursion event in her engine. As we discussed many centuries ago, *Silver Wings* could not contain such an energy release.'

I could only focus on the practicalities of what he was suggesting, not the brutal emotional truth of it.

'The opener's inside an impasse. Will it survive?'

'Unlikely. The impasse is strong enough to resist weapons, but not the energies associated with an engine failure.'

'There's no other way, is there?'

'No outside agency can stop us. Only we have that means now.'

My mind flashed through all the options we had already tried or rejected. 'Can we abandon ship and trigger the engine remotely?'

'Abandoning ship is not an option for me, I'm afraid. It would take me much too long to reshape myself, and we have little time left.'

'I'm sorry.'

'Regretfully, it is also not an option for you. I cannot disengage the curtain on the cargo bay, nor persuade the door to open. You could exit via one of the passenger locks in a suit, but without a ship, you would not survive long.'

'It's all right. I wouldn't leave you here alone.'

'That is considerate of you, Purslane.'

'What would it take? Do you have to make any preparations?'

'All it needs is a word from you. Tell me to do it, and the ship will cease to exist.'

'You shouldn't have woken me. You should have just done it.'

'I owed you the dignity of choice.'

I fell silent. I knew he was right. Every path I had taken in my life, from the moment Madame Kleinfelter removed the growth inhibitor from my forearm, had been of my own choosing. Absurd as it was to speak of feeling resentment from the perspective of being dead, that is how I would have felt had I been denied this final say in my affairs.

'I hope I would have extended you the same courtesy, Hesperus. We're sentients. We deserve that much.'

'I sense that your mind is settled.'

I felt more weary than saddened. 'What choice do we have? It's simple. Every other option has already been exhausted. You can't slow us down. That cordon won't stop us. The Line couldn't stop us – good shatterlings have died trying, when we could least afford to lose any more of them. I'll be one more death, but that's a small price to pay, isn't it? I'm not even sure why we're debating it. One human life, one robot life, to spare the galaxy a macro-war between the machine and the organic? I shouldn't hesitate. I should have already told you to do it instead of talking about it.'

'I thought you might like to send a final message to Campion. His ship will keep a record of it until he awakes.'

'Thank you.'

'You may speak at your leisure, Purslane.'

There was less to say now, but the words came with even greater difficulty. 'This is Purslane. You've followed me all this way, and I'm more grateful than you'll ever realise. I'm sorry about what happened to the others, to Betony and the rest – we did everything we could, but in the end it wasn't enough. I'm going to destroy *Silver Wings* now – it's the only thing left for us to do. It'll be fast and I won't feel anything. Clean and bright – a good way to go. Turn around and find the Line again, Campion. Speak for me at my funeral, make me a memorial, and then get on with your life. I love you, and I will always love you.'

Hesperus lowered his face. 'It's done. The signal is transmitted. *Dalliance* will receive it shortly.'

'You're certain of that?'

'Beyond all doubt.'

I looked at the displayer again, with the black circle of the stardam and the red icons of that useless, soon to be decimated cordon. There was no sense asking if anything had changed. The message I'd already sent would still not have reached them, and there would be precious little time for them to act even when it did.

'I don't think there's much point in delaying this, is there? The longer we drag things out, the more chance there is of the opener triggering.'

'That is always a possibility. But I wish to make one suggestion. The likelihood of you surviving the excursion is not good, but you may maximise your chances be re-entering stasis. By some great good fortune, your casket may come through unscathed.'

'Great good fortune. That's encouraging.'

'I do not wish to overstate your chances.'

'Point taken, Hesperus. But how would you rate yours?'

'Rather unpromising, if I am compelled to be truthful. But that changes nothing. If our roles were reversed, I feel certain that you would want me to do all in my power to survive, even if the likelihood of that survival was small.'

I could not argue with that, as much as I would have liked to.

'I'll go back to the ark. I can set the stasis casket myself.'

'No – that would achieve nothing. To stand a chance of surviving, you would be better off as far from the ark – and *Silver Wings*' own engine – as circumstances allow. Fortunately, there is such a place. During my peregrinations, I found a secret room containing an armoured stasis chamber, protected by multiple impassors. It is very near the bows, not far from our present position. You must have built it as a precaution against just such a situation as this – your being compelled to remain aboard during a catastrophic engine failure.'

I had no conscious recollection of doing such a thing. 'I built it?'

'There's no question, Purslane. I may only have known you for a fraction of your existence, but I recognise your handiwork. You did well to think ahead.'

'Just as I did well to stop anyone tampering with the opener.'

'You cannot blame yourself for that. You never envisaged that you would be the person trying to sabotage it.'

'You'd better tell me how to get to this secret room.'

'I programmed it into the go-board. Enter "terminus". The whiskway will carry you there.'

'A secret whiskway as well as a secret room?'

'This is a big ship. It has space enough for a few surprises.'

'Thank you, Hesperus. It won't help, but it'll give me something to pin my hopes on. At least when I go into stasis, it won't be in the absolute and certain knowledge that I'm going to die. There'll be a chink of light, for me anyway.'

'I have had my share of lucky escapes. There is nothing to say I will not profit from another. Go, Purslane.'

There were a thousand things I could have said to him, a thousand questions I wanted to ask. But every second that passed was another second in which the opener might activate, sending its irrevocable command to the stardam.

I said goodbye. I left the bridge and went to the whisking chamber. I punched in the command Hesperus had given me and steeled myself. In the last instant before the field engaged, it occurred to me that he might have been lying; that there might be no such thing as a secret room, and that the whiskway was going to send me into painless oblivion by dashing me against a sealed wall. But the field snapped, the whiskway transported me, swerved onto a track I did not know existed, and after a confusion of blurred, rushing spaces I arrived . . . *somewhere*.

It was a room, but not one I recognised. As I stepped out of the chamber, darkness yielded to light. The space was smaller even than *Silver Wings'* bridge – little larger than a lounge or kitchen. The walls were square and metallic, with bolt-like reinforcements. The room contained nothing except the emergency survival device Hesperus had already described.

I recognised it.

It was a green cube, densely patterned with mouldings depicting castles and palaces, knights and princesses, ponies and dragons and sea-serpents. It was Palatial, or at least a clever replica of that ancient game. I must have brought it with me all the way from the Golden Hour, across six million years.

It was exactly as I remembered it.

I walked in through the portal in one green face of the cube. Instead of the glowing holographic landscape of the Kingdom, with the Palace of Clouds centremost, there was only a stasis casket, surrounded by multiple impasse generators.

'Why here?' I asked myself. But if I did not have the answer, it was unlikely anyone else would.

I settled myself into the seat. In an emergency situation, there was no sense in selecting anything other than the highest possible stasis ratio. I moved the controls to a million. If *Silver Wings* was destroyed, I might be rescued by one of the ships of the cordon within months or years of planetary time. On the other hand, I might sail right past them, destined to fall through space for tens of thousands of years. This time at least I was prepared for an extended stay. Before the restraints tightened, I dropped Synchromesh into my eyes. The combination of 'mesh, stasis and relativistic time dilation would keep me alive until I was on the other side of the galaxy.

'Hesperus?' I asked, as the chamber warned me that stasis was about to be initiated. 'Can you hear me?'

'Of course, Purslane.'

'I'm about to go under. I just wanted to say—'

'There is no need to say anything. I was, and will remain, your friend.'

'I hope you can forgive us for the things we did.'

'Machines may do awful things to the organic if we are not successful. One day, we may both need forgiveness. Until then, you have both my forgiveness and my thanks.'

'Hesperus?' I asked.

But there was no answer. The restraints began to tighten. Before they bound me into immobility I set my chronometer and let the Synchromesh take effect. Then I was in stasis, and I had time for exactly two coherent thoughts.

The first was that I was still alive.

The second was that we had almost certainly failed.

CHAPTER FORTY-ONE

Hesperus had a message for me when I emerged from abeyance. I had intended to come out when *Silver Wings* was approaching the stardam, just before I expected the opener to activate. As it was, I came back to the living during a major space battle, almost a microwar, between the cordon around the stardam and the ship they were trying to stop. To call it a 'battle' implies a certain even-handedness to the affair, but in fact it was a ruthlessly one-sided bloodbath. *Silver Wings* brushed aside the local civilisations' efforts as if it was almost beneath her dignity to acknowledge them at all. But they did not give up, even when they had thrown dozens of ships against that hopelessly invulnerable target. The humans and machines kept coming. I watched with horrified, dumbstruck fascination.

'I failed,' Hesperus told me, after I had heard Purslane's final message to me, the one she had recorded before entering abeyance. He was signalling me from an hour ahead, calm despite the horrific destruction that was taking place all around him. 'I told Purslane that we had one chance of stopping this ship, by destroying the white ark. I believed it was in my power to do so, but I was mistaken. Unfortunately, I could not know for sure until I sent the final command. There was no way to gauge its effectiveness until that moment.'

He told me everything that had happened – how he and Purslane had come to a mutual decision to destroy the ship, thereby preventing the massacre of the cordon and the subsequent opening of the stardam. He told me how he had persuaded Purslane to take refuge in a stasis casket, so that she might have some slim but measurable chance of surviving the destruction of the ark, the opener and the larger ship in which both were contained.

'Satisfied that I had done all I could, that Purslane was as safe as I could make her, I issued the command. A moment later, when I found myself still conscious, I knew that it had been unsuccessful.

Purslane had been cleverer than both of us, Campion – cleverer than me, cleverer even than her future self. She had already taken measures to protect the opener against sabotage, so I suppose it was only natural that she would have considered this possibility as well. The command was intercepted and neutralised by fail-safe screens I had not detected until that moment. But it is much worse than that. The opener has triggered – I sensed the graviton pulse, racing ahead of *Silver Wings*. I do not know whether my command precipitated the activation of the opener, or whether it was simply time for it to happen, but ... we have failed.' Hesperus paused long enough for me to think his message had ended. Then he said, 'We are slowing. You will have detected that already, but I may as well confirm it in case you doubt your instruments. This will make it simple for you to catch up with us, but since the opener has already activated, nothing would now be gained from destroying *Silver Wings*. You may, of course, choose to regard this message as unreliable. I would not blame you if you did. But you may also wish to consider the implications of our deceleration. Left on its present course – and we have not begun to deviate from it – *Silver Wings* will run into the stardam only a few hours after the arrival of the opener transmission. At our previous velocity, the dam would not have opened sufficiently to allow a ship to slip between two of the ringworlds. But we are slowing, and that changes everything. The margin will still be narrow, but I believe that the additional time before our arrival will allow *Silver Wings* to enter the dam. This velocity correction was locked in thirty centuries of shiptime ago, Campion – I believe it was always the robots' intention to pass through the stardam, and to encounter whatever lies at its heart. The purpose of their mission was to release the First Machines, but they must also have been desirous of making contact with those machines in Andromeda. The robots were intending to make a wormhole traversal, and I do not believe anything can now stop that from happening.' He was silent again, giving me time to reflect on the scraps of intelligence we had learned from Galingale before we packed him off back to Neume and the tender mercies of Mezereon. The door, the aperture, the mouth – the macroscopic wormhole connection between our galaxy and Andromeda.

I finally realised why Hesperus was telling me this.

'The stardam may not stay in its open configuration for ever. I cannot promise you that *Silver Wings* will survive the transition –

this is not a journey any human ship has ever completed – but if you do not follow, you may never get another chance. It is a long way to Andromeda by the other route.'

I transmitted my reply. 'If the cordon lets me through, I'm going to keep on following.'

The Line's instructions to the local civilisations had been precise about the nature of the objective, and although the ships and defence stations of their cordon had been devastated, no one tried to take their revenge out on *Dalliance*. They understood that I had been chasing *Silver Wings* for sixty-two thousand years; they understood that I meant them no harm.

Silver Wings had dropped down to eighty per cent of the speed of light; I followed suit after allowing myself to fall within five minutes of the other ship. The cordon made a last effort to stop *Silver Wings* even though the opener had already activated. Their weapons barely grazed her, even at her reduced speed.

Ahead, the dark, nested machinery of the stardam began to respond to the signal. The ringworlds, held in place by pushers, began to tilt away from their existing inclinations. It was a deathly slow adjustment, but the monitoring devices around the stardam confirmed that the change was real and ongoing. No alarm was raised, for the monitoring devices knew only that an authenticated Gentian opener had sent that command. A widening, lens-shaped aperture was appearing along the circumference of the stardam, as if a dark marble was slowly opening its single, lazy eye. Over the course of hours, *Silver Wings* continued her deceleration, falling to fifty per cent of light, then to a third. She was still aimed precisely at the opening eye.

If there was one scant piece of consolation to be drawn, it was in the absence of hellish light pouring through that gap. No supernova had been contained by this stardam; the local civilisations were at least safe from that particular hazard. There was every likelihood that Galingale had been telling the truth.

I watched *Silver Wings of Morning* fall through the gap, into the black clockwork of the stardam. She held her course for several light-seconds then began to veer hard, passing out of my line of sight. A few minutes later a signal came through, staggered as it arrived from multiple reflection points. *Dalliance* sorted through the jumbled puzzle and dragged out a coherent message.

'This is Hesperus. I trust you can still receive me, Campion. We have begun to execute a series of increasingly violent course adjustments so that we may pass through the gaps between the interior ringworlds. These adjustments are of such severity that the inertial compensation is no longer working properly. Unshielded forces have been in excess of five hundred gravities and are still rising. Purslane is safe in stasis, but she would not have survived had she still been in realtime. I urge you to take similar precautions. *Silver Wings* is still out of my direct control, but I can transmit a record of our trajectory to *Dalliance* so that you may maintain your pursuit. With foreknowledge of the interior conditions, you may be able to ease the stresses on your ship.'

'Thank you,' I said. 'I'll go into stasis. Good luck, Hesperus. I hope you make it.'

'I'll see you on the other side, Campion. We'll have much to discuss, I think.'

'I expect we will,' I said, wondering why he suddenly sounded so much more human.

Presently *Dalliance* informed me that she had a lock on *Silver Wings'* trajectory. She was zigzagging deeper and deeper into the stardam, squeezing between gaps that were in some cases only a few thousand kilometres wide. Hesperus had been right to warn me into abeyance. It would be difficult enough for *Dalliance* to follow, let alone do so in a way that would protect her fragile human cargo.

There was just time to transmit a message to the Line, aimed in the rough direction of Neume, telling them of my plans. I also fired a copy towards the nearest node of the private network, deciding that it no longer mattered whether or not the network had been compromised. I did not even know for certain that there were any other Gentians alive. We had travelled so fast that only a few centuries' worth of information had managed to catch up with us from Neume.

Satisfied that I had done all I could, I left *Dalliance* to follow Purslane's trail and whisked to the abeyance chamber. I dialled the casket to a million, set the expiration clock to one hundred hours of shiptime (a wild guess, since I had no idea how long it would take to reach the heart of the stardam or complete the subsequent wormhole transition) and allowed the field to enfold me.

Four seconds of consciousness later, I was back in realtime.

I emerged from the casket. The room was exactly as I had left it; gravity was normal, the ride smooth. Deep inside the ship as I was, there was no visible evidence of damage or trauma to her systems.

For a moment I wondered if Hesperus had tricked me, by guiding *Dalliance* onto a trajectory that caused her to miss the stardam completely, placing a higher premium on my survival than on keeping his word. I quickly dismissed the thought: he knew that I would sooner die than not follow Purslane all the way in. According to the clock in the head portion of the casket, ten days really had passed.

I whisked back up to the bridge, feeling as if I had only just been there. When I arrived I found all superficial indications normal, as if *Dalliance* was just floating in space, becalmed in flat vacuum. But the displayer was very reluctant to show me anything. It would not relay an external view, claiming that it was having trouble achieving a consistent description of our surroundings. Nor would it hazard a guess as to *Dalliance*'s present position. Its last reliable astrogation fix had been just before we entered the stardam, but according to the ship's memory of her own motions, she should have passed through the stardam nearly a hundred hours ago. Yet it was still unable to get a reading from any navigation pulsars or beacons, or locate a pattern of stars that it recognised. In fact, it could not locate any stars at all.

So we were somewhere else – not necessarily in the Milky Way any more. Maybe we were inside the dark envelope of the Andromeda Absence, floating in a starless void that had once been a galaxy. I settled into my control seat and tugged down the floating console, punching commands to force the displayer to give me *something*, even if it was against its better judgement. *Dalliance* was so protective of me that she would rather withhold data than show me something she regarded as highly suspect, possibly distorted by the machine equivalent of hallucinatory delirium. But in the end I prevailed.

It was a mistake.

I cannot adequately describe what I saw. I was aware that I was seeing only *Dalliance*'s attempt to translate her perceptions into a form that might be comprehensible to me, an echo of an echo, but it was still too much, too strange, too alien. Vast and luminous structures were rushing past in too many directions for my mind to process, approaching and receding at the same time, shifting from one shape to another in a constant fluid progression that made me think less of machinery, of some natural phenomenon, than of a protean creature inverting itself, turning itself inside out over and over again. I had an impression of appalling speed and appalling motionlessness, as if *Dalliance* was being swept along at the mercy of a storm and at the same time creating that storm around herself, sitting in perfect tranquillity in the calm eye of her own making. Unless what I was seeing represented conditions inside the Absence, then I had to accept that we were still riding the wormhole.

The Priors made this, I thought. We had assumed that their science was superior to ours when we contemplated their ringworlds and the ancient, sphinx-like machines floating around the Milky Way's central black hole. In truth, we had understood nothing of their true capabilities. Faced with such a gulf of comprehension, my mind wanted to curl up inside my skull and hope that the universe would go away. In six million years, we had not even scratched the surface of the possible. We had barely recognised that there was a surface to scratch.

I thought of returning to abeyance, but since I still had no idea how much longer would be required, I chose to administer Synchromesh. I dialled myself up to ten, maintaining enough of a grip on external time to be able to respond to outside events. After three hours of consciousness, thirty hours of shiptime, I received a message from what *Dalliance* tentatively identified as 'ahead'.

It was from Hesperus. His signal dopplered in and out, as if *Silver Wings* was experiencing absurd changes in velocity – one instant moving away from me at half the speed of light, the next surging closer at a quarter. I could only assume that the spacetime between our two ships was highly elastic.

'I hope you can still hear me, Campion. I have a hailing fix on your ship, which suggests you have retained at least some basic functionality. The timelag between us is shifting unpredictably – it may be that we will move out of signalling range at any moment. I am afraid *Silver Wings* suffered damage during the latter stages of the passage through the stardam and the insertion into the wormhole. I am doing what I can to stabilise the ship and consolidate her basic functions, but I am fighting against the system blockades Cascade installed. I cannot say how much longer it will be before we emerge back into conventional space, but I believe the exit transition will be no less violent than the entrance transition. You may fare better, for your ship is smaller and perhaps more agile. I will do all in my power to protect Purslane, but I cannot promise that I will succeed.'

'I'm in one piece,' I said. '*Dalliance* is struggling to orientate herself, but otherwise she's in good shape.'

His response took forty minutes to arrive. 'That is welcome news, Campion. I would nonetheless recommend that you return to abeyance at the earliest opportunity. Set your apparatus in such a way that I may bring you out, when I have deemed that our ships are safe.'

'Thanks, Hesperus, but I'm fine as I am.'

This time his answer arrived within ninety seconds. 'It must be your decision, Campion. Regardless, the instant I detect the transition back to normal space I will send warning of it. You may still have time to protect yourself before *Dalliance* runs into difficulties.'

'Have you seen anything coming the other way?'

'The concept of "other way" is a problematic one, given the confused state of our surroundings.' This time I had to wait eleven minutes for his reply, and his message was redshifted almost to the point of incomprehensibility. 'But if I take your meaning correctly, I have detected no other physical objects occupying the wormhole. The only two ships appear to be ours. You are doubtless wondering about the First Machines.'

'It crossed my mind that if there are invasion fleets waiting to escape back into our galaxy, we aren't seeing much sign of them.'

Five seconds later he said, 'You were gone a very long time then, Campion – I began to worry about you. It is a great relief to find that you are still alive. Concerning your observation, you have a point. It may still be too soon to form ready judgements, but the absence of any traffic, let alone indirect evidence of the First Machines ... it is indeed puzzling.'

'I wonder what Cadence and Cascade would be saying now if they were still around.'

'I imagine they would be ... vexed,' Hesperus said, two and half hours later.

'We know the First Machines existed. That's not in dispute – is it?'

Eleven minutes: 'I met them, Campion. It was a long time ago, but I don't think my memory is playing tricks with me.'

'I'm not sure how you can have met them, but I know there's a lot you and Purslane haven't been able to tell me. I'm burning with questions, but the most important one is: where are they?'

Fifteen seconds: 'Perhaps when we emerge, we will have a better idea.'

'What do you think we'll find when we reach Andromeda? Are we even going to be able to exist inside the Absence?'

Nineteen hours, twenty-two minutes: 'Cadence and Cascade must have expected to continue to exist or they would not have set *Silver*

Wings on this course.' After a moment he added, 'Of course, they were robots. That may have factored into their thinking.'

I smiled at this far from comforting answer. 'What do you think they were hoping to achieve?'

Six hours: 'To meet the First Machines. To be welcomed as pilgrims unto God. I saw into Cadence's mind, Campion. That is how it felt to her, as if this was a pilgrimage, with a sacred destination.' Then Hesperus added, 'I am detecting something – a change in the local conditions. Perhaps you feel it as well. I think we may be approaching the emergence point. You should hasten to abeyance, Campion. I cannot—'

Something cut him off. It was sudden and total. There was no longer even a carrier signal from *Silver Wings*.

'Hesperus?'

Nothing returned. I waited a minute; ten more. Then I whisked to the abeyance chamber, dialled in one hundred hours at a stasis level of a million and submitted myself to the mercy of the casket.

A spine of stars arced across the sky, hazy with the light of a billion suns, none of which had ever been given human names. I thought back to the amplified sky over the Centaurs' world, the taste of strong wine on my lips as Purslane and I sat by the bay at night, watching Doctor Meninx take his swim, waiting with nervous anticipation for Mister Nebuly to deliver his verdict on my trove. I had seen the Milky Way then, daubed across the sky. I was seeing it again now, except that this was another Milky Way – another spiral arm – arcing across the sky of a different galaxy. It looked achingly familiar, but I was two and half million years from home. One grove of stars may look much like another, but I was not even in the same forest.

I knew I had travelled, rather than simply being ejected back into the galaxy at some other point in space or time. Although the surroundings were familiar, the specifics were not. *Dalliance* listened for the tick of a thousand pulsars and heard none that she recognised. There were pulsars in the galactic disc, but none of them were rotating at the right frequencies. Even allowing for a million years of slowdown, even allowing for ten million, none of the pulsars could be matched against the fixed clocks she had come to expect. The same could be said for the brightest stars in the sky – those that we would have shrouded with stardams back home. None of them fitted the maps. I was in Terra Incognita.

Not quite. It was not as if Andromeda had gone unobserved during all the millions of years before the Absence. There was data in the troves concerning Andromedan stellar populations, Andromedan pulsars, Andromedan globular clusters, even the positions and stellar types of individual stars. Given time, *Dalliance*'s navigation system might have been able to sift through that jumble of ancient data, extrapolate it forwards, correlate it against its current observations and come to some rough and ready estimate of our present position.

Sooner or later I would have an idea where I was, even if it did not depend on any nearby galactic landmarks. I was still in the Local Group, after all. I told *Dalliance* to locate the Milky Way and any other Local Group galaxies she could find, and triangulate our present position. It did not have to be accurate to more than a few thousand lights in any direction. I would settle for knowing which spiral arm I was in.

Dalliance attended to the task. While I was waiting for her answer, I set about looking for anything of interest nearby. Of Hesperus and *Silver Wings* I found no evidence at all. I did not know whether to take this as a good sign or not – it was better than finding wreckage, but only slightly. I tried omni-directional hails, but even after a hundred hours nothing came back. The sky was silent except for the mindless squawking and whistling of radio stars and quasars. The galaxy I knew was a-thrum with human babble. This was a mausoleum.

Dalliance was still cogitating.

There was a planet behind me, falling away at a third of the speed of light. The planet had no sun – it had either been moved into interstellar space deliberately or ejected from its solar system during some ancient gravitational encounter. The planet was an airless, cratered husk, illuminated by starlight alone, but there was something orbiting it: a smudge of spatial distortion, the open mouth of the wormhole that had carried me here. The Prior machinery propping that shaft open was so unthinkably advanced that it was not even contained in the visible dimensions of macroscopic space. I told *Dalliance* to calculate an accurate reading of the planet's course so that we could find it again. Then I asked her why it was taking so long to triangulate on the Local Group.

She told me she was having trouble finding the galaxy where I had been born. In the direction where it should have been (based on the assumed identities of the other galaxies in the group), there was only a black oval, peppered with a scattering of stars lying just outside its boundary.

It was a second Absence.

Dizzy with the implications of this discovery, my preconceptions unhinged, I told *Dalliance* to assume that the second Absence was indeed the old galaxy, and to triangulate on that basis. This time it did not take long at all.

I was in Andromeda. My position was defined to within a cubic volume a thousand lights along each side. Now *Dalliance* could even make a stab at identifying some of the celestial landmarks surrounding us. Six thousand years in the direction of the galactic centre was a stellar nursery known to the trove, still birthing suns and worlds. Thirty thousand lights beyond that was a whipping star, a close cousin to our galaxy's own SS433.

I struggled to grasp how everything could look so familiar. In all directions I saw normal-looking stars, drifting in normal associations, following normal orbits. Beyond the stars, I could see globular clusters, satellite galaxies of Andromeda, and other, more distant galaxies. I could see beyond the Local Group, into the sparse immensity of the Local Cluster. And beyond the Local Cluster, the deep structure of creation – galactic voids and galactic superclusters. Beyond the furthest superclusters, I heard the warble of high redshift quasars and the kettledrum hiss of cosmic background radiation. Nothing was out of place. Nothing was abnormal.

There was no sign of the Absence. No black fog enveloping everything. No black curtain wrapped around the galaxy, shielding it from the rest of the universe.

I knew then that every assumption we had made about the Absence had been wrong. It was not what we imagined, not in the slightest. It appeared that we had been wrong about the First Machines as well. They were nowhere to be found.

But someone had reactivated the wormhole, I reminded myself.

Shortly afterwards I picked up a Gentian signal. It was dismayingly faint, but because it was the only made thing in all that random hissing and squawking of cosmic noise, it was trivial to isolate. If its spatial direction was to be believed, it appeared to be coming from a solar system more than three thousand lights from my present position. Before my hopes rose, I assured myself that it could not possibly be Purslane. Unless she had emerged from a different wormhole throat, she could not possibly have travelled so far, so fast.

But with nothing better to do, no other clues to follow, I told *Dalliance* to follow the signal anyway.

Stasis compressed the hundred and fifty years of shiptime of the voyage to a few minutes of consciousness, scarcely worth the bother of Synchromesh. The signal grew in strength as I neared, unwavering except for a cyclical frequency shift caused by the orbit of a planet around its sun. Occasionally the signal dimmed, as if being blocked by some occluding structure. Whoever was generating that transmission was moving with the planet, either on its surface or in a spacecraft following the same orbit. Time and again I crushed any hope that Purslane might have been responsible, while simultaneously wondering how a Gentian signature had ever made it to Andromeda. It could not be that someone had detected one of our ancient transmissions across intergalactic space, for the signal protocol was much too modern for that.

I had still seen no evidence of the First Machines, and only indirect evidence of the Andromeda Priors. But as I approached the solar system, still travelling close to the speed of light, *Dalliance* began to make out awesome structures hanging in space near the star, as large as any Prior artefacts documented in the trove. Prudence dictated a slow approach. I reduced my speed when I was still half a light-year from the signal's origin, assessing the awesome, humbling spectacle awaiting me. I did not know whether this was the work of machines or organics. What I did know was that it made the grandest works of the Line look like the rudimentary creations of cavemen scratching around a fire. We were proud of our stardams, but they were constructed from someone else's components – all we did was move the pieces around. We thought we were clever with our wormhole taps, whereas in fact we scarcely understood the first detail about how they functioned.

The solar system I was approaching was a monument to godlike intellects, godlike abilities. It took the lofty ambitions of the Lines and crushed them underfoot. It told us to come back when we were serious.

It was a three-dimensional representation of the nested solids of the Platonic cosmos. Each of the five polyhedra – octahedron, icosahedron, dodecahedron, tetrahedron, cube – was inscribed and circumscribed by a sphere, represented by a latticework orb. The spars of this enormous construct were thicker than a sun; a hundred times thicker than a world. They were many light-minutes in length, so that the outermost sphere was wider than the largest stardam Gentian Line had ever constructed. The polyhedra were rotating, each layer in the opposite direction to the one it encompassed. The system's solitary planet circled inside the vast construct, almost lost in that dark, ticking orrery. As I slowed down even further, I watched the planet pass through slots in the spars, its orbit undeflected. The structure was opaque enough to block the planet from view and mask the transmission from its surface, but it must have massed almost nothing. Hazily, I wondered if it had been made from a stable form of the lesion matter left behind by the Homunculus weapons.

I dropped *Dalliance* to twenty per cent of light, then ten per cent, then five. I had been sending a corresponding Gentian identifier since my departure, alerting the signaller to my arrival, but there had been no response. The transmission had not changed its nature in six thousand years.

At one-hundredth of the speed of light, *Dalliance* passed through the shell of the largest orb. I had been anticipating a response as I transgressed the outer layer, but there was no change in the structure, the planet or the signal originating from it. By now I had established that the point of origin was on or near the surface, within the world's atmosphere. There was blue water and green life on the planet and oxygen in the atmosphere. Subject to certain caveats, *Dalliance* had already assured me that I would be able to survive on the surface.

I fell through the cube, through the tetrahedron, into the interstitial space of the dodecahedron. It was there that the planet's orbit was threaded, passing through the struts like wire through wood. The sun was six light-minutes further in, nestling within the two smallest polyhedra and their surrounding shells. It was a lantern fretted by dark moving bars, throwing a shadow theatre across the universe.

I concentrated my attention on the planet, notching *Dalliance* down to an approach speed of only one thousand kilometres per second. I had glimpsed continents and seas from interstellar space, but now I made out the detailed topography of the surface. As the planet completed a rotation – it had been adjusted to exactly twenty-four hours, implying a human connection – *Dalliance* refined her maps and scrutinised the data for signs of technological activity.

That was when she found the orbiting wreck of *Silver Wings of Morning*, circling just above the point where atmospheric friction would have brought her down.

My heart stalled in recognition. I had watched this lovely ship shrug off the attentions of interstellar civilisations, barely deigning to notice their weapons. I had struggled to chase her as she dived into the stardam, oblivious to the ferocious course she had to follow. I had watched her rise and fall above the seas of a thousand worlds. I had come to associate her so strongly with the woman I loved that seeing her in this state was almost unbearable.

Her last act must have been to bring Purslane to this world. The damage she had sustained was so extreme that I could not imagine her travelling at more than a small fraction of the speed of light. Whole kilometre-long sections of the ship had been ripped away, including much of the hull region where her engine was contained. The curved, uplifted wings were buckled on one side and torn away on the other. The tarnished silver of her hull was now mostly black, except where previously hidden machinery showed through. *Dalliance* sniffed and tasted, finding only a dead wreck, devoid of power. I could send search probes through that twenty-five-kilometre-long wreck, but I knew they would not find life. Perhaps Purslane was tucked deep inside, cocooned in abeyance, but my instincts said otherwise. For the sake of thoroughness I knew I ought to search, but I did not know if I had the strength of mind to wait for the result.

I tried hailing again. 'Hesperus. Hesperus or Purslane. It's Campion. Talk to me.'

There was no answer. I kept trying, for ten hours.

At last I turned my attention to the surface, and the origin of the Gentian signal. It was not that I had forgotten it, but *Dalliance* had already examined the focus of the transmission and found no signs of organised activity. Something was generating that signal, but I could only assume that *Silver Wings* had dropped one of our beacons as her last functioning act, claiming this nameless world for the Line.

I still felt obliged to investigate.

I pulled *Dalliance* into the atmosphere, touching breathable air for the first time since the Centaurs' world. I dropped through billowing tropical clouds until I was overflying a quilt of dense green jungle stretching from horizon to horizon and for thousands of kilometres beyond. I wondered about the origins of this solitary little planet. Perhaps it was the only world in the system that had not been taken apart and reforged into the ethereal matter of the Platonic solids. Or perhaps it had been born orbiting another sun entirely, somewhere else in this empty galaxy. I wondered who had scaped it to its present state of biological fecundity; whether it had happened millions or billions of years ago.

The origin of the Gentian signal could not be localised more accurately than to an area encompassing several square kilometres – it was as if it was being created by a transmitter that large, even though no such machinery was visible. I slowed *Dalliance* to less than a kilometre a second and quartered the area, searching for something that might not have been visible from space. The jungle had thinned out, the terrain changing to a series of flat, rocky plateaux intersected by plunging ravines. The sheer-sided plateau rose from dense, dark jungle, but their sides were rocky and devoid of vegetation. Some of them had micro-ecologies on their upper surfaces, watered by pools fed by rainfall, draining via ribbon-thin, rainbow-banded cataracts. Others were arid and seemingly lifeless. Insofar as it could be pinned down, the Gentian transmission was originating from the surface of one of these barren plateaux.

I brought *Dalliance* to a hovering posture one hundred metres above the table-flat surface of the formation. My ship was much too large to land; she would overhang the plateau to a worrying degree. Foregoing a suit, trusting the ship's judgement that nothing in the atmosphere was likely to kill me quickly or irreversibly, I lowered a ramp and walked down, dressed only in the black clothes of Gentian funeral garb. Once I was clear, *Dalliance* pulled the ramp back in and rose until she was only a hand-sized shape in the sky. Wind snapped at me, warm and fragrant. The atmosphere was thick with pollen and micro-organisms, goading my body's ancient defences. I wiped my nose on my sleeve and walked towards the edge of the cliff, until my toes were only a foot's length from the drop. The plateau terminated in a crumbling overhang. I thought of Cyphel's long fall. It was a long way down, and *Dalliance* would not be able to react quickly enough to save me if I lost my balance. As the breath-hot wind shifted direction, threatening to push me over rather than away from the edge, I took a hasty, undignified step backwards.

'Sit with me a while, Campion.'

The voice startled me on two counts: I had not been expecting company; nor had I been expecting to hear a human voice, speaking Trans, that I did not recognise. It was not Hesperus; it was also not Purslane. I turned around very slowly, for the speaker had come up behind me from what I had assumed was a completely deserted plateau. I was glad that I had not brought an energy-pistol, for if there had been one in my hand I would surely have used it.

It was a man and it was not a man. A figure was walking towards me, strolling in a relaxed and unthreatening manner, raising one arm in welcome. It was assembling out of the air as it moved, gaining form and solidity. As it neared I saw that it was composed of thousands of glass spheres, the same size as the marbles that had entertained me in the playroom when I had been Abigail. The marbles were flying in from all directions, sticking together to form the approximate shape of a walking man. They had been in the air until then, undetected except for the signal I guessed they had been transmitting. An aggregate of machines, much like the Spirit of the Air.

'Who are you?' I asked.

'Like I said, sit with me a while.' The figure strolled to the very edge of the cliff and sat down with its legs dangling over the precipice. It was sitting to my left, a few metres from me. With a hand made of marbles it patted the stony ground, making a chinking sound of glass on rock, encouraging me to join it. 'Go ahead,' it urged, still in a casual and welcoming manner, although there was something beneath that too-human, too-avuncular voice that absolutely forbade me from doing anything but obey it. 'It's not as if you have anything *else* to do, is it, shatterling?'

The glass man was right. I had come here looking for Purslane, and for answers. Denied Purslane, I would settle for just the answers. Warily I lowered myself to a sitting position and dangled my legs over the edge, acutely aware of how little rock there might be below me.

'I'll ask again. Who are you?'

'You already know. You expected to find us in this galaxy, but when you arrived we were gone. I am the only one left; the last of the First Machines.'

'Only Purslane called them that.'

'But she spoke to Hesperus, and Hesperus remembered what she had said,' the glass man corrected me.

'Then you've spoken to Hesperus.'

'Not exactly. He was very damaged when he arrived. It had been a difficult crossing. You've seen the ship.'

'And Hesperus?'

'He fell to earth. He'd had time to regather himself into a more compact form, but not much of his mind was left by the time I reached him. I took his memories, such as they were. There was little I could do for his personality. He had already discarded much of it

494

of his own volition.' The figure fell silent, as if a moment of respect was necessary after discussing the death of the other machine. I looked out across the chasm that separated us from the sheer wall of the next plateau, waiting for him to continue. Mist cloaked the forested ground, muffling the distant sound of a waterfall. 'It was a pity,' my companion continued eventually. 'He and I would have had much to talk about. Much to catch up on, after so much time. I always enjoyed his company.'

'You couldn't have known Hesperus. He was a Machine Person. You were dead and gone for millions of years before he came on the scene.'

'You're mistaken, shatterling – but I can't blame you for not being in full possession of the facts. Hesperus was also a man, once upon a time. His name was Abraham Valmik. He was human, born in the Golden Hour. When the First Machines emerged, Valmik was a great friend to us. We called him the Intercessor. We thought highly of him, and hoped that he might broker trust between our two orders of existence. We were mistaken, but it was not Valmik's fault. He did everything he could for us, and we have always been grateful for that.'

'Is it true that we killed the First Machines?'

'You sought to be able to kill us, to hold a dagger against our hearts. Unfortunately, the dagger slipped. It was an accident, but that does not lessen the repugnant fact of the dagger being put there in the first place.' The glass man touched a hand to his chest. 'Some of us were fortunate – far enough away from the hub of First Machine society that we could run, or adapt ourselves to eliminate the threat. I was one of those that ran. We sought sanctuary in Andromeda, imagining that the organics would leave us alone if we let them have their galaxy in peace.'

'We forgot the crime,' I said. 'Then the Machine People arose.'

'Yes. Promising, aren't they? Do you think much will come of them?' He asked this confidingly, as if my answer was of genuine interest to him. 'We have hopes and fears.'

'I think they'd like to destroy us all.'

'And would you blame them if they did? You have, it must be said, demonstrated a distinct propensity for killing machine intelligences. The Machine People would have every right to take defensive measures, wouldn't you say?'

'I don't know. The Lines committed that atrocity and then covered it up afterwards. Should all the other cultures in the meta-civilisation be held responsible for something they had no hand in, and don't even know happened?'

'Now there's a question.'

'We thought the First Machines would come through the wormhole and assist the Machine People. That's what Cadence and Cascade were counting on.'

'Yes – Cadence and Cascade,' he said with a measure of distaste. 'I know of *them* from Hesperus's memories. Well, what do you think, shatterling? Do you see evidence of First Machines gathering en masse to storm through the wormhole and exact a blood toll for the manner in which they were wronged? Do you see us slavering for revenge, that most pointlessly biological of imperatives?'

'Apart from this system, I haven't seen much evidence of anything. Andromeda appears completely deserted.'

'Not what you expected, then?'

'We assumed that the Absence was the result of organised activity by Andromeda Priors. When I learned about the First Machines, I assumed they'd been responsible for it. But there's nothing here – just millions of empty systems. You could be hiding, you could be disguising yourselves, but if you are, it's very well done. And now I don't even understand the Absence. This is Andromeda – I know that from *Dalliance*'s positional fix – but everything here looks absolutely normal. I can see all the way out to the edge of the universe. And yet when I look in the direction of our galaxy, I see another Absence there.'

'You are right in one regard,' the glass man said. 'The Absence was the result of organised activity. Reactivating the wormhole link was one of the last acts of the First Machines, before we left.'

'I still don't get it.'

'It's about the preservation of causality. What you perceived as the Andromeda Absence was nothing but a barrier, permitting information to flow one way but not the other. It's still there. When you look into the sky, out to the edge of the universe, you are recording photons that have travelled through this barrier in the permitted direction. By the same token, no photons – no information-carrying entities of any kind – may leave Andromeda. You see a lightless envelope, encompassing the entire galaxy except for those outlying stars that happened to fall beyond it at the time it came into existence. The galaxy's gravitational field reaches through the barrier, but it is essentially static, conveying no information.'

'And our galaxy?'

'The same thing applies. From the moment the wormhole link was reactivated and superluminal information flow between the galaxies became possible, the galaxies had to be screened off from the rest of the universe. You are seeing the Milky Way Absence from the outside now, but it has been in existence for as long as the one around Andromeda. But because information was free to reach you from outside, you had no idea of its existence.'

'But we could never have left. No ship or signal would ever have been able to pass through that barrier.'

'And have the Lines ever sent envoys into intergalactic space, shatterling?'

'No one ever reported back.'

'Now you have your answer. The Absence is a barrier that permits faster-than-light travel between two points in space, millions of light-years apart, without violating the causal ordering postulate. The wider universe never observes superluminal travel.'

'Did you do this, or just make it work again?'

'Have some perspective, Campion. Machine intelligences have only been around for five million years. The Priors who put the wormhole link in place had been manipulating matter and energy on a cosmological scale for billions of years. Even to them, it must have been a daunting task. We still don't understand how they did it, only that it functions.'

'But the price of intergalactic travel is that we can't go anywhere else. Is that what you're saying?'

'I said nothing of the kind. Do you imagine that you arrived by the only wormhole link in and out of Andromeda? There are others, Campion – many others. We've spent much of our time here record-ing their positions, and guessing as to their destinations.' He extended a hand to the sky, pointing in a particular direction, close to the west as measured by the slowly setting sun. 'If it were night, you would be looking in the direction of the Boötes Void, about two hundred and fifty million light-years away – a hundred times as far as you've already travelled, in other words. It's one of the largest empty spaces in the visible universe – a great region of space devoid of galaxies, the most perfect vacuum in creation. Yet suppose that there *are* galaxies in that darkness, but each hidden behind its own Absence, each linked to the next by a superluminal wormhole? Imagine it, Campion – a vast, lunglike network of galaxies, thousands or tens of thousands of them – the equivalent of an entire super-cluster?'

'You'd see the Absences. They'd block the light from the microwave background.'

'Perhaps.' The glass man waved his hand, as if he considered my point profoundly uninteresting. 'There are other theories, developed by the First Machines, which say that Absences may be tuned to a kind of invisibility, if the supercivilisation deems it useful. We haven't reached that degree of understanding yet, but who knows what may become possible in a million or a billion years? The wormhole link is still settling down after a long period of dormancy – you'll have noticed the unpredictable nature of the spacetime medium during your transit. The Absence may also still be converging on its end-state condition.' I started to speak, but he cut me off. 'The point is, there's a lot out there. I told you that I am the last First Machine. That is only because I chose to remain behind when the others departed. They've left Andromeda via the outgoing wormhole links, intending to follow them as far as they are able. I don't doubt that they are already far beyond the Local Group, if they haven't already reached the Boötes Void.'

'What do they hope to find when they get there?'

'Something bigger and better than themselves. You've seen what we can do with matter, when the fancy takes us. Kepler's Platonic model – did you like it?'

'It frightened me, more than anything.'

'That's how we feel about the Boötes Void supercivilisation, if it exists.'

I watched the mist rising from the depths. 'Will you go?'

'Now that I'm done here – why not? I've seen enough of Andromeda for one lifetime.'

'And us? Are we going to be punished for what we did?'

The glass man put a marbled hand against my back, between my shoulder blades. 'Do you really imagine punishment is of the slightest interest to us?'

'We nearly killed you all.'

'You did, and it was unforgivable. Nonetheless, we offer our forgiveness. What is the point in being a superior civilisation if you can't do that once in a while? I could push you off this cliff now, watch you fall all the way to the bottom. I might gain some barely measurable degree of satisfaction from seeing you die, knowing what you did to us, but would any higher purpose be served by that act?'

The pressure on my back eased; I was able to lean back a little.

'It's not what I expected.'

'Surprises are always good. It's what we live for, sentients like you and me.' The glass man pushed himself to his feet. 'I think we're about done here, shatterling. You can have this galaxy. I suggest you refrain from following us deeper into the wormhole network – just for a few million years. Give it five million, ten, maybe. Then perhaps we'll be in a position to talk, meta-civilisation to meta-civilisation. In the meantime, try not to mess this one up. That thing you humans do – the turnover? There has to be a better way, don't you think?'

'I don't know,' I said, in all truthfulness. 'We're still fumbling in the dark, trying to find out how to live on a galactic scale.'

'You're right. It's still early days. I shouldn't be too harsh.'

'Is there going to be a war? Between us and the Machine People, I mean.'

'If there is, it may already have started. Nothing has emerged from the wormhole since your arrival, but since you reached this world at only slightly less than the speed of light, that's not to say someone hasn't come through after you. They may be on their way, they may be delayed by thousands of years, or the stardam may have closed again. Whatever happens, I think it safe to say that you are in for exceedingly interesting times.'

'Macro-war, taking in the entire Milky Way.'

'It doesn't have to happen like that. Even if the war has begun, it may still be contained. You have enemies amongst the Machine People, that's for certain. But you also have allies and sympathisers, like Hesperus. He wasn't the only one of his kind. The best thing would be for progressive elements in the human meta-civilisation to reach out and embrace their counterparts in Machine Space. The Lines could play a role – even a depleted, worn-out Line that has blood on its hands.'

'Gentian Line?'

'Exactly.'

'We're finished. For all I know, I'm the last one left.'

'I don't think so, shatterling.'

Parts of him had begun to detach. Marbles were peeling away, taking flight, vanishing into the air. He touched a diminished hand to his forehead, absent-mindedly. 'I should have mentioned it already. You exited the wormhole a little over three thousand years ago, by your reckoning?'

I nodded uneasily. 'Give or take.'

'*Silver Wings of Morning* came out much earlier. She was damaged by the transit, incapable of fast flight. She reached orbit around this world seventeen and a half thousand years ago.'

I felt as if the rock had finally given way beneath me – all hope gone. It had been there for a second, like the sun breaking through a crack in the clouds, bringing a glint of daylight. Now the clouds had closed over, heavier than before.

'I don't understand.'

'I told you that the wormhole is still settling down. That's what happens. You'll just have to live with it, until things stabilise. You'll cope. It's not as if you haven't already had some experience with deep time.'

'You told me you found Hesperus. What happened to Purslane? Did you find her in stasis?'

'I found the robot. He had fallen from space, abandoning the dying ship. Nothing could survive aboard her any more – with the threat of an engine detonation it would have been too hazardous even to remain in stasis. From what I could gather from his memory, it was not possible to land or take a shuttle.'

Hesperus must still have been locked out of vital control functions, even after the ship had brought him all the way here. Since she could not have been homing in on the Gentian signal, I could only presume that *Silver Wings* had steered towards the first hint of intelligent activity she found – the Platonic model solar system, with its strangely occluded star.

'Did he bring Purslane with him?'

'I'll show you the robot, shatterling – you may find it of interest. It won't take a moment – he's down in the jungle, at the base of this plateau.' The glass man beckoned out across the edge of the plateau. 'Step off.'

'What?'

'Unless you can think of another way to get down there. I wouldn't look to your ship – she would never fit. Don't worry – I'll be there to catch you.'

'I only have your word for that.'

'Yes,' the glass man said, 'that's rather the point. There's going to have to be a lot more trust from this time forward. Why don't we start as we mean to go on?'

I closed my eyes. It occurred to me that perhaps *this* was the punishment; that the First Machines had left behind the glass man to torment just one member of the human species, enacting their vengeance on me alone, rather than the rest of the meta-civilisation.

But, like Hesperus had said: revenge was for biologicals. Machines did things differently.

I stepped off.

There was a moment of weightlessness, time enough for me to begin to think that I had indeed been tricked. Then the pieces of the glass man caught up with my falling figure and supported me, just as the Spirit of the Air had supported me when we visited it on Neume. Marbles pressed under my arms, under the curve of my back, under my legs.

I was lowered through mist, towards the roaring cataract and into the green-canopied gloom of the jungle. There was life there but no animal life; nothing with a mind or a mouth. The forest was silent except for the swish of leaf on leaf, the creaking of old tree trunks and the static hiss of falling water, like the radio simmer of a million quasars. Still being buoyed aloft, we came to a clearing near the base of the cliff. The mist was a white ceiling that occasionally thinned out to reveal bluer sky or the sheer edifice of the plateau.

I landed softly. The clearing was floored with something like grass, thick-bladed and damp with condensation. Grass was universal, even in Andromeda. The clearing was empty except for a glass sphere three metres across, with a golden form suspended inside.

'He's still in stasis,' the glass man said as he gathered his pieces back into human form. 'He's been here seventeen and a half thousand years, but he's experienced less than six days of subjective time.'

'Where's the apparatus? I don't see any stasis-generating machinery.'

'You wouldn't,' the glass man said. He raised a hand and made the stasis bubble collapse, the barely recognisable form of Hesperus lowering slowly to the grass, on his back. 'There's a much simpler way of slowing time. You'll work it out eventually, and then wonder what all the fuss was about.'

Hesperus's body was in a bad way. The gold armour was fused and blackened, as if he had been melted and then allowed to cool again. In places it was leathery, cracked like an old painting; in others it was as glassy as amber. He was larger than I remembered – less like a gold man than a gold sarcophagus in the shape of a man. His arms were fused with the sides of his body, his legs joined together into a single mass. His head, which was swollen, showed no indications of life. His features had been melted together, leaving only a half-formed approximation of a human face. His eyes were gone. The dark windows of his skull were scorched, but I could see no lights moving beyond them.

'You already told me he was gone,' I said. 'You told me he was dead, that there was nothing left of his personality.'

'That's still true.'

'So why did you put him into stasis?'

'Because of what he contained. I told you that he sacrificed his higher functions, discarding much of his own personality. He did that for a reason. He had to make room inside himself, to protect the thing he cared for most.' The glass man nodded at my thoughts, as if they were transparent to him. 'He became armour, Campion – altered himself so that he could protect Purslane during the fall to earth. Deciding to protect her would have been one of his last conscious acts as a fully formed sentience.'

I had felt strong until then, but now I fell to my knees, next to the golden form.

'She's inside him?'

'There is a female human within the armour. The human is alive, albeit in a state of coma. I am no expert in these matters, but I believe the human to be unharmed. Of course, it may not be Purslane, but given the weight of evidence ...'

I closed my eyes, sobbing with the force of the unseen cataract, all my worst fears draining out of me in a silvery rush. 'I have to get the armour off,' I said, when I could speak again. I was racked by remorse for Hesperus, racked by desperate, intoxicating gratitude for the cargo he had kept safe.

'Then I'll help you,' the glass man said as my fingers dug their useless nails into the fused seams of that golden mask. 'After which, with regret, I shall have to be on my way.'